7

The African American West

The African American West

A CENTURY OF SHORT STORIES

EDITED BY

Bruce A. Glasrud & Laurie Champion

UNIVERSITY PRESS OF COLORADO

Published by the University Press of Colorado
5589 Arapahoe Avenue, Suite 206C
Boulder, Colorado 80303

The University Press of Colorado is a cooperative publishing enterprise supported, in part, by
Adams State College, Colorado State University, Fort Lewis College, Mesa State College,
Metropolitan State College of Denver, University of Colorado, University of Northern
Colorado, University of Southern Colorado, and Western State College of Colorado.

The paper used in this publication meets the minimum requirements of the American National
Standard for Information Sciences—Permanence of Paper for Printed Library Materials. ANSI
Z39.48-1984

Library of Congress Cataloging-in-Publication Data

The African American West : a century of short stories / edited by Bruce A. Glasrud &
Laurie Champion.
    p. cm.
    Includes bibliographical references and index.
    ISBN 0-87081-559-8 (cloth : alk. paper)
    1. Short stories, American—Afro-American authors. 2. Afro-Americans—West
(U.S.)—Fiction. 3. Short stories, American—West (U.S.) I. Glasrud, Bruce A. II.
Champion, Laurie.

PS647.A35 A38 2000
813'.01083278'08996073—dc21   99-058822

09 08 07 06 05 04 03 02 01   10 9 8 7 6 5 4 3 2

Contents

Preface

Life could be lived with dignity, that the personalities of others should not be violated, that men should be able to confront other men without fear or shame.

—*Richard Wright*

The ideas for *The African American West: A Century of Short Stories* germinated while we (Bruce Glasrud and Laurie Champion) were driving to a western social science conference in Albuquerque, New Mexico, and back to Alpine, Texas. As we drove, we began to discuss various political and social issues raised by the conference. Our discussion of social issues was also the result of the newly established Women's Program at Sul Ross State University. Having recently been appointed dean of Arts and Sciences, Glasrud had helped initiate the program, and Champion was its co-coordinator. We began to discuss various factors related to women's studies, such as race, class and gender. A sort of blending of our disciplines emerged (Glasrud specializes in African American history, specifically western African Americans, and Champion in literary studies, specifically the short story in the South and West) and we began to consider African American short stories set in the West. As we discussed short stories written by African Americans, we tried to think of those written about the West. We could only recall a few offhand.

When we returned from the conference, we started to research African American fiction set in the West. We started a bibliography tentatively entitled "African American Fiction in the West," which encompassed a broader approach than searching merely for short stories. At first, we found only a few works; but fortunately we were able to locate several general bibliographies that listed African American short stories or covered African Americans in the West. We gathered anthologies, novels, essays, short stories, and other works and checked to see what items might be added to our bibliography. After months of research, we narrowed our list to include only short stories and discovered we had amassed an entire body of African American short stories by western authors. We began writing a research paper, included here as an introduction, and decided to gather some of these stories in a single volume.

We established criteria for defining both the West and the African American short story. While the former was relatively easy because it lent itself to more concrete explanations, the latter was more complicated. Basically, we define the West as those states one removed westward from the Mississippi River, although more generally as any state west of the Mississippi. On occasion, we crossed the Mississippi eastward to garner a few stories that captured the western spirit. In other words, the West is a geographic entity, albeit with moving parameters; but (as these short stories demonstrate) it is also a state of mind, a sense of place, a community, and a dream and spirit: "I am a Westerner," "I enjoy studying the Wild West," "I am going West," or "Oh give me a home . . . where seldom is heard a discouraging word."

As far as what constitutes an African American short story, we first considered the problems inherent in defining a short story itself (e.g., length, story vs. essay, fiction vs. nonfiction, prose vs. poetry), but quickly decided issues related to genre definition went beyond the scope of our project—we would use normal guidelines as well as common sense to decide whether or not a piece of writing was a short story. Next, we considered what makes a short story an African American short story and concluded that for the most part it would be one wherein the point-of-view character is an African American; that is, if the story is told from the point-of-view of an African American or if the main character is an African American, we considered it an African American short story. Therefore, in general, for inclusion in our initial bibliography the story was set in the West and was told from the point of view of an African American or portrayed an African American as a major character. Most of the stories that met both criteria were written by African American writers, but we found a few by white authors; however, the author's race was not a factor when the stories were selected for our bibliography.

In regard to the criteria for selecting stories from our bibliography to include in our anthology, we considered factors such as the story's readability, the story's artistic merit, the message the story conveys, the development of the story, the political and social points the story makes concerning African Americans in the West, and the themes the story conveys concerning life in the West as opposed to that in the East. Because we wanted to provide a historical account of blacks in the West, we also considered chronology—when the story was written and during what time the story was set. We strived for a variety of geographical settings west of the Mississippi River in order to represent a broad spectrum of the West as a specific geographic region. Although we found stories set in almost every state, we did not discover any set in Alaska or Hawaii.

By gathering in a single volume stories we defined as African American short stories set in the West, we hoped to show the history of black Westerners through fiction, to examine why African Americans moved West, to place western African Americans in the more broad American short story tradition, and to explore the problems, skills, survival techniques, and daily lives of African Americans in the West.

During our research, we came across an appropriate quote by Richard Wright, the influential black author of *Native Son* and *Uncle Tom's Children*. As he remarked in *Black Boy*, when he left the South he was simultaneously "taking a part of the South to transplant in alien soil." He felt "full of a hazy notion that life could be lived with dignity, that the personalities of others should not be violated, that men should be able to confront other men without fear or shame, and that if men were lucky in their living on earth they might win some redeeming meaning for their having struggled and suffered here beneath the stars" (228). We thought this statement described well the motives for many of the characters in these stories to move to and remain in the West. Among other motives, they hoped to gain a life with dignity, find equal economic opportunities, strengthen personal and social relationships, acquire liberty and freedom, and celebrate their African American culture and heritage.

We hope that this collection of short stories provides insights about African Americans in the West and raises consciousness about various social and political issues—obviously we refer especially to sexism, discrimination, segregation, and racism. Together, the stories provide a range of ideas, themes, situations, and voices; they tell us a lot about the history of African Americans in the West. Perhaps on a lighter note, in different ways they all offer basic entertainment—one of the chief reasons we read any work of literature. Enjoy reading them while you learn from them.

Acknowledgments

Conceptualizing, researching, and preparing an anthology of this nature and magnitude took considerable effort, and obviously resulted in our incurring many debts. Because of space limitations, most cannot be acknowledged here, but suffice it to say that we send *thanks* to the many editors, authors, agents, publishers, and colleagues who answered our queries, led us to new sources, and kept encouraging our efforts.

A few individuals merit further mention. The library staff at Sul Ross State University never ceased to search one more time—thanks, Mike Robinson, Pam Spooner, and Eleanor Wilson. Luther Wilson of the University Press of Colorado listened, facilitated, and supported our proposal. The editorial staff at the press—Darrin Pratt, Laura Furney, and Stacy Zellmann—professionally and constructively facilitated the preparation and marketing of our work. We also profusely thank Sul Ross State University for providing us with a Research Enhancement Grant to help defray some of the expenses connected with preparing this work.

The initial reviewers of this proposal were thorough and warm in their responses to our early outlines and writings. Robert J. Mallouf, director of the Center for Big Bend Studies at Sul Ross State University, encouraged us to prepare an overview of the western African American short story tradition. Even though so many people helped us, any errors remain our own.

The African American West

Introduction
African Americans in the West,
A Short Story Tradition[1]

BRUCE A. GLASRUD & LAURIE CHAMPION

Along with other peoples of color, African Americans played a prominent and distinctive part in the exploration, settlement, development, and transformation of the western United States.[2] In the process their experiences provided the impetus for as well as the creation of a body of short stories that reflect their attitudes, sense of community, survival skills, personal and communal ties, and social concerns. One can learn much from a study of these frequently unrecognized stories—in particular, that there has been a century-long tradition of short stories that provide a clear understanding of western African American history and culture. Although hitherto unacknowledged in social and cultural assessments, an important way to view the aspirations, achievements, and lives of western blacks is through these stories that represent the emergence of a strong and vibrant short story tradition.

For a variety of reasons, the short stories that portray African Americans in the West are not well known, are frequently ignored, and are not used as a means of exploring black life in the West. Yet, some of the most prominent black (and a few white) American authors have used this genre effectively, and their stories enable us to discern the peopling, interacting, and settling of western black communities. Many stories speak to the question: why move west? Or, what was the lure of the West? It comes as no surprise that liberty and opportunity head the list, but other, more subtle, motives can also be found. These motives are reflected in the various subjects depicted in short stories about blacks in the West: oppression, social radicalism, struggle of women, resistance, religion, survival, geographic freedom, family, and friends. Contrarily, it is also noticeable from some of the stories that all was not well in the West, and some disillusioned African Americans moved back east.

For the most part, stories set in the West that portray blacks do not represent the traditional, or popular, western. It is important to distinguish them from those designated "western" as a genre. Black authors, characters, and situations are not discovered in, or considered part of, the "western" label. Editors Judy Alter and A. T. Row found this out while preparing *Unbridled Spirits: Short Fiction About Women in the Old West*; they "found no useable stories about black women."[3]

Because historically black Americans were denied publication in white journals, *because* American publishers frequently assumed an eastern bias, *because* western African Americans were too busy exploring opportunities for survival, *because* western writers were less likely to use condescending dialect and to depict stereotypes, and *because* the short story is among the least appreciated literary genres, short stories that portray blacks in the West have too often been neglected. Our purpose for preparing this study is to clarify this void.

Generally, the short story has been the most critically neglected literary genre even though Edgar Allan Poe's reviews of "tales" during the late 1830s and early 1840s and Brander Matthew's 1901 study, *The Philosophy of the Short-Story*, provided a firm foundation for the definition of the American short story.[4] The short story has been a legitimate genre for more than 100 years, but as William Peden noted recently in "The Black Explosion," "the short story writer in America—white or black or red or yellow—has always tended to be a kind of creative stepchild working for the most part in comparative obscurity and with very few financial rewards." African American short story writers have been neglected both because of the lack of interest in the genre and because blacks have been denied access to avenues of publication traditionally dominated by whites. Bill Mullen's assessment in his introduction to *Revolutionary Tales* rings true: "short story writing, more than any other genre, depends upon control of and access to the literary marketplace."[5]

Even though most stories of black westerners were written by African Americans, white authors also created stories depicting black Westerners. They faced a task fraught with problems. It seems especially difficult for someone of another culture or gender to "get inside" another group or person in order to create viable characters and accurate cultural renditions (read nonstereotypical). Some western stories by white authors are flawed by biased assumptions. Examples include Mark Twain's "Jim" in *Huckleberry Finn*, Theodore Dreiser's "Nigger Jeff," and John Ball's detective Virgil Tibbs. Other authors, such as Larry McMurtry, include black characters in minor roles as servants or as "oddities."[6] What can be accomplished, however, in terms of refuting stereotypes, can be ascertained in the skillful novel *The Wolf and the Buffalo* by Elmer Kelton.

The intriguing and absolutely ironic fact is that black and white western authors who defied depiction of race stereotypes were often overlooked by publishers and critics; nonetheless they usually have been at the forefront of short story creativity and experimentation. In fact, just by writing about the West, they were breaking with tradition. They also did not depict the stereotypes of black characters found in other fictional realms. Sterling Brown and Nick Aaron Ford developed a list of stereotypes (created mostly by white authors) that by the 1930s included the contented slave, the comic Negro, the wretched freeman, the brute Negro, the tragic mulatto, the local-color Negro, the exotic primitive, the worshipful servant, and the superstitious Negro.[7] Western characters, however, were usually forceful figures with depth and dimension who did not fit the stereotypes. Since white editors seemed to prefer portrayals of black stereotypes and an East Coast bias predominated in selecting and interpreting stories, the depiction of African American Westerners was not critically appreciated. For example, the African American editor of one "national" anthology asserted that "all of the stories in this book are about the young brothers and sisters. They are born in Southern rural areas and in Harlem. They grow and sing and love in Atlanta or New York or No Name, Missabama."[8] Obviously, however, not west of the Mississippi River.

Even though by the late 1890s the short story was established as a legitimate American genre, the short story as a literary form had "been intended primarily for popular magazine publication." As the editors of *The Negro Caravan* continued, "in this medium, more than in others, the black author faced the dilemma of the divided audience—that is, at whom to aim the story, whites or blacks. With a few exceptions, there have been no magazines with a primarily African American audience in which writers could place their short stories."[9] Because of such publishing and audience limitations the African American short story writer faced three unsatisfactory choices as outlined by Peter Bruck: (1) the writer could turn to protest fiction, as did Sutton E. Griggs; (2) the writer could stop writing because of limited reception, as did Charles W. Chesnutt, or (3) the writer could veil protest and present happy characters in the plantation tradition, as Paul Laurence Dunbar sometimes did.[10] Fortunately, the western setting allowed for more viable alternatives.

The first western short story writers to portray black Americans emerged around the turn of the twentieth century with stories that reflected the spirit, opportunities, and peoples of the latter nineteenth century. It is fitting, and certainly no surprise, that Paul Laurence Dunbar and Charles W. Chesnutt, the two earliest and best known western African American short story writers, resided in the Old Northwest. Slavery had been outlawed early by the Northwest Ordinance, and it was in this region that African Americans first ventured to seek the freedoms and opportunities associated with the West. Although Dunbar is sometimes criticized for creating black characters for white expectations, in "The Ingrate" he presents a slave who escapes to Canada by using the reading and writing skills his owner taught him. When the slave uses these abilities to escape, the owner considers him an "ingrate."[11]

Other authors who wrote during or about this period covered subjects such as the Buffalo Soldiers, a potential labor strike, and Jack Johnson's Reno boxing match against the "White Hope"; even Frank and Jesse James became side characters in a recent (1987) story set in the latter nineteenth century. Generally, in the earlier years African American authors either published a collection of their own short stories (with white support) or published in the *Colored American Magazine*, which for a time was edited by a black woman, Pauline E. Hopkins, who contributed a story about lynching in the West.[12]

By the 1920s another group of African American writers emerged. These writers, their topics, and the social climate of the twenties and thirties provide additional detail about the western short story. Stories with western settings were published in *The Crisis, Half-Century Magazine,* and *The Messenger;* a few appeared in the *Baltimore Afro-American* newspaper. The stories were often bitter, reflecting the state of white-black race relations as well as the influence of the "new Negro" who arrived after World War I. The great race crusader W.E.B. DuBois, for example, published a short story entitled "Jesus Christ in Texas." Although known primarily for his essays that advocate social equality, here DuBois portrays a lynching, a topic of immediate concern to black Americans during the first half of the twentieth century.[13]

In addition to DuBois, other writers of this era include Kansas-reared Langston Hughes, onetime Californian Arna Bontemps, and western-based Anita Scott Coleman. Noted for his realistic portrayal of African Americans, Hughes's short story "The Gun" depicts a young girl in Tall Rock, Montana, whose parents left Texas because of white racist pressures. Unlike many stories that demonstrate the lure of the West, Arna Bontemps's "Why I Returned" is an essay-like treatment of his decision to return to and remain in the South.[14] Anita Scott Coleman remained in the West and became one of its most prolific black writers. Born in Mexico and educated in New Mexico, she resided for much of her life in California and Arizona. Coleman frequently published short stories in the standard African American journals of the twenties and thirties. Her stories portray female protagonists either as newly married or independent of a male "protector." Her women are proud and frequently make choices that reflect independence. In some stories, the West as a geographical setting provides the central conflict or the more promising habitat. For example, in "Rich Man, Poor Man—" a young woman's father hopes that she will not leave the West when married.[15]

These writers, although not necessarily a part of the Harlem Renaissance, paralleled it and were often absorbed into it. A classic example of the influence of the Renaissance, albeit its rejection of the West—Harlem, remember, was as east as one can get—can be ascertained by the career of Wallace Thurman. Thurman wrote the highly successful and very skilled novel *The Blacker the Berry.*[16] Set in Idaho and California, it was an accomplished first novel. However, to seek his fortune Thurman traveled to New York, was extolled as a great editor and writer, and wrote nothing else about the West. Unfortunately, he died at an early age without returning in his stories to the western setting. Even Arna Bontemps, who early in his career wrote stories and a novel—*God Sends Sunday*—set in the West, is not known so much for his relationship to the Harlem Renaissance as are other representatives.

The Harlem Renaissance,[17] a significant movement for black artists and writers, began during the 1920s. The movement brought together in New York City writers such as Rudolph Fisher, Zora Neale Hurston, Jean Toomer, Claude McKay, Nella Larsen, Wallace Thurman, and Dorothy West. Black journals and magazines such as *Opportunity,* founded by Charles Johnson, and newspapers such as the *Baltimore Afro-American* offered outlets for black short story authors. Writing in an environment that included "a new feeling of ethnic identity and racial pride," blacks no

longer had to "succumb to the stereotyped habits of the white reading public." In his essay "The Negro Artist and the Racial Mountain," Langston Hughes provided an overview of the attitudes shared by black writers during the twenties and thirties: "an artist must be free to choose what he does, certainly, but he must also never be afraid to do what he might choose." According to Bill Mullen, the desire to express both individual and cultural identity along with an increase in markets available for the black short story allowed black writers to write short stories as a "vehicle for social protest and [as a] demand for self-definition."[18]

Not everyone agreed with Hughes's interpretation of this freedom of choice. As J. Saunders Redding pointed out, "a writer writes for an audience. Consciously or unconsciously," Redding argued, the writer "bears in mind the real or imagined peculiarities of the audience to whom he wishes to appeal." Referring to the black writer's continued struggle with audience during the Harlem Renaissance, James Weldon Johnson noted that the black author

> faces a special problem which the plain American author knows nothing about—the problem of the double audience. It is more than a double audience; it is a divided audience, an audience made up of two elements with differing and often opposite and antagonistic points of view. His audience is often both white America and black America. The moment a Negro writer takes up his pen or sits down to his typewriter he is immediately called upon to solve, consciously or unconsciously, this problem of the double audience. To whom should he address himself, to his own black group or to white America?[19]

Yet Johnson also advised black writers not to stereotype blacks for a white audience and, perhaps overoptimistically, asserted that blacks have "as fair a chance today of being published as any other writers."[20] Even though more writing and publishing opportunities for black writers occurred during the era of the Harlem Renaissance, they were still denied an audience who shared their personal and social concerns.

By the mid-thirties, the double audience conflict for black writers began to improve. Langston Hughes set an example of ways the black American short story could reach both black and white audiences. His 1934 collection of short stories, *The Ways of White Folk*, generally received favorable reviews and was somewhat successful commercially. Hughes's Simple tales began to appear in the *Chicago Defender* in 1942 and "marked, in socio-literary terms, an important development of black short fiction. . . . Hughes set a model of how to leave behind the ethnic province and the literary ghetto of the black short story writer."[21] But the conflict of the double audience was far from solved. In 1938, Richard Wright published his collection of short stories, *Uncle Tom's Children,* which was read more by whites than by blacks, his intended audience. Wright's reaction was instructive: "when the reviews of that book began to appear, I realized that I had made an awfully naive mistake."[22]

During the World War II, African Americans served in the U.S. armed forces moved to urban centers on the West Coast to acquire better-paying jobs in

burgeoning defense industries, and struggled against efforts to reduce their rights and deny them equal pay and equal housing. Short story writers reflected these trends and pointed to the continuing changes that transpired after the war. By the mid-1940s, the audience for these writers continued to increase. Both black and white authors who wrote about blacks without stereotyping published in "white" journals that offered increased marketing outlets and a larger audience. For example, *Harper's Magazine* and *The California Quarterly* published stories set in the West by Frank Yerby and John O. Killens respectively. *The Crisis, The Messenger*, and *Opportunity* continued to focus on black issues, and a new forum was established in the Chicago-based *Negro Story*. The presence of a few black women persisted; black midwestern women edited and published *Negro Story*. Also notable is that during and immediately after World War II, referred to as "the forgotten years" of the black revolution, protest became a principal part of the black experience.[23] The first stirrings of the national Civil Rights movement could be found in western settings, including the elimination of the white primary, a move led by Texans with the support of the NAACP.

During the 1940s, many African American writers created fiction that reflected naturalism,[24] a literary tradition that began in the late nineteenth century. Naturalism is part of the broader-based school of "literary realism," which focuses on the stark conditions of society. The naturalistic perspective is that humanity responds to environmental forces that cannot be controlled; hence, it frequently stresses biological or social determinism. Borrowing from this literary tradition, black writers emphasized the social environment as the root of such problems as racial tension, crime, and poverty. They looked to social activism as a primary solution to societal ills. Authors such as Chester Himes, John Oliver Killens, and Richard Wright followed this naturalist tradition to expose social ills.

Two of the most significant black American writers of this time, Ralph Ellison and Chester Himes, are critically acclaimed for their novels; however, both writers wrote short stories as well. They also acknowledged the influence of the West. While comparing himself (southwestern) to Richard Wright (southeastern), Ellison noted that they were "divided by geography and a difference of experience based thereupon." Significantly, Ellison's only collection of short stories, *Flying Home and Other Stories*, was published posthumously in 1996. It is equally significant that Himes's first collection of short stories, *Black on Black: Baby Sister and Selected Writings*, was not published until 1973 (*The Collected Short Stories of Chester Himes* appeared posthumously in 1991).[25] Although both Ellison's and Himes's stories were published in magazines during the 1940s, the individual stories were not published as a collection until much later. Both writers' novels were well received and commercially successful. However, the decades of waiting for publication of a collection of short stories reflect both the lack of interest in the short story genre and the commercial publishing perils of the black author in white America.

The fifties and sixties witnessed the eruption of the Civil Rights revolution, which coalesced into the Black Power movement, and became part of the total

reform effort referred to as the Struggle for Black Liberation. What most Americans, white and black, too often forget is that the Civil Rights movement began in the West and that most of the resistance strategies were first used in the West. Remember, the 1954 *Brown v. Board of Education* decision was a Kansas case. Western civil rights advocates pursued the age-old dream of freedom offered by the desegregation decision. "Freedom" and "Civil Rights" became watchwords in the West, and when sit-ins and peaceful demonstrations were too slow or insignificant, African Americans in Watts exploded in anger and in Oakland they formed the Black Panther party.

These developments became part of the short story tradition. It was an easy transition—minister of propaganda for the Black Panther party Ed Bullins became a prominent author. Eldridge Cleaver, somewhat like Chester Himes, grew up in poverty, spent time in prison, and became a writer. Cleaver's *Soul on Ice* became essential reading for anyone seeking to understand the young black radicals of the 1960s. His story "The Flashlight" is, to say the least, a poignant reminder of growing up as an African American youth. Perhaps the title of John R. Posey's short story set in 1971—"Ticket to Freedom"—best depicts the possibility, difficulty, and irony of the era.[26]

During the late fifties and early sixties the protest theme was revived in black American literature. The revival of interest in protest literature was combined with the Black Arts movement of the 1960s, the first major movement for African American artists since the Harlem Renaissance. Continuing through the mid-seventies, the movement also reflected attitudes associated with Civil Rights and Black Power. The movement marks a clear separation between the Harlem Renaissance idea of aesthetic art and the idea of political art. John O. Killens reviewed the movement's attitudes when he reflected: "the sixties saw a blossoming of the Black arts. Some hailed it as the new Renaissance. Others called it a cultural revolution. . . . Black writers were proclaiming their Blackness. Very seldom did you hear a writer say, 'I'm not a Black writer. I'm a writer who happens to be Black.'"[27]

Unlike the Harlem Renaissance, during the Black Arts movement the black American writer no longer struggled with the problem of the divided audience. As J. Saunders Redding argued in 1966, white audiences and black audiences "were kept apart by a wide socio-cultural gulf. . . . Now that gulf is closed and the writer can write without being either false to the one audience or subservient to the other."[28] Four years later, Al Young pointed out another key element of the Black Arts movement when he noted that until recently:

> Black writers were almost required to write something that was overtly angry, something that said, "Charley, Whitey, I'm gonna cut your throat." It gave the white reader a titillation, it sold, and publishers were pushing it because it did sell. It's reached the point now, though, where the public is no longer excited by clenched fists, by pseudo-black anger—I say "pseudo" because of the way Madison Avenue has been exploiting it.[29]

As in other art forms, western short stories written during the sixties used the ideology of the Black Arts movement. Yet, while the Black Arts movement gave black artists freedom to write for other blacks and to express their cultural identity, during the 1960s there was still a problem for the short story writer because of lack of interest in the short story genre.

The beginning of the 1970s clearly marked the end of the divided audience conflict. "Times have changed," Terry McMillan asserted in the introduction to *Breaking Ice*, her short story anthology; "we do not feel the need to create and justify our existence anymore. We are here. We are proud. And most of us no longer feel the need to prove anything to white folks. If anything, we're trying to make sense of ourselves to ourselves."[30] Although McMillan's assessment reflects the new freedom of writing about themselves for themselves that African Americans experienced in the seventies, the short story as a genre was still not a critically acclaimed or popularly read category.

Black women short story writers during the Black Arts movement, Mary Helen Washington observes, "replaced images of themselves as maternal, domesticated, sexually promiscuous, and helpless with empowering portraits of black women as warriors in the struggle for racial and sexual emancipation." These changes led during the 1970s to a renaissance of African American women writers. As Washington notes, "the women who had once been described as 'the mules of the world' chose for themselves some new imagery: the hardiness and resiliency of black-eyed susans, the hunger and yearning of the mysterious midnight bird; they are seeing themselves as reborn, creators of a new world in which new values prevail."[31] Like the second wave of an American feminist movement, much of black women's writing began to portray the effects of sexism and other forms of oppression. This feminist illustration of women frequently reflects strong women who confront anger caused by oppression and women who directly experience the effects of racism and sexism, such as poverty and physical abuse.

During the late seventies and early eighties, the American short story also experienced a renaissance, partially because of the teaching of creative writing classes across the country. This trend aided aspiring black writers who were denied access to universities. In Los Angeles, soon after the 1965 Watts riot, Budd Schulberg opened the Watts Workshop and published a volume entitled *From the Ashes*.[32] Such writers' workshops were also established in other cities. Unfortunately, as the short story in general began to gain more recognition, African American short stories in particular were often ignored or marginalized. Most short story anthologies were still edited by whites for whites, and collections of short stories by whites were published much more frequently than those by blacks. Moreover, critics who discussed the black American short story sometimes looked more at white authors who wrote about blacks than at black authors. To exacerbate the difficulty of presenting the black West through short stories, even African American short story anthologies generally neglected the West.

The short story resurgence influenced African American women writers and led to the emergence of the Third Black Cultural Renaissance of the twentieth century. Whereas during the 1970s, women writers such as Alice Walker, Toni Cade Bambara, and Rita Dove began publishing short stories, during the 1980s and 1990s even more black American women short story writers began to publish short story collections and anthologies. African American short story writers such as Wanda Coleman, Colleen McElroy, Terry McMillan, Maxine Clair, Carolyn Ferrell, and J. California Cooper set stories in the West during this fruitful period for African American women. Black women now published at least as much as black men. Attention to black women's short stories also motivated the publication of works written earlier but neglected or forgotten: collections of short stories such as those by Zora Neale Hurston, Dorothy West, and Alice Childress were either published for the first time or reprinted.[33] Anthologies such as Mary Helen Washington's *Black-Eyed Susans*, Bill Mullen's *Revolutionary Tales*, and Ann Schockley's *Afro-American Women Writers* provided much-needed attention both to contemporary black women short story writers and to those whose works have been neglected for decades.[34]

These women authors frequently pursue and emphasize feminism. Ntozake Shange's "Ridin' the Moon in Texas" and Wanda Coleman's "The Friday Night Shift at the Taco House Blues (Wah-Wah)" are two examples of western stories that reflect strong feminist issues. "Ridin' the Moon in Texas" celebrates black women's identity by illustrating women who defy traditional roles. "The Friday Night Shift at the Taco House Blues (Wah-Wah)" depicts a young woman in 1973 who works at a Los Angeles taco house. Among other themes, the story reveals the unfortunate struggles of families trying to survive on meager incomes.[35]

Stories set in the West and published in the nineties, such as J. California Cooper's "Vanity," Harryette Mullen's "Tenderhead," and Carolyn Ferrell's "Wonderful Teen," reflect to different degrees the humiliation experienced by women who have been conditioned to strive for, and value, physical beauty. In *Black-Eyed Susans*, Mary Helen Washington perceptively observes this concern for beauty:

> the subject of the black woman's physical beauty occurs with such frequency in the writing of black women that it indicates they have been deeply affected by the discrimination against the shade of their skin and the texture of their hair. In almost every novel or autobiography written by a black woman, there is at least one incident in which the dark-skinned girl wishes to be either white or light-skinned with "good" hair.[36]

Although, as Washington posits, the concept of physical beauty haunts both white and black women, "the idea of beauty as *defined by white America* has been an assault on the personhood of the black woman."[37]

The emergence of black women writers at the apex of western short story writing parallels the overall maturation of western African American short stories. *Although* conditions for black Americans relative to white Americans may not have improved, *though* black Americans still face discrimination, and *though* western states participate in the opposition to affirmative action and other means to ensure that people of color receive a more equitable stance in society, short story writing prospers while reflecting the problems of the past two decades. Remarkable writers predominate—Maxine Clair, Reginald McKnight, Terry McMillan, Walter Mosley, John Edgar Wideman—to name just a few.

These authors tell us much about the West as they explore such issues as why people come to the West, the significance of the past, the tribulations of families, the "Long Distances," the interactions among people, and the vital role of religion. They accomplish these tasks by traversing in their settings the entire West, from Washington to Arizona, from California to Minnesota, from Kansas City to Dallas, from ghetto to suburb, from rural to urban. The increasing importance of urbanism among African American writers is apparent in the recent publication of *Street Lights: Illuminating Tales of the Urban Black Experience*, which includes at least three stories set in the West (regrettably out of a total of forty-nine).[38] The theme appears that not all is well in the promising West. Former Wyoming resident John Edgar Wideman sets many of his stories in Pennsylvania, and the characters in his stories explain why they leave the West to return to Homewood.

The 1990s allowed more freedom for writers to explore hitherto taboo subjects such as homosexuality. The anthology *Go the Way Your Blood Beats: An Anthology of Lesbian and Gay Fiction by African-American Writers*, a collection of short stories that depict lesbian and gay African Americans, appeared in 1996. One western story that portrays gay blacks is Darieck Scott's "This City of Men," an epistolary story set in Kansas wherein the protagonist Julius writes his girlfriend Danielle to inform her that he is gay. Published the same year, another work, *Shade: An Anthology of Fiction by Gay Men of African Descent*, includes "Spice," a story by A. Cinque Hicks, in which the individual spices used to make gumbo represent ways that people as individuals come together to create a society. In 1997, Lisa C. Moore's *Does Your Mama Know? An Anthology of Black Lesbian Coming Out Stories* was published. Even in these anthologies, the pervasive influence of an East Coast bias is reflected, for very few stories are set in the West.[39]

Although by the 1990s, African American writers were finding markets for their short stories and access to publishing avenues, the black short story nevertheless remained somewhat marginalized. In his preface to Terry McMillan's 1990 anthology of African American short stories, *Breaking Ice*, John Edgar Wideman asserts:

> magazine editors know that their jobs depend upon purveying images the public recognizes and approves, so they seldom include our fictions, and almost never choose those which transcend stereotypes and threaten to expose the fantasies of superiority, the bedrock lies and brute force that sustain the majority's power over the *other*. Framed in foreign, inimical contexts, minority stories appear at best as exotic slices of life and local color, at worst as ghettorized irrelevancies.[40]

As late as 1993, one critic noted that Peter Bruck's 1977 assessment of the "critical void" concerning the black American short story continues as "short story histories either ignore black short stories . . . or contain them in a marginal position."[41]

Changes have occurred. Authors such as Ernest J. Gaines, Terry McMillan, and J. California Cooper are more likely to reside in the West than their predecessors who moved to New York—Langston Hughes, Wallace Thurman—or to Paris—Chester Himes. Some African American short stories demonstrate a peculiar avoidance of localization as a means of emphasizing the similarity of conditions for black Americans throughout the nation. For example, J. California Cooper's collection *A Piece of Mine* begins "where we live is not a big town like some and not a little town like some, but somewhere in the middle, like a big little town."[42]

African Americans are finding more publishing opportunities and recognition from both black and white critics for their work in the short story genre. This long-overdue recognition is evident in the appointment of former Wyoming resident John Edgar Wideman as guest editor for the 1996 edition of *Best American Short Stories*, an annual anthology that reprints the year's best twenty stories as selected by a guest editor; by the 1997 selection of *Epoch* (including short stories by black authors) as the inaugural recipient of the O. Henry Award (an annual Prize Stories anthology) for the American or Canadian magazine having published the best fiction for the year; and by the 1997 selection of Carolyn Ferrell's collection, *Don't Erase Me*, as *Ploughshares*' Zacharis First Book Award.[43]

It is important to note that authors who created stories with western settings represented in their approaches and their renditions the western black short story writer for the past century, an entire short story tradition, and the courage and conviction of those African Americans who ventured to the western United States over the past five centuries. They did not quibble, mince words, shy away from difficult topics or hesitate to take on causes. Although too often ignored, they asserted the rights of blacks more forcefully than their compatriots in the East (sometimes concerned about how whites would view the story), thereby establishing a creative and realistic standard for the portrayal of race issues and endurance. Western African Americans as portrayed in short stories survive, challenge, and encourage a multicultural, inclusive West. That is a fitting tribute to a century of effort.

NOTES

1. This essay was first published in a slightly different version in *The Journal of Big Bend Studies* 10 (1998). We thank the Center for Big Bend Studies at Sul Ross State University for permission to reprint the essay.

2. For information on the history of African Americans in the West see Quintard Taylor, *In Search of the Racial Frontier: African Americans in the American West, 1528–1990* (New York: W. W. Norton, 1998); and Bruce A. Glasrud, *African Americans in the West: A Bibliography of Secondary Studies* (Alpine, Tex.: Center for Big Bend Studies, 1998). By "western" we mean those states one removed westward from the Mississippi River,

including Alaska and Hawaii. We also cover the northern states along the Mississippi River—the First Tier states—as part of this study. Occasionally, in order to point to its history, we consider stories set in the states of the Old Northwest as western and add them to the study.

3. Judy Alter and A. T. Row, "Apologia," *Unbridled Spirits: Short Fiction About Women in the Old West*, edited by Judy Alter and A. T. Row (Fort Worth: Texas Christian University Press, 1994), xviii.

4. Poe's reviews appeared in the 1830s and 1840s and are reprinted in Charles E. May, *Edgar Allan Poe: A Study of the Short Fiction* (Boston: Twayne Publishers, 1991), 118–129; Brander Matthew, *The Philosophy of the Short-Story* (New York: Longmans, Green, 1901).

5. William Peden, "The Black Explosion," *Studies in Short Fiction*, 12 (1975): 231–241; Bill Mullen, "Introduction," *Revolutionary Tales: African American Women's Short Stories, from the First Story to the Present*, edited by Bill Mullen (New York: Laurel, 1995), xxv.

6. In *Anything for Billy*, McMurtry introduced Mesty-Woolah, a seven-foot-tall African who rode a camel and sliced the bad guys. On the issue of white portrayals of blacks, see Aya de Leon, "The Black Detective in the White Mind,"*Armchair Detective*, 25 (1992): 34–39.

7. Sylvia Lyons Render, "Introduction," *The Short Fiction of Charles W. Chesnutt*, edited by Sylvia Lyons Render (Washington, D.C.: Howard University Press, 1974), 3–56; Sterling Brown, "Negro Character as Seen by White Authors," *Journal of Negro Education*, 2 (January 1933): 180–201; Sterling Brown, *Negro Poetry and Drama and the Negro in American Fiction* (New York: Atheneum, 1969), 2; Nick Aaron Ford, "The Negro Author's Use of Propaganda in Imaginative Literature" (unpublished Ph.D. dissertation, State University of Iowa, 1945), 14.

8. Arnold Adoff, "Preface," *Brothers and Sisters: Modern Stories by Black Americans*, edited by Arnold Adoff (New York: Macmillan, 1970). Frequently in searching for western short stories, in an anthology of thirty stories at most two or three would be set west of the Mississippi River.

9. Sterling Brown, Arthur P. Davis, and Ulysses Lee, eds., *The Negro Caravan* (New York: Dryden Press, 1941), 10.

10. Peter Bruck, ed., *The Black American Short Story in the 20th Century: A Collection of Critical Essays* (Amsterdam: Gruner, 1977), 6.

11. Paul Laurence Dunbar, "The Ingrate," *The Strength of Gideon and Other Stories*, (1900; New York: Arno Press, 1969), 87–103; Charles W. Chesnutt, "The Averted Strike," 1899, *The Short Fiction of Charles W. Chesnutt*, edited by Sylvia Lyons Render (Washington, D.C.: Howard University Press, 1974), 383–390.

12. Colleen McElroy, "A Brief Spell by the River," *Jesus and Fat Tuesday, and Other Short Stories* (Berkeley: Creative Arts Book Company, 1987), 1–16; Michael Fultz, " 'The Morning Cometh': African-American Periodicals, Education, and the Black Middle Class, 1900–1930," *Journal of Negro History*, 80 (Summer 1995): 97–112; Pauline E. Hopkins, "'As the Lord Lives, He Is One of Our Mother's Children,'" *Colored American Magazine*, 6 (November 1903): 795–801. It should also be noted that a black midwestern woman—Katherine Williams-Irwin—edited *Half-Century Magazine*. Fultz described nine magazines that published materials for black Americans between 1900 and 1930: *Opportunity*, *The Competitor*, *Colored American Magazine*, *Voice of the Negro*, *Alexander's Magazine*, *Horizon*, *The Crisis*, *Half-Century Magazine*, and *The Messenger*.

13. W.E.B. DuBois, "Jesus Christ in Texas," *Darkwater: Voices from the Veil* (1920; New York: Schocken Books, 1969), 123–133.

14. Cary D. Wintz, "Langston Hughes: A Kansas Poet in the Harlem Renaissance," *Kansas Quarterly*, 7 (1975): 58–71; Mark Scott, "Langston Hughes of Kansas," *Kansas*

History, 3 (Spring 1980): 3–25; Langston Hughes, "The Gun," *Something in Common and Other Stories* (New York: Hill and Wang, 1963), 154–161; Arna Bontemps, "Why I Returned," *Harper's Magazine*, 230 (April 1965): 176–182. Also in *The Old South: "A Summer Tragedy" and Other Stories of the Thirties* (New York: Dodd, Mead, 1973), 1–25.

15. Mary E. Young, "Anita Scott Coleman: A Neglected Harlem Renaissance Writer," *CLA Journal*, 40 (March 1997): 271–287; Anita Scott Coleman, "Rich Man, Poor Man—," *Half-Century Magazine*, 8 (May 1920): 6, 14.

16. Wallace Thurman, *The Blacker the Berry, A Novel of Negro Life* (New York: Macaulay, 1929).

17. Cary D. Wintz, *Black Culture and the Harlem Renaissance* (College Station: Texas A&M University Press, 1992); Margaret Perry, *Silence to the Drums: A Survey of the Literature of the Harlem Renaissance* (Westport, CT: Greenwood Press, 1976); Charles Scruggs, " 'All Dressed Up but No Place to Go': The Black Writer and His Audience During the Harlem Renaissance," *American Literature*, 48 (1976): 543–63.

18. Bruck, *Black American Short Story in the 20th Century*, 7; Langston Hughes, "The Negro Artist and the Racial Mountain," *Nation*, 122 (June 23, 1926): 694; Mullen, *Revolutionary Tales*, xxvii.

19. J. Saunders Redding, "The Negro Writer and American Literature," *Anger, and Beyond: The Negro Writer in the United States*, edited by Herbert Hill (New York: Harper & Row, 1966): 19; James Weldon Johnson, "The Dilemma of the Negro Author," *American Mercury*, 15 (December 1928): 477.

20. James Weldon Johnson, "Negro Authors and White Publishers," *The Crisis*, 36 (July 1929): 228–229.

21. Langston Hughes, *The Ways of White Folks* (1934; New York: Alfred A. Knopf, 1973); Bruck, *Black American Short Story in the 20th Century*, 9.

22. Richard Wright, *Uncle Tom's Children* (1938; New York: Harper & Row, 1965); Richard Wright, "How 'Bigger' Was Born," *Native Son* (1940; New York: Harper & Row, 1966), xxvii.

23. Richard M. Dalfiume, "The Forgotten Years of the Negro Revolution," *Journal of American History*, 55 (June 1968): 90–106; Kristine McCusker, " 'The Forgotten Years' of America's Civil Rights Movement: Wartime Protests at the University of Kansas, 1939–1945," *Kansas History*, 17 (Spring 1994): 26–37.

24. See Donald Pizer, *Twentieth-Century American Literary Naturalism: An Interpretation* (Carbondale: Southern Illinois University Press, 1982); Lee C. Mitchell, *Determined Fictions: American Literary Naturalism* (New York: Columbia University Press, 1989).

25. Ralph Ellison, "Remembering Richard Wright," *Going to the Territory* (New York: Random House, 1986), 199; Ralph Ellison, *Flying Home and Other Stories*, edited by John F. Callahan (New York: Random House, 1996); Chester Himes, *Black on Black: Baby Sister and Selected Writings* (New York: Doubleday, 1973); Chester Himes, *The Collected Stories of Chester Himes* (New York: Thunder's Mouth Press, 1990).

26. Taylor Branch, *Parting the Waters: America in the King Years, 1954–63* (New York: Simon & Schuster, 1988); Ronald Walters, "The Great Plains Sit-in Movement, 1958–60," *Great Plains Quarterly*, 16 (Spring 1996): 85–94; Eldridge Cleaver, *Soul on Ice* (New York: McGraw-Hill, 1968); Eldridge Cleaver, "The Flashlight," *Playboy*, 16 (December 1969): 120–124, 287–302; John R. Posey, "Ticket to Freedom," *Texas Short Fiction: A World in Itself II*, edited by Mike Hennech and Billy Bob Hill (Redmond, Wash.: ALE Publishing, 1995), 203–217.

27. John Oliver Killens, "Introduction: The Smoking Sixties," *Black Short Story Anthology*, edited by Woodie King, Jr. (New York: Columbia University Press, 1972), xiv.

28. Redding, "Negro Writer and American Literature," 19.

29. Al Young, *San Francisco Sunday Examiner and Chronicle* (May 3, 1970), cited in Abraham Chapman, ed., *New Black Voices: An Anthology of Contemporary Afro-American Literature* (New York: New American Library, 1972), 31–32.

30. Terry McMillan, "Introduction," *Breaking Ice: An Anthology of Contemporary African-American Fiction*, edited by Terry McMillan (New York: Viking, 1990), xxi.

31. Mary Helen Washington, "New Lives and New Letters: Black Women Writers at the End of the Seventies," *College English*, 43.1 (1981): 3.

32. Budd Schulberg, ed., *From the Ashes: Voices of Watts* (New York: New American Library, 1969); Budd Schulberg, "Black Phoenix: An Introduction," *The Antioch Review*, 27 (1967): 277–284.

33. Zora Neale Hurston, *The Complete Short Stories* (New York: HarperCollins, 1996); Dorothy West, *The Richer, The Poorer: Stories, Sketches, and Reminiscences* (Garden City: Doubleday, 1996); Alice Childress, *Like One of the Family: Conversations from a Domestic's Life* (Boston: Beacon Press, 1986).

34. Mary Helen Washington, ed., *Black-Eyed Susans: Classic Stories by and About Black Women* (Garden City, N.Y.: Anchor Books, 1975); Mullen, *Revolutionary Tales*; Ann Allen Schockley, ed., *Afro-American Women Writers, 1746–1933: An Anthology and Critical Guide* (New York: Penguin Books, 1988).

35. Ntozake Shange, "Ridin' the Moon in Texas," *Ridin' the Moon in Texas: Word Paintings* (New York: St. Martin's Press, 1987), 5–11; Wanda Coleman, "The Friday Night Shift at the Taco House Blues (Wah-Wah)," *A War of Eyes and Other Stories* (Santa Rosa, Calif.: Black Sparrow Press, 1988), 103–116.

36. Washington, *Black-Eyed Susans*, xv.

37. Washington, *Black-Eyed Susans*, xvii. Emphasis added.

38. DorisJean Austin and Martin Simmons, eds., *Street Lights: Illuminating Tales of the Urban Black Experience* (New York: Penguin Books, 1996). The three stories are "My Father's Son," "The Elixir," and "Oda Rainbow"; they were written by Steven Corbin, Leslie Nia Lewis, and J. R. McKie respectively.

39. Shawn Ruff, ed., *Go the Way Your Blood Beats: An Anthology of Lesbian and Gay Fiction by African-American Writers* (New York: Henry Holt, 1996); Darieck Scott, "This City of Men," *Callaloo*, 17 (1994): 1035–1050; A. Cinque Hicks, "Spice," *Shade: An Anthology of Fiction by Gay Men of African Descent*, edited by Bruce Morrow and Charles H. Rowell (New York: Avon Books, 1996), 1–13; Lisa C. Moore, ed., *Does Your Mama Know? An Anthology of Black Lesbian Coming Out Stories* (Decatur, Ga.: Redbone Press, 1997).

40. John Edgar Wideman, "Preface," *Breaking Ice*, edited by Terry McMillan, vi.

41. Wolfgang Karrer, "Introduction: The History and Signifying Intertextuality of the African American Short Story," *The African American Short Story, 1970 to 1990: A Collection of Critical Essays*, edited by Wolfgang Karrer and Barbara Puschmann-Nalenz (Trier: WVT, 1993): 1.

42. J. California Cooper, *A Piece of Mine* (Navarro, Calif.: Wild Trees Press, 1984), 1.

43. John Edgar Wideman, ed., *The Best American Short Stories, 1996* (Boston: Houghton Mifflin, 1996); Larry Dark, ed., *Prize Stories 1997: The O. Henry Awards* (New York: Anchor Books, 1997), xiii–xiv; "Zacharis Award," *Ploughshares* 23 (Winter 1997–98): 222–224.

Turn of the Century

ESTABLISHING THE TRADITION

Although an African American presence has existed in the West since the sixteenth century, it was not until the latter nineteenth century that blacks settled there in significant numbers. They came seeking new opportunities as ranchers, farmers, soldiers, cowboys, miners, laborers, townspeople; and in the process they adapted, modified, created, and struggled. They lived in every state and territory and formed communities in each. Western African Americans refused to accept white stereotypes, often challenging false white perceptions. For those recently (five to thirty years) released from bondage, their westward movement epitomized the search for freedom promised in the American Dream; they assumed that hard work, loyalty, determination, ethical behavior, knowledge, and trust in God would enable them to persevere and succeed. Of course, they also realized that they needed to acquire new skills, to use the ones they had, and to challenge discrimination when and where it occurred.

At the same time the black presence in the West was increasing, short story authors emerged and established the tradition of capturing the lives and efforts of African Americans in the West. Short stories disclosed the nature of African American thoughts and actions during this period. This section begins with a story about slavery and ends with one about lynching. From beginning to end, these stories demonstrate various ways in which blacks used their skills to gain a foothold, to improve their status, to survive, and to seek justice. Although they realistically portray situations faced by western blacks, the stories, perhaps reflecting the promise of the American Dream, offer optimistic outcomes for western blacks. For example, one story suggests that religious faith can conquer racism (albeit after a black man is lynched).

In Paul Laurence Dunbar's "The Ingrate," a slave uses his newly acquired knowledge to overcome slavery and escape. "The Ingrate" depicts the paternalistic attitude of a slave owner toward his slave as well as the slave's desire for freedom. Mr. Leckler teaches his slave, Josh, to read and write so that the man for whom Josh works will not cheat him when the day's books are prepared. Leckler claims that he does not care if he is cheated, but that he does not want Josh to be denied the portion of earnings that is applied toward the purchase of his freedom. Josh uses his literacy to write a false freedom note and escapes to Canada, where he finds dignity, undergoes a new enthusiasm for life, and desires to help other slaves find freedom. When Leckler learns that Josh is now a military sergeant, he considers him an "ingrate" for misusing the reading and writing skills he was taught. This story uses irony to show that Leckler's "righteous" sense of principle is immoral and cruel.

Colleen McElroy's "A Brief Spell by the River" is set in Kansas and, more than any other story in this anthology, represents a western genre story. It takes place in a valley near Big Creek River, where Pap Thacher (undoubtedly a reference to the Exodust leader, "Pap" Singleton) has encouraged some blacks heading west to settle and develop a small community. The story is about the relationship between fifteen-year-old Cressy and the legendary Sam Packer (referring to Sam Bass). Cressy's grandfather warns her when she leaves the valley to be careful of violence against blacks. He tells her that folks "still remember how it is to put a branding iron on black skin." One day a mysterious man meets Cressy near the woods and rapes her. Amidst rumors of train robberies, the man continues to meet Cressy in the woods and have sex with her. The mysterious man, now the father of Cressy's four-year-old son and of the child with which she is pregnant, turns out to be Sam Packer. This story adds a folkloric quality to historical facts with its "what if" scenario for the personal life of a well-known outlaw. It blends history with myth to suggest that outlaws may have engaged in behaviors not represented in historical accounts.

"An Adventure in the Big Horn Mountains" also uses a historical background to the plot and characters of the story. Its author, Eugene Frierson, was a squadron sergeant-major in the 10th Cavalry of the U.S. Army, one of the soldiers known as "Buffalo Soldiers." In "An Adventure in the Big Horn Mountains," Frierson uses a framed narrative with several episodic adventures. Set in 1893, the story concerns a squadron of the 10th Cavalry stationed at Fort Custer, Montana. The squadron participates in a "practice march" to offer young soldiers experience. They march forty-five miles southwest of the fort to the Big Horn Mountains and return through Little Horn Valley by the Custer Battlefield, an adventure planned to take ten days. The narrator and two other men receive permission to explore a snowcapped mountain. Although not technically part of the march, their wanderings offer the soldiers the spirit they need for success in the Army, one that allows them to understand that danger is inevitable and that they can face it. The soldiers return to their comrades, feeling that they have become more than new recruits as the result of their experiences on the journey to the snowcapped mountain. Blacks, too, Frierson indicates, can overcome obstacles and become first-rate soldiers.

Charles Chesnutt's "The Averted Strike," set in the Midwest, is an allegory with lead characters named Strong and Walker. The story is told from the point of view of Strong, a high-ranking white administrator at the Strongville Rubber Works mill.

His daughter wants to take a friend on a tour of the mill, and he calculates how much time and money the visit will cost his corporation. Strong is considering appointing Walker, a black man, as foreman, and the other workers become disgruntled because they do not want a black man as their boss, and they threaten to strike. Strong explains to the white workers that they are asking him to deny the job to the best qualified man. He tells them that he is even more inclined to choose Walker because the other men would deny Walker the job solely on the basis of race. In the midst of Strong's deliberations, the mill catches on fire and he sees his daughter caught in the conflagration. Strong says he will give a huge monetary award to whoever can save his daughter and her friend. Acting boldly, Walker saves the girls and Strong calls him a friend. The other workers ask Strong to forget their comments about Walker and hire him as foreman. He becomes foreman and gains stock in the company but tells Strong he was only doing his duty. Thus Chesnutt seems to suggest that through good deeds, blacks can overcome racism—a vast contrast to the protest fiction of later black western writers.

Pauline Hopkins, in "As the Lord Lives, He Is One of Our Mother's Children," presents a lynching as the core of her story, told from the point of view of a white minister who plans a sermon that preaches a sympathetic answer to the "Negro question." While looking out the window, he witnesses a mob lynching a black man. Shortly afterward, Gentleman Jim, alias George Stone, comes to live with the minister, who discovers that Stone is the man whom the town has accused of helping the man they lynched murder a white man. Stone says that he and Jones had come west from Wilmington, North Carolina, where they were driven out because they were black. The minister's dilemma is whether to turn Stone in or hide him from the brutal mob. Later, a tree falls over a railroad track as a train approaches. Stone moves the tree, but in the process kills himself while saving the trainload of people. Jones and Gentleman Jim are publicly exonerated when the real murderer is found. As the minister preaches Jim's funeral sermon, the townspeople repent of their racist behavior when they hear the reverend say, "As the Lord lives, He is one of our mother's children." Once more a good deed leads to redemption; nonetheless, in Hopkins's story, both black characters are dead, one a victim of Judge Lynch.

As these stories illustrate, at the turn of the century even those blacks who ventured west with hopes of freedom met discrimination and struggled to survive. And survive they did: one escapes slavery, one escapes a lynching, others achieve acceptance through adventures in the military, one becomes a foreman. The stories also indicate the dilemma of the black author: for whom, black or white, to write the stories? Perhaps to entice white readers, these black authors sometimes use white narrators. Yet they realistically portray aspects of black life in the West and make their points carefully. To accomplish this, instead of confronting the reader, they use irony, and seemingly approach race-related issues with tongue in cheek.

The Ingrate

PAUL LAURENCE DUNBAR

Mr. Leckler was a man of high principle. Indeed, he himself had admitted it at times to Mrs. Leckler. She was often called into counsel with him. He was one of those large-souled creatures with a hunger for unlimited advice, upon which he never acted. Mrs. Leckler knew this, but like the good, patient little wife that she was, she went on paying her poor tribute of advice and admiration. Today her husband's mind was particularly troubled—as usual, too, over a matter of principle. Mrs. Leckler came at his call.

"Mrs. Leckler," he said, "I am troubled in my mind. I—in fact, I am puzzled over a matter that involves either the maintaining or relinquishing of a principle."

"Well, Mr. Leckler?" said his wife interrogatively.

"If I had been a scheming, calculating Yankee, I should have been rich now; but all my life I have been too generous and confiding. I have always let principle stand between me and my interests." Mr. Leckler took himself all too seriously to be conscious of his pun, and went on: "Now this is a matter in which my duty and my principles seem to conflict. It stands thus: Josh has been doing a piece of plastering for Mr. Eckley over in Lexington, and from what he says, I think that city rascal has misrepresented the amount of work to me and so cut down the pay for it. Now, of course, I should not care, the matter of a dollar or two being nothing to me; but it is a very different matter when we consider poor Josh." There was deep pathos in Mr. Leckler's tone. "You know Josh is anxious to buy his freedom, and I allow him a part of whatever he makes; so you see it's he that's affected. Every dollar that he is cheated out of cuts off just so much from his earnings, and puts farther away his hope of emancipation."

If the thought occurred to Mrs. Leckler that, since Josh received only about one tenth of what he earned, the advantage of just wages would be quite as much her husband's as the slave's, she did not betray it, but met the naïve reasoning with the question, "But where does the conflict come in, Mr. Leckler?"

"Just here. If Josh knew how to read and write and cipher—"

"Mr. Leckler, are you crazy!"

"Listen to me, my dear, and give me the benefit of your judgment. This is a very momentous question. As I was about to say, if Josh knew these things, he could protect himself from cheating when his work is at too great a distance for me to look after it for him."

"But teaching a slave—"

"Yes, that's just what is against my principles. I know how public opinion and the law look at it. But my conscience rises up in rebellion every time I think of that poor black man being cheated out of his earnings. Really, Mrs. Leckler, I think I may trust to Josh's discretion and secretly give him such instruction as will permit him to protect himself."

"Well, of course, it's just as you think best," said his wife.

"I knew you would agree with me," he returned. "It's such a comfort to take counsel with you, my dear!" And the generous man walked out onto the veranda, very well satisfied with himself and his wife, and prospectively pleased with Josh. Once he murmured to himself, "I'll lay for Eckley next time."

Josh, the subject of Mr. Leckler's charitable solicitations, was the plantation plasterer. His master had given him his trade, in order that he might do whatever such work was needed about the place; but he became so proficient in his duties, having also no competition among the poor whites, that he had grown to be in great demand in the country thereabout. So Mr. Leckler found it profitable, instead of letting him do chores and field work in his idle time, to hire him out to neighboring farms and planters. Josh was a man of more than ordinary intelligence; and when he asked to be allowed to pay for himself by working overtime, his master readily agreed—for it promised more work to be done, for which he could allow the slave just what he pleased. Of course, he knew now that when the black man began to cipher this state of affairs would be changed; but it would mean such an increase of profit from the outside that he could afford to give up his own little peculations. Anyway, it would be many years before the slave could pay the two thousand dollars, which price he had set upon him. Should he approach that figure, Mr. Leckler felt it just possible that the market in slaves would take a sudden rise.

When Josh was told of his master's intention, his eyes gleamed with pleasure, and he went to his work with the zest of long hunger. He proved a remarkably apt pupil. He was indefatigable in doing the tasks assigned him. Even Mr. Leckler, who had great faith in his plasterer's ability, marveled at the speed which he had acquired the three R's. He did not know that on one of his many trips a free negro had given Josh the rudimentary tools of learning, and that ever since the slave had been adding to his store of learning by poring over signs and every bit of print that he could spell out. Neither was Josh so indiscreet as to intimate to his benefactor that he had been anticipated in his good intentions. It was in this way, working and learning, that a year passed away, and Mr. Leckler thought that his object had been accomplished. He could safely trust Josh to protect his own interests, and so he thought that it was quite time that his servant's education should cease.

"You know, Josh," he said, "I have already gone against my principles and against the law for your sake, and of course a man can't stretch his conscience too far, even to help another who's being cheated; but I reckon you can take care of yourself now."

"Oh, yes, suh, I reckon I kin," said Josh.

"And it wouldn't do for you to be seen with any books about you now."

"Oh, no, suh, su't'n'y not." He didn't intend to be seen with any books about him.

It was just now that Mr. Leckler saw the good results of all he had done, and his heart was full of a great joy, for Eckley had been building some additions to his house and sent for Josh to do the plastering for him. The owner admonished his slave, took him over a few examples to freshen his memory, and sent him forth with glee. When the job was done, there was a discrepancy of two dollars in what Mr. Eckley offered for it and the price which accrued from Josh's measurements. To the employer's surprise, the black man went over the figures with him and convinced him of the incorrectness of the payment—and the additional two dollars were turned over.

"Some o' Leckler's work," said Eckley, "teaching a nigger to cipher! Close-fisted old reprobate—I've a mind to have the law on him."

Mr. Leckler heard the story with great glee. "I laid for him that time—the old fox." But to Mrs. Leckler he said, "You see, my dear wife, my rashness in teaching Josh to figure for himself is vindicated. See what he has saved for himself."

"What did he save?" asked the little woman indiscreetly.

Her husband blushed and stammered for a moment, and then replied, "Well, of course, it was only twenty cents saved to him, but to a man buying his freedom every cent counts; and after all, it is not the amount, Mrs. Leckler, it's the principle of the thing."

"Yes," said the lady meekly.

Unto the body it is easy for the master to say, "Thus far shalt thou go, and no farther." Gyves, chains, and fetters will enforce that command. But what master shall say unto the mind, "Here do I set the limit of your acquisition. Pass it not"? Who shall put gyves upon the intellect, or fetter the movement of thought? Joshua Leckler., as custom denominated him, had tasted of the forbidden fruit, and his appetite had grown by what it fed on. Night after night he crouched in his lonely cabin, by the blaze of a fat pine brand, poring over the few books that he had been able to secure and smuggle in. His fellow servants alternately laughed at him and wondered why he did not take a wife. But Joshua went on his way. He had no time for marrying or for love; other thoughts had taken possession of him. He was being swayed by ambitions other than the mere fathering of slaves for his master. To him his slavery was deep night. What wonder, then, that he should dream, and that through the ivory gate should come to him the forbidden vision of freedom? To own himself, to be master of his hands, feet, of his whole body—something would clutch at his heart as he thought of it, and the breath would come hard between his lips. But he met his master with an impassive face, always silent, always docile; and Mr. Leckler congratulated himself that so valuable and intelligent a slave should be at the same time so tractable. Usually intelligence in a slave meant discontent; but not so with Josh. Who more content than he? He remarked to his wife: "You see, my dear, this is what comes of treating even a nigger right."

Meanwhile the white hills of the North were beckoning to the chattel, and the north winds were whispering to him to be a chattel no longer. Often the eyes that looked away to where freedom lay were filled with a wistful longing that was tragic in its intensity, for they saw the hardships and the difficulties between the slave and his goal and, worst of all, an iniquitous law—liberty's compromise with bondage, that rose like a stone wall between him and hope—a law that degraded every free-thinking man to the level of a slave catcher. There it loomed up before him, formidable, impregnable, insurmountable. He measured it in all its terribleness, and paused. But on the other side there was liberty; and one day when he was away at work, a voice came out of the woods and whispered to him "Courage!"—and on that night the shadows beckoned him as the white hills had done, and the forest called to him, "Follow."

"It seems to me that Josh might have been able to get home tonight," said Mr. Leckler, walking up and down his veranda, "but I reckon it's just possible that he got through too late to catch a train." In the morning he said, "Well, he's not here yet; he must have had to do some extra work. If he doesn't get here by evening, I'll run up there."

In the evening, he did take the train for Joshua's place of employment, where he learned that his slave had left the night before. But where could he have gone? That no one knew, and for the first time it dawned upon his master that Josh had run away. He raged; he fumed; but nothing could be done until morning, and all the time Leckler knew that the most valuable slave on his plantation was working his way toward the North and freedom. He did not go back home, but paced the floor all night long. In the early dawn he hurried out and the hounds were put on the fugitive's track. After some nosing around they set off toward a stretch of woods. In a few minutes they came yelping back, pawing their noses and rubbing their heads against the ground. They had found the trail, but Josh had played the old slave trick of filling his tracks with cayenne pepper. The dogs were soothed and taken deeper into the wood to find the trail. They soon took it up again, and dashed away with low bays. The scent led them directly to a little wayside station about six miles distant. Here it stopped. Burning with the chase, Mr. Leckler hastened to the station agent. Had he seen such a negro? Yes, he had taken the northbound train two nights before.

"But why did you let him go without a pass?" almost screamed the owner.

"I didn't," replied the agent. "He had a written pass, signed James Leckler, and I let him go on it."

"Forged, forged!" yelled the master. "He wrote it himself."

"Humph!" said the agent. "How was I to know that? Our niggers round here don't know how to write."

Mr. Leckler suddenly bethought him to hold his peace. Josh was probably now in the arms of some northern abolitionist, and there was nothing to be done now but advertise; and the disgusted master spread his notices broadcast before starting for home. As soon as he arrived at his house, he sought his wife and poured out his griefs to her.

"You see, Mrs. Leckler, this is what comes of my goodness of heart. I taught that nigger to read and write, so that he could protect himself—and look how he uses his knowledge. Oh, the ingrate, the ingrate! The very weapon which I give him to defend himself against others he turns upon me. Oh, it's awful—awful! I've always been too confiding. Here's the most valuable nigger on my plantation gone— gone, I tell you—and through my own kindness. It isn't his value, though, I'm thinking so much about. I could stand his loss, if it wasn't for the principle of the thing, the base ingratitude he has shown me. Oh, if I ever lay hands on him again!" Mr. Leckler closed his lips and clenched his fist with an eloquence that laughed at words.

Just at this time, in one of the underground railway stations, six miles north of the Ohio, an old Quaker was saying to Josh, "Lie still—thee'll be perfectly safe there. Here comes John Trader, our local slave catcher, but I will parley with him and send him away. Thee need not fear. None of thy brethren who have come to us have ever been taken back to bondage.—Good evening, Friend Trader!" and Josh heard the old Quaker's smooth voice roll on, while he lay back half smothering in a bag, among other bags of corn and potatoes.

It was after ten o'clock that night when he was thrown carelessly into a wagon and driven away to the next station, twenty-five miles to the northward. And by such stages, hiding by day and traveling by night, helped by a few of his own people who were blessed with freedom, and always by the good Quakers wherever found, he made his way into Canada. And on one never-to-be-forgotten morning he stood up, straightened himself, breathed God's blessed air, and knew himself free!

To Joshua Leckler this life in Canada was all new and strange. It was a new thing for him to feel himself a man and to have his manhood recognized by the whites with whom he came into free contact. It was new, too, this receiving the full measure of his worth in work. He went to his labor with a zest that he had never known before, and he took a pleasure in the very weariness it brought him. Ever and anon there came to his ears the cries of his brethren in the South. Frequently he met fugitives who, like himself, had escaped from bondage; and the harrowing tales that they told him made him burn to do something for those whom he had left behind him. But these fugitives and the papers he read told him other things. They said that the spirit of freedom was working in the United States, and already men were speaking out boldly in behalf of the manumission of the slaves; already there was a growing army behind that noble vanguard, Sumner, Phillips, Douglass,

Garrison. He heard the names of Lucretia Mott and Harriet Beecher Stowe, and his heart swelled, for on the dim horizon he saw the first faint streaks of dawn.

So the years passed. Then from the surcharged clouds a flash of lightning broke, and there was the thunder of cannon and the rain of lead over the land. From his home in the North he watched the storm as it raged and wavered, now threatening the North with its awful power, now hanging dire and dreadful over the South. Then suddenly from out the fray came a voice like the trumpet tone of God to him: "Thou and thy brothers are free!" Free, free, with the freedom not cherished by the few alone, but for all that had been bound. Free, with the freedom not torn from the secret night, but open to the light of heaven.

When the first call for colored soldiers came, Joshua Leckler hastened down to Boston, and enrolled himself among those who were willing to fight to maintain their freedom. On account of his ability to read and write and his general intelligence, he was soon made an orderly sergeant. His regiment had already taken part in an engagement before the public roster of this band of Uncle Sam's niggers, as they were called, fell into Mr. Leckler's hands. He ran his eye down the column of names. It stopped at that of Joshua Leckler, Sergeant, Company F. He handed the paper to Mrs. Leckler with his finger on the place.

"Mrs. Leckler," he said, "this is nothing less than a judgment on me for teaching a nigger to read and write. I disobeyed the law of my state and, as a result, not only lost my nigger, but furnished the Yankees with a smart officer to help them fight the South. Mrs. Leckler, I have sinned—and been punished. But I am content, Mrs. Leckler; it all came through my kindness of heart—and your mistaken advice. But, oh, that ingrate, that ingrate!"

A Brief Spell by the River

COLLEEN McELROY

Early that morning before the sun could clear the line of scrub maple just east of the crab apple orchard, Cressy Pruitt had stepped into the shadowy area behind the hen house where the old biddy hen, Eelly, liked to nest. Cressy had shooed Eelly away from her cache of eggs, collected all but two of them and placed them in her apron pocket. Eelly cackled and defiantly settled back onto the two eggs. As Cressy walked through the barnyard, she'd selected a fat, lazy brown chicken, swooped it up with one hand and held it at arm's length. Mama Lou had already decided on a stew pot for supper and Cressy knew that taking one hen meant the others would get jumpy. The birds skittered in all directions. Before their harsh, frightened clucking could reach its full pitch, before Titbeak, the rooster, could squawk a second warning cackle, she'd snapped the hen's neck.

Later, as she walked along the edge of the railroad tracks, she noticed the red taint of blood staining the grit beneath her fingernails. Cressy frowned, then spit on her wide, blunt fingers and rubbed them through the woolly mass of hair behind her left ear where one of her thick braids had pulled loose. She'd have to redo her hair before she returned from Miz Greenlove's with the goose grease and witch hazel Mama Lou had sent her to fetch. But she was only half a mile from Big Creek River and she could wash her hands real good once she got there.

In the fringe of trees bordering the railroad tracks, she heard the cry of a redstart or a warbler. Cressy paused for a moment. The bird repeated its call. She heard a cow mooing in the pasture beyond the thicket of trees. Insects buzzed a shaded pool of stagnant water just beyond the gravelled edge of the railroad hump. There were other sounds, barely audible and indistinct. The bird trilled again and she heard a rustle of leaves as it left the tree area. She decided it must have been a redstart when she saw it flit into the next patch of elms, its flight as skitterish as a butterfly's.

She swung the croker sack of potatoes and onions onto her other shoulder. "Don't drag that sack through the mud," Mama Lou had warned. "Miz Greenlove won't take no chewed up roots in trade and your papa needs that medicine. He got the croup real bad."

Miz Greenlove's house was west of Pap Thacher's place. Miz Greenlove and Pap Thacher were the oldest folks in the valley. Some said Miz Greenlove was nearly ninety, but no one knew exactly how old Pap Thacher was. He'd always looked as grizzly and rusty black as he did now. Mama Lou said folks talked about Pap Thacher clear down in South Carolina. Pap Thacher had been one of the first black freemen in the valley. Twice he'd been run out of the valley by Quantrill's raiders; early in the Civil War, he'd helped slaves cross the valley on their way north to Canada, and when Cressy's family had moved into the valley from Alabama, the year Cressy was born and two years after the Civil War, Pap Thacher had helped them settle onto the craggy ten acres they now farmed. He was a wily old man and didn't really believe any presidential papers could keep one lone black man safe from the rebel raiders who'd crossed the Missouri border all too often. So he'd carefully culled a thin string of families from the many black people fleeing north or heading west across the Plains states. Six other families now farmed land around Pap Thacher's place and black folks dotted the shores of Big Creek River from Granville to Deepwater.

Pap Thacher knew everyone and everyone knew Miz Greenlove because at one time or another, everyone, including Pap Thacher, had been sick enough to visit Miz Greenlove for medicine. Sometimes Mama Lou just sent Cressy to Miz Greenlove's with food, but sometimes Cressy had to go fetch medicine like everyone else. At any rate, Cressy went to Miz Greenlove's every week and every week Mama Lou warned her to be careful.

For Cressy, the trip to Miz Greenlove's was a time for her to forget all the chores she had at home. She stepped onto the iron rail and for the next quarter of a mile walked the hot ribbon of tracks, balancing her pace against the bouncing weight of the croker sack and the burning strip of metal that connected all the towns behind her to Sedalia to the east and St. Joseph to the north. Then she felt the rumble of the afternoon train vibrate against her bare feet. Cressy walked the rails for a few more yards before she hopped clear of the cross-ties and gravel bed. She could hear the echo of the great lumbering thing as it entered the tunnel near Pap Thacher's farm. Cressy walked over to a fallen tree, sat down and waited. She swung the croker sack onto the ground in front of her feet and picked a few of the bright buttercups growing in a clump just behind the tree trunk. By the time she'd gathered five or six of the flowers, measuring each stem to make sure they were all the same length, the train was out of the tunnel and heading up the gorge toward the hill where she sat. She cocked her head, waiting for the whistle that signalled the train's journey across Big Creek River. The pulsing throb of the driving wheels let her know that the train had gathered speed. She could even see the billows of smoke as the engine plowed toward the uphill grade, but the whistle was silent.

Then she heard the gunshots.

They were muffled at first, but as the train drew nearer, she heard seven or eight shots in rapid succession. Cressy stood up. All of the sounds around her seemed to be sucked in to the space between the train tracks. She saw the engine slice through the shadows that marked the thicket of trees where she'd heard the redstart, then it barrelled past her, its funnel belching puffs of black smoke as it headed up the line toward Sedalia or St. Joseph. But there was no face in the cab window and no one pulled the whistle as the train sped by. She heard another gunshot, the sound so close she jumped, clutching the flowers until one or two of the stems broke. Then she saw him. A tall white man crawling the rim of the boxcar halfway down the length of the train. When he stood up, she could see the shotgun in his hand, long and evil as a snake.

The backwash of wind from the train lifted the edge of her cotton skirt. This movement must have drawn his attention, because at that moment he stood straight and stared at her. Cressy did not move. The whoosh of wind lifted her skirts again, this time pulling the hem from her dusty ankles and bare toes almost to the tops of her knees. The black-clad figure lifted his hat, nodded his head, then turned, dropped to his knees and swung into the car through a door on the other side of the train. But for that second, Cressy was sure his eyes had stared clear into her soul. Almost as soon as he'd disappeared, she heard more gunshots. Another figure loomed up over the edge of the first three passenger cars. Cressy heard someone shout, then a scream and more gunshots. She grabbed the croker sack and ran. She didn't stop running until she'd reached the footbridge at Big Creek River.

She didn't think her knees would stop trembling, but her chest was pumping air so hard, she had to stop. She fell to the ground at the edge of the creek and leaned forward to scoop water into her hands. That's when she realized she was still clutching the flowers. The reflection of her sweaty black face and that scraggly bunch of flowers trembling in her clenched fist caused her to laugh. She laughed so hard, she rocked back on her heels and toppled over. Then she released the flowers, righted herself into a kneeling position and looked into the water again. She was still laughing softly, but this time the face was familiar.

"Look at those little round cheeks," Mama Lou would say. "And that mouth. Lips stuck out like a poke-mouthed trout sucking scat flies," she'd laugh.

Cressy crossed her eyes, wrinkled her broad black nose and blew up her cheeks until they were round as fat purple plums. She grinned at the dusky image unfolding on the water's surface, then tried the face again. When she'd eased the tight knot in her stomach, she leaned forward and rippled the water to clear the scum. She was about to scoop a handful of the clear water when she saw the long thin line worming its way downstream. It was as bright red as a ribbon and Cressy remembered how she'd seen blood seep from the deer Papa had shot last winter. He'd caught it off guard sipping water from Indian Pond and when it fell, it had landed in the marshy shallows of the pond. Cressy remembered how the current had pulled the blood away from the body and how it had trailed into the deep part of the water like a finger of bright red vine.

She looked upstream. At the base of the railroad trestle, there was a clump of couch grass, its spiky blades mildewing at the edge of the wash. There, the line of blood muddied the water into a deeper shade of red. She squinted. The grass was dark and solid, waving slightly under the force of the river's current. Then she heard the horses.

Cressy was already into the trees on the other side of the footbridge when the men rounded the corner. She could see them clearly, but unless they moved to the middle of the footbridge, she was well hidden.

"Down here," one of the men called. The others followed him, one of them leading a riderless horse.

"I don't see him, Bradshaw," another yelled. Then Cressy recognized the man who'd stared at her from the top of the train.

The horses stopped and the men leaned forward. Cressy couldn't be sure how many there were. She hadn't learned to do her figures too well and she really had trouble anytime someone rushed her. But she recognized the man from the train and she knew where those men had come from.

Pap Thacher had worked on the railroad when it was being built. He'd told her how the train had to slow down when it reached the spur about two miles down the line. "That's when they got to make their move," he'd said. "East to Sedalia so they can dump the cattle heading for Kansas City, or north to St. Joseph. Up there in St. Joseph, they got a big de-pot. But they got to figure out which way they gonna go when they reach that spur down yonder by Big Creek."

Pap Thacher had told Cressy that the train slowed down enough when it reached the spur to allow a man to hop on or off. Cressy was sure the men had jumped the train down by the spur, and now they'd doubled back looking for whoever made that bloody line slide down the middle of the river.

"Bradshaw, you move on down there a piece," the man with the shotgun yelled. "Me and Clint gonna check further up."

Before they could swing their horses around, another man, the one leading the riderless horse, waved a purple scarf and yelled to them. He was standing at the base of the railroad trestle and Cressy knew he'd found what they were looking for. The others moved toward the trestle, but the man Cressy recognized swung off his horse and kneeled by the spot where she'd been only a few minutes before. The man's horse blocked her view, but when he stood up, she could see his head—that black wide-brimmed hat, the mustache, long and sleek, hanging to the edge of his chin, and those eyes narrowed to a slit. He was looking across the river, peering at the trail that led away from the footbridge.

The other men called to him again. Cressy could see them lift the limp figure of a man from the grassy bog. They propped him onto the horse and called to the man standing by the river bank. He waved to them but did not turn his head away from the trees where Cressy was hiding. She held her breath. Then she saw him swing back onto his horse. And she saw the tattered bunch of buttercups in his hand. He lifted his hat in her direction, smiled, replaced the hat and moved toward the marshy spot at the base of the trestle. Cressy snatched up the croker sack and ran. This time, she did not stop until she'd reached the porch of Miz Greenlove's house.

The whole valley was buzzing with the news of the train robbery. Some said the men had killed everyone on the train, while others said all of the robbers had been killed. A few even talked about how the train had been blown up before it left the tunnel at North Forks. Cressy didn't say a word. She knew better than to interrupt her papa when he was talking. Even though she was fifteen and "pret-near a woman," as Mama Lou was always saying, she knew her papa would swat her backsides before he'd let her sass him. But Cressy had seen the men and she closed her ears when she heard folks saying how many of them had been killed.

Pap Thacher took the buckboard over to Pittsville and talked to some of his railroad friends. He came back two days later and let everyone know that only one person had been killed on the train. "A young buck from Texas," Pap Thacher told them. "I hear tell he'd been causing trouble anyways. One of them fool Rebels still bragging about Sherman and how he's gonna make his darkies work twice as hard as his papa did."

All the old folks said um-hum and Lord-Lord and Thank-you-Jesus, so Cressy knew they didn't hardly mind hearing that man was dead. Pap Thacher's story shut up those who wanted to say everybody on the train had been killed and nobody paid any attention to that business about the train being blown up anyway, but Cressy was the only one who knew what happened to the robbers.

"They wanted in six states," Pap Thacher said. "Tell me they been robbing trains since they was nigh on to twelve years old."

"Tell me them James boys come back," Miz Ada's boy said. "Brung some of Isom Dart's boys with them."

Pap Thacher glowered at him. Everyone knew how Pap Thacher felt about Isom Dart. Pap Thacher lived by himself now. His wife had been dead for five years. His oldest son had been killed in a brush war up in the Dakota mining territory, and his only other son had run off to join the black outlaw, Isom Dart.

"Naw," Pap Thacher spat. "Weren't none of them more than ten or twelve years old. White bucks. Half growed, I hear."

Cressy smiled and counted buttercups.

But for the next few weeks, Mama Lou crossed her thick black arms over her chest and wouldn't let her go to Miz Greenlove's. Mama Lou was Cressy's grandmother. Cressy's mother had died the year she was born, when it was too cold to even find firewood, and Mama Lou would let Cressy do most anything she wanted to do. Cressy's papa yelled a lot and sometimes took a willow switch to her, but Mama Lou told her she looked too much like her mother for her papa to really get mad at her. Still, they both kept her away from Miz Greenlove's after the Wichita-Sedalia/St. Joseph train was robbed.

"Hear they still hanging round down by the spur," Mama Lou said, but after a new moon had passed, Cressy made the trip the way she always did and Mama Lou warned her to keep the croker sack out of the mud the way she always did.

Cressy thought she'd nearly forgotten the man with the shotgun until Mama Lou and Papa took her to Granville. They didn't go to Granville very often, so just the thought of going into a store or walking down the street where the houses were lined up against the road like buckboards when the travelling preacher set up his tent at North Forks, made her so excited Mama Lou threatened to leave her at home. Cressy tried to keep herself calm all morning, but by the time Papa had the horse harnessed to the wagon, she'd had to cross one foot over the other and knot her dress up in her hands so she wouldn't leap up on the seat before Mama Lou got comfortable.

They'd been in town nearly all day when Papa took her to Applegate's Feed and Grain store. Papa was buying a new curb bit for the hinny mule when she wandered down the street. If Papa had been paying attention, he would have told her to go back and sit in the wagon with Mama Lou. "Don't be forgetting who you are," Papa always told her whenever they went to town. "Folks don't think no more about stringing you up like a chicken than they do about getting up every morning. They still remember how it is to put a branding iron on black skin."

But Papa was busy looking at a box full of saddle rings, so she'd wandered down the street. She was staring at some pictures on the wall outside of the saloon when she saw his face. A white woman came to the door and fanned herself. When she saw Cressy looking at the pictures, she said, "Don't you be talking to none of those men, gal. They don't know good from bad. I reckon they shoot little darkies like you for practice," the woman laughed.

Cressy stared at the man's face. His picture was set dead center of a group of pictures, but none of the other men had a mustache as long as his and none of them had eyes that cut straight through her. She knew it was him even without the wide hat and shotgun. The woman began to tell her what all of the men had done.

"That one robbed a bank. And that one killed forty men over in Abilene. That one rode clear from Texas to Wyoming just to shoot a lawman. Think they'd have enough marshals in Texas. And that one, the one with the buck teeth, he done run clear out of new trouble. Now he's trying to make money on other folks' trouble." The woman held her stomach and fanned even faster, laughing at Cressy's wide-eyed stare.

Just then, Papa called her back to the feed store, his arms folded across his chest and his stocky black figure planted in the middle of the walkway like those tree stumps he was always pulling out of the fields.

"I got to go," Cressy told the woman.

"Don't you want to hear about them others?" the woman asked. Her finger was inching closer to the picture of the man Cressy had seen holding buttercups down by Big Creek River.

Cressy shook her head. "My papa be real mad if I don't come directly," she said. She took one last look at the picture, then walked away.

Papa yelled at her all the way home, and the next week Mama Lou said Papa didn't even want her to go to Miz Greenlove's cause she was so hardheaded, but after Mama Lou made her promise to be careful, she sent her to Miz Greenlove's anyway.

Cressy knew Mama Lou was watching her, so she hoisted the croker sack onto her shoulder and held the end of it with both hands. As soon as she'd rounded the bend in the road, she relaxed. She had just reached the clearing near Big Creek River when she remembered Mama Lou's warning. But it was a quiet day. She'd passed the edge of the fields, walked the length of railroad tracks and turned into the woods without causing even a flutter in the movements of the small animals and birds that made their home in the valley. Since the robbery, she'd learned to cross the river quickly and no matter how thirsty she became, she never stopped for a drink. When Cressy reached the other end of the footbridge, she turned and looked at the opposite shore.

She didn't hear him. He was just there, the air filled with the pungent odor of sweat, horseflesh and tobacco.

She knew who it was before she turned around. He had one hand on the horse's bridle and the other, extended toward her, was clutching a cluster of yellow flowers. The man was smiling. Cressy shifted her feet in the loose dirt of the path. She stared past him into the trees, the bushes beside the path and the dense woods beyond them.

"Ain't nobody," the man said. "Just me."

Cressy's head jerked as she tried to shy away from the sound of his voice, but his eyes held her still. He stabbed the air with the flowers, thrusting them to her as if she hadn't seen them. Cressy shook her head. The man sighed and dropped the horse's reins. He moved forward. Cressy moved back a step. It was as if her movement had startled him as much as his voice had startled her. They were both still for a moment, then the man threw back his head and laughed.

Cressy stared at him. She hadn't heard so much noise since the last time Mama Lou had taken her to the revival meeting at the travelling preacher's tent. A host of wood sparrows swirled away from the trees and squirrels chattered in the uppermost branches as the sound of his laughter billowed into the air like wash on a clothesline. When the man laughed, his mustache moved away from his lips in half circles like two thin black slivers of a dark moon. As abruptly as he had started, he stopped, swallowing the sound in large gulps as if he'd needed to swallow a hunk of dry corn bread. Then he looked at the flowers in his hand, grinned and tossed them in the bushes beside the path.

As he lifted his hat and wiped the sweat from his forehead where the band had bleached a ridge into his skin, Cressy turned to run. Before she'd managed three steps, he grabbed her around the waist and pulled her against him. She swung the croker sack over her head and heard it thunk as it slammed into his back. The man did not flinch. Instead he grinned. Cressy hit him again, swinging the sack over her shoulder and letting it take a full arc towards the small of his back. When she raised it the third time, he said, "Stop it," his voice as deep and strong as her papa's when he worked the horses around the tree stumps. Cressy let her arm go limp.

The man pulled the croker sack from her hand, then lifted her off the ground. He carried her easily, one hand around her waist, the other under her knees. Cressy felt her stomach churning up into her throat. The man smiled, his eyes never leaving her face. When they reached the bushes, he slowly eased her to the ground. Cressy wanted to move, to run, but she couldn't remember how. The man took off his hat and vest. Then he pulled the end of his shirt from his pants.

Cressy heard a small sound, like an animal mewing. The man put his hand over her mouth. "Hush," he said. Then he began to unbutton her blouse.

Cressy wanted to hide. No matter how many ways she moved her hands, they would not cover her body. The man moaned and drew her skirt up over her waist. She thought he would kill her. She wanted to die, to close her eyes and wake up on another morning in her own pallet in the corner of Mama Lou's room. But nothing was that easy. For that time, while the man pressed her against the prickly underbrush, she knew no other sound except that of his breathing. He smelled of tobacco and liniment, the dusty smell of horses who have run too long under the oil of saddle leather. He smelled of strong swamp smells like the trails possums leave when you surprise them at night. Cressy's stomach filled her throat and her mouth burned with the taste of bile as she heaved into the tangle of weeds beside her head. The man groaned and lay still. When he felt Cressy begin to heave again, he kneeled beside her and wiped the sour fluid from her lips with the tail of his shirt. Then he moved away. Cressy kept her eyes closed. She could hear him pulling and tugging at the rough material he wore, then she felt a damp coolness fall onto her bare chest and heard him move away.

Long after he'd gone, she opened her eyes. The buttercups lay against her bare black skin like the light gray moths she sometimes found in the morning lying on the dark wood of the kitchen table. Cressy turned away from the ugly pool of vomit next to her head and cried softly. Finally, she limped to the river and washed herself. She pulled the stickers from the thick braids of her kinky hair and dried her face with the hem of her skirt. When she saw that her skirt was stained with blood, she waded into the water until she was waist deep. After she located the croker sack, she hoisted it onto her shoulders and walked to Miz Greenlove's.

The man met Cressy in the woods on and off all summer. Each time he just appeared. Each time he brought a small bunch of flowers. At first she cried, but she did not run. Soon she no longer cried. He'd hold her hand and lead her back to the path. Once he explained why there had been blood the first time. Once he lifted her onto his horse and she'd ridden behind him almost to Miz Greenlove's door. After a while, Cressy learned to give Mama Lou new reasons as to why it took her so long to return from Miz Greenlove's.

All summer, news of train robberies reached the valley. Cressy said nothing. By mid-summer, Pap Thacher made another visit to Pittsville. He came back with the news of a bank robbery in Holden, a train robbery near Odessa and another one near Liberty. Cressy listened when the man told her about the hot dry fields near Odessa. She said nothing about Liberty and Holden, but when she didn't see him for several weeks and when she heard there'd been a series of hold-ups near Atchinson, she knew he was moving north.

Sometimes on her route to Miz Greenlove's, the afternoon train passed her as she made her way to the footbridge. She'd stop and watch it slide by, smiling at the gloved hand that waved to her from the cab. By mid-October, she grew listless and even the sound of the train's whistle couldn't cheer her up. Mama Lou sent her to Miz Greenlove's and although Cressy took the medicine Mama Lou had sent her to fetch, she didn't feel any better. One morning, Mama Lou saw Cressy heaving her breakfast into the trough behind the outhouse. Mama Lou began to watch the girl as if she expected her to grow larger by the minute. But it was November before Papa noticed any change.

"Musta been one of Miz Ada's boys," he yelled. "You gonna tell me which one?"

Cressy said nothing.

The next week, Papa sent for Pap Thatcher. Early one morning, Cressy saw the old man's buckboard round the bend of the road at the end of the yard. She walked to the front porch. Mama Lou was already standing in the yard and Papa was in the doorway behind her. By the time Pap Thacher had climbed down from the buckboard, Cressy had reached the barn. She fed the milk cow and cleaned its stall. When she heard Pap Thacher coming to the door, she was heading toward the shaded area behind the hen house where the old biddy, Eelly, liked to nest.

"Can't rightly say as I know what to tell you, chile," Pap Thacher muttered. He stroked the stubbly grey whiskers on his chin, cocked his head and looked at her so that his milky grey eye, the one that had been blinded by one of Quantrill's raiders, was in the shadows. "I spect you ought to stay clear of folks till the circuit preacher comes around next spring."

Cressy nodded.

"You the only child your Papa's got," he added. "Surely would hep him to know who you been seeing."

Cressy stared at him. After a while, he limped back to the buckboard and she saw him shake his head. Her papa looked across the yard at her, then Pap Thacher patted him on the back, climbed into the buckboard and rode out of the yard.

After that, her papa seemed to grow tired of asking her the same questions. By spring, Cressy was so heavy with child, she used all of her energy moving from her bed, the one Papa built once he found out what was wrong with her, to the kitchen where she sat most of the day sewing scraps of cotton onto a new bed quilt or into clean even squares for the baby. Mama Lou had collected material from all of the women who had it to spare, and Mama Lou sat in the opposite corner, sighing and singing gospels.

Miz Ada came to the house several times, even brought one or two of her boys with her. The boys looked at Cressy with new eyes, but Cressy said nothing. By spring, Miz Ada was visiting so often, it was as if she herself felt guilty about Cressy's condition.

Cressy got up every morning, dragged herself from her bed to the kitchen and, once the days turned warm, onto the front porch. One morning in late April when the sun was particularly bright, Cressy took up her post on the porch. The

sun was still cold, but if she placed her chair directly in its path, she could stay on
the porch for hours. She didn't want to go into the house anyway. Miz Ada had
come over with some chicken stock and one of Miz Ada's boys was sitting in the
wagon waiting for her to finish her visit. Cressy had not spoken to the boy although
she knew he'd been staring at her.

She was sitting on the porch, her head turned away from the boy, when she
heard them ride into the yard. The boy stood up in the wagon and yelled, "Yahoo,"
and Miz Ada ran to the door, Mama Lou close at her heels. Cressy could hear the
sound of Papa's hinny mule round the bend on the path below the house. She knew
he must have seen them when they passed the road bordering the field.

There were four of them, but the yard seemed to be filled with men. Mama Lou
brushed past Miz Ada and whispered, "Lord have mercy. What those white men
want?" Cressy pulled herself from the chair. When she moved, the horses pawed the
ground and whinnied, but the men reined them in and patted their necks until they'd
calmed. Cressy remembered the one with the purple scarf, but she didn't recognize
the other three. Then she saw another figure ride up the path.

The black hat was pulled down low over his eyes; his mustache drooped to the
edge of his chin and he cradled the shotgun in the crook of his arm. She was already
moving toward the stairs when she heard her papa call to her to stop. Mama Lou
just kept saying, "Lord have mercy. Lord have mercy," and Miz Ada motioned her
boy to get down off the wagon.

The man swung off his horse and handed the gun to one of the other men.
Cressy leaned against the supporting pole when she saw he was limping, but he
smiled and walked toward her. When he reached the porch, he tipped his hat to
Mama Lou, saying, "Ma'am" as if they'd met many times before. Cressy could see
her papa over by the barn, and when the man saw she was looking in that direction,
he smiled even wider.

"Bradshaw," he said, "y'all get down offa them horses. They needs a rest. Just
sit a spell. We be going directly." Then the man looked at Cressy again and raised
his hand to help her down the stairs.

Cressy had just managed to get to the foot of the stairs by the time Bradshaw
and the other men pulled their horses over to the elm tree in the corner of the yard.
Cressy took the man's hand and led him around the back of the house to a bench
near the well.

At first, he just looked at her and shook his head. Then he asked her if she was
doing alright, when the baby would come and if she needed anything. Cressy answered yes, soon and no, but for the first time in months, she smiled. He gave her a
brooch, an egg-shaped flat black stone with a flower carved in the center of it. "I'd
be pleased if you'd call the baby Sam," he said.

He told her how he'd been shot, the miles of country he'd seen, the harsh
winters in the Dakotas and the miles of trail they'd cut coming home across the
plains. Cressy let him hold her hand and listened to the sound of Titbeak clucking
the hens away from the horses' hoofs.

Then she saw her papa standing at the corner of the house staring at them. The man stood up. "I'm Sam," he said. "Sam Packer." Her papa nodded.

"I come to see. . . ." the man paused.

Cressy saw him frown, look at her, then back to her papa. "Cressy," she whispered. The man shook his head and frowned again. "I be Cressy," she told him.

Before he could say anything else, her papa said, "I spect them others want to go."

Cressy followed him to the front yard. She smiled when he pressed the small purse in her hands and watched him swing onto his horse, grimacing as the pain in his leg caused him to ease into the saddle. Then they were gone. Cressy moved back to the porch, the pin and leather pouch tucked into her skirt pocket. She heard Mama Lou and Papa questioning her, but she did not move. After a while, Miz Ada and her son got into their buckboard and rode off. They stared at her over their shoulders as they left the yard.

Before she went to bed, Cressy gave the money to Mama Lou. She pinned the brooch inside her blouse, and that night she slept soundly.

Some say that over the years, Sam Packer made regular visits to Cressy Pruitt's house. Some say that Cressy and Sam had a score of children, that Sam took some of them off to Oklahoma and Cressy never saw them again. Folks that live near Pap Thacher's, those who still talk to Miz Ada and don't believe one of her boys had anything to do with Cressy's baby, tell strangers they've seen a photograph of Cressy and Sam Packer. According to them, those two are standing on Mama Lou's porch with three, four, can't tell how many members of Sam's gang around them. Talk is those men are as ragged as teeth on a saw blade, lounging against the porch rail or sprawled in Mama Lou's chair like they own the house. Their guns are in plain sight and they're so relaxed, they're not wearing shirts, just long johns, dingy white and cut on each shoulder by broad suspenders. And Cressy is leaning against Sam Packer.

The way those folks tell it, Cressy is expecting another baby, or maybe it's because she's got that first baby straddling her waist as if he's riding a horse. They all agree that Cressy's round as a pumpkin and next to Sam Packer's lanky redbone figure, her walnut face is even darker.

Pap Thacher says he heard Sam Packer caught a marshal's bullet over in Bloomfield, Nebraska, the same week Cressy's child was born, but even though folks in the valley are inclined to believe Pap Thacher, they still wonder if Cressy Pruitt knows where Sam Packer is.

Anyone with patience could have asked Cressy herself.

Cressy's son was four years old the last time she saw Sam Packer. By that time, Jesse James had been dead for three years; Cole Younger and his boys had crossed the Kansas border; the railroad had hired Pinkerton men to guard their trains, and the Wichita-Sedalia/St. Joseph run had not been robbed all summer. Cressy had borrowed Pap Thacher's buckboard and she was riding into Granville to run some errands for Mama Lou. As she drew near the spur north of Big Creek River, she could hear the train chugging toward her in the distance. Pap Thacher's horses tended to be skittery and with the child beside her, she decided not to take any chances on the mare.

The train slowed as it reached the spur and when the engine moved past, pausing for a moment as if the train hadn't decided which fork to take, her son giggled and waved. The screeching whistle made the horse jump, but she reined it in and clucked until it was calm. When she looked up again, the last of the boxcars was sliding past, and the train was moving so slowly, no faster than a horse's gait, that she had a clear view of the passengers' faces in the windows.

He was sitting in the last passenger car, the wide-brimmed hat tipped back from his head as if he'd just shoved it away from his eyes. His mustache framed his mouth in flat, shiny arcs, but he was not smiling. He must have seen her before she saw him. Almost as soon as she spotted him, he raised one hand, then the other. The hand next to the window was as strong as she remembered, but the other was bound to the wrist of another man, the ugly glint of manacles flickering in the light. Then he was gone.

As soon as the train had passed, Cressy whipped the horse across the tracks. The wagon jerked, its wheels grinding against the soft dirt that bordered the railroad hump. The sudden movement caused her son to rock in the seat, but he caught himself and clutched her skirt before he toppled backwards. Cressy heard him giggle again, and in the scraggly tangle of trees on the other side of the road, she heard the angry chatter of startled birds. They flew from the thicket, scattering in all directions, but Cressy did not bother to see if she could recognize them.

An Adventure in the Big Horn Mountains; Or, the Trials and Tribulations of a Recruit

EUGENE P. FRIERSON

Early in October, 1893, a Squadron of the Tenth Cavalry, consisting of Troops B, E, G and K, stationed at Fort Custer, Montana, proceeded on its annual practice march under command of Lieut.-Col. D. Perry. "Practice March" is a march made by troops, foot and mounted, annually, for the purpose of giving "recruits" (young soldiers) an idea of field service, a knowledge essential to the duties of a soldier in time of actual warfare, and to give older soldiers more practice and experience in the duties and knowledge pertaining to the same.

Each troop, with but few exceptions, was filled with recruits who had never crossed the plains of that wild, historical country before. But all were filled with "field aspiration" and were as gleeful as their older comrades in taking the field. The course of march was to a point about 45 miles southwest of the fort leading along the Big Horn River to the Big Horn Mountains, thence by return through the Little Horn Valley, by the historical Custer Battle Field to post, traversing an entire distance of more than 120 miles. The period of the march was only ten short Montana days. The first day out from the fort found a great many of our "recruit aspirants" wishing that they were at home by their mothers' side, or at least in post, for their seating capacity was very much worn from fare, wear and tear, occasioned by their inability to maintain a firm seat in the saddle during several miles of the regulation gait of eight miles an hour. One of the most effected aspirants was, with much regret, the writer of this story.

The soldiers were, of course, a jollier set of men than their would-be recruit comrades, for some of them had "been there" many times before in actual warfare against hostile Indians.

Nothing was very certain with the younger soldier until after "Mess Call" (supper), when all were soon stretched out upon their improvised beds, having unconditionally succumbed to the effects of his first day's experience, leaving the old soldier awake to participate in the usual camp fire yarns. However, the recruit was persistent in his determination to accomplish the journey without casting discredit upon his ability as a cavalryman, the next day having closed with him in a far better condition to endure a long, continuous journey.

All went very well with the boys for several days. About the fifth day out from post the conmand remained over in camp a day to allow the horses and men to recuperate and to give to those who desired it, an opportunity to fish and hunt, and enjoy the full benefit of field life. It was on this very day that Privates Collins, Walden and I, all members of Troop K, obtained permission for an extensive hunt and general exploration of the Snow Capped Mountain that seemed only a few miles from camp. After the regular and customary duties were performed, armed each with carbine and revolver, we proceeded on our journey. The first two or three miles were made without incident. Upon arriving at what first seemed like the foot of the great range of mountains, we were surprised to find ourselves confronted by a great canyon that seemed to be habitated by nothing but game of the largest and most dangerous kind, such as bear, deer, wolves, coyotes, wild cats, and a number of other gentlemen and ladies of the animal species that would proudly welcome such adventurous young soldiers as we into their community. After a few minutes' pause of wonder we decided to descend into the great valley below that seemed, with the exception of a gentle breeze, as silent as death. Being armed with a 45-calibre carbine and revolver each, we thought we were as brave and defiant as a recruit could be under ordinary circumstances, each being extremely nervous and shaky under the weight borne upon his legs.

At any rate, we proceeded (after drawing lots to see who should precede) by file down a narrow trail that wound its way into the great canyon below. I have always been unlucky since, but I was fortunate enough that day to draw the lot that entitled me to "bring up the rear." When about two-thirds of the way down the trail Walden, who preceded, came to a sudden stop and looked around with astounding countenance, as though the next step would have precipitated him into eternity. Collins, who stood at his back, was apparently in the same predicament. After carefully and cautiously scrutinizing the country in the immediate vicinity, I saw to my surprise a large "Grizzly" standing upon his hind legs bowing to each and every one of us as gracefully as if by pre-appointment. Taking the situation in at a glance, I brought my 45-calibre to my right shoulder and without sighting (being extremely nervous) pulled the trigger. This seemed to be great sport for Mr. "Grizzly," who shook his head as an indication of a miss. At this stage of affairs Walden, who was by virtue of his lot, and owing to his inability to climb the cliffs on either side, still in front, fired the shot that caused our informal friend to drop to his all-fours and make a hasty retreat. Being inspired with what we thought was an accomplished feat we, or rather they,—for I remained a little in the rear to reload my rifle— proceeded to follow at a rapid pace. Collins being more inspired than either of us, succeeded by some way or another in getting in front of Walden, in order to claim the skin of the beautiful black bear.

After reloading my rifle I took up a fast gait, to at least be on hand at the "skinning," and had proceeded only a short distance when, to my surprise, I beheld Collins beating as hasty a retreat as circumstances would permit under emergency conditions, followed as closely as conditions would allow by Walden and our "friend," in the order named.

In some way Collins had succeeded in successfully giving Walden the "leap frog act" in his effort to reach the point of starting.

It wasn't long, however, before the situation was thoroughly comprehended by me, and as the vote seemed unanimous, it fell to my lot to lead, and having, at the point of starting, at least twenty feet advantage, I soon succeeded in coming out No. 1 at the top of the hill. It was soon apparent to our "friend" that he was no match for this fleet-footed trio, for Collins was second to top of hill, followed closely by Walden by at least a neck. We soon saw that it was time to try some of our knowledge acquired during target season. Although recruits, we were marksmen, but needed only a little staying quality, which is very essential to a soldier. We succeeded by our combined efforts in sending our "friend" to the "happy hunting ground."

After having accomplished this, we decided to resume our journey and accomplish our desire to reach the great snow capped mountain that seemed as far now as before leaving camp. Returning along the trail we were more enthusiastic and adventurous than ever. After reaching the valley we were in the midst of one of the most beautiful scenes in Southwestern Montana, being surrounded with wild flowers of every variety and a beautiful brooklet running gently by. After spending a short time there we proceeded across the valley to the foot hills that seemed only an outpost to the great mountain beyond. We successfully reached the table land, and sat down to partake of a small lunch that we had thoughtfully prepared before leaving camp. Having rested about fifteen minutes, we continued our tramp. When within what seemed a few rods of the mountain, we were even more surprised to find that the greatest valley in Montana laid between us and the lone Snow-Capped Mountain, being more than seven miles wide. However, we were determined, and carefully groped our way far into its interior. The greatest problem now remained to be solved: How could we reach the lone mountain that held a commanding position overlooking the entire country for hundreds of miles around.

The day had begun to close, the sun having long before crossed the meridian, and night was near at hand; but we pressed bravely on. At last we came to the base of the great mountain, which was very steep and appeared to be seldom frequented. After a short pause we attempted to climb to its summit, but without avail. Night having silently crept upon us a speedy return was necessary in order to reach camp, which was more than ten miles away. We at once began the return trip, and succeeded in crossing the great valley before darkness fell with all her dismal.

We were still adventurous and full of glee, and our hope of reaching camp was as strong as that of reaching the mountain, which now was our only guide; for by keeping the mountain directly behind us we were sure of landing safely at camp. All trace of trail or road having been lost, we were at the mercy of the howling wolves and crying coyotes that seemed almost upon our very heels. Having reached an unsurpassable cliff, we were obliged to detour our line of march, and by so doing laid ourselves liable to spending a night among the wild creatures.

By mere chance we came to the very stream that passed through our camp, and by keeping in touch with it were able to reach camp at about 10 o'clock that night, very much worn from our experience. We were aware of two calls that we had failed to respond to, and immediately proceeded to explain our absence to the 1st Sergeant, who was sitting in his tent smoking an old cob pipe. After listening attentively to our tale of woe he promptly took us over to explain the little incident to the Troop Commander, who immediately gave us orders for the next day, which meant to "take pains and walk."

After receiving our walking orders for the next day, and instructions to report before leaving camp for an idea only of about where the troops would camp; and to receive a compass to guide us, we returned to our tents to take a much needed rest. After laying aside our arms, we proceeded to look up the cook, who had by that time drawn his 240 pounds of avoirdupois into his bunk, but being a thoughtful old gentleman, had laid aside something that would, at least, maintain life until morning. After partaking of all that could be found, we returned to our tents and were soon in dreamland. The next morning we turned over our arms and equipment to the Quartermaster Sergeant, as previously directed, and proceeded to the Troop Commander's tent to receive the instructions pertaining to the itinerary of our march. After receiving instructions to the effect that the troops would march about thirty miles in a certain direction, armed with compass alone, we departed upon our journey.

We had not gone very far before the troops passed us at an eight mile gait. We received everything uncomplimentary from our comrades, and were soon left far behind in a cloud of dust, with nothing in sight but a broad prairie, a compass and a number of cattle. We were as adventurous as the day before and kept up courage by relating our experience the previous day with the "Grizzly."

But about thirty miles to walk seemed more than our contract with the government contemplated, and the first shade tree we came to we sat down to rest. While resting, we decided that we could "cut out" about ten miles by taking a more direct line, utilizing the compass for this purpose. Leaving the road entirely, we soon found ourselves in sight of the troops again, but had not gone very far in this direction, however, before we had a very frightful experience with a herd of cattle: An old bull of many years' experience upon the plains decided that trespassing upon his premises, without permission, was a direct violation of the rules and regulations of this command, and immediately displayed his contemptibleness by making a few acrobatic stunts, charging the right wing of our advance. Being armed with nothing but a compass and there being no trees in sight, the reader can imagine our predicament. We were trained athletes and were soon off in a 100-yards free-for-all dash, and after a few tree frog vaults succeeded in gaining the other side of a gulf that prevented our antagonist from carrying off all honors. I wished very much for the rifle that I had so nervously fired the day before at the "Grizzly," but of course I had just as well wished for my horse, for each was well out of my reach. We sat down for a few minutes to regain some of the compressed air that had escaped our bellows during the dash, after which we proceeded on our journey and were soon far out upon the prairie.

We had a small lunch and partook of it on our way and had soon forgotten about the latest incident, when, to our utmost dissatisfaction and surprise, we were greeted by a big brown wolf standing about thirty feet to our right front. He seemed very much carried away over the appearance of such healthy and tender looking youngsters. What should we do: What could we do? We were unarmed, except for the compass, and it wasn't designed to accomplish a one desire, that of having wings, so we moved on as though we had seen nothing, and soon our adversary advanced to extend formally his appreciation of our appearance at so opportune but unexpected time, but of course we were not civil enough to adhere to such formal proposals as were now in progress by the gentleman. We detoured a little from our original plans—that of keeping on a bee-line—but the wolf-gentleman seemed very determined in his desire to have us exchange a few friendly terms with him at a closer range, and was willing, if we hadn't the time to stop, to accompany us a short distance to accomplish this one desire. Seeing that we could not shake him easily, we turned and greeted him with a few stones that we had fortunately come in possession of and soon induced the intruder to return to his place of peace. There was no time to lose at this stage of affairs, and we pushed on, and had soon covered about fifteen miles.

After resting awhile at a small spring we continued our journey until within sight of the troops that were now in the act of bivouacking for the night. Seeing that the compass had served its purpose and had guided us almost on a direct line to the very sight of camp, we decided to remain on watch, at a safe distance, until camp had been pitched, wood and water supplied and horses groomed, and descend upon camp at the sounding of mess call, "just in time," but being a little wearied from our two days' experience were soon asleep, and failed to respond to mess call, tattoo or call to quarters. Well, after waking up and seeing that darkness had long ago stretched her folds over the earth, and the old soldier had crept away from the fireside into his resting place beneath the willows that are so numerous along the Big Horn and Little Horn rivers, we proceeded cautiously to camp. When within the limits of camp, and a few yards of our destination, we were shocked almost into insensibility by a challenge from a sentinel on post: "Halt! Who comes there!" The same being repeated several times, with the remark: "If you don't halt I will shoot."

After recovering our wits we halted and gave a half way satisfactory answer and were admitted into camp, with orders to report to the First Sergeant at once. We reported to the First Sergeant as directed and were called upon to explain the cause of our late arrival in camp.

We tried to explain the uncertainty of the location of camp and our long journey over the "take pains and walk" route, but were greeted with a stern look from the upper corner of the left eye of the "old top," which was sign sufficient to us that our story was of little credit. After a slight pause the old gentleman asked if we hadn't arrived upon the hill overlooking camp at about the same time the command arrived in camp. Well, we couldn't face the old man and deny it, and admitted that little fact under conditional circumstances, but were again directed to report to the Troop Commander the next morning for the usual orders over the "take pains and walk" route.

The next morning we were up bright and early, and after breakfasting, reported for our usual walking orders and were soon off upon the prairie. We were veterans over the walking route, and proceeded at quite a rapid pace and soon were far out from our last camp. The morning was a beautiful one; the sky was cloudless, except for a few white specks here and there; the wind was calm and, with the exception of a few risings here and there, the prairie was almost as smooth as the sky above. Everything seemed in our favor to accomplish the journey to camp without incident.

Having reached a large tree, we stopped for a few minutes' rest and were soon well upon our way again. The day passed away without incident and the close of it brought us safely in camp. After visiting the mess tent we received our equipments, turned in prior to our "take pains and walk" journey, with instructions to mount with the command on the following morning.

Our places were filled around the campfire that night and we held prominent, as well as worthy positions, among our older comrades in relating our three days' experience over the "take pains and walk" route. At 9 o'clock sharp tattoo was sounded, the fireside was vacated and our bones were soon resting in a small but comfortable improvised bunk. The next morning found us all in unusually good spirits. The day was an ideal one and three more days would find us back in old Fort Custer, so we were as prompt as possible, and were soon mounted upon our steeds alongside the other Cavalrymen enroute to the next camping place.

The boys were all busily engaged in something or another; some were singing, some whistling and others thinking of the girl "I left behind me." The Captain rode at the head of the column and seemed as cheerful as the enlisted men in returning to the good old post that was yet two days away, but would, in due time, appear upon the horizon slightly to the northwest, just as it had disappeared some ten days previous. The command was halted, and the men and horses were given about fifteen minutes in which to rest. "Attention" was sounded and we were off again for the camp that was to mark our eighth day from post. Having been out of the saddle for three days we were inclined to shift from one side to the other in search of an easy place, thereby causing several little risings under the seat known as the horse's back, the same having been discovered upon our first halt by the Troop Commander, who had made an inspection just for such a thing. We were cautioned that if our horses' backs were not in a normal condition upon reaching camp, we could make up our minds to "hoof" it the remainder of the distance—about seventy miles—so we were soon applying every known remedy to prevent any undue inflammation, and acting upon the advice received from an old soldier, I applied a remedy not known in veterinary science, and soon discovered, after making another halt, that in order to reach camp with a sound horse, it necessitated his being unsaddled and led. I looked around for an encouraging nod from some comrade, but was met on every side by a frown and an occasional burlesque from some more fortunate recruit, so I decided to make the best of it until I could communicate with my comrades. I would have been satisfied to finish the trip with them over the "take pains and walk" route. But the old "top" rode to the rear of the column and said: " 'Cruit, fall out." I obeyed.

He very abruptly ordered: "Unsaddle that horse, put your saddle upon the wagon train, turn your horse over to the Corporal here, and you can get to camp the best way you can. You 'cruits should be in a cotton field, for you are a menace to the government." Well, I was alone this time, for my other two comrades were more fortunate. I was soon left far behind upon the prairie at the mercy of all the wild creatures of the country, as well as a tribe of Crow Indians, who were harmless, and whose only aim in life was eating dogs, running horse races and gambling; yet I was not discouraged and was determined to make the very best of it, and to accomplish the journey in the best way and to gain the respect and confidence of my superiors. I soon reached camp again. After my arrival in camp alone I proceeded to look up my two comrades and enlist their sympathy to the extent of having two more companions for the next day; but they were more fortunate than I in the day's journey having arrived in camp with sound horses.

Finding that I could not enlist my comrades' sympathy to the extent of being passengers over my route, I proceeded to my old friend, the cook, and was soon capable of taking things as they were presented. During the evening the First Sergeant reported to the Troop Commander in regards to my (the writer's) journey over the usual route next day. During this conversation I was called upon for some kind of explanation in regards to the physical condition of my beautiful steed, whose name was Keptomania, and, of course, allowing me to be both counsel and jury, I soon had orders to mount the wagon next morning, which was to be the ninth day out from post. The tenth day was to find us back in the dear old fort.

I felt very much relieved and was soon telling my comrades about my latest success. After stables the regular meal was served, after which the troops attended retreat roll-call, and were soon free until morning to stroll up and down the banks of the Little Big Horn River and toss pebbles into the deeps. Some were hunting, some fishing, some bathing in the beautiful stream, and others doing various kinds of other things essential to field life. "Tattoo" found us all lying in a well-deserved bunk dreaming of the various incidents of the day. The next morning we were in an unusually good humor, and by 7 o'clock were ready to mount and begin the beginning of the end. One day only was left for us to spend upon the prairie, so all were imbued with the spirit and principle essential to good soldiers in time of actual warfare—a spirit that each and every soldier in Uncle Sam's Army has in him when he is about to embark upon some perilous mission; a spirit that moves him, causes him to feel that danger is one of the working tools of his profession; thereby relieving his frame from all fear or danger.

A number of beautiful scenes were passed during the day, the close of which found us camped upon that famous Custer Battle Field where, on June 26, 1876, more than three hundred brave soldiers of the 7th U.S. Cavalry lost their lives making a last brave stand; headstones mark their last positions; some stood alone; some more fortunate ones sacrificed their lives together; headstones appear in the position of a squad or platoon, showing that they had congregated together there to die for their country. The next morning all were up and stirring before day. This was to be our last day upon the prairie. The post could be seen slightly above the horizon and a little to the northwest, so the reader can imagine how full of joy was each heart. At exactly 7 A.M. "Boots and Saddles" were sounded and the command was soon jolting along toward the post. We halted to rest for a few minutes, but the march was soon resumed and quickly we were in plain view of the post. Another half an hour found us in line at a halt ready to dismount, unsaddle and prepare to the barracks. After unsaddling we were marched to the barracks, dismounted, and then and there called from labor to refreshments, to enjoy the pleasures of a well earned garrison life. There are few pleasures to equal the experiences of a new recruit.

The Averted Strike

CHARLES W. CHESNUTT

M r. Philetus Strong sat in his private office at the Strongville Rubber Works, about ten o'clock in the morning, looking over the mail that had been delivered a few minutes before. Some of the letters were pleasant reading—those enclosing checks, for instance—and especially one containing a very large order for an expensive grade of goods. One letter he tossed aside with a gesture of impatience. It was a notice from the municipal authorities requiring him to equip the main building of the factory with fire escapes of a prescribed design. Mr. Strong's first impulse was to ignore the notice, or to refer it to his lawyers.

"It's an imposition," he muttered, "an outrage. Fire escapes are not needed on the mill. It is of slow-burning construction, and our own apparatus will put out any fire in five minutes. It will be money thrown away. But it's the law," he decided, "and I suppose must be obeyed. It's cheaper to put them up than to fight the city."

Having reached this conclusion Mr. Strong opened the next letter. It was from the general foreman, or superintendent, of the factory, a naturalized Englishman named Armitage, announcing his resignation of the position. Armitage had been foreman of the factory for ten years, and had filled the place admirably; but a brother in England had died recently, and left him a small estate, and he wished to go to the old home to settle up the property, which would be sufficient, he said, to place him thereafter above the necessity for hard work.

Armitage had been away for a week on leave of absence, to consult a lawyer in an Eastern city. His place had been taken temporarily by one of the most experienced and capable workmen, a man by the name of Walker, the only colored man employed in the factory. As Mr. Strong had not expected to lose Armitage's services, the question of securing permanently another foreman had not until now presented itself.

So important a matter required careful consideration. Should he promote a man from the ranks of his own workmen, or would the ends of discipline be better subserved by employing an outsider? While Walker was a good workman, and an intelligent, steady fellow, did he possess the firmness, the judgment, the readiness of decision necessary in a man to be trusted with responsibilities so considerable, and would a colored man command the respect of several hundred white operatives to the extent necessary to maintain discipline among them?

While Mr. Strong was weighing this matter he became aware of a rustle of silken skirts, an odor of violets, and, as he looked up, of a couple of young ladies who had entered the office without ceremony.

"Papa," said one of them, a tall, stylishly dressed girl with blue eyes and fair hair, "I'm going to take Mabel through the factory and show her everything, and then we'll go up in the tower and look out at the view. Of course, I had to show Mabel first the center of the web—the office."

"Ah, I see," said Mr. Strong, as he shook hands with his daughter's friend, "where the old spider sits and sucks the life-blood of his victims. Thank you. But I'm afraid you two will interfere with the business," he added. "The operatives will stop to look at you for at least five minutes each. Two hundred times five minutes equals one thousand minutes. At sixty minutes to an hour that makes upwards of sixteen hours, which at eight hours a day amounts to more than two days' time your visit will cost me."

Alice bent over and kissed him. "That makes the loss good," she said, "and now we won't disturb you any longer."

"Shall I send a man with you?" asked her father.

"Oh, no, papa," said Alice, "it isn't at all necessary. I know the way perfectly."

Mr. Strong had scarcely resumed his train of thought, when a party of five or six men filed into the office. Mr. Strong looked up and saw they were operatives from the mill.

"Well, men," he asked, "what's the trouble? It must be something serious that would bring you from your work at this hour."

"One of the belts broke, sir, and while it was being repaired we thought we would come and speak to you. We are a committee of the workmen, sir, and we want to ask a question and perhaps make a suggestion."

Mr. Strong had been in business many years and had long ago learned that it was good business policy to treat his workmen courteously and fairly, and to consider suggestions they might make from time to time. If he did not always grant their wishes, he at least did not ignore them. As a consequence he seldom had any trouble with his workmen, and agitators who tried to stir up discontent among them met with but slight encouragement.

"All right, Ludlow," said Mr. Strong, addressing the spokesman of the party, "go ahead."

"Well, sir," replied Ludlow, "the question is whether you are going to appoint Walker foreman."

"Suppose I were going to do so—and I have been thinking of it—what then?"

"Then we should want to suggest," rejoined Ludlow, "that you don't do it."

"Humph!" said Mr. Strong, "and what objection have you to Walker?"

"Well, sir, we're not used to working under niggers—perhaps I should say colored men—and we don't like it, and don't want to keep it up. We didn't mind it so much for a week. But we've learned that Armitage is not coming back and we thought that we'd let you know our way of thinking, in case you might have any notion of giving Walker the job permanently."

"You've worked with Walker for several years," said Mr. Strong, "and no one has objected to him. He's the same color now that he has been all along."

"Yes, sir," rejoined the spokesman, "and we haven't objected to working *with* him; what we don't want is to work under him."

Mr. Strong did not reply for a moment. Meanwhile the men sat silently waiting.

"Have you seriously thought over what you are asking me to do?" Mr. Strong said, when he broke the silence. "Here you ask me to rob of well-earned promotion an experienced and competent workman in whom I may have found the very qualities that I need in a foreman. You are not only unjust to him, but you are doing me an injury. And you ask this for what reason? Simply because God has planted under Walker's skin the color you get on the outside of yours by the day's work. You talk of the rights of labor, and yet you come and ask me to deprive an industrious and faithful man of the highest right of labor—the right to an opportunity to do the best he is capable of, and to obtain the proper reward for it."

"Well, sir," replied Ludlow, somewhat shamefacedly, but not yielding the point, "we think you put it rather strongly. We don't object to his earning a living, or to his working with us. But we don't like the idea of having him over us. Put yourself in our place. You're a white man yourself. You've fought in the army. How would you have liked to have a black officer over you?"

"Whenever our government gives one of them an opportunity to demonstrate that he is a better soldier and more capable leader than I, then I will face the question. But this man has had his chance and proved his quality. I am willing to say that before you came in I doubted the expediency of appointing Walker foreman, although I had thought about it. But since you men, who ought to know what makes a good foreman, come in and frankly ask me to keep him back solely on account of his race, I feel even more strongly inclined to believe that I ought to appoint him. I'll take the matter under consideration. Perhaps he might not care to be foreman in a mill where the workmen were unfriendly to him. I'll only say now that I'll think about it."

"We hope you'll think our way, sir. There's a lot of us, and we've got our minds pretty well made up."

"Is that a threat?" asked Mr. Strong, sharply.

"Well, no, sir, not exactly. We haven't been authorized to make any threats, but merely to make a request and report your answer."

Mr. Strong was tempted for a moment to use harsh language. He resented the interference in the first place—the factory was not yet a union factory—and in the second place he revolted at the narrow prejudice displayed by the workmen.

Strongville was not in New England, but in the southern part of a state of the Middle West, and not far from the old line that in former years had separated free labor from labor enslaved; and while himself New England bred, Mr. Strong knew that old social customs and habits of thought are not easily changed, and that old prejudices need but a breath to revive them. He did not wish to precipitate a strike, in view of the large order he had received in the morning's mail. He did not wish to yield the point too easily, nor, if possible to avoid it without disaster, did he wish to yield it at all.

"I'll consider your proposition," he repeated, as the men rose to go, "and do what I think right, and best for all concerned."

"We hope, sir," said Ludlow, "that you'll decide this week. The Labor Day parade takes place next week, and our foreman is always appointed as one of the marshals. We don't want to change the rule, and we don't want to give you any trouble."

"You're giving me more than you think," replied Mr. Strong. "But as I say, I'll think the matter over."

Ludlow and his companions filed out, and left their employer seriously annoyed. He was entirely familiar with labor conditions and it had been his settled policy to consult the interests, and where possible, the wishes of his employees. But there was a higher principle involved in this question, which Mr. Strong could not ignore, the very principle, indeed, which had governed his dealings with his workmen. For he had been taught from his youth up to love justice and to try to do it. His father had been a pronounced abolitionist at a period when to help the oppressed was both a glory and a shame. He recalled how he had fed runaway Negroes in his father's attic, and how when a lad he had thrilled beneath the passionate eloquence of anti-slavery orators pleading the cause of the slave.

For a man of these antecedents, a fair-minded, just, and withal somewhat obstinate man, to treat an employee unjustly because of his color, was not a thing to be done off-hand. And yet the emergency was a serious one. In the event of a strike his business would be seriously embarrassed, for the workmen were skilled laborers, and the industry was one in which the supply of labor was not in excess of the demand. He could not fill the order just received if his working force should be disorganized by a strike, and unless he filled it he would probably lose what promised to become his best business connection. Mr. Strong realized with a sigh (and not for the first time) that wealth and position carried with them serious responsibilities; and that he had before him the somewhat difficult task of harmonizing his principles with the requirements of business.

Mr. Strong was occupied in the office until the whistle blew that marked the hour of noon. The operatives filed out of the mill and scattered, most of them, to their homes in the neighborhood for their midday meal, leaving in the mill only a few who had brought their lunches with them. Mr. Strong looked up at the clock, and was pulling down the top of his desk to go home for luncheon when a confused noise of voices in the yard caught his attention. As he rose from his chair a workman rushed into the office.

"Mr. Strong," he exclaimed excitedly, "the mill's on fire."

"Has the water been turned on from the tank?"

"No, the fire caught in the tower and we can't get to the levers."

The mill was equipped with a system of pipes extending along the ceilings of the various rooms, and connecting with a tank on the roof, from which by a system of levers the water could be turned on at any point desired, or over the whole of the factory at once. Unfortunately the location of the fire rendered the mechanism for working the apparatus unavailable. Besides this arrangement there were fire extinguishers and buckets about the mill with which an incipient fire could have been easily extinguished. But the fact that the mill was practically deserted at noon had given the flames an opportunity to gain some headway before any steps could be taken to fight them.

It was the work of a moment for Mr. Strong to turn in the city fire alarm from his office and place himself at the scene of the fire. The mill building which stood a few rods distant from the office was of brick, and the main portion of it of slow-burning construction. The tower, however, in which the fire had started, formed a sort of offset to the main building, and was less solidly built, and the rooms on the several floors were used largely for packing goods. There were quantities of pine boxes, filled and empty, and paper wrappers and packing material of various kinds, so that when the fire got under way it found plenty of inflammable material to feed upon. The fire engines, because, it was learned afterwards, of a fire elsewhere, were slow to respond to the call, and the fire had made considerable progress by the time the operatives, disturbed at their dinners, came flocking back to the mill.

Mr. Strong had scarcely begun to give directions about getting as much machinery, goods and material as possible out of the burning building, when he heard a shriek, and turning his eyes upward, simultaneously with two hundred other pairs of eyes, saw a sight that froze his blood. Standing on the edge of the tower, which had a flat roof above which the side walls projected upward for about eighteen inches, stood his daughter, and by her side her companion to whom he had spoken an hour and a half before. As he learned afterwards, they had been on the topmost floor of the tower, which was six stories high, when the ascending smoke warned them of the fire below. They had tried to descend the stairs, and had only just found their way through a trap door to the roof. Mr. Strong had supposed them gone an hour before.

"My God!" he exclaimed with agonized voice. "How can we get them down? Bring ladders, men, bring ladders!"

"There's no ladder long enough to reach up so far," said Ludlow, who happened to be standing near.

"Then someone must go up the stairs."

He made a rush for the door, but the interior of the first floor was a fiery furnace and the stair had already fallen. Even in his distraction he could see there was no possible way of rescue in that direction. He rushed back into the yard, glanced upward, and saw his daughter's friend weeping and wringing her hands, and Alice quietly looking downward to see what steps would be taken for their rescue. From the window in the roof the smoke was already pouring.

"Can nobody get them down?" cried Mr. Strong. "I will give a thousand dollars, ten thousand dollars—anything—everything—to anyone who will save them."

The men looked on eagerly. They would willingly have helped without reward if there had been any feasible way. And Mr. Strong was rich and generous, and the prospect of a liberal reward would have been an inducement to take desperate chances. But apparently every avenue of access to the tower was cut off; part by the flames, which were pouring out of the windows on one side, but the rest quite as effectively by dense volumes of smoke. While a dozen voices discussed so many wild plans of rescue, none of them practicable, a man came running through the crowd, with a coil of small rope in his hand. It was Walker, the foreman.

"Help me put this ladder at the corner of the tower," he said. "I'll go up there."

A dozen willing hands placed the ladder at the spot designated. The man fastened the coil of rope so that it hung at his back and would not interfere with his movements.

"You'll never get up, Walker," they cried, wondering what he meant to do. "The ladder doesn't reach within twenty feet of the roof."

"Never you mind," said the colored man, "I didn't sail the ocean seven years for nothing. I can almost climb a straight wall. Somebody get a stronger rope to tie onto this line when I let it down, and hurry!"

When Walker reached the top of the ladder, which he climbed with surprising agility, the plan which he meant to adopt was at once apparent. The end of the ladder rested against one side of an ornamental projection extending downward on the corner of the building from the roof for the depth of two stories. This projection was simply an extra course of brick four inches in thickness and lapping each side of the corner about a foot, resembling almost exactly the reinforcing pieces on the corners of a dry-goods box or packing case. Walker left the ladder, and clasping one arm and knee against the inner side of the projection and the others around the corner of the tower, began to work his way slowly upward.

The brick was common brick with a rough surface, so that he could get friction enough to hold on, though only by great effort, because of the very narrow space in which to move his right arm and knee. To those who watched him breathlessly from below, his position seemed one of extreme peril. Suppose he should lose his hold? Three lives would be sacrificed instead of two. Interest in the man and his daring attempt almost eclipsed anxiety for the position of the two girls, which was every moment becoming more perilous. When at length Walker reached the top and drew himself over the wall, the tension was relieved by a wild shout of joy and applause.

To fasten one end of the line to the flagstaff on the tower, and throw the coil down, was the work of a moment. Then while Miss Strong, who had never for a moment lost her nerve, pulled up the stout rope which was immediately tied on below, Walker ran to the water tank and released the mechanism that let the water into the fire-extinguishing pipes in the workrooms and storerooms of the building below. To tie the rope around the almost fainting form of Miss Strong's friend and with a turn of the rope around the flagstaff to lessen the strain, to lower her into the waiting arms below, took but a few minutes. Miss Strong's turn came next, and then the crowd saw Walker coming down the rope hand over hand, with the ease and rapidity of an old salt. As he touched the ground the fire-engine dashed into the yard.

"Walker," said Mr. Strong, as he grasped the panting but smiling rescuer by the hand, "I owe you more than my own life. I can never repay you."

"That's all right, sir, you don't owe me anything. Anybody that knew how to climb as well as I do could do what I did. I was in the Navy, sir; any able seaman could do as well."

By this time the fire engine had begun to play on the flames, and combined with the action of the extinguishing apparatus, and got the fire under control before any material damage had been done to the main part of the building.

"You have saved my daughter and saved the mill, Walker. I can only thank you now, but henceforth you are my friend, and friendship with me is not an empty name."

That evening, Walker dressed in his best clothes and, much to his discomfort, was overwhelmed with gratitude by two beautiful young ladies, who had partially recovered from the shock of their adventure, and lionized by his employer and his wife, and a host of their friends who had asked an opportunity to meet the brave rescuer. Some men are born heroes, some achieve heroism, and some have heroism thrust upon them. To Walker all these parts were assigned at once. Soft hands pressed his horny palm. Fair faces smiled into his, and sweet voices said flattering words, and he would have been less than human, as he went home that night, if he had not felt the world a pleasant place to live in, and himself a very acceptable member of its population.

About nine o'clock next morning the same committee of workmen, with Ludlow at their head, called on Mr. Strong at the office. The mill had been shut down for a few days, until the slight damage by fire and water could be repaired.

Mr. Strong had quite made up his mind as to the answer he would give them in reference to Walker.

"Well, my men," he said, "what can I do for you today?"

"You can forget what we said about Walker yesterday, sir," answered the spokesman, "and we hope you won't mention it to him at all. We've taken the sense of the mill-hands about it, and they all want you to make him foreman. We realize that he saved your daughter's life, and probably saved our jobs. And he's a good fellow, and we like him, and don't want any better man to work under. And next Saturday we're going to elect him one of the marshals of the Labor Day parade, and we'll be proud to march behind him."

"My friends," replied Mr. Strong, with emotion, "you do honor to yourselves, to humanity, and the cause of labor. I shall be glad to forget your visit of yesterday, and to remember only your appreciation of and desire to reward character and courage. I shall be happy to appoint Mr. Walker foreman, and shall tell him it was done at your request."

Walker was informed of his appointment the same day.

"I owe you more than I can repay, Walker," said Mr. Strong, "but I am going to give you some substantial evidence of my appreciation. The appointment as fore-man you have earned, and are entitled to by the rule of promotion. But my personal acknowledgment shall take a different form. I had a talk with the other directors last night. We are going to reorganize the company, and have decided to credit you with five thousand dollars of the new company's stock, in acknowledgment of your courage and coolness, and the service you have rendered us all."

Walker was overwhelmed. "I haven't done anything to deserve all this, sir. I only did my duty, and it was easy for me to do. You don't need to give me anything, sir."

"It is sometimes hard to do one's duty, Walker. You have a family to provide for and bring up, and you cannot afford to throw away your chances; and I certainly cannot afford, on my part, to do less than I think right in the matter. Your interest in the business will make you a better foreman and be to our mutual advantage."

And being a man of good, hard sense, whose chances in life had been few, Walker had no further objections to make, but thanked his employer and Another for the good fortune that had befallen him.

As the Lord Lives, He Is
One of Our Mother's Children

PAULINE E. HOPKINS

It was Saturday afternoon in a large Western town, and the Rev. Septimus Stevens sat in his study writing down the headings for his Sunday sermon. It was slow work; somehow the words would not flow with their usual ease, although his brain was teeming with ideas. He had written for his heading at the top of the sheet these words for a text: "As I live, he is one of our mother's children." It was to be a great effort on the Negro question, and the reverend gentleman, with his New England training, was in full sympathy with his subject. He had jotted down a few headings under it, when he came to a full stop; his mind simply refused to work. Finally, with a sigh, he opened the compartment in his desk where his sermons were packed and began turning over those old creations in search of something suitable for the morrow.

Suddenly the whistles in all directions began to blow wildly. The Rev. Septimus hurried to the window, threw it open, and leaned out, anxious to learn the cause of the wild clamor. Could it be another of the terrible "cave-ins" that were the terror of every mining district? Men were pouring out of the mines as fast as they could come up. The crowds which surged through the streets night and day were rushing to meet them. Hundreds of policemen were about; each corner was guarded by a squad commanded by a sergeant. The police and the mob were evidently working together. Tramp, tramp, on they rushed; down the serpentine boulevard for nearly two miles they went swelling like an angry torrent. In front of the open window where stood the white-faced clergyman, they paused. A man mounted the empty barrel and harangued the crowd: "I am from Dover City, gentlemen, and I have come here today to assist you in teaching the blacks a lesson. I have killed a nigger before," he yelled, "and in revenge of the wrong wrought upon you and yours, I am willing to kill again. The only way you can teach these niggers a lesson is to go to the jail and lynch these men as an object lesson. String them up! That is the only thing to do. Kill them, string them up, lynch them! I will lead you. On to the prison and lynch Jones and Wilson, the black fiends!" With a hoarse shout, in which were mingled cries like the screams of enraged hyenas and the snarls of tigers, they rushed on.

Nora, the cook, burst open the study door, pale as a sheet, and dropped at the minister's feet. "Mother of God!" she cried. "And is it the end of the wurruld?"

On the maddened men rushed from north, south, east, and west, armed with everything from a brick to a horse-pistol. In the melee a man was shot down. Somebody planted a long knife in the body of a little black newsboy for no apparent reason. Every now and then a Negro would be overwhelmed somewhere on the outskirts of the crowd and left beaten to a pulp. Then they reached the jail and battered in the door.

The solitary watcher at the window tried to move, but could not; terror had stricken his very soul, and his white lips moved in articulate prayer. The crowd surged back. In the midst was only one man; for some reason, the other was missing. A rope was knotted about his neck—charged with murder, himself about to be murdered. The hands which drew the rope were too swift, and half-strangled, the victim fell. The crowd halted, lifted him up, loosened the rope, and let the wretch breathe.

He was a grand man—physically—black as ebony, tall, straight, deep-chested, every fiber full of that life so soon to be quenched. Lucifer, just about to be cast out of heaven, could not have thrown around a glance of more scornful pride. What might not such a man have been, if—but it was too late. "Run fair, boys," said the prisoner, calmly, "run fair! You keep up your end of the rope, and I'll keep up mine."

The crowd moved a little more slowly, and the minister saw the tall form "keeping up" its end without a tremor of hesitation. As they neared the telegraph pole, with its outstretched arm, the watcher summoned up his lost strength, grasped the curtain, and pulled it down to shut out the dreadful sight. Then came a moment of ominous silence. The man of God sank upon his knees to pray for the passing soul. A thousand-voiced cry of brutal triumph arose in cheers for the work that had been done, and curses and imprecations, and they who had hunted a man out of life hurried off to hunt for gold.

To and fro on the white curtain swung the black silhouette of what had been a man.

For months the minister heard in the silence of the night phantom echoes of those frightful voices, and awoke, shuddering, from some dream whose vista was closed by that black figure swinging in the air.

About a month after this happening, the rector was returning from a miner's cabin in the mountains where a child lay dying. The child haunted him; he thought of his own motherless boy, and a fountain of pity overflowed in his heart. He had dismounted and was walking along the road to the ford at the creek which just here cut the path fairly in two.

The storm of the previous night had refreshed all nature and had brought out the rugged beauty of the landscape in all its grandeur. The sun had withdrawn his last dazzling rays from the eastern highlands upon which the lone traveler gazed, and now they were fast veiling themselves in purple night shadows that rendered them momentarily more grand and mysterious. The man of God stood a moment with uncovered head repeating aloud some lines from a great Russian poet:

"O Thou eternal One! whose presence bright
All space doth occupy, all motion guide;
Unchanged through time's all devastating flight;
Thou only God! There is no God beside
Being above all beings, Mighty One!
Whom none can comprehend and none explore."

Another moment passed in silent reverence of the All-Wonderful, before he turned to remount his horse and enter the waters of the creek. The creek was very much swollen, and he found it hard to keep the ford. Just as he was midway the stream, he saw something lying half in the water on the other bank. Approaching nearer, he discovered it to be a man, apparently unconscious. Again dismounting, he tied his horse to a sapling and went up to the inert figure, ready, like the Samaritan of old, to succor the wayside fallen. The man opened his deep-set eyes and looked at him keenly. He was gaunt, haggard, and despairing, and soaking wet.

"Well, my man, what is the matter?" Rev. Mr. Stevens had a very direct way of going at things.

"Nothing," was the sullen response.

"Can't I help you? You seem ill. Why are you lying in the water?"

"I must have fainted and fallen in the creek," replied the man, answering the last question first. "I've tramped from Colorado hunting for work. I'm penniless, have no home, haven't had much to eat for a week, and now I've got a touch of your d——— mountain fever." He shivered as if with a chill and smiled faintly.

The man, from his speech, was well educated and, in spite of his pitiful situation, had an air of good breeding, barring his profanity.

"What's your name?" asked Stevens, glancing him over sharply as he knelt beside the man and deftly felt his pulse and laid a cool hand on the fevered brow.

"Stone—George Stone."

Stevens got up. "Well, Stone, try to get on my horse, and I'll take you to the rectory. My housekeeper and I together will manage to make you more comfortable."

So it happened that George Stone became a guest at the parsonage and, later, sexton of the church. In that gold-mining region, where new people came and went constantly and new excitements were things of everyday occurrence, and new faces as plenty as old ones, nobody asked or cared where the new sexton came from. He did his work quietly and thoroughly and quite won Nora's heart by his handy ways about the house. He had a room under the eaves and seemed thankful and content. Little Flip, the rector's son, took a special liking to him, and he, on his side, worshipped the golden-haired child and was never tired of playing with him and inventing things for his amusement.

"The reverend sets a heap by the boy," he said to Nora one day in reply to her accusation that he spoiled the boy and there was no living with him since Stone's advent. "He won't let me thank him for what he's done for me, but he can't keep me from loving the child."

One day in September, while passing along the street, Rev. Stevens had his attention called to a flaming poster on the side of a fence by the remarks of a crowd of men near him. He turned and read it:

$1,500 REWARD!

The above reward will be paid for information leading to the arrest of "Gentleman Jim," charged with complicity in the murder of Jerry Mason. This nigger is six feet, three inches tall, weight one hundred and sixty pounds. He escaped from jail when his pal was lynched two months ago by a citizens' committee. It is thought that he is in the mountains, etc. He is well educated, and might be taken for a white man. Wore, when last seen, blue jumper and overalls and cowhide boots.

He read it the second time, and he was dimly conscious of seeing, like a vision in the brain, a man playing about the parsonage with little Flip.

"I knowed him. I worked a spell with him over in Lone Tree Gulch before he got down on his luck," spoke a man at his side who was reading the poster with him. "Jones and him was two of the smartest and peaceablest niggers I ever seed. But Jerry Mason kinder sot on 'em both; never could tell why, only some white men can't 'bide a nigger eny mo' than a dog can a cat; it's a natural antiperthy. I'm free to say the niggers seemed harmless, but you can't tell what a man'll do when his blood's up."

He turned to the speaker. "What will happen if they catch him?"

"Lynch him sure; there's been a lot of trouble over there lately. I wouldn't give a toss-up for him if they get their hands on him once more."

Rev. Stevens pushed his way through the crowd and went slowly down the street to the church. He found Stone there sweeping and dusting. Saying that he wanted to speak with him, he led the way to the study. Facing around upon him suddenly, Stevens said, gravely: "I want you to tell me the truth. Is your real name Stone, and are you a Negro?"

A shudder passed over Stone's strong frame, then he answered, while his eyes never left the troubled face before him, "I am a Negro, and my name is not Stone."

"You said that you had tramped from Colorado."

"I hadn't. I was hiding in the woods; I had been there a month ago. I lied to you."

"Is it all a lie?"

Stone hesitated, and then said: "I was meaning to tell you the first night, but somehow I couldn't. I was afraid you'd turn me out; and I was sick and miserable—"

"Tell me the truth now."

"I will; I'll tell you the God's truth."

He leaned his hand on the back of a chair to steady himself; he was trembling violently. "I came out West from Wilmington, North Carolina, Jones and I together. We were both college men and chums from childhood. All our savings were in the business we had at home, when the leading men of the town conceived the idea of driving the Negroes out, and the Wilmington tragedy began. Jones was unmarried, but I lost wife and children that night—burned to death when the mob fired our home. When we got out here, we took up claims in the mountains. They were a rough crowd after we struck pay dirt, but Jones and I kept to ourselves and got along all right until Mason joined the crowd. He was from Wilmington; knew us, and took delight in tormenting us. He was a fighting man, but we wouldn't let him push us into trouble."

"You didn't quarrel with him, then?"

The minister gazed at Stone keenly. He seemed a man to trust. "Yes, I did. We didn't want trouble, but we couldn't let Mason rob us. We three had hot words before a big crowd; that was all there was to it that night. In the morning, Mason lay dead upon our claim. He'd been shot by someone. My partner and I were arrested, brought to this city, and lodged in the jail over there. Jones was lynched! God, can I ever forget that hooting, yelling crowd, and the terrible fight to get away! Somehow I did it—you know the rest."

"Stone, there's a reward for you, and a description of you as you were the night I found you."

Gentleman Jim's face was ashy. "I'll never be taken alive. They'll kill me for what I never did!"

"Not unless I speak. I am in sore doubt what course to take. If I give you up, the vigilantes will hang you."

"I'm a lost man," said the Negro helplessly, "but I'll never be taken alive."

Stevens walked up and down the room once or twice. It was a human life in his hands. If left to the law to decide, even then in this particular case the Negro stood no chance. It was an awful question to decide. One more turn up and down the little room and suddenly stopping, he flung himself upon his knees in the middle of the room and, raising his clasped hands, cried aloud for heavenly guidance. Such a prayer as followed, the startled listener had never before heard anywhere. There was nothing of rhetorical phrases, nothing of careful thought in the construction of sentences; it was the outpouring of a pure soul asking for help from its Heavenly Father with all the trustfulness of a little child. It came in a torrent, a flood; it wrestled mightily for the blessing it sought. Rising to his feet when his prayer was finished, Rev. Stevens said, "Stone,—you are to remain Stone, you know—it is best to leave things as they are. Go back to work."

The man raised his bowed head.

"You mean you're not going to give me up?"

"Stay here till the danger is past; then leave for other parts."

Stone's face turned red, then pale; his voice trembled, and tears were in the gray eyes. "I can't thank you, Mr. Stevens, but if ever I get the chance you'll find me grateful."

"All right, Stone, all right," and the minister went back to his writing.

That fall the Rev. Septimus Stevens went to visit his old New England home—he and Flip. He was returning home the day before Thanksgiving, with his widowed mother, who had elected to leave old associations and take charge of her son's home. It was a dim-colored day.

Engineers were laying out a new road near a place of swamps and oozy ground and dead, wet grass, overarched by leafless, desolate boughs. They were eating their lunch now, seated about on the trunks of fallen trees. The jokes were few, scarcely a pun seasoned the meal. The day was a dampener; that the morrow was a holiday did not kindle merriment.

Stone sat a little apart from the rest. He had left Rev. Stevens when he got this job in another state. They had voted him moody and unsociable long ago—a man who broods forever upon his wrongs is not a comfortable companion; he never gave anyone a key to his moods. He shut himself up in his haunted room— haunted by memory—and no one interfered with him.

The afternoon brought a change in the weather. There was a strange hush, as if Nature were holding her breath. But it was as a wild beast holds its breath before a spring. Suddenly a little chattering wind ran along the ground. It was too weak to lift the sodden leaves, yet it made itself heard in some way and grew stronger. It seemed dizzy and ran about in a circle. There was a pale light over all, a brassy, yellow light, that gave all things a wild look. The chief of the party took an observation and said: "We'd better get home."

Stone lingered. He was paler, older.

The wind had grown vigorous now and began to tear angrily at the trees, twisting the saplings about with invisible hands. There was a rush and a roar that seemed to spread about in every direction. A tree was furiously uprooted and fell directly in front of him; Stone noticed the storm for the first time.

He looked about him in a dazed way and muttered, "He's coming on this train, he and the kid!"

The brassy light deepened into darkness. Stone went upon the railroad track and stumbled over something that lay directly over it. It was a huge tree that the wind had lifted in its great strength and whirled over there like thistledown. He raised himself slowly, a little confused by the fall. He took hold of the tree mechanically, but the huge bulk would not yield an inch.

He looked about in the gathering darkness; it was five miles to the station where he might get help. His companions were too far on their way to recall, and there lay a huge mass, directly in the way of the coming train. He had no watch, but he knew it must be nearly six. Soon—very soon—upon the iron pathway, a great train, freighted with life, would dash around the curve to wreck and ruin! Again he muttered, "Coming on this train, he and the kid!" He pictured the faces of his benefactor and the little child, so like his own lost one, cold in death; the life crushed out by the cruel wheels. What was it that seemed to strike across the storm and all its whirl of sound—a child's laugh? Nay, something fainter still—the memory of a child's laugh. It was like a breath of spring flowers in the desolate winter—a touch of heart music amid the revel of the storm. A vision of other fathers with children climbing upon their knees, a soft babble of baby voices assailed him.

"God help me to save them!" he cried.

Again and again he tugged at the tree. It would not move. Then he hastened and got an iron bar from among the tools. Again he strove—once—twice—thrice. With a groan the nearest end gave way. Eureka! If only his strength would hold out. He felt it ebbing slowly from him, something seemed to clutch at his heart; his head swam. Again and yet again he exerted all his strength. There came a prolonged shriek that awoke the echoes. The train was coming. The tree was moving! It was almost off the other rail. The leafless trees seemed to enfold him—to hold him with skeleton arms. "Oh, God save them!" he gasped. "Our times are in Thy hand!"

Something struck him a terrible blow. The agony was ended. Stone was dead.

Rev. Stevens closed his eyes, with a deadly faintness creeping over him, when he saw how near the trainload of people had been to destruction. Only God had saved them at the eleventh hour through the heroism of Stone, who lay dead upon the track, the life crushed out of him by the engine. An inarticulate thanksgiving rose to his lips as soft and clear came the sound of distant church bells, calling to weekly prayer, like "horns of Elfland softly blowing."

Sunday, a week later, Rev. Septimus Stevens preached the greatest sermon of his life. They had found the true murderer of Jerry Mason, and Jones and Gentleman Jim were publicly exonerated by a repentant community.

On this Sunday Rev. Stevens preached the funeral sermon of Gentleman Jim. The church was packed to suffocation by a motley assemblage of men in all stages of dress and undress, but there was sincerity in their hearts as they listened to the preacher's burning words: "As the Lord lives, he is one of our mother's children."

Meanwhile . . . ,

1920S AND 1930S

By the 1920s and 1930s, the western African American presence in the West, though small, was well established, and a new influx of African Americans during World War I increased their numbers and precipitated change. As had the majority of blacks for some time, they located in the cities of the West. They witnessed heightened black-white tensions and incidents of anti-black violence; concomitantly they fostered the rise of vibrant black communities. Organizations such as the National Association for the Advancement of Colored People (NAACP), the Universal Negro Improvement Association (UNIA), and Women's Clubs emerged to confront and challenge discrimination.

Short stories by those who covered the 1920s and 1930s black experience in the West are of two types: realistic and romantic. Some authors clearly portray the tense conditions that existed between the races. Others, perhaps to encourage white readers, perhaps to serve as escape literature, and perhaps reflecting the sentiments of the middle class, wrote "raceless" stories. The former attacked race-related problems and noted that virtue seldom overcomes racism. The latter presented stories focused on African Americans but emphasized ideal relations among people, and ended happily. The expanded number of stories indicated the growth of an educated middle class—who have time to read but do not always have the desire or energy to write about their experiences.

The persistence of lynching, and the refusal of whites to control and outlaw it, continued to anger black writers. This section begins, as the previous one ended, with the lynching of a black man by a white mob. In "Jesus Christ in Texas," W.E.B. DuBois portrays a lynching with a much more sarcastic tone than does Hopkins. In DuBois's version a black man in Texas is accused of attacking a white woman and is subsequently lynched. At the end of the story, the wife of the man for whom the black man works realizes that the mob lynched Jesus Christ. DuBois points out the hypocrisy of Christian racists.

Even though it is not a short story, William Pickens's biting essay, "Jim Crow in Texas," is purposely juxtaposed with DuBois's story. Renowned author Pickens taught and traveled in Texas; this essay is a clear explication of the psychological and physical aspects of segregation. The points of both pieces are clear: if segregation is not effective, blacks will be lynched.

The "Little Grey House," by Anita Scott Coleman, is a romance story. It is set in the small town of Hillsvale, where Timothy recognizes the charm of an unfinished grey house. He meets Opal Kent, who has recently moved with her employer to Hillsvale. With the insurance money from her father's death she has purchased land and builds a rental house. When her employers move again, Opal remains because of her obligation to her little grey house. She sells the house to Timothy, marries him, and they live together in the little grey house. Race is clearly not an issue.

Another "raceless" story, Julian Elihu Bagley's "Children of Chance," concerns Miss Mary Colser, who moves to California and discovers that two of her former students also live there. She is disappointed that they are not successful. The students have sacrificed teaching careers to become "children of chance," and work at a hotel and pursue dancing careers. After a magnificent performance in California, they are offered contracts to perform in Chicago. They get married the day they sign the contracts.

Nick Aaron Ford's "Let the Church Roll On" takes place in Iowa. The Reverend Doakes plans to deliver to his congregation, which includes some racist members, a sermon on "The Fatherhood of God and the Brotherhood of Man." An example of discrimination in the community is the university's denial of dormitory rooms to male minorities, although it has admitted two black women as a token of its nonsegregation policy. When the minister plans to baptize a black youth in the church, a woman announces that the congregation will not tolerate it. When she tells the minister that she will resign from the church and renounce her large monetary donation, he removes her name from the church register, concluding that she is the church's biggest financial asset but also its biggest spiritual liability. Instead of preaching on brotherhood the following week, the Reverend Doakes preaches on the verse that says if a hand or foot offends, cut it off.

Arna Bontemps's "Why I Returned" is an essay-like treatment of his decision to return to and remain in the South. The narrator feels guilty in the West, leaves San Francisco, and moves to Tennessee, where he stays because the South is where the "main action" is occurring in "the Negro's awakening and regeneration."

March Lacy, by contrast, vividly explicates the lure of the West, and the fantasies behind it, in "No Fools, No Fun." Black domestic servants in an eastern city seek various means to obviate the mundane nature of their existence: alcohol, dreams, pretend jobs, etc. One young woman dreams, and acts out in reality, that she works with a movie production company and that she may move to Hollywood.

Langston Hughes's "The Gun" is about a young girl in Tall Rock, Montana, whose parents left Texas because of racist antagonisms. However, she discovers that race relations are not much more progressive in Tall Rock. When her mother dies, she and her father move to Butte, then to Seattle. Finding peace in no location, the girl, now a young woman, moves alone to San Francisco and lives in various cities along the West Coast. She settles ultimately in Fresno, where she realizes that her unhappiness is not related to geography. She buys a gun and finds solace in knowing that she can choose to live or die at any moment.

"Grazing in Good Pastures," by Margaret Williams, is set in the East Texas town of Coonville. David Woods marries Rubye, a light-skinned woman from Dallas, and together they move to Coonville. Rubye is determined to acquire skills such as farming, and David's friends tell him he is grazing in good pastures. Rubye learns to grow beautiful black roses. Accepted neither by white nor black women, she sets out to prove her talents by entering her roses in the fair. When she tells David that if her roses do not win the contest she will go back to Dallas, he accuses her of trying to identify with white women. She believes he thinks more of his white cotton than he does of her black roses. When her roses win, the judges try to give credit to David, but he corrects them, informing them Rubye that raised the roses. Rubye realizes that David loves her.

These stories of the 1920s and 1930s involve landownership, varied employment options, the lure of the West, efforts of white sympathizers, effects of racism, return to the East, and (albeit romanticized) the nature of rural life. They still indicate that perhaps choices and opportunities are better in the West than in the East; the "New Negro" writers of the East coast–based Harlem Renaissance, who attack and confront race issues, turn to the South and the East for their settings. The emerging black community in Los Angeles or Seattle or Denver seems not to be an interesting topic to these authors. However, the brutality of the Great Depression permitted even less time for writing and reading. This smaller literary output also indicates that those who came west were more concerned with earning a living and exploring new opportunities than with writing. As Quintard Taylor remarks in his compelling book *In Search of the Racial Frontier: African Americans in the American West, 1528–1990* (New York: W. W. Norton, 1998), "the small African American population, its recent arrival in the region, its scant identification with the rural West, which was at that time the principal focus of regional writing, and the absence of regional outlets for black writers all weighed heavily against a western literary tradition."

Jesus Christ in Texas

W.E.B. DuBOIS

It was in Waco, Texas.

The convict guard laughed. " I don't know," he said, "I hadn't thought of that." He hesitated and looked at the stranger curiously. In the solemn twilight he got an impression of unusual height and soft, dark eyes. "Curious sort of acquaintance for the colonel," he thought; then he continued aloud: "But that nigger there is bad, a born thief, and ought to be sent up for life; got ten years last time—"

Here the voice of the promoter, talking within, broke in; he was bending over his figures, sitting by the colonel. He was slight, with a sharp nose.

"The convicts," he said, "would cost us $96 a year and board. Well, we can squeeze this so that it won't be over $125 apiece. Now if these fellows are driven, they can build this line within twelve months. It will be running by next April. Freights will fall fifty per cent. Why, man, you'll be a millionaire in less than ten years."

The colonel started. He was a thick, short man, with a clean-shaven face and a certain air of breeding about the lines of his countenance; the word millionaire sounded well to his ears. He thought—he thought a great deal; he almost heard the puff of the fearfully costly automobile that was coming up the road, and he said:

"I suppose we might as well hire them."

"Of course," answered the promoter.

The voice of the tall stranger in the corner broke in here:

"It will be a good thing for them?" he said, half in question.

The colonel moved. "The guard makes strange friends," he thought to himself. "What's this man doing here, anyway?" He looked at him, or rather looked at his eyes, and then somehow he felt a warming toward him. He said:

"Well, at least, it can't harm them; they're beyond that."

"It will do them good, then," said the stranger again.

The promoter shrugged his shoulders. "It will do us good," he said.

But the colonel shook his head impatiently. He felt a desire to justify himself before those eyes, and he answered: "Yes, it will do them good; or at any rate it won't make them any worse than they are." Then he started to say something else, but here sure enough the sound of the automobile breathing at the gate stopped him and they all arose.

"It is settled, then," said the promoter.

"Yes," said the colonel, turning toward the stranger again. "Are you going into town?" he asked with the Southern courtesy of white men to white men in a country town. The stranger said he was. "Then come along in my machine. I want to talk with you about this."

They went out to the car. The stranger as he went turned again to look back at the convict. He was a tall, powerfully built black fellow. His face was sullen, with a low forehead, thick, hanging lips, and bitter eyes. There was revolt written about his mouth despite the hangdog expression. He stood bending over his pile of stones, pounding listlessly. Beside him stood a boy of twelve,—yellow, with a hunted, crafty look. The convict raised his eyes and they met the eyes of the stranger. The hammer fell from his hands.

The stranger turned slowly toward the automobile and the colonel introduced him. He had not exactly caught his name, but he mumbled something as he presented him to his wife and little girl, who were waiting.

As they whirled away the colonel started to talk, but the stranger had taken the little girl into his lap and together they conversed in low tones all the way home.

In some way, they did not exactly know how, they got the impression that the man was a teacher and, of course, he must be a foreigner. The long, cloak-like coat told this. They rode in the twilight through the lighted town and at last drew up before the colonel's mansion, with its ghost-like pillars.

The lady in the back seat was thinking of the guests she had invited to dinner and was wondering if she ought not to ask this man to stay. He seemed cultured and she supposed he was some acquaintance of the colonel's. It would be rather interesting to have him there, with the judge's wife and daughter and the rector. She spoke almost before she thought:

"You will enter and rest awhile?"

The colonel and the little girl insisted. For a moment the stranger seemed about to refuse. He said he had some business for his father, about town. Then for the child's sake he consented.

Up the steps they went and into the dark parlor where they sat and talked a long time. It was a curious conversation. Afterwards they did not remember exactly what was said and yet they all remembered a certain strange satisfaction in that long, low talk.

Finally the nurse came for the reluctant child and the hostess bethought herself:

"We will have a cup of tea; you will be dry and tired."

She rang and switched on a blaze of light. With one accord they all looked at the stranger, for they had hardly seen him well in the glooming twilight. The woman started in amazement and the colonel half rose in anger. Why, the man was a mulatto, surely; even if he did not own the Negro blood, their practised eyes knew it. He was tall and straight and the coat looked like a Jewish gabardine. His hair hung in close curls far down the sides of his face and his face was olive, even yellow.

A peremptory order rose to the colonel's lips and froze there as he caught the stranger's eyes. Those eyes,—where had he seen those eyes before? He remembered them long years ago. The soft, tear-filled eyes of a brown girl. He remembered many things, and his face grew drawn and white. Those eyes kept burning into him, even when they were turned half away toward the staircase, where the white figure of the child hovered with her nurse and waved good-night. The lady sank into her chair and thought: "What will the judge's wife say? How did the colonel come to invite this man here? How shall we be rid of him?" She looked at the colonel in reproachful consternation.

Just then the door opened and the old butler came in. He was an ancient black man, with tufted white hair, and he held before him a large, silver tray filled with a china tea service. The stranger rose slowly and stretched forth his hands as if to bless the viands. The old man paused in bewilderment, tottered, and then with sudden gladness in his eyes dropped to his knees, and the tray crashed to the floor.

"My Lord and my God!" he whispered; but the woman screamed: "Mother's china!"

The doorbell rang.

"Heavens! here is the dinner party!" exclaimed the lady. She turned toward the door, but there in the hall, clad in her night clothes, was the little girl. She had stolen down the stairs to see the stranger again, and the nurse above was calling in vain. The woman felt hysterical and scolded at the nurse, but the stranger had stretched out his arms and with a glad cry the child nestled in them. They caught some words about the "Kingdom of Heaven" as he slowly mounted the stairs with his little, white burden.

The mother was glad of anything to get rid of the interloper, even for a moment. The bell rang again and she hastened toward the door, which the loitering black maid was just opening. She did not notice the shadow of the stranger as he came slowly down the stairs and paused by the newel post, dark and silent.

The judge's wife came in. She was an old woman, frilled and powdered into a semblance of youth, and gorgeously gowned. She came forward, smiling with extended hands, but when she was opposite the stranger, somewhere a chill seemed to strike her and she shuddered and cried:

"What a draft!" as she drew a silken shawl about her and shook hands cordially; she forgot to ask who the stranger was. The judge strode in unseeing, thinking of a puzzling case of theft.

"Eh? What? Oh—er—yes,—good evening," he said, "good evening." Behind them came a young woman in the glory of youth, and daintily silked, beautiful in face and form, with diamonds around her fair neck. She came in lightly, but stopped with a little gasp; then she laughed gaily and said:

"Why, I beg your pardon. Was it not curious? I thought I saw there behind your man"—she hesitated, but he must be a servant, she argued—"the shadow of great, white wings. It was but the light on the drapery. What a turn it gave me." And she smiled again. With her came a tall, handsome, young naval officer. Hearing his lady refer to the servant, he hardly looked at him, but held his gilded cap carelessly toward him, and the stranger placed it carefully on the rack.

Last came the rector, a man of forty, and well-clothed. He started to pass the stranger, stopped, and looked at him inquiringly.

"I beg your pardon," he said. "I beg your pardon,—I think I have met you?"

The stranger made no answer, and the hostess nervously hurried the guests on. But the rector lingered and looked perplexed.

"Surely, I know you. I have met you somewhere," he said, putting his hand vaguely to his head. "You—you remember me, do you not?"

The stranger quietly swept his cloak aside, and to the hostess' unspeakable relief passed out of the door.

"I never knew you," he said in low tones as he went.

The lady murmured some vain excuse about intruders, but the rector stood with annoyance written on his face.

"I beg a thousand pardons," he said to the hostess absently. "It is a great pleasure to be here,—somehow I thought I knew that man. I am sure I knew him once."

The stranger had passed down the steps, and as he passed, the nurse, lingering at the top of the staircase, flew down after him, caught his cloak, trembled, hesitated, and then kneeled in the dust.

He touched her lightly with his hand and said: "Go, and sin no more!"

With a glad cry the maid left the house, with its open door, and turned north, running. The stranger turned eastward into the night. As they parted a long, low howl rose tremulously and reverberated through the night. The colonel's wife within shuddered.

"The bloodhounds!" she said.

The rector answered carelessly:

"Another one of those convicts escaped, I suppose. Really, they need severer measures." Then he stopped. He was trying to remember that stranger's name.

The judge's wife looked about for the draft and arranged her shawl. The girl glanced at the white drapery in the hall, but the young officer was bending over her and the fires of life burned in her veins.

Howl after howl rose in the night, swelled, and died away. The stranger strode rapidly along the highway and out into the deep forest. There he paused and stood waiting, tall and still.

A mile up the road behind a man was running, tall and powerful and black, with crime-stained face and convicts' stripes upon him, and shackles on his legs. He ran and jumped, in little, short steps, and his chains rang. He fell and rose again, while the howl of the hounds rang louder behind him.

Into the forest he leapt and crept and jumped and ran, streaming with sweat; seeing the tall form rise before him, he stopped suddenly, dropped his hands in sullen impotence, and sank panting to the earth. A greyhound shot out of the woods behind him, howled, whined, and fawned before the stranger's feet. Hound after hound bayed, leapt, and lay there; then silently, one by one, and with bowed heads, they crept backward toward the town.

The stranger made a cup of his hands and gave the man water to drink, bathed his hot head, and gently took the chains and irons from his feet. By and by the convict stood up. Day was dawning above the treetops. He looked into the stranger's face, and for a moment a gladness swept over the stains of his face.

"Why, you are a nigger, too," he said.

Then the convict seemed anxious to justify himself.

"I never had no chance," he said furtively.

"Thou shalt not steal," said the stranger.

The man bridled.

"But how about them? Can they steal? Didn't they steal a whole year's work, and then when I stole to keep from starving—" He glanced at the stranger.

"No, I didn't steal just to keep from starving. I stole to be stealing. I can't seem to keep from stealing. Seems like when I see things, I just must—but, yes, I'll try!"

The convict looked down at his striped clothes, but the stranger had taken off his long coat; he had put it around him and the stripes disappeared.

In the opening morning the black man started toward the low, log farmhouse in the distance, while the stranger stood watching him. There was a new glory in the day. The black man's face cleared up, and the farmer was glad to get him. All day the black man worked as he had never worked before. The farmer gave him some cold food.

"You can sleep in the barn," he said, and turned away.

"How much do I git a day?" asked the black man.

The farmer scowled.

"Now see here," said he. "If you'll sign a contract for the season, I'll give you ten dollars a month."

"I won't sign no contract," said the black man doggedly.

"Yes, you will," said the farmer, threateningly, "or I'll call the convict guard." And he grinned.

The convict shrank and slouched to the barn. As night fell he looked out and saw the farmer leave the place. Slowly he crept out and sneaked toward the house. He looked through the kitchen door. No one was there, but the supper was spread as if the mistress had laid it and gone out. He ate ravenously. Then he looked into the front room and listened. He could hear low voices on the porch. On the table lay a gold watch. He gazed at it, and in a moment he was beside it,—his hands were on it! Quickly he slipped out of the house and slouched toward the field. He saw his employer coming along the highway. He fled back in terror and around to the front of the house, when suddenly he stopped. He felt the great, dark eyes of the stranger and saw the same dark, cloak-like coat where the stranger sat on the doorstep talking with the mistress of the house. Slowly, guiltily, he turned back, entered the kitchen, and laid the watch stealthily where he had found it; then he rushed wildly back toward the stranger, with arms outstretched.

The woman had laid supper for her husband, and going down from the house had walked out toward a neighbor's. She was gone but a little while, and when she came back she started to see a dark figure on the doorsteps under the tall, red oak. She thought it was the new Negro until he said in a soft voice:

"Will you give me bread?"

Reassured at the voice of a white man, she answered quickly in her soft, Southern tones:

"Why, certainly."

She was a little woman, and once had been pretty; but now her face was drawn with work and care. She was nervous and always thinking, wishing, wanting for something. She went in and got him some cornbread and a glass of cool, rich buttermilk; then she came out and sat down beside him. She began, quite unconsciously, to tell him about herself,—the things she had done and had not done and the things she had wished for. She told him of her husband and this new farm they were trying to buy. She said it was hard to get niggers to work. She said they ought all to be in the chain-gang and made to work. Even then some ran away. Only yesterday one had escaped, and another the day before.

At last she gossiped of her neighbors, how good they were and how bad.

"And do you like them all?" asked the stranger.

She hesitated.

"Most of them," she said; and then, looking up into his face and putting her hand into his, as though he were her father, she said:

"There are none I hate; no, none at all."

He looked away, holding her hand in his, and said dreamily:

"You love your neighbor as yourself?"

She hesitated.

"I try," she began, and then looked the way he was looking; down under the hill where lay a little, half-ruined cabin.

"They are niggers," she said briefly.

He looked at her. Suddenly a confusion came over her and she insisted, she knew not why.

"But they are niggers!"

With a sudden impulse she arose and hurriedly lighted the lamp that stood just within the door, and held it above her head. She saw his dark face and curly hair. She shrieked in angry terror and rushed down the path, and just as she rushed down, the black convict came running up with hands outstretched. They met in mid-path, and before he could stop he had run against her and she fell heavily to earth and lay white and still. Her husband came rushing around the house with a cry and an oath.

"I knew it," he said. "It's that runaway nigger." He held the black man struggling to the earth and raised his voice to a yell. Down the highway came the convict guard, with hound and mob and gun. They paused across the fields. The farmer motioned to them.

"He—attacked—my wife," he gasped.

The mob snarled and worked silently. Right to the limb of the red oak they hoisted the struggling, writhing black man, while others lifted the dazed woman. Right and left, as she tottered to the house, she searched for the stranger with a yearning, but the stranger was gone. And she told none of her guests.

"No—no, I want nothing," she insisted, until they left her, as they thought, asleep. For a time she lay still, listening to the departure of the mob. Then she rose. She shuddered as she heard the creaking of the limb where the body hung. But resolutely she crawled to the window and peered out into the moonlight; she saw the dead man writhe. He stretched his arms out like a cross, looking upward. She gasped and clung to the window sill. Behind the swaying body, and down where the little, half-ruined cabin lay, a single flame flashed up amid the far-off shout and cry of the mob. A fierce joy sobbed up through the terror in her soul and then sank abashed as she watched the flame rise. Suddenly whirling into one great crimson column it shot to the top of the sky and threw great arms athwart the gloom until above the world and behind the roped and swaying form below hung quivering and burning a great crimson cross.

She hid her dizzy, aching head in an agony of tears, and dared not look, for she knew. Her dry lips moved:

"Despised and rejected of men."

She knew, and the very horror of it lifted her dull and shrinking eyelids. There, heaven-tall, earth-wide, hung the stranger on the crimson cross, riven and blood-stained, with thorn-crowned head and pierced hands. She stretched her arms and shrieked.

He did not hear. He did not see. His calm dark eyes, all sorrowful, were fastened on the writhing, twisting body of the thief, and a voice came out of the winds of the night, saying:

"This day thou shalt be with me in Paradise!"

Jim Crow in Texas

WILLIAM PICKENS

The classics tell about the tortures invented by the Sicilian tyrants, but the Sicilian genius for cruelty was far inferior to that of the fellow who contrived the Jim Crow car system to harass the colored population of the South. There are tens of thousands of white people in this country who would be uncompromisingly opposed to this exquisite torture if they only understood it. But *they* are not "jim crowed," they have not the experience, and they do not and almost *cannot* understand what the colored brother finds to complain of. Have you noticed how difficult it is to explain a sensation or a pain to some one who never experienced it?

Fourteen States have Jim Crow car laws. Not one of them maintains "equal accommodations" for colored people, although the law generally calls for accommodations "equal in all points of service and convenience," so as to square with the Fifteenth Amendment. Nobody expects the railroads to go to the expense of duplicating their accommodations for the colored, non-voting, minority population. The result is that the colored traffic is usually attached to the general service with the least possible expense: a small waiting-room in one corner of the station, generally unswept and otherwise uncared-for; a compartment in one end of the white men's smoker for all the colored people—men, women, and children—to ride in; generally no wash basin and only one toilet for both sexes; with no privilege of taking meals in the diner or buying a berth in a sleeper. Colored passengers taking a journey of several days must either carry cold food enough to last or else buy the high-priced trash of the newsboy. A colored woman traveling three nights from El Paso, Texas, to Charleston, S. C., with a baby and small children, is compelled to carry cold food and to sit up on straight-backed seats for the whole trip. A colored woman of Portland, Oregon, editor of a paper there, bright, intelligent, and attractive, respected by the best-known white and colored people of the State, was visiting her parents in Texas, carrying her infant and a small child of three years. On their third night's ride, in Texas, she was compelled to get up, dress herself and babies, and vacate her berth because some short-distance white passengers objected to her presence in the car. A colored person who was hurrying from Florida to undergo an operation by an expert in Chicago had to risk death by a twenty-four-hour ride in a Jim Crow day coach. Sick colored people sometimes have to be carried on stretchers in the baggage car.

Let us look at an actual case of Jim Crow, which is typical of practically the whole South. This system is not designed to rid white people of the mere physical presence of the Negro, for a white man who objects to a colored person who rides in the other end of the car may have a colored servant with his family in his end of the car, and this colored servant may sleep in his house and be a wet-nurse for his baby. I shall use the first person singular and attempt to tell of Jim Crow experiences, without exaggeration and without abatement. I sit in a Jim Crow as I write, between El Paso and San Antonio, Texas. The Jim Crow car is not an institution merely to "separate the races"; it is a contrivance to humiliate and harass the colored people and to torture them with a finesse unequaled by the cruelest genius of the heathen world. The cruder genius broke the bodies of individuals occasionally, but Jim Crow tortures the bodies and souls of tens of thousands hourly.

In the last two months I have ridden many thousands of miles in comfortable Pullman reservations out from New York to the great Northwest, with many stops and side trips; then down from Tacoma and past the Golden Gate to the City of the Angels, from the red apples of Spokane to the golden apples of the southwestern Hesperides; and then on by the petrified forest, the great canyon, through the ancient cliff-dwellings of man to Albuquerque, New Mexico. In Albuquerque I had bought my reservation to El Paso, Texas. El Paso is where the train would enter Texas, and both my tickets terminated there. But so thoroughly is it understood that Jim Crowism is not designed merely to "separate," but also to humiliate, colored passengers that the thing is always in the consciousness of the railway employees, even those who operate in and out of Jim Crow territory, and they begin to "work on you" as soon as you buy a ticket that leads even to the limbo of this hell.

"Well, you can't ride in this car after you get into Texas. You'll have to get out of this car in Texas, and I suppose you know that?" This from the Pullman conductor, in a very gruff and loud voice, so that the whole car might hear him, while he and others stare and glare upon me. His speech is absolutely unnecessary since my tickets call only for El Paso, but the object is to "rub it in." I answered with not a word nor a look, save such mild and indifferent observation as I might bestow upon idiots who should spit at me or lick out their tongues as I passed by their cells of confinement.

In El Paso, because of the miscarriage of a telegram, my friends did not meet the train and I had to call them up and wait till they came down. I was meanwhile shown to the "Negro" waiting-room, a space of about twenty by twenty, away off in one corner of the station structure like a place of quarantine or a veritable hole in the wall. I had to traverse the entire length of the great main waiting room in order to reach this hole. This main waiting-room has all the conveniences, 'phone booths, ticket offices, and what not. And whom do you suppose I saw in this main waiting-room as I passed through? Not only the "white people," but all the non-American "colored peoples," yellow Chinese, brown Japanese, and the many-colored Mexicans, some dirty with red handkerchiefs around their necks and carrying baskets and bundles with fruits, vegetables, and live chickens. These Mexicans are the people whom the colored soldiers of the Twenty-fourth Infantry held off those white people some years ago. And if we should go to war with Japan the colored American will again be expected to rush forth from that hole in the wall to the defense of his white compatriot. I say all this without the slightest feeling of animosity toward any race, and absolutely without scorn of any human misfortune. I am only stating the case plainly. And when I reached the little humiliating hole assigned to "Negroes," I found there only four or five colored people, all intelligent, not one of the conspicuously unkempt like some of the Mexicans in the main waiting-room. Those Mexicans were being treated as human beings, as they should be treated. These colored people knew that this arrangement was not so much for their separation as for their humiliation and attempted degradation, and it formed the burden of their conversation.

I stayed in El Paso two nights and three days. Its colored people are alert to the situation. By means of their automobiles they protected me against the "rear-seat" treatment of the electric street cars. They took me across the shallow Rio Grande into Mexico, just a few hundred yards from Jim Crowism. And over there, bless you, white and black people come out of Texas and gamble at the same table, drink at the same bar, and eat in the same restaurant, while the dark and almost black Mexican stands around as the policeman and the law.

Then I went to buy a ticket for San Antonio. I did not expect to buy a Pullman ticket, but I did expect to buy a day coach ticket on any train. But I found that colored passengers are allowed to go to San Antonio on but one train a day, the one that leaves at night. The morning train carried only Pullmans, and colored folk are made to wait twelve hours longer for the train that carries a Jim Crow compartment. A colored man's mother may be dying in San Antonio, but he must wait. Any Mexican, however, whom the colored infantry fought on the border and did not happen to kill, can ride on any train. Any foreigner, or any foreign spy who happens to be loose in the land, can travel freely, but not the mothers or wives or sisters of the black Americans who fought, bled, and died in France. All the rest of the world, be he an unlettered Mexican peon, an untrammeled Indian, or a representative of the uncivilized "white trash" of the South, can get either train; but the Negro, be he graduate of Harvard or bishop of the church, can go only once daily. Now if the Negro can be limited to once a day while others ride on any train, the Negro can be limited to one day a week while others ride seven, or even to one day a month while others ride thirty.

I took the train that leaves at night. It is a ride of about twenty-four hours. Through friends it had been arranged that I be given a berth, late at night, after all the white people had gone to sleep and could not see me, and perhaps be called early before any of the whites were up. The money was accepted from my friends, even tips, but only the porter was sent to bring me a pillow into the Jim Crow car, and they still have the money. In the morning I went back to see if I could get some breakfast in the dining car, before 7 o'clock, before the whites got hungry. And what did I find as I passed through the whole string of Pullman cars in the rear? All the races of the world, as usual, save only the most loyal of all Americans.

In the Jim Crow car there was but one toilet and wash-room, for use of colored women and men. And the Jim Crow car is not a car, mind you, but only the end of a car, part of the white men's smoker, separated from the white smokers only by a partition that rises part of the way from the floor toward the ceiling, so that all the sickening smoke can drift over all night and all day. And yet what do you suppose the colored porter said as he swept out the Jim Crow end this morning? Nobody asked him, he volunteered as he swept: "Well, this is the cleanest floor I have to sweep every morning. Them white folks and Mexicans and things back yonder sho' do mess up the floors!"

When I reached the dining-car there was not another person there. I was asked did I "want anything." I replied briefly, breakfast. Then there was confusion and much conferring between the steward and several colored waiters at the other end of the car. The steward kept glancing at me meanwhile, as if endeavoring to "size me." Finally I was given a seat at the end of the car where the porters eat. Oatmeal, eggs, and postum were brought, and then a green curtain was drawn between me and the rest of the vacant dining-car! Remember, this did not all happen in some insane asylum, but in Texas. The check on which I was to order my food was a green check, a "porter's check," so that I should not need to be treated to such little formalities as an extra plate or a finger bowl. I deliberately wrote my name down in the blank for "porter," but I was charged a passenger's fare. It all meant that I would not eat any more that day, although I was not to reach San Antonio till eight or nine at night.

One must be an idiot not to comprehend the meaning and the aim of these arrangements. There is no such thing as a fair and just Jim Crow system with "equal accommodations," and in very human nature there will never be. The inspiration of Jim Crow is a feeling of caste and a desire to "keep in its place," that is, to degrade, the weaker group. For there is no more reason for a Jim Crow car in public travel than there would be for a Jim Crow path in the public streets. Those honest-souled, innocent-minded people who do not know, but who think that the Jim Crow system of the South is a bona-fide effort to preserve mere racial integrity on a plane of justice are grievously misled. Any man should be permitted to shut out whom he desires from his private preserves, but justice and Jim Crowism in public places and institutions are as far apart and as impossible of union as God and Mammon.

The Little Grey House

ANITA SCOTT COLEMAN

It was built of cement, of a lighter hue than most cement houses, so it was dubbed the little grey house.

Somehow, its builders pervaded every inch of its rough exterior with an inviting air. Even before it was finished—and we all know most incompleted houses are so mussy and dreary with daubs of paint and spattered lime and splotches of mud and shavings and blocks of wood and the workmen's tools lying all about—but this was different.

The unfinished windows suggested gauzy curtains and flowering plants. The littered interior with its yawning doorways revealing other unplastered chambers and yet more clutter, gave a cheery promise of clean-swept, cozy rooms. The little squat chimney that lifted its stubby nose into the air from the left-hand corner of its roof hinted with all its might, of the hearth-fire that would soon cast its rosy warmth over the inmates of the little grey house; while the chimney that poked its nose towards the sky at the rear of the roof, was a silent witness of many smokes it would exhale from the cooking of savory meals.

Timothy passed the little grey house every morning on his way to work and every evening on his way home—home to his untidy bachelor apartment, where he, himself, made the bed and cooked the meals and washed the dishes whenever they were washed, that was, when Timothy found his cupboard shelves were bare and his sink over-filled with plates and cups.

He was interested from the first—from the moment he saw the men laying off the site for the little grey house. Every evening he paused to take in what had been accomplished during the day. He inspected the foundation—noted the number of rooms there were to be—guessed boyishly just which would be the bed-room, living-room, and kitchen. He hoped heartily there would be an honest-to-goodness kitchen and none of your new-fangled, fool-notion kitchenettes.

"Even if they eat in the kitchen 'twill be better'n one of those fool kitchenettes," he soliloquized. "For now, what in heck is a home without a kitchen, if 'taint just like a ship without a rudder I'll be blowed." He passed on, his broad good-natured face wreathed in smiles at his own wit.

The little grey house was nearing completion when it happened the first time. At the next street crossing he met her. He remembered that she was just about to take the step up to the sidewalk.

Hillsvale was such an up and down hill little place—that each walk began or ended in a flight of steps—and he had politely stood aside to let her ascend.

She acknowledged the little courtesy with the tiniest scantiest acknowledgement that could be.

Friendly Timothy was made somewhat crest-fallen by her chilly manner, wondered if it was just her scant politeness or more of his "infernal, confounded knack at getting in bad with the ladies."

Leastways the encounter put an end to that day's pleasant musing about the little grey house. It made the boiled and steaming "hot-dogs" and the loaf of home-made bread still warm from the oven, that kind old Mrs. Bloomsay had given him for his supper, and the butter and the tea and the cabbage, he had prepared so painstakingly that morning, guided by a vivid memory of his mother's cold-slaw into a semblance of that dish, and the baker's blue-berry pie, which he meant to use as the climax of his evening's meal taste, as he said, "Like gol-darned saw-dust in his mouth."

"The truth is," he flayed himself further in comical petulance "you are plump put out because a cross old hen gave you the icy stare. Oh boy, she's got your goat."

He tried reading his evening's paper and found himself glaring menacingly at the front page whereon in great black type announced the sweeping victory of a political candidate, who was especially distasteful to him; he flung the paper from him disgustedly.

He tried smoking, but his cigar—one of the same brand he smoked invariably—was the rankest, vilest weed he ever put in his mouth. It was tossed vehemently into the fire.

He stood up then in the middle of his mussy kitchen and scowled at the littered supper-table and the sink full of dirty dishes, then suddenly rolled up his sleeves and gave battle to the disorder until everything shone tidy and neat. "Be blowed," he said and smiled, almost restored to his usual good nature, "if it don't look like a woman did it." But there . . . he had spoken the unlucky word . . . woman. As he uttered it, his thoughts reverted to the object of that species who was causing all the trouble.

"Who in the deuce is she anyhow?" he exclaimed wrathfully. . . . As there was no one to answer him, he presently went to bed, with a conscience as clean as any man's could be, who had lived forty years in this sin-filled world—re-enforced with a kindly good-nature, and a body keyed to the fatigue point by a full day of hard work soon brought refreshing sleep, accompanied by a dream, which he remembered vaguely, featured a plump little brown woman with a regular apple-dumpling sort of a face. For Timothy was certain that an apple-dumpling browned to a turn, and spiced and sugared to suit an epicure's appetite, was the neatest description for the little woman's soft full cheeks and rounded chin.

Altogether he was pleased with that face; until he remembered the eyes. "My stars," he would say, "some ice! Oh boy!" Only, he recalled through the indistinctness of his dream, those eyes had been soft and tender and he declared wonderingly, as he kicked off the covers and rolled out of bed next morning, "They got his goat."

With another day's work "neatly put over" and the makings of a nifty meal—a juicy steak, a package of potato-chips, a dozen freshly baked rolls all tucked into the curve of his arm; with nothing in the world to worry about; the incident of the evening before almost swept from his mind—Timothy paused almost from habit before the little grey house.

"I'll be blowed, if you ain't the prettiest little box of a house I've seen yet!"

Then beset with the thoughts of his yet-to-be-cooked steak, he hurried on—and there—almost in the same spot approached the woman. Timothy grinned broadly over the coincident and just as he had done the previous evening stood aside politely as she ascended. And again just to a T she acknowledged the little courtesy with the tiniest, scantiest acknowledgment, so scant, that only an intent—a very intent observer could have discerned it at all.

"Well, one thing's certain, old girl," thought Timothy, "you're sure no killer for looks. I reckon it's the old girl's way of pulling off the high and mighty that's got my goat. Anyhow," he announced quite spiritedly to himself, "I'll be blowed if I don't fry this steak and eat every scrap of it—old haughty one, you're not going to spoil my eats every single night, not on your life."

"I wonder," mused Opal Kent half angrily, who all unknowingly lived in Timothy's mind as the plump little lady with the apple-dumpling face, "who on earth that grinning Jacob of a man can be?"

Opal Kent had never received any marked attention from men, so Timothy's eager politeness was bewildering to her simple soul; and his broad smile, which she so contemptuously termed a grin, exasperated her to the limit and what made it worse, she could not reason why—and his intent scrutiny of her as she passed—it was maddening.

"The horrid, horrid thing!" she exclaimed aloud, then in an undertone which sounded cooingly soft as it wafted away on the breeze:

"But he isn't bad-looking a bit, not a bit."

Opal Kent was one of the jolliest, dearest little women in the world, good-hearted to a fault and responsive as a kitten to kindness and gentle treatment; but at present, she was all out of sorts. She was lonely and homesick—homesick as only a homeless woman can be and she was disheartened. Here she was already past the thirty mile sign in years, and as Timothy himself had concluded, "In no way a killer for looks." All in the world she could do was cook and keep house. Of course, there was her crocheting and tatting and knitting, but no valuation could be put upon that, thought Opal for where in the world could you find a homely old spinster fond of her hearth-fire who couldn't?

Poor lonely Opal; like all disheartened people she belittled her attainments, for her cooking was sheerest witchery and she belonged to those rare women who could, given the stimulation of having near her, those she loved, could convert a bare spot in a desert into a home.

To be sure, of this last attribute, none save old Joseph Kent could testify and since he had died a year ago, his testimony was hopelessly out of the question.

Opal had always kept house for her father. As far back as she could remember she had been the little woman of his household. A distant relative had helped old Joseph raise her to an early age of independence and since then, she had been the little mistress of their home.

"Old Joe Kent" had been a grim, forbidding old man, who repulsed rather than encouraged any friendships for himself and daughter. They had lived a bleak and lonely life, relieved only by the love they bore each other. Old Kent had uncanny success with his pigs and chickens and by supplying his neighbors' tables with these commodities, earned a livelihood. He looked forward a bit for Opal's sake and insured himself quite heavily and the payment of those premiums had eaten the heart out of his meagre income.

Opal had stinted and economized for every dress and every hat or ribbon she had ever possessed. So plus her cooking and house-keeping was an almost instinctive frugality that saved seemingly valueless things and cunningly contrived them into articles of value. She made cunning baby shoes from a man's old, cast-off hat. She saved the vinegar off the pickles to mix her salad dressings, saved turkey feathers and made her own feather dusters, could take a nearly clean-picked chicken carcass, a grain or two of rice, a cabbage leaf, a celery stalk and turn out soup with a savory odor that lingered in your nostrils for a fortnight and a pleasing taste that tickled your palate whenever you recalled it.

Almost simultaneously, with the sad occurrence of her father's death and the coming of the insurance money, old Judge Crowley prepared to move West for his wife's health. And Opal was prevailed upon to accompany them as cook.

"Why not?" reasoned Opal, for who in her little home town cared if she went or remained? It was enough to make one sour to think about it, for no one ever suspected how much Opal Kent longed for friendship and there was none among all her life-long acquaintances who could be called friend.

If someone had suggested to Opal that it was her father's fault, she would have been appalled. She would have repudiated it with every ounce of strength of her being. Her father, her dear, old, kind, indulgent dad! how she missed him! She could see him just as he used to be and it was sweet to remember how the lines of care faded from his face as he sat and watched her bustle about preparing the supper. His favorite place was beside the kitchen door, which faced westward. He always sat full in the golden shaft of sunlight. "It warms like nothing else on earth," had been his phrase. And Opal had come to time the evening meal with the fading of the sunlight from the door. Such had been their life together, replete with the nameless love tokens each had performed for the other, with no word of explanation to add to or distract their pleasure. "You are like your Ma, girl," had been his one form of endearment, and she perceived that those six words summed up the strength of a love that had lasted unto death and beyond the grave and lived again in all of its wondrous beauty for herself.

The Crowleys had settled in Hillsvale six months ago and Opal Kent suddenly decided to invest her insurance money in a home. Hillsvale would be as good a place as any in which to spend her life, since she had no friends or any tie to bind her elsewhere. And forthwith, she had bought the lots and had the little grey house built.

She would rent it at first, of course, and work on, saving every cent of her money until she had enough to allow her to become mistress of the little grey house in earnest.

Then she would raise chickens. Just supposing, if she had fifty hens and got fifty eggs a day, as the ads in the farm papers guaranteed was the simplest thing to do . . . and she would keep bees, the Government bulletins extolled their virtue to the highest . . . a pleasant and profitable industry . . . and she would have a few bunnies, another profitable and little known money-maker, she wouldn't go into that so deeply, but a few would add variety to her meat supply, providing she could kill and eat them after fondling them, as she knew she would do. They were such cunning creatures with their pink noses forever wiggling and their bright eyes constantly watchful. She would have a nice old tabby cat and a collie pup and maybe after she was known in Hillsvale, little children would come to see her and her pets. She would keep a well-filled cookie jar, and of course there would be honey, and perhaps, oh perhaps, she would be ever and ever so happy as mistress of the little grey house, even though she was alone and friendless and had nothing, nothing with which to challenge the coming lonely years. She was unable to suppress the shudder which came when she thought of that.

Taken from all angles, it is quite true that folks are the masters of their own destiny: only one must admit that catching hold of your own particular bit of destiny is nearly as futile a performance as a kitten swirling around trying to catch his tail. At least it appeared so to Opal all bolstered up with expectations over the little grey house.

The big "FOR RENT" sign which was tacked upon the little grey house as soon as it was finished failed to attract any notice whatever. It seemed that all the house hunters and all the disgruntled renters for once in their lives were happily settled and satisfied. Nobody rented Opal Kent's little place, by no means as soon as she expected and certainly not as soon as she had need for it to be.

The Crowleys, without any hint of their intentions, decided to move elsewhere. Opal, finding herself indefinitely linked to Hillsvale because of the little grey house, could not be induced to move with them.

Opal found another place and though it saved her from becoming stranded in a strange town, she did not like it. Not having learned how, she did not make friends readily and her work was confining, so she became acquainted with no one.

She was timid and self-conscious and oppressed by an overgrowing dread of loneliness, and like most homeless women, she was afraid, just afraid of everything.

"Suppose," ran her thoughts, "I should lose my health, what then? Suppose I do not save enough before I am old. . . ."

She grew more and more reticent and her plump, round face grew overcast with dread and her eyes grew sharp. She watched people, watched the expression of their faces and construed them to portend queer things concerning herself, when for the most part her dumpty little figure passed among the crowds unnoticed. She wondered over Timothy's good-natured smile. "Why does he laugh at me so? Oh, dear, I must be funny, and, oh . . . oh, queer."

The first time Timothy saw the "FOR RENT" sign he stopped and gazed at it incredulously. "Well now," he said, "what nut built a house like that to rent? I was as sure as pop that it was going to be somebody's home—somebody who'd love every inch of it and take care of it and plant flowers around it, and all such as that. Now look at that there sign, 'FOR RENT'; just spoils the whole thing, be blowed if it don't."

He continued to meet Opal. In fact, his interest was divided between the little grey house and these meetings with the plump little woman. Taken together, they afforded Timothy something pleasant with which to wind up his lonely evenings. He would think of the little grey house and wonder who'd rent it, and he would think about the little woman, wondering who she was. No one he questioned seemed to know. At bed time he would turn in and maybe dream that he was Lord and Master of both the little woman and the little grey house.

Then as unexpected as the "FOR RENT" sign had been was the "FOR SALE" sign which Timothy glanced up to see one evening as he passed. In smaller lettering the placard stated, further information secured from PITMAN'S RE-ALTY COMPANY.

It set Timothy to thinking. He was preoccupied when he passed the little dumpty woman.

So for once Opal failed to see him grinning, but with a woman's inconsistence, she found herself wondering what in the world had happened to chase his smiles away.

And if Timothy had not been so absorbed he would have been sure to notice the traces of tears which lingered in the little woman's eyes.

Opal was on her way to the little grey house. She had enjoyed so much to go there when her hopes were high. She had found grim satisfaction in seeing it after she knew that as a business venture it was a hopeless failure. And now, that she had decided to sell it, from necessity, she found a torturing delight in looking upon it.

Yes, the place she had was unendurable. She couldn't stand the contempt and the rude treatment, the family for whom she now worked, seemed to think was a cook's portion. She would sell the little place and get out of it whatever she could and write the Crowleys that she would join them.

That night, Timothy made up his mind. "Be blowed, if I won't buy it myself. . . ." 'Twas a shame for a house like that go to waste! "Who knows?" he questioned, "I might find me a wife, and even if I don't, 'cause a man's single is no sign he has to live like a pig. Gosh no! I'll set out a lilac bush and some flowers and plant some trees. Anyhow, I'll buy the dinged little place and get it off my mind."

Two days later, Opal Kent went to the realty office and transacted her portion of the business pertaining to the sale of the little grey house. She received her money—nearly as much as the little grey house had cost—minus the commission.

With the money in her possession, her plans changed again. She would stay in Hillsvale and see who had purchased the little grey house.

Timothy Martin stopped that evening to inspect his property thoroughly. He went from room to room, there were five, a nice spacious kitchen with built-in cupboards and cabinets, and one end which made an alcove built almost entirely of glass, a stationary table and chairs stood resplendent, invitingly coaxing one to eat. "Holy Pete!" ejaculated Timothy, "I'll plant honeysuckle to climb all over that there glass . . . and won't it be pretty?" In the other rooms, he found window seats with hinged covers and more built-in cabinets and book cases. "Gosh," he exclaimed, "mighty pretty, but it's just been built for a woman. A woman's the only creature on earth that can care for this sort of trick."

He was nearly through with his round of inspection, when he stopped short, startled by a sound. "Gee," he muttered and listened. Again the sound came. "Be blowed, it sounds like someone crying." Timothy quietly retraced his steps, finding nothing until he entered the kitchen.

And there, in the waning sunlight which poured into the glass-walled alcove, beside the table, with her head bowed on her arms, sat the little woman, his plump little apple-dumpling woman, crying, just crying, thought Timothy, "like a great big baby."

Timothy stood stock still and watched her, watched her with a mingled delight and dismay and consternation; delight to find her there, dismay that she was crying and at the very end of his wits for fear his presence would frighten her away.

What should he do? Then a quivering little voice restored him to his senses.

"Oh, it's you—it's you! Did you buy it?"

Timothy sensed that she was speaking of the little grey house, and nodded his head in assent. Then in an eager desire to cheer her up, he began to talk in his cheery booming voice.

"Though, I'll be blowed, Miss, the blame little box was intended for a woman and not for the likes of me. All these here fixings tells you that. Now if I had a wife . . . Say, now, you mustn't cry any more. Just you listen to me. I was saying that if I had a wife to putter around and fix this here trinket of a house like it ought to be fixed . . . I'd be the happiest man alive. Gee, Miss, I'm a demon when it comes to setting out vines and flowers and I'd have the yard out front looking like a bit of fairy land and we'd have chickens in the back and maybe a wee turnip patch."

"And," put in Opal, wholly unaware of the strangeness of it all, "I'd planned to have some bees too and just a handful of bunnies. Oh, don't you like to watch 'em wiggle their noses? . . . and I'd meant to have flowers too, holly-hocks and roses and lark-spurs growing everywhere, and a lilac bush under the bedroom window and honey-suckle and climbing roses over the ones in the dining room and I hadn't quite decided what I'd have over the windows in the living room, perhaps I'd have left 'em bare so's to look out and see folks passing . . ."

"Say you," burst in Timothy excitedly, "did you have this house built?" Thrust back into reality by his question, Opal could not speak, for tears choked back her words and her plump little shoulders heaved piteously.

In the wee interval in which he watched her second outburst, good-hearted, good-natured, forty-year-old bachelor, Timothy made a few swift calculations concerning his weeping companion. That in the main they were correct was not surprising for Timothy earned his livelihood by an ability to size up people. His heart jumped exultingly as he concluded she was not married and never had been. It clutched in pity, as he decided she wept thus because she was lonely and friendless and homeless, for he discerned from her tears that the little box of a house had been built to be her home. It took but a minute for his quick mind to ferret out this . . . then the blunt fashion that had ever been his custom that was the main spring of his "infernal, confounded knack of getting in bad with the ladies," expressed itself blurtingly . . .

"There . . . there . . . there," he punctuated each word with a bearish pat on Opal's heaving shoulder. "What in all heck, you crying about now, didn't I say I wanted a wife . . . ?"

And say what you will, the real mating among humans is like the birds, instinctive and unerring, for presently Opal's plumply rounded face was lifted to receive Timothy's smacking kiss; while the kindly sun, blinking his red-gold eye, like a jocose inebriate, slipped quietly away, out of the glass covered alcove, leaving them, master and mistress, in full possession of the little grey house.

Children of Chance

JULIAN ELIHU BAGLEY

It was a curious twist of fate that brought Miss Mary Colser and two of her former pupils together under the same roof at the fashionable Crest View Hotel in San Francisco. True it was that the former pupils—Hugho and Elnoma—had done some skillful and deliberate planning for their meeting at the Crest View, but they certainly had not included Miss Colser in this plan. Nevertheless she was there—there as a full-fledged guest and a woman of apparent wealth, while Hugho and Elnoma were there in quite another capacity. It had been some five years since this trio met or rather one should say parted, for the last time they saw one another was that day when Miss Colser reluctantly resigned her position as teacher in a colored missionary school in Virginia where she had taught some thirty years and returned to her native New England to pass the rest of her days.

But some how or other this idle empty life seemed desperately lonely to her. Always she longed to return to the school. The magic of the old songs, the warm sunny skies of the South, and the happy laughter of her former pupils—all bade her come back once more. But the missionary school had very politely intimated that she was too old for further service. So when a generous donor of the school offered her anything she might wish, she cast old memories aside and asked for and got a trip to California. Now she was living in splendor on the top floor of the Crest View where she spent her time reading and knitting and watching the ships bound from and to the various parts of the world pass in and out the Golden Gate. And had it not been for the discovery of Hugho and Elnoma Miss Colser might have gone on enjoying this sort of life.

But the presence of these two young people gave her an entirely different view of herself and the work she had given most of her life to. Heretofore she had thought of her life only in terms of success, for during her entire connection with the missionary school not one failure had been reported among her pupils. She was therefore very much chagrined in these last days to find two of her most recent and brilliant pupils at work in a hotel. She immediately labeled them failures. But Elnoma took up the cudgels of defense. Her story was a simple story of a country girl and boy who during the course of their training at the missionary school had come to themselves and discovered that they had more talent and liking for such things as singing and acting and dancing than for teaching. But they were poor and the custom or policy or whatever you want to call it of the school was to encourage teachers and not dancers. And so Elnoma and Hugho were "turned out" teachers only to be let out of a rural school in the middle of their first term because the patrons objected to their children being taught folk dances.

After this unfortunate and discouraging incident Elnoma went to New York where she sought and obtained a job with one Madame Dernier, a well-known dancer whom she had met one summer while working in a hotel on Long Island. Later on, an engagement to direct the ballet dancing in one of San Francisco's finest moving picture theaters had called Madame Dernier across the continent, and, of course, she had brought Elnoma with her. Now they were making their home at the Crest View. Hugho, Elnoma explained, had made his way to California and finally San Francisco by his own resources, being guided only by his admiration for her. Then one day there was a chance for a lobby porter at the Crest View and through Elnoma, Hugho got the job.

But this explanation followed by a statement from Madame Dernier that Hugho and Elnoma possessed unusual and original ideas about dancing and that she hoped to help them to success one day made no impression on the former missionary. She still referred to these former pupils as failures—shirkers of duty, children of chance. Elnoma who was more ready at argument than Hugho finally succeeded in convincing Miss Colser that there were two sides to this story; that if they were failures, shirkers of duty or children of chance, Miss Colser had played a conspicuous part in the game.

"I guess after all, though," added Elnoma thoughtfully, "none of us is wholly to blame. It's a sort of combination of pupils, teachers and policies. Of course there have been bigger failures than Hugho and I, but you've never seen them. Lacking the courage to break away from the traditional path, they've tucked their dreams away in their hearts and trudged on down the path of least resistance! We haven't lost the spirit of service which we found at the missionary school. Indeed we haven't. We'd help anyone right this moment, but still we think it best to try the thing that's nearest our heart. Maybe some day you'll understand what we mean, Miss Colser; maybe you'll come to see that if the missionary school had a more varied assortment of molds and the courage to blaze certain untraditional paths, there would be fewer blasted dreams among the people they serve. But understand us now," Elnoma concluded, "we are not complaining, only we do think that sculptors who shape rough stones into finished products should—"

"Well, I guess we won't talk about it any more for a while," Miss Colser broke in abruptly. And from that day on the subject was taboo. Yet, all along, a vigorous struggle went on in the minds of the former teacher and her pupils. Each side hoped and waited for the opportunity to prove the other side wrong. And finally one day the chance came. The generous donor responsible for Miss Colser's trip had died some time since without making provisions for her maintainence and now the little missionary was in acute need. Monsieur Jean Ferrier, the proprietor, had already allowed her some two or three months of grace, but with the coming of the Christmas season and the increasing demand for rooms he felt obliged to ask her either to make some provisions to pay her bills or to move, and since she could not do the former she was preparing to do the latter.

Miss Colser had made a careful attempt to keep these facts from Hugho and Elnoma and had it not been for Hugho's sudden discovery of her trunk and some of her most treasured articles in the held-for-charges section of the Crest View's store-room, they might have always believed her casual statement that she was "just moving to a smaller and less expensive hotel." But now that they had the real truth of the matter it was different. Something must be done to save the little missionary. They appealed to Monsieur Ferrier but he clung to his original stand. "Then what would you say to our making some provisions for paying her bills?" Monsieur Ferrier was asked.

"Oh you can't do that," he assured them. "Miss Colser doesn't even want you two to know she's in need."

"Oh yes we can do it too," Elnoma put in, "and we will—if you'll let us have the ball room Christmas Eve night. And Miss Colser needn't know anything about it until—until it's all over." Now Monsieur Ferrier had heard of Elnoma's ability as a dancer through Madame Dernier and he himself had seen Hugho do some fast stepping as he went about his work at the Crest View. So—

"I'll not only give you the use of the ball room Christmas Eve night," was his solemn promise, "but I will do all I can to help you make the affair a success."

What welcome news this was for Hugho and Elnoma. That same evening they set out and found talent enough to complete a tentative program calculated to satisfy the most exacting audience. There was, for instance, the Coleridge-Taylor Choral Club which would sing the old plantation melodies; a violinist who listed such exquisite gems as "Deep River" and an "Ave Maria." Of course, Hugho and Elnoma would dance. When Christmas Eve, the night for the affair, came every seat in the ball room was taken long in advance of the time set for the curtain and Monsieur Ferrier was scurrying about here and there trying to find chairs enough for those who continued to pour in.

Came the time for the curtain. There was no delay. The Choral Club, first on the program, began. How they did chant that plaintive old Christmas spiritual of their people—

> *Go tell it on the mountains,*
> *Over the hills and everywhere.*
> *Go tell it on the mountains,*
> *That Jesus Christ is a-born!*

The audience applauded the singers vigorously and they sang song after song all of which resounded with the Christmas Spirit. Then the violinist played and got an increasing amount of applause. But Elnoma was hailed as "a lithe brown girl with magic eyes who put more gusto, originality and insinuation into her dance 'Abyssinia' than any one we've ever seen. And," concluded the notice, "if the *blasé* theatrical producer whom we saw eating up this entertainment last night doesn't grab up these gifted steppers, some one else will."

Came the time when Hugho could snatch a moment from his work. Hurriedly he made his way to Miss Colser's room with the morning paper. But she had already read the story.

"How did you get a paper so early?" asked Hugho, for he knew in these last lean days Miss Colser had depended on his saving her a paper from the ones picked up in the lobby.

"The man who sat next me last night brought it in," said she. "He's a theatrical producer—from Chicago," she went on, "and I literally pulled him into the ball room last night to get his opinion on your dancing. He's an old friend of mine and I told him I hoped he'd say you and Elnoma couldn't dance, but he didn't. Says you both have a wonderful future and he's going to give you your first big chance in his show opening in Chicago in February."

Now this was the biggest and most welcome news Hugho had ever received and from that moment on his little romance took on a tempo that was decidedly swift, for the next day he and Elnoma gave up their respective jobs and signed two important contracts—the one to dance in the Chicago producer's show, and the other to serve and be true to each other to the end of their days! This then is the story of the Children of Chance. There is not much more to tell about them except to say that on New Year's Day a wistful brown maid with tear-dimmed eyes stood beside a picturesque and handsome youth on the rear of the observation car of the "Overland Limited" and waved good bye to California and a group of admiring friends, not the least of whom was Miss Colser.

"Elnoma," said Hugho as the train got under way for Chicago, "aren't you glad the Chicago producer is going to take care of our little missionary teacher?"

"Yes, I am," replied Elnoma, "but aren't you rather sorry that she still thinks we're just plain Children of Chance?"

Let the Church Roll On

NICK AARON FORD

The Reverend Jerome K. Doakes sat uneasily at the big oak desk in his study. The long Iowa winter had relaxed, and this was the first day since late October that the furnace in the parsonage needed no attention. The minister was pleased that he could give uninterrupted thought to the preparation of his sermon.

But the joy of spring was not in the minister's heart. The assignment before him was a tough one. He was going to preach next Sunday on "The Fatherhood of God and the Brotherhood of Man."

It was not that the Reverend Mr. Doakes did not practice what he was about to preach. He had always lived the gospel of brotherhood.

His five children, from the sixteen-year-old Marjorie to the five-year-old Jerome, Jr., sought opportunities to fraternize with members of minority groups. He had transformed part of the thirteen-room parsonage into living quarters for eight students. Among his roomers were a Chinese, a Japanese, a Jew, and a colored girl from Des Moines.

The University, located in the Reverend Mr. Doakes' home town, denied all charges of racial segregation. Yet no male member of minority races could secure rooms in the dormitories. Only recently the women's dormitories had admitted two colored girls, presumably as a token of the University's "official" policy of non-segregation.

Although there were only nine colored families in town, an insufficient number for any racial businesses, white barbers would not serve Negro customers. A few restaurants and several places of recreation also drew the color line.

For twelve years the Reverend Mr. Doakes had waged a quiet but active campaign against racial barriers in the seat of the renowned University. He had three colored members on the choir of the Second Baptist Church. He even encouraged Negro students to affiliate with his church as "watch care" members during their stay at the University.

But despite the minister's long record of aggressive work for equality and fraternity, the proposed sermon on "The Fatherhood of God and the Brotherhood of Man" made him uneasy.

He was certain that the events of the next Sunday would be a test of all that he had fought for since the beginning of his pastorate.

It wasn't the sermon itself that disturbed him so greatly, but the occasion for it, the event for which it was prepared.

He turned to the second chapter of I John, verse 9, and began to read: "He that saith he is in the light, and hateth his brother, is in the darkness . . ."

There was a light knock on the door. The minister looked up from his open Bible and told the intruder to come in.

"I am glad to find you alone," the visitor said in a frightened voice.

"Alone with God," the pastor suggested.

The tall, frail woman nervously walked over to the wicker chair pointed out by her host, and sat down. "I am sorry to interrupt you," she apologized, "but I had to come."

She hesitated. The words seemed to stick in her throat. A red flush rose in her left cheek and crept over her entire face.

"Is it a matter of life or death?" the minister asked calmly.

"Yes," she replied, "the life or death of the Second Baptist Church."

The pastor set himself for trouble. Mrs. J. Russel Spruce was an influential member of his church. Her husband was the president of the local real estate company. He had been warned when he accepted his present post that Mrs. Spruce could "make him or break him."

Quickly his mind ran over his twelve years of dealing with Mrs. Spruce. He remembered her distress when he accepted the Negro boarder in his home. He recalled her disapproving remarks when the colored singers joined the choir. He could never forget the scowl on her face when he had introduced the Chinese student to her at the church anniversary banquet.

"I am listening," he said in a hard, inflexible voice.

"I have come to warn you," she said, anger rising in her throat and overflowing in her voice. "You must not go through with this monstrous thing next Sunday."

The minister did not answer immediately. A storm of rage swept over his sainted countenance and wore itself out in dignified silence. "I presume," he finally replied, "you mean the baptism of Billy Jones."

"Yes," she shot back, "you know that's what I mean. The church will not stand for it. We reluctantly went along when you took colored members on the choir and when you accepted them under watch care of the church. But we will not stand for the baptism of a black boy in our church."

"And what is your objection?" the minister inquired.

"Don't be ridiculous, Dr. Doakes," she retorted. "If we had wanted an interracial church, we would have organized it before you came. But we don't want it, and we're not going to have it!"

"You want a Christian church, don't you?" the pastor asked.

"Of course," Mrs. Spruce agreed.

"Then you cannot logically object to Billy Jones," the minister explained. "Christ has no respect for race or color or national origin. He respects only the desires, the intents, the purposes, and the deeds of people."

Mrs. Spruce was not impressed. She rose in obvious anger. "You ignore my warning?" she shouted.

"I do," the pastor calmly replied.

"Then I withdraw my membership. And woe be unto you!"

"Just a minute, Mrs. Spruce," the minister said, as his visitor turned toward the door, "I have something further to say."

He pushed a button under his desk and his secretary appeared. "Bring in volume III of the ledger," he ordered.

During the interval, the man and woman faced each other in icy silence. The minister was standing now with his hand on the door knob, as if he feared his caller might take flight before he was ready.

When the secretary returned, he instructed her to find the name of Mrs. J. Russel Spruce.

"You'll find I'm the biggest financial asset you have in this church," Mrs. Spruce volunteered. She was trying to relax now, believing the pastor was about to yield.

"I know," replied the minister, "but you are also the biggest spiritual liability."

Turning to his secretary, he said, "Blot out her name with your red pencil. And may God have mercy on her soul!"

He opened the door, and Mrs. Spruce, chastened and bewildered, walked out.

The next Sunday the church was crowded for the baptismal services of Billy Jones. The Reverend Mr. Doakes did not preach his sermon on the Fatherhood of God and the Brotherhood of Man. Instead, he took his text from Matthew 18:8.

"Wherefore if thy hand or thy foot offend thee, cut them off, and cast them from thee: it is better for thee to enter into life halt and maimed, rather than having two hands or two feet to be cast into everlasting fire."

Why I Returned

ARNA BONTEMPS

The last time I visited Louisiana the house in which I was born was freshly painted. To my surprise, it seemed almost attractive. The present occupants, I learned, were a Negro minister and his family. Why I expected the place to be run down and the neighborhood decayed is not clear, but somewhere in my subconscious the notion had been planted and allowed to grow that rapid deterioration was inevitable where Negroes live. Moreover, familiar as I am with the gloomier aspects of living Jim Crow, this assumption did not appall me. I could reject the snide inferences. Seeing my birthplace again, however, after a considerable spread of years, I felt apologetic on other grounds.

Mine had not been the varmint-infested childhood so often the hallmark of Negro American autobiography. My parents and grandparents had been well-fed, well-clothed, and well-housed. One does not speak of ancestors who lived publicly—Creole style—with their colored families and gave proof of fealty to dark offspring. Some have called these genealogies unwritten history. I have come to feel that mine was fairly typical. I observe with more than mild surmise, for example, that all the Negroes in the Congress bear the mark of a similar tradition, that many faces conspicuous in government, in the United Nations, even among the Black Muslims, are so obviously of mixed ancestry that the bald expurgation of this fact from the history of the South becomes increasingly comical. The cold—or hot—fact is that down here there is a widespread kinship, sometimes unknown, generally unacknowledged. There are old folks from my home who say, knowing something about the background of the city, they would bet a hatful of money that some of those "white" women seen on television hooting and poking out their tongues and spitting at Negro children integrating New Orleans public schools a year or two ago were themselves as colored as Adam Clayton Powell. In any case, the Civil War and the violent disorders that followed Reconstruction tended to restrict, if they did not immediately end, such quaint companionship, so my birthplace was only indirectly connected with it.

In my earliest recollections of the corner at Ninth and Winn both streets were rutted and sloppy. On Winn there was an abominable ditch where water settled for weeks at a time. I can remember Crazy George, the town idiot, following a flock of geese with the bough of a tree in his hand, standing in slush while the geese paddled about or probed into the muck. So fascinated was I, in fact, that I did not hear my grandmother calling from the kitchen door.

It was after I felt her hand on my shoulder shaking me out of my daydream that I trumped up the absurdity that made her laugh. "You called me Arna," I protested, when she insisted on knowing why I had not answered. "My name is George." And so it became, where she was concerned, for the rest of her years.

I had already become aware of nicknames among the people we regarded as members of the family. Teel, Mousie, Buddy, Pinkie, Ya-ya, Mat, and Pig all had other names which one heard occasionally. Even the dog Major had a nickname. The homefolks called him Coonie. I got the impression that to be loved intensely one needed a nickname. My mother preferred to call these pet names, and I was glad my grandmother, whose love mattered so much, had found one she liked for me, *George*.

My hand was in hers a good part of the time, as I recall. If we were not decorating a backyard bush with egg shells, for my young uncles to come home from school, we were under the tree in the front yard picking up pecans after one of the boys had climbed up and shaken the branches. If we were not decorating a backyard bush with egg shells, we were driving in our buggy across the bridge to Pineville on the other side of the Red River. I never found out whether or not the horse had any name other than Daisy.

The serenity of my grandmother in those days was recognized by many who knew her, but it took me a number of years to find out what made it seem remarkable. All I knew then was that this idyll came to a sudden and senseless end at a time when everything about it seemed flawless. In one afternoon scene, my mother and her several sisters had come out of their sewing room with thimbles still on their fingers, needles and thread stuck to their tiny aprons, and were filling their pockets with pecans. Next, it seemed, we were at the railroad station catching a train, my mother, my sister, and I, with a young woman named Sousie.

The story behind it, I learned, concerned my father. His vague presence had never been with us under the pecan tree or on our buggy rides. When he was not away working at brick or stone construction, other things occupied his time. He had come from a family of builders. His oldest brother had married into the Metoyer family on Cane River, descendants of the free Negroes who were the original builders of the famous Melrose plantation mansion. Another brother older than my father went down to New Orleans, where his daughter married one of the prominent jazzmen. My father was a band man himself, and, when he was not working too far away, the chances were he would be blowing his horn under the direction of Claiborne Williams, whose passion for band music awakened the impulse that worked its way down the river and helped to quicken American popular music.

In appearance my father was one of those dark Negroes with "good" hair— meaning almost straight. This did not bother anybody in Avoyelles parish, where the type was common and "broken French" accents were expected, but later in California people who had traveled in the far East wondered if he were not a Ceylonese or something equally exotic. In Alexandria, Louisiana, his looks, good clothes, and hauteur seem to have been something of a disadvantage in the first decade of this century.

Returning home one Saturday night after collecting his pay and spending a part of it on presents for his wife and youngsters, he was walking on Lee Street when two white men wavered out of a saloon and blocked his path. One of them muttered sloppily, "Let's walk over the big nigger."

Frozen for a moment, my father felt his muscles knot. Inside the saloon the voices also sounded strangely belligerent. Was something brewing? Racial tension again? The two men on the sidewalk were unimportant. He was not afraid of their threat. But was this the time or place for a showdown? Assuming he could handle them two-on-one, what then? For striking a white man the routine penalty was mob vengeance, regardless of the provocation. Had a family man a right to sell his pride, or even his honor, in this way at the expense of his dependents? He was capable of fury, and he might have reasoned differently at another time, but that night he calmly stepped aside, allowing the pair to have the walk to themselves. The decision he made as he walked the remaining blocks to our home changed everything for all of us.

My first clear memory of him as a person was the picture he made standing outside the Southern Pacific Depot in Los Angeles. He was shy about showing emotion—he often seemed blunt—so he greeted us quickly on our arrival and let us know this was the place he had chosen for us to end our journey. We had tickets to San Francisco and were prepared to continue beyond if necessary.

We moved into a house in a neighborhood where we were the only colored family. The people next door and up and down the block were friendly and talkative, the weather was perfect, there wasn't a mud puddle anywhere, and my mother seemed to float about on the clean air. When my grandmother and a host of other relatives followed us to this refreshing new country, I began to pick up comment about the place we had left, comment which had been withheld from young ears while we were still in Louisiana.

For one thing they mentioned the house my father had just started building in Alexandria when he decided to drop everything and make his move. They talked about Joe Ward, my grandmother's younger brother, nicknamed Buddy. I could not remember seeing him in Louisiana, and I now learned he had been down at the Keeley Institute in New Orleans taking a cure for alcoholism. A framed portrait of Buddy was placed in my grandmother's living room in California. It pictured a young mulatto dandy with an elegant cravat and jewelled stickpin. All the talk about him gave me an impression of style, grace, éclat.

All of that was gone a few years later, however, when we gathered to wait for him in my grandmother's house and he entered wearing a detachable collar without a tie and did not remove his hat. His clothes did not fit. They had been slept in for nearly a week on the train. His shoes had come unlaced. His face was pock-marked. Nothing in his appearance resembled the picture in the living room.

Two things redeemed the occasion, however. He opened his makeshift luggage and brought out jars of syrup, bags of candy my grandmother had said in her letters that she missed, pecans, plus filet for making gumbo. He had stuffed his suitcase with these instead of clothes. He had not brought an overcoat or a change of underwear. As we lit into the sweets, he began to talk, and I became entranced. He was not trying to impress or even entertain. He was just telling how things were down home, how he had not taken a drink or been locked up since he came back from Keeley the last time, how the family of his employer and benefactor had been scattered or died, how the schoolteacher friend of the family, Mr. George O' Quano, was getting along, how high the Red River had risen along the levee, and such things.

Someone mentioned his employer's daughter. A rumor persisted that Buddy once had a dangerous crush on her. This, I took it, had to be back in the days when the picture in the living room was made. It was all mostly gossip, he commented with only a shadow of a smile. Never had been much to it, and it was too long ago to talk about now. He did acknowledge, significantly, I thought, that his boss's daughter had been responsible for his enjoyment of poetry and novel reading and had taught him perhaps a thousand songs, but neither of these circumstances had undermined his lifelong employment in her father's bakery, where his specialty was fancy cakes. Buddy had never married. Neither had the girl.

The dim rumor of interracial romance had an air of unreality, but it prompted one of my aunts to tell me later something Buddy had told her in confidence. One of the sons of Buddy's boss appeared to have strong feelings against Negroes. When this young man got married and brought a beautiful brunet wife home from New Orleans, some of his cronies taunted him by saying she looked as if she might have a drop or two of colored blood. He appeared to laugh it off, but Buddy found out that the boss's son promptly returned to New Orleans and hired an investigator to look up the records and find out whether there was anything to the innuendo about his bride. After a careful search the investigator reported cheerfully that her pedigree was clear: she had no Negro blood. However, in the course of his research, the investigator had found that the young husband *did,* on his mother's side. And this discovery, Buddy revealed, was the explanation of the young man's subsequent suicide, which publicly had remained a mystery.

When my mother became ill, a year or so after Buddy's arrival, we went to live with my grandmother in the country for a time. Buddy was there. He had acquired a kind of rusticity wholly foreign to his upbringing. Never before had he worked outdoors. Smoking a corncob pipe and wearing oversized clothes provided by my uncles, he resembled a scarecrow in the garden, but the dry air and the smell of green vegetables seemed to be good for him. Perhaps they were continuing the restoration begun at the Keeley Institute. In any case, I promptly became his companion and confidant in the corn rows.

At mealtime we were occasionally joined by my father, home from his bricklaying. The two men eyed each other with suspicion, but they did not quarrel immediately. Mostly they reminisced about Louisiana. My father would say, summarizing now and then, "Sometimes I miss all that. If I was just thinking about myself, I might want to go back and try it again. But I've got the children to think about—their education."

"Folks talk a lot about California," Buddy would reply thoughtfully, "but I'd a heap rather be down home than here, if it wasn't for the conditions."

Obviously their remarks made sense to each other, but they left me with a deepening question. Why was this exchange repeated after so many of their conversations? What was it that made the South—excusing what Buddy called the *conditions*—so appealing. Was it the same thing that made my father determined to keep his children away from it? Was this a lust, a craving, a kind of illicit love they were feeling?

There was less accord between them in the attitudes they revealed when each of the men talked to me privately. My father respected Buddy's ability to quote the whole of Thomas Hood's "The Vision of Eugene Aram," praised his reading and spelling ability, but he was concerned, almost troubled, about the possibility of my adopting the little old derelict as an example. He was horrified by Buddy's casual and frequent use of the word *nigger*. Buddy even forgot and used it in the presence of white people once or twice that year, and was soundly criticized for it. Buddy's new friends, moreover, were sometimes below the level of polite respect. They were not bad people. They were what my father described as don't-care folk. To top it all, Buddy was still crazy about the minstrel shows and minstrel talk that had been the joy of his young manhood. He loved dialect stories, preacher stories, ghost stories, slave and master stories. He half-believed in signs and charms and mumbo jumbo, and he believed wholeheartedly in ghosts.

When I told him on the authority of my schoolteachers that there were no such things as ghosts, he sneered, "That's pure nonsense. I seen one just last night. He was standing up yonder by the gate." He went on after that to recall hundreds of encounters he had had with ghosts since his childhood.

My father's opinion was that Buddy had probably been drunk when he saw most of them, and hence these did not count as authentic experiences. For the rest, my father had picked up in California an explanation about ghosts that I found even more dreadful than Buddy's amused acceptance of hants. Someone had proved to my father from the Bible that the devil could change himself into an angel of light and appear to people in various guises. This is what "ignorant" people were actually seeing when they thought they saw ghosts. He believed this "fact" should dispose of Buddy's "old fogy-ism." Whether it did or not, it nearly scared me to death.

I took it that my father was still endeavoring to counter Buddy's baneful influence when he sent me away to a white boarding school during my high school years, after my mother had died. "Now don't go up there acting colored," he cautioned. I believe I carried out his wish. He sometimes threatened to pull me out of school and let me scuffle for myself the minute I fell short in any one of several ways he indicated. He never did. But before I finished college, I had begun to feel that in some large and mighty important areas I was being miseducated, that perhaps I should have rebelled.

How dare anyone—parent, schoolteacher, or merely literary critic—tell me not to act *colored*. White people have been enjoying the privilege of acting like Negroes for more than a hundred years. The minstrel show, the most popular form of entertainment in America for a whole generation, simply epitomized, while it exaggerated, this privilege. Today nearly everyone who goes on a dance floor starts acting colored immediately, and this has been going on since the cake walk was picked up from Negroes and became the rage. Why should I be ashamed of such influences? In popular music, as in the music of religious fervor, there is a style that is unmistakable, and its origin is certainly no mystery. On the playing field a Willy Mays could be detected by the way he catches a ball, even if his face were hidden. Should the way some Negroes walk be changed or emulated? Sometimes it is possible to tell whether or not a cook is a Negro without going into the kitchen. How about this?

In their opposing attitudes toward roots my father and my great-uncle made me aware of a conflict in which every educated American Negro, and some who are not educated, must somehow take sides. By implication at least, one group advocates embracing the riches of the folk heritage; their opposites demand a clean break with the past and all it represents. Had I not gone home summers and hobnobbed with folk-type Negroes, I would have finished college without knowing that any Negro other than Paul Laurence Dunbar ever wrote a poem. I would have come out imagining that the story of the Negro could be told in two short paragraphs: a statement about jungle people in Africa and an equally brief account of the slavery issue in American history. The reserves of human vitality that enabled the race to survive the worst of both these experiences while at the same time making contributions to western culture remained a dark secret with my teachers, if they had considered the matter at all. I was given no inkling by them, and my white classmates who needed to know such things as much as I did if we were to maintain a healthy regard for each other in the future, were similarly denied.

So what did one do after concluding that for him a break with the past and the shedding of his Negro-ness were not only impossible but unthinkable? First, perhaps, he went to New York in the twenties, met young Negro writers and intellectuals who were similarly searching, learned poems like Claude McKay's "Harlem Dancer" and Jean Toomer's "Song of the Son," started writing and publishing in this vein himself, and applauded Langston Hughes when he wrote in the *Nation* in 1926:

> We younger Negro artists who create now intend to express our individual dark-skinned selves without fear or shame. If white people are pleased we are glad. If they are not, it doesn't matter. We know we are beautiful. And ugly too. The tom-tom cries and the tom-tom laughs. If colored people are pleased we are glad. If they are not, their displeasure doesn't matter either. We build our temples for tomorrow, strong as we know how, and we stand on top of the mountain free within ourselves.

At least that was how it was with me. My first book was published just after the depression struck. Buddy was in it—conspicuously—and I sent him a copy, which I imagine he read. In any case, he took the occasion to celebrate. Returning from an evening with his don't-care friends, he wavered along the highway and was struck by an automobile. He was sixty-seven, I believe.

Alfred Harcourt, Sr., was my publisher. When he invited me to his office, I found that he was also to be my editor. He explained with a smile that he was back on the job doing editorial work because of the hard times. I soon found out what he meant. Book business appeared to be as bad as every other kind, and the lively and talented young people I had met in Harlem were scurrying to whatever brier patches they could find. I found one in Alabama.

It was the best of times and the worst of times to run to that state for refuge. Best, because the summer air was so laden with honeysuckle and spiraea it almost drugged the senses at night. I have occasionally returned since then but never at a time when the green of trees, of countryside, or even of swamps seemed half so wanton. While paying jobs were harder to find there than in New York—indeed they scarcely existed—one did not see evidences of hunger. Negro girls worked in kitchens not for wages but for the toting privilege, that is, permission to take home leftovers.

Meanwhile, the men and boys rediscovered woods and swamps and streams with which their ancestors had been intimate a century earlier and about which their grandparents still talked wistfully. The living critters still abounded. They were as wild and numerous as anybody had ever dreamed; some small, some edible, some monstrous. I made friends with these people, heard their dogs at night, and went with them on possum hunts. I was astonished to learn how much game they could bring home without gunpowder, which they did not have. When the possum was treed by the dogs, a small boy went up and shook him off the limb and the bigger fellows finished him off with sticks. Nets and traps would do for birds and fish. Cottontail rabbits driven into a clearing were actually run down and caught by bare-foot boys. These were prized no more, however, than the delicious mushrooms which hunters and housewives had recently learned to distinguish from the poison-ous variety. The locations of the best fruit- and nut-bearing trees in the woods were kept as choice secrets by their discoverers.

Such carrying-on amused them while it delighted their palates. It also took their minds off the hard times, and they were ready for church when Sunday came. I followed them there, too, and soon began to understand why they enjoyed it so much. The preaching called to mind James Weldon Johnson's "The Creation" and "Go Down Death." The long-meter singing was from another world; the shouting was ecstasy itself. At a primitive Baptist foot-washing I saw benchwalking for the first time, and it left me breathless. The young woman who rose from her seat and skimmed from the front of the church to the back, her wet feet lightly touching the tops of the pews, her eyes upward, could have astounded me no more had she walked on water. The members fluttered and wailed, rocked the church with their singing, and accepted the miracle for what it was.

We lived in a decaying plantation mansion for a time, entertaining its ghosts in our awkward way. An ancient visitor from a snug little community folded between nearby hills came to call and told us that in his boyhood older folks often talked about Andrew Jackson's visits with the first occupants of the house. Later we moved into a tiny new cottage a stone's throw from an abandoned sawmill and within hollering distance of a wooded swamp. Night and morning we were aroused by sounds of bedlam among its flying, creeping, or climbing inhabitants. I set up my portable typewriter on the shady side of the cottage and began writing such children's stories as *You Can't Pet a Possum* and *Sad-Faced Boy.*

It was the worst time to be in northern Alabama because the big road between Huntsville and the Tennessee line was unpaved, rutted, and hard to traverse. If you came down from Nashville at night, pushing your little secondhand Ford briskly, you ran off the pavement with a jolt and automatically yelled "Bam!" That was also the year of the trials of the nine Scottsboro boys in nearby Decatur. Instead of chasing possums at night and swimming in creeks in the daytime, this bunch of kids without jobs and nothing else to do had taken to riding empty box cars. When they found themselves in one with two white girls wearing overalls and traveling the same way, they did not have to be told they were in bad trouble. The charge against them was rape, and the usual verdict in Alabama, when a Negro man was so much as remotely suspected, was guilty; the usual penalty, death. Several times I was tempted to go over and try my luck at getting through the crowds and into the courtroom to hear the trials. My wife did not favor this, and neither did I on second thought. We were not transients, as were most of the spectators, and that made a difference. The ghosts in the old mansion and the screams in the swamp were about as much of the horror as we could cope with while at the same time trying to write a little when the spirit moved.

To relieve the tension while we waited for a verdict, we drove to Athens one night and listened to a program of music by young people from Negro high schools and colleges in the area. A visitor arrived from Decatur during the intermission and reported shocking developments at the trial that day. Ruby Bates, one of the girls involved, had given testimony about herself that reasonably should have taken the onus from the boys. It had only succeeded in infuriating the throng around the courthouse. The rumor that reached Athens was that crowds were spilling along the highway, lurking in unseemly places, whispering, and threatening to vent their anger. After the music was over, someone suggested nervously that those of us from around Huntsville leave at the same time, keep our cars close together as we drove home, and be prepared to stand by, possibly help, if anyone met with mischief.

We readily agreed. Though the drive home was actually uneventful, the tension remained and I began to take stock with a seriousness comparable to my father's when he stepped aside for the Saturday night bullies on Lee Street in Alexandria. I was younger than he had been when he made his move, but my family was already larger by one. Moreover, I had weathered a northern as well as a southern exposure. My education was different, and what I was reading in newspapers differed greatly from anything he could have found in the Alexandria *Town Talk* in the early 1900s.

With Gandhi making world news in India while the Scottsboro case inflamed passions in Alabama and awakened consciences elsewhere, there was less inclination for me than there had been for him to restrict my thoughts to my personal situation. I could see, as I thought, something beginning to shape up, possibly something on a wide scale. As a matter of fact, I had already written a stanza foreshadowing the application of a nonviolent strategy to the Negro's efforts in the South:

> We are not come to wage a strife
> With swords upon this hill;
> It is not wise to waste the life
> Against a stubborn will.
> Yet would we die as some have done:
> Beating a way for the rising sun.

Even so, deliverance did not yet seem imminent, and it was becoming plain that an able-bodied young Negro with a healthy young family could not continue to keep friends in that community if he sat around trifling with a typewriter on the shady side of his house when he should have been working or at least digging in the yard and trying to raise something for the table. Luckily the tires on the Ford were almost new, and there was nothing wrong with the motor. I decided that this would be a good time to see what it would do on the road.

We did not learn till later (when I read *The Grapes of Wrath*) who all those people were that we saw headed for California as we went. Nor did we fall among them out there. We visited with my kinfolks, acquainted my old friends with our youngsters, and boarded with my father and stepmother till I could finish a book, collect an advance, sell the Ford, and move on to Chicago.

Crime seemed to be the principal occupation of the South Side at the time of our arrival. The openness of it so startled us that we could scarcely believe what we saw. In a few months my feeling ran from revulsion to despair. Twice our small apartment was burglarized. Nearly every week we witnessed a stick-up, a purse-snatching or something equally dismaying on the street. Once I saw two men get out of a car, enter one of those blinded shops around the corner from us, return dragging a resisting victim, slam him into the back seat of the car, and speed away. We had fled from the jungle of Alabama's Scottsboro area to the jungle of Chicago's crime-ridden South Side, and one was as terrifying as the other.

I woke from these nightmares and began dreaming of a beachcomber's island, complete with mango tree and thatched hut. A summer trip to the Caribbean, made possible by a fellowship grant, may have abetted the fantasy, but it also convinced me that my only real option was to continue racking my brain.

Despite literary encouragement, the heartiness of a writing clan that adopted me and bolstered my courage, and a gradual adjustment to the rigors of the depression, I never felt I could settle permanently with my family in Chicago. I could not accept the ghetto, and ironclad residential restrictions against Negroes situated as we were made escape impossible. Thus we were confined to neighborhoods where we had to fly home each evening before darkness fell and honest people abandoned the streets to predators. Garbage was dumped in alleys around us. Police protection was regarded as a farce. Corruption was everywhere.

A precinct worker promised that if we registered to vote, we would receive Christmas boxes for the children. We registered, since she represented the party of our choice, and tried to forget the implications of that second remark. We were astonished not only that she kept her word but that the boxes she showed up with were so large and contained clothes of such excellent quality. We learned later that these boxes had been prepared for the "needy" and went to those who had registered as we had been advised. When I inquired about transfers for two of our children to integrated schools more accessible to our address, I was referred to a person not connected with the school system or the city government. He assured me he could arrange the transfers—at an outrageous price. These represented ways in which Negro leadership was operating in the community at that time and how it had been reduced to impotence.

I did not consider exchanging this way of life for the institutionalized assault on Negro personality one encountered in the Alabama of the Scottsboro trials, but suddenly the campus of a Negro college I had twice visited in Tennessee began to seem attractive—somewhat of a prose equivalent of that beachcomber's island. There, one should be able to relax at least enough to entertain his own thoughts. A measure of isolation, a degree of security seemed possible. If a refuge for the harassed Negro could be found anywhere in those days, it had to be in such a setting. If there was any way to count on higher educational opportunities for a family growing as fast as mine, this appeared to be it.

Even so, waiting on a beach—a temporary expedient—is one thing; settling down for the best years of one's life is another. We had made the move, and I had become the Librarian at Fisk University when a series of train trips during World War II gave me an opportunity for reflections of another kind. I started making notes for an essay to be called "Thoughts in a Jim Crow Car." Before I could finish it, Supreme Court action removed the curtains in the railway diners, and the essay lost its point. While I had been examining my own feelings and trying to understand the need men have for such customs, the pattern had altered. Compliance followed with what struck me, surprisingly, as an attitude of relief by all concerned. White passengers, some of whom I recognized by their positions in the public life of Nashville, who had been in the habit of maintaining a frozen silence until the train crossed the Ohio River, now nodded and began chatting before it left the Nashville station. I wanted to stand up and cheer. I did not, of course, and when on the same impulse the Army began to desegregate its units, I was sure I detected fatal weakness in our enemy. Segregation, the monster that had terrorized my parents and driven them out of the green Eden in which they had been born, was itself vulnerable and could be attacked, possibly destroyed. I felt as if I had witnessed the first act of a spectacular drama. That I would want to stay around for the second went without saying.

Without the miseries of segregation, the South as a homeplace for a Negro of my temperament had clear advantages. In deciding to wait and see how it worked out, I was also betting that progress toward this objective would be more rapid in the southern region, and the results more satisfying than could be expected in the metropolitan centers of the North where whites were leaving the crumbling central areas to Negroes while they themselves moved into restricted suburbs and began setting up another kind of closed society.

Down here, in addition to the fact that some of us are unrecognized kin, we know each other pretty well. We know more about each other than we tell. During slavery, the South filled this country with mulattoes much as the Snopes family filled the Faulkner country with spotted horses. Working with Negroes in some relationship or other is part of the experience of nearly every Southerner and, with many, cooperation on higher levels is nothing new. Will Alexander told me in 1943 that he was convinced the South was ready to settle the race problem for fifty cents on the dollar. As a dyed-in-the-wool southern liberal, however, he was not recommending that Negroes should be enticed by such a deal. He favored holding out for one hundred cents on the dollar, if that was the way to put it.

Many Negroes owned property close to the finest white residences under the old regime. Apparently the southern gentry felt more secure with Negroes nearby. The idea that Negroes devaluated the property was one of the carpetbaggers' swindles. The change came as the upper class whites, like the European aristocracy, became ineffective. The Negro lost his place and security as the middle class assumed dominance. Nevertheless, many white southerners continue to have Negro neighbors, as some had always had, and complaints are seldom heard on this score.

Segregation as a racket promoted by carpetbaggers found ready adherents, of course, because of the ways in which it lent itself to the economic squeeze. Banks, real estate operators, insurance companies, politicians, and many others found ruses by which to make it turn an unrighteous profit. Few but the ignorant or the naïve could have believed deeply that the practice was moral, and certainly none of the people with whom I have been associated have ever been willing to compromise on this principle. We were and are here to oppose segregation and try in every way to undermine it. Charles S. Johnson had this continuing effort in mind, no doubt, when he talked about "intensive minority living."

The second act of the spectacular on which I had focused began with the 1954 decision of the Supreme Court that cut down the old separate but equal façade behind which inequality was perpetuated. While this was a landmark, it provoked no wild optimism. I had no doubt that the tide would now turn, but it was not until the freedom movement began to press itself that I felt reassured. We were in the middle of it in Nashville. Our little world commenced to sway and rock with the fury of a resurrection. I tried to discover just what it was that made it shake, how the energy was generated. I think I found it.

The singing that broke out in the ranks of protest marchers, in the jails where sit-in demonstrators were held, and in the mass meetings and boycott rallies, was gloriously appropriate. The only American songs suitable for a resurrection—or a revolution, for that matter—are Negro spirituals. The surge these awakened was so mighty it threatened to change the name of our era from the "space age" to the "age of freedom."

Some literary work appeared in the course of these events, and there were those who thought that travail such as this called for a latter day Thomas Paine. In the North a clutch of sensational books, plays, and magazine pieces profited from the foment, perhaps, but they were irrelevant to the movement itself. The momentum of the marchers came from the sermons of Martin Luther King, Jr., and his co-horts. The lineage of this kind of expression is well-known to devotees of Negro folk preaching. It has its own style. Evoking audience response and participation, it is not unrelated to the call and response pattern of some Negro spirituals—a pattern which scholars have traced to Africa.

One was obliged to notice that Negroes in the South seemed better armed for a struggle with spiritual overtones than their kinfolk in the North. I suspected, and I still believe, that they are less likely to go berserk than the Harlemites. Willing to sacrifice, even to take risks, they are more apt to keep their cool, as the college kids say. Perhaps the word is morale. Moreover, you can communicate with them because you know where to find them. Often that will be in church—a good place for them to catch the beat of the call and response and slip in a hot lick now and then during the gospel singing.

The southern Negro's link with his past seems to me worth preserving. His greater pride in being himself, I would say, is all to the good, and I think I detect a growing nostalgia for these virtues in the speech of relatives in the North. They talk a great deal about "Soulville" nowadays, when they mean "South." "Soulbrothers" are simply the homefolks, "Soulfood" includes black-eyed peas, chitterlings, grits and gravy, and all are held in the warmest esteem. Aretha Franklin, originally from Memphis, sings, "Soulfood—it'll make you limber; it'll make you quick." Needless to say, vacations in Soulville by these expatriates in the North tend to become more frequent and to last longer since times began to get better.

I was interested a year or so ago in a tiff between a group of militant Negro intellectuals in New York and "white liberals." It was not clear to me just who constituted the group under attack, but I assumed the others were really disturbed by what they saw as hypocrisy. Of course, hypocrisy is everybody's affliction, and its presence in race relations could become a problem in the South at a future time. At present, however, the southern situation does not lend itself to hypocrisy of this kind. Some Negroes in personal service may have retained attitudes traditional to that occupation, but southern whites, alas, do not yet have enough incentive to feign liberality when they do not feel it. A greater problem at this stage is the encourage-ment of timid liberals whose hearts are on the right side to stand up and be counted.

Colleagues of mine at Fisk University who, like me, have pondered the ques-tion of staying or going have sometimes given other reasons. The effective young dean of the Chapel, for example, who since has been wooed away by Union Theo-logical Seminary, felt constrained mainly by the opportunities he had here to guide a large number of students and by the privilege of identifying with them. John W.

Work, the musicologist and composer, found the cultural environment more stimulating than any available to him in the North. Aaron Douglas, an Art professor, came down thirty-odd years ago to get a "real, concrete experience of the touch and feel of the South." Looking back, he reflects, "If one could discount the sadness, the misery, the near volcanic intensity of Negro life in most of the South and concentrate on the mild almost tropical climate and the beauty of the landscape, one is often tempted to forget the senseless cruelty and inhumanity the strong too often inflict on the weak."

For my own part, I am staying on in the South to write something about the Negro's awakening and regeneration. That is my theme, and this is where the main action is. Also, there is this spectacular I'm watching. Was a climax reached with the passage of the Civil Rights Act of 1964, or was it with Martin Luther King's addressing Lyndon B. Johnson as "my fellow Southerner"? In any case, having stayed this long, it would be absurd not to wait for the third act.

No Fools, No Fun

MARCH LACY

S he slapped the leather stool and the noise was loud in the quiet bar.
I had said, "Still holding up Eddie's bar?"

She slapped the empty stool next to her and invited me to have a seat. A cigarette hanging from her lips sent gray smoke against her dark face. "I see you do all right by Eddie's, too," she smiled. "Doesn't she do all right, Carter?"

Carter grinned and went on with his work. He was a quiet bartender and people liked him.

Patsy took a long last puff on her cigarette and immediately lit another one from it. She crushed the butt, the whole process a smooth, practiced routine. You wouldn't call her pretty nor very young, but she wore the kind of clothes and hairdress that gave a smart touch to her tall figure and thin face.

She said, "I had a hard day on the set. Nothing went right. Had to retype pages of the script. Mr. Golding almost tore his hair, what's left of it; and my God, how the actors kept blowing their lines."

Her voice was too crisp and a little loud. Several beer drinkers stopped to listen. Who had ever heard of a colored script-girl?

"What picture are you making now?"

"'Blow Horn, Blow I' with Edith Flowers and that pansy, Ted Strong. Mr. Golding planed in from the Coast yesterday to begin shooting."

"You're lucky having a job like that, working in a studio with all those big stars. It must be exciting."

"In a way, but it's pretty much of a grind. Golding depends on me to doublecheck every little detail. Like today we were finishing a scene we started yesterday and I noticed that Ted Strong was wearing a different tie. If I hadn't caught that boner, all today's footage would have been wasted—thousands of dollars."

Patsy's talk, mixed with the drinks, the soft lights, and the hot juke box music, almost made me feel a part of the glamor that is the movies.

We talked until my boy friend came in, nodded to Patsy, and said to me, "Let's catch an early show. Got to get to bed. There's a mess of cars to wash tomorrow." He always talked in a quick, jerky manner.

I had to work late all the next week preparing my people for the country. I didn't go with them because I hate the country quiet, and it turned out pretty lucky.

The same day the family left, one of the madam's friends gave me a part-time job for the summer. It didn't look bad, only two rooms and no kids. The people weren't the stay-at-home type.

I felt like celebrating, but the boy friend was strictly a Saturday night good-timer. I took a walk down the avenue to see who was around. I walked into a girl I used to room with. After we finished the small talk, I invited her to have a drink with me.

"You know this is the middle of the week," she apologized, "and I'm broke."

"Don't let that worry you," I said. "It's on me."

We walked into Eddie's, and Patsy was at the bar like a fixture. I said, "Patsy, this is Lucy," and to the bartender, "Bring us a shorty of rye with ginger ale chasers."

"Patsy is a script girl at the Paramount Studios in Astoria," I said to Lucy. "How's the picture coming, Patsy?"

"We've been shooting pretty fast. Mr. Golding wants to finish the picture ahead of schedule and well within the budget. You know, he's one of the few directors who like to work in the East. It means a lot to him to make a successful picture in New York."

"You going back to Hollywood with Mr. Golding?" I asked.

"I don't know whether I'll make the trip again," Patsy answered, her voice undecided. "I've been back and forth so many times. There is nothing in Hollywood for me. I won't make the trip this time unless he insists."

"Then you'll be out of a job," I said.

Patsy blew out a mouth full of smoke. "I get paid just the same. When Mr. Golding isn't here, I read for him—report on the latest books."

"Girl, hasn't she got some racket!" I said to Lucy.

"Sounds good," Lucy said.

Patsy got up. "Sorry I have to go now. We've a call for seven in the morning. You know, the studio is out in God's country, and I have to get up at the crack of dawn."

As soon as she left, Lucy said, "Is that the girl you were telling me about?"

"Sure. She's been a script-girl with Mr. Golding, the big movie director, for the last couple of years."

"That's her story," Lucy said. "She works in the same building with me on East Seventy-Second Street. Works for a family on the fifteenth floor. I saw her in the laundry no longer than yesterday."

"Doing house work? That's not the same girl."

"Oh, yes it is." Lucy's voice took on a positive tone. "I know her. See her almost every day. Puts on a lot of airs. Never socializes with the rest of the girls."

"But she know all about the studios and the stars."

Lucy laughed. "Any fool can read the movie magazines."

I thought about it for a moment. Somehow I felt hurt and disappointed, as if my bluff had been called.

Saturday night I dropped into Eddie's again to wait for the old man. I sat down next to Patsy.

Patsy said, "Hello. Tell Carter what'll it be, a long or a short beer."

"I could do with a rum-cola," I said. "Getting to be a big girl now. Knocking myself out slowly by degrees. How is the picture getting along?"

"Oh, we'll finish shooting by Tuesday," she answered casually, watching me out of the corner of her eye. "Mr. Golding is staying East for another picture."

"That'll work out fine for you."

"Means I don't have to make up my mind right away about going to the coast." Patsy lit a cigarette.

I looked at her, and understood her perfectly. We all dream—that's why I need an occasional drink. Only she went further, acting out her dream, almost believing it was real. Anything to rise out of the lonely, blind alley of a housework job. I knew exactly how she felt.

I suddenly grinned at her. "Let me buy you a drink, Patsy."

The Gun

LANGSTON HUGHES

Picture yourself a lone bird in a cage with monkeys, or the sole cat in a kennel full of dogs. Even if the dogs became accustomed to you, they wouldn't make the best of playmates; nor could you, being a cat, mate with them, being dogs. Although, in the little town of Tall Rock, Montana, the barriers were less natural than artificial (entirely man-made barriers, in fact), nevertheless, to be the only Negro child in this small white city made you a stranger in a strange world; an outcast in the house where you lived; a part of it all by necessity, and yet no part at all.

Flora Belle Yates, as a child, used to shield herself from the frequent hurts and insults of white children with tears, blows, and sometimes curses. Even with only one Negro family, the Yateses, in Tall Rock, race relations were not too good. Her father and mother had come up from Texas years ago. Flora Belle had heard them tell about the night they left Texarkana, looking back to see their hut in flames and a mob shouting in the darkness. The mob wanted to lynch Flora Belle's father. It seemed that, in an argument about wages, he had beaten up a white man. Through some miracle, her mother said, they had gotten away in the face of the mob, escaping in a rickety Ford, crossing the state line and driving for three days, somehow making it to the Northwest. Her father had an idea of getting to Canada, fleeing like the slaves in slave days clean out of the United States, but gas and money ran out. He and his wife stopped to work along the way, and finally ended up by staying in Tall Rock. Flora's father had gotten a job there, tending to the horses and equipment of a big contractor. Her mother worked in the contractor's house as cook, maid, and washwoman. Shortly after their arrival, Flora Belle was born in a large room over the contractor's stable.

She was never a pretty baby, Flora Belle, for her parents were not beautiful people. Poor food and hard work had lined their faces and bent their bodies even before she was born. The fear and strain of their hegira, with the mother pregnant, did not help to produce a sweet and lovely child. Flora Belle's face, as she grew up, had a lugubrious expression about it that would make you laugh if you didn't know her—but would make you sorry for her if you did know her.

Then, too, from helping her mother with the white folks' washing and her father to tend the horses, Flora Belle grew up strong and heavy, with rough hands and a hard chest like a boy's. She had hard ways, as well. A more attractive colored girl might have appealed to the young white men of the town for illegitimate advances, but nobody so much as winked at Flora Belle. She graduated from high school without ever having had a beau of any kind. The only colored boys she had ever seen were the ones who came through Tall Rock once with a circus.

Just before her graduation, her mother laid down and died—quite simply "worked to death," as she put it. Tired! A white preacher came to the house and preached her funeral with a few white neighbors present. After that Flora Belle lived with her aging father and cooked his meals for him—the two of them alone, dark souls in a white world. She did the contractor's family washing, as the new Irish maid refused to cook, clean—and then wash, too. Flora Belle made a few dollars a week washing and ironing.

One day, the second summer after she came out of high school, her father said, "I'm gonna leave here, Flora Belle." So they went to Butte. That was shortly after World War I ended, in the days of prohibition. Things were kind of dead in Butte, and most of the Negroes there were having a hard time, or going into bootlegging. Flora Belle and her father lived in the house with a family who sold liquor. It was a loud and noisy house, with people coming and going way up in the night. There was gambling in the kitchen.

There were very few Negroes in Butte, and Flora Belle made friends with none of them. Their ways were exceedingly strange to her, since she had never known colored people before. And she to them was just a funny-looking stuck-up ugly old girl. They took her shyness to mean conceit, and her high-school English to mean superiority. Nobody paid any attention to Flora.

Her father soon took up with a stray woman around town. He began to drink a lot, too. Months went by and he found no steady work, but Flora Belle did occasional housecleaning. They still had a little money that they had saved, so one day Flora Belle said, "Pa, let's buy a ticket and leave this town. It's no good."

And the old man said, "I don't care if I do."

Flora Belle had set her mind on one of the big cities of the coast where there would be lots of nice colored people she could make friends with. So they went to Seattle, her and Pa. They got there one winter morning in the rain. They asked a porter in the station where colored people could stop, and he sent them to a street near the depot where Negroes, Filipinos, Japanese, and Chinese lived in box-like buildings. The street had a busy downtown atmosphere. Flora Belle liked it very much, the moving people, the noise, the shops, the many races.

"I'm glad to get to a real city at last," she said.

"This rain is chillin' me to the bone," her father answered, walking along with their suitcases. "I wish I had a drink." He left Flora Belle as soon as their rooms were rented and went looking for a half-pint.

In Seattle it rained and rained. In the gray streets strange people of many shades and colors passed, all of them going places, having things to do. In the colored rooming house, as time went by, Flora Belle met a few of the roomers, but they all were busy, and they did not ask her to join them in their activities. Her father stayed out a good deal, looking for a job, he said—but when he came back, you could smell alcohol on his breath. Flora Belle looked for a job, also, but without success.

She was glad when Sunday came. At least she could go to church, to a colored church—for back in Tall Rock there had been no Negro church, and the white temples were not friendly to a black face.

"I'm A.M.E., myself," the landlady said. "The Baptists do too much shoutin' for me. You go to my church."

So Flora Belle went to the African Methodist Episcopal Church—alone, because the landlady was too busy to take her. That first day at services quite a few members shook hands with her. This made Flora Belle very happy. She went back that evening and joined the church. She felt warm and glad at just meeting people. She was invited to attend prayer meeting and to become a member of the Young Women's Club, dues ten cents a week. She in turn asked some of the sisters, with fumbling incoherence, if they knew where she could get a job. The churchwomen took her phone number and promised to call her if they heard of anything. Flora Belle walked home through the rain that night feeling as if she had at last come to a welcome place.

Sure enough, during the week, a woman did call up to let her know about a job. "It's a kinder hard place," the woman said over the phone, "but I reckon you can stand it awhile. She wants a maid to sleep in, and they don't pay much. But since you ain't workin', it might beat a blank."

Flora Belle got the job. She was given the servant's room. It was damp and cold; the work was hard, and the lady exacting; the meager pay came once a month, but Flora Belle was thankful to have work.

"Now," she thought to herself, "I can get some nice clothes and meet nice people, 'cause I'm way behind, growing up in a town where there wasn't none of my color to be friends with. I want to meet some boys and girls and have a good time."

But she had only one night off a week, Sunday evening to go to church. Then Flora Belle would fix herself up as nice as she knew how and bow and bow in her friendliest fashion, fighting against shyness and strangeness, but never making much of an impression on folks. At church everybody was nice enough, to be sure, but nobody took up more time with her than brotherly love required. None of the young men noticed her at all, what with dozens of pretty girls around, talkative and gay—for Flora Belle stood like she was tongue-tied when she was introduced to anybody. Just stood staring, trying to smile. She didn't know the easy slang of the young people, nor was she good at a smart comeback if someone made a bright remark. She was just a big, homely, silent woman whose desire for friends never got past that lugubrious look in her wistful eyes and that silence that frightened folks away.

A crippled man after Sunday services tried to make up to her once or twice. He talked and talked, but Flora Belle could manage to say nothing more than "Yes, sir" or "No, sir" to everything he said, like a dumb young girl—although she was now twenty-five, and too unattractive to play coy.

Even the sporting men—to whom women give money—used to laugh about Flora Belle. "Man, I wouldn't be seen on the streets with that truck horse," was their comment in the pool halls.

So a year went by and Flora Belle had no more friends than she had bad back in Butte or Tall Rock. "I think I'll go away from here," she said to herself. "Try another town. I reckon all cities ain't like Seattle, where folks is so cold and it rains all the time."

So she went away. She left Pa living in sin with some old Indian woman and shining shoes in a white barbershop for a living. He had begun to look mighty bowed and wrinkled, and he drank increasingly.

Flora Belle went to San Francisco. She had a hard time finding work, a hard time meeting people, a hard time trying to get a boyfriend. But in California she didn't take up so much time with the church. She met, instead, some lively railroad porters and maids who gave parties and lived a sort of fast life. Flora Belle managed to get in good with the porters' crowd, mostly by handing out money freely to pay for food and drinks when parties were being arranged.

She was usually an odd number, though, having no man. Nevertheless, she would come by herself to the parties and try her best to be a good sport, to drink and be vulgar. But even when she was drunk, she was still silent and couldn't think of anything much to say. She fell in love with a stevedore and used to give him her pay regularly and buy him fine shirts, but he never gave her any matrimonial encouragement, although he would take whatever she offered him. Then she found out that he was married already and had four children. He told her he didn't want her, anyway.

"I'm gonna leave this town," Flora Belle said to herself, "if the bus station still sells tickets."

So the years went on. The cities on the coast, the fog cities of fruit trees and vineyards, passed in procession-full of hard work and loneliness. Cook in a roadhouse, maid for a madam, ironer in a laundry, servant for rich Mexicans—Monterey—Berkeley—San Diego—Marysville—San Jose. At last she came to Fresno. She was well past thirty. She felt tired. She wanted sometimes to die. She had worked so long for white folks, she had cooked so many dinners, made so many beds.

Working for a Fresno ranch owner, looking after his kids, trying to clean his house and keep things as his wife desired, passing lonely nights in her room over the garage, she felt awful tired, awful tired.

"I wish I could die," she said to herself. By now she often talked out loud. "I wish I could die."

And one day, she asked, "Why not?"

The idea struck her all of a sudden, "Why not?"

So on her Thursday afternoon off from work, she bought a pistol. She bought a box of bullets. She took them home—and somehow she felt better just carrying the heavy package under one arm along the street.

That night in her room over the garage she unwrapped the gun and looked at it a long time. It was black, cold, steel-like, heavy and hard, dependable and certain. She felt sure it could take her far away—whenever she wanted to go. She felt sure it would not disappoint her—if she chose to leave Fresno. She was sure that with the gun, she would never again come to an empty town.

She put in all the bullets it would hold, six, and pressed its muzzle to her head. "Maybe the heart would be better," she thought, putting its cold nose against her breast. Thus she amused herself in her room until late in the night. Then she put the pistol down, undressed, and went to bed. Somehow she felt better, as though she could go off anytime now to some sweet good place, as though she were no longer a prisoner in the world, or in herself.

She slept with the pistol under her pillow.

The following morning she locked it in her trunk and went down to work. That day her big ugly body moved about the house with a new lightness. And she was very kind to the white lady's children. She kept thinking that in the tray of her trunk there was something that meant her good, and would be kind to her. So the days passed.

Every night in her little room, over the garage, after she had combed her hair for bed, she would open the trunk and take the pistol from its resting place. Sometimes she would hold it in her lap. Other nights she would press the steel-black weapon to her heart and put her finger on the trigger, standing still quite a long time. She never pulled the trigger, but she knew that she could pull it whenever she wished.

Sometimes, in bed in the dark, she would press the gun between her breasts and talk to it like a lover. She would tell it all the things that had gone on in her mind in the past. She would tell it all that she had wanted to do, and how, now, she didn't want to do anything, only hold this gun, and be sure—*sure* that she could go away if she wanted to go—anytime. She was sure!

Each night the gun was there—like she imagined a lover might be. Each night it came to bed with her, to lie under the pillow near her head or to rest in her hand. Sometimes she would touch that long black pistol in the dark and murmur in her sleep, "I love . . . you."

Of course, she told nobody. But everybody knew that something had happened to Flora Belle Yates. She knew what. Her life became surer and happier because of this friend in the night. She began to attend church regularly on Sunday, to sing, shout, and take a more active part in the weeknight meetings. She began to play with her employer's children, and to laugh with his wife over the little happenings in the house. The white lady began to say to her neighbors, "I've got the best maid in the world. She was awfully grouchy when she first came, but now that she's gotten to like the place, she's simply wonderful!"

As the months went by, Flora Belle began to take on weight, to look plump and jolly, and to resemble one of those lovable big dark-skinned mammies in the picture books. It was the gun. As some people find assurance in the Bible or in alcohol, Flora Belle found assurance in the sure cold steel of the gun.

She is still living alone over the white folks' garage in Fresno—but now she can go away anytime she wants to.

Grazing in Good Pastures

MARGARET WILLIAMS

Handsome young David Woods made a mistake when he fell in love with a bright-skinned gal. At least all of Coonville thought so. He was fair to rue the day he brought home a woman like that. A farmer had no more use with a light-eyed wife than a monkey had with a side-saddle. Why, her hair was too yellow and straight and her skin too fair for her to hoe in the field.

That would mean that David must hire all his work.

That was what all of Coonville was saying when young David brought his bride home to the little farm in the pines down in East Texas. He had found her in Dallas. Being city-bred and practically white, she would have ideas, of course, that would soon ruin any hardworking man. That was to be expected.

But Rubye was determined to prove to the settlement that no matter how bright was her skin she could make a farmer a good wife.

She had a good education, better than that of any of the white folks around there. Before she had left she had gathered all the information she could about farming in East Texas. Her fancy had been struck when she learned that roses was one of the main crops.

"I love roses!" she told David. "Roses teach us that everything must have a purpose for coming to this earth. A rose's duty is to be beautiful and to smell sweet. He starts out being beautiful, and the older he grows the sweeter is his expression. I'm going to love growing roses. I'll cross them. I bet I find one no one else has ever found."

David's expression was non-committal. No doubt, though, he was wondering how he could break the news to her easy-like that the farm was for cotton and corn. That was all that had ever been raised on it.

"Why, when business gets good, we'll even get a tractor to work the roses. I read that people have acres and acres of roses down there."

"I'se afraid, honey, we can't never have no tractor. The stumps is so bad. We have to use a hand plow so we can pull up from around the stumps."

"We can get the stumps out."

"Too hard a work, honey."

"Nothing is going to be too hard now, David. We're going to progress. In a year you won't know the place."

"Don't expect too much."

But Rubye had expected more than she found. Just a two-roomed log cabin with one lone pine at the back. The stumpy field surrounded the house. The dump ground for generations was to the right of the low front porch in a sand hollow. She tried hard to hide her disappointment when she climbed out of the model T in front of the fallen-down abode.

"Why, it can be made so pretty. Trees surround the farm. Those trees yours?" She pointed to the distant wood.

"Sure, honey. A creek runs through the entire place. And them woods is sho' full of hogs."

"I hope you don't mean those funny-looking skinny long-nosed things resembling the hog we saw always running across the road?"

"Them is the piny-woods rooter. They make the best lean bacon."

"That'll be all right for the present until we get our roses started. Then I'll make a pretty park in the wood, with bridges winding across the creek. I am somewhat of a landscaper myself."

"Uh-huh. 'cuse me. I see Evvy, my hired boy," said David, as his black eyes shifted bewilderedly from his wife's pretty face.

He strode on off to have a chat with his hired hand at the barn, which was to the left of the cabin. Rubye wanted her husband to carry her across the threshold, and so she sat down on the edge of the porch to wait for his return. She could see that the hired-hand was only about sixteen and of a skin the color of good liver. She heard him say to her husband:

"All of Coonville is sayin' you sho' is grazin' in good pastures, and I see yo is."

"Yeah. But she may find country life disappointin'," replied David.

"Most city womens gits crazy notions when they come to the country. Jest put her off, Pa says iffen she does. That's what Pa always done. Oncet Ma went to town and seen some wallpaper and takened a notion to paper the cabin. She even went as fur as to borrow the catalog and see how much buildin' paper was. Pa agreed, but kept puttin' her off givin' her the money. Finally Ma give up the idea and the bare walls done her jest as much good."

The next morning David wanted to get the cotton in the ground, but Rubye told him that he must first plow up an acre in one corner so that she could start on her roses.

"That can rest, honey. Jest as soon as I git this cotton in the ground. It might rain. Yo know we gots to eat."

So he was taking Evvy's advice!

"My roses will bring more money."

"I don't know roses, but I do cotton."

"That is why so many people remain in the same rut: afraid to try the new. You'll see if you'll only do as I say."

"Jest as soon as I gits the cotton in the ground, honey. Besides I don't wants yo in the field alone. A black runner might attact yo."

"A black runner? What's that?"

"A snake here in East Texas. It ain't poisonous, but the male snake attacts womens or girls and iffen she don't git help he'll injure her fur life. I had to cut one off my cousin oncet."

"You're just trying to scare me. Besides I can watch out and carry my hoe."

Then she tried putting her arms about her husband's neck. He always softened under her kisses. But he pulled her back, no doubt realizing he might give over if he once let her touch him.

"Please," she begged.

He just shook his head and promised as he started toward the barn.

Rubye let him hitch up. When he came by in front of the cabin on the way to the field, she ran out to beg him again. He only waved his hand to her and told Pete to get hisself on down the trail before he skinned his head.

Rubye stood there and watched him. She didn't know that David could be so stubborn. Her pride was hurt.

"All right," she told herself, "I'll show him. I'll show all of Coonville. They think—they think—I don't care what they think. It is what I think that counts."

As Rubye hadn't yet felt the effects of coming from a high altitude to this low altitude, she found the shovel and walked down to the acre she had picked out and began spading it up.

All morning she worked, so long in fact that she forgot to see about getting dinner. When she saw David coming in for lunch, she wiped the perspiration from her brow, and fled for the cabin where she found a pile of dirty dishes. The sound of bacon frying on the wood stove was the only hope for a dinner when her husband came in.

A half-hour later she sat him down to bacon, gravy, and cold biscuits. He said not a word of complaint, but ate in a strained silence.

That night it was the same thing, and the following day. The third morning he said:

"I see I ain goin' to git any dinner if I don't plow up that land. Yo stay here and I'll git that done."

Rubye was thankful. Already she was beginning to feel tired and without energy to lift a shovel. But she didn't mention the fact to her husband. Really they had little to say to each other.

That day Rubye forced herself to sweep the house, wash the dishes, and to cook. Between work she fell down on the bed and sighed what time she was not sleeping.

Finally her husband had the acre plowed, and still Rubye did not feel like setting out her roses she had placed in a dirt box under the big pine tree. About five that afternoon she went out under the tree and looked at them. That tired feeling had her gripped so hard that she only sat down on a rusty bucket and groaned.

"This sun is so hot. Is this the reason these people never have flower yards nor paper their walls? But I won't give up. I'll keep on and on and show them. I'll whip myself to it."

The next morning Rubye dragged out to the rose field and managed to set out two rows of bushes. She was so tired when she came in to cook dinner that she sobbed as she fixed a fire and made up bread.

After dinner she dragged herself again to the field, but spent most of the time on her knees or sitting down, groaning from aching muscles and from that terrible feeling of depression.

Time dragged on. Though their days were strained, their nights were filled with love; for after all they were young and very much in love. They would lie awake and kiss and forget about the cotton field and the rose garden and listen to the cry of the whippoorwill or to the silly talk of the hoot owl.

"Listen, honey," David would say, as he held his wife in his arms, "can you make out what he's sayin'?"

> "Rubber boot
> shoe boot
> chicken soup
> so good."

Then they would kiss good-night and sigh. And she would go to sleep with her small fist doubled up in his big palm.

One year passed. Rubye had become accustomed to the low altitude, but she had never regained the feeling for a desire to progress. Still she stubbornly fought with the rose idea. She wanted to show David and all of Coonville that she knew what she was talking about. She would stand by a rose bush and gaze down upon its pretty bloom, trying hard to feel something beautiful for the flower.

"It's this hot sun pouring down upon this red sand which does something to people," she would sigh.

At last fall came, the time for the county fair at Pinecrest. Both the colored and the white were welcome. The biggest stalk of cotton, the finest ear of corn, the best pickle, and the sweetest tasting jar of jelly were to be brought there. Everyone was guessing that David's wife would not be represented, because she did not belong to the Home Cooking Club. She never canned. In fact she never stayed in the house long enough for her to cook David a decent meal.

Rubye knew what they were saying about her. The white folks, of course, would have nothing to do with her, even though they did take time off to have their say. A drop of nigger blood was nigger to white folks in Texas. They never stopped to weigh one's soul. The colored folks treated her nice, but they openly showed her that they felt sorry for David. He should have married a dark brown-skinned gal from the South, someone who would have made a hand in the field. Then all of that extra hiring could be saved.

"He wouldn't of lost his cotton in the east field if she'd throwed in there with him," she heard one woman tell another.

What David thought the young man kept to himself. He had grown depressingly silent. He and his wife hardly spoke a word a day now. Even at night they forgot to listen to the hoot owl say his silly ditty.

That last day before the fair opened Rubye tried to draw her husband into conversation as she took the noon meal from the stove to the small pine table across the room.

"Tomorrow, David, the fair starts. Aren't you going to take something?"

He shook his head. She could see tears in his eyes. He was undergoing some terrible emotion, she saw. Was he sorry he had married her?

"I've crossed three different roses and have discovered the prettiest rose I ever saw in my life. It is sort of an orange rose. The bush grows about four feet tall, and the blooms are as big as a saucer. I am taking that."

She started to tell him about her black rose, but he didn't seem to be listening, and so she retorted:

"I know all of Coonville is feeling sorry for you, and I can see you are even sorry for yourself now. If I don't make good with my roses this year, I'll quit and go home."

Still David did not reply.

"And this is the last word I'll say to you until I find out tomorrow."

David's black eyes held resentment for his wife.

"I darsent say a word or I'll git my head skinned."

"How can you say that! I only try to show you the sensible side of things, and you act like a child, believing all of Coonville rather than me."

"The onliest way we have of knowin' a thing is to take it from experience."

"Then we would never progress. There is always someone to start things first."

"Then why in the devil did it have to be my wife! Yo color is enough to make folks take notice to yo. Why couldn't yo have been like others of our race? Why did yo have to try and show us a lot of white folks' notions?"

Rubye rose from the table. It was all so useless. Well, she would go on with her roses this fall, and then leave David. She could never make him happy. They were as different as a pea and a bean. But why did that ache in her heart grow worse upon considering such a thing as leaving him? He had stopped loving her; he thought her a failure as a wife.

Just as she left the kitchen, her husband said:

"Don't expect me to carry you in to town tomorrow. I got work in the field to do. No money to hire hands with."

David had long ago sold his model T. Their first year had been a crop failure, due to so much rains. There had not been enough hands to chop out the grass. And he had to use the team in the field.

It was five miles in to Pinecrest, but Rubye did not let this stop her. She got up at three in the morning, hastily cooked up some bread for David, and fried meat. She left his breakfast on the stove and then lit the lantern. She did not want a bite herself, for she felt sort of weak and tired.

She closed the door behind her, and went straight to the rose field to cut her orange roses. Not until she was nearly there did she remember that she had not got her hoe. Well, surely the black-runner would not be out at night.

When she reached her prize roses, she let out a pitiful gasp. She could hardly believe her eyes. All the leaves had fallen off during the night. Or had they been plucked? She sank down beside them, broken-hearted, weeping:

"I can't believe it! He wouldn't have done such a horrible thing to me. But the leaves were too firm to have dropped off. Oh, he knew if I failed, I would leave. That's it! He wants me to leave. He really wants me to leave."

She sat there in the dew for at least twenty minutes, sobbing out her heart. Suddenly she became aware of a long black thing beside her. A black-runner! Before she could rise the snake was across her lap. She grabbed out at it, every drop of her blood seeming to have turned to ice. As she tugged and struggled to get up, the snake only wound himself tighter about her, drawing her back to the ground.

"David! Oh, my God! David!"

But he was at the house. He could not hear her. Still she emitted one scream after another.

Then she heard:

"Comin'!"

And she fainted.

When she came to, she was lying on the bed in the fireplace room. David was bathing her face.

"He didn't git time to hurt yo, honey," he was saying. "I killed him with my knife first. I cut him off yo. Yo is just scared, not hurt."

Rubye suddenly sat up.

"No, I'm not hurt. Just scared. Please leave me alone so I can rest."

She had remembered how he had destroyed her prize roses that night. She did not want him even in the room with her ever again.

David gave her a funny look, but obeyed and left. Soon she saw him hitching up and going out to the field.

"He actually thinks more of his cotton than he does of me. He's got to get that precious white stuff out of the field before a rain."

Rubye was not to be beaten. She remembered her black roses. Though the black rose had before been grown, she knew it had not in this section. She rose and hastily dressed.

It was noon before Rubye reached the fair grounds. She was thankful to find that she was in time to enter her roses. In fact hers were the only ones at the fair. She learned that a man from the A. and M. was to judge the plants. She waited with bated breath. Maybe he would appreciate her roses. No one in Coonville did.

As she waited there on the hard bench, she realized that she had not had a bite to eat that day. Still she was not hungry. She felt sort of sick at her stomach. Cold chills ran up and down her spine. Then hot flashes passed over her. She thought it was due to her scare. She prayed that she could stand it until her plants were judged.

It was four that afternoon before the man came to judge her plants. Rubye had held on somehow, but she hardly realized what was going on until a man said:

"Whose roses are these? By George, I never saw such roses! I've seen the black ones before, but not such large specimens. Judging by the stalk they must grow six feet tall."

Rubye rose.

"They're from David Woods' farm out in Coonville Community. He—he raised them."

The man turned to the young woman.

"You representing him?"

"I am his wife."

"How did he do it, lady?"

"I—he is keeping that a secret. He hopes to sell cuttings. He also has found the orange rose. And some of the biggest pink and yellow ones you ever saw."

"That's a damn' lie!" said a voice behind them.

Rubye turned and saw David stumbling up, his black eyes filled with both resentment and anger.

"She done it by herself. I raise cotton and corn."

"Well, she's done something, man. She'll win five hundred dollars for just this black rose. And I can fill as many orders for her orange rose as she can supply. Probably some of these others, too."

David looked at his wife in time to catch her as she fell in a faint.

When Rubye came to, David had the doctor with her. She was at the Pinecrest Hospital. David was sitting beside her crying.

"Why are you crying?" Rubye asked her husband. "Am I that bad off ? Or is it because I am not going to die?"

"Mrs. Woods, you have the malaria fever. Nothing to worry about. I'll have you fixed up before long. I'd better be going now. See that she takes her medicine, young man." Then the doctor picked up his case.

"Yes, suh."

As soon as the doctor had left the room, David looked sorrowfully at his wife and said:

"Honey, I wish yo'd take a gun and kill me."

"We'll forget all about it, David."

"No, we won't until yo understand it was the cotton I was so stubborn about, not that I didn't love yo. Folks first thought I was grazin' in good pastures when I brung yo home, and then soon they got to sayin' I wasn't. I wanted to win out, win by myself, even if yo wouldn't help. But yo won without my help. I'm a fool!"

"If you are, you are the sweetest one I ever saw. David, you can't drive me off now that I know you love me. That is all that matters to my heart. Tonight take me home and let's listen to the hoot owl quarreling again."

"Sho' will. He says somethin' new now, honey. I heard him last night."

"Work done
no done
night come
go home."

Then Confront World War II

AND AFTERMATH

African Americans by the thousands migrated to the West during World War II, and their migration acted as a catalyst for populating western cities, for abetting racial tensions, for changing economic conditions, and for uniting black Westerners. The western urban centers boomed, but the arrival of blacks coincided with an influx of white Southerners seeking the same opportunities that attracted blacks. Crowded housing, job competition, and whites' refusal to associate with African Americans led to unsavory behavior. Discrimination was rampant. Blacks protested in a number of ways; for example, by successfully challenging discrimination via the courts: white primaries were overturned, all-white juries were declared unreasonable, restrictive covenants were unenforceable, and miscegenation laws were struck down. This spirit and the effects of these developments, together with the personal pain and pathos of segregation, were captured by short story writers.

The stories in this chapter demonstrate the personal, social, and political ramifications of racism. Many of them show ways in which racism occurs through the perpetuation of stereotypes. "Mister Toussan," one of several stories by Ralph Ellison wherein the young Oklahoma boys Buster and Riley appear, shows that promoting stereotypes and a segregated educational system denies blacks a proper history. While listening to a song, Riley and Buster imagine where they might go if they could fly. They decide they would fly north, or above the stars, or to Africa—someplace where blacks are free. They have inaccurate, stereotyped ideas of Africa that they have learned from history books. Thinking about the stereotypes that are perpetuated through "education," Buster tries to remember what he has learned about Africans. He recalls one story his teacher told him that celebrates blacks, and tells it to Riley. It is about a black leader named Toussan (Toussaint L'Ouverture), who lived in Haiti and fought Napoleon's troops. Buster tells the story enthusiastically, making it come alive. When Riley questions some of Buster's bold claims about Toussan, both boys agree that adults cannot tell a story correctly. Buster realizes that historical accounts that celebrate black identity and defy stereotypes are not found in history books. Blacks have traditionally been excluded from discussions not only in the discipline of history, but also in other disciplines such as literature and art.

Frank Yerby, in "Health Card," considers the consequences of following stereotypes on a personal level. The story introduces Johnny, a young soldier, and his wife, Lily, who visits him where he is stationed. When Johnny asks the corporal for special permission to leave the base so he can meet his wife, it is granted. While Johnny is walking with Lily, the police ask her for her health card (prostitutes must carry one) and Johnny tells them she is his wife. An argument ensues and Lily begs Johnny not to fight the police. The police walk away and Johnny feels inadequate because he cannot defend Lily against their racism. The assumption that Johnny's wife is a prostitute upholds the stereotype of the black woman as prostitute and has tremendous consequences for both Lily and Johnny—she is insulted personally and he is unable to protect his wife's dignity.

John Wesley Groves's "Stop, Thief!" demonstrates discrimination in terms of a black man who is denied medical attention in a life-threatening situation. Jimmy Hughes escapes from a California prison for the fifth time and is determined to fight social inequality. He is shot during a police chase, and when a white doctor refuses to treat his injured arm, he threatens him with a gun. Hughes is refused treatment not because he is a hard-core criminal, but because he is black. "Stop, Thief!" reveals how discrimination goes beyond emotional consequences: when blacks are denied medical treatment, they are denied survival. The story demonstrates that Hughes's plight is caused not by his own actions but by racism and social inequality.

Unlike "Mister Toussan," "Health Card," and "Stop, Thief!", Chester Himes's "Lunching at the Ritzmore" seems to show that blacks are not the victims of discrimination. However, Himes uses irony to convey a Pyrrhic victory. The story begins with two white men who make a bet about whether a black man will be served in a restaurant, as a test to determine whether racial discrimination still exists. As the two white men and the black man look for a restaurant in which to conduct their test, people begin to follow. Finally, a crowd awaits outside the Ritzmore, a fashionable Los Angeles restaurant, where the black man attempts to be served. When he is served, some onlookers assume that racial discrimination is not practiced in Los Angeles. Ironically, the onlookers may deduce that the black man would be served in any restaurant, but he knows otherwise. In classic Himes irony, by winning the bet the white man fails to show that discrimination is still practiced and must pay the bill because he is the only one with money.

John O. Killens, in "God Bless America," uses irony also. "God Bless America" is one of many stories by African Americans that portray racism as practiced in the military. Here, the black protagonist wants to join the Army during the Korean War because he is convinced that racial equality exists in the military. Despite his wife's objections, he enlists, goes to California for training, and experiences prejudice while boarding the plane to fly to combat. The story demonstrates that black soldiers must fight for a country that not only tolerates but encourages racism.

Malvin Wald's "Keys to the City" uses irony in terms of poetic justice. The story focuses on an election for the mayor of Stanley, a small Texas town. The incumbent, Ed Horton, fears he will lose the election because the wealthy town residents support his challenger. Attempting to win his political enemies' votes, he invites Ernest Johnson, a local war hero, to Stanley for a war bond drive. Horton is to present a huge set of painted "keys to the city" to Johnson. When Johnson arrives, Horton and the townspeople see that he is black. During his acceptance speech, Johnson says that he is proud of his race. Trying to appease the racist citizens, Horton claims that he acted in Stanley's best interest when he invited Johnson to speak. One man acknowledges that, although Horton did provide Stanley with welcome publicity, he also insulted the town when he publicly acknowledged Stanley as a racially tolerant place. Horton believes that Johnson should be lynched even if he is a war hero. When the American Council for Tolerance awards Horton a medal, he knows he has lost the race for mayor.

Losing a race for mayor because an inadvertent, yet affirmative, action taken by a candidate leads to an award for tolerance epitomizes the state of race relations during and after World War II. It also epitomizes the successful way in which irony is used by authors to portray the lives of western African Americans. Other writers pursue a more confrontational approach, such as in John Wesley Groves's "Stop Thief!" and in Ralph Ellison's "Mister Toussan." But also important about these stories is their personal nature. One can feel the slights, the affronts, the anguish, and the danger of segregation induced by racism. Later writers will capture the effort to eradicate segregation.

Mister Toussan

RALPH ELLISON

Once upon a time
The goose drink wine
Monkey chew tobacco
And he spit white lime

—Rhyme used as a prologue to Negro slave stories

"I hope they all gits rotten and the worms git in 'em," the first boy said.

"I hopes a big wind storm comes and blows down all the trees," said the second boy.

"Me too," the first boy said. "And when ole Rogan comes out to see what happened I hope a tree falls on his head and kills him."

"Now jus look a-yonder at them birds," the second boy said. "They eating all they want and when we asked him to let us git some off the ground he had to come calling us little nigguhs and chasing us home!"

"Doggonit," said the second boy. I hope them birds got poison in they feet!"

The two small boys, Riley and Buster, sat on the floor of the porch, their bare feet resting upon the cool earth as they stared past the line on the paving where the sun consumed the shade, to a yard directly across the street. The grass in the yard was very green, and a house stood against it, neat and white in the morning sun. A double row of trees stood alongside the house, heavy with cherries that showed deep red against the dark green of the leaves and dull dark brown of the branches. The two boys were watching an old man who rocked himself in a chair as he stared back at them across the street.

"Just look at him," said Buster. "Ole Rogan's so scared we gonna git some a his ole cherries he ain't even got sense enough to go in outa the sun!"

"Well, them birds is gitting their'n," said Riley.

"They mockingbirds."

I don't care what kinda birds they is, they sho in them trees."

"Yeah, ole Rogan don't see *them*. Man, I tell you white folks ain't got no sense."

They were silent now, watching the darting flight of the birds into the trees. Behind them they could hear the clatter of a sewing machine: Riley's mother was sewing for the white folks. It was quiet, and as the woman worked, her voice rose above the whirring machine in song.

"Your mama sho can sing, man," said Buster.

"She sings in the choir," said Riley, "and she sings all the leads in church."

"Shucks, I know it," said Buster. "You tryin' to brag?"

As they listened they heard the voice rise clear and liquid to float upon the morning air:

"I got wings, you got wings,
All God's chillun got a wings
When I git to heaven gonna put on my wings
Gonna shout all ovah God's heab'n.
Heab'n, heab'n
Everbody talkin' 'bout heab'n ain't going there
Heab'n, heab'n, Ah'm gonna fly all ovah God's heab'n . . ."

She sang as though the words possessed a deep and throbbing meaning for her, and the boys stared blankly at the earth, feeling the somber, mysterious calm of church. The street was quiet, and even old Rogan had stopped rocking to listen. Finally the voice trailed off to a hum and became lost in the clatter of the busy machine.

"Wish I could sing like that," said Buster.

Riley was silent, looking down to the end of the porch where the sun had eaten a bright square into the shade, fixing a flitting butterfly in its brilliance.

"What would you do if you had wings?" he said.

"Shucks, I'd outfly an eagle. I wouldn't stop flying till I was a million, billion, trillion, zillion miles away from this ole town."

"Where'd you go, man?"

"Up north, maybe to Chicago."

"Man, if I had wings I wouldn't never settle down."

"Me neither. Hecks, with wings you could go anywhere, even up to the sun if it wasn't too hot . . ."

". . . I'd go to New York . . ."

"Even around the stars . . ."

"Or Dee-troit, Michigan . . ."

"Hell, you could git some cheese off the moon and some milk from the Milky Way . . ."

"Or anywhere else colored is free . . ."

"I bet I'd loop-the-loop . . ."

"And parachute . . ."

"I'd land in Africa and git me some diamonds . . ."

"Yeah, and them cannibals would eat the hell outa you, too," said Riley.

"The heck they would, not fast as I'd fly away . . ."

"Man, they'd catch you and stick some them long spears in your behin'!" said Riley.

Buster laughed as Riley shook his head gravely: "Boy, you'd look like a black pincushion when they got through with you," said Riley.

"Shucks, man, they couldn't catch me, them suckers is too lazy. The geography book says they 'bout the most lazy folks in the whole world," said Buster with disgust, "just black and lazy!"

"Aw naw, they ain't neither," exploded Riley.

"They is too! The geography book says they is!"

"Well, my ole man says they ain't!"

"How come they ain't then?"

" 'Cause my old man says that over there they got kings and diamonds and gold and ivory, and if they got all them things, all of 'em caint be lazy," said Riley. "Ain't many colored folks over here got them things."

"Sho ain't, man. The white folks won't let 'em," said Buster.

It was good to think that all the Africans were not lazy. He tried to remember all he had heard of Africa as he watched a purple pigeon sail down into the street and scratch where a horse had passed. Then, as he remembered a story his teacher had told him, he saw a car rolling swiftly up the street and the pigeon stretching its wings and lifting easily into the air, skimming the top of the car in its slow, rocking flight. He watched it rise and disappear where the taut telephone wires cut the sky above the curb. Buster felt good. Riley scratched his initials in the soft earth with his big toe.

"Riley, you know all them Africa guys ain't really that lazy," he said.

"I know they ain't," said Riley. "I just tole you so."

"Yeah, but my teacher tole me, too. She tole us 'bout one of the African guys named Toussan what she said whipped Napoleon!"

Riley stopped scratching in the earth and looked up, his eye rolling in disgust: "Now how come you have to start lying?"

"Thass what she said."

"Boy, you oughta quit telling them things."

"I hope God may kill me."

"She said he was a *African?*"

"Cross my heart, man . . ."

"Really?"

"Really, man. She said he come from a place named Hayti."

Riley looked hard at Buster and, seeing the seriousness of the face, felt the excitement of a story rise up within him.

"Buster, I'll bet a fat man you lyin'. What'd that teacher say?"

"Really, man, she said that Toussan and his men got up on one of them African mountains and shot down them peckerwood soldiers fass as they'd try to come up . . ."

"Why good-God-a-mighty!" yelled Riley.

"Oh boy, they shot 'em down!" chanted Buster.

"Tell me about it, man!"

"And they throwed 'em off the mountain . . ."

". . . Goool-leee! . . ."

". . . And Toussan drove 'em cross the sand . . ."

". . . Yeah! And what was they wearing, Buster? . . ."

"Man, they had on red uniforms and blue hats all trimmed with gold and they had some swords all shining, what they called sweet blades of Damascus . . ."

"Sweet blades of Damascus! . . ."

". . . They really had 'em," chanted Buster.

"And what kinda guns?"

"Big, black cannon!"

"And where did ole what you call 'im run them guys? . . ."

"His name was Toussan."

"Toozan! Just like Tarzan . . ."

"Not Taar-zan, dummy, Toou-zan!"

"Toussan! And where'd ole Toussan run 'em?"

"Down to the water, man . . ."

". . . To the river water . . ."

". . . Where some great big ole boats was waiting for 'em . . ."

". . . Go on, Buster!"

"An' Toussan shot into them boats . . ."

" . . . He shot into 'em . . ."

". . . shot into them boats . . ."

"Jesus! . . ."

". . . with his great big cannons . . ."

". . . Yeah! . . ."

". . . made a-brass . . ."

". . . Brass . . ."

". . . an' his big black cannonballs started killin' them peckerwoods . . ."

". . . Lawd, Lawd . . ."

". . . Boy, till them peckerwoods hollowed, *Please, Please, Mister Toussan, we'll be good!*"

"An' what'd Toussan tell 'em, Buster?"

"Boy, he said in his deep voice, *I oughta drown all a you bastards.*"

"An' what'd the peckerwoods say?"

"They said, *Please, Please, Please, Mister Toussan . . .*"

". . . We'll be good," broke in Riley.

"Thass right, man," said Buster excitedly. He clapped his hands and kicked his heels against the earth, his black face glowing in a burst of rhythmic joy.

"Boy!"

"And what'd ole Toussan say then?"

"He said in his big deep voice: *You all peckerwoods better be good, 'cause this is sweet Papa Toussan talking and my nigguhs is crazy 'bout white meat!*"

"Ho, ho, ho!" Riley bent double with laughter. The rhythm still throbbed within him and he wanted the story to go on and on . . .

"Buster, you know didn't no teacher tell you that lie," he said.

"Yes she did, man."

"She said there was really a guy like that what called hisself Sweet Papa Toussan?"

Riley's voice was unbelieving, and there was a wistful expression in his eyes that Buster could not understand. Finally he dropped his head and grinned.

"Well," he said, "I bet thass what ole Toussan said. You know how grown folks is, they caint tell a story right 'cepting real old folks like Granma."

"They sho caint," said Riley. "They don't know how to put the right stuff to it."

Riley stood, his legs spread wide, and stuck his thumbs in the top of his trousers, swaggering sinisterly.

"Come on, watch me do it now, Buster. Now I bet ole Toussan looked down at them white folks standing just about like this and said in a soft easy voice: *Ain't I done begged you white folks to quit messin' with me? . . .*"

"Thass right, quit messing with 'im," chanted Buster.

"But naw, you all had to come on anyway . . ."

". . . Just 'cause they was black . . ."

"Thass right," said Riley. "Then ole Toussan felt so damn bad and mad the tears came a-trickling down . . ."

". . . He was really mad."

"And then, man, he said in his big, bad voice: *Goddamn you white folks, how come you all caint let us colored alone?*"

". . . An' he was crying . . ."

". . . An' Toussan tole them peckerwoods: *I been beggin' you all to quit bothering us . . .*"

". . . Beggin' on his bended knees! . . ."

"Then, man, Toussan got real mad and snatched off his hat and started stompin' up and down on it and the tears was tricklin' down and he said: *You all come tellin' me about Napoleon . . .*"

"They was tryin' to scare 'im, man . . ."

"Said: *I don't give a damn about Napoleon . . .*"

". . . Wasn't studyin' 'bout him . . ."

". . . Toussan said: *Napoleon ain't nothing but a man!* Then Toussan pulled back his shining sword like this, and twirled it at them peckerwoods' throats so hard it z-z-z-zinged in the air!"

"Now keep on, finish it, man," said Buster. "What'd Toussan do then?"

"Then you know what he did, he said: *I oughta beat the hell outa you peckerwoods!*"

"Thass right, and he did it too," said Buster. He jumped to his feet and fenced violently with five desperate imaginary soldiers, running each through with his imaginary sword. Buster watched him from the porch, grinning.

"Toussan musta scared them white folks almost to death!"

"Yeah, thass 'bout the way it was," said Buster. The rhythm was dying now and he sat back upon the porch, breathing tiredly.

"It sho is a good story," said Riley.

"Hecks, man, all the stories my teacher tells us is good. She's a good ole teacher—but you know one thing?"

"Naw, what?"

"Ain't none of them stories in the books. Wonder why?"

"Hell, you know why, Ole Toussan was too hard on them white folks, thass why."

"Oh, he was a hard man!"

"He was mean . . ."

"But a good mean!"

"Toussan was clean . . ."

". . . He was a good, clean mean," said Riley.

"Aw, man, he was sooo-preme," said Buster.

"Riiiley!!"

The boys stopped short in their word play, their mouths wide.

"Riley, I say!" It was Riley's mother's voice.

"Ma'm?"

"She musta heard us cussin'," whispered Buster.

"Shut up, man . . . What you want, Ma?"

"I says I want you all to go round the backyard and play. You keeping up too much fuss out there. White folks says we tear up a neighborhood when we move in it and you all out there jus provin' them out true. Now git on round in the back."

"Aw, Ma, we was jus playing, Ma . . ."

"Boy, I said for you all to go on."

"But, Ma . . ."

"You hear me, boy!"

"Yessum, we going," said Riley. "Come on, Buster."

Buster followed slowly behind, feeling the dew upon his feet as he walked up on the shaded grass.

"What else did he do, man?" Buster said.

"Huh? Rogan?"

"Hecks, naw! I'm talkin' 'bout Toussan."

"Doggone if I know, man—but I'm gonna ask that teacher."

"He was a fightin' son-of-a-gun, wasn't he, man?"

"He didn't stand for no foolishness," said Riley reservedly. He thought of other things now, and as he moved along, he slid his feet easily over the short-cut grass, dancing as he chanted:

Iron is iron,
And tin is tin,
And that's the way
The story . . .

"Aw come on, man," interrupted Buster. "Let's go play in the alley . . ."

And that's the way . . .

"Maybe we can slip around and get some cherries," Buster went on.

. . . the story ends, chanted Riley.

Health Card

FRANK YERBY

Johnny stood under one of the street lights on the comer and tried to read the
letter. The street lights down in the Bottom were so dim that he couldn't make
out half the words, but he didn't need to: he knew them all by heart anyway.

"Sugar," he read, "it took a long time but I done it. I got the money to come to
see you. I waited and waited for them to give you a furlough, but it look like they
don't mean to. Sugar, I can't wait no longer. I got to see you. I got to. Find a nice
place for me to stay—where we can be happy together. You know what I mean.
With all my love, Lily."

Johnny folded the letter up and put it back in his pocket. Then he walked
swiftly down the street past all the juke joints with the music blaring out and the
G.I. brogans pounding. He turned down a side street, scuffing up a cloud of dust
as he did so. None of the streets down in Black Bottom was paved, and there were
four inches of fine white powder over everything. When it rained the mud would
come up over the tops of his army shoes, but it hadn't rained in nearly three
months. There were no juke joints on this street and the Negro shanties were neatly
whitewashed. Johnny kept on walking until he came to the end of the street. On
the corner stood the little whitewashed Baptist Church, and next to it was the neat,
well-kept home of the pastor.

Johnny went up on the porch and hesitated. He thrust his hand in his pocket
and the paper crinkled. He took his hand out and knocked on the door.

"Who's that?" a voice called.

"It's me," Johnny answered; "it's a sodjer."

The door opened a crack and a woman peered out. She was middle-aged and
fat. Looking down, Johnny could see that her feet were bare.

"Whatcha want, sodjer?"

Johnny took off his cap.

"Please, ma'am, lemme come in. I kin explain it t' yuh better settin' down."

She studied his face for a minute in the darkness.

"Aw right," she said; "you kin come in, son."

Johnny entered the room stiffly and sat down on a cornshuck-bottomed chair.

"It's this way, ma'am," he said. "I got a wife up Nawth. I been tryin' an' tryin' t' git a furlough so I could go t' see huh. But they always put me off. So now she done worked an' saved enuff money t' come an' see me. I wants t' ax you t' rent me a room, ma'am. I doan' know nowheres t' ax."

"This ain't no hotel, son."

"I know it ain't. I cain't take Lily t' no hotel, not lak hotels in this heah town."

"Lily yo' wife?"

"Yes'm. She my sho' nuff, honest t' Gawd wife. Married in th' Baptist Church in Deetroit."

The fat woman sat back, and her thick lips widened into a smile.

"She a good girl, ain't she? An' you doan' wanta take her t' one o' these heah ho'houses they calls hotels."

"That's it, ma'am."

"Sho' you kin bring huh heah, son. Be glad t' have huh. Reveren' be glad t' have huh too. What yo' name, son?"

"Johnny. Johnny Green. Ma'am—"

"Yas, son?"

"You understands that I wants t' come heah too?"

The fat woman rocked back in her chair and gurgled with laughter.

"Bless yo' heart, chile, I ain't always been a ole woman! And I ain't always been th' preacher's wife neither!"

"Thank you, ma'am. I gotta go now. Time fur me t' be gettin' back t' camp."

"When you bring Lily?"

"Be Monday night, ma'am. Pays you now if you wants it."

"Monday be aw right. Talk it over with th' Reveren', so he make it light fur yuh. Know sodjer boys ain't got much money."

"No, ma'am, sho' Lawd ain't. G'night, ma'am."

When he turned back into the main street of the Negro section the doors of the joints were all open and the soldiers were coming out. The girls were clinging onto their arms all the way to the bus stop. Johnny looked at the dresses that stopped halfway between the pelvis and the knee and hugged the backside so that every muscle showed when they walked. He saw the purple lipstick smeared across the wide full lips, and the short hair stiffened with smelly grease so that it covered their heads like a black lacquered cap. They went on down to the bus stop arm in arm, their knotty bare calves bunching with each step as they walked. Johnny thought about Lily. He walked past them very fast without turning his head.

But just as he reached the bus stop he heard the whistles. When he turned around he saw the four M.P.s and the civilian policeman stopping the crowd. He turned around again and walked back until he was standing just behind the white men.

"Aw right," the M.P.s were saying, "you gals git your health cards out."

Some of the girls started digging in their handbags. Johnny could see them dragging out small yellow cardboard squares. But the others just stood there with blank expressions on their faces. The soldiers started muttering, a dark, deep-throated sound. The M.P.s started pushing their way through the crowd, looking at each girl's card as they passed. When they came to a girl who didn't have a card they called out to the civilian policemen:

"Aw right, mister, take A'nt Jemima for a little ride."

Then the city policemen would lead the girl away and put her in the Black Maria.

They kept this up until they had examined every girl except one. She hung back beside her soldier, and the first time the M.P.s didn't see her. When they came back through, one of them caught her by the arm.

"Lemme see your card, Mandy," he said.

The girl looked at him, her little eyes narrowing into slits in her black face.

"Tek yo' hands offen me, white man," she said.

The M.P.'s face crimsoned, so that Johnny could see it even in the darkness.

"Listen, black girl," he said, "I told you to lemme see your card."

"An' I tole you t' tek yo' han' offen me, white man!"

"Gawddammit, you little black bitch, you better do like I tell you!"

Johnny didn't see very clearly what happened after that. There was a sudden explosion of motion, and then the M.P. was trying to jerk his hand back, but he couldn't, for the little old black girl had it between her teeth and was biting it to the bone. He drew his other hand back and slapped her across the face so hard that it sounded like a pistol shot. She went over backwards and her tight skirt split, so that when she got up Johnny could see that she didn't have anything on under it. She came forward like a cat, her nails bared, straight for the M.P.'s eyes. He slapped her down again, but the soldiers surged forward all at once. The M.P.s fell back and drew their guns and one of them blew a whistle.

Johnny, who was behind them, decided it was time for him to get out of there and he did; but not before he saw the squads of white M.P.s hurling around the corner and going to work on the Negroes with their clubs. He reached the bus stop and swung on board. The minute after he had pushed his way to the back behind all the white soldiers he heard the shots. The bus driver put the bus in gear and they roared off toward the camp.

It was after one o'clock when all the soldiers straggled in. Those of them who could still walk. Eight of them came in on the meat wagon, three with gunshot wounds. The colonel declared the town out of bounds for all Negro soldiers for a month.

"Dammit," Johnny said, "I gotta go meet Lily, I gotta. I cain't stay heah. I cain't!"

"Whatcha gonna do," Little Willie asked, "go A.W.O.L.?"

Johnny looked at him, his brow furrowed into a frown.

"Naw," he said, "I'm gonna go see th' colonel!"

"Whut! Man, you crazy! Colonel kick yo' black ass out fo' you gits yo' mouf open."

"I take a chanct on that."

He walked over to the little half mirror on the wall of the barracks. Carefully he readjusted his cap. He pulled his tie out of his shirt front and drew the knot tighter around his throat. Then he tucked the ends back in at just the right fraction of an inch between the correct pair of buttons. He bent down and dusted his shoes again, although they were already spotless.

"Man," Little Willie said, "you sho' is a fool!"

"Reckon I am," Johnny said; then he went out of the door and down the short wooden steps.

When he got to the road that divided the colored and white sections of the camp his steps faltered. He stood still a minute, drew in a deep breath, and marched very stiffly and erect across the road. The white soldiers gazed at him curiously, but none of them said anything. If a black soldier came over into their section it was because somebody sent him so they let him alone.

In front of the colonel's headquarters he stopped. He knew what he had to say, but his breath was very short in his throat and he was going to have a hard time saying it.

"Whatcha want, soldier?" the sentry demanded.

"I wants t' see th' colonel."

"Who sent you?"

Johnny drew his breath in sharply.

"I ain't at liberty t' say," he declared, his breath coming out very fast behind the words.

"You ain't at liberty t' say," the sentry mimicked. "Well I'll be damned! If you ain't at liberty t' say, then I ain't at liberty t' let you see the colonel! Git tha hell outa here, nigger, before I pump some lead in you!"

Johnny didn't move.

The sentry started toward him, lifting his rifle butt, but another soldier, a sergeant, came around the corner of the building.

"Hold on there," he called. "What tha hell is th' trouble here?"

"This here nigger says he want t' see tha colonel an' when I ast him who sent him he says he ain't at liberty t' say!"

The sergeant turned to Johnny.

Johnny came to attention and saluted him. You aren't supposed to salute N.C.O.s, but sometimes it helps.

"What you got t' say fur yourself, boy?" the sergeant said, not unkindly. Johnny's breath evened.

"I got uh message fur th' colonel, suh," he said; "I ain't s'posed t' give it t' nobody else but him. I ain't even s'posed t' tell who sont it, suh."

The sergeant peered at him sharply.

"You tellin' tha truth, boy?"

"Yassuh!"

"Aw right. Wait here a minute."

He went into H.Q. After a couple of minutes be came back.

"Aw right, soldier, you kin go on in."

Johnny mounted the steps and went into the colonel's office. The colonel was a lean, white-haired soldier with a face tanned to the color of saddle leather. He was reading a letter through a pair of horn-rimmed glasses which had only one earhook left, so that he had to hold them up to his eyes with one hand. He put them down and looked up. Johnny saw that his eyes were pale blue, so pale that he felt as if he were looking into the eyes of an eagle or some other fierce bird of prey.

"Well?" he said, and Johnny stiffened into a salute. The colonel half smiled.

"At ease, soldier," he said. Then: "The sergeant tells me that you have a very important message for me."

Johnny gulped in the air.

"Beggin' th' sergeant's pardon, suh," he said, "but that ain't so."

"What!"

"Yassuh," Johnny rushed on, "nobody sent me. I come on m' own hook. I had t' talk t' yuh, Colonel, suh! You kin sen' me t' th' guardhouse afterwards, but please, suh, lissen t' me fur jes' a minute!"

The colonel relaxed slowly. Something very like a smile was playing around the corners of his mouth. He looked at his watch.

"All right, soldier," he said. "You've got five minutes."

"Thank yuh, thank yuh, suh!"

"Speak your piece, soldier; you're wasting time!"

"It's about Lily, suh. She my wife. She done worked an' slaved fur nigh onto six months t' git the money t' come an' see me. An' now you give th' order that none of th' cullud boys kin go t' town. Beggin' yo' pahdon, suh, I wasn't in none of that trouble. I ain't neber been in no trouble. You kin ax my cap'n, if you wants to. All I wants is permission to go into town fur one week, an' I'll stay outa town fur two months if yuh wants me to."

The colonel picked up the phone.

"Ring Captain Walters for me," he said. Then: "What's your name, soldier?"

"It's Green, suh. Private Johnny Green."

"Captain Walters? This is Colonel Milton. Do you have anything in your files concerning Private Johnny Green? Oh yes, go ahead. Take all the time you need."

The colonel lit a long black cigar. Johnny waited. The clock on the wall spun its electric arms.

"What's that? Yes. Yes, yes, I see. Thank you, Captain."

He put down the phone and picked up a fountain pen. He wrote swiftly. Finally he straightened up and gave Johnny the slip of paper.

Johnny read it. It said: "Private Johnny Green is given express permission to go into town every evening of the week beginning August seventh and ending August fourteenth. He is further permitted to remain in town overnight every night during said week, so long as he returns to camp for reveille the following morning. By order of the commanding officer, Colonel H. H. Milton."

There was a hard knot at the base of Johnny's throat. He couldn't breathe. But he snapped to attention and saluted smartly.

"Thank yuh, suh," he said at last. Then: "Gawd bless you, suh!"

"Forget it, soldier. I was a young married man once myself. My compliments to Captain Walters."

Johnny saluted again and about-faced, then he marched out of the office and down the stairs. On the way back he saluted everybody—privates, N.C.O.s, and civilian visitors, his white teeth gleaming in a huge smile.

"That's sure one happy darky," one of the white soldiers said.

Johnny stood in the station and watched the train running in. The yellow lights from the windows flickered on and off across his face as the alternating squares of light and darkness flashed past. Then it was slowing and Johnny was running beside it, trying to keep abreast of the Jim Crow coach. He could see her standing up, holding each other, Johnny's arms crushing all the breath out of her, holding her so hard against him that his brass buttons hurt through her thin dress. She opened her mouth to speak but he kissed her, bending her head backward on her neck until her little hat fell off. It lay there on the ground, unnoticed.

"Sugah," she said, "sugah. It was awful."

"I know," he said. "I know."

Then he took her bags and they started walking out of the station toward the Negro section of town.

"I missed yuh so much," Johnny said, "I thought I lose m' mind."

"Me too," she said. Then: "I brought th' marriage license with me like yah tole me. I doan' wan th' preacher's wife t' think we bad."

"Enybody kin look at yuh an' see yuh uh angel!"

They went very quietly through all the dark streets and the white soldiers turned to look at Johnny and his girl.

Lak a queen, Johnny thought, lak a queen. He looked at the girl beside him, seeing the velvety nightshade skin, the glossy black lacquered curls, the sweet, wide hips and the long, clean legs striding beside him in the darkness. I am black, but comely, O ye daughters of Jerusalem!

They turned into the Bottom where the street lights were dim blobs on the pine poles and the dust rose up in little swirls around their feet. Johnny had his head half turned so that he didn't see the two M.P.s until he had almost bumped into them. He dropped one bag and caught Lily by the arm. Then he drew her aside quickly and the two men went by them without speaking.

They kept on walking, but every two steps Johnny would jerk his head around and look nervously back over his shoulder. The last time he looked the two M.P.s had stopped and were looking back at them. Johnny turned out the elbow of the arm next to Lily so that it hooked into hers a little and began to walk faster, pushing her along with him.

"What's yo' hurry, sugah?" she said. "I be heah a whole week!"

But Johnny was looking over his shoulder at the two M.P.s. They were coming toward them now, walking with long, slow strides, their reddish-white faces set. Johnny started to push Lily along faster, but she shook off his arm and stopped still.

"I do declare, Johnny Green! You th' beatines' man! Whut you walk me so fas' fur?"

Johnny opened his mouth to answer her, but the military police were just behind them now, and the sergeant reached out and laid his hand on her arm.

"C'mon, gal," he said, "lemme see it."

"Let you see whut? Whut he mean, Johnny?"

"Your card," the sergeant growled. "Lemme see your card."

"My card?" Lily said blankly. "Whut kinda card, mister?"

Johnny put the bags down. He was fighting for breath.

"Look heah, Sarge," he said; "this girl my wife!"

"Oh yeah? I said lemme see your card, sister!"

"I ain't got no card, mister. I dunno whut you talkin' about."

"Look, Sarge," the other M.P. said, "th' soldier's got bags. Maybe she's just come t' town."

"These your bags, gal?"

"Yessir."

"Aw right. You got twenty-four hours to git yourself a health card. If you don't have it by then we hafta run you in. Git goin' now."

"Listen," Johnny shouted; "this girl my wife! She ain't no ho'! I tell you she ain't—"

"What you say, nigger—" the M.P. sergeant growled. "Whatcha say?" He started toward Johnny.

Lily swung on Johnny's arm.

"C'mon, Johnny," she said; "they got guns. C'mon, Johnny, please! Please, Johnny!"

Slowly she drew him away.

"Aw, leave 'em be, Sarge," the M.P. corporal said; "maybe she is his wife."

The sergeant spat. The brown tobacco juice splashed in the dirt not an inch from Lily's foot. Then the two of them turned and started away.

Johnny stopped.

"Lemme go, Lily," he said, "lemme go!" He tore her arm loose from his and started back up the street. Lily leaped, her two arms fastening themselves around his neck. He fought silently but she clung to him, doubling her knees so that all her weight was hanging from his neck.

"No, Johnny! Oh Jesus no! You be kilt! Oh, Johnny, listen t' me, sugah! You's all I got!"

He put both hands up to break her grip but she swung her weight sidewise and the two of them went down in the dirt. The M.P.s turned the corner out of sight.

Johnny sat there in the dust staring at her. The dirt had ruined her dress. He sat there a long time looking at her until the hot tears rose up back of his eyelids faster than he could blink them away, so he put his face down in her lap and cried.

"I ain't no man!" he said. "I ain't no man!"

"Hush, sugah," she said. "You's a man aw right. You's my man!"

Gently she drew him to his feet. He picked up the bags and the two of them went down the dark street toward the preacher's house.

Stop, Thief!

JOHN WESLEY GROVES, IV

Jimmy Hughes was a young, thin Negro who had served time in prison and who would knife you in a minute if you riled him. Five times the state of California had sent him to prison and five times he had escaped. Some of the crimes he had been charged with and convicted of he had perpetrated and some he hadn't. However, the fact that he had been unjustly convicted didn't mean that he was incapable of committing the crime with which he was charged. There wasn't any crime he wouldn't commit if the opportunity presented itself.

His mother had died of tuberculosis when he was six. By the time he had reached seven his father was gone too. So he was left to roam the streets of the ghettos and make it as best he could. Shortly after his father died the landlord put a padlock on the two-room apartment because the rent had not been paid. Jimmy made a shoeshine box and started to work on his own. The shoeshine business wasn't bad, but you had to work so hard and take so low just to make a nickel that it soon became distasteful to him. He wanted more money and he wanted more respect from his fellowmen. When he couldn't get enough money by shining shoes he started stealing; when he couldn't get respect by soliciting it peacefully he started fighting. So began the criminal career of Jimmy Hughes.

After he got the name of being bad it wasn't hard to live up to it, nor was it hard to feel mean and vindictive. He learned the lessons of the underworld well and soon he was schooled in every underhand art in existence. He was an excellent pickpocket, a remarkable shoplifter, a clever card shark and a good liar. He had only one weakness and that was his inability to control his temper. He couldn't stand to be stepped on, not even by members of the underworld without fighting back. He wasn't sent to reform schools the first time by the tax-paying citizens of San Francisco, but by certain members of the underworld to whom he just wouldn't bow.

Jimmy was thirteen when he received his first sentence. He and two white boys had stolen a car for a fence who hired willing youths especially for that purpose. The fence had good contacts and therefore experienced little or no trouble in disposing of the stolen goods. Jimmy had planned the job and taken most of the risks. The two white boys had just followed instructions.

The car was a '47 Nash and belonged to one of the wealthy families of San Francisco. It wasn't hard to steal the car after they had persuaded the boy at the parking lot where the owner left it every morning to loan them the key long enough to have a duplicate made, after which they gave the original back to the mechanic so that no suspicion would fall on him. They didn't steal the car from there because they wanted to use the place again in future jobs. They waited until the car was driven to the house of the owner and parked. Then, when the owner had gone into his house, they got into the car and drove away.

The man for whom they were working was having trouble getting keys to cars; however, Jimmy's idea of having duplicates made when the cars were left at the garage with the keys in them revolutionized the car-snatching. He could just plant two or three mechanics in the best garages in town, have them tend to the business of the duplicate keys and then the car-snatchers could steal the automobiles at their leisure.

That idea and the Nash job should have paid off good and Jimmy knew it. However, when he went to collect, the go-between working for the fence counted out twenty-five dollar bills to the two white boys and fifteen dollars to Jimmy.

"What's the big idea?" Jimmy asked

"What do you mean?" the man replied.

"I should git more than a lousy fifteen bucks for a job like that. I did most of the brainwork on this ——ing job and I ain't takin' the short end of the deal for nobody. That job we turned in is worth every bit of two thousand dollars, if it's worth a cent. And this all I git out of it? ——, no! I ain't takin' this crap."

"You'd better watch your mouth," one of the boys said. The other one silently backed up his friend's statement.

"You might as well accept the fact, sonny," the agent said. "That's all you get."

Jimmy looked at the agent then at the two boys who had helped him pull the job.

"I'd advise you to take what you got," the agent said, "and beat it before I change my mind and don't give you nothin'."

"You sonsofbitches," Jimmy said. "You no good, stinkin' sonsofbitches, pullin' a low-down, rotten trick like that! Well, you just wait. I'll tell every cop in this town what you've been up to and have the whole ——ing bunch of you thrown in the can, even if I've got to go myself."

"Careful there, sonny," the agent said. "Them's dangerous words."

Jimmy threw the money in his face and turned to go when the two white boys and the agent jumped him. The last thing he remembered before he woke up in jail was going into his pocket for his switch blade and then feeling something heavy and blunt hit him on the head.

At the police station they booked him for petty larceny. A man whom Jimmy had never seen before claimed he had picked his pocket. Jimmy thought of telling them about stealing the car and being gyped and beaten up by the agent and his two accomplices, but he knew they would only laugh at him and that he would receive all the blame for stealing the car. Besides, he didn't even know where he could find the agent and the two boys who had helped him. Every time they had met it had been in a back alley somewhere, not even always the same alley. He could guess what had happened. They had turned him in and gotten the man who claimed his pocket had been picked to file charges against him. The whole thing was so cleverly arranged there wasn't even any use in protesting. Jimmy took the conviction calmly, knowing that he was going to jail not because he had committed a crime, but because he was unfortunate enough to be a Negro. Underworld or upperworld, the codes of discrimination and white supremacy still held true.

That was what might be called the beginning of Jimmy's career. About five years after he got out of jail he had another encounter with the law. This time it was much more serious. Jimmy had graduated. He was now planning to hold-up a bank.

It was a big job for one man but he needed the money for his aunt's operation. She had cancer and the doctor said she would die if she wasn't operated on immediately. Jimmy liked his aunt because she had sheltered him when he escaped from prison. He had stayed with her all during the weeks the police had been looking for him, and now that the search was ended and he wanted to leave he found he couldn't walk out and leave her in that condition. When he told the local authorities that his aunt was sick and needed money for an operation, the reply was, "Banks have a lot of money. Why not try one of them?" That wasn't a bad idea, Jimmy thought. He would try a bank.

The next morning he stood across the street from the Citizens' Commercial Bank and waited for the doors to open. It was cold that morning and he had to walk up and down to keep his toes from getting frostbitten. The bank was on Market Street in one of the busiest sections of the street. He was thankful for the crowds of people on the street for they would conceal him from anyone who would be looking for him. His keen eyes examined the crowd. They were mostly housewives who obviously were waiting to draw on their husbands' accounts to buy some unnecessary articles of luxury.

As he watched the domesticated-looking women waiting there he could not help but compare them to parasites. He had never liked the leech type of woman who attached herself to a man and drained him dry of everything he had. He had never liked the type of woman who grew fat while her husband grew thin, who grew smug while her husband grew nervous. He thought his girl was not that kind. Thank God, she was the kind to help a fellow out of a jam. He couldn't help but feel that he was very lucky in having a girl like Pearl. She was the kind of woman a man could live for. If he got away with this he would devote the rest of his life to making her happy.

The doors of the bank opened and the crowd rushed in. Jimmy waited until they were all in and then he hurried across the street and entered the bank. There was a short line in front of most of the tellers' windows. Those which did not have a line in front of them were closed.

"I'd like to close out my account," Jimmy said when it was his turn at the window.

"Very well, sir. Do you have your bank book with you?"

"No," Jimmy said, "but I've got something else."

The teller looked puzzled.

Jimmy put his hand inside his coat and said, "I've got a gun in here and I'm willing to shoot if you don't gimme all the cash in that drawer."

Nervously the teller reached into the drawer which contained paper currency, took it out and laid it on the counter.

When it was all there Jimmy reached out, got the money and pocketed it. "Now you just keep right quiet until I'm out of that door. If you so much as make a move I'll let you have it. They might get me but that won't do you much good."

Slowly Jimmy backed away from the teller's window. The lady behind him walked up to the window.

"I'd like to draw out twenty-five dollars, please. Here's my book."

The teller looked at her as if he was paralyzed.

"Young man, did you hear what I said?" the querulous middle-aged woman asked.

The teller still stood motionless.

Meanwhile Jimmy was walking slowly to the door of the bank. When he got to the door he coolly lit a cigarette and looked back at the teller, put out the flame of the match with a puff of smoke and then rushed out of the doorway and into the crowd of people on the street. He heard the teller holler, "Get that man!" Then he heard an alarm go off. But by that time he was blocks away.

The chase didn't start until that night when two detectives found him in his aunt's house. They tried to arrest him but he ran out the door and into the street. His heart throbbed fiercely. His nerves were drawn tight and he could feel his thoughts rushing through his head. Where to go? Where to hide? Where would they look for him? Was there some hole, some corner in San Francisco where he would be secure? All of his life he had been hounded by them. They would never let him alone and now again they pursued him. He was the Negro, the black man, the undesirable, the unwanted. He was alone in the night with nothing but the darkness and the spotlight moon to keep him company. The cold air rushed in and out of his lungs as he put block after block between himself and the detectives.

But no matter how far and how fast he ran he could not lose the sinister figures that followed him. He could not get beyond the hearing of the footsteps behind him. No matter how many corners he turned nor how many alleys he ducked through they were always behind him, hounding him, stalking him, driving him. They had always driven him. Never once had he felt safe from them. Always, always they had driven him.

There were no shadows. There was nowhere to hide. He couldn't go on much longer. His breath was giving out. His legs were becoming limp and rubbery. More than once they gave away beneath him and he stumbled to the cold, hard cement, scraping the flesh off his hands and knees. He could hear the violent voices of the two agents:

"Stop thief!"

"Stop thief!"

"Halt!!"

"Halt or we'll fire!!!"

They were going to shoot, Jimmy thought. Perhaps they would hit him and kill him. Perhaps he should stop to save his life. Save his life, he repeated to himself in his thoughts. What kind of life did he have to save? No, there was no use in his halting. What did he have to halt for? Was prison any better than death? He might as well die now. He might as well die quickly and violently as to die slowly and painfully in prison. He'd prefer that to being humiliated and encaged. No, he wouldn't halt. He'd never halt. He had only two alternatives in this life—one was to fight, the other was to die fighting. There was no inbetween. There had never been any inbetween.

And so through the night he ran. On through the thick black night he forged his way and now the very night and the atmosphere seemed to be against him. The force of the wind blew him back and the blackness of the night pushed against him so hard that he seemed to come to a standstill. It was no use, Jimmy thought. He couldn't fight all of them . . . the wind, the night, the moon, the law, and America.

He heard the detectives call halt again and then a loud bang and the whistle of a bullet as it shot by his head. He began to zigzag so that he would not be an easy target for their intention. Once again he heard the report of a fired pistol and once again the bullet breezed past his head. He stopped long enough to take aim and fire twice at the two shadows behind him. Then he ran on.

For a while he no longer heard footsteps trailing him. Perhaps he had hit one or both of them. Perhaps he had put an end to this incessant hounding once and for all. He was not a killer. He had never desired to deliberately murder anyone but out of self-defense he had returned the fire of those who would have felled him. Having done it, he was glad. He hoped he had killed them. He wanted to kill now. He would never be rid of them unless he did kill, so the only thing to do was kill, kill, kill, kill until his hands were bloody and his heart reeked of murder.

He heard the footsteps again and knew that his shots had gone wild. He had missed them and the chase was still on.

The wind continued to beat against him like the collective tongues of a thousand whips, striking across his face and into his eyes. He felt he could go on no longer and so began to slow down. He was aware the two were gaining on him. He tried to resume speed but continued to slow down instead. He had almost given up when he heard the judge's voice sentencing him to another prison term.

He saw them taking him aboard a train and shipping him off to a federal prison. He saw the gray stone walls. He pictured himself in a cell. He saw the burly prison guards standing over him. The walls seemed first gray and then white. The white walls seemed to imprison him as did the white world. He saw it all. He saw the little groups of prison guards that hated Negroes and took advantage of them. He saw them standing around him with clubs in their hands. He saw himself fighting against them in vain. He felt their clubs pounding against his skull. They were trying to break him. He had come into prison as a man, afraid of no one and demanding his rights as a man and they were trying to break him. They were trying to take away his spirit. They were trying to make him one of the shadows of men who inhabited the prison cells and walked about slowly with their heads bowed and their wills bent, jumping when the guard raised his voice and fawning at his feet. This was what they wanted to make of him.

All of these thoughts ran through his mind and for that reason he called upon the last bit of energy in his legs and lungs so that he could spend that energy in one final attempt to escape. He looked behind him and saw that the agents were not more than twenty-five yards off. Just at that moment a truck came speeding up the street. It passed the two detectives and was about to pass Jimmy when he dashed out into the street, latched onto the end of it and climbed aboard. After getting on the truck he looked to see what had happened to the detectives. He saw the sparks flying from their pistols and heard the loud blasts as they stood in the middle of the street firing at him.

The truck began to pick up speed. The driver probably thought they were attempting to hold him up. Jimmy was about to duck down behind the half door out of sight of the detectives. He ducked just a second too late for a hot piece of lead shot into his right shoulder just before he hit the floor. He grabbed his shoulder and felt the warm blood oozing out of the wound through his clothing. Lines of pain and grimace streaked his face and fear filled his heart. In the darkness he played with the wound, trying to determine the seriousness of it. He was not altogether sure whether the lead had gone into his shoulder or had just nicked him. If that were so, it was a pretty bad nick. He reached into his pocket and brought out his handkerchief. After opening up the collar of his shirt he stuck the handkerchief in next to the wound. He could feel the cold wind coming through the opening of his shirt and chilling the blood which was running down his chest and arm. The damn thing hurt like hell. Best to forget it, he thought, best to forget it. Best to try to think about something else. Forget the pain. One could forget pain by thinking about other things. That's what he'd done all of his life, forgot the pain. He'd always forgotten the pain by thinking of something else.

He sat there on the floor breathing heavily, panting and gasping at times. The blood upon his chest and arm began to coagulate and he could feel the clothing in the region of the wound sticking to his flesh. The truck hit a bump in the road and bounced him up into the air. He wondered where the truck was going. He knew that sooner or later he would have to get off. That moment he dreaded because then he would be faced with the task of finding security in the black night. He'd be confronted with the job of concealing himself from the authorities. He'd be tortured by his own imagination. Around every corner the law might be lurking to reach out with its long arm and lay hold of him. Every shadow might be a detective. The police were sure to broadcast his description over the radio. How many Negro-haters would hear that description and go out seeking him? How many mobs would be waiting to tear him to pieces? He didn't want the truck to stop. He wanted it to go on forever. He wanted to just keep riding. He wanted to ride out of San Francisco. He wanted to ride out of the world. They had been driving him out of the world for years. It may well be that he was now traveling his last mile.

The wound seemed to be biting into his shoulder. Blades of pain cut into him like electrical shocks. The pain raced through his body, burning up the network of his nervous system. The only thing worse than pain was loneliness. God, he thought in despair, where can I go?

The truck was approaching a large garage where were stored a number of its counterparts. Jimmy surmised that this was the end of the driver's journey and as the truck slowed down he jumped off and ran over to the sidewalk. He walked along very rapidly, keeping in the shadows as much as possible. When he got to the corner he looked up a sign on a post to see where he was. The name of the street was strange to him but he could tell that he was well out of the city proper because the nearby large stone houses had intervals between them. In the city all of the houses were crowded together in rather crooked lines. They were so close together you could sit in one house and through the walls hear the people talking in the house adjacent. It wasn't like that out here. He could tell from the lawns and the beautiful porches of the homes that fairly wealthy tenants and home-owners lived here.

He began to feel weak. He guessed he had lost more blood than was good for him. He knew that if he did not see a doctor and get the wound attended to, he might bleed to death. He made up his mind to find a doctor and make him dress the wound at the point of a gun. He began to look at the houses for one with a doctor's sign on it. His legs were no longer steady and so he stumbled along the block as he looked up at the houses.

He bumped into a white couple. "Excuse me," he said, regaining his balance. The man shoved him out of the way.

"Of all things!" the girl said. "What on earth is a nigger doing out here?"

"The drunken fool," said the man. "I've got a mind to call the police."

"Oh, fiddlesticks," the girl said.

They walked on up the street and Jimmy watched them with his hand on the automatic stuck under his belt. When they were out of sight he continued on his way. As he staggered along looking at the large, expensive houses for one where a doctor might live he mumbled to himself, "rich folks. Fat American rich folks with Negro maids and butlers to wait on them hand and foot, with Negro cooks to prepare them delicious meals. They'd better be glad I'm not working for them, the bastards."

His thoughts were interrupted by a pang of pain that started at the bullet wound in his shoulder and went through the rest of his body. I've got to find a doctor. Damn it, he thought, tightening the muscles of his body, I've got to find a doctor.

He walked about a half block more. Then he looked up and saw a doctor's shingle on one of the houses. He walked up the path to the porch, dragging his feet and holding his shoulder. When he got to the porch he rang the bell. After waiting a while he heard someone coming to the door. The door opened and a chic white maid stood looking at him inquisitively.

"The delivery section is around the back," she said.

"I'm not the delivery boy. I want to see—" He paused to look at the shingle again. He read the name on it. "I want to see Dr. Kenneth Clifford."

"I'm sorry, but Dr. Clifford only receives patients at his downtown office. Besides, I don't think he has a colored clientele. There is a colored doctor over in the colored section. I'm sure he'll attend to you."

"I—I couldn't go another block," Jimmy said.

"Who is it, Mary?" These words were projected from the rear of the house by a dignified male voice.

"It's no one, Dr. Clifford," the maid said.

"What do you mean it's no one?" Jimmy snapped angrily.

"I'm sorry, mister," the maid said, "but will you please get off this porch and go on to where you belong, or do I have to call the police?"

"Step aside," Jimmy said, pulling out the pistol and pointing it at her narrow mid-section. The maid yelped like a puppy whose paw had been stepped on. "Don't scream," he said, threatening her. "Don't you dare scream."

The maid moved out of the doorway and Jimmy stepped inside the house, shutting the door behind him. "Take me to the doctor," he ordered.

She led the way to Dr. Clifford's office. When they got to the office door Dr. Clifford was just coming out to see what was the matter. When he saw Jimmy holding a gun on his maid he did not seem surprised at all. He looked as if strange men broke into his house every night and had his maid lead them to his office at the point of a gun.

After he had analyzed the situation, the doctor said: "Oh? What's this?"

"Dr. Clifford," the maid said, "this man said he wanted to see you. When I told him you don't receive patients at your home and that you don't treat colored patients he pulled out that gun and threatened me."

"I'm wounded," Jimmy said. "I'm soaked and wet with blood. You've got to do something, doctor."

"Well," the doctor said, "it is true that I don't receive patients at my home except on very special occasions. It is also true that I don't have Negro patients—but. . . ."

"Cut the talk and do something, will you?" Jimmy's shoulder twitched with pain. He couldn't pay the doctor because he had hidden the money he had stolen.

"I'm sorry, young man," the doctor said, "but you'll have to see me in my office tomorrow or else go to the emergency room of the San Francisco General Hospital."

"Look, doctor," Jimmy said, pointing the gun at him, "this gun is loaded and I'm not afraid to fire it."

"Then go on and shoot," said the doctor. "But remember, if you shoot me you'll surely bleed to death."

"You're right. I can't shoot you, but I can shoot her." Jimmy pointed the gun at the maid's foot and pulled back the hammer.

"Please, Dr. Clifford," said Mary with tears welling up in her eyes, "do something."

"She'd look awfully bad with one foot," Jimmy said.

"All right," said the doctor. "Come into my office."

He led the way. Jimmy told Mary to follow the doctor and then he followed her. When he got into the office he shut the door and locked it from the inside.

"You'll have to take off your coat," the doctor said.

Jimmy began to get out of his coat. It pained him to move his arm. Dr. Clifford began to prepare the necessary bandages for his wound. He saw that Jimmy was having trouble.

"Mary, help the gentleman with his coat," he said.

Mary looked frightened as reluctantly she approached Jimmy. He pointed the gun at her and she stopped.

"Don't try anything funny," Jimmy said.

"If you want me to help you, you'll have to put that gun down," the doctor told him.

Jimmy looked at him. In the doctor's eyes was an unmistakable look of sincerity. Jimmy put the gun away and the maid helped him off with his coat. The doctor came over to attend him. He cut open the sleeve of his shirt and began to examine the puncture made by the bullet.

"The slug is still in your shoulder and I'm afraid I'll have to dig for it. You'll have to take an anesthetic."

"What do you think I am, crazy? Do you think I'd let you put me to sleep and then turn me over to the police?"

"I have little to gain from turning you over to the police. You can either trust me or lose your arm. Which is it?"

Jimmy thought for several seconds. He had to trust someone, he knew. However, he was wondering if the doctor wouldn't turn him over to the authorities as soon as he was unconscious? Dr. Clifford had every reason to do so. Wasn't he white and wasn't he a capitalist? Wasn't Jimmy black and poor? Didn't all whites hate Negroes and didn't all capitalists hate the poor? Wasn't that the way life was in this world? Wasn't life just one great battle between races and classes, between nations and ideals? Wasn't that life?

But Jimmy had no time to weigh these facts. He was aware of one thing and one thing only. That was: he was growing weaker every minute and he needed help very badly. He had to trust someone. All of his life he had lived among white people, and all of his life he had been on guard against them. He had mistrusted them and feared them. But now he was weak. He did not have the strength to mistrust. Earlier, his nerves had been so taut with fear and anger that when the climax of the ordeal was over his nerves had relaxed and were now limp and no longer responsive. They were like rubber bands which had been stretched so much that they had lost their elasticity.

Jimmy saw the doctor pour some ether out of a bottle onto a piece of cotton. When this was done Dr. Clifford approached as he held the cotton in his hand.

"I said I wasn't going to let you put me to sleep and I meant it. I'm warning you," he said as the doctor continued to approach him, "you'd better keep away from me."

The doctor paid no attention to the threatening words. He just continued walking slowly towards him. The closer he came the larger he seemed to grow in Jimmy's sight until he was a giant who loomed over and dwarfed his victim. The hand which held the cotton moved up to Jimmy's face. He tried to raise his arms in protest but they were much too heavy. He was tired. He wanted to sleep forever. He no longer struggled nor wanted to struggle. He knew that when he woke up he would be in the hands of the police and they would carry him off to jail, but he didn't care. He was tired of running. He would rather face it and take the consequences. He was tired, so tired. . . .

He felt the wet cotton covering his nose and mouth. He gasped for breath and every breath he took he sank farther and farther into a deep sea of sleep. He felt himself floating upon the waters and gradually sinking beneath the surface. He could hear the ocean's undercurrents roaring in his ears. He could feel the darkness about him as he sank deeper into the black waters. He could feel the enormous weight of this sleep pressing upon him. In a futile effort he told his mind to lift his arms so that they could push the sleep off. However, there was no longer any coordination between his mind and his body. No matter how hard his mind tried to dictate to his body, his inert limbs would not take heed to the will of his mind. Soon his mind itself lost the will to will and he was unconscious.

When he awoke his arm felt much better. The pain was gone. In its place he could feel the tight bandages about his shoulder holding the tissues in place. He was lying on an operating table. Suddenly he felt that he was at the mercy of the world and had been at the mercy of it during the whole time he was unconscious. He had been at the mercy of the thing he feared most. For years he had been afraid to fall sound asleep for fear the beasts in the world would move in upon him and tear him to pieces while he slept.

Now that he was conscious again the old feeling of mistrust returned and he felt for his gun. It was not there. Suddenly he felt even more unsafe.

"Is this what you want?" Dr. Clifford asked.

The doctor was on the other side of the room pointing the gun at him. Jimmy looked at him and thought, he is going to turn me in now. He is going to hold me here at the point of the gun until the police come and then he will turn me over to them. Jimmy knew what was coming. He had known all along that the doctor hated him. When he woke up unharmed he had felt that he had been wrong about the doctor, but now he knew he had been right in the first place. The doctor was a Negro-hater just like the rest. They were all alike. He had been a fool to think that this doctor was any different from the others.

"You are looking for this?" the doctor said, walking toward him with the gun still pointed at him.

Jimmy watched, waiting for a chance to get the gun away from him, waiting for a chance to overpower him. There might still be an opportunity for escape. If there was, Jimmy was going to take it.

"These things always make me nervous," the doctor said, coming closer to him. "I wish you would take it and put it away for good. You might hurt someone with it and I'm sure you don't want to do that." He handed the gun to Jimmy.

Jimmy snatched it and for a second felt that he had outsmarted the doctor. Then he saw how foolish the doctor was making him seem and it was like looking in a mirror. Suddenly he realized that in a sense he *was* a fool.

"I should have called the police," the doctor said, "but I didn't feel like being bothered with a lot of questions."

"O.K. Doc," Jimmy said, "I'll be seeing you."

Jimmy backed out of the room with one eye on the doctor and one eye on the door. Once outside he was again confronted with the problem of finding concealment. He couldn't go back to his aunt's place because the police would surely be looking for him there. He couldn't just roam the streets. Eventually someone would pick him up. He couldn't leave the city because he didn't have enough money on his person. In short, he was stranded. What was even worse, he was lonely. He wanted to see his girl. Realizing that he couldn't go to see her, he wanted to talk to her. He decided to call her on the phone and tell her that he was all right and that she should not worry about him.

In the distance he saw a gasoline station. There was sure to be a public phone there, he reasoned. He hurried to the station and dashed into the phone booth in the office. He fumbled in his pocket searching for a nickel. All he had was some pennies and paper money. He didn't want to ask the station attendant to change a dollar for him but he had no alternative. He got out of the booth and went over to the man in the office.

"Can you change a dollar for me?" he asked in a voice none too steady. "I want to make a phone call."

The man looked at him suspiciously. "I don't know if I have it."

"O.K.," Jimmy said, about to rush out of the place. He was glad the man didn't have it. That gave him an excuse to make a break. He didn't like the man's looks.

He was just about to hurry through the doorway when the station attendant said, "Wait a minute!"

Jimmy wheeled around with his hand inside his coat, ready to draw the pistol he had stuck behind his belt. He didn't want to shoot anybody—God knew he didn't want to shoot anybody—but he had to get away from the man if he recognized him.

"On second thought, I think I do have change for a dollar."

"That's all right. Forget about it."

"Nonsense; no trouble at all. Glad to do it." He opened the cash register. Jimmy heard the jingle of coins as the man counted out a dollar's worth of nickels, dimes and quarters. "Here you are," he said, holding the money out to Jimmy.

Might as well take it, he thought. If I don't he will think something is funny and call the police. "Thanks," Jimmy said, handing him the dollar and taking the change.

He went back into the telephone booth, dropped a nickel into the money slot and dialed Pearl's number. He waited with impatience as he heard the phone ringing several times. Perhaps she wasn't at home. Perhaps the police had arrested her, thinking she had had something to do with his escape. Perhaps a thousand things. . . . Hell, why didn't someone answer? Finally he heard the receiver lifted off the hook.

"Hello," a girl's voice said.

"Hello, Pearl. This is Jimmy."

"Jimmy, where are you? I just came from your aunt's house. Jimmy, she's worried to death over you."

"Yes," he said, "I know. That's why I called you. I want you to do something for me."

"What, Jimmy? I'll do anything I can, sugar."

"I've got the money I stole stashed away. I'm going to get it now. I want you to keep most of it and see that my aunt gets the operation she needs. Will you do that?"

"Yeah. Swell, Jimmy. Anything you want, sugar. Anything."

"Good; then meet me at the corner of Twelfth and U in about an hour. Do you think you can make it?"

"Yes, Jimmy, I can make it. I'll call a cab right now."

"O.K., then, I'll see you there. Goodbye for now."

"Goodbye," she said softly.

He hung up, hurried out of the gas station and to the corner, where he boarded a bus back to the heart of the city. At the appointed time he was at the corner of Twelfth and U. The corner was not crowded, which was what he had expected. He waited, pacing back and forth. It was more than an hour now since he had spoken to her and he began to imagine all sorts of things because she wasn't there on time. Perhaps the police had overheard their phone conversation and had apprehended her. No, they wouldn't do that. They would be more likely to follow her until they met and then arrest both of them at the same time. But something must have happened to delay her. She was usually very punctual. He had never known her to be late for an appointment.

Suddenly she was there beside him. "I'm sorry I'm late," she said, "but I had to wait such a long time for a cab."

"It's all right, sugar. Let's get off this corner. Do you still have the cab?"

"No. I paid him and sent him away."

"That's all right. There's a cab over there."

They told the driver to take them out to the park. After settling in the back seat of the cab Jimmy embraced Pearl, holding her very tightly and kissing her tenderly, telling her how much he had missed her and whispering over and over again in her ear that he loved her and would always love her. She returned his kisses at first and then broke off suddenly.

"What are you going to do?" she asked him.

"What do you mean?"

"I mean, where are you going and how do you intend to keep out of their way?"

"I don't know," he answered frankly. "All I do know is that they're not going to get me if I can help it."

"Oh, darling," she said, hugging him tightly and resting her head upon his shoulder.

"Take it easy, sugar," he said, drawing back his shoulder. "That still hurts a little."

"What?"

"My shoulder. Had a bullet in it."

"How did it happen?"

"One of the bullets the detectives fired at me didn't miss."

"You've been wounded?"

"It's nothing serious. I went to a doctor and had it fixed up."

"Why don't you give up? You'll only make things worse by running away."

"I know what they would do. I know what kind of trial they would give me. The jury's mind would be made up even before my attorney spoke a word. You've never had them against you, sugar. You don't know what they're really like."

"Then let me go with you."

"Do you think I want to mess your life up too?"

"My life is already messed up. You'll only mess it up more if you go running off without me."

"It's no good, Pearl. What happens to me now isn't important. There are some people who, although they were born on the wrong side of things, seem to get right as time goes by. Then there are some who are born on the wrong side and who stay on the wrong side all of their lives. That's the way I am. You're straight. You've adjusted yourself to conditions I cannot accept. You can live and be contented. You don't know when you're well off. Take my word for it you're better off without me. I'll never be satisfied. I'll never be contented. The best thing to do is to shoot me before I get you. I'm like a mad dog. There's no reasoning with me. That's the way I am, sugar. I didn't make myself like that. They made me like that, but I'm content to play the part. Perhaps I could have been just like everybody else if they had given me half a chance, but they didn't. So let's just leave it at that. No, Pearl—it's no good. That's all there is to it. I'll just go on the way I've been doing for years. Your best bet is to let me go on alone."

He gave her the money for his aunt's hospital expenses and told the driver to stop the cab. On the edge of the park he got out, paid the driver, kissed the girl goodbye, and slammed the door. He watched the cab drive away and then turned to face the night and the darkness. He felt in his pocket. It was there, safe and secure. He had enough money left from the hold-up to take him some place far from where he was.

Then suddenly it occured to him that some day they were sure to catch him. A space cleared somewhere in the misty hereafter and he saw himself being shot down in a gun battle by the same two detectives who had trailed him. He saw it as clear as day and he knew that it was a certainty, but he didn't care about that. As a matter of fact he knew that his life was over. It had ended the day he had lost respect for himself. The bullet that took his life would find no happiness in his heart. That was all there was to it.

He turned his collar up against the cold of the night and started to run.

Lunching at the Ritzmore

CHESTER HIMES

If you have ever been to the beautiful city of Los Angeles, you will know that Pershing Square, a palm-shaded spot in the center of downtown, is the mecca of the motley. Here, a short walk up from 'Skid Row,' on the green-painted benches flanking the crisscrossed sidewalks, is haven for men of all races, all creeds, all nationalities, and of all stages of deterioration—drifters and hopheads and tbs' and beggars and bums and bindle-stiffs and big sisters, clipped and clippers, fraternizing with the tired business men from nearby offices, with students from various universities, with the strutting Filipinos, the sharp-cat Mexican youths in their ultra drapes, with the colored guys from out South Central way.

It is here the old men come to meditate in the warm midday sun, and watch the hustle and bustle of the passing younger world; here the job seekers with packed bags wait to be singled out for work; here the hunters relax and the hunted keep vigil. It is here you will find your man, for a game of pool, for a game of murder.

Along the Hill Street side buses going west line up one behind the other to take you out to Wilshire, to Beverly Hills, to Hollywood, to Santa Monica, to Westwood, to the Valley; and the red cars and the yellow cars fill the street with clatter and clang. On the Fifth Street side a pale pink skyscraper overlooks a lesser structure of aquamarine, southern California architecture on the pastel side; and along Sixth Street there are various shops and perhaps an office building which you would not notice unless you had business there.

But you would notice the Ritzmore, swankiest of West Coast hotels, standing in solid distinction along the Olive Street side, particularly if you were hungry in Pershing Square. You would watch footmen opening doors of limousines and doormen escorting patrons underneath the marquee across the width of sidewalk to the brass and mahogany doorway, and you would see hands of other doormen extended from within to hold wide the glass doors so that the patrons could make an unhampered entrance. And after that, if your views leaned a little to the Left, which they likely would if you were hungry in Pershing Square, you would spit on

the sidewalk and resume your discussion, your boisterous and heated and surpris-
ingly-often very well-versed discussion, on defense, or on the army, or the navy,
or that 'rat' Hitler, or 'them Japs,' or the F.B.I., or the 'so and so' owners of
Lockheed, or that (unprintable) Aimee Semple McPherson; on history and geography, on life and death; and you would just ignore the 'fat sonsaguns' who entered
the Ritzmore.

On this particular day, a discussion which had begun on the Soviet Union had
developed into an argument on discrimination against Negroes, and a young University of Southern California student from Vermont stated flatly that he did not
believe Negroes were discriminated against at all.

'If you would draw your conclusions from investigation instead of from agitation, you would find that most of the discrimination against Negroes exists only in
communistic literature distributed by the Communist Party for organizational purposes,' he went on. 'As a matter of plain and simple fact, I have yet to visit a place
where Negroes could not go. In fact, I think I've seen Negroes in every place I've
ever been—hotels, theatres, concerts, operas . . .''

'Yass, and I bet they were working there, too,' another young fellow, a drifter
from Chicago, argued. 'Listen, boy, I'm telling you, and I'm telling you straight,
Negroes are out in this country. They can't get no work and they can't go nowhere,
and that's a dirty shame for there're a lot of good Negroes, a lot of Negroes just as
good as you and me.'

Surveying the drifter from head to foot, his unshaven face, his shabby un-
pressed suit, his run-over, unpolished shoes, the student replied, 'Frankly, that
wouldn't make them any super race.'

'Huh?'

'However, that is beside the point,' the student continued, smiling. 'The point is
that most of what you term discrimination is simply a matter of taste, of personal
likes and dislikes. For instance, if I don't like you, should I have to put up with your
presence? No, why should I? But this agitation about Negroes being discriminated
against by the Army and Navy and defense industries and being refused service by
hotels and restaurants is just so much bosh.'

'Are you kidding me, fellow?' the drifter asked suspiciously, giving the student
a sharp look, 'Or are you just plain dumb? Say, listen—' and then he spied a Negro
at the edge of the group. 'Say, here's a colored fellow now; I suppose he knows
whether he's being discriminated against or not.'

'Not necessarily,' the student murmured.

Ignoring him, the drifter called, 'Hey, mister, you mind settling a little argument for us.'

The Negro, a young brown-skinned fellow of medium build with regular features and a small mustache, pushed to the center of the group. He wore a pair of
corduroy trousers and a slip-over sweater with a sport shirt underneath.

'Say, mister, I been tryna tell this schoolboy—' the drifter began, but the Negro interrupted him, 'I know, I heard you.'

Turning to the student, he said, 'I don't know whether you're kidding or not, fellow, but it ain't no kidding matter with me. Here I am, a mechanic, a good mechanic, and they're supposed to be needing mechanics everywhere. But can I get a job—no! I gotta stand down here and listen to guys like you make a joke out of it while the government is crying for mechanics in defense.'

'I'm not making a joke out of it,' the student stated. 'If what you say is true, I'm truly sorry, mister; it's just hard for me to believe it.'

'Listen, schoolboy,' the drifter said, 'I'll tell you what I'll do with you; I'll just bet you a dollar this boy—this man—can't eat in any of these restaurants downtown. I'll just bet you a dollar.'

Now that a bet had been offered, the ten or twelve fellows crowded about who had remained silent out of respect for the Negro's feelings, egged it on, 'All right, schoolboy, put up or shut up!'

'Well, if it's all right with you, mister,' the student addressed the Negro, 'I'll just take this young man up on that bet. But how are we going to determine?'

They went into a huddle and after a moment decided to let the Negro enter any restaurant of his choice, and if he should be refused service the student would pay off the bet and treat the three of them to dinners on Central Avenue; but should he be served, the check would be on the drifter.

So the three of them, the student, the Negro, and the drifter, started down Hill Street in search of a restaurant. The ten or twelve others of the original group fell in behind, and shortly fellows in other groups about the square looked up and saw the procession, and thinking someone was giving away something somewhere, hurried to get in line. Before they had progressed half the length of the block, more than a hundred of the raggedy bums of Pershing Square were following them.

The pedestrians stopped to see what the commotion was all about, adding to the congestion; and then the motorists noticed and slowed their cars. Soon almost a thousand people had congregated on the sidewalk and a jam of alarming proportions had halted traffic for several blocks. In time the policeman at the corner of Sixth and Hill awakened, and becoming aware of the mob, rushed forth to investigate. When he saw the long procession from the square, he charged the three in front who seemed to be the leaders, and shouted.

'Starting a riot, eh! Communist rally, eh! Where do you think you're going?'

'We're going to lunch,' the student replied congenially.

For an instant the policeman was startled out of his wits. 'Lunch?' His face went slack and his mouth hung open. Then he got himself under control. 'Lunch! What is this? I suppose all of you are going to lunch,' he added sarcastically.

The student looked about at the crowd, then looked back. 'I don't know,' he confessed. 'I'm only speaking for the three of us.'

Shoving back among the others, the policeman snarled, 'Now don't tell me that you're going to lunch, too?'

A big, raw-boned fellow in overalls spat a stream of tobacco juice on the grass, and replied, 'That's right.'

Red-faced and inarticulate, the policeman took off his hat and scratched his head. Never in the six years since he had been directing traffic at Sixth and Hill had he seen anyone leave Pershing Square for lunch. In fact, it had never occurred to him that they ate lunch. It sounded incredible. He wanted to do something. He felt that it was his duty to do something. But what? He was in a dilemma. He could not hinder them from going to lunch, if indeed they were going to lunch. Nor could he order them to move on, as they were already moving on. There was nothing for him to do but follow. So he fell in and followed.

The Negro, however, could not make up his mind. On Sixth Street, midway between Hill and Olive, he came to a halt. 'Listen,' he pointed out, 'these guys are used to seeing colored people down here. All the domestic workers who work out in Hollywood and Beverly and all out there get off the U car and come down here and catch their buses. It ain't like if it was somewhere on the West Side where they ain't used to seeing them.'

'What has that got to do with it?' the student asked.

'Naw, what I mean is this,' he explained. 'They're liable to serve me around here. And then you're going to think it's like that all over the city. And I know it ain't.' Pausing for an instant, he added another point, 'And besides, if I walk in there with you two guys, they're liable to serve me anyway. For all they know you guys might be some rich guys and I might be working for you; and if they refuse to serve me they might get in dutch with you. It ain't like some place in Hollywood where they wouldn't care.'

When they had stopped, the procession behind them which by then reached around the corner down Hill Street had also stopped. This was the chance for which the policeman had been waiting. 'Move on!' he shouted. 'Don't block the sidewalk! What d'ya think this is?'

They all returned to the square and took up the argument where they had dropped it. Only now, it was just one big mob in the center of the square, waiting for the Negro to make up his mind.

'You see, he doesn't want to do it,' the student was pointing out. 'That proves my point. They won't go into these places, but yet they say they're being discriminated against.'

Suddenly, the drifter was inspired. 'All right, I'll tell you, let's go to the Ritzmore.'

A hundred startled glances leveled on him, then lifted to the face of the brick and granite edifice across the street which seemed impregnated in rocklike respectability. The very audacity of the suggestion appealed to them. 'That's the place, let's go there,' they chimed.

'That's nonsense,' the student snapped angrily. 'He can't eat at the Ritzmore; he's not dressed correctly.'

'Can you eat there?' the Negro challenged. 'I mean just as you're dressed.'

The student was also clad in a sweater and trousers, although his were of a better quality and in better condition than the Negro's. For a moment he considered the question, then replied, 'To be fair, I don't know whether they would serve me or not. They might in the grill—'

'In the main dining room?' the drifter pressed.

Shaking his head, the student stated, 'I really don't know, but if they will serve any of us they will serve him.'

'Come on,' the drifter barked, taking the Negro by the arm, and they set forth for the Ritzmore, followed by every man in Pershing Square—the bindle-stiffs and the beggars and the bums and the big sisters, the clipped and the clippers, the old men who liked to sit in the midday sun and meditate.

Seeing them on the move again, the policeman hastened from his post to follow.

They crossed Olive Street, a ragged procession of gaunt, unshaven, unwashed humanity, led by two young white men and one young Negro, passed the two doormen, who, seeing the policeman among them, thought they were all being taken to the clink. They approached the brass and mahogany doorway unchallenged, pushed open the glass doors, and entered the classical splendor of the Ritzmore's main lounge.

Imagine the consternation among the well-bred, superbly clad, highly-heeled patrons; imagine the indignity of the room clerk as he pounded on his bell and yelled frantically, 'Front! Front! *Front!*' Had the furniture been animate, it would have fled in terror; and the fine Oriental rugs would have been humiliated unendurably.

Outraged, the house officer rushed to halt this smelly mob, but seeing among them the policeman, who by now had lost all capacity for speech, stood with his mouth gaped open, wondering if perhaps it wasn't just the effects of that last brandy he had enjoyed in '217,' after all. Stupidly, he reached out his hand to touch them to make certain they were real.

But before he could get his reflexes together, those in front had strolled past him and entered the main dining room, while, what seemed to him like thousands of others, pushed in from the street.

The student and the Negro and the drifter, along with ten or twelve others, took seats at three vacant tables. In unison the diners turned one horrified stare in their direction, and arose in posthaste, only to be blocked at the doorway by a shoving mass of men, struggling for a ringside view.

From all over the dining room the waiters ran stumbling toward the rear, and went into a quick, alarmed huddle, turning every now and then to stare at the group and then going into another huddle. The head waiter rushed from the kitchen and joined the huddle; and then the *maître d'hotel* appeared and took his place. One by one the cooks, the first cook and the second cook and the third cook and the fourth cook on down to what seemed like the twenty-fourth cook (although some of them must have been dishwashers), stuck their heads through the pantry doorway and stared for a moment and then retired.

Finally, two waiters timidly advanced toward the tables and took their orders. Menus were passed about. 'You order first,' the student said to the Negro. However, as the menus were composed mostly of French words, the Negro could not identify anything but apple pie. So he ordered apple pie.

'I'll take apple pie, too,' the student said; and the drifter muttered, 'Make mine the same.'

Every one ordered apple pie.

One of the fellows standing in the doorway called back to those in the lobby who could not see.

'They served him.'

'Did they serve him?'

'Yeah, they served him.'

'What did they serve him?'

'Apple pie.'

And it was thus proved by the gentlemen of Pershing Square that no discrimination exists in the beautiful city of Los Angeles. However, it so happened that the drifter was without funds, and the student found himself in the peculiar situation of having to pay off a bet which he had won.

God Bless America

JOHN O. KILLENS

Joe's dark eyes searched frantically for Cleo as he marched with the other Negro soldiers up the long thoroughfare towards the boat. Women were running out to the line of march, crying and laughing and kissing the men good-by. But where the hell was Cleo?

Beside him Luke Robinson, big and fat, nibbled from a carton of Baby Ruth candy as he walked. But Joe's eyes kept traveling up and down the line of civilians on either side of the street. She would be along here somewhere; any second now she would come calmly out of the throng and walk alongside him till they reached the boat. Joe's mind made a picture of her, and she looked the same as last night when he left her. As he had walked away, with the brisk California night air biting into his warm body, he had turned for one last glimpse of her in the doorway, tiny and smiling and waving good-by.

They had spent last night sitting in the little two-by-four room where they had lived for three months with hardly enough space to move around. He had rented it and sent for her when he came to California and learned that his outfit was training for immediate shipment to Korea, and they had lived there fiercely and desperately, like they were trying to live a whole lifetime. But last night they had sat on the side of the big iron bed, making conversation, half-listening to a portable radio, acting like it was just any night. Play-acting like in the movies.

It was late in the evening when he asked her, "How's little Joey acting lately?"

She looked down at herself. "Oh, pal Joey is having himself a ball." She smiled, took Joe's hand, and placed it on her belly; and he felt movement and life. His and her life, and he was going away from it and from her, maybe forever.

Cleo said, "He's trying to tell you good-by, darling." And she sat very still and seemed to ponder over her own words. And then all of a sudden she burst into tears.

She was in his arms and her shoulders shook. "It isn't fair! Why can't they take the ones that aren't married?"

He hugged her tight, feeling a great fullness in his throat. "Come on now, stop crying, hon. Cut it out, will you? I'll be back home before little Joey sees daylight."

"You may never come back. They're killing a lot of our boys over there. Oh, Joe, Joe, why did they have to go and start another war?"

In a gruff voice he said, "Don't you go worrying about Big Joey. He'll take care of himself. You just take care of little Joey and Cleo. That's what you do."

"Don't take any chances, Joe. Don't be a hero!"

He forced himself to laugh, and hugged her tighter. "Don't you worry about the mule going blind."

She made herself stop crying and wiped her face. "But I don't understand, Joe. I don't understand what colored soldiers have to fight for—especially against other colored people."

"Honey," said Joe gently, "we got to fight like anybody else. We can't just sit on the sidelines."

But she just looked at him and shook her head.

"Look," he said, "when I get back I'm going to finish college. I'm going to be a lawyer. That's what I'm fighting for."

She kept shaking her head as if she didn't hear him. "I don't know, Joe. Maybe it's because we were brought up kind of different, you and I. My father died when I was four. My mother worked all her life in white folks' kitchens. I just did make it through high school. You had it a whole lot better than most Negro boys." She went over to the box of Kleenex and blew her nose.

"I don't see where that has a thing to do with it."

He stared at her, angry with her for being so obstinate. Couldn't she see any progress at all? Look at Jackie Robinson. Look at Ralph Bunche. Goddamn it! they'd been over it all before. What did she want him to do about it anyway? Become a deserter?

She stood up over him. "Can't see it, Joe—just can't see it! I want you here, Joe. Here with me where you belong. Don't leave me, Joe! please." She was crying now. "Joe, Joe, what're we going to do? Maybe it would be better to get rid of little Joey—" Her brown eyes were wide with terror. "No, Joe, No! I didn't mean that! I didn't mean it, darling! Don't know what I'm saying . . ."

She sat down beside him, bent over, her face in her hands. It was terrible for him, seeing her this way. He got up and walked from one side of the little room to the other. He thought about what the white captain from Hattiesburg, Mississippi, had said. "Men, we have a job to do. Our outfit is just as damn important as any outfit in the United States Army, white or colored. And we're working towards complete integration. It's a long, hard pull, but I guarantee you every soldier will be treated equally and without discrimination. Remember, we're fighting for the dignity of the individual." Luke Robinson had looked at the tall, lanky captain with an arrogant smile.

Joe stopped in front of Cleo and made himself speak calmly. "Look, hon, it isn't like it used to be at all. Why can't you take my word for it? They're integrating colored soldiers now. And anyhow, what the hell's the use of getting all heated up about it? I got to go. That's all there is to it."

He sat down beside her again. He wanted fiercely to believe that things were really changing for his kind of people. Make it easier for him—make it much easier for him and Cleo, if they both believed that colored soldiers had a stake in fighting the war in Korea. Cleo wiped her eyes and blew her nose, and they changed the subject, talked about the baby, suppose it turned out to be a girl, what would her name be? A little after midnight he kissed her good-night and walked back to the barracks.

The soldiers were marching in full field dress, with packs on their backs, duffle-bags on their shoulders, and carbines and rifles. As they approached the big white ship, there was talking and joke-cracking and nervous laughter. They were the leading Negro outfit, immediately following the last of the white troops. Even at route step there was a certain uniform cadence in the sound of their feet striking the asphalt road as they moved forward under the midday sun, through a long funnel of people and palm trees and shrubbery. But Joe hadn't spotted Cleo yet, and he was getting sick from worry. Had anything happened?

Luke Robinson, beside him, was talking and laughing and grumbling. "Boy, I'm telling you, these peoples is a bitch on wheels. Say, Office Willie, what you reckon I read in your Harlem paper last night?" Office Willie was his nickname for Joe because Joe was the company clerk—a high-school graduate, two years in college, something special. "I read where some of your folks' leaders called on the President and demanded that colored soldiers be allowed to fight at the front instead of in quartermaster. Ain't that a damn shame?"

Joe's eyes shifted distractedly from the line of people to Luke, and back to the people again.

"Percy Johnson can have my uniform any day in the week," said Luke. "He want to fight so bad. Them goddamn Koreans ain't done me nothing. I ain't mad with a living ass."

Joe liked Luke Robinson, only he was so damn sensitive on the color question. Many times Joe had told him to take the chip off his shoulder and be somebody. But he had no time for Luke now. Seeing the ship plainly, and the white troops getting aboard, he felt a growing fear. Fear that maybe he had passed Cleo and they hadn't seen each other for looking so damn hard. Fear that he wouldn't get to see her at all—never-ever again. Maybe she was ill, with no way to let him know, too sick to move. He thought of what she had said last night, about little Joey. Maybe . . .

And then he saw her, up ahead, waving at him, with the widest and prettiest and most confident smile anybody ever smiled. He was so goddamn glad he could hardly move his lips to smile or laugh or anything else.

She ran right up to him. "Hello, soldier boy, where you think you're going?"

"Damn," he said finally in as calm a voice as he could manage. "I thought for a while you had forgotten what day it was. Thought you had forgotten to come to my going-away party."

"Now, how do you sound?" She laughed at the funny look on his face, and told him he looked cute with dark glasses on, needing a shave and with the pack on his back. She seemed so cheerful, he couldn't believe she was the same person who had completely broken down last night. He felt the tears rush out of his eyes and spill down his face.

She pretended not to notice, and walked with him till they reached the last block. The women were not allowed to go any further. Looking at her, he wished somehow that she would cry, just a little bit anyhow. But she didn't cry at all. She reached up and kissed him quickly. "Good-by, darling, take care of yourself. Little Joey and I will write every day, beginning this afternoon." And then she was gone.

The last of the white soldiers were boarding the beautiful white ship, and a band on board was playing *God Bless America*. He felt a chill, like an electric current, pass across his slight shoulders, and he wasn't sure whether it was from *God Bless America* or from leaving Cleo behind. He hoped she could hear the music; maybe it would make her understand why Americans, no matter what their color, had to go and fight so many thousands of miles away from home.

They stopped in the middle of the block and stood waiting till the white regiment was all aboard. He wanted to look back for one last glimpse of Cleo, but he wouldn't let himself. Then they started again, marching toward the ship. And suddenly the band stopped playing *God Bless America* and jumped into another tune— *The Darktown Strutters' Ball* . . .

He didn't want to believe his ears. He looked up at the ship and saw some of the white soldiers on deck waving and smiling at the Negro soldiers, yelling "Yeah, man!" and popping their fingers. A taste of gall crept up from his stomach into his mouth.

"Goddamn," he heard Luke say, "that's the kind of music I like." The husky soldier cut a little step. "I guess Mr. Charlie want us to jitterbug onto his pretty white boat. Equal treatment. . . . We ain't no soldiers, we're a bunch of goddamn clowns."

Joe felt an awful heat growing inside his collar. He hoped fiercely that Cleo was too far away to hear.

Luke grinned at him. "What's the matter, good kid? Mad about something? Damn—that's what I hate about you colored folks. Take that goddamn chip off your shoulder. They just trying to make you people feel at home. Don't you recognize the Negro national anthem when you hear it?"

Joe didn't answer. He just felt his anger mounting and he wished he could walk right out of the line and to hell with everything. But with *The Darktown Strutters' Ball* ringing in his ears, he put his head up, threw his shoulders back, and kept on marching towards the big white boat.

Keys to the City

MALVIN WALD

The city of Stanley, Texas, has a population of 78,485 people. It is located in the southeast part of the state, between Dallas and the border.

Last fall the mayor was Edward J. (Big Ed) Horton, former sheriff of the county. A huge brawling man with thinning brown hair and a perennially reddened face, he still wore a revolver as if to remind the citizenry that he stood for law and order.

His proudest boast was that he killed "four Mexicans and five nigras in the performance of duty." On such a platform of fearlessness and civic protection, Ed had been elected to head the city government of Stanley.

But after two sluggish years in office, Ed didn't seem to be the right man for the job. That was the opinion of the members of the Stanley Businessmen's League. And those stalwart leaders of industry and thought owned and ran the city as they pleased.

Tall, easy-going Pete Hunter, Stanley's leading insurance agent and president of the league, was being sponsored by his associates to oppose Ed Horton in the coming elections.

"Ed is a good fellow," admitted Pete generously. "He was a fine sheriff. But he makes a mighty poor mayor."

"Ed's bungled so many chances to improve Stanley that he should be booted out of the mayor's chair," added barrel-shaped Henry Lewis, Pete's partner.

"You boys are dead right," agreed Roy Gradey, silver-haired editor of the local paper. "Remember when those airplane manufacturers were here? Wanted to build a bomber plant. Ed got so flustered that he let 'em get away—saying we couldn't supply the labor."

In his office at City Hall, Big Ed Horton was well aware of the talk around town. Despite his husky, six-foot frame, he felt alone and frightened. He nervously picked his yellow-stained teeth with a pen-knife blade.

Was his political career to end here? When he started his public life as deputy sheriff eleven years ago, he had pictured himself as another Huey Long. He had fought hard in the years that followed. He had done his job well, managing to please the big men in town—the wealthy ranchers, the local business men, the men high in political circles.

And now after only two years as a mayor, these same important men who had put him in office were against him. Ed knew, with a fear deep inside of him, that he'd lose the election if he didn't do something to take their minds off his past failures.

Pinky Hawkins, Ed's middle-aged, red-headed secretary, ambled in with the afternoon paper.

"Anything new today, Pinky?" asked Ed, snapping the knife blade shut.

"At last Stanley's got itself a first-class war hero," said Pinky. "Name's Johnson."

Ed snatched the paper. His watery blue eyes widened and his thick, hard lips formed a smile as he read.

A P-51 Mustang pilot, Lt. Ernest Johnson, had shot down four Messerschmitts over Italy, though wounded himself. He had been awarded the Distinguished Flying Cross and the Purple Heart. Born in Stanley, Texas, Lt. Johnson expected to return to America on sick leave.

"Hallelujah!" shouted Ed. "This is the answer!"

Pinky started at the mayor's stout, excited face. "What's the answer?"

"This war hero," roared Ed happily. "Lieutenant Johnson. We'll invite him here for our war bond drive next month. Get me Sam Walters on the phone!"

"Congressman Sam Walters? In Washington?" asked Pinky.

"Sure," snapped Ed, a sudden dynamo of action. "Can't waste time. I want Sam to get word through the War Department to the lieutenant that his old home town wants to honor him."

During the next month, Ed and Pinky worked at fever pitch. No trace of Johnson's family could be found. However his cable of acceptance arrived a few days later. A welcoming committee of Stanley's most prominent citizens, including Pete Hunter, Henry Lewis and Rob Gradey, was formed to help greet the returning hero.

Rob Gradey's newspaper and Jerry Hendrix, owner of the local radio station, both cooperated in publicizing the event which would put Stanley on the map.

The Main Street stores decorated their fronts with flags and bunting for the occasion. Phil Anderson, the leading locksmith, made a huge set of gilt-painted keys.

"Here's the keys to the city for the lieutenant, Ed," said Phil, handing them to the beaming mayor.

"Thanks a lot," said Ed with great enthusiasm. "It's about time Stanley had some."

A month later, on the day of Lt. Johnson's reception at the Stanley airport, Mayor Ed Horton was busy, happy, smiling. A brand new Stetson hat adorned his head. He was everywheres at one time—shaking hands, receiving congratulations, smoothing out last minute details.

The entire program was working out perfectly. A Dallas newspaper had even sent a reporter and a photographer. Jerry Hendrix had set up a microphone for his radio station. In connection with the national war bond drive, he had managed to get a nation-wide hook-up for the event.

The fire department band was on hand. Its uniforms, like its melodies, were loud and bright. Its brass instrument shone in the morning sun. The band was followed by the local boys' club with a banner, "Welcome Home—Stanley's Hero—Lt. Johnson."

Suddenly a shout went up from the waiting crowd. A silver transport plane came into sight. The big plane circled the field and made a smooth landing. It taxied up to the fence behind which the mayor and his committee craned their necks anxiously.

An airport attendant rushed a ladder-runway up to the door of the plane. The fire department band blared forth with "He's a Jolly Good Fellow." The crowd started to cheer.

The plane door opened and only one passenger stepped out. He was a Negro—handsome, young, and erect in an army officer's uniform. His chest was covered with pilot's wings and campaign ribbons.

The keys to the city faltered in the mayor's hand. He caught his breath in horror. The crowd stopped cheering. The band choked its music. The sound of its horns died off as if they had been strangled.

Lt. Johnson studied the scene before him. Then he calmly proceeded down the runway onto the ground. The crowd was strangely silent, as if attending a funeral.

The young pilot noticed Horton's pudgy lips snarl the words, "A nigra!" Johnson deliberately walked over to the startled mayor, quickly took the keys to the city with one hand and shook hands with the other. The Dallas photographer photographed the event with great glee.

Even the radio announcer, Jerry Hendrix, was speechless. Johnson noticed the microphone. Before Jerry could stop him, the guest of honor spoke into it.

"My presence here, ladies and gentlemen, has caused much excitement. Both the mayor and the radio announcer seem too startled to introduce me, so I will perform that duty myself. My name is Ernest Johnson, second lieutenant, United States Army Air Corps. I'm a Negro. I'm proud of my race."

Mayor Horton's normally red face took on a purplish hue. But he was too shaken and stunned by the Negro officer's actions to do anything. The crowd stared and listened.

Johnson continued, looking straight ahead, his voice clear and even. "I'm proud to be fighting for a country which has cities like Stanley, Texas, my birthplace. A city kind enough to invite me to participate in its bond drive. It makes me feel good to meet a man like Mayor Horton who practices racial tolerance—who showed his belief in equality between the white man and the Negro by sending for me. I know you will all back him up and buy war bonds. Thank you."

The astonished crowd gradually regained its voices and slowly drifted away, buzzing with talk. Soon only Horton and his reception committee was left.

Horton finally managed to speak. "This was a big surprise to us," he spluttered. "That is . . ."

Johnson finished it for him. "You didn't expect a Negro." He smiled without bitterness. "I guess you don't want to carry out your original plans."

"Under the circumstances, no," mumbled Horton. He looked to the committee members for support. They gave him none. Cold-eyed and relentless, they watched his squirming.

Johnson looked at the faces of the white men. "Thanks, anyway," he said. "I'll catch the next train out of town. That is, if you allow Negroes on trains."

A week later, the Businessmen's League meeting was going full blast. Ed Horton was speaking. His words were desperate. They spurted out of his mouth nervously.

"You boys got to realize I was tricked. I only had the interest of the city at heart."

"And get yourself re-elected," boomed a heavy voice from the back of the room.

"Fellows," persisted the mayor, holding up a trembling hand. "I wanted to put Stanley on the map."

"You put it on the map as a nigro-loving town," shouted Jerry Hendrix.

"I didn't know he was a nigra," said Horton. "Even though he's a war hero, he orter be lynched!"

"What about him shaking hands with you?" demanded Phil Anderson, the locksmith.

Horton feigned indignation. But he couldn't control the beads of perspiration forming on his brow. "Ain't I always kept the nigra in his place. There never was an uppity black boy in this town until Johnson came here under false pretenses."

"False colors, you mean," suggested Pete Hunter. The businessmen burst into roars of laughter. Big Ed tried to grin but only managed to look sick instead.

"What about his radio speech?" asked Henny Lewis.

"And those newspaper pictures," said Rob Gradey. "All over the country. Reprinted in 'Life'."

"It's a good thing for Stanley there's an election coming up," commented Henny Lewis.

Perspiration was streaming down Horton's face. He clinched and unclinched his huge hands. "People'll forget the whole business. It'll blow over."

An errand boy from Rob Gradey's paper came in and handed the editor a note. Rob stood up.

"This dispatch just came from New York. 'The American Council for Tolerance has awarded a medal to Mayor Edward J. Horton of Stanley, Texas, for practicing fellowship between whites and Negroes in his city. His recent honoring of a Negro war hero is commended as the act of a courageous public official who dares to fight the Jim Crow customs of the South'."

The heavy voice in the back of the room boomed out, "What do you say to that, Ed?"

Ed sank weakly into his chair, wiping his brow.

"Okay, boys," he gulped in desperation, "I'm licked!"

We Too—

FREEDOM AND CIVIL RIGHTS

Among the key reasons for African American migration to the West was the search for freedom, opportunity, and justice. However, sometimes freedom was denied, opportunity was elusive, and justice did not equally prevail. Beginning with the first black western settlers, there was a struggle for freedom and democracy to correct these wrongs. Before the Civil Rights revolution in the fifties and sixties, it was in the West where the original battles emerged. As a result, the West offers a unique focal point for examining this era. Civil rights activity in the West took three distinct forms: (1) direct-action protest, including demonstrations, sit-ins, and boycotts; (2) legal challenges culminating with the 1954 Supreme Court decision in *Brown v. Board of Education of Topeka*; and (3) Black Power confrontation that challenged both the tactics and goals of the earlier efforts to eliminate job discrimination, housing bias, and school segregation. The architects of western civil rights action shared a foundation of poverty, alienation, and anger and formulated distinct brands of civil engagement.

The stories in this section concern western issues that led to the Civil Rights movement and the issues it challenged. The festering racial tensions that lay behind the drive for civil rights and freedom are exceptionally well developed in John A. Williams's "Son in the Afternoon." Pay attention to Williams's prescient ending: at least five years before Watts exploded, the black protagonist hates "the long drive back to Watts." "Son in the Afternoon" depicts Wendell, an African American in Los Angeles, who visits his mother at the house where she does domestic labor for a white woman. Wendell becomes infuriated when he sees the affection his mother shows the white woman's young son and the way the white son disrespects Wendell's mother. He recognizes his mother's degrading position and feels her humiliation, so he avenges her by allowing the boy to see him sensuously hugging the boy's mother. Because the white child has developed the racist attitudes passed down through his family, Wendell knows that seeing his white mother hugging a black man will make him disrespect his own mother in the same way he disrespects Wendell's mother because she is black.

Mike Thelwell's "Direct Action" depicts a more direct way to confront racist tactics than the ironic means used by the narrator in "Son in the Afternoon." "Direct Action" concerns integration, as shown by the diverse racial origins of five young men who share a house in a midwestern college town and by their plan to fight racial segregation. They decide to take "direct action," to cross the Missouri state line and, using an intriguing tactic, occupy white-only restrooms so the whites will have to use the ones designated for blacks.

The father of the young narrator of Johnie Scott's "The Coming of the Hoodlum" moved to the Watts district of Los Angeles in search of a job opportunity when the narrator was a small boy. This story deals with police brutality and other forms of violence against blacks. The narrator, Hoodlum, attends Harvard University, experiences alienation, and returns to Watts with the realization that Watts would burn before he would be able to make sense of his experiences. And it did; Watts erupted in 1965, prior to the writing of Scott's story.

John R. Posey's "Ticket to Freedom" takes place in Dallas, Texas. Stephen, the adolescent narrator, describes his mother's childhood in Lubbock, where poverty and segregation plague black Texans. The Ku Klux Klan killed Stephen's uncle because he acquired an education and worked to integrate the schools. The narrator's grandfather once headed the local NAACP. Stephen has always been taught to resist racism. When he is accepted into an all-white Catholic school, his mother encourages him to attend as a means to fight segregation. While at the school, Stephen is the victim of racism, including racial slurs painted on his locker. When he politely asks a priest about a grade that has been recorded incorrectly, the priest calls him a "nigger." After Stephen attacks the priest and gets expelled from school, he realizes that his "opportunity" to attend the school was not the ticket to freedom that his mother had hoped for. Although schools in the United States were eventually desegregated, blacks did not receive the same educational opportunities as whites because of prejudice.

"Judah's a Two-Way Street Running Out," by Jack Burris, demonstrates how blacks were not given equal opportunity in the labor force. A young black man moves from the South to San Francisco in search of a job. He meets a friend while waiting for a job interview and realizes, after neither receives the job, that the interview was merely an attempt to make it appear as if the employer were acting according to equal opportunity.

Job constraints are also emphasized in "Water Seeks Its Own Level," a story from Maxine Clair's collection *Rattlebone*, set in the 1950s Rattlebone district of Kansas City. In this story, James Wilson has returned home after a year's separation from his family. He recently quit his construction job because whites were given all the overtime work. After a day looking for work, he volunteers to spend the evening sandbagging a levee in an effort to save the city from flooding. When the river begins to flood, the volunteers leave. James thinks about his family while working at the river and contemplates his situation. He knows his wife will be angry because he has been gone too long. At the end of the story he learns he will be home even later because the bridge is flooded and he must drive through Missouri to get home.

In "The Flashlight," Eldridge Cleaver shows the consequences of segregation in terms of the unequal living conditions of minorities and whites. Stacy, who lives in the housing projects of Crescent Heights near Los Angeles, is the leader of a gang who breaks into the houses of El Serrano, a thriving community where the privileged live. Stacy is bored and looks for adventure. He finds a flashlight during one of his raids, and using it to antagonize the Marijuanos, shines it on their faces while they attempt to hide their drug deals. Stacy feels empowered when he harasses the Marijuanos, who represent older and more powerful men. Finally, one of the Marijuanos, Chico, tells Stacy that he will buy the flashlight from him because he does not want Stacy to be harmed by the Marijuanos. After Chico promises Stacy that the Marijuanos will not hurt him, Stacy reluctantly sells the flashlight. However, one of the Marijuanos tries to attack Stacy, Chico stops him, and Stacy joins the group by smoking marijuana with them. At the end, Chico helps Stacy find his way home. This story clearly shows the consequences of segregated housing districts and the unequal distribution of power and money. As Chico tells Stacy, the Marijuanos could kill him and the police would not care because Stacy is black. In tragic irony, Stacy has sold his symbol of freedom, the flashlight.

"Support Your Local Police," by Ed Bullins, involves a black man who hitchhikes from New York to California in order to see one of his plays performed in Los Angeles. Different political ideologies are expressed in various regions of the country through bumper stickers, road signs, and his conversations with the people who give him rides. He tells most of them that he is a janitor or works at a car wash, for he is afraid to admit that he is a playwright and that he supports the black revolution. He knows that most of the people have a stereotyped image of him, so he acts out the script and exaggerates the stereotype. Bullins uses humor to show how stereotypes are inaccurate.

Western authors such as Bullins clarify the difficulty of being black in the West at the same time they create a more inclusive West. Although their efforts were not entirely successful—even after the Civil Rights movement, blacks and other minorities were still segregated and did not have equal opportunity—the western movement furnished new techniques and strategies, posed new questions, and established a firm foundation for the national Civil Rights movement. These authors, many of whom were participants, poignantly report on these developments in their stories.

Son in the Afternoon

JOHN A. WILLIAMS

It was hot. I tend to be a bitch when it's hot. I goosed the little Ford over Sepulveda Boulevard toward Santa Monica until I got stuck in the traffic that pours from L.A. into the surrounding towns. I'd had a very lousy day at the studio.

I was—still am—a writer and this studio had hired me to check scripts and films with Negroes in them to make sure the Negro moviegoer wouldn't be offended. The signs were already clear one day the whole of American industry would be racing pell-mell to get a Negro, showcase a spade. I was kind of a pioneer. I'm a *Negro* writer, you see. The day had been tough because of a couple of verbs—slink and walk. One of those Hollywood hippies had done a script calling for a Negro waiter to slink away from the table where a dinner party was glaring at him. I said the waiter should walk, not slink, because later on he becomes a hero. The Hollywood hippie, who understood it all because he had some colored friends, said that it was essential to the plot that the waiter slink. I said you don't slink one minute and become a hero the next; there has to be some consistency. The Negro actor I was standing up for said nothing either way. He had played Uncle Tom roles so long that he had become Uncle Tom. But the director agreed with me.

Anyway . . . hear me out now. I was on my way to Santa Monica to pick up my mother, Nora. It was a long haul for such a hot day. I had planned a quiet evening: a nice shower, fresh clothes, and then I would have dinner at the Watkins and talk with some of the musicians on the scene for a quick taste before they cut to their gigs. After, I was going to the Pigalle down on Figueroa and catch Earl Grant at the organ, and still later, if nothing exciting happened, I'd pick up Scottie and make it to the Lighthouse on the Beach or to the Strollers and listen to some of the white boys play. I liked the long drive, especially while listening to Sleepy Stein's show on the radio. Later, much later of course, it would be home, back to Watts.

So you see, this picking up Nora was a little inconvenient. My mother was a maid for the Couchmans. Ronald Couchman was an architect, a good one I understood from Nora who has a fine sense for this sort of thing; you don't work in some hundred-odd houses during your life without getting some idea of the way a house should be laid out. Couchman's wife, Kay, was a playgirl who drove a white Jaguar from one party to another. My mother didn't like her too much; she didn't seem to care much for her son, Ronald, junior. There's something wrong with a parent who can't really love her own child, Nora thought. The Couchmans lived in a real fine residential section, of course. A number of actors lived nearby, character actors, not really big stars.

Somehow it is very funny. I mean that the maids and butlers knew everything about these people, and these people knew nothing at all about the help. Through Nora and her friends I knew who who was laying whose wife; who had money and who *really* had money; I knew about the wild parties hours before the police, and who smoked marijuana, when, and where they got it.

To get to Couchman's driveway I had to go three blocks up one side of a palm-planted center strip and back down the other. The driveway bent gently, then swept back out of sight of the main road. The house, sheltered by slim palms, looked like a transplanted New England Colonial. I parked and walked to the kitchen door, skirting the growling Great Dane who was tied to a tree. That was the route to the kitchen door.

I don't like kitchen doors. Entering people's houses by them, I mean. I'd done this thing most of my life when I called at places where Nora worked to pick up the patched or worn sheets or the half-eaten roasts, the battered, tarnished silver—the fringe benefits of a housemaid. As a teen-ager I'd told Nora I was through with that crap; I was not going through anyone's kitchen door. She only laughed and said I'd learn. One day soon after, I called for her and without knocking walked right through the front door of this house and right on through the living room. I was almost out of the room when I saw feet behind the couch. I leaned over and there was Mr. Jorgensen and his wife making out like crazy. I guess they thought Nora had gone and it must have hit them sort of suddenly and they went at it like the hell-bomb was due to drop any minute. I've been that way too, mostly in the spring. Of course, when Mr. Jorgensen looked over his shoulder and saw me, you know what happened. I was thrown out and Nora right behind me. It was the middle of winter, the old man was sick and the coal bill three months overdue. Nora was right about those kitchen doors: I learned.

My mother saw me before I could ring the bell. She opened the door. "Hello," she said. She was breathing hard, like she'd been running or something. "Come in and sit down. I don't know *where* that Kay is. Little Ronald is sick and she's probably out gettin' drunk again." She left me then and trotted back through the house, I guess to be with Ronnie. I hated the combination of her white nylon uniform, her dark brown face and the wide streaks of gray in her hair. Nora had married this guy from Texas a few years after the old man had died. He was all right. He made out okay. Nora didn't have to work, but she just couldn't be still; she always had to be doing something. I suggested she quit work, but I had as much luck as her husband. I used to tease her about liking to be around those white folks. It would have been good for her to take an extended trip around the country visiting my brothers and sisters. Once she got to Philadelphia, she could go right out to the cemetery and sit awhile with the old man.

I walked through the Couchman home. I liked the library. I thought if I knew Couchman I'd like him. The room made me feel like that. I left it and went into the big living room. You could tell that Couchman had let his wife do that. Everything in it was fast, dart-like, with no sense of ease. But on the walls were several of Couchman's conceptions of buildings and homes. I guess he was a disciple of Wright. My mother walked rapidly through the room without looking at me and said, "Just be patient, Wendell. She should be here real soon."

"Yeah," I said, "with a snootful." I had turned back to the drawings when Ronnie scampered into the room, his face twisted with rage.

"Nora!" he tried to roar, perhaps the way he'd seen the parents of some of his friends roar at their maids. I'm quite sure Kay didn't shout at Nora, and I don't think Couchman would. But then no one shouts at Nora. "Nora, you come right back here this minute!" the little bastard shouted and stamped and pointed to a spot on the floor where Nora was supposed to come to roost. I have a nasty temper. Sometimes it lies dormant for ages and at other times, like when the weather is hot and nothing seems to be going right, it's bubbling and ready to explode. "Don't talk to my mother like that, you little—!" I said sharply, breaking off just before I cursed. I wanted him to be large enough for me to strike. "How'd you like for me to talk to *your* mother like that?"

The nine-year-old looked up at me in surprise and confusion. He hadn't expected me to say anything. I was just another piece of furniture. Tears rose in his eyes and spilled out onto his pale cheeks. He put his hands behind him, twisted them. He moved backwards, away from me. He looked at my mother with a "Nora, come help me" look. And sure enough, there was Nora, speeding back across the room, gathering the kid in her arms, tucking his robe together. I was too angry to feel hatred for myself.

Ronnie was the Couchman's only kid. Nora loved him. I suppose that was the trouble. Couchman was gone ten, twelve hours a day. Kay didn't stay around the house any longer than she had to. So Ronnie had only my mother. I think kids should have someone to love, and Nora wasn't a bad sort. But somehow when the six of us, her own children, were growing up we never had her. She was gone, out scuffling to get those crumbs to put into our months and shoes for our feet and praying for something to happen so that all the space in between would be taken care of. Nora's affection for us took the form of rushing out into the morning's five o'clock blackness to wake some silly bitch and get her coffee; took form in her trudging five miles home every night instead of taking the streetcar to save money to buy tablets for us, to use at school, we said. But the truth was that all of us liked to draw and we went through a writing tablet in a couple of hours every day. Can you imagine? There's not a goddamn artist among us. We never had the physical affection, the pat on the head, the quick, smiling kiss, the "gimmee a hug" routine. All of this Ronnie was getting.

Now he buried his little blond head in Nora's breast and sobbed. "There, there now," Nora said. "Don't you cry, Ronnie. Ol' Wendell is just jealous, and he hasn't much sense either. He didn't mean nuthin'."

I left the room. Nora had hit it of course, hit it and passed on. I looked back. It didn't look so incongruous, the white and black together, I mean. Ronnie was still sobbing. His bead bobbed gently on Nora's shoulder. The only time I ever got that close to her was when she trapped me with a bearhug so she could whale the daylights out of me after I put a snowball through Mrs. Grant's window. I walked outside and lit a cigarette. When Ronnie was in the hospital the month before, Nora got me to run her way over to Hollywood every night to see him. I didn't like that worth a damn. All right, I'll admit it: it did upset me. All that affection I didn't get nor my brothers and sisters going to that little white boy who, without a doubt, when away from her called her the names he'd learned from adults. Can you imagine a nine-year-old kid calling Nora a "girl," "our girl?" I spat at the Great Dane. He snarled and then I bounced a rock off his fanny. "Lay down, you bastard," I muttered. It was a good thing he was tied up.

I heard the low cough of the Jaguar slapping against the road. The car was throttled down, and with a muted roar it swung into the driveway. The woman aimed it for me. I was evil enough not to move. I was tired of playing with these people. At the last moment, grinning, she swung the wheel over and braked. She bounded out of the car like a tennis player vaulting over a net.

"Hi," she said, tugging at her shorts.

"Hello."

"You're Nora's boy?"

"I'm Nora's son." Hell, I was as old as she was; besides, I can't stand "boy."

"Nora tells us you're working in Hollywood. Like it?"

"It's all right."

"You must be pretty talented."

We stood looking at each other while the dog whined for her attention. Kay had a nice body and it was well tanned. She was high, boy, was she high. Looking at her, I could feel myself going into my sexy bastard routine; sometimes I can swing it great. Maybe it all had to do with the business inside. Kay took off her sunglasses and took a good look at me. "Do you have a cigarette?"

I gave her one and lit it. "Nice tan," I said. Most white people I know think it's a great big deal if a Negro compliments them on their tans. It's a large laugh. You have all this volleyball about color and come summer you can't hold the white folks back from the beaches, anyplace where they can get some sun. And of course the blacker they get, the more pleased they are. Crazy. If there is ever a Negro revolt, it will come during the summer and Negroes will descend upon the beaches around the nation and paralyze the country. You can't conceal cattle prods and bombs and pistols and police dogs when you're showing your birthday suit to the sun.

"You like it?" she asked. She was pleased. She placed her arm next to mine. "Almost the same color," she said.

"Ronnie isn't feeling well," I said.

"Oh, the poor kid. I'm so glad we have Nora. She's such a charm. I'll run right in and look at him. Do have a drink in the bar. Fix me one too, will you?" Kay skipped inside and I went to the bar and poured out two strong drinks. I made hers stronger than mine. She was back soon. "Nora was trying to put him to sleep and she made me stay out." She giggled. She quickly tossed off her drink. "Another, please?" While I was fixing her drink she was saying how amazing it was for Nora to have such a talented son. What she was really saying was that it was amazing for a servant to have a son who was not also a servant. "Anything can happen in a democracy," I said. "Servants' sons drink with madames and so on."

"Oh, Nora isn't a servant" Kay said. "She's part of the family."

Yeah, I thought. Where and how many times had I heard *that* before?

In the ensuing silence, she started to admire her tan again. "You think it's pretty good, do you? You don't know how hard I worked to get it." I moved close to her and held her arm. I placed my other arm around her. She pretended not to see or feel it, but she wasn't trying to get away either. In fact she was pressing closer and the register in my brain that tells me at the precise moment when I'm in, went off. Kay was very high. I put both arms around her and she put both hers around me. When I kissed her, she responded completely.

"Mom!"

"Ronnie, come back to bed," I heard Nora shout from the other room. We could hear Ronnie running over the rug in the outer room. Kay tried to get away from me, push me to one side, because we could tell that Ronnie knew where to look for his Mom: he was running right for the bar, where we were. "Oh, please," she said, "don't let him see us." I wouldn't let her push me away. "Stop!" she hissed. "He'll *see* us!" We stopped struggling just for an instant, and we listened to the echoes of the word *see*. She gritted her teeth and renewed her efforts to get away.

Me? I had the scene laid right out. The kid breaks into the room, see, and sees his mother in this real wriggly clinch with this colored guy who's just shouted at him, see, and no matter how his mother explains it away, the kid has the image— the colored guy and his mother—for the rest of his life, see?

That's the way it happened. The kid's mother hissed under her breath, *"You're crazy!"* and she looked at me as though she were seeing me or something about me for the very first time. I'd released her as soon as Ronnie, romping into the bar, saw us and came to a full, open-mouthed halt. Kay went to him. He looked first at me, then at his mother. Kay turned to me, but she couldn't speak.

Outside in the living room my mother called, "Wendell, where are you? We can go now."

I started to move past Kay and Ronnie. I felt many things, but I made myself think mostly, *There you little bastard, there.*

My mother thrust her face inside the door and said, "Good-bye, Mrs. Couchman. See you tomorrow. 'Bye, Ronnie."

"Yes," Kay said, sort of stunned. "Tomorrow." She was reaching for Ronnie's hand as we left, but the kid was slapping her hand away. I hurried quickly after Nora, hating the long drive back to Watts.

Direct Action

MIKE THELWELL

We were all sitting around the front room the night it started. The front room of the pad was pretty kooky. See, five guys lived there. It was a reconstructed basement and the landlord didn't care what we did, just so he got his rent.

Well, the five guys who lived there were pretty weird, at least so it was rumored about the campus. We didn't care too much. Lee was on a sign kick, and if he thought of anything that appeared profound or cool—and the words were synonymous with him—wham! we had another sign. See, he'd write a sign and put it up. Not only that; he was klepto about signs. He just couldn't resist lifting them, so the pad always looked like the basement of the Police Traffic Department with all the DANGER NO STANDING signs he had in the john, and over his bed he had a sign that read WE RESERVE THE RIGHT TO DENY SERVICE TO ANYONE. Man, he'd bring in those silly freshman girls who'd think the whole place was "so-o-o bohemian," and that sign would really crack them up.

Anyway, I was telling you about the front room. Lee had put up an immense sign he'd written: IF YOU DON'T DIG KIKES, DAGOS, NIGGERS, HENRY MILLER, AND J. C., YOU AIN'T WELCOME! Across from that he had another of his prize acquisitions; something in flaming red letters issued a solemn WARNING TO SHOP-LIFTERS. You've probably seen them in department stores.

Then there was the kid in art school, Lisa, who was the house artist and mascot. Man, that kid was mixed up. She was variously in love with everyone in the pad. First she was going with Dick—that's my brother. Then she found that he was a "father surrogate"; then it was Lee, but it seems he had been "only an intellectual status symbol." Later it was Doug "the innocent." After Doug it was Art—that's our other roomie—but he had only been an expression of her "urge to self-destruction." So now that left only me. The chick was starting to project that soulful look, but hell, man, there was only one symbol left and I wasn't too eager to be "symbolized." They should ban all psychology books, at least for freshman girls.

Anyway, I was telling you about the room. When Lisa was "in love" with Dick she was in her surrealist period. She used to bring these huge, blatantly Freudian canvases, which she hung on the walls until the room looked, as Doug said, like "the pigmented expression of a demented psyche." Then Lisa started to down Dick because of his lack of critical sensitivity and creativity." She kept this up, and soon we were all bugging Dick. He didn't say too much, but one day when he was alone in the pad, he got some tins of black, green, yellow, and red house paint, stripped the room, and started making like Jackson Pollock. The walls, the windows, and dig this, even the damn floor was nothing but one whole mess of different-colored paint. Man, we couldn't go in the front room for four days; when it dried, Dick brought home an instructor from art school to "appraise some original works."

I was sorry for the instructor. He was a short, paunchy little guy with a bald patch, and misty eyes behind some of the thickest lenses you ever saw. At first he thought Dick was joking, and he just stood there fidgeting and blinking his watery little eyes. He gave a weak giggle and muttered something that sounded like, "Great . . . uh . . . sense of humor. Hee."

But Dick was giving him this hurt-creative-spirit come-on real big. His face was all pained, and he really looked stricken and intense.

"But, sir, surely you can see some promise, some little merit?"

"Well, uh, one must consider, uh, the limitations of your medium, uh . . . hee."

"Limitations of medium, yes, but surely there must be some merit?"

"Well, you must realize—"

"Yes, but not even *some* spark of promise, some faint, tiny spark of promise?" Dick was really looking distraught now. The art teacher was visibly unhappy and looked at me appealingly, but I gave him a don't-destroy-this-poor-sensitive-spirit look. He mopped his face and tried again.

"Abstractionism is a very advanced genre—"

"Yes, yes, advanced," Dick said, cutting him off impatiently, "but not even the faintest glimmer of merit?" He was really emoting now, and then he started sobbing hysterically and split the scene. I gave the poor instructor a cold how-could-you-be-so-cruel look, and he began to stutter. "I had n-no idea, n-no idea. Oh, dear, so strange . . . Do you suppose he is all right? How d-do you explain . . . Oh, dear."

"Sir," I said, "I neither suppose nor explain. All I know is that my brother is very high-strung and you have probably induced a severe trauma. If you have nothing further to say, would you. . . ?" and I opened the door suggestively. He looked at the messed-up walls in bewilderment and shook his head. He took off his misty glasses, wiped them, looked at the wall, bleated something about "all insane," and scurried out. He probably heard us laughing.

Man, these white liberals are really tolerant. If Dick and I were white, the cat probably would have known right off that we were kidding. But apparently he was so anxious not to hurt our feelings that he gave a serious response to any old crap we said. Man, these people either kill you with intolerance or they turn around and overdo the tolerance bit. However, as Max Shulman says, "I digress."

The cats in our pad were kind of integrated, but we never thought of it that way. We really dug each other, so we hung around together. As Lee would say, "We related to each other in a meaningful way." (That's another thing about Lee. He was always "establishing relationships." Man, if he made a broad or even asked her the time, it was always, "Oh, I established a relationship today.") Like, if you were a cat who was hung up on this race bit, you could get awfully queered up around the pad. The place was about as mixed up as Brooklyn. The only difference, as far as I could see, was that we could all swear in different languages. Lee's folks had come from Milan, Dick and I were Negro, and Art, with his flaming red head and green Viking eyes, was Jewish.

The only cat who had adjustment problems was Doug. He was from sturdy Anglo-Saxon Protestant stock; his folks still had the Mayflower ticket stub and a lot of bread. When he was a freshman in the dorm, some of the cats put him down because he was shy and you could see that he was well off. And those s.o.b.'s would have been so helpful if the cat had been "culturally deprived" and needed handouts. Man, people are such bastards. It's kind of a gas, you know. Doug probably could have traced his family back to Thor, and yet he had thin, almost Semitic features, dark brown hair, and deep eyes with a dark rabbinical sadness to them.

Anyway, we guys used to really swing in the pad; seems like we spent most of the time laughing. But don't get the idea that we were just kick-crazy or something out of Kerouac, beat-type stuff. All of us were doing okay in school—grades and that jazz. Take Art, for instance: most people thought that because he had a beard and was always playing the guitar and singing, and ready to party, he was just a campus beatnik-in-residence. They didn't know that he was an instructor and was working on his doctorate in anthropology. Actually, we were really more organized than we looked.

Anyway, this thing I'm telling you about happened the summer when this sit-in bit broke out all over. Since Pearl Springs was a Midwestern college town, there was no segregation of any kind around—at least, I didn't see any. But everyone was going out to picket Woolworth's every weekend. At first we went, but since there was this crowd out each week and nobody was crossing the line anyway, we kind of lost interest. (Actually, they had more people than they needed.)

So we were all sitting around and jiving each other, when I mentioned that a guy we called "The Crusader" had said he was coming over later.

"Oh, no," Dick groaned; "that cat bugs me. Every time he sees me in the cafeteria or the union he makes a point of coming over to talk, and he never has anything to say. Hell, every time I talk to the guy I feel as if he really isn't seeing me, just a cause—a minority group."

"Yeah, I know," Art added. "Once at a party I was telling some broad that I was Jewish and he heard. You know, he just had to steer me into a corner to tell me how sympathetic he was to the 'Jewish cause' and 'Jewish problems.' The guy isn't vicious, only misguided."

Then Lee said, "So the guy is misguided, but, hell, he's going to come in here preaching all this brotherly love and Universal Brotherhood. And who wants to be a brother to bums like you?"

That started it.

Dick was reading the paper, but he looked up. "Hey, those Israelis in Tel Aviv are really getting progressive."

"Yeah, them Israelis don't mess around. What they do now?" Art asked. He was a real gung-ho Zionist, and had even spent a summer in a kibbutz in Israel.

"Oh," said Dick, "they just opened a big hydroelectric plant."

Art waded in deeper. "So what?"

"Nothing, only they ain't got no water, so they call it The Adolf Eichmann Memorial Project."

Everybody cracked up. Art said something about "niggers and flies."

"Niggers and kikes," I chimed in. "I don't like them, either, but they got rights . . . in their place."

"Rights! They got too many rights already. After all, this is a free country, and soon a real American like me won't even have breathing room," cracked Lee.

"Hey, Mike," someone shouted, "you always saying some of your best friends are dagos, but would you like your sister to marry one?"

"Hell no, she better marryink der gute Chewish boy," I replied.

"And for niggers, I should of lynched you all when I had the chance . . ." Art was saying when The Crusader entered. This was the cat who organized the pickets—or at least he used to like to think he did. A real sincere crusading-type white cat. He looked with distaste at Lee's sign about kikes and niggers.

"Well, fellas, all ready for the picket on Saturday?"

"Somebody tell him," said Lee.

"Well, you see," I ventured, "we ain't going."

"Ain't going!" The Crusader howled. "But why? Don't you think—"

"Of course not. We are all dedicated practitioners of non-think. Besides, all our Negrahs are happy. Ain't yuh happy, Mike?" Art drawled.

"Yeah, but I don' like all these immigran's, kikes, dagos, an' such. Like, I thinks—"

"And Ah purely hates niggers: they stink so," Lee announced.

The Crusader didn't get the message. "Look guys, I know you're joking, but . . . I know you guys are awful close—hell, you room together—but you persist in using all these derogatory racial epithets. I should think that you of all people . . . I really don't think it's funny."

"Man," said Dick, "is this cat for real?"

I knew just what he meant: I can't stomach these crusading liberal types, either, who just have to prove their democracy.

"Okay, can it, guys. I think we ought to explain to this gentleman what we mean," Art said. "Look, I don't think I have to prove anything to anyone in this room. We're all in favor of the demonstrations. In fact, nearly half the community is, so we don't think we need to parade our views. Besides, you have enough people as it is. So we're supporting the students in the South, but why not go across the state line into Missouri and really do something? That's where direct action is needed."

"Oho, the same old excuse for doing nothing," The Crusader sneered.

I could see that Lee over in his comer was getting mad. Suddenly he said, "So you accuse us of doing nothing? Well, we'll show you what we mean by direct action. We mean action calculated to pressure people, to disrupt economic and social functions and patterns, to pressure them into doing something to improve racial relations."

"Very fine, Comrade Revolutionary, and just what do you propose to do, besides staying home and lecturing active people like me?" The Crusader's tone dripped sarcasm.

Lee completely lost control. "What do we propose to do?" he shouted. "We'll go across the state line and in two weeks we'll integrate some institution! That'll show you what direct action means."

"Okay, okay, just make sure you do it," said The Crusader as he left.

Man, next day it was all over campus that we had promised to integrate everything from the State of Georgia to the White House main bedroom—you know how rumors are. We were in a fix. Every time Lee blew his top we were always in a jam. Now we had to put up or shut up.

The pressure was mounting after about a week. We were all sitting around one day when Doug proclaimed to Lee, "We shall disrupt their social functions, we shall disrupt their human functions—You utter nut, what the hell are you going to do?"

Lee was real quiet, like he hadn't heard; then he jumped up. "Human functions! Doug—genius. I love you!" Then he split the scene, real excited-like.

About an hour later Lee came back still excited, and mysterious. "Look," he said, "we're cool. I have it all worked out. You know that big department store in Deershead? Well, they have segregated sanitary facilities."

Dick interrupted, "So? This is a Christian country. You expect men and women to use the same facilities?"

"Oh, shut up, you know what I mean. Anyway, we're going to integrate them. All you guys have to do is get ten girls and five other guys and I'll do the rest."

"Oh, isn't our genius smart," I snarled. "If you think that hot as it is, I'm going to picket among those hillbillies, you're out of your cotton-chopping little mind."

"Who's going to picket?" Lee said. "Credit me with more finesse than that. I said direct action, didn't I? Well, that's what I meant. All you guys have to do is sit in the white johns and use all the seats. I'll do the rest."

"And the girls?" I asked.

"They do the same over in the women's rest rooms. Oh, is this plan a riot!" The cat cracked up and wouldn't say any more. Nobody liked it much. Lee was so damn wild at times. See, he was a real slick cat. I mean, if he had ten months with a headshrinker he'd probably end up President. But, man, most of the jams we got into were because the cat *hadn't* seen a headshrinker. Anyway, we didn't have any alternative, so we went along.

The morning we were ready to leave, Lee disappeared. Just when everyone was getting real mad, he showed, dragging two guys with him. One was The Crusader and the other cat turned out to be a photographer from the school paper. So we drove to Deershead, a hick town over in Missouri. All the way, Lee was real confident. He kept gloating to The Crusader that he was going to show him how to operate.

When we arrived at the "target," as Lee called it, he told everyone to go in and proceed with stage one. All this means is that we went and sat in the white johns. The girls did the same. Lee disappeared again. We all sat and waited. Soon he showed up grinning all over and said:

"Very good. Now I shall join you and wait for our little scheme to develop." He told The Crusader and the photographer to wait in the store for our plan to take effect. Man, we sat in that place for about an hour. It was real hot, even in there. The guys started to get restless and finally threatened to leave if Lee didn't clue us in on the plan—if he had one.

Just as he decided to tell us, two guys came into the john real quick. We heard one of them say, "Goddamn, the place is full." They waited around for a while, and more guys kept coming in. All of a sudden the place was filled with guys. They seemed real impatient, and one of them said, "Can't you fellas hurry up? There's quite a line out here."

"Wonder why everyone has such urgent business?" drawled Lee. "Must be an epidemic."

"Must be something we ate," the guy said. His voice sounded strange and tense. "Hurry up, fellas, will you?"

I peeped through the crack in the door and saw the guys outside all sweating and red in the face. One cat was doubled up, holding his middle and grimacing. I heard Lee say in a tone of real concern, I tell you what, men, looks like we'll be here for some time. Why don't you just go down to the other rest room?"

"What!" someone shouted. "You mean the nigger john?"

Then Lee said ever so sweetly, "Oh, well . . . there's always the floor." And he started laughing softly.

The guys got real mad. Someone tried my door, but it was locked. I heard one guy mutter, "The hell with this," and he split. For a minute there was silence; then we heard something like everyone rushing for the door.

Lee said, "C'mon, let's follow them." So we all slipped out.

Man, that joint was in an uproar. There was a crowd of whites milling around the door of both colored johns. The Crusader was standing around looking bewildered. Lee went over to the photographer and told him to get some pictures. After that, we got the girls and split the scene.

In the car coming back, Lee was crowing all over the place about what a genius he was. "See," he said, "I got the idea from Doug when he was saying all that bit about 'human functions.' That was the key: all I had to do then was figure out some way to create a crisis. So what do I do? Merely find a good strong colorless laxative and introduce it into the drinking water at the white coolers—a cinch with the old-fashioned open coolers they got here. Dig? That's what I was doing while you guys were sitting in."

Just then The Crusader bleeped, "Hey—would you stop at the next service station?"

The guy did look kinda pale at that. I thought, "And this cat always peddling his brotherhood and dragging his white man's burden behind him all the time." Oh, well, I guess I might have used the cooler, too.

Well, there was quite a furor over the whole deal. The school newspaper ran the shots and a long funny story, and the local press picked it up. Deershead was the laughingstock of the whole state. The management of the store was threatening to sue Lee and all that jazz, but it was too late to prove any "willful mischief or malice aforethought," or whatever it is they usually prove in these matters. The Negro kids in Deershead got hep and started a regular picket of the store. Man, I hear some of those signs were riots: LET US SIT DOWN TOGETHER, and stuff like that. The store held out a couple of months, but finally they took down the signs over the johns. Guess they wanted to forget.

That's the true story as it happened. You'll hear all kinds of garbled versions up on campus, but that's the true story of the "sitting" as it happened. Oh, yeah, one other thing: the Deershead branch of the N.A.A.C.P. wanted to erect a little statue of either me or Dick sitting on the john, the first Negro to be so integrated in Deershead. You know how they dig this first Negro bit. We had to decline. Always were shy and retiring.

The Coming of the Hoodlum

JOHNIE SCOTT

The coming of the Hoodlum was not an entirely unpremeditated affair. Characters within characters took part: Harvard, Watts, and I. It was in the form of a journey, a traveling from the teeming black heart of Los Angeles, Watts, to the pulse of America's intellectual showplace, Harvard: a journey that took only a year in which to begin the gradual eroding away of all former attitudes toward life: an experience that carried its pilgrim beyond his concepts of educational, racial, and social attitudes, that was to find at the culmination of that eventful year's passage a new, albeit embittered and disenchanted, man where before there had been but a child of promise.

At the war's end, the Hoodlum was born: 1948, in Cheyenne County Memorial Hospital. The month of May, of May and sunshine, of a world finally breathing again, of the ending of the spilling of blood on the land, on the birth of a new generation, on the coming of the nuclear bomb, and the passing of a collective hysteria that had produced the bloodiest holocaust in mortal history.

The war's end had found his father, our father, father of the Hoodlum, a soldier awaiting his leave orders, a Negro who had left the South after a painful youth of his own: a son who had to leave school in the fifth grade, the Old South, deepest Lousiana, picking cotton so that a family might survive: a son of sharecroppers and former slaves, a man who longed to be free, free of the bonds all Southern Negroes felt, free to work where he loved—he got his leave orders, his discharge, honorably, all the returning heroes of the war got honorable discharges and all war veterans were called heroes. From Cheyenne to the South to Los Angeles: from the war to the Old South to the West: from death to birth to chance: but then, all men felt a new promise in the air—children were being born, I was born, the Hoodlum was born, the War Babies all were born. Not born into happiness, but into hope, some of the hope to be disillusioned, some of the hope to be fulfilled: the growing years of the child born in a country hospital were to be spent in the teeming ghetto of black folk, Southern emigrants, a dozen dialects, to be known as Watts: its old name, the name of history, was Mudtown.

When Father first brought me to Watts, he had found work in an airplane plant: North American Aircraft: the Korean war, a newer war, going on, the old veterans now sheetmetal workers and engineers while younger men went on to die: Negroes flooding Los Angeles and other western towns, in search of these jobs that took Negroes. He had been fortunate, had saved his money, had bought a small wooden frame house: worked night shifts and, come the light of day, was out in the streets looking for more work, more money, had to have it, the family was growing larger: soon there were two children, three children, four, then five, then six.

In the meanwhile, the wooden structure caught fire and burned completely down. His dreams burned down with it—we moved into the housing projects, the old Jordan Downs Housing Projects. Roaches carpeted the floor at night, a black floor that moved up and down and around the walls, if one woke in the middle of the night to see this shifting blackness in the blackness moving inevitably a scream would escape the lips: we learned to live with them, however; in time man learns to adjust to anything, anyone, any fear, even the fear of insects, the fear of filth: that is, if man wants to live.

Those years in the "old" projects, for newer ones were built late in the 1950s, were changing years, full of growth as Watts grew and the city grew. Negroes continued to come into Los Angeles, Negroes continued to look for those jobs in the West: some, my father, were laid off, others were hired, then fired, more came in their place: it was a cycle, as complete a cycle as one could hope. The ghetto had become more than roaches, or buildings that stank both day and night, more than the oppressive summer heat that left us rasping for breath along with the flies that zipped in and out of the houses—the ghetto had become the people. It was the people: their wishes, their dreams, their forgotten homes, their hopes, starved and starving hopes, and the coming of the bitterness. In this world, a world of darkness, churches were built. Into this world was I born, a half-complete angel.

Those years saw the scars come, scars from fights. Fights that took in neighbors, roaches, broken bottles, brickbats, saw gangs chase people blocks, saw men hop fences six feet tall in one bound, saw bricks barely miss bashing skulls in, saw knives, saw the erection of the churches, saw the night, and the darkness, and the unlit streets: these were the lightless streets, streets that saw bar-b-que joints like Page's on 103rd and Grape, that saw a person's mother get her purse snatched at night if she walked home without a stick in her hand: to become a man and know that there is not that much happiness in the world: to know that you can cry because you have grown old in such a short span of time.

You see police beat people on the streets, in their cars; you hear the mothers cursing the police, calling them "White Crackers!"; you wonder in confusement, What are these words? and then you see the skins: all the white skins clothed in black, all the shiny badges: association of forms, the white skins become the black uniforms, Police, and the voices, the curses, the People—your People, dark as you, fathers and mothers, friends.

And just as suddenly, your consciousness expands. Poverty is not just withered bodies, flesh lost in weeks of hunger, but something else; as an inner Presence, poverty is far greater and menacing. The Spirit of Christmas To Come leading Scrooge before a dead Tiny Tim. Or, something else; more personal—The Poverty had led *you* back in time to your childhood. All of the voices were the voices of friends—a comradery within Watts.

To have a father carried from his home, you the Watcher and the child, away for questioning: you wonder and you see, the handcuffs, memories of the police on television handcuffing the bad guys: the Law and the wrong-doing: again, white versus colored: if the beginning of racism didn't set in by then, it only took the isolation to come, isolation from the white world: the streets and Us against the markets, the cars, the dealers, the other world, Them. We learned, fought off fear against, the white boys, going to the Opera on public school excursions: seeking culture, and found it—found it one's own balled hand smashing against a face you would never see because you had never seen it: smashing out against a blind prejudice: the orphan if you were taken for what you were: wanting to be loved, but in the middle of an unnamed world, alone. I ran out of the house crying, but ran into my neighbors: out in their yards, listening—there never was privacy in a housing project.

But somehow, out of wanting a place into which I could withdraw, I found a refuge in books: I would read, would go to the old library by myself, seven years old: a walk that took me past savage dogs, saw me running by some of the yards with rotting wood fences: on into the quiet, the book: would read of a Round Table, and could see myself in a land where honor was upheld, where men were as free as their pride would carry them.

Would it matter that our Hoodlum could look back on those years and think of how he stood on streetcorners like everyone else; that taunts flowed as swiftly from his mouth when someone could be seen carrying books home from school, or going to the library to do some homework? He didn't think so. That is why, during those years, the beginning of a cleavage began to be felt within himself: a strange and troubling turmoil, born out of the chaos that refused to be shaped in the image of education: a world that refused any sort of understanding, brutal and brutalized, the feelings of the rejected: a time when life came to a standstill for him as he surveyed the great emptiness of his own heart, dissatisfied with the answers streets would whisper into his ears—no less dissatisfied with the chalkboards of the schools, where numbers remained numbers and never became a thought more: while his thoughts sank into memories, wishes.

A cleavage was born that would be nourished by the bitter spirit of the ghetto even though our Hoodlum tried to hide this tear from the eyes of all: include Mother and Father, who soon were to break apart as so many of the neighbors had broken apart: who soon were to become numbers that remained numbers, statistics in the files of the divorce courts and the long rows of Vital Statistics in the newspapers. The pulse of the nation beat swiftly, but not as swiftly as that young heart racing even further into the Hell that was to come. It was a Hell that would see blood flow, his own, and those dear to him—a Hell that would see disputes rise, a family divide against itself and send each member out flying into the streets of that world. Was it any wonder that he sought refuge in books? Was it any wonder that his spirit grew ever more divided? There existed truth, it could be found in the world if only he became a part of it. All that could be found in books were dreams, high and full of mystery. But he wanted dreams.

And so he entered school, the alienated. Alienated out of his own frustration, that longing to resolve the incoherent patterns of a world in which all intemperate attitudes might survive: from ultraracism to Uncle Tomism, from the fear of God to the police-fearing pimps and petty racketeers. His own resolution was simply to survive: to survive and laugh, for it was sheerly by being able to laugh that the horrors could be compromised, that sanity could be maintained. Mayors and governors entered office and then left office. Nothing changed.

What was Watts like?

The year the Hoodlum (we can forget that name, he was no hoodlum, but his friends were, even though they shared his feelings, what made him different?) was elected president of the student body at his junior high school many things happened: inter-school council meetings were held, speeches given, a girl found raped in a classroom during a lunch break, the accent given to good oral hygiene, a seventh-grade girl stabbing her math teacher seventeen times with a butcher-knife because he called her "stupid." But he survived, as the class dwindled in number from 750 to 550, but on the day of graduation this was said:

> Lives of great men all remind us
> We can make our lives sublime;
> And, departing, leave behind us
> Footprints on the sands of Time.

I *apologize,* Mr. Longfellow.

> Leave Markham knowing you left
> Far more than mere footprints,
> Leave Markham knowing you helped
> Begin a brighter future for us all.

From seventh grade to ninth grade, from 750 to 550, from small children to wide-eyed adolescents. But, three days later, they had all matured: 250 were left, the "largest incoming class in Jordan's history," or so it went according to the head counselor: the following years would see larger classes, to be sure, more babies were born each year, illegitimacy and wedlock both strove to rise higher even as people married younger and lives broke up faster. Had the Hoodlum changed in this time?

Yes. He had learned to feel. He had learned that there was no love in this world. He had learned, three years later, as 97 men and women walked across an auditorium stage to receive diplomas, that of the forgotten and the fallen, of those empty 153 "other" diplomas that were not given, there could be no crying. They

had not asked for remorse. Even now, they sat in the audience, among the spectators, silent when the speeches were given, laughing when the clowns tripped over
their gowns, crying as a brother finally made it, gone when it was over: gone as
surely as Death leaves when faced with an attitude of toughness. For the Hoodlum
had grown a shell of toughness, that resisted both the hate of the streets, and the
love that he tried, wanted, to release. It would have been futile for him to relate
these emotions.

Instead, the toughness grew harder, making communication with him all but
impossible. But of what, from where, had this bitterness come? Surely not from
the mere presence of failure, from the odor of death! One would have thought
that the scene of dying hardened one to the facts of life, but this was a different
sort of hardening: you went out for sports, wrote on the school paper, became
active in student government, studied diligently. Then, you were the biggest prankster in class, the loudest mouth, the silent antagonist of affairs between student and
teacher: when in the streets these conflicts were magnified, distorted, the image of
truth was purposely turned inside out, hoping to make the true false in order to
make things for oneself more bearable. Inside the soul, the pressure was mounting: the days of waiting in outer offices on disciplinary actions, of hearing teachers
pass the rumor that you were a "smart-alecky" kid that could think quickly when it
came time for assignments but even more quickly when it came time to lie. You
went home with him, saw his mother as she went through her daily motions, trying
to make a bearable existence out of living, playing the blues. B. B. King, Blind
Lemon Jefferson, Billie Holiday, Charles Brown, the old Lowell Fulsom: sounds
from his home and from the streets, no longer from Page and Page's Bar-B-Que
Pit, it had burned down in the years before. Nothing had been built there, but then,
what had ever been built there. Only roasted meat had been sold, and ice cream on
hot summer afternoons, and the sound of music where there would only have
been the oppressive stillness of one's own thoughts brooding.

At one time, like most of his friends, the Hoodlum hated school, hated Jordan
High especially for what it had done to him: *nothing*. That was the reason for all
hatred toward the school: his class read no better than sixth-graders and this showed
in its average gradepoint: 1.8, the equal of the bottom fifth of the intellectual
cracker barrel. His hatred did not last long, a break came, the big break in his life—
accepted into Harvard College, the acme of the East, the springboard of Presi-
dents and businessmen; most of all, the place from which decent homes came:
homes like they didn't exist in his world. Had he been a brilliant student to be
admitted? Not if his grades were looked at—3.03. Had he exceptionally high college board scores? Not especially—1096. What had he done in school to earn
entrance into a Harvard class which claimed an average I.Q. of 128, was selective
enough to pick 1,200 people from over 6,000 applicants from the best schools and
training institutes in the world?

Nothing, nothing except survive those years of his childhood. Nothing, nothing except remember what those years were, except make it his purpose to some-

how do something about it. Nothing, nothing save start out on a career that soon would see him thrown into an even graver crisis: to decide between one's environment, one's home, and the atmosphere of Academia.

Not too many survived that regimen our Hoodlum went through. He had a friend, a member of the 99th percentile, as sensitive and as introspective as anyone, *a human being like we all are,* who never got past the tenth grade. That friend came to class one day, (a science course handled by a man who doubled as a gym teacher in the high school) with a cigar, puffing away as conspicuously as he could. Asked to put it out, he replied, "No. Not if you have to be my teacher. Not if I have to stay here and 'learn' like everyone else. Because I care. I care enough to not give a damn whether you kick me out of school or not." And he was kicked out. Like so many others were kicked out. For reasons of caring. For reasons of wanting something that was neither at home nor in the school. For reasons that still exist in every school even now. For want of a true friend. For want of love. For reasons incomprehensible to used textbooks and second-rate equipment, reasons that surpassed inadequate school facilities.

It is very simple. Have a sister and have her an unwed mother. Close your eyes, blush with secret shame, hide the secret, live on as though nothing happened. Bury that scar with the other scars. And then, at an airport, pose for pictures as the first Negro to enter Harvard with her and your other sisters. With teachers that did not know her but looked away when looked to for answers why: the pictures were taken, the plane took off, and you sat on the plane remembering the past: "I'm surprised you aren't going to Pomona or Whittier College, or somewhere like that! You could have been something but you talked too much. You could have done something with your life. *I thought you were different from the rest!*"

It is not easy to make a happy world when your diet has been tragedy. The tragedy of having to see how much hate, and being hated, of ignorance, and being unknown, of wanting, and being unwanted, the sheer tragedy of being a human in this world. A stigma if you dare to care: the withdrawing into your soul; the thought of another way of life. The ghetto has a way of reaching into your life just when you think you have climbed to the top of the mountain, and bringing everything crashing down. Sisyphus pushing a rock to the top of the mountain, seeing it roll to the bottom again. Laughing while accepting his fate, walking down again to begin over: this, in the real world, was not a myth or a treatise on why not to take death over a half-emptied bottle of sleeping pills: pill-taking had begun far earlier for so many of us, of Them, of the Others who were not on that jet flying across the country to Cambridge in search of a new life as well as an education. But what was education?

It was not so easily defined. It couldn't be: not if, in the process, one knows that only in rebelling against a system that consciously seeks to stifle the creative instinct one rises to the fore, is regarded by one's equals in that environment as a leader that will never be seen or known or heard over airwaves as the representative. Representative! Of what, and then—why? Why, if being representative meant having as one's constituents aged and aging whores, homosexual preachers whose antics sooner or later hit the presses and, when they did, made an even greater mockery of the Church; what if one's constituents were little half-clothed kids who would never be more than half-clothed throughout life, if they got to be any older, they threw away instinctively the protective shell of insulated education for the more existentialist proposition of freedom Now, or Never! Representative of friends and enemies, of those who had not learned their "ABC's" until the seventh grade, who, when they left school, still read at fourth- and fifth-grade levels yet who could, when asked, make the fastest dollar simply by jacking up a car, taking all four tires, the battery, and selling them at dirt-cheap prices to small garages in and around the neighborhood. You stayed penniless those years not because you had no father, or because your mother was on welfare: you were penniless because you were afraid, afraid of being killed out there on the streets, ashamed of being ashamed if you were caught. You remembered bullets, had seen guns pointed and heard them fired at human beings in your world, had seen men die in the streets and it was not called War by the press.

But you got off that plane. With two suitcases, a shaving kit, an open-flight back home for Christmas, and the determination to be something you had only seen in books. A man in love with his dreams. Was it any wonder, then, that the Hoodlum found it so easy to read Herman Hesse's *Steppenwolf*?:

> I cannot understand or share these joys, though they are within my reach, for which thousands of others strive. On the other hand, what happens to me in my rare hours of bliss, what for me is bliss and life and ecstasy and exaltation, the world in general seeks at most in its imagination; in life it finds it absurd. And in fact, if the world is right, if this music of the cafes, these mass enjoyments and Americanized men who are pleased with so little are right, then I am wrong, I am crazy. I am in truth the Steppenwolf that I often call myself; that beast astray who finds neither home nor joy nor nourishment in a world that is strange and incomprehensible to him.

For him, for that Hoodlum, it had been with a near-attitude of revenge that he had walked into the offices of Jordan High, when he had shown each one the letters of acceptance from different schools, had shown them all and had announced his intentions of attending Harvard: and then had come home, had sat with friends who were both awe-stricken and now, in the face of this turn of events, respectful: a distance was growing between the Hoodlum and his world, a distance that soon was to become as marked as that cleavage within his own soul, the division between the ugliness of reality and the bliss of his own imaginations, his wildest dreams for the future. Unless a person fights back with all he has and believes in, the social and academic world of the school system in the ghetto will crush him. But, the fight within our Hoodlum became distorted—transfigured; it was now a short-lived revenge. And, in this especial, bitter cup of emptiness, of tightly wound despair, he knew his own truth—he had found no solace in a sneering attitude, only wanting again to let them know that there existed within each man such a temper of life that, with its own drive, it could surmount the obstacles, it could climb the mountain.

It *had* to climb the mountain for it was the fear of dying lonely, without a soul around, that pushed, that inspired the fearful drive: strange, but during the summer which preceded the Harvard adventure, there was no inkling really of what was to come up, of what the intellectual challenge would be: nor, of how the Harvard *Crimson* would run articles on the stiff competition the freshmen offered upperclassmen in studies, of the new vitality in the class, of its expanding representation of the masses, nor of how his mind would look once he left, a year later. All of that was forgotten, just as all thoughts of the future were forgotten: put aside, the attention was given to parties held in honor of him, held in honor of his achievements, to the beaches where he went to sit and stare at the sand, the sound of the waters flooding into his ears, his mind, his eyes closed. The scent of new life was like a long hungered-for resurrection of the spirit—the total mood was one of enjoyment within the Now, within the real senses of the present, for time had come to a standstill and all that the eye could conceive and comprehend was there before it. Much plainer than the nose of Cyrano's face. But then, that nose caused Cyrano no end of grief, it was the cause of his blushings, his stammerings when faced with the reality of his existence. Eugene O'Neill had said that, "stammering is the native eloquence of us fog people." And this tongue-tied Hoodlum tried to break out of that habit, as fiercely as he had been reared to break habits.

He sought out his father, going into the heart of south Los Angeles, for reasons why he should continue to live, though that purpose was hidden under another guise: he was worried about the pregnancy of his sister, her being left stranded in the world after bravely venturing out on her own to sample it, her rude shock at being discovered without knowledge of refuges within herself so that she was left marooned on a sea of leering faces. For three hours that conversation lasted. It spoke of the draft, of what the Army had meant to him as he sought out purpose in life. It spoke of how lonely a man can be who has no home to call his own, no family to call his own: though his children come to see him, he is not theirs, not like "Ozzie and Harriet and David and Rickey," not like singing stars or glamour queens divorcing one husband and picking up another one. As his father said, "I wouldn't marry a woman for her money. She'd have to be a little more than pretty, too. She'd have to understand some of the facts about life."

But the Hoodlum did not want to understand some of the facts of life. He wanted to see where there was some justification for these facts, and so the conversation ended as suddenly as it had begun, for the mind of the man had closed and it trailed off again.

His eyes opened again and he was in Boston. He was in Harvard Square, in the Old Commons, the day bright and the opening of school still three days off. Thoughts reeled in of childhood and growing up. The sight of Mama waving good-bye. My sisters laughing. Irvin's crooked grin concealing his devilish heart. Mr. Anderson and Mrs. Trotter, former high school teachers and friends. Both of them, standing there beneath the plane, so small and yet, so BIG. Watts was just as big as they were. Where was everybody? But then, he wasn't lost. He was in Harvard Square, away from ties he had always hated. He had begun to wonder why he was here, who he was, most of all, why Harvard had let someone with the mark of the ghetto, with the sign of the outcast, into its ivied walls. It was as though Cain had slipped unawares into the Garden of Eden again, but this was a Cain that did not know what his crime was, nor where he was, but only that he did not belong here: neither Harvard, nor Watts would ever be personal worlds for him, and yet they were, because he lived within them.

Now there had been those along the way who sought to look after him. People like Christopher Wadsworth, Senior Advisor at Harvard, and Dr. Dana Cotton, member of the Admissions staff. To him, all of eighteen years old, much of what he saw and felt inspired fear: fear as the voices of the past came into his ears, voices that had predicted failure along the route toward self, voices that never stopped singing in his ear: the voices of the Serpent, the man who wore so much clothing until his body could not be seen and yet who, with but a single question, three words, could disrupt all of his life. *Who are you?* The fear was not of Harvard, but of Watts: a much stronger force than books. He could sit down in dining halls, he could talk with any of a number of people, he could try to study. And then, his sister's face floated across the pages. Here, and then gone. But he could not articulate. He only stammered before the judges, his advisors, these kindly men who sat in on him when he came to them for help: for a help that could not be named, a help that welled up from the bottom of his being, a need that had been there for so long until it was becoming painfully obvious that there could be no life inside of that world. No life was in education if that life had to be shared with the voices of a dead past—a past of Death, whose presence never failed to make itself felt. A presence so overpowering as to draw tears when he sat in his room, isolated, and played the muted trumpet of Miles Davis, played "It Never Entered My Mind," and then turned his gaze outward, into Harvard Yard, into tradition, and history, into all that he had ever read of as a young child striving to find values in life: and could not see because he was blind.

Hello, Mr. Wadsworth, I understand you want to see me?

Yes, I do. How are things here at Harvard for you?

Oh. They're all right, I guess.

Like the way they've been treating you here?

Yes. Everything's all right, I guess. It's an all right place. It hasn't done anything wrong to me I can think of.

Guess it's kind of different from Watts, eh?

Yes. It is a little different from Watts.

How's that?

Well, it ain't anything you can put your finger on. It's like, well, it's like this is a new life, a different place, with different people. It's the kind of thing I expected (seeing surprise on his face), so I don't feel out of place in the sense of running into prejudice.

But then, conversations always ran through those currents for him: he sought to express the difference. It would have been easy to say that he *felt* two different people within him, but he was afraid that someone might overhear and call him crazy. For expressing fears. But this wasn't the simple case, it went much deeper, much further, than an alienation from Harvard society.

Ghettoes are built within the mind, and in one part of the Hoodlum's mind he was *black,* which meant apart from all that is white and stands for white, which meant the faces and opinions of his former friends, those that now were in Watts, behind him and yet in front of him, in front of his face as he sat and talked with Wadsworth: while there was its opposite, that part which had seen the humanity of all men because it had seen the humanity within itself, and known that love could be if only men dedicated their minds to liberation. But to express this was difficult. He would slow down in his speech, some of his Cambridge comrades noticed an overly drawn-out drawl, while at the same time injecting a hatred of white society, a hatred that carried itself into his living quarters. There, walking in late at night from drunken sprees, he found his two white roommates listening to Bach, Mozart.

What is this Mozart *shit?* he would holler, and then, striding to the record player, place atop it jazz albums that were freedom songs: the songs of protest, that spoke out against all the injustices, that were in themselves reflective of the black position, of the position of Watts and black life as it had to reach out for breath in an all-white, and all-dominated superstructure largely unknown to it. A super-society that was predicated upon a foundation of books, of knowledge: the same books that had fed the Hoodlum's soul at night when he was a child. His mind would roll back: there was Dale and Jack and J. C., finally reading *Baldwin* after I've been through King Arthur and so much more of other things until it's almost pitiful. But then, he would be glad at the same time, glad to see the hunger for truth in the faces of others. He had begun to wonder to himself about the possibility of communication amongst peers. That Christmas of 1964, he sat in an old garage in Watts, talking with some of his former childmates, deep in the depth of Harvard and what Veritas might mean for Us.

That's right! They have got so much to read, to see, to understand! IT'S LIKE THEY GOT THE POWER AND THEY DON'T REALLY KNOW IT BUT AS LONG AS WE SIT HERE TALKING ABOUT IT INSTEAD OF GETTING UP AND DOING SOMETHING *WE GONNA ALWAYS BE ON THE BOTTOM, FELLAS!* Yes, he had styled himself a revolutionary. He had majored in African History, would sortie and frequent with the foreign exchange-students. Much of what they said and much of their humor he couldn't understand. But he could sense their own feeling of desolation in this great community, a sense of aloneness that was very much within him, too, and as homing devices are attracted to one another, he came to know of those customs. But he was also a Negro, a fact he couldn't, didn't, escape from: he did sort out other Negroes on the campus and together they formed a group which centered its interests, aspirations, on a black culture: the scene was established for a black dialogue, meetings were called in which other Negroes of the freshman class discussed racial sorespots on the Cantabrigian scene. Then, though no resolutions were ever reached, they always ended the meetings with firm declarations on the strength of black peoples, of their right to survive, of their pride in themselves as future leaders, and on the beauty of the black woman, a beauty that could not be marred in its sensuality—not even by the stated four-hundred-year rape of Prospero.

That was a year of many changes. From revolutionary, the Hoodlum went to mystic. His religion had become one of Godhood, though it concerned no Christian God. He found himself in his room again many nights, questioning his belief in life. Am I a Muslim? Can I, do I, I know that in *some* ways I hate white people, but then there are some that are all right! I can't be a Muslim! But that doesn't make me an Uncle Tom! It was a term that had come to be feared, as many people were becoming aware of the yet-carpetbagging ghost of Uncle Tom stealing in and out of the nights with caches of cash while whites walked away smiling, thinking communication had been established with *comprehensible* Negroes. But nothing is so reprehensible as an Uncle Tom, or the smug face of the white collar that tells of working for everything he's ever gotten in life. As if life wasn't a struggle in the ghetto, but rather, a mere question of survival! What was the difference? What had Harvard become that he thought like this? He lay on his bed into the waking hours, looking at the sun flood the room, the bed, the body, his mind: standing up, he would shiver with the first cold, and then, smile almost ritualistically. To think that I can be here anyway, be here and be mad and be free! Walking into the Co-Op, he bought records, books, gloves, paper, pencil, letterheads, anything he could buy: he charged it willfully, beyond his allowance, wanted to break himself completely, knew that destruction loomed just ahead but rushed on pell-mell.

There was a continued interest in his plans, his future, his life. Many worked with him. Not much was said in those meetings of what impressions were being made. The talk centered around Harvard, Watts, clothes, studies, anything, in fact, but who was talking to who. And why, in the first place! It should have seemed natural to believe that sincerity surrounded every meeting, that this sincerity provoke a concern in his wishes. But the Hoodlum would not have sensed this, nor would he have responded. His world was too clouded, too filled with the spectres of his world, *that* world which now included Harvard as well as Watts, which began to space time and memories: so that there were times when he was afraid of going home, afraid of going there and finding that he wanted Cambridge instead. The exact fear he had when first arriving of wanting Watts more than he wanted Cambridge. The Hoodlum *knew* that he was changing, in name and form as well as in belief. The Hoodlum was dying, he was fighting, kicking, yes, but he was also dying. And this is why he was so sad. No one is happy, not very happy, when a part of them dies, when a fragment of the past begins to recede into the mists.

To be sure, he had encountered prejudice. But it was a subtle kind unknown even to its perpetrator. He had gone to the B'Nai B'Rith House at Harvard, for example, for a party given there one evening by the Hillel Foundation. The place was packed. Of the group he was with, there were six altogether, four whites and two Negroes, not much in the way of overt attention was paid. But then, as our Hoodlum stood away from even this group, in a corner, watching the people, hearing the sounds of the party, listening to the wonderment in his own eyes, a small, bespectacled Caucasian fellow strode up to him and, there, from the top of a drink, asked, "Do you feel a little uncomfortable here, if you don't mind my asking?"

"Only if you feel uncomfortable." To know that he did not know that I would not know until the morrow that the B'Nai B'Rith was a Jewish Foundation. Or that Jews had suffering in common with us Negroes, and that they, too, were meeting injustice in the present world.

There were questions that could not be so easily answered, though: What does *your* father do for a living? No, he wasn't a Civil Service employee. Then, he was not unemployed. He could not answer that question. He did not know the answer. My father is a laborer. The hardest kind of worker, because to hustle in the streets, knock someone in the head and take their money, run away, that would be so much easier a way to survive. Always in fear of capture. If it wasn't the police who were after you, it was your wife: Why don't you go out and get a job? Oh, I suppose there ain't any work that's *good enough* for you? Things that prep school kids would not understand, had not been raised to understand, might not ever understand. Why were black men so concerned about being black men? Why did they insist on making things so difficult to explain, making civil rights the perpetual subject of discussion—Watts was forever on the lips of white boys, wanting to know what it was like. Is it really that bad? Have you ever seen anyone shot? Is there really police brutality? Have you ever been shot at?

They had never seen the lonely unlit streets of Watts. Had never been afraid at night, typing or reading, of the animal sounds. Look out the window and see the dog packs roaming the streets of the projects, knock over and then forage through garbage cans, no one chasing them away but only watching. Green beast eyes glowing in the night, out of the night, and the moon, the moon's pale light, above your head as you gazed back into those eyes, into their unthinking depths, and heard the low guttural growls of the beast. He feared dogs, a feeling quite unlike even his closest friends on that campus, in that world. Negroes from middle-class backgrounds who had attended prep schools and achieved glowing records. Negroes from South Side Chicago housing projects who taught him how to light matches against the wind. Harvard Negroes, who believed in themselves and looked on life, all of life, as part of the game. The Education Game: to play it you have to seem it, have to become so much a part of the accepted stereotyped portraiture of the aspiring Negro that you finally become accepted. But acceptance was not really this feeling. It would have been as easy to accept the dog packs. Thoughts of Harvard, of the long-haired, well-groomed dogs that strode, romped through the Freshman Yard—friendly dogs, *cared for* by their owners. Could it be that in the dog packs, in Watts, he saw himself and his friends? So close to fighting over garbage, the garbage that life dumped out to you, in trash cans called haunted schoolyards and wind-swept playgrounds: where the only sound was the continual grating of the rings, the iron rings, suspended by chains, swinging back and forth over the sandpit, the housing projects silhouetted in the gray stormy weather against the horizon—one's face turned toward the projects above the buildings into the gray-ness of God's Heaven. Where little kids fought over games, spilled blood, and ran in gangs while inside those buildings, locked away from sight of the world, fought the owners of the children: to have the love of a child.

But what did they say whenever faced with this Hoodlum? Of course, thoughts arose concerning his maturity: what is a man that he tells of youth and youth's own fears, of dogs and people and the hardships, the tragedies. Not as if he were singing a song, but because he simply believed that he had lived this way and that in this survival, he had a particular influence which had to be realized sooner or later. There was fear of a growing rift in that Cambridge. Because he feared the eyes of man, the Hoodlum withdrew, regardless of their interest in his story. Tragedy had withdrawn as it only knew how: the universal had been tapped, no matter how slightly or unseemingly, in the lives of all who had grown to know him, and within that human shell another life was being born: I stepped forth, aware that a man can create a ghetto within the confines of his own mind. Stake out the preposed bor-derlines of blackness and whiteness: move at that instant into the outside world, itself both black and white, a world of externals and appearances: become two people, black and white, not Good and Evil. Learn to immerse oneself into the plights, the stories, of other people because you can tap the extent of sorrow in the lives of all you meet. Tell Negroes to beware of their blackness: it may be but another white man's values. Tell whites of how books, of how *Bleak House,* can become real, the fog a part of your nostrils: your sister pregnant and your mind totally detached from this reality: that you moved intermittently between Harvard and Watts, afraid of committing yourself to one or the other completely. No one could tell me anything. I knew what the answers were. There was only one question that had everyone confused.

It was the middle of the school year. It was the beginning of spring, Christmas was over and so, too, was much of the light-hearted air that had atmospherized Harvard Yard during its opening three months. Now, education had set in and our Hoodlum raised himself from his bed to look out of the window, to take stock of that change in the air, and then, to walk out of the door into the crisp thirty-degree weather before quickly retiring to his room. Damn, it's colder than hell out there! he would mutter—though, of course, the winter had been much colder. He was simply looking for an excuse not to go to class and this coldness was the best excuse he could find. Of course, it would soon be warm, but that did not matter. His bookshelf would always be there, big and with each day's trip to the Harvard Bookstore growing bigger (though we must remember that these book-buying ex-cursions took place in the late afternoon when it had grown commensurately warmer). There was no thought in his mind of attending classes. Was he an ingrate, or a rebel, or a reactionary, some radical, perhaps, if it might not be asking too much, could he well have been simply involved in finding out what life was all about, or is that too simple? If he was a product of the slums, then of what slums, and what sort of product was he?

Did his eyes see Harvard: the Yard and the Yale Game behind, the counseling sessions over with, his position in the movement of things firmly established? No, not really that kind of world. It was too artificial, too involved with the processes of trying to make a better living when all be wanted was to simply let time pass by. He didn't know who Norman Mailer was, though *The Naked and the Dead* was out. Nor had he read James Joyce. *Finnegans Wake*: what was that? Or if one knew who Samuel Beckett and the race-screaming LeRoi Jones (who could sink down into the limpid surfaces of reality and come out with some pretty valid insights into the nature of homosexuality, which scares most college kids) were—then it was just as easy to assume a literary superiority, a greater racial awareness. He was not that involved, in other words, with the world situation at large. You had on your hands a kid who was genuinely wrapped up in trying to make meaning out of a wrecked life instead of scrapping all remembrances of it completely, then having the courage to admit this rejection consciously to himself, and then moving on to restructure a new world. Nothing unusual at all.

To then be aware of what life exacts of you, if one is concerned with this whole business of dying, and it was not the easiest task in the world for the Hoodlum. Many times he found himself using a borrowed joke from a friend to express his morning breakfast greetings in the old freshman dining quarters: "It's your world, squirrel. I'm just trying to get a nut!" And he was, he was in search of an orgasm of physical and spiritual revelation that could not be his consciously during that year because he had not opened himself up to the possibility of there existing other worlds of existence than his own. The typical white rebels were met, these rich kids who had turned away from their parents and those Cadillacs, black (as opposed to the loud whiteness, the white-on-white-in-white Cadillacs of Watts and any other Negro ghetto in America) which used to turn into the Yard on weekends, parents bringing candy and cookies and other various foodstuffs which sooner or later were eaten by everybody but the parents' kid. Like most poor kids, our man would see these goodies and say nothing. "You'll get tremendous cultural exposure!" one former Jordan teacher had told him before he left for Harvard. He did. In sarcastic, biting ways that might have been seen by others but was felt, registered internally, and then left there to realize itself days, weeks, hours, months, years later: perhaps as a sudden laugh, perhaps as a bitter cursing, perhaps a shame, perhaps, and then in greater proportions, as a concern with the twin shingles of the social measuring-scales upon which poverty and affluence are doled out: some suffer, some die, all of us learn what it is to want more. Another teacher had said, "Do you know what *enough* is?—just a little bit more!"

He was on academic probation—make up your grades or flunk out. Only nine out of that class of twelve hundred flunked out. A lot of others took leaves of absence to study themselves, and there were the perpetual Radcliffe cases: those unnamed medical leaves of absence so that some girl could have her illegitimate baby in peace. A world that was, in retrospect, quite similar to Watts. And yet, because of its tremendous freedom, there were the canoe rides on the Concord

River where cold was the name of the air and pretty was the color of the fish, a great deal more warming. Most of the time life back home was cold. Parents here were people you could see and appreciate. Made you wonder why white kids would rebel. If you had the chance, you surely wouldn't walk out on a million-dollar inheritance.

The shocking realization was that this was me, JOHNIE, who had grown up in Watts and had seen policemen literally crack skulls open while women fell to their knees crying like babies at seeing their babies carried off to jail, who had seen his father's house burn to the ground, who had almost become inured to death and blood and tears. Too much of it spoils the novelty. My own morality was not based on a Western system of good and evil, traceable to Plato and Hesiod, Jesus and St. Augustine. Rather, it was a social and cultural orientation to the slums—in which evil was taken for granted and upon it erected a value system of happiness and terror. I knew that I was not alone. My friends, all of us who have been nursed on this world, live according to this system of values. This was something neither Chris Wadsworth, nor Dr. Cotton, nor anyone else in that entire place would have gathered, no farther than seeing a bit of the sun just before it sinks into the sea, and then, until the next day, is lost. They only saw the moon, good people for all that they were, showing human characteristics of love and warmth and sincerity in their work that make definite impressions but which could not at that time be extended into this many-surfaced world.

Some might run the risk of calling it all a dreamworld and they would be wrong, as wrong as those who would call the Hoodlum a racist when all he was, in truth, was a bearer of the imprint from that world. He was beyond even looking back upon his world and calling it sordid, brutal, with a frankness that at times had left him overwhelmed, typical advertising adjectives of revealing books. No, this for him was a dynamism that time and again cost him, cost him friendships and relationships that might have offered a way out of this reality into another: an escape. And he would have been glad for a hand toward escape, though now, when Harvard is superimposed over Watts, though the Hoodlum is placed above my own reflection in the mirror, I suppose there truthfully could have been no escape. Harvard had become a ghostyard, empty. There were animal sounds in the air. The snow had become brown and slushy. Snow was not pretty, it acted as an obstruction. In his way of travel, in my way, and everyone else's. People were laughing and looking real because they tasted joy denied to me. A man can flunk out of school for many reasons.

A man looking into himself must not look too hard, or the reflection will be encased within Reality's mirror. I saw mine, the entire story called the coming of the Hoodlum. I began to wonder if I might ever escape, so that I would come closer to my own salvation. That is right, for I had become a spiritualist, not a mystic. I had entered Harvard an atheist, who went home Christmas and sat in his mother's church taking notes on the Reverend's sermon and then, at the end of the services, when everyone went up and congratulated the minister on his ministerings, had shown where his dialectics differed considerably from his own exhortations to the good and plenty of the land.

On June 7, 1965, exactly nine months later, I returned to Watts. This time it was for keeps, if anything in life can be applied that label. But the Hoodlum was fired, fire: he believed in God. He had believed in the possibility of all men finally coming together, in truth, he had dedicated himself to some personal ministering of his own to the needs of his friends and companions, with whom he had shared the living experience, Watts. There, within that jet, the mind's eyes traveled both back and forth in time, seeing Harvard before arriving that September 21, 1964, and leaving that June day, seeing Christmas and seeing Jordan High, seeing all that he was. Most of all, understanding that things would have to be different from here on out. Something had happened, he did not know what. But there was one thing that had to be true: he was more than a year older, he had done a lot more than party late at night, or lose his virginity, or take Chinese Philosophy. He had changed. Back home.

The last thing he remembered reading in the Harvard *Crimson* was that applications this year for those 1,200 spots had risen to 6,500. To be sure, there would be more Negroes. It has been getting like that all across the country. But then, that was progress. This, 1965, would be the year, His year: his resolution. And in August of that year, Watts and all of Los Angeles would burn before he began understanding why life was so much dearer than death.

Ticket to Freedom

JOHN R. POSEY

"Boy, you act like you been here before," announced my father at the dinner table. "And that ain't good." He shook his head in frustration like he knew that I would someday pay a heavy price for that character trait.

"What you mean Pop?" I asked, knowing that this conversation was going to lead to a point of no return. It always did when he started speaking in that cryptic fashion like he was an old, African griot slapping one of life's lessons upside my thick head as part of my rites-of-passage to black manhood.

I slapped two chicken legs on my plate, waiting for him to take me on this journey to only he knew where. I knew one thing for certain; I was the passenger and he was driving this train and we weren't stopping until he dropped his size eleven's on the brake.

"It ain't good for a young, black man to be so wise. It scares white folks," he advised as he reached for the bowl of collard greens and piled four, gigantic spoonfuls next to the mound of corn bread on his plate. "And scared white folks is bad for your health."

"Huh?"

"Son, I've watched you look white folks square in the eyes. You walk around huffin' and puffin' like you and they equal." He splashed hot sauce on his greens, heaped a stack in his mouth and let out an ear-shattering belch. "You sportin' that wild Afro and talkin' like them young fools at CORE and SNCC. That scares me son, 'cause white folks ain't got no problems takin' an uppity nigger on that final journey to meet his maker."

Another tremor roared from the bowels of his vast midsection. "This is Dallas. And some things ain't gonna ever change in the Big D," he offered with the resignation of a man beaten down by life.

"Billie Dahhden. Say excuse me," scolded my mother in her chicken-fried voice. "Raght now. I mean it."

She plunked her hand on a plush, round hip and whipped her neck and gave Pop that "I'm-pissed-off-and-you-better-get-your-house-in-order" look that makes a smart black man change his ways.

Momma Darden was a petite woman, with smooth, muted brown skin, cat eyes and caramel-colored hair. Her legs bent in opposite directions—no doubt inherited in the genetic sweepstakes. Lillie Mae was a proud woman with regal air that filled a room when she graced it with her presence. Momma taught me that style was a matter of mindset, rather than money.

"You settin' a bad example for that boy and ah don't like it." She pushed her glasses up her slender nose. "Ah'm tryin' to raise him to be a gentlemen. Ah don't want him actin' like he don't have no home trainin' just cause you don't know no better."

"I'm sorry baby," Pop mumbled as he ducked his head to avoid another frontal assault from Momma. "Scuse me Son," slipped out between Pop piling another mound of greens in his mouth.

Pop and Momma had been married for eighteen uneventful years. I wondered if they ever really were in love or just got tired of searching for the ideal partner and settled on each other—warts and all. Over time, they developed a quiet love, based on mutual respect and trust. Nothing fancy, but solid. I should be so lucky.

Pop learned from experience that Momma could kick your butt with her razor-sharp tongue. When Lillie Mae Darden's mouth went to work, it was like watching a surgeon performing an operation. Momma could talk about you so bad all you wanted to do was find a hole, crawl into it, and heap dirt on yourself. Nobody messed with momma, unless they wanted their feelings hurt.

Lillie Mae was a piece of work. She escaped from a hard scrabble life in Lubbock, Texas. Times were tough for black folks in Lubbock back then. Schools were bad. Good jobs were scarce as hen's teeth. Everything was segregated. And blacks served as little more than indentured servants for white folks as their nannies, butlers, maids, porters, cooks, and sharecroppers.

Momma liked to say that "slavery is alive and well in Lubbock. I don't care what Mr. Lincoln did. They only lets black folks have a taste of freedom on Juneteenth. Then they snatch it back at the first hint of midnight."

Life was even tougher for Momma since she was a bastard, a half breed. It seems the county sheriff infected Grandmomma's essence one night after she cleaned the jail's toilets. Oh, they gave Grandmomma her day in court. Then the grand jury threw the case out. Something about "two adults and mutual consent." Justice is a capricious beast in West Texas.

Black folks laughed at Momma and called her all kinds of half-breed names. There's no doubt in my mind why Momma was so color conscious. "Black is a state of mind not a shade of color," she drummed into me whenever people made fun of my cream colored skin.

Lubbock white folks avoided her like she carried the plague in her bosom. She might as well have been a ghost because people looked right past her. Lillie Mae Darden was a living reminder of the double standards of justice that existed between black and white folks. But people don't discuss those things in the "genteel South." It's not proper.

When Momma graduated from high school, she packed up her meager belongings, headed for Dallas, married Pop, and never looked back. Lillie Mae built up a nice little seamstress business making clothes for the rich, white ladies in Highland Park. She made enough money to get me a private tutor to compensate for the inferior education of the public schools. Ms. Lillie was a retired principal and smart as they come. I learned more in three hours a week from her than from all my teachers combined.

Whenever somebody challenged Momma, she jumped on them like they had stolen something. The only thing Lillie Mae Darden was afraid of—outside of the Almighty—was going back to Lubbock, Texas. Momma wouldn't even go back for Grandmomma's funeral. Just sent flowers. Everybody in the family begged her, but she was stubborn as a mule about it.

I don't blame her. Lubbock left nothing but shattered glass in the windows of her mind. The Klan killed her oldest brother, Willie. He had gone off to Howard and gotten his law degree, and his life looked bright as the sun in full force.

When Uncle Willie came back home, he was different. Living in the North had changed his perspective and heightened his expectations.

At first nobody thought anything unusual about Uncle Willie spending time at the library reading all those law books until he decided to sue the Board of Education to integrate the schools. Why did he want to do that? White folks didn't take too kindly to educated black folks challenging their system of laws.

One day, on his way to the courthouse reality snatched him by the back of the shirt. When it turned him loose, the black folks in Lubbock understood the consequences of speaking up for equality. I believe that's what the think tank intellectuals call an object lesson.

That was in 1945. Momma was eight. She never forgave my Grandmomma for staying in Lubbock. Things like that have a way of sticking in your mind—kinda like white on rice.

Pop always followed his mysterious statements with more confusion. He'd take a draw on his cigarette, swirl the smoke in his lungs and ask me, "Didn't you learn anything in your first life?" Then he'd wait for my answer while he was quietly killing us both with his bad habit.

What was I supposed to say? I was thirteen and the most challenging thing that crossed my mind was how to get Freda Jones on her daddy's couch. Like most teenagers I couldn't remember what I did last week. And he's asking me to recall a previous first life? Please.

But I wasn't going to bring it to him like that because Pop cast a big shadow in my world. We're talking huge. Pop just walking into a room put fear into most people. He had hands as large as Virginia hams. When we horseplayed and he clutched my peanut head, it felt like someone had covered it with a salad bowl. He could blot out the sun with his huge body.

After dinner and a couple of shots of Gordon's Gin, he would take me into the living room to finish our one-sided, man-to-man talk. He'd put his hand on my shoulder and tell me to sit on the cold, plastic-covered couch that Lillie Mae only let her children sit on during holidays.

Pop rambled on about how, at birth, I wore the look of someone who had graced this earth at another point in time. Wisdom dominated my cherubic, bronze face and steel forged my heavyset eyes. "I saw the sadness in your face—you wore the look of a man who had witnessed great tragedy and injustice. You must have been black in that life too," he added taking a long pull on the gin.

He told me the nurses nicknamed me "little man" because I only weighed five pounds at birth. I was two months premature. The doctors didn't think I'd survive the night. Guess I was too evil to die. He said he knew then that I would always have a special way with women. Pop swore, through his tobacco-stained teeth, that he saw a couple of them stick their phone numbers in my diaper bag. If lying was a profession, Pop would have made a hell of a lawyer. I guess that's why he drove a cab in South Dallas. Looking back through the prism of time, I think Pop was trying, in his uniquely convoluted fashion, to get me to understand what it meant to be a strong, black man in a society that penalizes you for your skin color.

Pop's lying aside, I come from proud stock on his side also. We can only trace my family back five generations to a sugar plantation in Louisiana. But judging from the stories my great aunts told me, it's not hard to imagine my ancestors being from the great Yoruba tribes that dominated the plains of Africa and refused to bend to the oppression of slavery on South's plantations.

Grandpa Darden carried on the family tradition in compelling fashion. He was an octoroon. Blood was blended with more white than black. He could have passed like his sister did, but chose to exist in the world of living color.

Grandpa died two months before I was born. From all accounts, he sounds like one part Malcolm X and one part Adam Clayton Powell. All the elders in my family say that I'm the spitting image of him because of my fiery spirit.

As family legend has it, the year was 1920 when destiny changed his life. Grandpa was walking with his family along the broad boulevard leading to Fair Park during the State Fair. Black folks weren't welcome on the grounds in those days.

A white man, riding in his buggy, flashed by Grandpa and cursed him for blocking his path. Grandpa told him where he could put his buggy. He thrashed Grandpa with his horsewhip. Being a strong black man or a damned fool, depending on who you ask, Grandpa pulled out his .22, shot him in the chest, and left him staining the ground.

Imagine shooting a white man in Dallas in 1920? Grandpa gathered the Darden clan and caught the first thing smoking due north. The freedom ride ended on the east side of Cleveland. Pop came back to Dallas after serving in World War II.

Grandpa set a civil rights standard for the family. He headed the local NAACP Branch for 29 years. We were taught not to take anything from white folks. "Look 'em in the eye and don't back down," was the family motto. Momma used to say "You just as good as they are." I believed what she told Me. I'm still waiting for them to come around to my way of thinking.

"Momma. I don't wanna go to no all-white, Catholic school," I argued and slammed my acceptance letter from Saint Phillip's on the kitchen table.

"Those white people don't want me there. And I don't want to go." I poured a glass of milk and sucked it down to quench my anger. "I want to go to Lincoln."

It was an official looking envelope with a red crest at the top of the page like the ones the Christians used during the crusade. The words Saint Phillip's were in bold letters underneath. The motto *We mold boys into men* was in italics at the bottom of the page. The letter was very direct and cold, like it was written by a man who had pledged a life of celibacy. A life without knowin' a woman's love will take the emotion out of a man, I guess.

Dear Mr. and Mrs. Darden:

The Board of Trustees of Saint Phillip's Academy is pleased to inform you that your son Stephen has been accepted for the incoming class of 1969. We look forward to his matriculation and have every reason to believe that he will uphold the high academic and moral standards of this institution. If you have any questions, please don't hesitate to call me.

Sincerely,

Father John J. O'Conner
Principal

I stalked around the room waiting for Momma's inevitable response. She had been oddly silent during my tantrum, sewing together a quilt for the Van Patton family. I should've known that was the quiet before the storm.

Momma slammed her fist on the table knocking the colorful fabric and needles across the room. "Sit down young man! Raht now," she demanded as her gray-green eyes narrowed to two, beady dots. " 'Fore you do. Please pick up my material from off the floor."

I stooped down and collected the fabric up and put it in her basket. As I walked over to the table and moved the *Dallas Post Tribune* and cereal bowl over to the counter, the headline caught my attention, "Blacks Boycott Downtown Diner." Hundreds of young blacks circled the store with their picket signs singing "We Shall Overcome."

Momma touched my hand to salve the pain of her harsh words. Momma's soft, finely manicured hands smelled like cocoa butter. "Honey. I wants you to go to that school so you can have the opportunity to do things your father and me can only dream about."

"Momma, nobody black ever went to that school," I heatedly protested. "Why do I have to go?"

"Baby, things is changin' all over the United States because of Dr. King," smiled Momma as she leaned back in her chair and pushed the sleeves up on her blue sweater. "Black people can eat where they want and go to schools with white children."

"Momma. They can pass all the laws they want. White folks ain't gonna accept us as their equals." My eyes bounced off of hers. "Why you think we were slaves for over three hundred years? Besides, things are changing cause black folks are burning down cities and listenin' to what Malcolm X preached. He's the prophet for young people, Momma. They're tired of all this praying."

"That may be," she replied coyly setting the trap as she cupped my arm. "But they ain't burnin' down nothin' in Dallas."

"That's cause all the black preachers have been bought and paid for by the Citizen's Council."

"Say that again boy," Momma challenged indignantly. "What you know about that kinda thing?"

"It's true Momma," I countered with attitude. "Everybody knows it."

"Then men from the Citizen's Council is some of my best customers," Momma yelled. Her eyes were glaring with anger. "If it wasn't for them, you wouldn't have this ticket to freedom," Momma said as she violently shook the admission letter in my face. "They done more for us than our own people."

"Momma. Wasn't it you that said don't trust white folks that want to give you something for nothing?" I challenged. My heart hung in the balance. I had never taken Lillie Mae on, but I could tell that my words cut deeply. No one had ever questioned her loyalty to the white men who ran Dallas.

Momma slowly dragged over to the stove and poured a cup of chickory-laced coffee into the scarred brown cup. She turned around and looked right through me. I pulled eyes away from her to avoid her intense gaze. I just knew Momma knew what I was thinking. And she knew I knew. And I knew that she didn't give a good damn that I knew. Lillie Mae was tryin' to will me into going to that school. But I wasn't buying her freedom ticket argument, if I could help it.

"How you know 'til you tried? Or are you jes plain old scared?" she hissed across the table.

Momma had played her trump card. She knew that a Darden couldn't back down from a challenge.

"I'm not scared of them white boys," I said in an angry whisper.

Momma smiled and slowly moved her lips. "Then what's your problem honey?" She lifted the letter and fanned it back and forth in my face. "This is your ticket to freedom. Are you going to cash it in? Or do you want to spend the rest of yo' life drivin' a cab like yo' daddy?"

I squirmed in the chair trying to find the right words to deflect Momma's attack. I watched the birds hunting for worms in the grass. The cool wind brushed the tree limbs against the house. I was silent for a long time. I knew Momma was sizing me up for the kill.

"Momma. All my friends are going to Lincoln," I weakly shot back. "I don't know anybody at that stupid school."

"Honey, you can make new friends," she laughed. " 'Sides, you'll find out that they really ain't your friends, only acquaintances." Momma pulled the needle through the taffeta fabric and propped her elbows on the table. "Let somethin' bad happen to you and see how quick they scatter for cover. Like roaches when the light goes on." Then Momma said softly, "Will you go for me?"

After I heard Lillie Mae say that, I tried to draw a mental picture of the school and the sea of white faces that would flood the halls every day. And wearing a necktie every day. Could I make friends with white boys, I wondered? How would I act when they called me nigger, which they surely would? Damn her. I turned toward the refrigerator and nodded my head weakly. I suddenly felt older than the banks of the Nile.

"Hey nigger," shouted the red-headed boy. "Why don't you go back to the jungle with the rest of the monkeys?"

A banana landed at my feet as I walked toward my locker. So this is what freedom was like?

"I don't like you people," snarled Moose Burnett, the huge guard on the football team, as he knocked the books from under my arms. Moose wore a crew cut that was so short you could see what he was thinking. His red letter sweater, with the big gray "P" perched over his chest, was bursting, barely concealing his powerful arms. "Why should I have to block for a nigger. You ain't smart enough to learn the plays. Why don't you go back to South Dallas and be with your own kind."

A crowd quickly gathered as I carefully stooped down to pick up my books. Watching Moose out of one eye, I stood up and looked at him. "And why don't you kiss the raw part of my black ass you fat pig?"

Moose descended on me. I moved to the left and gave him a push. He crashed into the lockers. He charged me and tried to tackle me waist high. I smashed my algebra book into his broad, flat nose. He fell and I kicked him hard in the ribs once, then a second time for good measure. Moose groaned.

I began to laugh hysterically. Moose got up holding his ribs, "If you don't block for me, I'ma kick your ass again."

Moose limped off to his next class.

Molly Flaherty's face was covered with freckles that highlighted her strawberry blonde hair and ended long past her shoulders. The golden orb of morning bounced off her freshly scrubbed face. Molly's hair was pulled back in a neat ponytail. She had a ready smile that brought joy to everyone.

Molly went out of her way to speak to me every morning on the school bus that we shared with the girls who attended our sister school, Sacred Heart. She was one of those rare people who didn't see a color when she looked in your face.

One clear, November morning, Molly plopped down in the seat next to me. Her leg felt warm and vibrant. I had never been this close to a white female. Her hair smelled of lilacs. My stomach turned flips as I thought about how many black men had met an untimely end for less.

"You played a wonderful game on Saturday. How many touchdowns did you score?" She asked and elbowed me playfully. Molly winked oblivious to the cold stares that knifed her in the back. My heart hummed like an airplane motor.

Lord, what was this white girl up to, I wondered? The silence was earsplitting. It grew louder and louder until it filled the bus. I looked past her reflection gleaming in the window and counted the tops of the elm trees guarding the elegant homes along majestic Swiss Avenue.

"Three," I mumbled.

Someone got up and offered her his seat. She waved him away. "Three? Wow, that's fantastic." She moved a little closer and asked me if I wanted to be her date for homecoming.

The bus slammed to a stop.

The driver, Barney, was a gruff old man about sixty who had stuttered and stammered his way through life. I had once heard him say that he was originally from Mount Pleasant in East Texas. He wore Dickey jeans and T-shirts with a pocket over his heart. A can of Red Man always peeked out of his shirt pocket. Tobacco juice stained the floor mat under his eelskin boots

Barney had never called me nigger before, at least not to my face. But he said it in his fierce, gray eyes every morning when I walked past him to my seat. There was a fierceness borne of a tradition that reached back to his parent's parents. The hate was drawn on his eyelids and formed an invisible shield, like the white robe I'm sure he wore on his night rides terrorizing decent, black folks.

"G . . . G . . . G . . . Get in the f . . . front of the . . . the b . . . b . . . bus," he ordered as he pulled me by my sleeve.

"What did I do?" I asked as I got up and walked with him. I decided there was no sense in confronting him. When I got to the front, all the seats were taken. I turned to him. "Where do you want me to sit?" I asked.

He jerked open the front door. "I . . . I . . . d . . . d . . . don't wantchu . . . t . . . t . . . to . . . s . . . sit anywhere. G . . . get y . . . your b . . . black ass off m . . . m . . . m . . . my b . . . bus," and shoved me down the stairs.

"Mr. Darden, please hand me your demerit card," demanded Father O'Rourke, the stern-faced vice principal. His wrinkled skin looked like a well-worn ballet. He was an ex-boxer who had some moderate success in New York's tough CYO tournaments. Father kept a pair of boxing gloves hanging in his office to convert the hardheaded to the ways of Saint Phillip's. A real tough guy in the John Wayne tradition.

I reached into my wallet and handed him my card. He snatched it and deftly punched two holes through the numbers four and five. Bingo.

"Mr. Darden, it appears you will be my guest for Jug this Saturday morning," he sneered. "Please make sure you bring your dictionary." He turned. I hesitated. Now was the time to stop him.

Jug was Saint Phillip's way of instilling fear and ensuring conformance to their rigid code of conduct. Once you got your fifth demerit, you were Father O'Rourke's guest for a day of memorizing a page of the dictionary, sanding desks, and doing any other odd jobs that needed to be done.

"Er . . . excuse me Father O'Rourke," I asked, "What did I do?"

"Look on your locker," he told me and abruptly headed for his office. He turned and said sharply, "You'll be painting it on Saturday."

I ran down the hall and slid around the corner. I stared at my locker for a long time. I pushed back my anger. The noise and the people no longer mattered as the words *Nigger, Coon, Darkie, Jungle Bunny,* and *Tar Baby* screamed at me. I twisted the lock and the latches clicked. I yanked the door open quietly and dropped my English book in the locker.

Father Fahey was my Latin teacher. A crinkly, orange shock of hair served as sort of a barricade protecting the broad, empty space on his head that cast a shadow on his glassy eyes. Years of tossing down cheap bourbon had sucked the life out of his cheeks and carved dark circles in his face. He eased around the classroom with short painful steps, like he had a permanent case of hemorrhoids.

He ran his classroom like a marine drill instructor—which he had been. Conjugating verbs was our daily military exercise. Failure to complete an assignment earned the offender a stern backhand upside the meaty part of the head and fifty sit-ups. The wonders of a Catholic education.

Father Fahey was a small man, with an even smaller mind. He made it clear to me that he didn't like black people from day one. However low his opinion of me was as a person, his expectations for my performance were even lower.

"Calvin, I don't expect much from you," he told me. "My experience with Negro students, in the North, is that they don't do well in Latin. It's not your fault. You people don't excel academically," he pontificated before the entire class. Everyone exploded into laughter.

Embarrassed, I slid deep into my seat until shoulders were level with the desk top. A fly landed on my lip. The thought of what Momma would do to me if I smacked this arrogant white man helped me slam my mouth shut before I could tell him where he could stick his opinion. It was eerie. Suddenly I felt my grandfather's hand stroking my shoulder and holding me back. As I turned my head, I swear I heard him say, "Not now. It'll be okay." Damn if it was okay.

It was a windy, May morning. This was the final week of the semester. Track season was ending on Monday. The fresh bluebonnets were sprinkled around the base of the broad-shouldered cedar tree outside the classroom. The housing projects loomed large off in West Dallas. I stared out the window at the small airplane that buzzed in and out of the clouds headed toward Love Field.

Father Fahey handed me my weekly test back. The grade eighty-four, in red jumped off the page. I checked his corrections carefully. Once. Then a second time. My calculations showed I scored a ninety-five. This was the third time he had made an "error."

Momma had been into visit with Father Fahey about this problem on two other occasions: once with Pop and once by herself. He reassured Momma that it was an honest mistake. Lillie Mae was a normally skeptical person, but each time his flimsy excuses left her appeased. Momma wanted me in this school so bad she could taste it. She was living her dreams through my eyes. I guess she wanted white folks to accept her through my accomplishments.

I raised my hand and asked if I could come up to his desk. Putting my paper gently on the desk, I politely asked, "Father, could you please review my score? I think my grade should be a 95, not an 84."

The gold cross swung carelessly about his neck. His head shot up from his grading book. Anger clouds formed in his sallow eyes and he was still—like he was frozen in time. Father Fahey turned living color red. I guess you'd call it crimson. He slammed his pencil against the desk and fragments shot across the room. One hit me in the eye.

"How dare you challenge me, *nigger*," he shouted. "You shouldn't even be in this school." He pointed to my desk and ordered me to, "Sit your black ass down."

I clutched my eye and felt my morning meal of two scrambled eggs and bacon climbing up my throat. I could see Father Fahey, through my tears and snot, from the corner of my other eye. I brushed my sleeve across my runny nose. No one can talk like that to me, not even a priest, I thought. My eyes turned directly on his. Steel met glass. The window panes shattered under the intensity of my gaze. Anger surged through me like lightning.

I can't remember what happened first, but it was the way he looked at me that set me off. Maybe it was everything that had happened since I began this long journey to freedom. The locker. Jug. Moose. The bus driver. White people. Sell-out ministers. Racism.

Grandpa's spirit flashed before me, dark on darkness. I thought I heard him say, "Okay, now." My head was pounding. I shifted my weight and began to run blindly in Father's direction. My mouth was open far wider than I imagine possible. I never heard sounds like those that came out of my mouth. He tried to shield himself from my vicious punches and kicks. I looked into his eyes one last time.

"Who's the *nigger* now?" I shouted clutching his throat with the rage of a man gone mad.

"Who?"

"I am," he murmured. "I am," he cried and then he fainted.

The ghost was exorcised.

I spent the afternoon sitting uncomfortably in the supply closet, surrounded by mountains of textbooks, rulers, pens, and paper, waiting for the board of advisors to determine my future. The room was dark. Darker than any room that I had ever been in. I could hear the second hand sweeping, sweeping, sweeping its eternal journey. If only I could turn back the hands of time and erase this nine-month nightmare that had descended upon my head like a swarm of locusts, devouring everything in sight. This had been no ticket to freedom Momma. It was more like a passport to hell.

An uneasy tension gripped my stomach so hard that I doubled over in pain. I suspect it was the anticipation of a man who is about to be executed. My only question was how was I going to die? There was a familiarity about this experience. Maybe Pop was right. Maybe I had traveled this path before. As Crispus Attucks. Or Nat Turner. Or John Brown. Or Garvey. Or Paul Robeson.

Someone turned the handle of the door. When he entered, a sudden light burst into the room. It scalded my eyes. This stranger was tall and thin and his white collar rode tightly on his red, chapped neck. His jaw was set. The small, black eyes told me everything I needed to know. He handed me an envelope and ordered me to clean out my locker. The rest of his speech I did not hear. I folded my hands, shifted my head down and said a little prayer of thanks.

The school bus shook violently to a halt at Sacred Heart. The drab, red bricks served as an appropriate backdrop for the tight-lipped nuns, shrouded in their white and black costumes, guarding the horde of giggling, bubble gum-chewing girls. Among the phalanx of plaid uniforms, I spotted a shimmering, blonde pony-tail bobbing back and forth through the crowd. Molly Flaherty scurried to the front of the line.

She leaped on the bus. Molly's brilliant blue eyes blinked off and on like turn signals. Her face full of distress creased her even, polished forehead. "What happened?" Molly asked as she dropped down next me, her cheeks stained from sobbing.

I noticed the panicked look on her face. "What happened?" she demanded. Molly shook me hard, "Please tell me," she pleaded.

"Got expelled," I admitted quietly. Someone yelled out, "nigger lover," but it bounced off Molly harmlessly into the afternoon breeze.

"Why?"

"It's . . . it's," I stumbled out, "sorta . . . uh complicated."

I explained the incident as best I could to this sweet girl who didn't see a color, but simply judged me as a human being. I showed her the letter and watched Molly closely as she read it several times. She seemed to deliberate over every word searching for any subtle implications. Molly carefully folded it and expressed her sympathy and disgust at the hate and viciousness of her people toward blacks. I told her not to worry, god just didn't make me to be a pioneer. To be a pioneer, you have to be an early settler I explained. And I didn't have the meek personality that the job description called for.

A sheet of lightening discharged and severed my words into one thousand shreds of sound. Thunder boomed across the low, gray clouds; I rested my head against the window and watched the wet pellets bouncing crazily off the ground. It was something about rain that comforted me. The steady beat of the raindrops hypnotized me and made me relax. Maybe I enjoyed the rain because the clouds protected me from the rest of the world.

I reached for the smeared, crumpled envelope buried in my jacket pocket. I watched a squadron of crows buzz over the even row of trees. Beyond the angry sky, I could barely see an orange ball of light that helped shed the revelation that I lived in a land that was not my own. I smiled at Molly, let the window down, and cast my letter to the wind. It was spring. A time for new beginnings.

Judah's a Two-Way Street Running Out

JACK BURRIS

Clay looked up from the newspaper when the figure passed, recognized it as a woman from his neighborhood, and started to smile, but then he saw the ice in her eyes, remembered he was a city-boy now, and reraised the newspaper. *"That's the trouble with them niggers,"* he thought, addressing to himself the words he had so often heard spoken about himself and others. *"They don't stick together. Ain't got no gumption, 'less you wave a relief check at 'em."* *"Who, me, boss?"* he answered his own charges, amused by the game, now that he no longer had to play it.

"Heck, boss, not me. All I wants to do is sit here in the back of the bus and ride out to Judah street so I can get me a job. That's all I want, honest, boss. Then, I'll go home and eat my watermelon and dance in the mud and sing my happy songs for you and then maybe tonight I'll poke a pickaninny up the old lady if she ain't too tired from scrubbin' yore floors an' stealin' yore food. Honest, boss, that's all I want."

Except that wasn't all he wanted, and they would spot the lie quickly enough and bring him to account. Or maybe not. Maybe this time they wouldn't. Or maybe they wouldn't even care. That card was due to come up, too. Claire Mae had promised. The least he could do for her was sit there in the back of the bus and ride it out, even to the last stop, if he had to go that far.

Only he wasn't really on the back of the bus, of course. He was sitting in the front seat of a street-car, where he always sat, or at least as often as he reasonably could. Claire Mae had teased him about it, had asked him if he thought he was proving something to somebody, and he had answered that the only thing it proved was they were living in San Francisco now, and he supposed any black-ass fool could tell that quickly enough just by looking out the window. He still sat at the front of buses, though, knowing that there would be time enough later for indifference.

Looking through the hair-oil smeared window, he carefully checked the address given in the newspaper against those painted on the windows of the stores they were passing. *Two more blocks,* he decided, and lifted his arm, preparing to pull the cord that would signal his desire to stop. He hesitated, though, not knowing exactly where the streetcar's next stop was and not wanting, in his eagerness, to be forced to walk those last two blocks just because he'd signaled too early.

While he waited, undecided, he felt the cord sliding through his slippery fingers and heard the bell tinkle in front of him. Surprised, and even mildly disappointed, he stood up immediately and walked toward the doors at the back, even though he had to fight against several people who were forcing their way to the front. *There's time enough for me to do that later, too,* he thought, pausing to let an old woman step before him. *Today I'm going to obey all them dumb ofay's rules.*

Stepping down, he quickly spotted the building in the next block that was his destination. Claire Mae had described it well that morning, just as she had carefully described the whole neighborhood for him. She had done so partially to avoid his getting lost again, as he had done when he first went downtown to look for work, but he knew her detailed description had also come from her nervousness, her unspoken desperation. He'd spotted that quickly, right at the start, when she'd looked up from ironing his shirt and said, in all seriousness, "You'll recognize Judah easily enough. It's a two-way street running out to the ocean."

He'd wanted to stop her then, to ask her mockingly how many ways the street ran when it came back from the ocean, but she was too painfully intent to interrupt, still too aware of the fact that it had been at her suggestion that they had moved to San Francisco, back to the city of her childhood. Anyway, it was because San Francisco was her city that he had been willing to listen, too grateful for any information she might offer, however humorously expressed, to risk losing it and the security it might later give him. *One thing you can say about me, I never tease the hand that's feeding me. "No Sir, not me, boss."*

Thinking about hands he took out his handkerchief and wiped the sweat from his own hands while he was walking. *"Look, Ma, how good you taught me,"* he thought, remembering now without any real resentment how his mother had told him to always wipe his hand on the inside of his pocket before shaking hands with a white man. She hadn't said it in words, but she made him understand that even a simple thing like sweat, which on another white man would be ignored, on him would be magnified. Once, after she'd died and before Claire Mae had found him, he'd worn pocketless pants, carefully cutting the right, front pocket out of each new pair that he bought, willingly sacrificing the convenience for the sake of the joke. But that was before Claire Mae. She wouldn't see anything funny in it, at least not as long as she was working in a white man's house every day to pay for those pants. So now he left the pockets in and carefully wiped his hands on a handkerchief. *Lo, how the mighty has fallen.*

The door was locked when he tried it. He gave it a second try to make sure, then checked his watch. The ad had said ten o'clock, so he had almost twenty minutes to wait. He considered going to search for a coffee shop, but then balanced that against the impression he might give if he were standing there when the owner arrived. *"Yes, suh, boss, ah's always early. Yes, suh, and no cavities, either."* He decided, instead, to have a cigarette, even though there were only five left in the pack and they had to last the day. He was still standing there in the doorway, enjoying the smoke and the warmth of the early sun, when he saw the other man approaching.

He recognized the man as a neighbor of sorts, in that he lived somewhere in the same overfilled apartment building. Clay had seen him sometimes when he was climbing the stairs or emptying the garbage and the man, usually dressed up as though for Saturday night, would pass silently by, their eyes always failing to make contact. It wasn't that the man was unfriendly, he knew, but simply that in that house the only privacy to be had was in refusing to recognize people. Maybe you had to listen to your neighbor's television and kids and fights and screwings, but you didn't have to recognize those neighbors when you saw them, not even in broad daylight on the stairs.

The man had stopped, looked first at the address on the door, then at Clay, and finally nodded.

"Hi, man."

"Hi," Clay answered, smiling, and offered his hand. "I'm Clay Carter. Live on the third floor, back apartment."

The man nodded again and gave him a smile in return. Clay noticed the mishapen, gold-capped teeth. "Thought I recognized you! I'm William Potter. Only call me Billy, like in goat. I'm staying with my sister and her old man. Up on the top floor." He smiled again, this time without the show of teeth. "Only I won't be tomorrow, 'less something turns up."

Clay nodded this time then watched as the man lit a cigarette. He'd already noticed the man's frayed shirt, dirty at the neck, and the lack of a crease in the trousers of his black suit. "Been looking long?"

"Four months," Billy said. "Before that I had unemployment so I took it easy. Man, I didn't know when I was well off. I had this job deliverin' diapers, see, only I didn't think it was good enough. Not for a college man. So I quit. Hell, I had to learn. Now, man, I'd pick up them dirty diapers with my teeth, they'd let me."

"This is only my second month," Clay said, "but I know what you mean. I got a wife working, so I guess it ain't as bad, but we're just gettin' started out here. So far it ain't been much of a start."

"Man, don't you worry none. Ain't you heard about the Pres-e-dent's new bill? He gets that passed, man, we're gonna' have rights up the ass. Won't even have to work. Just go pick us some money off that money-tree marked 'Niggers Only.'"

"Sure. Only watch out for The Man. He's behind that tree somewhere, and he's got him a shaft marked 'Niggers Only' too."

"Don't you believe that, man! Why, I heard Gov'nor Wallace just last night. Said them dirty coons'll be pickin' the money and the white folks'll have to pick the cotton. Ain't that a shame? Man, I cried all night!"

Clay laughed, enjoying his new friend's gestures as much as the words. "Wonder who they'll burn their crosses for then."

"Why, them dirty commies, of course. They're the ones startin' all this fuss anyway. Them cotton-pickin' niggers wasn't causin' no trouble until them Yankee commies started in."

"I thought the niggers and the commies were one and the same."

"No," Billy said. "They're different. Them commies are sort of bleached-out niggers, see. Didn't you hear about Dr. Dejone? He's the head of the science department down there at good old Georgia U or someplace like that and he wrote this book provin' that all commies are just washed-out niggers. Something about the curse of God and Ham and small heads. I didn't read all of it, but it was something like that."

Clay flicked the butt of his cigarette out over a parked car and into the street. He checked his watch, saw that they still had almost five minutes to wait, and leaned back against the wall of the building. Billy was trying to look through the windows, cupping his hands around his eyes to shut out the outside light.

"I think there's somebody in there."

"Must of come in the back door," Clay said. "You think we have much of a chance?"

"Yeah, man, the best! Ain't we niggers, man? And ain't this old nigger-lovin' San Francisco? Hell, soon as that old white boss looks at us he's gonna' say, 'Coons, you're both hired!'"

Clay laughed, trying to hide his nervousness. "I guess we can always threaten to picket them."

"Picket, hell I'm gonna' tell them if I don't get this job I'll have old buddy Marty come in and pray for them. Hey, watch out, man! Here comes that little old white chick to let us in. Um, um, wouldn't my brother like a piece of that!"

The secretary who had let them into the office also explained to them that Mr. Robertson would be a little late and then helped them fill out the application forms. Then, when these were completed, she showed them two chairs where they could wait. At first Clay had found her attractive, but the more she talked in her phony, dead voice, the more he lost interest. He was grateful to her for her kindness, but he wondered how soon he would hate her if he had to work in the same office. *"Don't worry about that, man. You ain't got the job yet!"*

Although she had given them some magazines to look at while they waited, Clay couldn't get interested in them. Instead he watched the men moving back and forth in the back part of the office. He noticed that there were no Negroes, but he couldn't decide if that were a blessing or a curse. Maybe they would hire him, just to prove their tolerance, but on the other hand maybe they were planning to wait until they absolutely had to before they gave in.

Three other men, all of them white, had come in since he had been sitting, and the secretary was helping them through the problems of the application forms. Clay watched them closely, trying to balance his own qualifications against theirs. They were obviously in less dire need—otherwise they couldn't have afforded such clothing—but he refused to think about that for long, having given up the idea of poetic justice along with his diapers. He overheard them listing some of their qualifications, but not enough to influence him one way or the other. He finally gave up the game, concluding only that two of them might give him some serious competition. The third man, who was still a pimple-scarred youth, he threw into the "Reject" file in his mind, where he had much earlier placed Billy Potter.

"Mr. Carter?"

Clay tried to locate the source of the voice. Turning his head slightly, he saw a large, middle-aged man in a grey, double-breasted business suit. He was holding an application form, and Clay recognized it as his own.

"Yes, sir," Clay answered quickly, standing up and moving toward the man.

"I'm Mr. Robertson," the man said, offering his hand.

"Oh! Sorry, Mama, but this cat ain't goin' to give me no time for wipin'. Okay, ofay, have some sweet sweat!" "How do you do, sir."

"Would you come this way, please."

Clay followed him. The office door had the name Mr. Abraham Robertson printed on it in gold lettering. *Abraham, huh? Like from the Bible. "Well, Abraham, I ain't your Isaac, so don't go gettin' no ideas. I done played that game, Abe. All my life. Honest, Abe, I just want a job, Honest Abe."*

Clay sat down on the edge of the politely-offered chair, refused the cigarette that he needed so badly his mouth watered at its sight, and smiled, thanking God, that there weren't any gold caps on his teeth. Mr. Robertson pretended a fascination with the application form letting him cool his heels, Clay supposed. *"Hey, you dumb ass, I'm over here, not on that piece of paper."*

The message must have been received, for Mr. Robertson looked up, startled. "I see you have an M.A."

"Yes, sir."

"You realize, of course, that the job which is open doesn't require that kind of ability. It's only an accounting position."

"Yes, sir, I know that. But I thought that perhaps it would be a good place for me to start."

The ofay smiled. "You're not too humble to start at the bottom?"

"Don't give me that jazz, man! You want me to clean your toilets for openers? Show me the brush!" "No, sir. To be quite, frank, I need a job. I've only recently moved to San Francisco from the South, and I'm finding it a little difficult to get started."

"Is that begging, Mama?" Okay, so now I'm a beggar. Next week I start peddlin' the dope.

"Yes, I see that on your application form. I don't recognize your college, Mr. Carter."

"It's a Negro college in Alabama, sir."

"Oh."

Clay felt the irritation rising in him like an erection, hard against his gut. *"'Oh.' Is that all it's going to be white man, just 'oh?' One little word not even of sympathy but merely*

*indifference and then the door? You think I wanted to go to that friggin' little school? You think
I couldn't have made it at Harvard if I'd had the chance?"* His fingernails cutting into his
palms brought him back to realize he had missed a question. "I beg your pardon,
sir?"

"I asked if what you've listed here is your total work experience."

"Yes, sir, it is. You see I only finished college last year, and then moved out
here."

"Oh, yes, I see."

Four words this time, but they amounted to the same. Clay could even feel the
irritation now. It had dissolved, blending with a thousand past irritations, leaving
him only with a sour taste in his mouth. The interview was over, he knew, and he
was out, as usual. Now all that was left was the long ride to the end of the line, that
long line he had to take for Claire Mae, not for himself, because he already knew.
"Yes, sir," he said quickly answering another useless question. *"Yes, sir, Mr. Robertson.
Yes, sir, you are absolutely right, cap'n. Only come on, daddy, don't drag it out. Kill me quick,
Abe. Ain't no sense messin' around. Ain't gonna' be no savin' message from God this time!"*

When he phoned Claire Mae from the bar later, she took the news pretty hard.
She didn't agree with him as she usually did—"But you don t know yet, Clay. Not
really"—nor did she bother asking him what he was doing in a bar when he could
be looking for work in other places. She just said "All right" as though it was a kind
of vocal shrug, and then said she'd see him that night. When she finally came
home, though, she was feeling better. Evidently her work that afternoon had
smoothed away the edge of her disappointment, just as the liquor had smoothed
away his, because she listened patiently to the details of his explanation, then embraced him and said, "It doesn't matter, hon. Something'll turn up tomorrow. Maybe
right here in Fillmore. Can't every boss in this city be a white two-faced bastard."

She fixed him a steak for dinner, singing all the time she was cooking to show him
she still had faith, and while they ate they talked confidently of the future, of the
house they would someday buy and the children they would raise and the trips they
would take. *And if anybody can make it all happen, I guess Claire Mae can,* he thought,
smiling inwardly at the strength of her determination.

When they were watching television the newscaster mentioned that the President's
civil rights bill was having trouble in the House, but that it still seemed a sure thing
to pass. He felt Claire Mae touch his arm while the man was talking, but whether
it was to give him confidence or to seek some from him he couldn't determine.
They sat there, huddled together, as though for protection, while the little white
men danced in black-and-white before them, laughing together when the occasional lone Negro passed by in the background. *They can hire me 'for show' too if they
want. If I ain't black enough for them I'll even put on a little Man-Tan.* Claire Mae, as
though sensing his thoughts, leaned against him. He unbuttoned her blouse and
rested his hand beneath it. When she didn't pull away he started working on the bra
as well.

"Clay?"

There was no warning note in her voice, only a kind of questioning. "Yeah?"

"I thought you wanted to watch this show."

"Screw that show. Let's go to bed."

She sat upright then, forcing his hand away, but she was smiling. "I ain't done the dishes yet."

"Screw them, too."

She laughed. "Man, you do all that screwing, you ain't going to be much use to me!"

"You try me," he said, reaching again for her. She caught his hand and kissed it.

"I got to get that kitchen cleared up first. Them cockroaches'll carry the whole house off if I don't. And I need me a bath, too."

"You hintin' at something?"

"Me? Course not! Makes sense though, that if you took care of the kitchen while I was taking me a bath, we'd both get to that bed faster. Don't it?"

He lunged for her, laughing, but she beat him again, jumping up and heading for the bathroom. "You ain't out of that tub time I get ready, I'm climbin' in with you!" he yelled after her. She paused long enough to give him a smile, then disappeared behind the bathroom door.

Clay turned the television off, finding some consolation in shutting up some stupid ofay right in the middle of a sentence. The kitchen really wasn't too bad. There were only a few dishes on the table to clear away. He knew there wouldn't be enough hot water to wash them, since Claire Mae was running it for a bath, and so he only wiped at them the best he could. He heard her singing in the tub, and he tried to hum the tune along with her as he worked, but he heard himself go off-key and quit. *"Here's one nigger that can't carry a tune, boss." Can't do much of anything else either, seems like.*

He was looking out the kitchen window and down onto the half-lit street while he rinsed and stacked the dishes. He saw the figure of a man get off the bus at the corner. He thought it was Billy Porter, but it wasn't until the man started to cross the street that he was sure. He'd forgotten about his neighbor, just as he'd forgotten the interview, during the long, drinking afternoon, but now that he saw him again he wanted to talk with him, if for no other reason than to compare notes on the morning's embarrassment. He searched for some excuse, saw the sack of garbage heaped to the level of spilling, and, grabbing it, rushed out into the hall. He was too quick. He heard Billy just starting to climb the stairs as he dropped the bag down the chute, and so he had to wait empty-handed.

So maybe he'll think I'm waiting for him. I don't give a damn. I am. He'll want to see me, too. Only natural. He's probably just as disappointed as I am, and he doesn't have a wife fixing herself up just for his pleasure.

Clay heard the song then, the tune climbing up the stairway like an echo of the footsteps, and it bothered him. He heard in it not sadness, not disappointment, but a quiet joy of contentment.

What if he got the job?

The question rattled inside his head, knocking aside all the old defenses, spawning other questions in its flight. *What if Billy, the rejected of Clay, had been the accepted? What would Claire Mae find to say in consolation then? How could an ofay be a bastard if . . .*

Clay clutched the end of the handrail and watched the figure of the man climbing like a black Christ rising from a tomb to announce—*What? What will he announce? What new joyous disaster. . . .* The tune danced in the still air to the rhythm the footsteps beat out in warning. *No! Oh, my God, not that, too!*

The black face was first to reach the level of the hallway, looking like a dark moon against a pale horizon, and as Clay watched in fear the tiny, internal smile spread broadly in recognition.

"Hi, man!"

"Hi," Clay answered, forcing his voice to sound casual. "Hey, you sure sound happy enough."

"Hell, why not? I got me a job, man!"

So the drum warnings had been of doom, and he hadn't prepared in time. What did it matter, though? He had built the only defense he had, the only kind he knew, and if it wasn't enough. . . . "Yeah? Hey, that's great! Man, I didn't think that dumb ofay could even see us niggers there in that dark office."

"Him? Mr. Robertson? Hell, man, he couldn't. That ain't where I got my job. I got back on at the diaper factory."

Clay laughed, chasing the terrors away again by his sheer volume. "Yeah? Hell, I thought for a minute you'd gotten the other job!"

"Nah," Billy answered, smiling. He seemed puzzled by Clay's outburst. "Hell, I called them this afternoon. Pretended I was somebody new, you know, like I hadn't been there this morning. They told me it was already filled. They must have taken one of them dumb ofays that was standin' there when we was there."

Clay smiled, finished with the topic now that he had found his fears to be groundless. "Well, I'm glad you got you a job, anyway."

"Thanks. It ain't much, but it'll pay the rent."

They stood there quietly, as though neither of them was sure how to break away. Clay looked past Billy, down the stairs, looking intently at the door, as though the outside world were waiting there, like a puppy, whimpering to be let in.

"Fog must be coming in," he said. "I felt it a minute ago."

"Nah, it's clear out," Billy answered. "Clear as a virgin's conscience."

They shared a laugh, and then Clay shrugged. "Must be me then. I sure thought I felt it coming in."

Billy didn't answer. He stood quietly another moment, still a few stairs from the top, then started climbing again, moving past Clay. "Well, guess I better get on up. That sister of mine may even feed me tonight, she hears the news 'fore she starts throwin' things."

"Okay, man. See you."

Clay watched the back of his friend as he climbed the stairs on up to the next floor, sharing with him for a moment a genuine pleasure for his new job. *Tomorrow may be my turn,* he thought, promising himself and Claire Mae. *Or at least the next day. It's got to come, sooner or later, if we can only wait long enough.*

The footsteps, if they were an omen, were fading fast now, so they no longer seemed threatening. They stopped; a door opened and then closed quickly again.

Clay smiled, wiped his sweating hands down across his trousers, and started back to his own apartment, back to Claire Mae, who he knew was still waiting, in the dark and wide bed, to give him comfort.

Water Seeks Its Own Level

MAXINE CLAIR

This is what he saw: two muddy rivers coursing toward each other, rushing as if they were drawn by the axis of a great Y, then their headlong crash and the furious confusion over which river would prevail. Beyond this junction, the Kaw ceased to exist, and the Missouri flowed on. Such tides were not easily turned.

All day James Wilson had sat on the steps outside Union Hall, waiting to be sent on a job. Any job. But preferably to the subdivision in Olathe where, for several months, Cordon Construction had been laying foundations, and he had been bricking them in. The pay was good. Better than good. But the white boys were getting even better than that. Two days earlier he had protested—not so respectfully—the foreman's scheme of sending all the men home and letting the white boys sneak back for overtime. He admitted to himself that if he could have just ignored it, just let it go, he would be working in Olathe instead of standing on a hill in Rattlebone watching the river rise.

The long whine of the late-shift whistle from Armour's packing house stirred him. He was sure it was only a little past six. He took in the Kansas City smell of manure and bacon, strongest in Rattlebone across and downriver from the stockyards. For the late whistle to blow now meant that the workers were quitting early—locking pens, switching off conveyor belts, and hurrying home. At Union Hall all afternoon radios had broadcast warnings to the low-lying communities along the rivers. Evacuations were imminent, the levee might not hold. Since Rattlebone was on high ground, it was probably safe, but James thought he ought to be heading home too. He went down the hill.

And he ought to take the kids something—candy, soda pop. Or ice cream. It wouldn't hurt to sweeten Pearlean up a little. Through the glass front of the A&P he could see folks jam-packed and laying hold of groceries like everything was free. The commotion drew him in.

He heard one of the cashiers yell, "We all out of bread!" As he started down the aisle he saw that the milk and egg refrigerators were empty too. The checkout line extended nearly to the rear of the store.

It didn't matter that the river made no direct threat to their end of the city, people in Rattlebone took all natural disasters—wherever they happened—as personal warnings. *There, but for the grace of God, go I.* They fortified themselves with meat and canned goods. James thought he'd be better off stopping at Doll's Market where he wouldn't have to stand in line.

There too, as he pushed through the swinging door, he heard Doll's husky voice announcing, "No bread, no lunch ham, and no more candles!" to the twenty-odd customers waiting to pay for their groceries. Soda pop and candy were no big thing, but he felt like killing more time before going home to deal with Pearlean. He spotted Thomas Pemberton in the line—Old Uncle he called him—and waved.

"Shorty—boy, what you doin down here?" Thomas called to him.

"Just messin 'round, fixin to go home," James said, noting the weariness in his own voice. Thomas motioned for him to come closer.

"I guess you heard about the levee and all," Thomas said. Before James could answer, Thomas gave up his place in line and launched into his account of the record-breaking water levels the river had reached, all the little towns and whistle stops it had washed away in the past four days, including hollows and creek bridges he had known as a boy. Finally he gave James the latest news, that the Civil Defense was calling for volunteers to sandbag the levee on the south side of the city.

"They ain't payin, but they sayin that they need a lot of people," Thomas told him. "Soon as Wes closes the barbershop, me and him are thinkin 'bout goin out there to see what's what."

It had its appeal. Still, James said, "I guess I'll head on in. Pearl'll be wondering where I am." He told Thomas to "say hi to Miss Lydia," and fished around in the bin of penny candies.

It felt good to be out rushing around in the streets. This desire to be unfettered in the world came down on him sometimes like rain on an arid field. He drank it in, imagining the streets of Chicago or Harlem, places he had never seen. He pictured the wide ocean he had crossed to New Guinea during the war. Whenever he felt this way, he let the imaginings swell, and when they reached the point of forming themselves into ideas, he turned them loose, let them fly to be recaptured at any time he chose.

If he hadn't had to sell the truck, he could drive out to Armourdale just to see the river at the levee. Since he had moved back home, Pearl watched him like a hawk, he couldn't take a single breath on his own. All of what he knew to be her anger, and all of what he guessed was her hope, had crystallized in the single thing she must have repeated to him every day. Whether it was about his money, his time, or his attitude in general, she kept it constantly in his face.

"I have to come first in your life, James. Me and the kids, we have to come first."

She was justified, he couldn't argue. In her eyes he had up and left her for October Brown, and when he had gotten himself in way over his head and had to sell his truck, only then did he crawl back home. It would be a long, long time before Pearl would get over it.

He turned down Seventh Street toward Wes's Barber Shop. A six-bottle carton of Nehi's and a handful of Tootsie Rolls weren't going to cut him any slack tonight, either, when Pearlean found out about the Cordon job.

He crossed over to the Texaco station. Maybe it would be better for them both if he took his time getting home. He dropped a dime in the slot. He would call and tell her he'd be late. But why have a big blowout? Maybe for once he could take the time to clear his head, figure out what he needed to say to get her to understand him. He hung up the receiver and retrieved his dime.

When he got to the barbershop, Thomas was there waiting for Wes to lock up.

"You mean Pearlean's gonna let you go out to the river tonight?" Thomas said and winked at Wes.

If anyone else had said it, James might have bristled, but this was Thomas. Thomas Pemberton wasn't kin, and he wasn't James's ace-boon-coon, but James knew that despite the difference in their ages, Thomas would always be in his corner. He could count on Thomas to loan him money, and Thomas even gave him odd jobs in the pretense of letting him earn it. Of course he stayed on his back about going to church and saving for a house he could buy for Pearl and the kids. But that came with the territory.

"So you goin out there with us?" Wes asked him.

"What does it look like?" James said.

"Aw, so now, all of a sudden, you the man," Wes joked. "I saw you callin up to get permission."

And Thomas put in, "Don't you be gettin me on the outs with Pearlean. Next thing you know, Lydia'll be getting on my case 'cause Pearlean is upset about your foolishness. I ain't said you can ride in my truck yet," he said, but he was grinning.

As the sun gradually sank, they climbed into the cab of Thomas's truck and crept with the traffic out Seventh Street toward the bridge. At the wheel Thomas hummed a piece of a hymn. Wes hung his arm out the other window and sucked on one Lucky Strike after another. James wedged his shoulders between the two of them and distracted himself with memories. October Brown. His schoolteacher woman. His chocolate-covered cherry. The way she would walk with him into the semidarkness of Shady Maurice's after-hours place. *"Chez de,"* she told him every time. *"It's Chez de Maurice, not Shady."*

He could see himself smile as he looked into her face. She had a way of hooking her arm through his, touching his shoulder, leaning in for him to plant his kiss on the pink-white spot of her cheek. Always, then, her sweet muskiness would blind him.

Up ahead, taillights red-studded the road. Wes leaned farther out the window to get a clearer view. Thomas concentrated on the stop-and-start of the cars in front of him. By the time they caught sight of the bridge, night and river had come full into bloom.

It begins sometime in late September. The snows of Montana, Iowa, Minnesota sift down, layer after layer, undisturbed except in streets of cities like Bismarck and Dubuque. All over the plains the snows go on falling through November, Christmas, the dull of February. In March, when the earth changes its angle and thaws, the Kaw and Missouri join the fluid rampage down the Mississippi's grand troughway to the Gulf of Mexico. And if the Mississippi swells beyond the pores of its ample bed, every river, every creek, brook, and pond up through the Midwest to the Canadian line confirms the law that water seeks its own level.

James was restless. The force of the river and the excited air above it captivated him as he looked out from the cab of Thomas's truck into the deceptive sheen on the black water.

At the other side of the bridge a highway patrolman waved them out of the line of cars and onto a hastily made gravel road through overgrowth and marshes. After a while James saw a series of floodlights and heard the hum of the generator punctuated by the "Over here!" shouts of men.

They followed the gravel road to the work site made brighter than daylight by the floodlights strung makeshift to a tree. The men looked flat, unreal. The colors of their shirts and overalls were bleached in the bright light, and sharp shadows danced around them. The entire area was a theater enveloped by featureless dark. The trooper who directed the activity at the solid mountain of sandbags explained that they should move quickly to load Thomas's truck with bags. Then, following the gravel and the lights, haul them "up the line," closer to the river.

"One vehicle at a time," the trooper said. "The road is narrow. We can't have nobody getting out into the marshes."

After a whole day of sitting James was primed for action. Judging from the slow ride out to the levee, it was probably after nine. Pearlean and the kids would have gone on and had supper by now.

Once when his daughter had surprised him at the supper table and asked him about his stay away from home, he had managed to say some tired something about people needing time. But that wasn't it, not really. October Brown? Well she was something else again. Sure, he wanted her. A man would have to be a fool not to want her. But more and more it wasn't about her or any other woman. Whatever it was that had kept him in that rented room for a year had something to do with the satisfaction he got from following his mind out to the rising river on a dark night when all of Rattlebone, all of Kansas City, huddled in their houses.

And suppose he wanted to see the coast, say, and decided to take a trip alone, or even with Pearl? He hadn't come to that bridge yet, and when he did, he would cross it. Although they had never talked about leaving Kansas City, he could imagine Pearlean saying, "Name one thing they got in California that we can't get here."

The men had loaded up the truck and had driven so close that James could hear water rushing. He and Thomas let down the tailgate and lifted sandbags into pairs of hands. James worked up a sweat. He watched the double line of long shadows swing sand pillows from one set of hands to the next. These men were probably scared, or at least nervous. But if he didn't know better, he would think he was at any one of a hundred construction sites he'd seen. The artificial light, the generator noise, men hauling sand—none of this looked dangerous. If he was going to get any sympathy from Pearl, he was going to have to exaggerate a few of the details.

"They're sayin they closed the bridge down soon as we come off it," Thomas said. "Guess they got to be careful. Who knows, the bridge could go too."

When they emptied and refilled the truck with bags next time, James thought he might walk up closer to the river, see what there was to see, maybe sandbag on the actual levee for a while. On the white gravel, he followed the line of men until he could hear the river roaring over the generator's hum. Just ahead, the levee—a hill of sandbags now—rose ten or twelve feet. Men had stationed themselves like steps to toss the bags on the topmost layer. A trooper paced the ground at the base and kept constant dialogue with the crackle from his walkie-talkie.

"What's the word?" James asked the trooper.

"Don't know much yet," he said. "We got men strung out for two miles, and the river is supposed to crest here in another couple of hours. The Civil Defense will tell us when the time comes to pull out. Unless they do, we'll probably be here all night and we better hope it don't start raining."

James climbed up a few feet. This was better. Right on the other side of this wall the torrent of water rushed past. He could feel it when he stood stock-still, the rumble, the pull.

"They evacuated Lenexa earlier, you know," one of the men said. He swung a sandbag into James's hands. "Good thing, too. The trooper said it's gone under."

"I guess Bonner Springs is next," James said. He passed one bag and readied his hands for the next.

"Yeah, some parts of it," the man said, and slung the bag of sand into James's hands. "I've got family waiting," he said. "I'm thinking about pulling out before too long."

The man had said it with such a note of delight that James wanted to see his face. When the man turned again, his expression revealed little. Within the next hour, groups of men came and went. Then as midnight approached, a commotion broke out in the direction of the bridge—James thought he saw the flash of a red light against the dark.

Soon the sound of revving engines faded in. Then a loudspeaker boomed: "Evacuate the area! Evacuate! All personnel leave this area!"

The voice said something else about Shawnee Mission and the bridge, but James couldn't hear it for the noise of the gravel stampede. Men leapt from their perches on the sandbags and ran toward the generator-light. As James scrambled to get his footing, the light went out. A collective cry issued from the men.

James struggled to keep his footing. He thought if he could just head straight for the generator where the light had been, he would find his way out of there. But blinding darkness disoriented him. Straight ahead from here, he thought, but, then, hadn't he seen trees between the levee and the generator? Stay on the gravel, he thought, but already there seemed to be no gravel under his feet, or was there?

"The levee is out! Run!" somebody shouted.

With his eyes open to pitch black, he groped the air in front of his face like a sleepwalker and ran in the direction of the car engines. But they too had moved farther away. He heard the footfalls of men far ahead of him. He closed his eyes to gain balance, and ran faster.

Just run, he told himself. Don't try to see. A crashing sound, a tree falling? Were men laughing or crying? Surely the river wasn't taking them already. Making time now, he's making time. Don't try to see. Run. His heart rumbled in his chest, his ankle buckled. Was that gravel under his feet? Keep your balance, run straight. Behind him a roaring like a train. Faster. Pressure in his eyes, in his ears. Like a train churning up trees! His chest burned. He can run faster than this. His arms pumped. Water! His legs. Water! His hands. Mud! Men thrashed around him. All of them lost! No air! His nose, his chest exploded. Got to hold on. Swim. Got to.

His head went light. After what seemed like ages, he came to. At his own door. Pearl opens it. "We waited," she says. She leads him to the supper table and they sit down with Irene and Junie and her sister's children. She makes them all hold hands while she says the blessing. She sounds young, like a girl, like when he first met her. She finishes grace with "Good bread, good meat, good Lord, let's eat!" and they all laugh freely. She watches them eat, sprinkles more sugar on Junie's rice, and when Irene runs her bread around her plate for the last drop of gravy, Pearl pulls bits of meat from the neckbone on her plate and gives them to her daughter. "Eat up. You've got ten more years to grow." Her hands are quick. *What?* her eyes say when she sees him watching. *Who me?* they say. She tests his thoughts with a smile.

A sharp pain shot through his shoulder. His arm.

"Open up your eyes, fool! Shorty! Stand up! Open your eyes!"

James coughed and gagged on water and river slime. Thomas and Wes held him up, pounded his back. The three of them stood thigh-deep in marsh water.

"You all right, Shorty?" Wes said. "You almost drowned yourself hollering like something got a hold of you."

James nodded his head yes. When he wiped away some of the mud, he could make out only dark and darker, then forms—sky, trees, pale gravel. The river's rumble oriented him, and he shook the two men off.

"They're sayin the river is crestin. No need to take no chances. Let's get on home," Thomas said.

They joined other men on the gravel path to Thomas's truck and began the slow drive out. James thought he must have looked some kind of crazy, like a scared kid wallowing around, drowning his own fool self in the marshes. He was grateful that no one spoke. Once he could see the lights from the Seventh Street bridge he could not bear to be closed in.

"Let me out, Thomas, I'll walk the rest of the way."

"You can't walk, Shorty. You a mess and they ain't lettin nobody use the bridge. We got to go clean 'cross the state line through Missouri to get home," Thomas said, but he pulled over.

"You sure you all right? What you want us to tell Pearlean? You know she's gonna be lookin for you."

"Don't tell her nothin," James said.

Maybe by nearly drowning him in the marshes, God was telling him something. That this one life was the only life he would ever have. Maybe he should simply walk away. The gulf between the kind of life he sometimes imagined and his life with Pearl seemed as uncrossable as a wild river.

That night, furious though it was, the Kaw swept away many a sandbag but kept within its banks. All night James walked—out through Armourdale, across the Missouri line, past houses filled with people who waited in the dark for someone to return to them, then back across to Kansas and the hill above the natural collision of two rivers—in a roundabout circle home.

The Flashlight

ELDRIDGE CLEAVER

From each obstacle encountered and conquered, Stacy sapped fresh strength with which to confront the next; and from that next conquest, his depleted drive was again restored and poised to meet the latest oncoming task. Life to him was an endless series of regularly spaced hurdles he had to leap over. This was the form of his imagination—not that he was in any big hurry to reach some particular goal in life. But life was motion and motion required a direction and Stacy was young and saw the years stretched out before him as he sprinted down the track of his days. He hated dead ends and stagnation and wanted always to see ahead ample room for maneuver. He thought of himself as having no fear, as a strong, rough cat who would become even more so, because in the world he knew, strength seemed to have the edge.

He was lord of his gang and his word was law. He was light and quick on his feet, and a fierce, turbulent spirit drove him on, like a dynamo imprisoned in the blood, flesh and bone of his body. He set the pace. It was not that his gang did only the things Stacy did best but that everything they did he seemed to do better. The others deferred to him as though he were a prince among them, with mysterious powers of a higher caliber than theirs, as if somehow he was born with a built-in gun and they with built-in knives. They did not question or resent this. To them, it was life, nature. They were glad to have Stacy as one of their own and they followed his lead.

Stacy was conscious of the role he played, but he did not prance before the grandstands. It could be said that he was humble in his way and bowed low before the others even as he bullied them about, because there was always absent from this bullying that ultimate hostility of which they all knew he was so capable when up against cats from other neighborhoods. Among them, there was knowledge of each other, the thick glue of the brotherhood of youth, of their separate selves bound into one. If Stacy made a decision, it was only the summation of their interests as a whole, because as far as they wanted anything, they all wanted the same things. He was the repository of their youthful collective sovereignty. Perhaps, then, it is incorrect to say that Stacy's word was law. Their law was that of a roving band owing allegiance to itself alone. Stacy occupied his peculiar place among them precisely because he knew the restraints and sanctions implicit in the mechanics and spirit of a functioning gang. Had he been less skillful in his choices, less willing to risk all on the curve of his instincts, it would have been their loss as much as his. Together they formed a unit, clinging to one another for support. What he had he gave to them and the others did the same. There was nothing premeditated about it. It just happened that Stacy had the power of the endearing smile, the rebuking frown, the assenting nod, the admonitory shake of the head.

Of late, however, Stacy was growing friendlily disgusted with the others, primarily because they seemed content to continue in the same rut. He was beginning to feel miserably trapped and hemmed in by the thick futility of the very things he had loved and pursued with satisfaction and a sense of fulfillment. Only a few weeks ago, he could still draw delight and deep contentment from the raids they threw on El Serrano, from kicking in a window and ransacking a store, from stripping the hubcaps, wheels and accessories from cars, from stealing the clothing from clothes-lines or from breaking into a restaurant or café after it had closed and eating up as much food as they could hold in their guts and taking away with them all they could carry. These things no longer filled him with a warm glow after they were all over; rather, he would feel dejected and somehow disappointed in himself and the oth-ers, as if it all had been a big waste of time. When he went on a raid now, it was only because he knew the others depended upon him and that they would be angry and confused if he refused to go with them. Besides, he did not have anything else in mind to do, and he was not the type to enjoy doing nothing.

Stacy liked the money and the extra clothes that thievery brought him, but he was burned out on the ritual of these raids. As far back as he could remember, they had been a part of his life, and he knew from neighborhood lore that the practice of the raids existed as a tradition in Crescent Heights long before he or the others came along. It seemed natural for the youth of Crescent Heights to steal whatever they could from the white people of El Serrano. At this time in Stacy's life, Crescent Heights was separated from El Serrano by two miles of unimproved vacant lots that ran up to the top of a hill, so that from Crescent Heights, El Serrano could not even be seen. The long slope of the hill was a wall between the Negroes and Mexicans who lived in Crescent Heights and the whites of El Serrano.

On a clear night, the lights of El Serrano could be seen against the sky from Crescent Heights; but from El Serrano, the sky over Crescent Heights looked black and unbroken, even by the moon and stars. Stacy was fascinated by this contrast. Many times, either when setting out on a raid or on his way back, Stacy would pause at the top of the hill and brood over it. The darkness in which Cres-cent Heights was wrapped seemed familiar and safe to him, warm and protecting, while the lights of El Serrano held both a fascination and a terror for him. He was principally aware of the lights because they were central to the ritual of the raids.

It was a maxim to his gang that "where there is light there is wealth." They often repeated this to each other when searching through El Serrano for things to steal.

Each neighborhood had its own school. The police station and department servicing both areas were located in El Serrano. El Serrano was a thriving community with a frisky business section, while Crescent Heights was a residential slum devoid of any business except for a few corner grocery stores, liquor stores, gas stations and beer joints.

The only swimming pool and motion-picture theater in the region were in El Serrano, and during the summer, the kids from Crescent Heights hiked over the steep hill, paid their money and went in for a swim. On Saturday and Sunday, they'd go to the movies and, on their way home, fan out through El Serrano, looking for loot. By bedtime, the wealth of Crescent Heights was certain to have increased in proportion to a corresponding decrease in that of El Serrano's. Stacy's gang not only picked up things on the way back from the swimming pool or movies but two or three times each week, they'd wait for nightfall and then trek over the hill to throw a raid.

All this seemed so futile to Stacy now. He could feel that a change had to be made—just what, he could not tell. But he knew that something would happen and a way would open up for him. In the meantime, he continued to lead the raids and, although he would be just as systematic and cautious as ever, it was no longer a pleasure. It was a task.

Stacy loved Crescent Heights. He did not feel comfortable or secure anywhere else. When he ventured out of the neighborhood, on infrequent trips downtown or to the East Side or to Watts, he was always relieved when the trip was over and he was back among the familiar sights and sounds of Crescent Heights. Even school was still far enough away from his part of Crescent Heights that he felt alien and uncomfortable until he was away from the school and back in his own stamping grounds. He hated the teachers at Crescent Heights School for their way of talking down to the Negro and Mexican students and the superior attitude he saw reflected in them. He hated most of all the discipline they imposed upon him, the authority they tried to assert over him, to which they wanted him willingly to submit but which he resisted and rebelled against. The school seemed to him more like a prison than a school, the teachers seemed more like custodial guards than instructors and the atmosphere seemed more like that of a battlefield than of a place of learning. Stacy never got into fights with the teachers, as some of the others did, but he let it be known that if any of the teachers ever hit him—if the boys' vice-principal, for example, ever took him into his office and tried to force him to bend over and look at the rainbow colors drawn on the lower part of the wall, while the v.p. swatted him on his ass with his huge perforated paddle, as he did some of the others—there would be blood. Understanding this, the teachers would turn their heads from certain infractions when committed by Stacy, while they would pounce on other students for precisely the same transgressions. Sometimes, in the dreams of his heart, Stacy longed for one of the teachers to lay a hand on him, so that he could work him over. In his mind, he saw himself grabbing a teacher and beating him down to a bloody pulp. The teachers, sensing something of this desire in him, left him alone. Stacy loved the freedom he found in Crescent Heights. He felt he was losing it each time he set foot on the school grounds. It was not that he found the schoolwork difficult—he found it easy and was quick to catch on—but the whole situation repelled him. He felt that books and the knowledge in them were part of a world that was against him, a world to which he did not belong and which he did not want to enter, the world of which the hateful teachers were representatives and symbols. After school each day, it took several blocks of walking before he was free of its field of force. Then he blossomed, felt himself. His pace quickened and became his own again.

Stacy's loyalty went to Crescent Heights. To him, his neighborhood was the center of the world. Isolated somewhat from the rest of Los Angeles, in the way that each part of that scattered metropolis is isolated from every other, Crescent Heights was a refuge. If Stacy had been captured by beings from another planet, who cast him into a prison filled with inhabitants from all the planets, and if he were asked by the others where he lived, he would have said, "I'm Stacy Mims from Crescent Heights."

"Crescent Heights?" they would ask, puzzled.

"Oh," Stacy would remember, "Crescent Heights is the name of my neighborhood. I'm from Planet Earth. Crescent Heights is on Earth. It's in the United States of America, in the state of California."

The nucleus of the neighborhood was the Crescent Heights housing project, a low-rent complex of 100 units, laid out in long rows. They looked like two-story elongated boxcars painted a pale yellow or a weak pink, the colors alternating row by row. At the center of the project was the administration building and in back of it was a large playground. Behind the playground was a huge incinerator with a chimney that towered high above the buildings of Crescent Heights. Tenants from all over the project brought their trash to the incinerator to burn. The project sat down in sort of a valley formed by hills on three sides, with the fourth side wide open and leading down to Los Angeles. All traffic entered Crescent Heights through this side. As one traveled farther up into the valley, the streets ran out of pavement and asphalt and became dirt roads. The dirt roads turned into well-worn footpaths; the paths tapered into intermittent trails; the trails evaporated into the rolling hills, which the people of Crescent Heights regarded with a peculiar love. And while the county of Los Angeles had built the housing project with its drawn-to-scale playground laid out scientifically—basketball court here, volleyball court there, horseshoe pits here, swings there, slide over there, monkey bars and ladder here, tetherball, there, hopscotch here—Stacy's playground and that of the members of his gang had always been the hills of Crescent Heights.

Scattered throughout the hills surrounding the project were the ramshackle houses of the old families, the houses Stacy and his gang grew up in. There was a subtle distinction between the old families, who lived in the hills, and the inhabitants of the project. It was not that the houses in the hills had been there long years before the project; there had been similar houses on the site where the project now stood. The owners of those houses had been evicted by the county and state authorities after a bitter fight, which was lost by the homeowners before it ever began. The memory of it was still fresh, and there was a lingering undercurrent of resentment at this encroachment. The project itself was a symbol of the forces that had gutted the old neighborhood against the will and desire of the people, breaking up lifelong friendships and alliances, demolishing the familiar environment and substituting a new one. Although this prejudice was not as strong as in former times, it lingered on in the lore of the people.

The major point of difference was that most of the inhabitants of the project were women with small children, women who had not grown up in Crescent Heights but who had come there from other areas of Los Angeles, whose ties were with friends and relations who were strangers to the people who had lived in Crescent Heights all their lives. The names of these women had popped up on the housing authority's long waiting list downtown and, eager to get the apartment for which they might have been waiting for a year or more, they accepted a vacancy in Crescent Heights, sight unseen. These were unwed mothers on state aid, divorcées, women who had been abandoned by their men and the waiting wives, living on allotment checks, of servicemen stationed always somewhere far away. The turnover was rapid among residents of the project; someone always seemed to be moving in or out. But no one ever moved out of the surrounding hills. There, whole families lived. Most of them, like Stacy's family, owned the little plots of ground on which they lived.

After school each day, and after they had eaten their evening meals and performed whatever chores they had to do Stacy's gang used to meet at the playground in the project, pouring down from the hills, drawn there like moths to a light. On weekends and holidays, they usually hiked deep into the hills. They would take along their slingshots to shoot at the doves, pigeons and quail, which were plentiful in those hills. Sometimes they would return home in the evening with fowl for their mothers to cook. Or they would give the birds to women in the project, who always received them gladly, sometimes giving the boys some small change in return. In season, they would collect wild walnuts from the trees, and there were wild peaches, apricots, pears, figs, loquats and quince. Wild berries grew in patches here and there. Old Mexican men plowed sections of the hills and sowed them with corn, squash and sugar cane. There was always plenty for all who took the trouble to help themselves. Stacy and the others would sometimes harvest large quantities of this corn and sell it to the women of the project.

Those hills were the soul of Crescent Heights. Old-timers spun out legends concerning them. They told how somewhere in those hills was hidden an ancient Indian burial ground and that the graves were filled with priceless treasures. There was gold, intricately worked by artisans and set with splendid jewels, goblets encrusted with precious stones. The old-timers would talk and the youngsters would listen. A curse would fall on anyone who went looking for the treasures; to reach them, one had to disturb the sleep of the dead. It was said that many people had gone into those hills and were never seen or heard from again. Under this ominous cloud, Stacy and the others would test their courage by roaming deep into the hills, their eyes peeled for signs of an Indian grave, half expecting to be pounced upon by supernatural guardians of the dead, deliciously savoring the sweet taste of fear defied. With a gentle breeze waving the tall grass, they walked barefooted under the sun, drawing strength from each kiss of the soil on the soles of their feet.

Once in a while, shepherds from out of nowhere would appear, bringing huge herds of sheep to pasture and graze there for a few months. From his house, Stacy sometimes looked out to see the dark, undulating mass of shaggy creatures sweeping in a rolling wave across the hills, the bells tinkling around the necks of the leaders and the sheep dogs running back and forth, keeping the strays in line. The shepherds would be seen with long sticks, trudging along with their flocks. It always reminded Stacy of scenes from the Bible. Only the style of clothes had changed.

During summer, when the grass on the hills dried out, sometimes it would catch on fire, by the working of the sun through the prism of a broken wine bottle. Sometimes Stacy and the others grew impatient with the sun and would, out of sight of everyone, toss a match or two and wait for the fire trucks to come racing over from El Serrano. They would hear the sirens screaming in the distance, listening tensely as they came closer and closer until finally the huge red engines would swing into sight and the firemen would go into action. With guilty knowledge or not, Stacy and the others would watch the firemen and sometimes would even help them. Sometimes, to avoid inconvenient surprises and possible disasters, the county would send out crews and deliberately set a fire and control it, burning all the grass near the houses and back for about a mile into the hills as a safety measure. The whole neighborhood would turn out to watch a fire, to see the flames walk across those hills, leaving a black sheet of ash in its wake. It was always something of a shock to Stacy to see those hills transformed in an instant from tall grass to burned-out cinders. Black and barren, the hills were no good for walking barefooted, and there was no hope of finding any fowl concealed in a clump of grass. The youngsters of Crescent Heights did not enjoy the hills when the grass had burned. Fortunately for them, the fires never succeeded in burning all the grass, and they could always go deep into the hills until they found a point to which the flames had not penetrated.

One time the hills were so burned out that the gang had to hike a long way before reaching the green grass. Mitch, characteristically, set the grass on fire to spoil their day. Helplessly, Stacy and the others watched as the fowl took to the air.

Turning on Mitch, they punched and kicked him until he cried. Stacy did not tell them to stop. Mitch was mean as a dog. From him, the others learned early that a human being is full of surprises and capable of evil improvisations.

Mitch was full of peevish taciturnity. He was sullen and vicious. The others watched him, waiting for each new manifestation of his scurviness. Many times, Stacy had sat mystified in Mitch's back yard and listened with astonishment as he cursed out his mother. He would hurl at her the most vile names, in English and Spanish and combinations of both languages, and his mother, who seemed not at all surprised or shocked, would never raise her voice. She would ask him in very gentle tones, how he could talk to his own mother that way, inspiring an infuriated Mitch to a new torrent of epithets. She would stand there, at the top of the stairs, gently, calmly drying her hands on her apron, waiting for him to finish, never interrupting him. If she had started to speak and he cut her off, she would stop in mid-sentence, half apologetically, and let him finish; then she would start again, very slowly, cautiously, kindly.

"I'm your own mother," she would say to him in Spanish, or, "Come inside and talk to me, son; you can bring Stacy with you, too, if you like."

Mitch would only curse her more.

After a while, Stacy, unable to stand it any longer, would make Mitch come away with him. Stacy liked Mitch's mother. He saw her as a sweet old woman who always gave the neighborhood kids little Mexican goodies to eat, which she made up and kept on hand for when they came around. Big and fat, she went to Mass every Sunday morning, rain or shine, with a black shawl over her head and shoulders, her small children trailing behind her. These small children were one of the mysteries of Crescent Heights and the subject of endless rumors. Mrs. Chapultapec had children who were over forty years old, while Mitch was fourteen. There were always new children being added to the household. Around the yard, they followed her like tiny shadows. Nobody seemed to know just which of the children were her own or, in fact, if any of them were actually hers. If asked, she would only smile and say that all the children in the world were her own, and refuse to discuss it further. The older people understood that she had had, all her life, a great love and tenderness for children, and she would take in anybody's unwanted child and raise him as her own. Nobody knew how many children she had actually raised. Some she would keep for a few years, then their parents would come and take them back. At the bottom of Mitch's rage lay the fact that he did not know who his parents were, because he did not believe anything Mrs. Chapultapec told him.

Once, a new little face showed up in the house, and it so happened that Mitch knew that the little boy belonged to one of the women who lived in the project. Overhearing Mrs. Chapultapec telling someone, in her way, that the little boy was her own, Mitch was suddenly blasted by a vision that Mrs. Chapultapec was not really his own mother and that he did not know who his real mother was. When he asked Mrs. Chapultapec about it, she just told him that he was her very own. He accused her of being a notorious liar.

Mitch used to threaten to kill his father, or, rather, Mr. Chapultapec, whom Mitch always had believed to be his father but whom he later "disowned." A small, stooped, white-haired old man with quick, birdlike movements, he would never scold or correct the children. He was terrified of them. He would go straight to work and come straight home in the evening, except on Friday evening, when he would stop off at the Cozy Corner Café, down a few beers with the old-timers and listen to a few Spanish records on the juke box. Tipsy from the beers, his spirits charged from the music and the few moments spent in the company of the gents he had known all his life, he would walk crisply home, speaking to all he met.

"*Buenas noches, Señor Chapultapec,*" Stacy and the others would say to him on Friday evenings.

"*Salud, muchachos,*" he'd answer with extreme good feeling.

If Mitch was there, he would hurl a curse at the old man, who would cast a frightened look Mitch's way and continue on without a pause.

On Sunday evenings, Mr. Chapultapec could be found down at the Catholic church across the street from the project, sitting in the little area set aside for fiestas, sanctioned by the Church, which were held several times each year. There were booths set up where bingo was played; where darts three for a dime were tossed at balloons to win a Kewpie doll or a piggy bank; where washing machines and sets of silverware were raffled off; where kids, their eyes blindfolded, took turns trying to burst the piñata with a stick, then scrambled over the ground to retrieve the prizes that had been inside. At fiesta time, the whole neighborhood would turn out, drop by the church to look, to be seen, to participate. And although the church belonged more to the people of the hills than to those of the project— most of whom seemed to be Protestants or atheists or people who did not belong to anything—they, too, came around.

But on these Sunday evenings, the churchyard would be quiet; and while Mr. Chapultapec sat outside with one or two old men, watching the cars going up and down Mercury Avenue, watching the people passing by, Mrs. Chapultapec would be in the little kitchen in the back of the church with four or five other old women. They would make tacos, tamales, burritos and chili with fried beans, which they sold over a counter through a slitted window, like tellers in banks. The customers would mostly take their purchases with them to eat from paper napkins like hot dogs; but if they chose, as often happened if a fellow had a girl with him they spread their orders on a table in the yard and enjoyed the serene atmosphere Stacy could recall that when he was very little, he and the others would go to the window and the old women would give them a taco or a tamale free, with a kind word and a smile. After he was older and had the money, Stacy would still drop by Sunday evenings to purchase these warm goodies. He loved these old women and their quiet Mexican dignity. They asked no questions and condemned no one and seemed always to have their inner eyes fixed on a distant star.

It was from these old ladies that Stacy first heard the legend of the *Llorona*. He had been younger and the story fascinated him. In the long, long ago, the old women had said, in a small village deep in old Mexico, a wicked woman murdered her three children in a jealous rage, to get revenge on her unfaithful husband, who had run off with a beautiful señorita. She hid their tiny bodies so well that even she could not find where she had hidden them. Sometime later, an angel from God visited her to deliver a divine sentence. Until she found the bodies of her children and took them to the priest for a proper burial, she would know no peace. The wicked woman searched all over but could never find her little ones. Her doom was to wander the world over—in vain!—searching for her lost *niños*. When the wind, blowing down from the hills, whistled through the trees, or when a coyote or a dog howled mournfully, or when there was any other strange noise in the night, it was said to be the *Llorona* crying for her lost *niños* and for mercy from God. The mothers of Crescent Heights kept their kids in line by saying that if they were bad, the *Llorona* would come carry them away. That was why, when Mitch cursed Mrs. Chapultapec, sometimes he would put in, "Fuck the *Llorona* up her ass!" At this, Stacy would feel a chill down his back. One day, Mitch screamed at Mrs. Chapultapec, "You're the *Llorona!*"

Stacy's would be the last generation to grow up in the old Crescent Heights, the Crescent Heights of the hills. They sort of felt that. They felt themselves to be part of something that was passing away. The world of the housing project would conquer in the end. Along with the houses, which were succumbing to decay, Crescent Heights was dying. An image of its death was reflected in the decaying bodies of the old men and women. The younger people were moving deeper into the central city, drawn from the outskirts of town to the inner core by the same forces that attracted other generations of Americans into the new cities from off the farms and out of the countryside. Like all those other great neighborhoods of Los Angeles of the first half of the twentieth century, Crescent Heights had commanded a fierce tribal loyalty from its inhabitants and, along with Maravilla, Flats, Temple, Clanton, The Avenues, Hazard, Happy Valley, Alpine and Rose Hill, it had achieved a greatness and a notoriety in the folklore of Los Angeles. But the glory of these neighborhoods was of a genre alien to that inscribed in the official histories of the city. These were outlaw neighborhoods inhabited by Negroes and Mexicans, viewed by the whites in the core of the city as a ring of barbarians around their Rome, a plague of sunburned devils raging against the city gates. But the people of these neighborhoods had their lives to live. They were born and they died, they loved and they hated, they danced and mated with each other and fought against each other and won their reputations by day and by night.

A clue to the unimportance with which the city fathers regarded Crescent Heights is the fact that during election campaigns, the candidates never bothered to visit there in search of votes. They neither needed nor wanted those tainted votes. In turn, the people of areas such as this viewed the metropolis with distrust and hostility, if not hatred and scorn. Their sons were inducted into its army and were locked into its jails and were channeled, along with their daughters, into its factories. But it could not claim, nor did it seem to want, their loyalty and respect. The metropolis asked no such tender sentiments of the peripheral neighborhoods: it asked only for their sons and daughters.

After the heart had been cut out of Crescent Heights and the housing project built in its place, the inhabitants of the old neighborhood, or what was left of it, lived on in an uncertain wind, under the threat that at any moment, county and state authorities would take over their land, invoking eminent domain. There were all kinds of rumors, inspired by uncertainty and the memory of how suddenly and without warning the other homes had been condemned. One would hear of secret plans to build a country club and golf course in the hills, that the hills would be the site of a huge new campus of the University of California, that the Brooklyn Dodgers were coming to L.A. to build a stadium in the hills or that the housing authority would extend the project, covering vast areas of the hills with concrete, with the pink and yellow rows of apartments designed to official specifications. The only sure thing about these rumors was their effect on the people. No one bothered to lay plans, because they might be forced to move at any moment. No one bothered to improve or repair their houses and land, because they did not want to go to the trouble and expense, only to see their work rolled down the hills by bulldozers—just as they had seen the other houses and dreams demolished to make way for the project. All that was left of the old Crescent Heights were the old people and the last of their children. And in the new, the Crescent Heights of the project, there were only the women with their fatherless children—and the Marijuanos.

In that underground world, psychologically as far beneath the consciousness of a city's solid citizens as a city's sewerage system is beneath its streets, in the subterranean realm of narcotics peddlers and users, marijuana peddlers, gamblers, pimps, prostitutes, the thugs and the cutthroats, the burglars and the robbers, and the police—Crescent Heights had long been known as the marijuana capital of Los Angeles. If the old Crescent Heights was dying, the marijuana traffic did not feel the sting of its death, and it was not the odor or decay that the marijuana pushers smelled but the aroma of folding greenbacks. Even before the project, there was marijuana in Crescent Heights, grown in the hills in modest quantities. But the demand so vastly exceeded the supply that could be cultivated with safety in the hills that of the tons of marijuana flowing into Los Angeles from Mexico, hundreds of pounds of the weed found their way to Crescent Heights. The project became the base of operation, and the weed was controlled by the outlaws of old Crescent Heights, known by the local people as the Marijuanos. They were the alienated sons, in their twenties, of the people of the hills, those sons whom the metropolis had found indigestible. They had criminal records or had dropped out of school without acquiring any skills to fit into the economy. And they were either unfit or disinclined to enter the armed forces. They had fallen back on the skill of the hills, the knack of eluding the police while trafficking in contraband.

While he was very young, Stacy had the exciting experience of knowing a neighborhood hero who happened also to be one of Mitch's older "brothers." Known as Flamingo, his heroism consisted of the fact that he was the first guy from Crescent Heights to go to San Quentin. Surprised in the act of robbing a liquor store in El Serrano, he was wounded in a blazing gunfight with police. His crime partner was shot dead. When, years later, he got out of prison, Flamingo joined the Marijuanos and started dealing in weed. Soon, however, he disappeared from the scene. No one seemed to know where he had gone, but it was said, with knowing winks, that he had gone to Mexico and bought a fabulous hacienda from which he directed the flow of marijuana into Crescent Heights.

In Stacy and his gang, the Marijuanos inspired a romantic apprehension just short of fear. Not that they had anything to fear from the Marijuanos, whom they had known all their lives and to whom they were connected by memories and, in some cases, by blood. But the presence of the Marijuanos infused Crescent Heights with an aura of danger and mystery. At night, while Stacy and the others would be down at the playground, loafing, they would see the strangers who came to Crescent Heights furtively, after dark, and who would sometimes ask them, "Are any of the guys around?"

Stacy had directed many an inquirer to the spot where the Marijuanos might be. But if, when out at night, Stacy's gang was always aware of the whereabouts of the Marijuanos, it was more for the purpose of keeping out of their way than anything else. If the Marijuanos came too near, Stacy and his gang, with the excited feeling of being brushed by danger, would run away to another part of the project. But the Marijuanos kept generally to the darker sections of the project and Stacy and the others had the playground and other lighted areas to themselves. It was commonly known that the Marijuanos sometimes knocked out streetlights to make it darker in certain favored spots; it would be a couple of months before the county sent someone around to fix them.

If Stacy or the others ever saw a policeman, they'd run tell the Marijuanos. "The narcs are over there," they'd say, and the Marijuanos would melt away into the shadows. But every so often, Stacy would hear that one of them had gotten caught by the narcs and was put in jail.

Stacy wanted something to happen. The gang was beginning to seem like a prison and, although he continued to play his role, he went through the steps mechanically, his mind drifting, looking for somewhere to lodge. He had toyed with the idea of quitting school to look for a job somewhere, but it did not occur to him that he would really do this; it was more or less his way of threatening himself. He did want profoundly for his life to change. He felt that he could no longer endure school, the gang and the endless round of throwing raids on El Serrano. Now, when he burglarized a building, he would come away feeling disappointed, no matter what the haul. He no longer had the patience to search out all the hiding places, and so if things were not left out in plain sight, he would miss them. And this had been Stacy's main function in the gang. He was known to have a nose for sniffing out the valuables hidden by the owners in some secret cranny. Now he could feel a growing dissatisfaction among the others and, although no one criticized him, he knew they were watching him, wondering. How could he explain to them what was going on inside himself, when he himself didn't know? How could he explain that his pride was offended by what they were doing? How could he make them understand that if they carried off everything in El Serrano, it would not be enough to satisfy what he was beginning to feel inside?

He did not voice these questions; they were the ghosts behind his changed attitude toward the others. It began to bother him that when they burglarized a place, he was always the first one to go in, to look around and make sure it was safe before the others entered. If he didn't go in first, they'd just stand there and scare each other, and the fear would travel around the circle until panic set in. But even after he had crawled through the window, searched the whole place for hidden danger—a night watchman, a dog—they were still afraid, it seemed to him, of the dark, of what they could not see in the dark if something were there. It was easy for them to imagine anything being there: a squad of policemen crouching in the comer, waiting until they were all inside before switching on the lights to mow them down with shotguns or to capture them and take them to Juvenile Hall; or a pack of menacing Doberman pinschers or German shepherds too cool to bark that would leap on them from behind and rip their flesh to shreds. This fear had always been with them and, in the past, they all used to laugh at it. But now it seemed totally unacceptable to Stacy.

Mitch, though, was never afraid. The danger with him was that, spurred on by his total contempt for everything, he would crawl through a window as if he owned the place and, once inside, while shaking it down to see if it was safe, would growl viciously to attract any dogs, kick over packing crates, upset tables and chairs, in an effort to smoke out something. He'd open closets and store rooms. Unable to see in the dark, he would not hesitate to yell into the void, "Hey, you in there, I see you! Get the fuck out of there!"

The first time he did that, pandemonium broke loose among the others and they took off, running. Stacy had to run after them, overtake them, shake some sense into them before they could understand that it was only Mitch who had shouted. It had been a hard job persuading them to go back with him and impossible to get them to crawl through the window into the dark room, because Mitch, when Stacy called to him to prove to the others that it was safe, refused to answer. Stacy pictured him, leering at them through the dark, that sullen, scornful scowl on his face. In that moment, Stacy wanted to kick that face. He knew that Mitch was probably looking right at them, at the window that was a patch of light silhouetted against the night sky, but would not answer.

"You lousy bastard, Mitch!" Stacy said into the dark window. But in another sense, Stacy thought it was beautiful of Mitch not to answer, especially at a time like this, when he himself was absolutely serious and the others were afraid and they all were a long way from home and in danger of being shot or taken to jail. It took real dedication for Mitch to remain perverse in such circumstances. The others refused to precede Stacy through the window.

"Well, fuck all of you, then," he said, exasperated, and went swiftly through the window.

The others hesitated at first, decided all at the same time that they'd rather be inside than out, and they all tried to squeeze through the window at once, making a ton of racket, cursing and scratching each other as they fought to get through.

Then Mitch, somewhere in the darkness, hissed at them, "Shut the fuck up!"

Guided by his voice, Stacy caught Mitch in the dark and, bringing up his knee with just slightly less than hostile force, he shook Mitch up and shoved him to the floor. "Next time, you better answer me, you stupid shit!" he said. And, extending his foot in the dark, he made contact with Mitch, jarring him with a stiff thrust. It felt like he got him in the side.

Now that they were inside, Stacy could hear the others as they scuffled about in the dark, searching for objects of value with which to fill their gunny sacks. Stacy did not even unroll his sack. He leaned against a wall and let his mind drift as he waited for the others to finish. He was thinking of what had happened the previous week, when he had first made up his mind that this could not go on, that something had to change, that he had to find himself a new life.

The thought had come to him during a raid on a school cafeteria a week before. After eating all they could hold and filling their sacks, they had thrown all the other food on the floor, gutted the refrigerator, smashed all the cups, salt and pepper shakers and glasses, scattered the silverware, bent the trays out of shape and overturned the tables..

"Stacy, make Mitch stop!" Turtle said.

Mitch had turned all the jets of the gas range up full blast. Flames leaped at the ceiling. Shoving Mitch aside, Stacy began spinning the knobs to shut off the flow of gas. Screaming, Mitch came at him with a fork. Stacy feinted at him and, when Mitch slashed at him with the fork, Stacy stepped back and caught his arm, twisting it behind his back.

"Drop it!" Stacy demanded, applying pressure.

"You cocksucker!" hissed Mitch, defeated, holding the fork just long enough to register his defiance.

Stacy turned all the burners down.

"Let's burn this motherfucker down!" Mitch pleaded. "Then the *gavachos* won't have a school to go to!"

"That's going too far," the others protested in a chorus.

"That did it. That nauseated Stacy. *That's going too far.* The words burned into his mind. What did they mean by that? That's when Stacy really knew that he was finished, that he had to cut all this loose. Like a sailor locking the hatches on a submarine, he twirled the knobs, opening all the jets all the way, and the range burst into flames again.

"Let's go!" he shouted. He helped the others out the window. Looking around, he saw Mitch in front of the range, jumping up and down, laughing hysterically and cursing the flames in Spanish. Stacy rushed back and dragged him away by his belt.

"Leave go! Leave go!" Mitch yelled, as he struggled to free himself, straining toward the flames.

The building was mostly of wood and in a minute it would be one raging inferno. Stacy, seeing that Mitch would not relent in his efforts to return to the fire, hit him in his gut and shoved him up and out through the window. As Stacy came through the window, just as he expected, Mitch tried to kick him in the face to knock him back into the burning room. Catching Mitch's foot in the air, Stacy hurled himself backward into the dark night air, landing him on his ass; and as Stacy ran past Mitch, he was very careful not to miss stepping on him. He heard curses behind him in the night as he ran to catch up with the others.

The idea, voiced by the others, that Mitch had been "going too far" bothered Stacy. It sounded like the belief that if one sailed far enough over the open seas, one would eventually sail off the edge of the world. He found solace in repeating to himself: The world is round; you can sail on and on and end up where you started. It was as if the others were saying to him that the world is flat. His mind seized upon this incident to justify breaking with his gang. He was only waiting for the right moment.

The next time the others asked him to go on a raid, Stacy said no. After the others resigned themselves to inactivity for the night, Mitch and he stole away from them, leaving them sitting around the playground looking dejected, and the two of them headed for El Serrano by themselves. They prowled around for hours, without spotting anything worthwhile. It was Saturday night and every house seemed occupied; every business establishment, though they saw some that were obviously deserted and closed down for the weekend, seemed strangely forbidding and whispering of threat, crawling with hidden danger. They both felt this, without speaking about it, tacitly deciding there was no chance for action that night. Walking through alleys, down dark streets, always in the shadows, cutting back, zigzagging, to avoid the glow of streetlights, they trekked to the heart of El Serrano. They knew they could not afford to be seen by anyone, because only whites lived there and one look at them and it would be all over. If a car headed their way, they scrambled for cover, crouching behind parked cars, lying flat behind trees, kneeling down in the shrubbery near houses. The police would know, upon seeing them, that their only business there was to steal. El Serrano was their happy hunting ground. They had been hunting there for years, and for as long as he had been doing it, not one of his gang had got caught. The cops would lie in wait for them, leaving a bait of valuables out in clear sight, but they always passed it up. "That's a fishhook," they'd whisper to each other in the dark, gliding through the shadows. Sometimes they'd sneak noiselessly right past the cops sitting in their patrol car parked in the shadows. Once, Mitch had crawled up to their car on his belly, like a commando, and removed the valve from a rear tire. By the time the cops detected the flat, Mitch was well away.

"Let's hit a few cars, if nothing else," Stacy said to Mitch, as they crept silently down an alley.

"OK," Mitch said.

With their screwdrivers, they jimmied the vent windows on the passenger side of a few cars, sticking in an arm to roll down the window, then shoving their heads through the window to look around inside the car. It was their habit to take anything of value. They'd take coats, binoculars, guns, tools, radios, groceries, anything they could use or sell. Most of their loot they sold to the people of the project at cheap prices. They didn't care; all they wanted was a little something to keep them going from day to day. Goods in hand, they'd go from door to door and show what they had. The people would jokingly call them bad boys, but they were always glad to see them. They'd let them in, pull the curtains and examine the display. Clothes for their children, for themselves, cooking utensils, lamps, clocks, radios—everything went. If they could not sell something, the gang would give it away. If nobody wanted it, they'd throw it away. But most of the time, if they had something that wouldn't sell, they'd let Mitch keep it. His cellar contained a wealth of worthless loot.

Their pockets and sacks filled, Stacy and Mitch had almost called it quits when Stacy saw another car that seemed to beckon to him. That car, he was to think later, communicated with him. He had already got himself a nice leather jacket that, because he was big for his age, was not a bad fit. He got to the car and opened the window. On the front seat was the long, snaky body of a five-battery flashlight and a fifth of whiskey in a bag. Good for a few bucks, Stacy thought. He fell in with Mitch and they headed for home.

As soon as they were a safe distance away, Stacy tested the flashlight, playing it down a pitch-black alley, fascinated by its powerful beam.

"Put out that fucking light, man!" Mitch growled curtly. "You trying to signal to the cops where we are, or something?"

Stacy shined the light in Mitch's face. Mitch tried to stare the beam down, but it wounded his eyes, forcing him to turn his head.

"You crazy fucker," he said in disgust.

Stacy felt giddy about the flashlight, his new possession. Its properties he seemed to appropriate and incorporate into his own being. The light, he felt, was a powerful extension of himself.

The next night, when they all met at the playground, Stacy took his flashlight with him. It was an instrument that had to be used, a charge that by its potency refused to lie idle. As he left his room, it all but leaped into his hand, guiding itself into his palm. He had taken it completely apart several times, feeling a flush of triumph each time he reassembled it, flicked the button and saw the bulb glow. It seemed to him that when he assembled the parts, he was creating the light. And he had the strange feeling that this light would be the instrument by which great change would come into his life.

He loved his light. When he broke it down, he would caress the five batteries with his fingers, and the bulb, the gaskets, the spring in the cap. So closely did he examine each part that he had no doubt that out of a mountain of similar parts, he could easily select his own.

He would use the power of the batteries sparingly. As they all lay on the grass of the playground, the others kept urging him to turn it on, to show them how powerful was its beam. Stacy stood up and cast the beam into the hills, and a patch of light could be seen dimly sweeping the surface of the hills at a great distance. The others were impressed. Stacy lay on the lawn, fondling the metallic tube that held the mysteries of his future.

"Where did you score it?" asked one of the others.

"El Serrano," Stacy answered.

"When?"

"Last night."

"Last night?" Turtle perked up. "I thought you said last night you weren't going?"

Stacy made no reply. A heavy silence ensued. The others, not looking directly at Stacy, were nevertheless watching him closely, waiting for an answer to clarify what looked now like a betrayal.

Stacy said nothing.

A few minutes passed in this silence.

Then Mitch said, "Don't you punks know when you're not wanted along? Can't you take a hint?" Mitch spoke in a harsh, contemptuous tone, which was not directed to Turtle alone but to all the others. "Me and Stacy ducked you suckers last night and we scored heavy by ourselves. I got myself a flashlight, too, just like that one." After a significant pause, he added, "Who needs you guys with them? All you ever do is make noise."

Stacy was embarrassed, for he could feel himself how Mitch's words were hurting the others. He smothered an impulse to smash Mitch's face, to make him shut up, to make him retract that lie about his own flashlight—but he held back. Inside, he was glad that Mitch had spoken these things, for now something was done that could never be undone, and he had the intimation that Mitch was setting him free. Then he said, "You've got a big, dumb mouth, Mitch."

"It's my mouth," Mitch snapped back," big or not."

Suddenly, Stacy felt a deep loathing for the position he was in. He hated the necessity of giving them an explanation. If he acknowledged that he owed them an explanation, he would be sucked back in and lose this chance. Jumping up, he kicked Mitch in his side, and as he ran off into the night, he could hear Mitch's laughter following him.

He ran until he was exhausted, then walked until he found himself at the other end of the project. Around him, it was quiet and dark. The apartment windows were yellow squares where the shades stopped the light. He sat down on the lawn, propped himself up against a tree and closed his eyes. His heart still raced in his chest from running. He clung to his flashlight, glad to be alone.

Sometime later, he became aware of the sound of movement near him; he heard the muffled rustling of paper. Opening his eyes, at first he could make out nothing, then just below him, where the lawn on which he sat sloped down to meet the sidewalk, he saw a shadowy form kneeling and reaching into the hedge next to Mrs. Chapman's front door. Stacy realized it was a Marijuano, but he couldn't make out which one. As he sat there watching, it seemed to him that he was becoming aware of the Marijuanos for the first time. Then he wondered, What would the Marijuano do if he shined the flashlight on him? This thought, this possibility of making something happen, already had fastened upon his imagination; and even as he hesitated, he knew that he would end up by doing it. He perceived, in a flash, that such a step would set in motion forces of which he was not even aware. What will happen? he wondered. Am I afraid to do it? By putting the question to himself in terms of his courage, he knew that he had to do it.

Silently, he got to his feet and squatted on his haunches. Aiming his flashlight at the phantom, he savored the keen edge of the moment before the action, anticipating it with sharp exhilaration. Then he pressed the button. It was Chango! Chango froze, all lit up, his face contorted, eyes wide with panic. For the briefest moment, Chango remained motionless, his arm buried in the hedge up to his shoulder. Then he exploded, scooting backward on his knees, stumbling to his feet, tripping, falling down, crawling, looking over his shoulder to see if he was being chased, his face hysterical. Stacy kept the light on him till he turned the corner on the hump, then he flicked off the light and ran toward the playground. When he came to another dark spot, he fell onto the lawn and laughed till he could hardly breathe, rolling on the ground. The way Chango had looked when the beam first split his face, how he had flown! For long after, just the thought of it would send him chuckling.

That night, he dreamed that the world was inside a box with steep sides and no top, like the walls of a frontier fort, and the sun was a huge flashlight of a billion batteries with a tube so long it never ended; and some kid in the sky watching the people groping in darkness below pressed the button and the people said "Day" and he released the button and the people said "Night." Stacy woke up in a sweat, clutching his flashlight, keenly appreciative of the powers of light.

The next day, time seemed to slow down on purpose to torture him. It was with a keen foretaste of pleasure that he awaited the setting of the sun. All during school, he could think of nothing but his flashlight, the Marijuanos and how he would terrorize them again tonight. He saw himself chasing them all over the project. They would be there tonight, he had not the slightest doubt. They were always there. When it rained, they donned heavy coats and plastic slickers and did business as usual. The only time the Marijuanos would leave was when the cops came; and when the cops went away, the Marijuanos reappeared, like air drawn into a vacuum. That evening, Stacy hid in the bushes around the square at the end of the row of apartments in which Mrs. Chapman lived, not far from the spot where he had surprised Chango. The square was one of several located at strategic intervals throughout the project, placed there by the architects to add beauty to public housing. It was a concrete-covered clearing thirty feet by forty feet, surrounded with hedges and flowers and shaded by a tall tree. The tree's rich foliage hung over the square like a giant umbrella. It could actually stop rain. On each side of the square were four cement benches of the type often seen in public parks: a flat slab resting on two upright stays. During the daylight hours, the little kids scampered and romped in the square, riding in their wagons and on tricycles, catching and bouncing big rubber balls, jumping rope, playing jacks and hopscotch. At night, the Marijuanos took it over, using it to contact customers who came to Crescent Heights from all over Los Angeles to score their weed.

Stacy waited for the right moment. Hidden in the shadows of the square, the Marijuanos were smoking weed and making transactions. The acrid aroma tantalized Stacy's nostrils. He had smelled burning marijuana before, but never from so close. He knew that what he was doing was very dangerous and this knowledge, coupled with the intrigue of the night, the smell of the burning marijuana and the sight of men moving back and forth, talking in low voices and laughing now and then, gave it all a touch of adventure. Stacy felt keenly alive. He was doing something none of the others had ever dreamed of doing. He knew also that if a bush moved, the Marijuanos noticed it. Like him, they were all neighborhood boys who had spent their entire lives in the immediate area. They knew every tree, every hole in the ground, every rock, every bush and everybody. They could feel a cop coming. No cop could have snuck up on them as Stacy had done. It would not have been natural. But Stacy, who knew and loved every inch of the earth of Crescent Heights, had crept right up on the Marijuanos. With a little effort, he could have reached out and touched them. When he could bear it no longer, Stacy aimed his flashlight into the square. Before pressing the button, he gave the bushes a violent shake, drawing the Marijuanos' attention to him, then let go with the light. The Marijuanos gave up the square in a mad stampede, crashing through the bushes and running over each other. Stacy then dashed off in the direction the Marijuanos were least likely to take: He sprinted to the well-lit playground.

Three days later, at school, Mitch said, "The Marijuanos are after you."

"After me for what?" Stacy asked, a look of surprise on his face.

"You know for what," Mitch said curtly. "You and that flashlight, that's what."

"What about my flashlight?" Stacy asked, hungrily wanting to hear any details.

"You won't be playing dumb when they catch you," said Mitch. "Cutie, Chico and Chango said they're going to catch you and fuck you up. You know better than to fool around with those guys."

Stacy had not expected the Marijuanos to send him congratulations, but he did not really feel in danger; just as when he went on raids to El Serrano, he had not regarded the dangers as real. They were part of a game, like a penalty in football. If one made no mistakes, it was as if the penalties did not even exist.

"Fuck the Marijuanos, " Stacy said.

"That's easy to say," said Mitch, "but wait till they get their hands on you. The Marijuanos don't play around when they mean business."

Stacy had assumed that each time he turned on his light, the Marijuanos would automatically react the same way—run. But now that they knew it was he and not the cops, he knew their reactions would change. Whereas their main purpose had been to flee from a cop, it was now an angry desire to extinguish Stacy's light.

"The Marijuanos said you're putting the heat on them," Mitch had said.

"Later for them," Stacy said. But he was joined by that charge. In Crescent Heights, only a rat would knowingly put the heat on someone. And a known rat couldn't last five minutes in Crescent Heights. It was unheard of. Stacy had not expected such a charge. He threw it from his mind as too absurd and unpleasant to think about. He continued to creep up on the Marijuanos and flash his light on them. And when he did, it was he who had to take off, running, because the Marijuanos would be right on his heels. It was easy for Stacy to outdistance them. They laid traps for him. Some of them hid in the bushes while the others tried to sucker him in. They laid up a store of bricks, bottles and beer cans. Once, they hid near Stacy's home to ambush him on his way home. Stacy laughed at them and outflanked their every maneuver. Their battle, the Marijuanos' efforts to catch Stacy and his efforts to escape, became notorious in Crescent Heights. Everybody knew they were after him. Everyone waited for news that Stacy had at last been caught. Eluding the Marijuanos became his full-time occupation. He defied them with pride.

But underneath it all, Stacy had some regrets that the feud had ever gotten started. He would have liked nothing better than to be out of the spot he was in, which was becoming more difficult to occupy. He wished that he could just leave them alone and drop the whole thing, to be done with the whole affair, to be free from worrying about how to get away from the Marijuanos in a given situation. But he continued to force the issue, convinced that he would somehow come through it all unscathed. The Marijuanos became marksmen with bricks and bottles and it took some prize footwork by Stacy to keep from getting his brains knocked out. Even so, they hit him in the side once with a heavy rock that took the wind out of him, and the only thing that kept him from collapsing on the spot was the sure knowledge of what they would do to him if they caught him.

The Marijuanos sent people to talk to Stacy, but he refused to listen. They repeated that he was ruining their business.

Stacy's mother said to him, "Son, you better mind your p's and q's. I know what you been doing and you'd better stop it."

"I know what I'm doing," Stacy said.

Now the other members of the gang shied away from Stacy. They said he had gone crazy and they saw nothing positive in his keen thrill of excitement in outwitting the Marijuanos. They didn't know how it felt to be hunted by them, to elude their traps, to spring out of the bushes unannounced with a blazing torch and scare the pants off of the Marijuanos. The Marijuanos were all in their twenties and

Stacy, who felt neither old nor young, enjoyed this relationship with individuals already grown. He was a factor in their existence, whether they liked it or not. He had chosen them, like some gadfly in a dangerous game. They were stuck with Stacy and it was up to them to solve the problem. For his part, Stacy's course was clear. He would continue to bug them with his light.

One night, he climbed up a tree and from his perch saw Polio, a fat, phlegmatic Mexican, hide a little bag behind a bush. Several times, Polio returned to the bush, extracted from the bag, replaced it and went away. Stacy shinnied down the tree and chose a spot ten feet away from Polio's stash. The next time Polio came back, Stacy waited until he had gotten the bag and stuck his hand into it, then he hit him in the face with the blinding beam of the light. Dropping the bag, Polio uttered a cry and was in full flight before he realized it was Stacy, himself already running through the night in the opposite direction. He had scored again. It was coups like that that egged him on.

The Marijuanos tried a new trick. As Stacy walked home from school with the others one evening, two cars, one in front of him and one behind, pulled sharply into the curb and out poured the Marijuanos. They had not, however, counted on the speed of Stacy's legs. Stacy leaped over a fence into someone's yard and, before the startled dog in the yard realized what was happening, ran out the back way, was over the back fence and cutting out up the hill. Looking back, he saw the Marijuanos pile into their cars, burning rubber getting out of there. The stakes were going up. Such desperation!

When Stacy was in his classrooms, he was careful to sit near a window, in case the Marijuanos burst in to trap him. He suffered through his third-period class, because it was on the second floor and there was no ledge outside the windows. He felt trapped in that room. He fully expected the Marijuanos to know all about this particular room, and he would not have been surprised to look up one day and find them there. He watched for them in the halls, on the stairways, in the schoolyard, behind lockers in the gymnasium. During lunch hour, he often saw the Marijuanos drive by the school, their faces sweeping the crowd with Stacy-seeking eyes.

One day, the Marijuanos stopped chasing him and they stopped throwing things at him. When he crept up on them and flashed his light, they'd just look at him, in his direction. Stacy couldn't figure it out, but he didn't hang around waiting for answers. He ran away, as usual. One evening, Stacy was down at the playground, loafing, with his flashlight stuck in his belt like a knife or a gun. Turtle walked up to him.

"Chico wants to talk to you," Turtle said, pointing to another part of the playground, where, dressed in blue denims and wearing dark glasses, Chico stood waiting on the other side of the Cyclone fence. Warily, Stacy walked over, staying on his side of the fence, continually looking over his shoulder to see if the other Marijuanos were sneaking up on him while Chico held his attention.

"What do you want?" Stacy asked, mistrustfully.

"Say, Stacy," Chico began, "this shit has got to stop, man."

Stacy could see that Chico was burning with anger but trying also to conceal it. It shone like flaming coals in his black eyes. His mouth was set in a fixed, down-thrusting scowl. Through the fence, Stacy got the same feeling he had had when, at the Griffith Park Zoo, he had stood outside the cage of a lion and stared into its huge cat eyes. He was thankful for the fence between them. He said nothing, only stared into Chico's dark glasses, at the fire in those eyes, and he saw something there besides anger and hatred, something that surprised him: he saw the embryo of a smile.

"I want to make a deal with you," Chico said.

"What kind of a deal?" Stacy asked, regarding Chico narrowly. His anxiety was that the other Marijuanos were sure to try something.

"Here," Chico said, and he shoved a ten-dollar bill into a square of the fence. Stacy let it lie there, wedged in the wire.

"What's that for?" asked Stacy.

"For your flashlight," Chico said.

"For ten dollars, you can buy three or four like this one," Stacy said, patting his flashlight on his side.

"I want yours," said Chico.

The flashlight weighed heavily on Stacy's side. The full realization of what a burden it had become flowed in upon him. He wanted with all his heart to be rid of it.

"Listen to me, Stacy," Chico said. "You're a young cat and you don't realize what's going on. But you'd better think fast, because you don't have much time left. You know what the other guys want to do? Look." He lifted the corner of his shirt and showed Stacy the handle of a pistol stuck in his belt. "They want to just kill you. Because you're ranking our play. You're messing with our bread and butter, man."

Strangely, Stacy was not afraid. But he felt a knot in his chest, to think that the Marijuanos had been discussing his death.

"Listen, man," Chico went on. "We could kill you and bury you up on Walnut Hill and nobody would ever find your body. It would be no trouble at all. The cops wouldn't even look for you. You're just another nigger to them and they don't give a fuck about you. You know why we haven't done you up?"

Stacy stared at him impassively, not trusting himself to ask why, for not wanting to sound too urgent.

"Because you're one of us. You're from Crescent Heights." Chico paused. "So we decided to give you the respect of letting you make a choice. But maybe you're too fucking wild to see what's happening. We never like to fight with each other in Crescent Heights, Stacy, you know that. Because by sticking together, we can all make it, maybe. At least better than by fighting ourselves. At least we'll have a better chance. I'm a married man and I have my family to look out for. I don't have time to fuck around with you or anybody else. This is strictly business with me. If I get caught, I'm going to the can, and I don't look forward to that. I'm going to do everything in my power to see to it that I never get caught. Right now—" Chico paused, then went on—"right now, you are more of a problem than the narcs. So we've got to settle this right now. Right now. You know what, Stacy?" Chico looked at him and seemed to be measuring him. "You're getting to be about that age . . . Do you get high? Do you blow weed?"

"No," Stacy said.

"Well, pretty soon . . ." he paused. "It won't be long before you're going to get tired of running around in a pair of dirty Levi's, fucking off your time with those other young cats. I've dug you and I know that you've got something on the ball. Pretty soon, you're going to want some nice clothes and some money in your pocket, some of that folding money, and you're going to want a little car of your own to ride around in with the bitches. But then you're going to find out the world is not a—" he broke off, looking around him, and swept the area with his arm—"a playground. You're going to find out the world is not a merry-go-round. It's hard, hard, Stacy. But we've got a good thing going for us here in Crescent Heights, and we intend to keep it working for us. You guys call us Marijuanos . . . Yeah, we're Marijuanos, all right. But there are lots more Marijuanos in L.A., and lots of them come to us to score their jive. And you, with your flashlight, are fucking with all of that. I used to think like you and act like you. You know my brother Black Jack, don't you?"

"Yeah," Stacy said. "Everybody knows Black Jack."

"He used to control the action in Crescent Heights," Chico went on. "And he used to try getting me interested, but my mind was locked somewhere else. I was about your age and I used to call him Marijuano. Now I've got the bag and you're calling me Marijuano. It goes around and comes around; you take it a little way and then pass it on. Pretty soon, the little kids will be calling you Marijuano and, some-day, kids that are not even born yet will be calling them Marijuanos. It will never end. But it's going to end for you unless you straighten up your hand.

"Take the money," Chico said, "and we'll forget the whole thing. We'll forget it all happened."

Stacy hesitated for a long moment, then said, "What about the others?"

"Same with them," Chico said. "Nobody will bother you. I give you my word. But you have to give me your word that you won't fool around anymore. I'm not giving you the money to buy you off. I'm giving it to you to wake you up."

"What good is your word?" Stacy asked. "How do I know you're not just setting me up?"

Chico looked at Stacy fiercely. "I never break my word when I give it like this. If I say I won't bother you, I won't. If I say I'm going to kill you, you're as good as dead."

Stacy walked down to the end of the fence, where it was lower. As he jumped over, he saw Mitch and the others watching. He walked up to Chico and handed him the flashlight. Chico pulled the ten-dollar bill from the fence and placed it in Stacy's hand.

"Play it cool," Chico said, and walked away.

Stacy did not turn around to look after Chico. It felt good. It was a relief not to have to look over his shoulder anymore. The others walked over to Stacy. They all understood what had happened. They were all glad it was over. They all laughed and punched each other lightly to the body.

"You punks are crazy," said Mitch, off to the side.

"Let's throw a raid on El Serrano tonight," Turtle suggested.

"Count me out," Stacy said with mock astonishment, "I might find another flashlight!"

That night, Stacy walked into the square. When they saw who it was, the Marijuanos quickly surrounded him. There was murder in the intense way they crowded him.

"What the fuck you want?" Cutie snapped, fuming, his voice menacing, with overtones of blood.

"Nothing," Stacy said. He felt crushed, confused.

"Leave him alone," Chico spoke up. "Forget about it. I gave him my word that it was all over.

"You gave him your word," said Cutie, "but I didn't give him mine."

Stacy heard the click of Cutie's knife as it sprang open, although he couldn't see it in the darkness. He was afraid. Cutie was breathing in his face. The others stepped back. Stacy calculated his chances of running. All Cutie had to do was thrust upward with the blade to do damage.

"When I gave him my word, I gave him yours," Chico said. "And nobody's going to make me out a liar. Leave him alone, Cutie." Chico spoke with force and authority and he added, lowering his voice ominously, "Or are you going to make me out a liar?"

Cutie stepped back from Stacy and put his knife up. Tension evaporated from the square. The Marijuanos lit up joints of the weed.

Chico offered Stacy a joint.

"Never mind," Stacy said halfheartedly.

Chico fumbled with the joint and then lit it from the one being smoked by Gato. After he had taken a couple of drags, he passed it to Stacy.

"Here," he said.

Stacy took the joint between his fingers and raised it to his mouth, puffing in and immediately coughing out the acrid smoke. It felt like breathing over a burning rag. He was amazed at how the others could be smoking it if it tasted so bad.

"Do it like this," Chico said, taking the joint from Stacy. Chico took a long, powerful drag. Stacy watched the coal of fire travel up the joint as Chico consumed about half of it in that one drag. "Take it down into your lungs and hold it," he said. "You'll get used to it. The main thing is to hold it in your lungs as long as you can."

Stacy struggled over the remainder of the joint, coughing and choking occasionally, his throat getting raw, his eyes running, his heart racing. He was confused and a little apprehensive but continued to inhale the weed and hold in the smoke until his lungs expelled it. Then it was as if he ceased to exist. He was confronting a stranger in a body he recognized as his own but with which he was out of touch. His former state was now a memory; his new state was a soft, jet-smooth present fact. He had the sensation of being two disembodied beings fighting to inhabit one yielding body. His body, offering no resistance, became a battlefield on which two rival armies contended. The pitch of the war escalated as he took in more marijuana from the joints being passed around the circle of Marijuanos. Stacy accepted every one offered to him, and once he ended up with a lit reefer in each hand, puffing first one and then the other. He no longer cared or tried to keep track of how the war inside him was progressing. No matter which way it went, he thought, he'd still be the winner. He lost track of time. Everything seemed to occur without sequence, as if it was all happening simultaneously and spontaneously, separated rather by space than by time. He was dimly aware of people furtively entering the square, engaging one or another of the Marijuanos in short, snappy conversation. He watched as the Marijuanos collected money and disappeared from the square for a few moments, to return and hand something to the customer. These furtive shadows would brace up and, in a moment, fade from the square into the vast Los Angeles night.

Stacy was so high off the weed that the center of his vision was blotted out, although he could see perfectly well around the edges; and through these clear edges, he was trying to see into the center, around the dark spot. He had the impression that someone had taken a bottle of liquid shoe polish and, using the dauber, painted his eyeballs down the center. He did not notice that everyone was leaving, had drifted out of the square and gone for the night—except Chico, who was talking. At first, Stacy could make no sense of what he was saying.

"What? What?" Stacy kept asking him, over and over again.

"Go home, Stacy."

"What?"

"Go to your pad, man. I'm going to split."

"What?"

"It's one o'clock, man. You got too high."

Chico was laughing in Stacy's face. He was really having a big laugh. Stacy laughed, too. His face felt like rubber and he couldn't control his expression, though is was very dark in the square and Chico could not tell. Stacy's face seemed to be sagging and he was flexing his facial muscles to hold it in place, but it kept sliding down again. "I'm not high," he said.

"No, you're not high," Chico said, laughing. "You're wasted!"

Stacy was laughing, too.

"Do you think you can find your way to your pad?" Chico asked.

"Sure," Stacy said. "Who could forget that?" Even as he spoke, he experienced the panic of having no idea where he lived. "Where are we right now?" he asked Chico.

Chico knew that, although it was funny, it was also a serious phase Stacy was going through; and if he had not been there, Stacy might have wandered around Crescent Heights all night, looking for his house.

"We're in the square by Mrs. Chapman's house," Chico said.

"Where is Mrs. Chapman's house?" Stacy asked.

Chico turned Stacy to his right and he recognized Mrs. Chapman's apartment at the end of the row. From there, traveling like a beam of light, his mind raced off into infinity, reconstructing that portion of the universe of which he was aware . . . There is Mrs. Chapman's pad, this is the square, the playground is down there, that's Boundary Avenue up there. Florizel Street over there, Mercury Avenue over there, downtown L.A. is that way, Pasadena is that way, Lincoln Heights is over there, El Serrano and Alhambra are over there—I live down that way. Stacy felt serene, lucid, triumphant, peculiarly masterful and at peace.

"I'm going home," he said to Chico.

"Think you can make it?"

"Sure," he said. "Ain't nothing to it."

"I'll see you around," Chico said.

Stacy had started to walk in the direction of home when he missed something. He stopped, wondering what it was he was forgetting. Then he remembered the flashlight and laughed to himself. He did not know yet whether a Marijuano had any use for a flashlight. As he walked dreamily home, he had no doubt that he would soon find out.

Support Your Local Police

ED BULLINS

S UPPORT YOUR LOCAL POLICE!!! the bumper sticker read. And I should have known
better. From the way he slowed in front of me before he got to the toll gate,
and from his hesitation and his annoyed, "Ahhh, the hell with it," gesture that he
gave me crouched over from the cold. But I should have known not to relax as I
ran up behind the car after it stopped, my eyes on that bumper sticker. SUPPORT
YOUR LOCAL POLICE!!!

But then the Harrisburg exit of the Pennsylvania Turnpike seemed a gateway
to the below-freezing winds, and I had been trying to get any kind of lift for all of
two hours.

"Thanks," I said when I got into the car.

"Where you comin' from?"

"New York."

"Been waitin' long?"

"About two hours."

"It's a lousy spot. Where you goin'?" the driver asked.

"San Francisco."

"Boy! You really got a trip ahead of you, haven't you?"

"Yeah, I guess I have."

"Well, I'm only going a few exits down and then I'm going south."

That's how I ended up in Lexington, Virginia. Route 60 goes right through
there, and that's where my driver was going, to Lexington.

"The radio says there's a snowstorm comin' from the Midwest."

"Yeah, that's what I heard this morning."

After that it didn't take much prodding from him to get me to take the swing
below the Mason Dixon and out of the path of winter. I entered the South almost
without looking back.

I told him that I was going to San Francisco to get married, and find a good
job. He seemed to believe that my fiancee's name was Patsy Mae and that she
worked in a laundry, pressing shirts, and that I usually found work as a janitor or in

a car wash.

That's the story I usually use when hitchhiking all over the country, to everyone. Marriage, and janitor or car wash. I've learned that that story works on nearly all of them. For hours I can spin out fantasy about my Patsy Mae and how good life is going to be for us, especially if I get work in a good firm out west, like Dow or Lockheed or Boeing. And how California is famous with us colored people all across the country for them wonderful lifetime jobs. I tell these stories with a straight face and sometimes talk so much about Patsy Mae that the more brainy of my benefactors become bored with my conversation.

But I know better than to tell them that I am a writer, especially a playwright, and that I'm going to the West Coast this particular occasion to see one of my own plays in Los Angeles and to see and make love to an old girlfriend of mine in San Francisco. People get upset when you tell them the truth, some might even be hurt, especially those who have strange stickers on the bumpers of their cars. Now, what if I had said, "I'm a playwright involved in the Black Revolution and I'm hitchhiking to California to see one of my black revolutionary plays?" Or, "I'm going to see my ex-girlfriend. She's white, you know. (Winking as I say it.) And I don't honestly know truthfully whether I'm going to see my play out there, 'cause I've seen it already, or to see her. (Smiling at my own candor.) She's very nice and white, being Jewish and raised in St. Louis, but actually born in Texas, so more than likely you have much in common with her."

Now, I couldn't say that, could I? Those answers shouldn't come from black hitchhikers, writers or no. And since I knew this, I changed my speech accordingly.

"Yeah, Patsy Mae and me are gonna have a mess of kids. Maybe six or more."

"Well boy, if you and your little lady ever get down to Lexington, I got a friend who can always use a good presser."

"Oh thanks a lot."

Night closed in on the road and the Southern Pennsylvania hills and a sign came up: WELCOME TO MARYLAND—NO HITCH-HIKING!

"I thought Colorado was the only state that outlawed hitchhiking," I said.

"Well, you never know, boy, now do you?"

And his speedometer was at 95.

"Don't feel like we goin' ninety-five, do it, boy?"

"Nawh."

"Well we are. I'll have it up to a hundred and five before the night's over."

"You will, huh?"

"This is a special car, you know, boy. I guess you've guessed that by now, huh?"

"Oh, yeah, I did."

"Don't see many floor shifts like this, huh? This is a test model. That's about all I do now. Test special cars. But I used to be a truck driver."

"It must be interesting."

"Oh, it is, boy. It is."

"It seems that way."

"You ever hear of the John Birch Society, boy?"

"John Birch?"

"Yeah, the John Birch Society."

It was black outside. The road was straight and deserted ahead and winter had raped the trees that bordered and bent over us. We were in West Virginia.

"Yup. That's all I do, mostly. Just go around and check and see. My job in the New Jersey chapter of our group is to collect information. My territory is Jersey, Pennsylvania, part of Maryland and Delaware and southern New York. Sometimes I travel all weekend."

"It must be an interesting job."

"It is, boy. It is. I really work for the Ford Motor Company but I get enough time off and travel expenses to get around. This is the special car they give me. It's hopped up."

"Do they give you a new one every year?"

"No, every other. It's got a supercharger and a lot of stuff you probably never heard of."

"Yeah, that's right."

We entered Virginia and his speedometer read 110.

"Things are really getting bad," he sighed. "Commies taking over everything. You go to church, boy?"

"Oh, yes, I do. Yes, I do."

"You do, huh? What kind?"

"Baptist."

"Baptist, huh?"

"Yeah, Baptist."

"Do you know about Martin Luther King?"

"Who?"

"King! Martin Luther King . . . the freedom marcher."

"Ohhh . . ."

"Yeah, him."

"Well, I've heard about him but I ain't one of his followers."

"Good. The damned Commie. You know that's all that's behind him, don'cha?"

"Well, I don't keep up with that kinda stuff too much."

"It's just as well that you don't. It's really a mess. 'Cause he can't get things to go as fast as how he thinks it should go he comes in, gets good colored people like you, boy, all riled up and just makes trouble. Damned Commie. That's my job—to see what's going on and to spread information. If it wasn't for groups like us I don't know how long this country would last."

"Yeah, I see what you mean."

"The Commies infest this country. From the White House on down. There's a lot of things you don't know, boy. It was a colored man in 1914 that wrote a paper describing the coming Commie take-over. He was a Commie. Way back then was when they started planning and working, the Commies, the Jews and the niggers . . . no offense to you, boy, but some of your people just act like they are."

"You come from Lexington?" I asked.

"Naw, not originally. My father teaches down there. Virginia Military Institute. He's one of those that got me first interested in our group. My dad's a real fireball. I've tried to join the service over a dozen times but they won't take me. Me with college and all, but they don't take me . . . I got ulcers."

"That's strange they won't take you and you test out these high-powered cars."

"Yeah, they thought I'd get in and cost them a lot of money. Ulcers sure are expensive. My dad's done spent over twenty thousand dollars on his in the last six years."

"Where do you drive your test cars?"

"Oh, around the country. On tracks sometimes. I race them too, you see. And I can drive anything, boy, anything that's got wheels. Drove for Smith Brothers Trucking in Virginia for years, still take out a load for them when they get pressed. Damned good outfit, and I'm studying for my pilot's license when I ain't driving."

"You gonna fly a jet?"

"Naw, helicopters. That's where the money is. Ferry around executives."

A small dish-rag grey carcass lay in the road. My driver told me it was a skunk, that skunks infested that part of the country. The temperature rose and we cracked the windows, sniffing warmer air and an occasional unfortunate skunk.

"Yeah, I was married once," the driver said. "But that didn't work. Damned American women don't want their men to be individuals anymore. Want them never to get out of high school. I don't smoke or drink and I'm a hard worker. I believe in this country, boy, and its women . . . and its men too, but I just ain't going to bed with just any tramp that comes along. I'm savin' myself for a real woman. I was reared in the seat of the Confederacy."

We entered Lexington about nine.

"Damn, this is the best time I ever drove that stretch in my life. This new highway system they putting in really gets us here. Four states in half the time. I left New York only hours ago. The good old Army's behind it. Sees the need of staying mobile and ready."

"Your father teaches college?" I asked.

"Yeah, Dad was in business a long while but the Commies and ulcers drove him out. Now he's back to what he really wants to do."

"I wish I had gone to college," I said.

"Listen, boy. I got two degrees and I can tell you that you ain't missed a damned thing, let me tell you."

He showed me the college and told me that Jefferson Davis was born in Lexington. Then he pointed out Route 60.

"Well, we just passed a Baptist church. One of yours, boy. But it's for white folks. This is the real South, you understand? It's a lot different if you never been here. Now, this is the way you go. Keep on this road out of town. I wouldn't stop and try to get a ride before I got out of town, if I was you."

"Thanks," I said.

"Oh, before I forget it." He handed me a John Birch Society pamphlet. "Don't want you to get away clean, now do I, boy?" He smiled. "I feel kinda guilty 'cause all my heavy artillery is locked in my trunk but this is enough to get you started."

"Thanks, I really appreciate it."

"Now, that's all right. Just wait 'til you get out of town before you try and get a lift. It's dark out there but it's warm."

On my way out of town, a group of five black boys passed me and each said, "Hi," when passing, and they smiled as a group.

On the edge of town, five cars passed me, one stopping so that the driver could peer at me, then accelerating with a tearing of tires, the tail lights dissolving in the night.

Five minutes later, a car stopped. The driver was heavy and black.

"Where the hell you goin'?" he said.

"West."

"How goddamn far west?"

"California."

"Get in. I'm goin' all the hell the way to Cincinnati and you goddamn better keep me awake."

"Thanks, I will."

"Don't say another word, sport. What the hell you goin' to California for? You go to school or somethin'?"

"Nawh. I'm going get married and I usually work as a janitor."

I didn't feel too bad telling him that; I have been a janitor at times and who knows, maybe one day I'll get married again.

"Well, I'm in the Army, myself, youngster. Twenty-three goddamn years' worth. Just re-enlisted and bought this brand-new Impala. Yeah, spent my leave with my girl before I go to Korea! She's eighteen, my girl, and the prettiest little thing in this man's Army. Can't see what she sees in my old ass.

"Well, Sarge, there's more to it than looks."

"Sure is, son."

"Now take my Patsy Mae for a case. I'm the family man type and I shy away from those lookers but the moment I laid eyes on Patsy Mae . . ."

And that's how it was across a lot of the country. Next time I might fly, except that there's a lot of stories to hear and see between here and there.

SUPPORT YOUR LOCAL POLICE!!!

WELCOME TO MARYLAND—NO HITCHHIKING!

SUPPORT YOUR LOCAL POLICE!!!

95 M.P.H.

SUPPORT YOUR LOCAL POLICE!!!

SPEED LIMIT IS POSTED.

SUPPORT YOUR LOCAL POLICE!!!

SLOW DOWN AND LIVE!

SUPPORT YOUR LOCAL POLICE!!!
110 M.P.H.
SUPPORT YOUR LOCAL POLICE!!!
SPEED CHECK BY RADAR
SUPPORT YOUR LOCAL POLICE!!!
END OF FREEWAY
SUPPORT YOUR LOCAL POLICE!!!
FARM LABOR INFORMATION
SUPPORT YOUR LOCAL POLICE!!!
SUPPORT YOUR LOCAL POLICE!!!
SUPPORT YOUR LOCAL POLICE!!!

Women Need

APPLY HERE

Until the 1970s, African American women who wrote about their western experiences had few outlets for publication of their short stories. Reflecting the spirit of the second wave of American feminism that occurred during the sixties and seventies, women in general finally received recognition as writers. Partially because of their actions during the Civil Rights movement, African American women established a long-overdue voice and wrote and published stories based on their unique perspective, stories about issues relevant to women in general and to African American women in particular. Their portrayals of strong female characters who defy stereotypical notions about black women demonstrate feminist concerns. One motif that frequently recurs throughout these stories is women who achieve economic independence, which frees them from dependence on men. As these writers illustrate, because of the increased availability of jobs for African American women during this time, they were able to conceive of and take control of their lives, to attain personal and professional goals, and to succeed in a broad range of new opportunities.

Reflecting these new options, Ntozake Shange's story "Ridin' the Moon in Texas" portrays young black women who participate in the women's rodeo in Navasota, Texas. The beginning of the story provides a brief historical account of black Texans who participated in trail rides. Shange reveals that blacks truly understand the image rodeo participants should convey and that they feel at home on the prairie. Her story celebrates both black identity and female identity by depicting black women who participate in rodeos and by establishing a black female perspective on the rodeo profession. Her characters defy traditional roles both in their professions and in their personal lives. One of the rodeo participants, Twanda, who wins first place in the barrel-racing competition and discovers a man who appreciates her for her rodeo skills, succeeds both in the rodeo competition and in experiencing personal freedom.

New opportunities for black women were also achieved in the religious profession, where women began to take the previously male-dominated role of preacher.

Joyce Carol Thomas's "Young Reverend Zelma Lee Moses," set in Oklahoma, depicts a female preacher who plays a significant role in the church and the community. Eighty-year-old Mother Augusta, the community prophet, recognized Zelma Moses's spiritual gifts years ago when Zelma sang as a preschooler. Mother Augusta takes Zelma as her protégée and Zelma is soon offered a recording contract to sing gospel music. After Zelma gains a national reputation as a gospel singer, she announces that on Easter Sunday she will fly like an angel. If she successfully flies, Zelma plans to marry Daniel, a man who has recently moved into the community. People travel from considerable distances to attend the event, but when she attempts to fly, she fails. Feeling that she has failed her spiritual community, Zelma retreats to the woods. Mother Augusta correctly prophesies that Zelma will return—Christlike—in three days. Upon her return, Zelma sings gospel praises and "flies" away with Daniel.

Aya de Leon also describes women employed in careers formerly considered male professions. "Tell Me Moore" is a framed narrative wherein one of four African American women who are playing spades tells a story. The story explores lesbian relationships, strong friendships between women, and female bonding. The women are all employed as professionals in Oakland, California; Madeline Moore, the narrator of the framed narrative, is a private detective. She tells a story about a black woman who hired her to find out whether her husband was having an affair. When Madeline met her client to expose pictures of her husband entering a motel with another woman, the client screamed racial slurs about black women who try to seduce men. At the end of the framing story, Madeline looks at her cards and says, "Black is back," referring to the spades in her hand, which symbolically celebrate black identity. De Leon's characters are educated and professional women who do not need a man to feel fulfilled and who are emotionally and financially independent. She also juxtaposes these women's emotional independence against that of the woman who hired the detective. The client, instead of getting angry at her own husband, accused black women in general of seducing her husband, thus making women instead of men responsible for women's pain and suffering.

Pain and suffering are also an issue in "Quilting on the Rebound," by Terry McMillan, which is set in Los Angeles where Marilyn works as a chief underwriter for an insurance company. The story outlines her relationship with her coworker, Richard, who is younger than she and believes he can satisfy her more than can men her own age. Marilyn gets pregnant, Richard proposes to her, and she plans a big wedding. However, Marilyn has a miscarriage, and Richard breaks up with her shortly before the wedding. Trying to heal from romantic rejection, she begins quilting and takes a leave of absence from work to visit a friend in Arizona. She decides to move to Scottsdale, where she takes a lower-level position in an office amidst "rednecks" insulted at working under a black woman. Marilyn begins a successful quilting business. When Richard marries another woman, she sends him a quilt. Marilyn develops from a woman conditioned to marry and have children to someone who finds fulfillment as a successful businesswoman and entrepreneur.

Whereas Terry McMillan shows a woman who overcomes her dependence on romantic encounters and discovers self-respect and dignity, Rita Dove, in "Damon and Vandalia," portrays a woman who finds romance but loses her self-respect. "Damon and Vandalia" is structured as a series of brief summaries that alternate between Damon's and Vandalia's points of view. The story reveals the complex relationships among Damon, Vandalia, and Clark, who have come to Texas for job opportunities. Vandalia, who attended college on a track scholarship, now has a job as a filmscript editor and reviewer. Damon has held several menial jobs, such as waiting tables and gardening, as well as professional positions such as translating, but he is currently unemployed. Clark, a curator at the University of Texas, and Damon are lovers, while Vandalia dates a university professor. Eventually, Damon and Vandalia act upon their unacknowledged romantic feelings for each other despite the other romances in which they are involved. However, Vandalia wonders whether their sexual encounters are real or whether she will be punished for them.

"Tenderhead," by Harryette Mullen, is told from the point of view of Mimi, a ten-year-old African American girl. Every Saturday Mimi has her hair styled for church the next day. She must cope with the new social rules that dictate how a young girl, as opposed to a child, is supposed to look. She is told she needs to stay out of trees, carry a purse, and keep her skirt down. Most symbolically, Mimi, whom the hairdresser refers to as "tenderhead," is to have her hair pressed to appear more mature. On one Saturday while Mimi is visiting the beauty shop, Dot, the town outcast, who has poor hygiene and has never had her hair styled professionally, arrives at the shop. Dot challenges Mimi to a game of dominos and wins a soda from Mimi, who becomes upset. When Mimi begins to cry, Dot reacts by exposing her breast and telling Mimi that since she bought her a soda, she will in return offer her a drink. Finally, the hairdresser intervenes and asks Dot to leave. The hairdresser then curls Mimi's hair for the first time, symbolic of the initiation experience Mimi has just had. "Tenderhead" demonstrates how women are conditioned to strive for unreasonable standards that define women in terms of their physical attraction. Dot is an "outcast" because she does not conform to these standards.

"The Friday Night Shift at the Taco House Blues (Wah-Wah)" and "Emerald City: Third & Pike" both involve women who, rather than elusive physical beauty, seek professional opportunities such as those gained by women in some of the earlier stories. In "The Friday Night Shift at the Taco House Blues (Wah-Wah)," Wanda Coleman depicts two young women who work at a Los Angeles fast-food chain. Throughout the story, the narrator's dreams of better opportunities are revealed. She plans to get a job as a government secretary and gain financial independence before she marries. The narrator's situation is compared to that of Shurli, her coworker, who struggles to support six children and their three fathers. Among other themes, the story shows the difficulties of single mothers who must exist on meager incomes. It also demonstrates a powerful bond between two women whose relationship exemplifies female camaraderie.

Charlotte Watson Sherman's "Emerald City: Third & Pike" is about a homeless woman, Oya, who sits in front of McDonald's and tells people her family history. The story is told from the point of view of a woman who one day sits down next to Oya. She notices that no one pays attention to the two of them. They have become twice invisible because they are black and because they are women. Oya tells the narrator that there are no real black people in Seattle because they have become spineless. She claims she was imprisoned for protecting her dreams because she hit a white woman who employed her as a housecleaner after the woman told her she could never be an astronaut. Oya has a fighting woman's spirit that requires more than prison to discourage and tells the narrator that she too had better learn to fight for her dreams. This story shows a woman who is determined not to provide domestic service for whites, one of the few jobs available to black women in the first half of the century. Oya fights for equal opportunity and refuses to accept her mother's fate.

Perhaps Oya, as much as any of the characters in these stories, most accurately reflects the travails, excitement, challenges, interconnectedness, and spirit of western African American women in the latter twentieth century. Fresh opportunities, independence, and dreams epitomize the themes in these stories; but they are also about friendship, introspection, pride, romance, self-fulfillment, religious beliefs, concepts of beauty, community, and maturing. They emphasize the black female presence in the African American community, and above all the ability to survive, all while bringing meaning and integrity to African American women and their lives in the West.

Ridin' the Moon in Texas

NTOZAKE SHANGE

Houston Rodeo & Livestock Show ain't never seen the same since we come riding in from Arcola. All colored and correct. Long-sleeved shirts, cowboy hats, chaps, spurs, covered wagons, and a place all our own in Memorial Park. Ain't never seen that many niggahs in Memorial Park no way, least not at 4:30 in the morning. Perking coffee over open fires and warming each other with bourbon and one rodeo yarn after another. Ain't nothing white folks can do bout it, even Sam Houston enlisted this black fella could talk five Indian languages—five and English, of course. Even Sam Houston had enough sense to ask this niggah to go talk some sense to them Cherokees, so's they wouldn't fight gainst Texas independence. Well, we independent now and riding proud right down Hwy. 59 to Texas Avenue. Don't understand why that woman didn't buy those boys some hats. She knows cain't no man be in a trailride or a rodeo without a hat. Shame, too. They came all the way from Abilene to sit by the wayside with them other folks. Just looking. And I'll say one thing. That flock of niggahs on them gorgeous horses and them wagons, now that was something to look at! Must be why ain't none of us forget it. The trailride and all. And the rodeos. The black ones, of course, white folks don't quite have the hang of it. I mean, how you sposed to look, your image, on your horse. It takes a colored point of view.

"Twanda, whatcha gone do tonight? Louisiana Red is up for everything from bronc-busting to steel-dogging!"

"Oh go on, gal, you know I cain't do nothing but barrel racing. Sides, I've got some business out yonder."

"Whatchu mean, you got some business out yonder? You ain't plannin' on messin' with me or them hard-head cowboys come to laugh at us tonight. You know this is our night, the All-Women's Rodeo, Navasota, Texas, honey. We the stars this evening, girl, even if you do gotta itch in your twat—them races come first—you got some business out yonder—huh!—you better check Dallas—you really gonna let that Jamaican chick use your horse for calf roping?"

"Her horse is sick. She's an allright broad. You know she was champion two years in a row."

"But not with your horse."

"You know you can be one petty bitch when you wanna."

"I spose that's why you gonna investigate your business out yonder?"

"Listen, honey, I'ma see about Dallas. He misses me if I'm gone more than a hour and before a race he just gets beside himself and I gotta sweet talk him and snuggle up to him, specially fore I put that bridle thru his mouth—he don't like that thing at all—I sure do like them Oak Ridge Boys. Listen, can't ya hear it?"

"Hell, no. Why don't cha just ride bareback."

"I might—"

"Sure."

"No, I might saunter thru the night bare back on Dallas; naked as a jay bird."

"Oh yeah, where?"

"Out yonder, I told ya."

"Girl, you know you don't make no sense sometimes. Did you pay up for the bronc-busting and barrel racing?"

"Course I did. Cost me seventy dollars. That's why I gotta get Dallas feeling high and sweet. We gotta win alla that money back and then some."

"You signed up for the breakaway?"

"Hell, no. That ain't no rodeo. That's some real bullshit. Call you rope a run-away calf?"

"Some folks cain't."

"Well, that ain't shit to me. Rope the damn thing and tie it in eight seconds. That I can understand. Breakaways just some other way for the 'pro-mo-tors' to make some more dough."

"So what? There's money in it."

"And a lotta fools, too."

"Go on now. See bout Dallas. I'ma get me a beer and some barbecue. Thank God, they finally playing Charlie Pride. I Just love how that man can sing. Love me some Charlie Pride."

The night was fresh, more like morning should be. The grass and brush beyond the rodeo arena were moist and seductive, begging to be touched or lain on. The moon sat up in the sky like a hussy in red with her legs wide open. So what if all the women riders from Muskogee to Lubbock, Marshall to Lafayette, showed for the All-Women's Rodeo? Just last year, Susie Louise won bronc-busting and she was four months pregnant. Her momma won calf-roping and her daughter ran away with the steel-dogging. Shit. What a night that was. Take a look at those men come to look at us. I can't believe Lee Andrew had the nerve to tell me he came out here cuz he likes to see the expression on my face: see me change from pretty to ugly. Talk about nerve. I'ma bring me one of my pretty cowboys right on back here. It's so quiet. Most like there wasn't no rodeo going on. Maybe I'll ride Dallas by that rhiney boy with those dogging arms, the one in the black and red satin shirt with white fringe and red suede chaps dangling silver coins. He's the one whispered "I'm a black man who wants to ride off on a filly." Yeah, mister. I got something for your ass. God, I wonder how James is doing? I forgot to call the hospital once the ambulance carried him off. That bull stamped all over his ass and he ain't but so big. Big as a minute actually. Not much bigger than a minute. Jesus. That gore was more than I could handle. And that fool Joe-Man had the gall to say I didn't have no heart cuz I was paying up for calf-roping instead of seeing to James. Shit. James finished his event. How was I gonna calf-rope and see to James. Humph. That's awright, Dallas. We're just warming up, that's all. Getting a feel for the wind and the ground round here. Come on, I'ma kick it up! See if we can get neath these tree limbs and over that stream without hurtin' ourselves. Whatchu say, baby? That's a boy. Do like momma say and she'll give you a bright shiny apple. That's a boy. Let's get it. Go for it. There ain't nothing out here but prairie and me and you and the wind. So that makes it the moon, the wind and a little satisfaction. Those folks crazy now, they playing Otis Redding. Come on, now. Show momma whatcha can do. She needs some satisfaction too. Right, baby? Do it for momma.

"Breakaway:

"Nancy Bourdan—Houston—Score 57.

"Sally Johnson—Midnight, Mississippi—Score 55.

"Molly Hanks—Conroe, Texas—Score 52."

"No, man, just give me a beer from that cooler in your truck. I ain't out here to compete tonight. How can I do that? This a All-Women's Rodeo—ain't it? Well, ain't it?"

"Yeah, that why I'm out here, cain't really tell if a woman's a woman til you see how she could ride a horse."

"You right bout that, bro!"

"Gimme that beer and a joint."

"I'ma get some more barbecue but I'ma say one thing. Just one thing. The ladies is the horses. If you get my meaning. But the way my lady friend ride is fantastic. All that tension and excitement from the Diamond L all the way out here to Navasota or Madisonville. Now they got some great rodeo in Madisonville, but you know I got three daughters and I'ma black man and I'd rather have my girls here than anywhere else."

"Oh, man, go and get the barbecue."

"Whatever you say, Bubba. Watch the horses all right. These gals ain't got no more scruples than that white bitch whatcha call it, Belle Starr?"

"Yeah, man. I got it covered. Just get the beer, man, and let me know if you see that sassy gal what races barrels."

"There's Bo-Beep with those damned armadillos in a pond of draft beer. When these guys gonna learn armadillos get drunk. They chasing beer. They ain't racing. That's all right, Dallas. We'll just ignore that. Okay, baby."

"Hey, Twanda."

"Huh?"

"Ain't that what they call you, Twanda?"

"Some do, some don't. What's it to you?"

"That's a nice-looking animal you got there."

"I know that. You got a nice-looking face too."

"It's just a cowboy's face."

"I know that. Come on, Dallas."

"Hey, don't ride off like that."

"Whatcha think I'm on a horse for, to stay still somewhere? Let's go, Dallas."

"All right, everybody, clear the arena—it's time for the Cotton–eyed Joe."

"Well, cain't you dance, gal?"

"Whatchu mean? Of course I can!"

"Twan, let's me and you gone and do the Cotton-eyed Joe."

"Shit yeah. If you can keep up with me."

"Watch me, baby. Careful how you do that horse and you'll see what all I could do. What all I could do for you, baby."

"Sure, hot stuff."

"Calf-Roping:

"Agnes Moralez—San Antonio, Texas—Score 7.6.

"Sally Johnson—Midnight, Mississippi—Score 8.1.

"Louisiana Red—Lafayette, Louisiana— Score 7.2."

I cain't exactly explain how it happened, but out there somewhere how the prairie snapped up the last bits of night. Bubba and Twanda raced free as sepia roses on their horses' bare back. Holding the manes and each other the way you'd have to when you're dealing with a steer and you come out grinning and then be screaming. They fell out near a smooth mossy cloud neath a cypress tree. "Guantanamera" blasting from the arena.

Guantanamera, Gaujiro, Guantanamera.

Twanda was murmuring, "I'm in the rodeo cuz my momma was and my first night out I won ninety dollars just for running round barrels. You cain't beat that, for running round barrels." Bubba somehow quieted her. He was unsettled by her drive. She had to win. She was one with her horse. She had no sense of anything sides speed and her animal, but that was when she was racing. She said. She liked he was a champion. She said, "Look a heah, I'm a champion too," when she wrapped that huge silver buckle round her slight waist. The hairs from her thighs creeping like ferns from her navel. Women and horses. Black women and horses. An all-women's rodeo. What next? Bubba slapped his thigh and reached for that joint and Bud.

Twanda pulled him to her and let him play with a piece of grass she slipped tween his lips. Then she lay back on his shoulder. Let the sky celebrate her victory: Twanda Rochelle Johnson—Barrel-racing—17.5—First Place—$532.

She smiled, contented; remembered that business she'd had out yonder. Out on the prairie where black folks have always felt at home. She pulled the straw outta Bubba's mouth. He didn't know what was happening til she sang a cowgirl's song / sweet & tough / soft and rough:

let me be a chorus of a thousand / tongues
and your lips dance on a new moon / while
Daddy Cool imagines synchopated
niggafied erotica on Griggs Road

We'll have skimmed the cream off the milky way/made a permanent ellipse by the yet uncharted tail of Halley's Comet/these tongues and lips make a time step of Bojangles in fast forward/merely slow motion in a sultry dusk/so natural/ is the tone of your chest under the gaze of the wild stallions by the waterfalls, enveloped by scarlet blossoms like a woman's heart/your sweat seeps into my mouth/we sleep/deep/deep/like in Texas.

"Hey, ain't that the Judds—ain't that something."

"We gone sleep/deep/deep like in Texas."

Young Reverend Zelma Lee Moses

JOYCE CAROL THOMAS

A hoot owl feasted round eyes on the clapboard building dipped in April shadow at the edge of a line of magnolia and redbud trees.

The owl peered through the budding branches until he focused on the kitchen, in which a mother, brown and fluffy as buttermilk biscuits, stood by the muslin-draped window, opening glass jars of yams, okra, tomatoes, spinach, and cabbage and stirred the muted colors in a big, black cast-iron pot. Then she raised the fire until she set the harvest green and red colors of the vegetables bubbling before fitting the heavy lid in place and lowering the flame.

She watched the blaze, listening to the slow fire make the food sing in low lullaby.

When it was time, she ladled the stew onto warmed platters, sliced warm-smelling red-pepper corn bread into generous wedges, and poured golden tea into three fat clay mugs.

"Dinner!" her voice sang.

"Coming, Mama," said tall Zelma, who was leaning over stoking the fire in the wood fireplace. Her shadow echoed an angular face, backlit by the light from the flames.

When she turned around, her striking features showed misty black eyes in a face which by itself was a chiseled beauty mark. Indeed, she gave the phrase "colored woman" its original meaning. She was colored, with skin the sugar brown of maple syrup.

At the kitchen table she sat between her aging parents. Her father, his earthen face an older, darker, lined version of Zelma's, his hair thick as white cotton and just as soft and yielding to Zelma's touch, started the blessing.

"We thank thee for this bountiful meal. . . ."

"May it strengthen us in our comings and goings," Zelma continued.

"Lord, do look down and watch over us for the work that lies ahead," chanted the father and daughter together.

"And bless the hands of the cook who prepared this meal."

"Amen," said the mother.

They ate as the quiet light outside their window began to fall in whispers. Zelma told time by how long the fire in the fireplace at their backs danced. She counted the dusky minutes in how long it took to clear the table, to clean and place the dishes in their appointed places in the cabinet, to scrub the black cast-iron pot until it gleamed black as night.

Then it was the hushing hour, the clock of the trees and the sky and the flying crickets said, "Come, let us go into the house of the Lord." And they started out, hands holding hands, down the red clay dusty road together.

Before long they were joined by Mother Augusta, a pillar of the community and cornerstone of the church.

The eighty-year-old Mother Augusta, who like a seer was frequently visited by psychic dreams, enjoyed a reputation as the wrinkleless wonder because her face was so plump no lines could live there, causing folks to say, "She either a witch or she been touched by God." Today Mother Augusta kept up a goodly pace with her wooden cane. Augusta and her late husband had broken the record for the longest continuous years of service as board members to the church. She was a live oak living on down through the years and keeping up the tradition now that her husband was gone on.

Today as the family walked along, Mother Augusta smiled at Zelma, thinking it was just about wedding time for the young woman. The older Mother Augusta's head flooded with memories of Zelma and how she had always been special, but one memory stood out from the rest. One April memory many years back.

The Bible Band of preschoolers had come marching into the church that Easter looking so pretty, and all the children serious, strict-postured, the girls with black braids laced with ribbons like rainbows. A few with hot-iron curls.

Each of the ten children had stepped forward and given a biblical recitation, a spring poem, a short song. The church house nodded, a collection of heads in a show of approval as one child with pink ribbons sat down.

Another reciter in a little Easter-egg-yellow child's hat stood up and delivered an age-old poem. Finishing, she gave a sigh of relief, curtsied, and took her seat.

Then Zelma, pressed and curled, stepped forward, her maple hands twisting shyly at the sleeves of her lavender-blue and dotty-green organdy dress. In white cotton stockings and ebony patent leather shoes so shiny and carefully walked in no mud scuffed the mirror bright surface, her feet just wouldn't stay still. Zelma couldn't get settled; she nervously listed from one foot to the other.

She started her speech in an expressionless, sing-song tone. No color anywhere near it. It was a typical Bible Band young people's performance that the whole church endured, as yet another duty, as yet another means of showering encouragement upon the young.

Zelma recited:

"It's raining, it's raining;
The flowers are delighted;

The thirsty garden greens will grow,
The bubbling brooks will quickly flow;
It's raining, it's raining, a lovely rainy day."

Now instead of curtsying and sitting herself down, Zelma stared suddenly at the crucifix above the sanctuary door.

She stared so hard until every head followed her gaze that had settled on the melancholy light beaming on the crucifix.

Then in a different voice she started to speak.

"And Jesus got up on the cross and He couldn't get down."

Mother Augusta had moved forward in her seat as if to say, "Hear tell!"

And Zelma went on like that, giving her own interpretation of the crucifixion, passion making her voice vibrate.

An usher moved forward to stop her, but Mother Augusta waved the usher back.

"Well?" said Mother Augusta.

"If He could have got down, He would've," Zelma supposed.

Zelma talked about stubbing her toe, about how much it hurt, and she reported the accident she had of once stepping on a rusty nail.

"If one nail could hurt so bad, how painful the Christ nails piercing Him in His side must have been," Zelma decided.

"And so I think He didn't get down, because you see," she added in a whisper, "something was holding Him there.

"It was something special."

"Yes?" called Mother Augusta just as a deacon moved to herd the child to her pew. Bishop Moses waved the deacon back.

"I know He wanted to get down. Why else would He have said, 'My Lord, my Lord, why hast Thou forsaken me?'"

"Amen," said the first usher.

"But you see," said Zelma, "something was holding my Lord there, something was nailing Him to that old rugged cross, and it wasn't just metal nails."

Now the entire church had gotten into the spirit with young Zelma.

"Wasn't just metal nails," sang the church in response.

"It was nails of compassion."

"Nails of compassion," repeated the church.

"He was nailed with nails of sorrow," Zelma preached.

"Nails of sorrow," the church rang out.

"Nailed for our iniquity," Zelma called.

"Nailed," the church responded.

"He was nailed, he was bruised for our transgression."

Then Zelma let go. "The nail, the nail that wouldn't let Him down, the nail that would give Him no peace, the nail that held Him there was the nail of love."

"Love," shouted the church.

"Jesus," Zelma said, in a lower muted voice, "Jesus got up on the cross and He couldn't get down, and because He couldn't get down, and because He couldn't get down, He saved a world in the name of a nail called Love!"

It was all told in rhythms.

As the church went ecstatic with delight, somebody handed Zelma her guitar. Another child hit the tambourine.

And the music started talking to itself.

"She been called to preach," announced Mother Augusta.

Bishop Moses, scratching his getting-on-in-years head, was as thunderstruck as the other members of the congregation. He flitted from one to the other as they stood outside in the church yard to gossip and to appraise the service.

One of the elder deacons opened his mouth to object, starting to say something backward, something about the Bible saying fellowship meant fellows not women, but the eldest sister on the usher board proclaimed, "God stopped by here this morning!"

Who could argue with that?

This evening as Augusta walked along with Zelma's family skirting the honeysuckle-wrapped trees of the Sweet Earth woods, they eagerly approached that same church, now many years later. Two mockingbirds singing and chasing each other in the tulip trees just by the tamed path leading into the church house reminded Mother Augusta that it was almost Easter again.

Spring was lifting her voice through the throats of the brown thrashers and the wood thrushes and the wild calls coming from the woods.

And in the light colors of bird feathers, beauty spread her charm all over the land.

Inside the church a wine-red rug stitched with Cherokee roses led the way down the center aisle around a pot-bellied stove and continued up three steps. Behind the lectern sat three elevated chairs for Bishop Benjamin Moses, Zelma Lee Moses, and any dignitary who might come to visit. Then behind the three chairs perched seats for the choir members who filled them when the singers performed formally and on Sundays.

The church had been there so long that the original white paint on the pew armrests had been worn and polished by generations of the members' hands until in spots the pure unadulterated rosewood peeked through.

The Bishop opened the weeknight service by saying a prayer. All over the building the members stood, knelt, sat, waiting for the rapture.

Soon Testimony Service was over and the congregational singing had been going on for some time before they felt that special wonder when the meeting caught fire. First they felt nothing and then they all felt the spirit at one time.

The soul-thrilling meters, the changing rhythms, the syncopated tambourine beats trembled inside every heart until they were all of one accord.

Stripes of music gathered and fell across the people's minds like lights.

Melodies lifted them up to a higher place and never let them down.

The notes rang out from the same source: the female, powerhouse voice of Zelma Lee Moses. She bounced high on the balls of her feet as she picked the guitar's steely strings, moving them like silk ribbons. The congregation felt the notes tickling from midway in their spines and on down to the last nerve in their toes.

Zelma gave a sweet holler, then lowered her voice to sing so persuasively that the people's shoulders couldn't stay still, just had to move into the electrifying rhythm and get happy.

Zelma gospel-skipped so quick in her deep-blue robe whirling with every step she took, somebody had to unwrap the guitar from around her neck. She was a jubilee all by herself.

And the people sang out her name, her first two names, so musically that they couldn't call one without calling the other: *Zelma Lee.*

Perfect Peace Baptist Church of Sweet Earth, Oklahoma, sat smack-dab in the middle of a meadow near the piney woods. This zigzag board wooden building with the pot-bellied stove in its center served as Zelma Lee Moses's second home.

Here she sang so compellingly that shiny-feathered crows from high in the treetops winged lower, above the red clay earth, roosted on black tupelo tree branches, peeked in the church window and bobbed their heads, flapped their glossy feathers, cawing in time to the quickened-to-perfection, steady beat.

Reverend Zelma Lee Moses closed her eyes and reached for the impossible note made possible by practice and a gift from God. Row after row of worshippers commenced to moaning watching her soul, limited only by her earthly body, full and brimming over, hop off the pulpit. She sang, "Lord, just a little mercy's all I need."

And she didn't need a microphone.

"Look a yonder, just a skipping with the gift and the rhythm of God." Mother Augusta over in the Amen Corner clapped her hands in syncopated time. At home Sister Moses, Zelma's blood mother, was the woman of the house, but in the sanctuary Mother Augusta, the mother of the church, was in charge.

Zelma began and ended every sermon with the number "Lord, Just a Little Mercy's All I Need."

The sound tambourined and the Sweet Earth sisters swooned and swooned, the ushers waved their prettiest embroidered handkerchiefs under the noses of the overcome, but they couldn't revive the fainting women as long as young Reverend Zelma Lee Moses dipped into her soul and crooned,

"Lord, just a little mercy's all I need.
If I have sinned in any way,
Down on my knees I'll stay and pray,
Lord, just a little mercy's all I need."

How her silver voice swooped over the words, coloring them a mystery color that did not exist except in the mind which received it, forgot it, then gave it back.

Daniel, a newcomer who'd only been in town for one year, wanted Zelma to pay him some attention; how she had stayed unattached puzzled him. He knew the statuesque Reverend Zelma Lee Moses easily attracted men. On this third visit to church Daniel saw how men flocked like butterflies to Zelma's color-rich flower garden, to the sunbows in her throat every time she opened her mouth to preach or sing. Out flew the apricot hues of hollyhock. The gold of the goldenrod, the blue pearl of Jacob's ladder. Daniel got a little jealous watching Zelma study the fellows, her camera eyes pausing on one young man's skin that rivaled the brown feather colors of a red-tailed hawk. Her admiring gaze directed briefly at the young man made Daniel itch around the collar. He turned neon red inside watching her watching him.

But it was on Daniel that Zelma's camera stopped scanning and focused. She saw his skin flirting with light, his inky hair accepting the brilliance like a thirsty canvas accepts a crown of black beads dabbed by a painter's shimmering brush.

His eyes shone with such a joy-lit intensity of sparkling double black flecked with the silver crescents of the moon that looking into them made her want to die or live forever.

Now Zelma, already so touched with talent that limousined producers from New York came down and waved rock and roll contracts in front of her, wanted to ask Daniel his opinion of the intricate offers.

"What do you think about this here music contract," she asked him one night after service.

"Rock and roll? I don't know. Seems to me you ought to keep singing gospel. But take your time," he advised after studying the papers.

"Time," she said thoughtfully, and when she looked in Daniel's eyes, she knew he was just thinking about what was best for her.

"Think I'll write gospel right next to rock and roll," she said.

"Makes sense to me," said Daniel.

"What you studying to be?" she asked.

"How do you know I'm studying anything?" he teased.

"You're getting lots of books in the mail."

"Oh that! I'm studying to be an electrician or a bishop like your daddy," he said, handing the music recording agreement back to her.

"So that's why you're always carting the Bible and those big mail-order books around!"

"That's the truth," he acknowledged with a grin.

"An electrical bishop."

"An electrician-bishop," said Daniel.

"Uh-hm," said Zelma Lee in her most musical-speaking voice.

When she took her time about signing the contracts, the producers resorted to recording her mellifluous gospel voice to see if they could find someone else to match it who wouldn't study too long over the words in their contracts. But they never could.

Nobody else had that red clay memory in her throat, fat gold floating in the colored notes.

So they returned to try again and again until the young singer, after understanding as best she could all the small print and inserting the part about gospel, took pen in hand and signed the document.

That night her voice rivered out melodies so clear that when the music company visitors from the outside world heard the rhythms rinsed in some heavenly rain, they either thought of art or something dangerous they could not name.

Since the producers were coming with music on their minds, they only thought of songs and never perceived the threat.

The producers seemed so out of place in that place that welcomed everybody, common and uncommon, that they sometimes giggled suddenly without warning and thought that instead of stained glass they saw singing crows dressed in polka dot hats looking in the windows.

When they packed up their recording gear and stood on the outside of the church by the side of the road where the wild irises opened their blue mouths, Mother Augusta, leaning on her cane, bent an ear to the limousine and commented, "Say, good sirs, that motor's running so soft on this long machine you can hear the flowers whisper. Urnph, umph, umph!"

"What?"

The music merchants leaned back in their accordion cars and waved the chauffeur forward. They eased on down the road shaking their heads, couldn't figure out what she was talking about.

One said to the other, "Whispering flowers? Another one of those old Oklahoma fogeyisms."

"No doubt," agreed his partner, hugging the hard-earned contract to his breast.

Reverend Zelma Lee Moses only sang so the people could rejoice.

"A whole lot of people will rejoice when you sign this contract," the producer had said.

"Will?" said Zelma.

"Of course I'll be one of them." The record company man smiled as he extended the pen.

And more people did rejoice about a year after she'd signed the contract.

The echo of colors flew across the airwaves. The song "A Little More Mercy" made women listening to the radio as they pressed clothes still their irons in the middle of rough, dried collars, watching the steam weave through the melody.

Daniel, in his pine thick backyard chopping wood, his head awash in the sound, wondered at the miracle of vinyl, catching a voice like that and giving it back so faithfully, reached inside the open kitchen window and turned up the homemade radio he had assembled with his own hands. The sound flowed out to him even more distinctly. He raised the ax, chopping more rhythmically, clef signs scoring the wood.

More and more people rejoiced.

Both Zelma's mothers, Augusta and her natural mother, ended up with limousines, if they wanted them, turning the dials to their favorite gospel stations, which always played their favorite artist to the additional accompaniment of limousine tires dancing down the road.

Zelma only sang so the people could rejoice.

And therein lay the danger. Preachers who had that kind of gift had to be around folks who loved them, for the devil stayed busy trying to stick the old pitchfork in. Zelma kept herself too wrapped up with her gift to notice the devil's works; those around her had to be aware, wary, and protective.

She preached one Sunday 'til her voice rang hoarse with power and her guitar hit a note so high it rang heaven's doorbell. And all up and down the rows, women stood up, their tambourines trembling like rhinestones.

Palm Sunday, the Sunday when visiting congregations from as far away as New Orleans, Louisiana, arrived with their clothes speckled with the Texas dust they passed through to get to Sweet Earth, Oklahoma, and the new gospel recording star; the visiting Louisiana choir, hot from their journey, crowded the choir stands to overflowing and mopped sweat from their curious brows.

Palm Sunday in Sweet Earth at Perfect Peace Baptist Church, the deacons with trembling hands, babies sucking blisters on their thumbs, folks so lame they had to wheel themselves in in wheelchairs, eyeglassed teachers, and farmers with weed cuts persisting around their scrubbed nails, all stepped out, in shined shoes, pressed suits, spring dresses, and assorted hats, coming to hear the female preacher perform on Palm Sunday, and she didn't disappoint them; she preached until her robe stuck to her sculptured body, wringing wet. She preached until dear Daniel, in an evergreen shirt of cotton and linen, Daniel so handsome she could squeeze the proud muscles straining against his shirt sleeves, until Daniel who had been tarrying for a year on the altar, dropped his tambourine and fell out in the sanctuary overcome by the holy spirit.

A cloud of "Hallelujah's" flew up like joy birds from the congregation when Daniel got religion. Still the Sweet Earth saints in front of Zelma with their mouths stretched open on the last syllable of Hallelujah, had not *shouted*, had not danced in the spirit.

Only one mover shook loose in the whole flock of them. And that was dimpled Daniel, an earth angel dressed in light and leaf green and smelling of musky sweet spring herbs, stepping all up and down and inside the gospel beat, a human drum.

It was just about time for Zelma to wind up the sermon and finish with the song "Lord, Just a Little Mercy's All I Need."

And she felt as if she hadn't done her job at all if she couldn't get ten sisters and several deacons moved from their sanctified seats.

The visiting choir voices behind her had sunk and their volume diminished. She was used to more call and response and certainly much more shouting.

"Why's this church so cold?" she asked.

Stopped in the middle of her sermon and asked it.

What she could not see behind her were the visiting choir members being carried off the stage one by one. The entire soprano section of the New Orleans

New Baptist Church Youth Choir had danced until they fainted, until only one or two straggly alto voices were left.

The Sweet Earth congregation gazed so amazed at the rapture and the different shouting styles of the Louisiana choir that they settled back and, instead of joining in the commotion, sat transfixed on their chairs like they were in a downtown theater watching a big city show on tour.

Nobody told Zelma she had preached so hard that she had set a record for the number of folks falling out in one sermon.

She wasn't aware of the record she'd just broken because she couldn't see the Louisiana choir behind her, she only saw dear Daniel in a golden trance, speaking in tongues, Daniel who made her feel like an angel every time she beheld his face.

When she pronounced Daniel "saved" and accepted him into the church, she made a silent promise, looking into Daniel's deep dark gaze, finding her passion in the curve of his molasses colored lips.

Before the week-long revival was over Daniel would be proud of her.

And then it came to her, not from God but from the soft place in the center of her soul-filled passion.

She would do what nobody else had done.

Come Sunday, the crowning day of the revival, young Reverend Zelma Lee Moses would fly.

"On Easter Sunday," she announced, talking to the Church but looking Daniel in the eyes, "on the last day of the revival, on the day Christ came forth from the tomb, Church, it's been given me to fly."

Their opened mouths opened even wider.

The New Orleans New Baptist Youth Choir, scheduled to be in concert in Louisiana on Easter Sunday, took a vote and sent back word that their Oklahoma stay would be extended and that the Sunday School Choir would have to sing two extra numbers instead to make up for their absence.

Since the Reverend Zelma Lee Moses's voice had moved over them like a mighty wind, knocking them from their perches in the choir stand and rendering them senseless from the mighty impact of her spirit, they could not leave, even if they wanted to.

"Young Reverend Zelma Lee Moses's gonna fly come Sunday evening," the ecstatic choir director chanted over the Oklahoma-to-Louisiana telephone wires.

That very night, beneath her flower garden patched quilt, Mother Augusta dreamed. First she saw Zelma Lee inside the church, making the announcement about flying, then she saw a red-dressed she-devil down in her hell home listening to Zelma's promise to fly on Sunday. Slack-jawed, the devil looked up at the church and the people being moved like feathers and got jealous.

"Flying on Sunday? Zelma Lee's gonna fly!" The next day these two phrases lit up the telephone wires in Sweet Earth.

The funny thing about all of this, of course, was that passion was playing hide-and-seek.

Daniel wanted Zelma as much as Zelma wanted him, but she did not know this.

"I want this Zelma," Daniel whispered to himself in the still hours of the night when the lightning bugs flew like earth stars outside his window. It was then he spoke, forgetting his Sweet Earth enunciation, in the lyrical thick accent of the swamp place from which he came.

As experienced with women as Daniel was he had never seen anybody like Zelma, and so he studied her carefully; he slowly wondered how to approach her. He didn't want to make even one false move.

Just seeing her was sometimes enough to take his breath away. Zelma had already stolen his heart when he saw her sitting in the pulpit between the visiting evangelist and Bishop Moses that first Sunday he visited Perfect Peace.

Because the visiting evangelist preached, Zelma was not required to speak or sing. It was her presence alone that had attracted him. He didn't even know she could talk, let alone sing. Even quiet she was a sight.

Hearing her sing on his second Sunday visit brought him to his knees. Folks thought he had fallen down to pray.

Eventually he did kneel to pray all the subsequent Sundays, but his belly still quivered like Jell-O even now remembering what the woman did to his mind.

And Zelma had never had so much as one boyfriend before. Since she was a preacher's daughter, she was expected, when it came to passion, to wait 'til her appointed time. Music had been her passion; music had been enough.

Then came Daniel. When she looked at Daniel, her heart opened on a door to a God she had not known was even there.

Daniel she wanted to impress even though he was already smitten.

Anything she did beyond being who she already was was needless, was superfluous, but young Zelma didn't know this.

As Mother Augusta might have said, "Humph. The devil found work."

The first thing Zelma did wrong was she built a short platform out of the wrong wood and didn't ask the deacons of the church to help her out.

"Didn't ask nobody nothing," complained Deacon Jones, he was so mad his trembling bottom lip hung down almost to his knees. "Got to drive a nail in at the right angle or it won't hold!"

Second thing Zelma did wrong was she went downtown to some unsanctified, whiskey-drinking folks and had them sew some wings onto her robe; looking like vultures roosting, they sewed crooked, leaving tobacco smoke lingering in the cloth.

"You don't tell sinning people nothing sacred," Mother Augusta clucked in a chastising voice to whoever's ears were free to listen.

"Sinning people! They nature is such that they misunderstand the mysteries.

"If they see trumpets on your head, they refer to them as horns.

"Now and then you run across an exception, but half the time they don't know *what* they looking at," said Mother Augusta.

And too, the seasoned women in the church primped their mouths and got offended, because for as long as they could remember they had personally sewn the sacred robe with the smoke blue thread that had been blessed and sanctified in a secret ritual that nobody discussed, lest a raven run away with their tongue.

"Who knows what them drunk people put in them wings?"

Mother Augusta, the human *Jet* and *Ebony* combined, kept a running oral column going among the older people all the revival days approaching Easter Sunday.

In the meantime Mother Augusta wanted to have words with the young preacher, but the members of the New Orleans New Baptist Youth Choir kept Zelma so occupied the female preacher didn't even have time for her own Sweet Earth congregation.

Even her own father, the retired Bishop Benjamin Moses, couldn't get a word in edgewise. Between counseling the New Orleans young folk, Zelma studied the Bible in the day and slept in the church house at night after falling out exhausted from continuous prayer. In the wee hours of the morning she slipped home, where her mother had prepared steaming hot bathwater and laid out fresh clothes. She refused her mother's platters of peppergrass greens, stewed turkey wings and Sunday rice, including her favorite dewberry biscuits. She was fasting and only took water.

But the community fed the Louisiana visitors. The gray-haired, white-capped mothers of the church, mothers of the copper kettles and porcelain pans, kept their kitchens bustling with younger Sweet Earth women. They instructed these sisters of the skillet in the fine art of baking savory chicken-and-dressing and flaky-crusted peach cobblers.

"Put a little more sage in that corn bread.

"Make that dumpling plumper than that," Mother Augusta ordered, throwing out to the birds a pan of dough that didn't pass her inspection.

She personally turned over each peach, seeing with her farsighted eyes what stronger, younger eyes often missed.

The young Louisiana people stood around, underfoot, mesmerized by Zelma, but Mother Augusta saw what they couldn't see and what Zelma's mother's eyes wouldn't see.

She prayed, Mother Augusta did.

Zelma prayed, but her love for Daniel had her all puffed up and half-drunk with passion.

Come Easter Sunday she would fly, then after church she would offer Daniel her hand, and if he held it much longer than friendly, they would be companions.

Every night she preached and promised to fly on Sunday.

Every night the crowd got thicker.

By Sunday night the standing-room-only audience pushed and elbowed each other in competition with the cawing crows for a low, window-level place on the tupelo branches above the clay by the window.

Oh, the crowd and the crows!

The church house sagged, packed to the rafters. And Mother Augusta ordered the carpenter to check the floor planks because they might not be able to take the whipping she knew Zelma was going to give them once she got started stomping the floor and making the Bible holler.

"Tighten that board over yonder," she ordered.

Another sound that added to the clamor was the hum of more buses arriving from New Orleans. Some members back home in the Louisiana church were so intrigued by the choir's decision to remain in Sweet Earth that they boarded yet another bus and struck out for northeast Oklahoma to see what the excitement was all about, driving on through the sleepless night so they could reach Perfect Peace in time for Sunday service and the promised night of miracles.

The New Orleans contingency was so glad to have made it in time, they entered the church swaying down the aisle, fingers circling circles in the air, uncrossed feet whipping up the holy dance.

As the evening lengthened, something softened in the air. Maybe it was the effect of the full moon.

The Reverend Zelma Lee Moses preached about wings that Sunday night.

The soft shadows cast by the full moon looked like veils hanging over the sanctuary.

She took her text from Psalms.

"Read, Brother Daniel!"

Daniel opened his Bible and quoted, "Keep me as the apple of thy eye, hide me under the shadow of thy wings.

"And He shall cover thee with his feathers, and under his wings shalt thou trust: his truth shall be thy shield and buckler."

"Read!"

Daniel found the next Psalm and continued, "Be merciful unto me, O God, be merciful unto me: for my soul trusteth in thee: yea, in the shadow of thy wings will I make my refuge. . . ."

"Read!"

". . . Who layeth the beams of his chambers in the waters; who maketh the clouds his chariot: who walketh upon the wings of the wind."

Now the great flying moment the Sweet Earth people had been anticipating for a whole week arrived. The spectacle that the New Orleans visitors awaited was here at last.

As she approached the platform, the young Zelma Lee Moses began to sing the closing number, "Lord, just a little mercy's all I need."

One sister let out a long, low holler. Transfigured, a ghost took over her throat, and it was like a special spirit had flown in through the open church window; like the miracle of the cross, Christ ascending into heaven would be repeated in another way.

It was too crowded for the people to cut loose. They swayed backward, swooned; and the crush of their numbers held each member up.

Now Zelma Lee Moses approached the foot of the launching platform, the platform built without consulting the deacons.

She mounted it and spread the arms of her robe, revealing the drunk-people-made wings.

And the congregation hushed.

Neither crowd nor crows flapped.

Young Zelma Lee Moses leaped!

But instead of being taken up by a mighty wind into the rafters above the gaping crowd, she plopped, sprawled, spread out on the oak floor at the feet of the frowning deacons, under the scrutinizing gaze of Mother Augusta, dragging her wings in the sawdust.

"The hem's crooked. And the thread's red wrong." Mother Augusta pointed, almost choking.

"Caw!" sang a crow.

Zelma scrambled back up, sure that the Lord had not forsaken her.

Maybe all she needed was a little speed to prime her wings: Recalling the way kites had to be hoisted, remembering her long adolescent legs running down the weed fields fast and far enough before the kite yielded to the wind and took off, she opened her hands and spread her wings.

And with her long arms out as far as she could fling them, she ran, up and down the aisles, her arms moving up and down, her hands making circles. Up and down the aisles.

Up. Down.

Fast, faster.

Up. Down.

Fast. Faster.

She ran past her future sweetheart-to-be and Daniel saw that she could not fly. And she could not fly.

Finally her mother said, "Daughter?"

And the people got mad.

"Limp-winged!" somebody said in an un-Christian voice.

They chased her on out of the church house. Out across the weed field like a carnival of people chasing a getting-away kite. They ran her under the full moon, under the crows shadowing and cawing above them and on into the woods. She disappeared right through a grove of white oak and yellow pines. The last thing Daniel saw was Zelma's left foot, looking like a wing as she slipped farther into the piney woods.

The people stopped right at the lush wildness, which was a curtain of green forest pulled like a secret against the place where unknown lakes and streams flowed and where wild foxes and all sorts of untamed creatures roamed.

Daniel was the only one who could have followed her there into the wildness, for he knew wild places like the back of his hand. But the look Zelma had shot him had said No.

And then he remembered that the piney woods was a natural bird refuge. There also doves flew in the thicket, marsh hens strutted proud, and quail called across the muddy and winding Sweet Earth River. He saw Zelma trembling there among the white and golden lilies and the singing crows. And Daniel knew this red earth of willow trees, dogwoods, and redbuds could hypnotize a person like Zelma who had wings in her feet, until it would be difficult for her to leave its allure.

As the church people ended their chase, he also stopped. It seemed as if she had been gone for weeks already. But instead of following her, he did the best thing: He turned back with the others.

Mother Augusta now raised her trembling hand and directed the choir to sing Zelma's favorite number, "Lord, Just a Little Mercy's All I Need," which they began singing softly, and she conducted the song so that it slowed down to a soothing pace. Finally the Louisiana choir dispersed, gathered their belongings, got on board and continued their sweet, wafting music on the midnight bus as they started out for home and Louisiana.

"She'll be back," Mother Augusta promised Daniel, who was sitting by the altar, head sadly bowed, looking long-faced, sifting the sawdust through his fingers, sawdust Zelma Lee Moses made rise by pounding the oak into powder while doing one of her gospel-skipping holy dances.

"She'll be back," Mother Augusta repeated in a knowing voice, then added as she took apart the launching platform, "This church is full of God's grace and mercy. Zelma's seen to that." She was remembering Zelma's invisible flight of the soul every time she looked at Daniel.

"When?" asked Daniel in that deep baritone voice.

"In three days," Mother Augusta answered, mumbling something about God making humans just a little bit lower than the angels.

"Being a little spryer than a timeworn woman, she didn't know she couldn't fly," sighed Mother Augusta. "Yet we hear her flying every Sunday morning on the radio."

"Well then why did the people come if they knew she couldn't fly?" asked Daniel, forgetting the miracle of the sawdust in his hand and the clef notes in the wood he chopped that radio afternoon when Zelma's first record came over the airwaves.

"Listen," said Mother Augusta.

"I'm listening."

"They came for the same reason they got mad," answered Mother Augusta. "They didn't want to miss it just in case she could." The elderly woman paused, then added, "When she realizes she already can fly, she'll be back. Take a lesson from the crow. Why should a bird brag about flying—that jet bird just spreads two easy wings. When Zelma knows that lesson, and she will know it, she'll return, she'll sure enough return. "

The next day the women gathered in the morning pews and Mother Augusta offered up a prayer of early thanks.

The deacons joined in, serving the women broomwheat tea, gathering the cloth to help the sisters in the sanctuary sew a new gown fit for a child of God.

Somebody started lining a hymn.

It started out as a low moan.

Then it grew until it was full to bursting.

It exploded and the right word dropped from a mouth, scooted along the floor, lifted its head, flapped in place, flew up and became a note hanging from the light bulb in the rafters of the church.

A moan. A lyric.

And it went on like that, from moan to lyric.

Until the song was fully realized.

Three long days passed with the people sitting, waiting, sewing, singing.

Mother Augusta was lining a hymn and she was lining a hem.

And on the third day, and on the third day they heard the crows gathering around the church.

But they did not open their beaks.

The hymn stopped, circled the light bulb above their heads.

The sound of silence.

The sound of waiting.

Then the next sound they heard was the door of the church opening softly.

"Who is it?" Daniel asked.

"Sh!" Mother Augusta whispered.

Nobody turned around except the waiting silence.

The silence stood up and opened its welcome arms.

Zelma.

Zelma Lee.

Zelma Lee Moses.

On the third day Zelma Lee Moses, looking a little down at the heel, stepped through Perfect Peace, paused and put on her long sanctified robe of invisible wings, picked up her guitar, mounted the steps to the pulpit, opened her mouth, and began to sing a crescendo passage in a higher voice with light wings glittering in the fire-singed notes, "Lord, just a little mercy's all I need."

And she looked at Daniel with a look that some folks claimed she got from talking to the devil for three days. But this was not true.

The look was all mixed up with angels, mockingbird flights, burnished butterflies, and tree-skimming kites.

After the service Daniel took her hand and held it longer than friendly.

When Zelma glanced up at the crucifix it seemed to her that Jesus, through a divine transformation, was winking through His pain. Or maybe it was just the effect of the morning sun kindling His expression, beaming only on those muscles of the mouth that brightened the corners of His lips.

As they left the church they walked under the crucifix over the doorway.

As if he too saw the same expression on the Christ, Daniel squeezed Zelma

Lee's hand tighter. And she could feel electricity pulse back and forth from his fingers to hers.

And they flew away to a place where wings grew from their ribs.
    And they were standing still flying.

Tell Me Moore

AYA DE LEON

"So how was your first week of self-employment?" Liz asked.

"I bought a gun," I said.

"What?!" Liz asked, putting down the deck of cards she had been shuffling. Liz could do those crazy tricks where you stream the cards from one hand into the other from about a foot apart.

"I'm really not happy about this," Yamile said. On the one hand, it was none of her business, but on the other hand, it was. She was my best friend and we lived under the same roof, but in separate apartments.

"Wait a minute," Liz said, "is this the same Madeline Moore who refused to let me give her a gun for the two years she worked for me? 'I don't need one,' she mimicked me in a high voice that sounded nothing like me, 'I just don't feel comfortable with guns.'"

"And you shouldn't feel comfortable with guns," Yamile said. "It just lulls you into a false sense of security, and you're more likely to get hurt yourself than deter an attack with it."

"Yeah, well," I said, "I got into some potentially life-threatening drama."

"Domestic case?" Liz asked, dealing the cards.

"How did you know?" I asked.

"Just a feeling. Wait 'til you've been in the investigation business twenty years. Sometimes you just know."

After my experience that week, I didn't know if I wanted to be in the investigation business twenty years. But I certainly hadn't found anything I liked better. Then again, in my six years out of college, the only other things I had been were a research assistant and a paralegal.

Liz dealt smoothly and with lightning speed. "Come on now," she said as she dealt. "Baby needs a new pair of shoes!"

"Liz," Yamile pointed out, "we're not playing for money."

"Doesn't matter," Liz said, "I say it for luck."

I had a hunch that before she was in the investigation business, Liz was into some gambling racket, but she didn't talk about it, and I didn't ask.

"Black is back," Liz gloated as she arranged her hand. The game was spades, and it was time to bid.

"I got four," I said.

"I got seven," Liz said.

"I got . . ." Yamile began.

"Watch old sandbag Sally over there underbid again," Liz said to me.

"I am not gonna underbid," Yamile said defensively.

"Whenever I'm her partner, I always jack up my bid," Liz said to me.

"I can't believe it!" Yamile said, indignant.

"And don't we win?" Liz asked.

"Sometimes," Yamile said, "and other times, we go down in flames because we can't make our bids. Then Liz tries to talk me into those crazy blind sevens."

"And doesn't it work?" Liz asked.

"*One* time. It worked *one* time. And we probably would have won anyway," Yamile said.

"Liz," I said, "would you stop harassing the girl so she can bid."

"Sorry," Liz said, taking a sip of her wine.

"I got . . . five," Yamile said defiantly, and took a swig of her mango juice.

There were only three of us—Liz, Yamile, and me, so we were playing spades. Usually, we played bid whist or spades with partners, but Liz's girlfriend, Ronetta, was out of town.

"You miss your honey?" Yamile asked Liz.

'Girl, I miss that fine brown woman every day when I have to go to work," Liz said with a grin.

"I heard that," said Yamile.

Ronetta was at Princeton for the graduation of her son, Gus junior.

"When is she coming back?" I asked.

"Next week," Liz said with a sigh.

Liz and Ronetta had been together over ten years. They were still madly in love, but it was an open kind of love. Not the kind where the lovers lock themselves away and hoard it only for themselves. They played cards with Yamile and me every other week and went out with friends.

But don't think for a minute that Liz and Ronetta weren't tuned into each other. They had that serious lovers' telepathy, and we had to break them up when we played cards. Yamile and I had only been neighbors and best friends for a year and a half, and we were no match for those two. To keep it even, we switched off when we played partners. One week it would be me and Liz versus Yamile and Ronetta. The next week, it would be me and Ronetta against Yamile and Liz.

We also switched locations; that day the game was at Liz's apartment in Oakland. Her dining room looked out onto Lake Merritt, which was beautiful at night. It was too dark to see all the pollution, and the perimeter was surrounded by a string of yellow lights.

I took a sip of my root beer, and looked at the Tobe Correal original sculpture across from me. It was the bodice of a nude, glazed in glossy black with flecks of copper. Her breasts seemed to disagree, one pointing directly forward, and the other upward, as if one of her invisible arms was raised. Her full buttocks jutted out behind her in counterpoint to her round stomach. The sculpture sat on top of a 1940s-style radio with a front panel that swung open to reveal a Denon stereo. From the speaker within a speaker came the sounds of Billie's voice, telling us that we didn't know what love was.

"So what happened with this dramatic case," Yamile said as she started the game with the ace of hearts.

"I thought you'd never ask," I said. "I put this ad in the *Tribune* . . ."

"That rag," Liz said.

"It's better than the *Chronicle*," Yamile said.

"Please," Liz shot back, "those fools took the Oakland out of the *Oakland Tribune.*"

"Yeah," Yamile said defensively, "but at least we got Brenda Payton. Name one Black female perspective you get in the *Chronicle*—"

"Enough of the battle of the newspapers," I said. "*I'm* telling this story." It had all just ended the day before, and I needed to get it off my chest. "So my ad came out on Monday. 'M. Moore Investigations,'" I quoted, "'affordable, effective.'" It had also included my private investigator's license number and phone number. "Those three lines cost me $41.10 for two days," I said. "I sat around on Monday and Tuesday thinking I had wasted my money. Finally, on Wednesday, I got a call."

"Oh, damn," Liz said as she watched Yamile cut her queen of clubs with a three of spades.

"Anyway," I said, "this woman calls and says she wants me to follow her husband, she suspects him of having an affair."

"And what did you tell her?" Liz asked.

"I said I would shadow him, I would be willing to photograph him in public places or on the street, but not inside any private buildings, and no video."

"That's right, honey, 'cause you don't need no photo or video of nobody doing the do, to know somebody's doing the do. And you don't need no B and E rap to get 'em," Liz said.

"What's B and E?" Yamile asked.

"Breaking and entering," Liz said, reaching for a buffalo wing. She had made them, and they were good and spicy.

"Will you give me some of those wings?" I asked Liz and passed my plate to her. "Oh, and give me some of that sweet potato pudding while you're at it," I added.

"Oh, you like that, huh?" Yamile asked.

"It's not bad," I said, "considering it's probably good for me."

"Well," Yamile said, "it has no sugar, no flour, no butter, and no milk, but I'd be glad to give you the recipe."

"No thank you," I said, "telling me all the healthy soybean ingredients will just spoil it for me. Besides, what am I gonna do with a recipe? I'm no chef." For our card parties, I always brought the soda, juice, and wine.

"One of these days we gonna make you cook something," Liz said.

"And you'll be sorry," I told her.

"I'm a witness," Yamile said, tossing out the ace of diamonds.

"So this woman comes down to my office," I began again.

"How did she look?" Yamile asked.

"Well, she was about your color," I said. Yamile's skin was the color of butter-scotch, midway between her Black father and her Puerto Rican mother. Her dark hair was twisted into little ropes and pulled back in a ponytail. Her oval face rested on the knuckles of her fist and her forearm was covered in brightly colored beaded bracelets. Yamile is a tall, kinda pear-shaped woman.

"But the similarity ended there," I continued. "You're kind of the young, earthy, artistic type. This woman was a Jack and Jill type, with real long sandy-colored hair, and she was petite and slight. She had on this black and white tuxedo coatdress, high heels, expert makeup—you know, not a hair or a thread out of place. The girl looked like she had walked out of an *Essence* magazine 'fierce looks for winter' layout."

"Like something I would wear?" Liz asked. At that moment Liz was wearing a pair of red denim jeans and a plain white button-down shirt. This was very unusual for Liz, who had most of her clothes custom made for her voluptuous figure. At work she wore form-fitting suits and high heels. Liz took seriously all those studies about "power colors," and wore a lot of red. Liz was a milk-chocolate brown, and conservative folks might say she shouldn't wear red, but any fool could see that it worked on her. Besides, I'm a shade darker than Liz, and I wear any color I feel like.

"No, this woman wasn't like you at all," I said to Liz. "I think of you as a sort of urban diva. She acted like she wanted to pull the white silk handkerchief out of the pocket of her coatdress and wipe the chair off before she sat in it."

"It was like that, huh?" Liz asked as she cut Yamile's jack of diamonds with a spade.

"Yeah," I said, "and I told you I scrubbed that office from floor to ceiling."

"I don't understand why you're paying alla that rent when you know you can see clients at Front Rowe," Liz said.

I had worked for her at Front Rowe Investigations for two years. Liz Rowe was somewhere in her early forties and was basically my mentor. I had thought that seeing a client there would be like spending a night with a man at my mother's house. Even if I had permission, I would still feel inhibited; it wouldn't be *my* house. But with the rent they had me paying at that run-down office building, and the drama of this case, I was reconsidering.

"Miss Essence must have raised a sandy eyebrow at your short afro," Yamile said.

"That's right," Liz said, "and I'll bet you were dressed in let's see, was it sweats or blue jeans?"

"Jeans," I said defensively, "with a new burgundy turtleneck, thank you." Liz and Yamile were always trying to get me to *diversify* my wardrobe. Shoot, no one told Coffin Ed and Grave Digger Jones to stop wearing those rumpled suits.

"So was she impressed with your outfit?" Yamile asked.

"No," I said, "but she handed me a photo of her man and told me where to find him. And she wrote me a rather large check for a retainer, which didn't bounce."

"Good sign," Liz said.

"I wish it had been," I said.

"Hey, wait a minute," Liz said to me. "I thought you was cuttin' clubs."

"No," I said, "Yamile's cutting clubs. I threw the club."

"Dang, just set her up, why don't you," Liz said and tossed out a four of clubs, only to be cut by Yamile's six of spades. "Go on back to your story," grumbled Liz.

"Well, it was about three o'clock in the afternoon when the wife left, so I drove out to the husband's business. Ken's Men's Emporium on East Fourteenth street— they sell suits and stuff."

"Let me clarify here," Liz said, "you mean real suits, or the kind of low quality, buy on credit, wear it to the nightclub to impress the ladies type suits they sell in the 'hood."

"Well, I didn't go in," I said, "but I think it was pretty mediocre stuff. When I drove by, I could see him through the plate-glass window of the store handling a transaction. I parked my car in the supermarket lot across the street and watched him through my binoculars.

"Now, I must say," I went on, "the photo she gave me didn't do the man justice."

"Was he foyne?" Yamile asked in her best New York Puerto Rican girl imitation.

"He was a very good-looking man," I said. "Not my type at all, mind you. Tall, broad-shouldered, nice build, but he had that kind of light-skinned slick look. First of all, you could tell he didn't buy his suits at his own store."

"I know that's a fact," Liz said.

"And he looked like he was right out of an ad for Dax," I went on. "My man's head was waved *up.*"

"I'm surprised you couldn't see the mark on his head from the do-rag," Liz said.

"No," I said, "this guy was definitely not the do-rag type. He was more upscale, like his wife. I could imagine her saying something like 'Kenneth and I frown upon that kind of ghetto mentality,' in her prim voice."

"Hold up," Liz said. "What did you just throw out?" she asked me.

"The five of hearts," I said.

"Hearts led, and you threw the diamond?" Liz asked Yamile.

"I'm afraid so," Yamile said.

"Aw, sookie sookie," Liz said, grinning, and took the book with a four of spades.

"But anyway," I went on, "the brother is easy on the eyes, which is good, because I'm watching him all afternoon. Folks going in and out, buying mostly on layaway, but nothing to suggest any fooling around on his part. Then, at seven o'clock, he closes down, pulls the metal gate over the front of the store, and leaves. I follow him to their two-story white house. She had given me the address as being in Piedmont, but really it's on the Oakland side of the Oakland/Piedmont border."

"Who does she think she's fooling?" Liz asked.

"I hate that," Yamile said. "Let a city get too many colored folks, and everyone starts trying to disassociate themselves, even the colored folks."

"Look," Liz said, "if colored folks wanna do the upscale thing, do it. But if you can't really afford it, don't perpetrate."

"Well, I don't understand why Black folks can't just stay in the community," Yamile said. "Like this is a great apartment. There are plenty of really nice places to live, right here in Oakland."

"Hey, you two," I broke in, "I'm trying to tell this story, so will you stop interrupting me?"

"Well," Liz said, "It's okay with me, if it's okay with Miss Power-to-the-people over here."

"Don't start with me, Shelby Steele," Yamile said. "Go ahead, Madeline."

"Well anyway," I said, "I go home and check my messages. She's on my work machine, asking me to call. When I call the house, he answers, and, girls, I must say the man is really Barry White in disguise." I said "hello," in my deepest, suavest voice, just to give them the idea.

"Oh," Yamile said, "I love a man with a nice voice." She fanned herself facetiously, and took a long swallow of her mango juice.

"Yes, he had a *very* nice voice," I continued. "So then she gets on the phone, and I tell her who it is. So she says, 'Oh, hello, how did the meeting go?' and I say, 'There wasn't any meeting, but I'll be back tomorrow.' And she says, 'Okay, ciao!'"

"She didn't say 'ciao'!" Yamile said.

"Right on the Oakland/Piedmont border," I said. "So the next day, I'm down at the spot bright and early. I see him open up at nine o'clock. Same deal, I wait in the parking lot; folks buy suits on layaway. Then, at twelve-thirty, the man strolls out of the store, leaving his trusty assistant in charge. The assistant is a slightly younger and browner version of himself, maybe his brother or his cousin. Then he rolls out in his late-model BMW convertible—"

"He drove a convertible BMW?" Liz asked.

"A red one," I said. "I didn't tell you that?" They shook their heads. "Oh, well, while I was following him, I felt like *Ebony* was gonna have to feature the husband and wife team at any moment."

"I can see it now," Yamile said, "'Raveen Relaxer woman meets the S-Curl man; love at first sight.'"

"Yeah," I said, "either that or 'Young Black entrepreneur and lovely wife lead dream life in Piedmont, California.' Then there's a photo of them in front of the car parked by the house, and another photo of him in front of his business."

"Or there's the other angle," Liz said. " 'All the good men are married, gay, or in jail: one woman's struggle to keep her marriage together and to keep her good Black man from going astray.'"

"Hold that thought; it gets deeper," I said. "I follow him for a while, and it becomes apparent that he's not just going to the local deli for lunch. Instead, he drives out to San Leandro and goes by this apartment building. He rings the bell and I get a photo of him in the foyer. He gets back in his car and out comes this woman."

"Hold up," Liz said. "What did you just throw out?" She pointed to Yamile with the cards in her hand facedown.

"The two of spades," Yamile said.

"You threw out the highest spade in the deck to take a four and eight of hearts?" Liz asked.

"Oh, oops," Yamile said, "I forgot that the two was high."

"We said we were playing Madeline's crazy Back East way," Liz reminded her.

"Well I got distracted by Madeline's story," Yamile said. "Can I take it back?"

"Take it back? Girl, you must be from Berkeley," Liz said. "I been to card games where folks'll pull a knife just for *asking* to take something back."

"Yeah, but we're all unarmed here," Yamile said. "At least I hope so." She glanced at me disapprovingly. "So can I take the card back or what?" she asked Liz.

"What do you think?" Liz asked me.

"Well, I do tell a good story if I say so myself," I said, grinning. "I think she has a good excuse."

Liz rolled her eyes. "Go ahead, Yamile."

Yamile eagerly snatched up the two and took the book with a ten of spades.

"I think this California living is making me soft. Folks back home in Texas would be scandalized that I let that go by, just scandalized," Liz said. "So, Master Storyteller, go back to your tale of woe."

"Where was I?" I asked.

"The woman was coming out of the building," Yamile prompted, reaching for a buffalo wing.

"Yeah, right. So the woman was coming out of the building. I photograph her coming out and getting into his car. Now she's another *Essence* model type."

"Like me?" Liz asked.

"Yeah, this sister was a little more like you," I said. "A little darker than you, with a thicker build. Her hair was cut real short in the back, but was full on top, and pressed super-ultra straight like yours. Makeup for days, killer nails like yours. She had on this cream-colored pantsuit with flared legs, and a pair of brown patent leather pumps, with a matching brown patent leather bag. And I must say, the girl was wearing the pantsuit."

"Was she wearing it?" Liz asked.

"Yeah," I said, "she was just strutting to the car."

"Large and in charge," Liz said. "You gotta love that."

"Well, I don't know about in charge," Yamile said. "She is involved with a married man."

"Good point," Liz conceded, taking a sip of her wine.

Yamile was a counselor, and had heard every crazy story from "he's been gonna leave her any day now for years" to "I know he has another woman but he loves me more." "I mean, even if he lied," Yamile said, "she'd have to be blind not to know. With a wife like he's got, Ms. San Leandro can't be calling the house or coming by the job. If she doesn't know he's married, it's like the way white folks don't know Egypt is in Africa. 'Cause it's all about de Nile!" She laughed at her own joke. Liz chuckled.

These girls were not gonna let me tell this story. "Anyway," I said when their laughter subsided, "they drive out to a motel in San Lorenzo, and I photograph them going in, and then I wait. And it was weird, sitting there. I mean, I know at some level that even as we're here playing cards, someone is sleeping with someone else's man or woman. But to be in the parking lot while they're at it. That was another thing entirely. I felt a little cheap and tawdry, I must admit. But mostly, I felt like a voyeur."

"Honey," Liz said, "this business is about voyeurism. You investigate people's dirty laundry."

"Yeah, but the sexual part was just too personal for me," I said. "I didn't like it. So I just sat there feeling uncomfortable until they came out an hour later—"

"Only an hour?" Liz asked.

"Hey," Yamile said, "if he's gonna make it into *Ebony*, he can't afford to waste too much time."

"Yeah," I said, "but the wildest thing was, when they came out an hour later they were both immaculate, like nothing had happened. Not a wave or a curl out of place."

"Maybe they didn't have sex," Vamile suggested.

"Are you kidding me?" Liz asked. "There are a million ways to do the do without messing up your do. And you can also best believe that her matching brown patent leather bag had every styling implement and makeup accoutrement known to womankind," Liz said, laying down the little joker.

"Damn," said Yamile, grudgingly tossing out the king of spades. "You know that means she has the big joker." I nodded my agreement.

"Not necessarily," Liz said, scooping up the book.

"Watch," Yamile said.

"Go on with your story," Liz said and threw out the big joker.

"See!" Yamile said, and threw out the two in disgust.

I had no more spades anyway; my hand had been mostly clubs. I tossed out the five of clubs and went on with my story.

"I photographed them getting back into the car, him dropping her off at her apartment, and him back at work by two-thirty. I wait until four o'clock, but it's all quiet. So I go to a one-hour photo place to get the film developed.

"While I'm waiting, I go get a burger, then I come back and the film is out. I'm no brilliant artist, here, but I've got good, clear photos. I love that zoom lens; you can see him, you can see her, you can see them in the car, going into the motel, his arm around her waist. You can even see them kiss in one shot."

"Like I told you," Liz said, "you don't need to be in the room to know what went on."

"Yeah," I said, "that was my problem. I realized a little too late that I didn't want to know. But it was my job, so I was gonna finish it.

"I get home around six o'clock," I went on. "I pick up my work messages. She wants me to call her at home. This time I don't get Barry White; I get her. I tell her I got the photos. She's quiet for a minute, then she says she's on her way to my office, will I meet her there. I say yeah.

"My office is locked after six o'clock, so I stand around in the lobby waiting for her. She shows up a little after seven, this time in a geometric print dress, and she's smoking. We take the elevator up to the third floor, and I tell her not to smoke in my office. She mumbles how she's sorry, how she doesn't usually smoke, and she puts the cigarette out in the ashtray in the hall.

"I present her with the bill and ask for the final check before I release the photos."

"I taught you well," Liz said.

"Yeah," I continued, "and she says, 'Sure, whatever.' When she signs the check, there's a little tremor in her hand. I turn over the photos, prints and negatives, like I promised in the contract.

"I don't think I knew what to expect," I said, taking a sip of my root beer. "I mean, I had never done domestic investigation before. Maybe she would break down and cry, or get angry and run out, but never in my wildest dreams could I have imagined what she did."

"So what did she do?" Liz asked impatiently.

"I'm trying to tell you," I said. "She picks them up and looks at the photo of him in the foyer of the apartment building in San Leandro. Then she looks at a shot of him with his arm around the woman, taken from behind. Then she looks at a shot of them kissing, and in that photo you can see the woman's face much more clearly. Then the wife's eyes get all wide and crazy. I'm thinking fire is gonna come shooting out of them at any time. She just sits there for a minute, shaking. Then she says, 'Mother . . . fucking . . . Black . . . BITCHES! Black bitches! Black bitches!' I mean, the woman is screaming. She just goes *off*. 'I'll kill you, motherfucking Black bitches! All you Black bitches trying to take my man.'" I looked at Yamile and Liz; both of their mouths were hanging open.

"Whaaat?!" Yamile asked.

"Yes! I mean she just loses it," I said. "I tell her, 'I think you'd better—' but before I can even say 'leave now,' she reaches for her pocketbook. Now I don't know what she's carrying, and my heart is already jumping from her initial out-burst, and now I'm really scared, so I go for the door.

"By the time I yank it open, I look over my shoulder, because I am aware that I will be leaving a crazy woman alone in my office. Do you know she has pulled out *a huge meat cleaver?*" I gestured for them, with my hands about a foot and a half apart. "Mind you, all the time this woman is screaming about *you* Black bitches who want to take her man, meaning me, I guess, 'cause I was the nearest Black woman, and in reality I'm the only person anywhere nearby, and I am terrified.

"So by now, I'm out the door, but this woman is stepping on my shadow, screaming at the top of her lungs, waving this huge knife, and calling me everything but a child of God.

"I take off, with her right on me! It's seven o'clock, and there's no one left in the building. I'm screaming, 'Help! Help!' She's screaming, 'I'm a kill you bitch! I'm a kill you, hoe!' I'm running for the stairs, praying she doesn't throw the knife at me. I hit the stairwell, close the door behind me, and lean on it. Now I know I'm skinny, but I'm six feet tall, and she's a thin five feet two. There's no way she can force the door open, so I figure I've bought a little time, maybe she'll even calm down or wear herself out.

"She's banging on the door screaming at me to open it up so she can kill me, screaming, screaming, 'You ugly nasty nappy head bitches need to keep your dirty black hands off my man!' I swear the woman did not take a breath. Meanwhile, I'm trying to figure out which floors I can get out onto.

"The super had told me somthing about the stairwell doors getting locked at such and such a time, and I wasn't paying all that much attention when he said it, but with this crazy woman on the other side of the door, it suddenly seems very important, and I'm trying to figure it out. So I think I've got things somewhat under control, when all of a sudden glass shatters right by my ear, and the square top of the huge knife comes through the window."

"*¡Ay Dios!*" Yamile said.

"You got that right," I said. "I jump away from the door, scared out of my mind. It takes her half a second to get the door open. By now, I'm halfway down the stairs and *praying* the first-floor door is open. If I'm trapped in the stairwell with this woman, she's gonna hack me to death.

"I tear down the stairs and reach for the doorknob. *Please, please, please, don't be locked.* Praise God it opens! Now you all know I practically made the Olympic team, so I figure I can get away from this psychopath if I can just get outside.

"So I come flying out of the building, and she comes flying out of the building right behind me. I'm screaming, 'Help, help, call the police!' She's screaming she's gonna kill me. She has the knife in one hand, and her purse in the other hand. We musta looked so crazy, but there's no one around to see it. No one. I told you my office is on Third Street in that sort of warehouse district near Jack London Square. Well it's dead at seven o'clock. I mean *dead.* So she chases me for four blocks. But because she's got the heels, the knife, the purse, and the dress, she's no match for me.

"When I come around a corner onto Second Street, I've got about a half-block lead on her. I see that we're headed toward that club, Cherie's, at Second and

Broadway right? Well, there are a whole bunch of Black people standing outside, and they've all turned to look and see what the noise is about.

"Do you know that when the woman came around the corner and saw those people, she lowered her weapon and slowed down to a walk? A casual *walk?*" I gestured for them, my hand with a buffalo wing in it, raised over my head. Then slowly, I lowered my arm down and dropped the wing on my plate. "Yes she did, and she put that meat cleaver back in her purse so nonchalant, like it was just a big old lipstick."

"No," Liz said, finding her voice for the first time. "No, she didn't!"

"I am not lying," I said. "I was backing away from her, my eyes wide, panting, all out of breath, and she was just strolling, cool as you please, down the street. That woman ran her fingers through her sandy hair, smoothed down her dress, pulled out her handkerchief, and wiped her brow. Then she walked the remaining twenty yards to Broadway at a leisurely pace." Liz and Yamile were shaking their heads in disbelief. "The girl was just strolling along like it was a spring day.

"Now, I crossed the street and kept a good distance between us, in case she went off again. Do you know that woman hailed a taxi and got in it? She drove off, and there I was, standing on the street, with all these suited up Black people in front of this club staring at *me!* Do you hear me?

"Well, at first I was almost embarrassed, but then I realized that I was alive— that a crazy woman had tried to kill me, but I was alive. And I started laughing. Somehow, it was just so funny to me. She was acting like she was sane, because she didn't want those people to think she was crazy, and I didn't care if they thought I was crazy, just as long as I was alive. I've never felt so . . . elated. I just walked down the street, laughing hysterically."

"And called the police, I hope," Yamile said.

"Damn skippy," I said. "I dialed 911 at the first phone booth I saw. That woman was out of her Black mind. I believe she really would have killed me, and was liable to kill someone else.

"When they picked her up," I went on, "she acted all surprised and calm. She said she didn't know what they were talking about. But when they took her down to the station, there was this Black woman cop there, and the woman went off on *her.*"

"On the cop?" Liz asked.

"Yes, ma'am," I said. "That's what the other cop told me."

"That is such epic drama," Yamile said.

"Oh, it was *drama,*" I said.

"All this happened yesterday?" Yamile asked.

"Yesterday," I said.

We were quiet for a moment. The cards lay in undisturbed piles in front of us where Liz had dealt them. The game had stopped long ago. I took a sip of my root beer. In the silence, Billie took to telling us how she was crazy in love.

"Well damn," Liz said. "That's quite a story."

"Yeah," I said, "I'm just glad I lived to tell it."

"I'm glad, too," Yamile said.

"Folks are to' up," Liz said.

Yamile scooted her chair next to mine. "Are you okay, sweetie?" she asked, putting her arm around me.

"Yeah," I said hastily, "I'm fine."

"Are you sure?" she asked me pointedly. "That was really traumatic."

"Well," I admitted grudgingly, "I kind of broke down and cried for a little while at the police station." I had thanked God that it was a Black cop, because I hate to cry in front of white folks. And he was really nice about it.

"So you bought a gun?" Liz asked.

"Yeah, and, uh, I'm even thinking of taking you up on your offer to use office space at Front Rowe," I said. "I'd do most of my work at home, but only use Front Rowe when I needed to see a client. That is, if the offer still stands."

"Of course it does," Liz said, "I know it's a drag paying that high rent."

"It's not so much the rent," I said. "It's more that a client could go off on me and no one would have my back."

"I got your back," Liz said.

"Me, too," said Yamile.

"I know," I said. "Both of you always have."

"That poor woman," Yamile said. "Imagine how much pain she must be in to act like that. I hope she gets some help."

Liz just shook her head.

I was kind of mad at Yamile for sympathizing with the woman. I guess it's hard to sympathize with someone who tries to kill you.

Did I hope she would get help? I guessed so. It was hard for me to see her as someone who needed help. Mostly I thought of her as crazy and dangerous. But I guessed people weren't just born crazy. It's not like as a kid she said, "I want to grow up to be out of my mind." Maybe I could sympathize with her, just so long as she stayed the hell away from me.

Now that I'd finally gotten the whole story out, I didn't want to think about it anymore. I changed the subject. "Now excuse me, but weren't we playing cards?" I asked.

Yamile scooted her chair back, but gave me that best friend we'll-talk-later-when-we're-alone look.

"Well, come on then," Liz said, picking up her hand, "baby needs a new pair of shoes."

I picked up my cards. "Aw, sookie," I said, arranging them. "Black is back."

Quilting on the Rebound

TERRY McMILLAN

Five years ago, I did something I swore I'd never do—went out with someone I worked with. We worked for a large insurance company in L.A. Richard was a senior examiner and I was a chief underwriter. The first year, we kept it a secret, and not because we were afraid of jeopardizing our jobs. Richard was twenty-six and I was thirty-four. By the second year, everybody knew it anyway and nobody seemed to care. We'd been going out for three years when I realized that this relationship was going nowhere. I probably could've dated him for the rest of my life and he'd have been satisfied. Richard had had a long reputation for being a Don Juan of sorts, until he met me. I cooled his heels. His name was also rather ironic, because he looked like a black Richard Gere. The fact that I was older than he was made him feel powerful in a sense, and he believed that he could do for me what men my own age apparently couldn't. But that wasn't true. He was a challenge. I wanted to see if I could make his head and heart turn 360 degrees, and I did. I blew his young mind in bed, but he also charmed me into loving him until I didn't care how old he was.

Richard thought I was exotic because I have slanted eyes, high cheekbones, and full lips. Even though my mother is Japanese and my dad is black, I inherited most of his traits. My complexion is dark, my hair is nappy, and I'm five six. I explained to Richard that I was proud of both of my heritages, but he has insisted on thinking of me as being mostly Japanese. Why, I don't know. I grew up in a black neighborhood in L.A., went to Dorsey High School—which was predominantly black, Asian, and Hispanic—and most of my friends are black. I've never even considered going out with anyone other than black men.

My mother, I'm glad to say, is not the stereotypical passive Japanese wife either. She's been the head nurse in Kaiser's cardiovascular unit for over twenty years, and my dad has his own landscaping business, even though he should've retired years ago. My mother liked Richard and his age didn't bother her, but she believed that if a man loved you he should marry you. Simple as that. On the other hand, my dad didn't care who I married just as long as it was soon. I'll be the first to admit that I was a spoiled-rotten brat because my mother had had three miscarriages before she finally had me and I was used to getting everything I wanted. Richard was no exception. "Give him the ultimatum," my mother had said, if he didn't propose by my thirty-eighth birthday.

But I didn't have to. I got pregnant.

We were having dinner at an Italian restaurant when I told him. "You want to get married, don't you?" he'd said.

"Do you?" I asked.

He was picking through his salad and then he jabbed his fork into a tomato. "Why not, we were headed in that direction anyway, weren't we?" He did not eat his tomato but laid his fork down on the side of the plate. I swallowed a spoonful of my clam chowder, then asked, "Were we?"

"You know the answer to that. But hell, now's as good a time as any. We're both making good money, and sometimes all a man needs is a little incentive." He didn't look at me when he said this, and his voice was strained. "Look," he said, "I've had a pretty shitty day, haggling with one of the adjusters, so forgive me if I don't appear to be boiling over with excitement. I am happy about this. Believe me, I am," he said, and picked up a single piece of lettuce with a different fork and put it into his mouth.

My parents were thrilled when I told them, but my mother was nevertheless suspicious. "Funny how this baby pop up, isn't it?" she'd said.

"What do you mean?"

"You know exactly what I mean. I hope baby doesn't backfire."

I ignored what she'd just said. "Will you help me make my dress?" I asked.

"Yes," she said. "But we must hurry."

My parents—who are far from well off—went all out for this wedding. My mother didn't want anyone to know I was pregnant, and to be honest, I didn't either. The age difference was enough to handle as it was. Close to three hundred people had been invited, and my parents had spent an astronomical amount of money to rent a country club in Marina Del Rey. "At your age," my dad had said, "I hope you'll only be doing this once." Richard's parents insisted on taking care of the caterer and the liquor, and my parents didn't object. I paid for the cake.

About a month before the Big Day, I was meeting Richard at the jeweler because he'd picked out my ring and wanted to make sure I liked it. He was so excited, he sounded like a little boy. It was beautiful, but I told him he didn't have to spend four thousand dollars on my wedding ring. "You're worth it," he'd said and kissed me on the cheek. When we got to the parking lot, he opened my door, and stood there staring at me. "Four more weeks," he said, "and you'll be my wife." He didn't smile when he said it, but closed the door and walked around to the driver's side and got in. He'd driven four whole blocks without saying a word and his knuckles were almost white because of how tight he was holding the steering wheel.

"Is something wrong, Richard?" I asked him.

"What would make you think that?" he said. Then he laid on the horn because someone in front of us hadn't moved and the light had just barely turned green.

"Richard, we don't have to go through with this, you know."

"I know we don't *have* to, but it's the right thing to do, and I'm going to do it. So don't worry, we'll be happy."

But I *was* worried.

I'd been doing some shopping at the Beverly Center when I started getting these stomach cramps while I was going up the escalator, so I decided to sit down. I walked over to one of the little outside cafés and I felt something lock inside my stomach, so I pulled out a chair. Moments later my skirt felt like it was wet. I got up and looked at the chair and saw a small red puddle. I sat back down and started crying. I didn't know what to do. Then a punkish-looking girl came over and asked if I was okay. "I'm pregnant, and I've just bled all over this chair," I said.

"Can I do something for you? Do you want me to call an ambulance?" She was popping chewing gum and I wanted to snatch it out of her mouth.

By this time at least four other women had gathered around me. The punkish-looking girl told them about my condition. One of the women said, "Look, let's get her to the rest room. She's probably having a miscarriage."

Two of the women helped me up and all four of them formed a circle around me, then slowly led me to the ladies' room. I told them that I wasn't in any pain, but they were still worried. I closed the stall door, pulled down two toilet seat covers and sat down. I felt as if I had to go, so I pushed. Something plopped out of me and it made a splash. I was afraid to get up but I got up and looked at this large dark mass that looked like liver. I put my hand over my mouth because I knew that was my baby.

"Are you okay in there?"

I went to open my mouth, but the joint in my jawbone clicked and my mouth wouldn't move.

"Are you okay in there, miss?"

I wanted to answer, but I couldn't.

"Miss," I heard her banging on the door.

I felt my mouth loosen. "It's gone," I said. "It's gone."

"Honey, open the door," someone said, but I couldn't move. Then I heard myself say, "I think I need a sanitary pad." I was staring into the toilet bowl when I felt a hand hit my leg. "Here, are you sure you're okay in there?"

"Yes," I said. Then I flushed the toilet with my foot and watched my future disappear. I put the pad on and reached inside my shopping bag, pulled out a Raiders sweatshirt I'd bought for Richard and tied it around my waist. When I came out, all of the women were waiting for me. "Would you like us to call your husband? Where are you parked? Do you feel light-headed, dizzy?"

"No, I'm fine, really, and thank you so much for your concern. I appreciate it, but I feel okay."

I drove home in a daze and when I opened the door to my condo, I was glad I lived alone. I sat on the couch from one o'clock to four o'clock without moving. When I finally got up, it felt as if I'd only been there for five minutes.

I didn't tell Richard. I didn't tell anybody. I bled for three days before I went to see my doctor. He scolded me because I'd gotten some kind of an infection and had to be prescribed antibiotics, then he sent me to the outpatient clinic, where I had to have a D & C.

Two weeks later, I had a surprise shower and got enough gifts to fill the housewares department at Bullock's. One of my old girlfriends, Gloria, came all the way from Phoenix, and I hadn't seen her in three years. I hardly recognized her, she was as big as a house. "You don't know how lucky you are, girl," she'd said to me. "I wish I could be here for the wedding but Tarik is having his sixteenth birthday party and I am not leaving a bunch of teenagers alone in my house. Besides, I'd probably have a heart attack watching you or anybody else walk down an aisle in white. Come to think of it, I can't even remember the last time I went to a wedding."

"Me either," I said.

"I know you're gonna try to get pregnant in a hurry, right?" she asked, holding out her wrist with the watch on it.

I tried to smile. "I'm going to work on it," I said.

"Well, who knows?" Gloria said, laughing. "Maybe one day you'll be coming to my wedding. We may both be in wheelchairs, but you never know."

"I'll be there," I said.

All Richard said when he saw the gifts was, "What are we going to do with all this stuff? Where are we going to put it?"

"It depends on where we're going to live," I said, which we hadn't even talked about. My condo was big enough and so was his apartment.

"It doesn't matter to me, but I think we should wait a while before buying a house. A house is a big investment, you know. Thirty years." He gave me a quick look.

"Are you getting cold feet?" I blurted out.

"No, I'm not getting cold feet. It's just that in two weeks we're going to be man and wife, and it takes a little getting used to the idea, that's all."

"Are you having doubts about the idea of it?"

"No."

"Are you sure?"

"I'm sure," he said.

I didn't stop bleeding, so I took some vacation time to relax, and finish my dress. I worked on it day and night and was doing all the beadwork by hand. My mother was spending all her free time at my place trying to make sure everything was happening on schedule. A week before the Big Day I was trying on my gown for the hundredth time when the phone rang. I thought it might be Richard, since he hadn't called me in almost forty-eight hours, and when I finally called him and left a message, he still hadn't returned my call. My father said this was normal.

"Hello," I said.

"I think you should talk to Richard." It was his mother. "About what?" I asked.

"He's not feeling very well," was all she said.

"What's wrong with him?"

"I don't know for sure. I think it's his stomach."

"Is he sick?"

"I don't know. Call him."

"I did call him but he hasn't returned my call."

"Keep trying," she said.

So I called him at work, but his secretary said he wasn't there. I called him at home and he wasn't there either, so I left another message and for the next three hours I was a wreck, waiting to hear from him. I knew something was wrong.

I gave myself a facial, a manicure and pedicure and watched Oprah Winfrey while I waited by the phone. It didn't ring. My mother was downstairs hemming one of the bridesmaid's dresses. I went down to get myself a glass of wine. "How you feeling, Marilyn Monroe?" she asked.

"What do you mean, how am I feeling? I'm feeling fine."

"All I meant was you awful lucky with no morning sickness or anything, but I must say, hormones changing because you getting awfully irritating."

"I'm sorry, Ma."

"It's okay. I had jitters too."

I went back upstairs and closed my bedroom door, then went into my bathroom. I put the wineglass on the side of the bathtub and decided to take a bubble bath in spite of the bleeding. I must have poured half a bottle of Secreti in. The water was too hot but I got in anyway. Call, dammit, call. Just then the phone rang and scared me half to death. I was hyperventilating and couldn't say much except, "Hold on a minute," while I caught my breath.

"Marilyn?" Richard was saying. "Marilyn?" But before I had a chance to answer he blurted out what must have been on his mind all along. "Please don't be mad at me, but I can't do this. I'm not ready. I wanted to do the right thing, but I'm only twenty-nine years old. I've got my whole life ahead of me. I'm not ready to be a father yet. I'm not ready to be anybody's husband either, and I'm scared. Everything is happening too fast. I know you think I'm being a coward, and you're probably right. But I've been having nightmares, Marilyn. Do you hear me, nightmares about being imprisoned. I haven't been able to sleep through the night. I doze off and wake up dripping wet. And my stomach. It's in knots. Believe me, Marilyn, it's not that I don't love you because I do. It's not that I don't care about the baby, because I do. I just can't do this right now. I can't make this kind of commitment right now. I'm sorry. Marilyn? Marilyn, are you still there?"

I dropped the portable phone in the bathtub and got out.

My mother heard me screaming and came tearing into the room. "What happened?" I was dripping wet and ripping the pearls off my dress but somehow I managed to tell her.

"He come to his senses," she said. "This happen a lot. He just got cold feet, but give him day or two. He not mean it."

Three days went by and he didn't call. My mother stayed with me and did everything she could to console me, but by that time I'd already flushed the ring down the toilet.

"I hope you don't lose baby behind this," she said.

"I've already lost the baby," I said.

"What?"

"A month ago."

Her mouth was wide open. She found the sofa with her hand and sat down. "Marilyn," she said and let out an exasperated sigh.

"I couldn't tell anybody."

"Why not tell somebody? Why not me, your mother?"

"Because I was too scared."

"Scared of what?"

"That Richard might change his mind."

"Man love you, dead baby not change his mind."

"I was going to tell him after we got married."

"I not raise you to be dishonest."

"I know."

"No man in world worth lying about something like this. How could you?"

"I don't know."

"I told you it backfire, didn't I?"

For weeks I couldn't eat or sleep. At first, all I did was think about what was wrong with me. I was too old. For him. No. He didn't care about my age. It was the gap in my teeth, or my slight overbite, from all those years I used to suck my thumb. But he never mentioned anything about it and I was really the only one who seemed to notice. I was flat-chested. I had cellulite. My ass was square instead of round. I wasn't exciting as I used to be in bed. No. I was still good in bed, that much I did know. I couldn't cook. I was a terrible housekeeper. That was it. If you couldn't cook and keep a clean house, what kind of wife would you make?

I had to make myself stop thinking about my infinite flaws, so I started quilting again. I was astonished at how radiant the colors were that I was choosing, how unconventional and wild the patterns were. Without even realizing it, I was fusing Japanese and African motifs and was quite excited by the results. My mother worried about me, even though I had actually stopped bleeding for two whole weeks. Under the circumstances, she thought that my obsession with quilting was not normal, so she forced me to go to the doctor. He gave me some kind of an antidepressant, which I refused to take. I told him I was not depressed, I was simply hurt. Besides, a pill wasn't any antidote or consolation for heartache.

I began to patronize just about every fabric store in downtown Los Angeles, and while I listened to the humming of my machine, and concentrated on designs that I couldn't believe I was creating, it occurred to me that I wasn't suffering from heartache at all. I actually felt this incredible sense of relief. As if I didn't have to anticipate anything else happening that was outside of my control. And when I did grieve, it was always because I had lost a child, not a future husband.

I also heard my mother all day long on my phone, lying about some tragedy that had happened and apologizing for any inconvenience it may have caused. And I watched her, bent over at the dining room table, writing hundreds of thank-you notes to the people she was returning gifts to. She even signed my name. My father wanted to kill Richard. "He was too young, and he wasn't good enough for you anyway," he said. "This is really a blessing in disguise."

I took a leave of absence from my job because there was no way in hell I could face those people, and the thought of looking at Richard infuriated me. I was not angry at him for not marrying me, I was angry at him for not being honest, for the way he handled it all. He even had the nerve to come over without calling. I had opened the door but wouldn't let him inside. He was nothing but a little pip-squeak. A handsome, five-foot-seven-inch pip-squeak.

"Marilyn, look, we need to talk."

"About what?"

"Us. The baby."

"There is no baby."

"What do you mean, there's no baby?"

"It died."

"You mean you got rid of it?"

"No, I lost it."

"I'm sorry, Marilyn," he said and put his head down. How touching, I thought. "This is all my fault."

"It's not your fault, Richard."

"Look. Can I come in?"

"For what?"

"I want to talk. I need to talk to you."

"About what?"

"About us."

"Us?"

"Yes, us. I don't want it to be over between us. I just need more time, that's all."

"Time for what?"

"To make sure this is what I want to do."

"Take all the time you need," I said and slammed the door in his face. He rang the buzzer again, but I just told him to get lost and leave me alone.

I went upstairs and sat at my sewing machine. I turned the light on, then picked up a piece of purple and terra-cotta cloth. I slid it under the pressure foot and dropped it. I pressed down on the pedal and watched the needle zigzag. The stitches were too loose so I tightened the tension. Richard is going to be the last in a series of mistakes I've made when it comes to picking a man. I've picked the wrong one too many times, like a bad habit that's too hard to break. I haven't had the best of luck when it comes to keeping them either, and to be honest, Richard was the one who lasted the longest.

When I got to the end of the fabric, I pulled the top and bobbin threads together and cut them on the thread cutter. Then I bent down and picked up two different pieces. They were black and purple. I always want what I can't have or what I'm not supposed to have. So what did I do? Created a pattern of choosing men that I knew would be a challenge. Richard's was his age. But the others—all of them from Alex to William—were all afraid of something: namely committing to one woman. All I wanted to do was seduce them hard enough—emotionally, mentally, and physically—so they wouldn't even be aware that they were committing to anything. I just wanted them to crave me, and no one else but me. I wanted to be their healthiest addiction. But it was a lot harder to do than I thought. What I found out was that men are a hard nut to crack.

But some of them weren't. When I was in my late twenties, early thirties—before I got serious and realized I wanted a long-term relationship—I'd had at least twenty different men fall in love with me, but of course these were the ones I didn't want. They were the ones who after a few dates or one rousing night in bed, ordained themselves my "man" or were too quick to want to marry me, and even some considered me their "property." When it was clear that I was dealing with a different species of man, a hungry element, before I got in too deep, I'd tell them almost immediately that I hope they wouldn't mind my being bisexual or my being unfaithful because I was in no hurry to settle down with one man, or that I had a tendency of always falling for my man's friends. Could they tolerate that? I even went so far as to tell them that I hoped having herpes wouldn't cause a problem, that I wasn't really all that trustworthy because I was a habitual liar, and that if they wanted the whole truth they should find themselves another woman. I told them that I didn't even think I was good enough for them, and they should do themselves a favor, find a woman who's truly worthy of having such a terrific man.

I had it down to a science, but by the time I met Richard, I was tired of lying and conniving. I was sick of the games. I was whipped, really, and allowed myself to relax and be vulnerable because I knew I was getting old.

When Gloria called to see how my honeymoon went, I told her the truth about everything. She couldn't believe it. "Well, I thought I'd heard 'em all, but this one takes the cake. How you holding up?"

"I'm hanging in there."

"This is what makes you want to castrate a man."

"Not really, Gloria."

"I know. But you know what I mean. Some of them have a lot of nerve, I swear they do. But really, Marilyn, how are you feeling for real, baby?"

"I'm getting my period every other week, but I'm quilting again, which is a good sign."

"First of all, take your behind back to that doctor and find out why you're still bleeding like this. And, honey, making quilts is no consolation for a broken heart. It sounds like you could use some R & R. Why don't you come visit me for a few days?"

I looked around my room, which had piles and piles of cloth and half-sewn quilts, from where I'd changed my mind. Hundreds of different colored thread were all over the carpet, and the satin stitch I was trying out wasn't giving me the effect I thought it would. I could use a break, I thought. I could. "You know what?" I said. "I think I will."

"Good, and bring me one of those tacky quilts. I don't have anything to snuggle up with in the winter, and contrary to popular belief, it does get cold here come December."

I liked Phoenix and Tempe, but I fell in love with Scottsdale. Not only was it beautiful but I couldn't believe how inexpensive it was to live in the entire area, which was all referred to as the Valley. I have to thank Gloria for being such a lifesaver. She took me to her beauty salon and gave me a whole new look. She chopped off my hair, and one of the guys in her shop showed me how to put on my makeup in a way that would further enhance what assets he insisted I had.

We drove to Tucson, to Canyon Ranch for what started out as a simple Spa Renewal Day. But we ended up spending three glorious days and had the works. I had an herbal wrap, where they wrapped my entire body in hot thin linen that had been steamed. Then they rolled me up in flannel blankets and put a cold wash cloth on my forehead. I sweated in the dark for a half hour. Gloria didn't do this because she said she was claustrophobic and didn't want to be wrapped up in anything where she couldn't move. I had a deep-muscle and shiatsu massage on two different days. We steamed. We Jacuzzied. We both had a mud facial, and then this thing called aroma therapy—where they put distilled essences from flowers and herbs on your face and you look like a different person when they finish. On the last day, we got this Persian Body Polish where they actually buffed our skin with crushed pearl creams, sprayed us with some kind of herbal spray, then used an electric brush to make us tingle. We had our hands and feet moisturized and put in heated gloves and booties and by the time we left, we couldn't believe we were the same women.

In Phoenix, Gloria took me to yet another resort where we listened to live music. We went to see a stupid movie and I actually laughed. Then we went on a two-day shopping spree and I charged whatever I felt like. I even bought her son a pair of eighty-dollar sneakers, and I'd only seen him twice in my life.

I felt like I'd gotten my spirit back, so when I got home, I told my parents I'd had it with the smog, the traffic, the gangs, and L.A. in general. My mother said, "You cannot run from heartache," but I told her I wasn't running from anything. I put my condo on the market, and in less than a month, it sold for four times what I paid for it. I moved in with my mother and father, asked for a job transfer for health reasons, and when it came through, three months later, I moved to Scottsdale.

The town house I bought feels like a house. It's twice the size of the one I had and cost less than half of what I originally spent. My complex is pretty standard for Scottsdale. It has two pools and four tennis courts. It also has vaulted ceilings, wall-to-wall carpet, two fireplaces, and a garden bathtub with a Jacuzzi in it. The kitchen has an island in the center and I've got a 180-degree view of Phoenix and mountains. It also has three bedrooms. One I sleep in, one I use for sewing, and the other is for guests.

I made close to forty thousand dollars after I sold my condo, so I sent four to my parents because the money they'd put down for the wedding was nonrefundable. They really couldn't afford that kind of loss. The rest I put in an IRA and CDs until I could figure out something better to do with it.

I hated my new job. I had to accept a lower-level position and less money, which didn't bother me all that much at first. The office, however, was much smaller and full of rednecks who couldn't stand the thought of a black woman working over them. I was combing the classifieds, looking for a comparable job, but the job market in Phoenix is nothing close to what it is in L.A.

But thank God Gloria's got a big mouth. She'd been boasting to all of her clients about my quilts, had even hung the one I'd given her on the wall at the shop, and the next thing I know I'm getting so many orders I couldn't keep up with them. That's when she asked me why didn't I consider opening my own shop. That never would've occurred to me, but what did I have to lose?

She introduced me to Bernadine, a friend of hers who was an accountant. Bernadine in turn introduced me to a good lawyer and he helped me draw up all the papers. Over the next four months, she helped me devise what turned out to be a strong marketing and advertising plan. I rented an 800-square-foot space in the same shopping center where Gloria's shop is, and opened Quiltworks, Etc.

It wasn't long before I realized I needed to get some help, so I hired two seamstresses. They took a lot of the strain off of me, and I was able to take some jewelry-making classes and even started selling small pieces in the shop. Gloria gave me this tacky T-shirt for my thirty-ninth birthday, which gave me the idea to experiment with making them. Because I go overboard in everything I do, I went out and spent a fortune on every color of metallic and acrylic fabric paint they made. I bought one hundred 100 percent cotton heavy-duty men's T-shirts and discovered other uses for sponges, plastic, spray bottles, rolling pins, lace, and even old envelopes. I was having a great time because I'd never felt this kind of excitement and gratification doing anything until now.

I'd been living here a year when I found out that Richard had married another woman who worked in our office. I wanted to hate him, but I didn't. I wanted to be angry, but I wasn't. I didn't feel anything toward him, but I sent him a quilt and a wedding card to congratulate him, just because.

To be honest, I've been so busy with my shop, I haven't even thought about men. I don't even miss having sex unless I really just *think* about it. My libido must be evaporating, because when I *do* think about it, I just make quilts or jewelry or paint T-shirts and the feeling goes away. Some of my best ideas come at these moments.

Basically, I'm doing everything I can to make Marilyn feel good. And at thirty-nine years old my body needs tightening, so I joined a health club and started working out three to four times a week. Once in a while, I babysit for Bernadine, and it breaks my heart when I think about the fact that I don't have a child of my own. Sometimes, Gloria and I go out to hear some music. I frequent most of the major art galleries, go to just about every football and basketball game at Arizona State, and see at least one movie a week.

I am rarely bored. Which is why I've decided that at this point in my life, I really don't care if I ever get married. I've learned that I don't need a man in order to survive, that a man is nothing but an intrusion, and they require too much energy. I don't think they're worth it. Besides, they have too much power, and from what I've seen, they always seem to abuse it. The one thing I do have is power over my own life. I like it this way, and I'm not about to give it up for something that may not last.

The one thing I do want is to have a baby. Someone I could love who would love me back with no strings attached. But at thirty-nine, I know my days are numbered. I'd be willing to do it alone, if that's the only way I can have one. But right now, my life is almost full. It's fun, it's secure, and it's safe. About the only thing I'm concerned about these days is whether or not it's time to branch out into leather.

Damon and Vandalia

RITA DOVE

DAMON

They came out of the darkness past the bamboo patch so like a fistful of spears, and as they threaded a path between Clark's battered yellow Volkswagen and my blue Peugeot, I saw she was carrying a plastic bag filled with some sort of grain—rice, perhaps. Clark rose to meet them; wind swooped from the incline and blew the kerosene lamp out. I stood up, a reflex I didn't know I had—old world charm surging in this colonial, barrel chest—and stumbled over the ice bucket. Drunker than I realized. Bourbon and Texan heat go devilishly well together, a gentle pair passing practically unnoticed, leaving one languid and curious.

But all this unexpected activity. I stumbled, fell to one knee; in the warm, vegetal dark I stayed, palms pressed tight around the sweating aluminum bucket until they ached from the cold. What seemed to take centuries: a male drawl, then her voice, upbeat, saying *birdseed;* Clark's laugh I *must give both of you a hug come here.* Then I was on my feet again and walking towards them, unsummoned, hands dripping and a chest spiked with gasps. It was a scene to be repeated in endless variations—she await, earth's bounty in her arms; I bowed, my hands cupping all I had to offer—gifts that changed their form even as I held them out to her, stones melting to tears.

VANDALIA

That evening of high wind and heat, I was finely tuned to every sound, every movement, merry and skittish as a school girl without knowing why. My mood pleased Michael, and he smoothed his neat afro, and tried on his new smile, the one that went so well with his professor's pipe. The bamboo stood guard, a pale green organ in shadows.

We drank a lot. Somewhere around midnight, Clark ran out of ice and the trays lay forgotten on the back steps, condensation spreading in an ever darkening stain. The creek sang its ghost song, calling for a sign from the sky. Lukewarm whiskey, now, in tall glasses. The wind gushed, diving into the chimney of the lamp.

We took turns lighting the wick; my fingers shook as I slid the wooden match from its box. Damon began to chatter in Japanese—I thought he was talking gibberish, until Clark said he had spent his childhood in Japan—and then I found him pretentious. Without saying so. And each matchstick a long-stemmed, unopened rose.

DAMON

Protons and electrons—barometers of the human body, scientifically proven aphrodisiacs and depressants: the heavy, dragged-out feeling before a summer storm—and afterwards, the air discharging and you with it, purpling ions, all is electricity. More and more often she came from the city, escaping the proton-laden skyscrapers and traffic, her hair crinkling from sweat, her brown skin as glossy, each day a bit darker, as the bark of a cherry tree. By the time she reached our place the negatively-spiced air of the countryside had taken effect, and she showed no sign of exhaustion or tension. It was as if she were high. She told me that she was frightened of cacti—the flat peppery lobes, the tufted spikes—and that she found the drive through the mesquite wasteland strangely exciting, like the exhilaration of a soldier after surviving a battle.

VANDALIA

Michael, his pipe and his southern inferiority complex. Talk right, learn to play tennis, never lose control. Make something of yourself. There's a way to "go about" everything.

We were to meet after his faculty meeting and I had chosen the bar. I should have known The Diamond Cowboy could only be what it was, booths of black leather and men in tight jeans dancing with each other, their tooled boots shuffling across the dark red floor. I ordered a Carta Blanca and sat down to wait. Then Clark came up. He danced expertly, Mr. Cool, just like a black dude. He was cruising and I was waiting for Michael; we bolstered each other, ignoring the others so as to appear more desirable.

Then Michael had come, and I could tell Clark liked him and that Michael was jealous. I didn't explain, not at first. Clark bought a round; Michael began to loosen. *You'll have to come visit me,* Clark laughed, his arms around both of us, *in my love nest in the country. And meet my boyfriend, naturally.*

DAMON

I was born in Japan of a father who loved all that wasn't England and a mother doomed to follow him, but determined to take England with her wherever she went. We travelled throughout the Far East in service of the Company. It was a childhood of seas and pine woods and mountains, of inscrutable manners before all adults and spankings when I slipped out to play with the Japanese children. Those children bullied me mercilessly. I was Gulliver among the Lilliputians; they expected danger in my robust British frame and so they struck before I could or would, or so they thought. (But I was tame—oh, I was tame and stupid with my rosy cheeks.) I loved them so, those children, and I wanted to be like them—small and dirty and full of abandon and laughing as they pinched and kicked me. In the English school, haven for diplomats' sons, I excelled in running and in debate; alone, in bed, watched by the chill pine, I spoke Japanese like a sailor, cursing fiercely into the crisp pillow.

Vandalia

Our neighborhood was a garden of smells—the rank smoke of the rubber factories, the grapey breeze that passed for spring, the witch-water bitterness of collard greens—all these thick scents mingled and clung to the skin in silent collusion.

And in the endless alternating shifts in the tire factory, six to two to ten to six, I was born—a change of pace, a breath of fresh air in the lives of my parents. And in the accepted custom of lower-class black families, they chose for their daughter a name that would stand out, a name suited for the special fate awaiting this child, their contribution to history, and so they named me Vandalia. Vandalia the vivacious, the valiant, the vibrant. A lightness and a treachery, like the beguiling flames of a snowstorm. Softly: Vandalia.

Until fourth grade geography, when a classmate went up to the map to point out Chicago and instead cried out *Look, here's Vandalia!*, and everyone wondered, and the teacher took me up to the map so I could see for myself. Later, in the public library, I looked it up in the encyclopedia: A city in south central Illinois, seventy-five miles southwest of Springfield, on the Kaskaskia River. Dairy and grain region. Founded 1809, enjoying the position as state capital *1819–39,* now the seat of Fayette county. Industry: cereal production and the manufacture of transformers, shoe heels, clothing and telephone booths. Population 5,160 (1960 census).

I thought you knew, the teacher said, and what I felt was shame. My parents and their neighbors had never ventured beyond the once-thriving canal town of their youth—one had only to look at my name to see. And I had thought I was unique, a fine joke. At least 5,160 people knew how ignorant we were.

Damon

When I was old enough I was sent—as a punishment, it seemed at the time— "home." Education in Eton. The neat quadrangles, the livid lawns boxed in by stone, grey and raw. At last to be dwarfed, to look up to Something. The autumn evenings, the deep and aching blue through the dormitory windows, booze and philosophy in small spaces, the sharp animal scent of wool and male bodies warming the room, their sweat as stimulating, as exciting as a strong black tea. My roommate moaned in his sleep; I dared not rise and comfort him.

Later I fled across the Atlantic to central Canada and its furred creatures, lakes to fish and woods to fell, enough wilderness to get lost in—for three years, when it spit me out and over the border to North Dakota, where I thought I'd die until I learned to turn my fear to good use and began to run—to train until the heart-muscle swoll to meet the fear, beating to the *tropp* of track shoes on cinder, *endure, endure.* Marathon runner. Time to think of nothing but the body's thunder.

I ran my way to the university; I knew I couldn't escape it all along. Track scholarship—and again the slap on the ass and the innocent guffaw, the slick knotted thighs and the gang showers and the hair in the eyes, stinging, and the smell of strong black tea, that cool lightning at the base of my spine. I trained. I ran until my chest threatened to burst; but when I finally collapsed into knees and elbows on the grass next to the high jump pit, he was waiting, smiling, with his boy's face and his long slim legs.

VANDALIA

My job—the job that buys my freedom from the industrial midwest, from factory smoke and acrid stink of simmering greens—is to type filmscripts into a computer. Green letters, squarish stencils poured through with light, appear on the darkened screen. When the screen's full, I read it for mistakes, type them over—and the computer inserts the corrections, the lines readjusting automatically to accommodate the addition. I type the entire script on an ever-rolling scroll of light impressions, and when it is finished I print it out—the laser printer spitting out a page every few seconds, perfectly typed pages of eight-and-a-half by eleven bond with the appropriate margins and numerated and italics where indicated, the whole shebang.

A job unrelieved by physical contact or mental strain, a job of our time. I devise ways of coping, I pretend I am a sculptor, gaze into a block of blackish green marble until my gaze meets resistance, and so defining contour. I type in obscenities, I invent dialogues between the barber and his philandering wife and erase them the moment before Print Out. Though increasingly I have to admit that I feel nothing while I am typing; it is no more probing the stone as it is writing in air.

DAMON

I change jobs like drinking water—and wherever I go, what the tap brings forth tastes different—smooth with fluorine, salty from the pump, sweet as the brook running through pine woods (or is it the brook that runs through childhood, the rush that comes when one is unfamiliar with the world, a not-yet-tiredness), the metal-sour smack of reservoir fluids pulled from pits on the outskirts of town and strained from one steel tank to another, the liquid flowing clearer and more anonymous with every filter. . . . And as I grow accustomed to the new flavor of a drink I regard as delicious, yes, vital, something fades, life balks. So I break camp; I shed skins.

The jobs I've had: waiter, lumberjack, student, gardener. Whenever I needed money I did free-lance translations—instruction booklets for Japanese imports, from cassette recorders to automobiles through to the inevitable cameras.

But since Clark, I've languished under a curious lassitude, content to let whatever happens happen, the demands of the moment sluicing over me like a sexual flush. When Clark got hired as a curator at the University of Texas, I followed him to Austin. I followed him to the garden house in the country and took the hammer he held out; I planted the herb garden *parsley sage rosemary and thyme*. I accepted the duties assigned me, cook and mechanic and romantic foreigner.

VANDALIA

Clark knew. And said nothing, silently accepting the gifts I brought, shamefaced tribute. It was a habit I had learned from Michael's friends, liberal white intellectuals who went to Europe each summer and brought back quaint rules of etiquette: they could never accept a dinner invitation without showing up with a box of chocolates under their arm or flower heads bobbing, distressed, over a horn of blazing tissue paper.

My gifts were unusual—a reflection, says Michael, of my trusting personality. Now I outdid myself. Seed for the bird feeder. An olive retriever, metal jaws on a long stem. A wicker jar for crickets. Crayons, forty-eight in a yellow flip-top box.

Damon did nothing, all day. Hung around. Whenever I came, my latest ornament carefully presented for Clark's carefully registered delight, he was lounging on the back terrace. Walked in casually, hands balled in the deep pockets of his khaki pants, shirtsleeves rolled loosely below the elbows and the collar open, revealing a reddened vee of skin and the first crisp curls of chest hair. How strange that a man who tanned so easily should burn right there. And he never took his shirt off.

Clark knew without asking what I wanted, running around the kitchen in his illfitting jogging shorts, chopping limes, sloshing tonic over a tower of ice cubes. A half hour, no more. Else Michael would worry something had happened to me on the road.

And everytime he appeared in the back door, fists in pocket, I knew he had been waiting.

DAMON

Clark is gone. He came back from the supermarket with a bag full of fruit, among them limes, a netted sackful. Said he couldn't stand it anymore, took a sharp knife and slit the throat of the net so the limes spilled all over. I scrambled for the rolling limes and Clark stood there, watching as I gathered them to my lap, a palette of fragrant green. Then he turned. *Get it over with,* he said, walking out.

VANDALIA

A cold fish, my mother frowned, following the flattened pear of a white woman's buttocks down the street. *Couldn't warm up an ice cube, much less a man.*

It was the morning after Labor Day and we went downtown to shop for last-minute school supplies—and maybe a dress for me, if any decent ones were on sale. I was ten and she thought I didn't understand. I didn't—but I remembered until I was old enough.

She said it in self-defense, unaware she was rubbing a little brighter the myth.
I think she was even proud, who knows . . . this woman who wanted so much to
learn that she taught herself French with the help of a tattered primer found at a
rummage sale, calling out the names as she laid the groceries on the table: *oeufs,
jambon, pommes de terre, poulet.* No word for turnip greens. No word for chitterlings,
for sweet potato pie. A woman with so much and nowhere to give it but her house
and family, what she'd been taught was enough. And I her daughter, cold.

DAMON

The third day. Again Clark did not come home after work; for two days he hadn't
returned before ten or even midnight. No words had passed between us; we were
both exhausted. The knife lay next to the bowl of limes, exactly where I had placed it.

All day the sky had weighed on the earth like a large sweating hand. And
suddenly, without warning, water loosened over the house—a wonder that flattened the weeds and released a cool, metallic perfume. The roar was deafening.
From sheer nervousness I ran outdoors, peeling off my shirt and throwing it into
the herb garden. Bare-chested I was monstrous, a Caliban; I held back my face for
the rain to pelt eyelids and cheeks, throat and forehead. I was a harpooned whale;
I wanted to be drummed blind.

VANDALIA

The cloudburst overcame me as I turned into the driveway; I switched off the
engine but kept the ignition on, watching the windshield wipers plough a dry space
that was promptly inundated again. All a matter of timing—if I blinked, counterpoint, to the blades' click, the windshield was always clear. I sat for five minutes or
so, blinking. On the seat beside me stood a birdcage constructed entirely from
toothpicks, each sliver individually stained and varnished. There was a ladder inside the cage, leaning against one side, and a tiny wooden swing. The swing moved
in time with the wipers. . . .

The yellow Volkswagen was nowhere to be seen but the Peugeot was there,
blue hood well into the bamboo patch. Had they gone away for the weekend? I
could walk up to the door and check. Or I could drive back. In this rain.

DAMON

All I remember is that I took the birdcage from her and set it on the table. I was
dripping, shivering; I asked her if I could get her something, a towel or a drink.
Then, of course, it was over too quickly—she moved slightly and I overran her; I
nearly swallowed those gasping lips in my efforts to find the contours inside the
skin. She drew back instinctively, her mouth and chin slick and glistening from my
kiss and I apologized; *forgive me* I said again and again, as I licked from her neck and
ears the salt and bitter of sweat and cologne. For an instant I thought of those cold
and wet Japanese winters spent whispering into the crook of a pillow; I had never
been more terrified.

VANDALIA

The thundering around us and the silence between. He stood in the door to the terrace, bare-chested, the red vee of collar skin an arrow pointing down, down, and his khakis soaked and wrinkled, clinging to his legs. It was as if I were there and not there at the same time; I watched and felt myself being watched, I closed my eyes to disappear.

When we had finished, he placed his palm between my legs, cupping and defining, his face as wondering as a child's, amazed that that's all there was—no magic, no straining muscular desire.

It is possible we have never met. It is possible that this is fiction and, though we are always moving towards each other, the scene will fade at the last moment. There are times when I have not left the car, when the birdcage of sticks does not swing, buffeted by the rain, when I have not entered the house with Clark gone and the limes waiting on the counter, exhaling their insidious perfume.

DAMON

When I am with Clark there is consolation—the same bones beneath the same skin, how they float around, or rest quiet, or tense.

Now I know I am not modest though I pretend to be. Now I know I did not follow Clark to Texas but led him there; we ran away together but I pointed out the way; I chose the spiked and prickling desert as our retreat, I pressed for a house in the countryside, I glimpsed the wild bamboo, luxuriant, beside the creek and said *This is mine.*

I could not make a move until Clark spilled the limes over the kitchen counter, but then I moved. Now Vandalia is the one who waits—and when it doesn't happen, the thing she was waiting for (but I'm not sure even she knows what it is), she begins to grow vague, her eyes looking only at the surface of the world, not the world itself, not me, and I've lost her, again.

What I think about when we make love: the blip fading on the screen. What I feel: Vandalia flattening, spreading into a map, the map of my longing. Her skin is taut as a mask and mine is loose over its bones like an elephant's. The small of my back curves into her until there is nothing left. And I am small, small when she touches me.

VANDALIA

It is summer; I have done something wrong. *Wait till your father gets home* my mother says, and sends me to my room. Instead, I wait for her to disappear down the basement to check on the laundry—then I slip through the door and down the front walk. Quiet. Asphalt softening in the sun, undulating like black greased waves. A tar smell.

Across the street is a vacant lot with a maple tree in it, the flat starred leaves casting an irregular circle of shade. I go to this tree and climb it; I swear never to come down again.

For a while nothing happens. The broad leaves are cool on my arms and legs. The tar smell mixes with the non-smell of air. What does it mean, to do something wrong? I am alive but I am never where I think I am—for instance, I am not in this tree, I am far away. The six o'clock whistle blows and father's Buick comes trundling down the street; now things will happen.

The screen door slams; *Vandalia* they call. I will not come down I am not here. Where I am the streets are swept and flowers line the windows. There is a Sears & Roebuck where I am and a soda fountain and in the center of town a grassy square with a white bandstand right in the middle, and around the bandstand green benches but no one is ever sitting on them. I walk down the glittering sidewalk and everybody knows my name. *Vandalia,* they say, again and again.

Tenderhead

HARRYETTE MULLEN

Saturdays they went to the beauty shop to get their hair fixed. Something was wrong with their hair, so Miss Pearl had to fix it before they could be seen in public. Naps and kinks had to be smoothed, the way the body shop ironed those dents out of the car after Marna got hit by that drunk white lady on Commerce Street.

If it wasn't Miss Pearl, it was Mama at the kitchen range, attacking the rough hair with a hot comb kept for touch-ups at home. On Sunday, they had to dress up for the Lord—and so nobody would say Mama was getting slack. Children are a reflection of their parents, and church was full of eyes watching and measuring. Calculating who was rising or falling, who was sitting pretty or barely keeping up. They'd approve of Mimi's shiny, unscuffed patent leather shoes and spotless, unsagging white socks, and Latricia's broad-brim straw hat with pink grosgrain ribbon. They'd award Mama extra points for the girls' white gloves with tiny pearl-like buttons.

Jeanne was proud of her knack for making the kids look special on a tight budget, and she didn't want the overall effect ruined by hair going back. Between the twin demons of perspiration and precipitation, kinky hair straightened with a hot comb was prone to return to its former condition—but Sunday hair had to be smooth and glistening. It was that newly pressed look that showed they'd just been to the beauty shop—sacrificing Saturday cartoons to sit in a spinning chair that Miss Pearl never let them spin in anyway; flinching when hot comb and blue grease met and sizzled on their scalps; Miss Pearl warning Mimi, "Honey, sit still now, before you make my hand slip with this hot comb. Hold your ear down, sweetie pie, so I can get these edges."

Miss Pearl rented space in her shop to two other beauticians: Miss Ruthie, who sipped RC's all day, and Miss Clara, who was the youngest of the three and who preferred to be called a cosmetologist. Miss Clara avoided the words "nappy" and "kinky." She would say, "Darling, your hair has a lot of *texture*." She rarely mentioned a hot comb outright, but spoke of "thermal treatment." In her lexicon, straightened hair never "went back." It "reverted." And, of course, the harsh chemical process that burned the scalp while straightening the hair "permanently" (at least until the next touch-up) was called "relaxing," but Mimi thought the women getting the treatment looked anything but relaxed.

Mimi had noticed that barbershops had plate glass windows, so the barbers and their customers could keep an eye on the happenings out in the street. But beauty shop windows always had curtains drawn, so nobody outside could see the women and girls while the transformation was taking place. Sometimes a white salesman would come into the shop to do business with Miss Pearl. They would stare at his back as he passed, but avert their eyes if he seemed to look at them directly. Best to be under the dryer if a stranger, or even somebody's daddy or husband, came in. A woman caught with kinks exposed might try to disappear behind a copy of *Ebony* or *Sepia,* which made better screens than the smaller *Bronze Thrills* and *Tan Confessions.*

Mimi had made it through first grade without any visits to Miss Pearl's. Mama washed her hair at home, both of them kneeling at the bathtub, Mimi blinking suds out of her eyes. But Jeanne complained that shampooing and rinsing the thick hair twice, then carefully combing the tangles out from ends to roots (with Mimi kicking and yelling the whole time), and finally parting the hair into sections to make four sausage-like braids, was becoming a tiresome ritual.

Besides, as Grandma Clinton said, "She's too old, anyhow, to be running around nappy-headed. She needs to get her hair pressed, like the other girls her age." Mimi had heard that in a few more years she would be "maturing," and this was the reason she had to change her ways, be more ladylike, which, as far as she could tell, meant keeping her skirt down, staying out of trees, and carrying a cute little purse with nothing in it but a stick of spearmint gum and a hanky. And with all of that, the visits to Miss Pearl's were supposed to tame her down, like ten-year-old Latricia, who broke Miss Ruthie's heart with her silent weeping as the big plastic comb tugged at her tangles or the hot metal came uncomfortably close to her scalp.

Miss Pearl usually insisted that Jeanne and her daughters come in first thing on Saturday, before the heavy traffic of the day, so they could tackle those three heads of impossible hair in the first cool freshness of the morning. They all had heavy, coarse, fast-growing hair, each with her own unique pattern of waves, kinks, and plain old naps. Latricia's was just a little too kinkish and thick to be "water wave" hair. Mimi had a weird combination of tangled waves and bushy kinks. Jeanne, in contrast to her mostly wiry, strong, springy hair, had a conspicuous patch of soft baby curls at the back of her head, just above a stubborn "kitchen" of crisp, tight naps.

Each of the ladies would take a head, marveling, as they shampooed and combed out and hot-pressed, at the length and bushiness of the girls' and their mother's hair, and the fierceness of certain kinky patches, which, combined with the tenderheadedness that ran in the family, made the job a challenge. Miss Pearl was sure she had never seen such tough hair together with such tender heads.

Miss Pearl and her associates were all graduates of the Ideal School of Beauty, as Mimi knew, since she had personally inspected their diplomas. When she went around the shop, reading each one, Miss Ruthie joked that their school motto had been "I deal, you deal, we all deal with nappy heads." Their various certificates and licenses hung on the walls, along with glossy magazine pictures of women with glossy hair. Most of the women in the pictures were so light they looked like slightly exotic white women, but a few of them were dark to show that a black-skinned woman with naturally nappy hair could get the same stylish results from hot combs and chemicals. Waves and curls. Feathery bangs and pageboy flips. Hair hanging long and straight or teased into a bouffant.

Each of the ladies had her station, with an adjustable chair for her customers, a mirror, and a small gas heater for the hot comb and curling irons. On Mimi's first visit they had all let her look into their drawers full of combs, brushes, clippers, and hairpins. One wall was lined with plain wooden chairs for women and girls awaiting their turn. A fat vinyl chair with dryer attached figured prominently in a corner. The three ladies tried to stagger their customers so that no one had to wait too long with wet hair before getting to the dryer. They dreaded the occasional head of unruly hair that took half an hour to dry, throwing them off the estab-lished rhythm of their work. Yet they were fascinated by Jeanne's and her daugh-ters' "semi-good" hair that managed to grow long and thick, even though it was undeniably nappy.

What a triumph for the beauty shop ladies when all three heads were shining with oil of bergamot and the wild, rough hair was finally pressed down and civi-lized! Now they were beautiful, with kinks and naps transformed into the sleek and gleaming locks of the magazine pictures. It was most satisfying because their hair was long. How many nappy heads had they transformed only to find the slick hair still woefully short, even after it had been stretched by the pressing. Most of their heads needed curls to give them any style at all. If Miss Pearl did Jeanne's hair, she would just curl the ends under a bit, then part it on the side and comb the hair over one eye. She'd show her the mirror with a grand flourish, saying, "Now tell me, sugarplum, if you don't look just like Veronica Lake!" Seeing them with their straight hair spread around their shoulders was a satisfying reward after all that work. It was the reason the ladies had decided not to charge extra for doing such headstrong hair.

Now, three years later, ten-year-old Mimi often went alone to Miss Pearl's, because Jeanne and Latricia had permanents, which meant more widely spaced appoint-ments. Miss Clara had talked Jeanne into trying a permanent once, and she'd been coming back for touch-ups ever since. At least she only had to come in about once a month instead of every other week. When Latricia turned twelve she had begged to get her hair relaxed too. Jeanne had made her wait until she turned thirteen.

This Saturday Mimi was to be dropped off at Miss Pearl's while Mama took Latricia to buy a dress for her first junior high school dance. Jeanne parked the car at the curb, gave Mimi three dollars for Miss Pearl, and made sure her daughter was inside the shop before starting the engine. Out of the corner of her eye, she noticed two laughing men leaning against another parked car, passing a brown-bagged bottle back and forth between them. One of them seemed to be pointing at the wide, rolling hips of a woman striding barefoot down the sidewalk. Even from a distance, Jeanne knew it was Dot. Her feet must be tough as horse's hooves, and she was nappy as a jaybird. Jeanne, headed in the opposite direction, started the car again for the trip to the new shopping mall.

"Here's my little Tenderhead!" Miss Pearl would greet Mimi now when she arrived on Saturday afternoons. And later, when she was fidgeting under the hot comb, "Try and sit still now, Tenderhead. You just make it harder on both of us with all this wiggling." "Tenderhead" was one of the nicknames given her by the ladies in the shop, because she still squirmed and flinched under the hot iron and yelled when her kinks were being detangled. Sometimes they reproached her for her immaturity in this matter, holding her sister up as an example. Miss Ruthie would say, "Sweetheart, I know for a fact your sister Latricia's just as tenderheaded as you is, but she still could always hold a good head."

Her other nickname was Big Eyes, not only because of her large, dark eyes that were envied for their long, curly lashes, but also because she was curious about people and had never broken her child's habit of staring. It was regarded as a gross sign of disrespect for a child to stare at a grown person, particularly to lock eyes with an adult as she sometimes did. She'd received many a threat from Mama and Grandma Clinton because of that unnerving stare.

There was so much more to see and hear in Miss Pearl's shop when she was dropped off alone these Saturday afternoons with business in full swing. She could read the confession magazines her mama had dismissed as "trash for idle minds." She could listen to the lively gossip, which was plentiful when the shop was full of customers, and stare at the sheepish-looking white salesmen who dropped by with sample cases of beauty supplies. There was another white man with a strange tattoo on his arm of a big snake wrapped around a heart, who came to fill up the soft drink machine with bottles of RC Cola, 7-Up, and Nehi.

Black men hawking produce in battered pickup trucks made a stop at Miss Pearl's to sell fresh corn, snap beans, tomatoes, okra, and watermelon to the beauticians and their customers. Camp Fire Girls and Girl Scouts in neatly starched uniforms, with ribbons on their plaits, and their legs and elbows shined with petroleum jelly, knew they could sell their quota of candy and cookies at Miss Pearl's shop, and many a winning raffle ticket was purchased there. Occasionally someone would come in trying to sell stolen watches or other hot merchandise, but Miss Pearl could always spot a thief and send him packing. Around lunchtime, the ladies would call out to order and someone would arrive with aromatic brown sacks full of hot link sandwiches from Mason's Bar-B-Q, huge cheeseburgers from Big Daddy's, or fried chicken and potato salad plates from Carla's Place. Mimi would have gagged trying to eat around all that hair, but the ladies were unfazed. What did it matter that the oil on their hands was equal parts Crisco and hair grease?

Then there were the famous domino tournaments. The beauticians were too busy to play, but customers waiting for a turn competed with one another—not for money because Miss Pearl allowed no gambling in her shop (not counting the raffle tickets sold for a good cause), but the loser traditionally bought the winner a soda from the soft drink case. That strange woman, Dot, who sometimes came to sell fresh eggs and goat's milk, was said to enjoy a good domino game. Some of the customers complained about her and thought Miss Pearl should keep her out of the shop, but except for known criminals, and a certain spectacularly obnoxious Jehovah's Witness she had put out after the woman told the ladies they were all sinners condemned to hell, no one was barred from entering. So long as they abided by her rules against cursing, gambling, fighting, or bringing alcohol into the shop, Miss Pearl welcomed everybody into her place—even Dot.

"Ought to be a rule against stinking up the place, Miss Pearl," was Lula Mae's opinion. "I sure would rather listen to the worst cursing than have to smell that funk. Miss Pearl, she make your shop look bad and smell worse."

They said she made her coarse-looking dresses out of flour sacks, but occasionally she was seen in a homemade dress of cheap cotton fabric, always in a bright floral print. Children had composed a jump rope song about her:

> There you go, feet so bare,
> All over town with your nappy hair.
> Wearing a sack and living in a shack,
> If you ain't ugly, tar ain't black.
> Heard your name but I forgot—
> All I remember was it rhyme with snot.

On the last word, the jumper would pinch her nose as if in disgust and dance away from the swinging rope to give someone else a turn. Although they sang this rhyme daily in their play, none of them ever taunted her directly. They all had been taught with belts and paddles and backhand licks to show at least an outward respect toward adults. It was in fact a kind of tribute to her eccentricity that she had inspired a new lyric in their repertoire.

Dot lived alone in her small, unpainted wooden house. Her front yard was a leafy vegetable garden fenced with chicken wire. Along with several beady-eyed hens and one dandyish rooster, she kept a few sturdy goats in her backyard. "Yeah, she smell like a goat, too!" A dark, musky, country smell. The serious underarm and between-legs funk of a grown woman who never bothered with deodorant or perfume or feminine hygiene products. She was neither dainty nor delicate. She took up space. When she sat, her thighs spread. When she walked by, men joked behind her back, "Must be jelly 'cause jam don't shake like that." If any of them had ever spent a night with her, he surely would have died before admitting it. Their jokes among themselves were intended to sound mock-sexual, since the usual half-joking, half-hopeful sexual banter—which was, after all, a precious part of their days and something to be savored—should not be wasted on a woman like her.

Her appearance was that of a character in a comic strip, buttons popping and seams strained. Flies buzzing around her head like electrons in a chemistry textbook. They lit on her thick arms and she slowly fanned them away, seeming hardly to notice that she had become fly furniture. Perhaps you have seen those full-page color photos in expensive coffee table picture books about Africa. Beautiful men, women, and children, whose faces have the dignity and formality of masks, faces perfectly composed while flies rest lightly on an eyelid or cheek, at the corner of a child's mouth. No one would call Dot beautiful, but she did attract flies.

As Mimi kicked a 4/4 beat against the leg of her hard wooden chair, reading Miss Pearl's stack of old *Jet* magazines, Lula Mae Bishop, enthroned in the shampoo chair awaiting the magic chemicals that would turn her thin black hair a rusty red, was holding forth, hard on Dot's case like white on rice.

"You *know* she don't wear no underwear, the way them titties be flopping when she walk, and the way her dress get caught in her crack 'cause she ain't got no draws on."

Mimi looked up from the bikini-clad model in the *Jet* centerfold, who'd been snapped as a soft breeze blew her long, straight hair across her full but not *too* full lips that curved in a seductive smile. Mimi had been examining the photograph to see if the model's belly button sank in or if it stuck out a little like hers did. The women were talking about the notorious Dot, who lived in the exciting neighborhood where Miss Pearl's was located (along with the Eight Ball Pool Hall, the Pink Flamingo Club, Shorty's Shoeshine Parlor, Carla's Place, Big Daddy's Drive-In, and other establishments with open doors leading to dark interiors she had often tried to peer into as their car passed on the street).

It was Jeanne's old neighborhood and she continued to drive to Miss Pearl's out of loyalty. Once, Miss Pearl had suggested that Jeanne buy goat's milk from Dot when Latricia was found to have an allergy to cow's milk. Jeanne had said, "No, Miss Pearl. I say live and let live, but I don't think I could feel peaceful with myself if I gave my child something from that woman's hands. She doesn't have clean enough habits to suit me."

Mimi remained curious about this woman who raised goats in the city, walked barefoot down paved streets, and never came into Miss Pearl's shop except to play dominoes or sell eggs and milk. Now she was hearing what people thought of Dot for all her strange behavior. Girlie Moore, wincing as the burning lye went to work on her nappy roots, fervently spoke her feelings on the subject: "She don't even bother to try and make herself decent. Just walks out on the street looking any old way. Don't try to fix herself up or nothing. This ain't the country either, but she walk down the middle of a paved city street like she on a dirt road out in the sticks."

"I mean, talk about *colored!* Do the woman ever go to the store and buy real clothes? I ain't never seen her wear nothing but them mammy-made sack dresses.

My Lord, the woman's so country she don't *never* straighten her hair. It's a sin and a shame that a full-grown woman can walk around looking so bad all the time," Peaches Johnson complained, her head bent under the teeth of the hot comb, the odor of her singed hair mingling with the harsh alkaline fumes of Girlie's permanent and the sharp smell of Lula Mae's bleach. "Well, it's like they say, you can take folk out of the country, but . . ."

The talk stopped short as the screen door swung open and a heavy, dark, barefooted woman stepped into the shop. Mimi heard Girlie Moore's low whisper, "Speak of the devil." It was true. Dot's scalp had never felt the heat of a straightening comb or curling iron, nor the sting of a lye-based permanent. She had never been dyed, bleached, streaked, tipped, or frosted. Her hair was black and had always been black. It was nappy and had always been nappy. She didn't even braid her hair to make it grow long. Braids on a grown woman could look country too, but at least they were neat. She just let her hair go wild like the brambles in Brer Rabbit's briar patch. She kept it short and nappy, cutting it with the same scissors she used to cut the coarse fabrics of her simple dresses.

"Afternoon, everybody, how you ladies doing?" were Dot's first words. "Ain't nobody playing dominoes today?" The two women waiting to have their hair done looked away pointedly, searching for magazines they suddenly wanted to read. Neither of them cared to play with someone who had just been ranked so low by Lula Mae, Girlie, and Peaches.

Miss Pearl, after returning Dot's greeting, suggested, "Why don't you play with old Big Eyes here? It'll be a while before I get to her head."

"But I don't know how to play dominoes" was Mimi's quick response as she stared up at the substantial figure.

"That's all right, it ain't hard. I'll teach you. We'll play a few warm-up games 'til you got the rules down. Then we can play for a soda, if you can afford to spend a dime."

"I got a dime." Mimi dug into the pocket of her shorts and pulled out the three crumpled dollars her mother had given her, and a dime saved from her allowance. She held out the dime in her hand. "What about you, ma'am?" She was suspicious. The woman carried no purse and the dress she wore had no pockets that she could see—and obviously she didn't have a dime in her shoe. Her eyes scanned the woman from head to foot and then returned to stare at the uncouth hair. The smell of the woman's body was strong, but not offensive to her. Mimi thought she smelled like damp earth and salty sweat, with something else mixed in: a furtive smell that reminded her of whispers behind a closed door.

Dot laughed until her whole body jiggled. "Big Eyes sharp, ain't she? I can tell she gonna learn this game fast." She eased into a chair at the scarred wooden table with the dominoes on it and started turning them all face down. "Hey, come on, Big Eyes! Pull up your chair so we can get this game started." Mimi didn't budge as Dot began divvying up the dominoes. Finally, when half were in front of her and the other half pushed to the opposite side of the table, Dot cast an amused glance at the girl. "Oh yeah, that's right. You wanna be sure I got my dime." Then she reached down into the front of her dress and pulled from the cleavage of her huge breasts a knotted handkerchief, which she untied to show a few dollars folded into a square and a handful of change. "There, you see. So—you gonna play or not?" She tied the money back in the handkerchief, and returned it to its hiding place as Mimi pulled up her chair.

In no time at all Mimi was slapping the dominoes down hard, just like she'd been playing all her life. "Look at my girl," Miss Pearl chuckled. "She really getting into this game. I just hope she gonna be ready to stop when I have to get to work on that tender head of hers."

After two warm-up games, with Dot coaching her so she won each time, she wanted to play for the soda. Dot grinned and said, "You sure you ready now? 'Cause I'm really thirsty by this time."

Dot played to win, using strategy not only to get rid of her dominoes fast, but also to block potential moves that Mimi might make. This was the part of the game that took experience. Mimi had thought it was simply a matter of matching sets, like in math class. She was so stunned when the game was suddenly over and she still had lots of dominoes left that her eyes filled instantly with tears.

"Let me see now, what kind of soda I want. I can't make up my mind between a orange or a grape." Dot's voice sounded loud and cruel. Mimi felt she'd been taken advantage of, but Dot exhibited no shame. "What would you pick, Big Eyes? I'll let you buy me what you like, since it's your treat. Just go ahead and put your dime in the machine and bring me my nice cool drank, if you please."

Half-blind with the hot tears brimming in her eyes, Mimi went to the drink cooler, found the coin slot and heard her dime fall in. She watched her hand emerge with a Nehi grape. She had always loved drinking them and then looking in the mirror to see her purple tongue.

"Oh, and while you're there, would you mind opening it for me?"

Mimi handed her the cold, moist bottle, Dot's calloused palm felt rough against her fingers as the woman took the Nehi and set it down on the table. For the first time, Dot appeared to notice her distress. "My goodness, look at this. Has Dot hurt your little feelings?" She seemed genuinely concerned. "You look like you gonna bust out cryin' any minute now." Not the most sensitive remark, but Mimi held the tears in her eyes, not yet wiping them, as she waited for some sort of apology. Dot leaned back in her chair, as Mimi stared at her.

"I thought you was a big girl. Didn't know I was playing with a *baby*." With that Mimi was beside herself. The tears she couldn't hold back any longer scalded her eyes and cheeks. She was shaking with anger at the humiliating insult.

"Oh Lord, see I done made this baby cry. What I'm gonna do now?" Dot looked around at the women in the shop, who seemed determined to be silent witnesses to the whole transaction between her and the child. Despite the malevolent gleam in the woman's eye, no one intervened. All seemed preoccupied with their work, or the magazines they were reading.

"Baby, maybe it was wrong of me to beat you at the game and take your dime and leave you with nothing to drank. It might've been unkind of me to do that." Mimi wiped her tears with the back of her hand and sniffled, looking up hopefully. At last the woman seemed to recognize the injustice she had committed against a mere child. Now she would tell her she was sorry. Indeed, as if to make reparation, Dot was already reaching into the front of her dress again, as she continued speaking.

"Since you was nice enough to go ahead and treat me, I guess I might as well get you something to drank, especially if it will make you feel better." So saying, she plopped out of her dress a melon-sized breast, which she cradled and bounced in her palms with a maliciously amused leer at the girl, whose eyes had widened with shock. "Yeah, here's what you need. A nice fat titty so the baby can git some titty milk." Mimi was lost. Her whole body crumpled as she hid her face in both hands, her breath coming in jagged sobs. "If you thirsty, here it is. I just hate to see a baby cry."

At last Miss Pearl broke in. "That's enough, Dot girl. You best go on home now. I got to do this child's head." She hurried Peaches Johnson out of her chair and beckoned to Mimi, who now wept silently.

When her mother returned to pick her up, instead of the usual plain braids Mimi had the big-girl curls she'd always been denied. "Don't worry, sugar," Miss Pearl assured Jeanne. "I didn't charge a thing for the curls. I just threw 'em in 'cause for the first time since she been getting her hair fixed, Mimi sat still in the chair and held a good head."

The Friday Night Shift at the Taco House Blues (Wah-Wah)

WANDA COLEMAN

Down at the Taco House is where we work, Shurli and me. Shurli's an old timer and was managing the night shift when I first came on the gig. The night shift starts at six in the evening. That's five-forty night people's time. We night folks go by bar time, which in Los Angeles means the clock is always twenty minutes fast. When 2 A.M. rolls around (booze curfew) that's about how long it takes for the customers to finish their drinks, for us to coax the hypes out of the john or jane and sober up the drunks with hot coffee and send them all out into the night and presumably home. Since most waitresses have been barmaids at one time or another, the process is essentially the same. Our night lives—shaped by complete boredom one minute and mayhem and murder (not to mention robbery) the next.

So like, Shurli's been working the Taco House off and on for ten years. Actually, Shurli daylights as a welfare mother supporting six kids, their three fathers (two kids per father, a pretty good ratio), a three-hundred-dollar-a-month car note on her customized Cadillac *Coupe de Ville* and her one-hundred-and-fifty-a-month note on that raggedy-ass crib she calls a house located in the neighborhood about twelve blocks away. Me—I'm just passing through, I hope, on my way to bigger and better things.

I got my eye on a government job—trying to get on as a receptionist/secretary as they say in the want ads. I struggled awake yesterday morning about ten o'clock just in time to keep my eleven o'clock appointment for the typing, math, memory and the rest of the aptitude tests they give you. Me—I live alone, having no kids. That's one mistake I refuse to make. Not me. I've got to make my fortune first.

The Taco House stays open twenty-four hours in order to catch the night trade. Some are decent folks who work nights. Some are professional hoods, gamblers, pimps, hypes, prosties and shit like that—and of course, the cops, narks and plainclothesmen who are after their asses, and inevitably, the customers they've hooked on one trick or another.

So like, Shurli gets in right at five-forty when Redd completes her run. Redd is a bright-skinned woman who runs the day shift. She's called "red" like most niggahs what got that kind of orangy skin tone and rust colored hair that usually comes from certain black/white combines. She's a good person, everybody likes her, but I don't really know her, with her working the day shift.

Shurli bounces over to the register and takes over as we other girls come in. I say bounce, because Shurli is five feet four and weighs about three hundred pounds. She's got the meatiest forearms—a lot of that just plain muscle. She works the register the way she drives that Caddy, smooth and with profound grace.

As me and the girls come in, Jesus hands us our aprons. There are four of us. Me, Kathy, Li'l Bit and Sharita. Sharita is a tall slender chick whose old man rides with Scarlet Fever, a raunchy all black lightweight version of the Hell's Angels. She thinks she has clout. We don't like each other and I'm waiting for the day when I have to get off into that bitch's ass.

So we check in while Chuck (that's the owner) runs through the one hundred and fifty dollar bank with Shurli. You see, the register always gets a bank. That way the boss knows if you're stealing or not and can gauge his profit and loss margin against the tape. Actually, the money never stays in the register long. Periodically, Shurli removes part of the take, locks it and moves most of the tens, twenties and fifties (we don't change ben franks) to the back where there's a safe built into the floor which is usually hidden under a mat. All the girls work the register.

So like, anyhow, we come in, and Jesus hands us our aprons, and we go in the back, hang up coats and sweaters and then duck our purses under the counter so we can keep our eyes on what few pennies we do have. The set-up here is the usual. Black girls on the counter, Mexicans do the cooking and the owner (who's either white or Jewish as the case may be) rakes in the bread.

Chuck, who speaks Spanish fluently, puts one girl (in this case, Shurli) in charge of the girls, cause he knows that won't no niggah bitch take orders from no Mexican cook. Jesus has two assistants, Don and Herman. They look like Castilians. Don speaks faulty English, and when he does, he talks like us blacks. Herman grins a lot and can only get through the basic hello and good-bye. Jesus speaks both and although his English is usually very simple, I often get the feeling that where he's from in Mexico, he's big shit and can rattle off the King's English as well as any Harvard grad. Of course, just as most of the waitresses (with the exception of myself and Sharita) are welfare mothers, the Latinos are all illegal aliens. But nobody ever says anything and it's cool.

Chuck, the boss man, has a rep for messing around with the girls. Chuck usually hangs around for an hour or so after changeover, then goes home. Shurli tells me that he's slept with everybody except me and Li'l Bit. About herself she don't say. I grunt and shrug. The turkey has pulled at my bra strap a couple of times, but that's as far as it got. He's a family man with one of those pale sickly blonde wives—a classic. And his children are dark haired, slenderer images of himself. I've never seen his son, but his daughter runs through occasionally. Rumor is she's a campus activist and that she and her old man don't get along too well when it comes to politics, but she keeps the books and records and runs that end of the business for him. Shurli says that she's heard 'em arguing a lot about her shacking with some dude he thinks is a shiftless creep. As far as I'm concerned it's their business. I'm just looking forward to the day when I can clear out.

At the changeover, when we hit the counter, business is fairly heavy with the dinner trade. At the Taco House, people have the choice of fast food service in or out. The counter is long and on a curve. The first and the longest arm of the curve is where all the food preparation takes place. The customer can clearly see the de-wormed tomatoes (diced well for color), the week-old onions, the bleached lettuce, pickle, relish, mayonnaise, refried beans, ketchup, hot sauce and chili as we apply it in varying degrees per order. They can even watch as Jesus and the boys fry a barrage of hot dogs, corn tortilla shells (soft, semi-crisp and crunchy), steam buns and flour tortillas, fry hamburger patties, taco meat patties (mainly pork and cereal), toast hot dog buns and boil wieners.

People come and go in a steady stream and then the tide breaks about eight o'clock. Usually things are sporadic during the weekdays. Work is on a six day schedule with alternating days off. All the girls work on Sunday. Days off usually fall on Mondays and Tuesdays. You work half a day on Christmas. On weekends the traffic is killing. The people never stop and periodically Chuck will take on a new girl for the summer just to keep the stream of cash flowing smoothly. But normally, things pick up again about ten o'clock, get spotty, and then around twelve get heavy again for about a half hour. Then from twelve-thirty to two-thirty it's nightmare time. People come and go so fast, time becomes a blur. From two-thirty until five o'clock time comes to a complete halt. It's usually during this period when we girls start to get bitchy with one another. But about five things pick up again, with people coming in for eggs, coffee, donuts and shit. I was surprised to see the number of people who like to eat tacos and stuff for breakfast. The days of ham and eggs are numbered.

I start in filling the orders. We mark abbreviations for each order on each bag, figure the prices and totals in our heads, mark the price on the bag and circle it. We hand the bags to Shurli or whoever's on the register at the moment. She rings it up, takes the cash, makes change and hands the bag to the customer.

So like, this night I'm preparing orders, my hands stinging from continual dippings into the tomatoes. It's cold and the middle of November. Outside, it's crisp and clear and the lights from the bar across the street shine brightly. The juke is blasting rhythm and blues. Shurli is leaning across the counter talking to one of the local dope dealers, trying to score some white folks (bennies) for her and her old man. Li'l Bit and Kathy are feeding their faces on their break, jawing over two plates heaped with burger meat and frijoles (none of the girls will touch the taco meat including me) and gulping down coffee. Sharita has slipped out to turn a trick with a don who stuck twenty dollars in her paw.

I reach for a towel to wipe my hands when a lone customer walks in. He's a tall, lanky guy in his mid-twenties. He's brownskinned, just a shade lighter than me, and has his grayish brown hair cut to a crew cut, a style that spells jerk on the black side of town. He looks like he's safe enough, orders a tostada and a cup of coffee.

I glance at the girls, know I'm elected, and wait as Jesus tosses a tortilla into the fat vat.

K.P. comes in and it's on me to take his order for two chili burgers heavy on the onion. K.P. is one of the regulars. He practically lives here and will come in two or three times a night. Shurli has jammed me that he and a couple of other old cronies are Chuck's paid spies. They give Chuck clandestine reports on the conduct of the girls. And it must be true, because Chuck always knows everything that goes down. The Latinos report on the girls, the girls report on the girls and the spies report on everybody.

Another dude comes in. He's dark-skinned, youngish, looks like a thug. He knows the lighter guy and yells, "Hey! Ray, mah man!" They slap hands between placement of his order. After Shurli rings them up, they take their plates and sit at the counter. By now K.P. has joined them and everybody is on the two extreme ends of the counter. I look and decide to join Shurli and the fine piece of meat she's now talking to, K.P. and the two dudes on their end. Everybody's listening to the dude called Ray tell what's apparently an interesting story. I come up and lean against the soda fountain.

"Yeah," Ray is continuing. "She was dead—just like that. I mean, I can't get over it. I went out and went down to Jack's to shoot some pool, hustle up a couple of bucks. She wanted a fifth and neither one of us didn't have no money, man. She hadn't got her check—you know how it is , , ,"

He talks like he's high on reds (seconal) slurring his words, stretching each syllable. But I know what that is. That is that high you get—the one I call Pain. Yeah, that's it all *reet*.

"She had come home and washed her hair. You know, she hadn't been feeling good lately and had been complaining a lot—but you know how womens are. Theys always complainin' about one thing or another." The men nod in agreement. Shurli grunts.

"And she was older than me, you know! I don't know how old she was, I guess about forty-five. And I'm only twenty-four, but to me that didn't make no difference. I loved the broad. You know what I mean?"

"Amen," snorts K.P. His crony shakes his head in agreement. I shift my weight to my left leg. Shurli grunts.

"She was good lookin' for her age too, you know how it is with us—we don't age like white peoples do. She had on her favorite wig, a brown one all done up in curls—kind of like yours only shorter." He's speaking to me and everybody turns to look at the wig I'm wearing. A sort of controlled afro.

"I really loved that woman. I mean—I had other girls, you understand me?" Everybody nods. "But she was my wo-man. She was my heart."

"Hey—bring yo' ass over here, Carol."

A shout from Li'l Bit interrupts the bemoaning. I look around to see that fifteen people have suddenly appeared from nowhere, Jesus and his boys are popping at the griddle and Li'l Bit and Kathy are tossing plates, tacos and beans as fast as they can move. I speed to the counter, pencil and bag in hand. "Next, please place your order." Shurli bustles over and helps out. The dude, Ray, and his partner take their plates from the counter and move to a table against the wall in the back. K.P. sips his coffee and picks at his plate, keeping a watch on us and the register.

I work, having trouble keeping the orders in my head as they come rapid-fire. I kind of have my eye on the dude Shurli was talking to. He is real clean cut, wearing a camel hair mack coat and brim to match, clean beige threads underneath. He's built smooth-skinned and muscular on a wiry frame, has even white, pearly teeth and heavy-lidded, sexy brown eyes. I jam Shurli between a chili tamale order and an enchilada plate.

"Who's that—he sho 'nuff fine."

"Oh, Tommy? He's like a baby brother to me. Him and his other brothers are in here all the time."

"Do they all look as good as him?"

She laughs. "Pretty good. I'll introduce you to 'em sometimes. They're nice too—and they all *work* for a livin'."

I look up suddenly and catch his eyes. He smiles slowly, slightly. He knows I'm asking about him. The smile goes through me and straight to my tenderloin. Whoowhee, baby!

"Get that order," Kathy barks and I'm back into the grind.

"Where in the fuck is Sharita?" Li'l Bit pipes.

Kathy sniggers. "That bitch puts a high premium on her pussy."

As if having heard the summons, Sharita shows up through the glass window, footing up the pavement. She pushes the door and enters, throwing off her coat and rushing behind the counter. She glances at K.P. for a second (all of us know Chuck's paid spies) and then slips into the grind.

We're on our feet three hours solid. Seems like a few people did get their county checks and it's Friday night anyhow. Fridays are always busy.

By one o'clock a hundred people have come and gone and we're cranky for another break. Sharita is eyeing my stud who briefly introduced himself to me when I maneuvered service at one of the tables which is strictly Shurli's domain (the tables leave better tips than the counter—sometimes a girl can add ten to fifteen dollars a night to her salary). I catch Sharita eyeing him as he talks to some old man who's taken the stool beside him. Sharita looks dead to me. I stare daggers. She shrugs and backs off.

At one, Tod comes in. Everybody calls Tod crazy.

"Here comes that crazy Tod," Chuck always said whenever he was around and spotted Tod coming in. Tod is a regular. Tale was that he worked for Chuck between jobs and good women. He is supposed to be the best fry cook Chuck has ever had. Everyone is fond of him and regrets the fact that Tod is a Viet Nam veteran.

"He was a fine boy, all right before he went into the Army, I tell you. I don't know what they did to him over there, Viet Nam. Ever since he's been out, he's been crazy like that. He's a good person, but nutty as a fruit cake." Tod won't eat the taco meat either.

Tod's wardrobe is limited (a sign of immense and extreme poverty among blacks) to denim overalls, the remains of his military uniforms replete with ribbons from numerous deeds of heroism and sharp shooting, karate, etc. and a raggedy trench-type overcoat he sports like a private eye. I had seen Tod several times before. He was in at least two or three nights a week on my shift. He knew I was a new girl, and made it a point to get to know me. I kept picking up the vibe that he lusted after me. But I'm ambitious and he doesn't suit my qualifications. The first of which is to have a car and every time I saw him, he was walking, which is a sin in Car City, Los Angeles.

Tod orders his usual, twenty tacos with hamburger meat and fifteen hamburgers. Jesus groans as he always does when Tod places his order. We only charge him half price as is the policy for Chuck's favorites (twenty percent off for the cops from the local precinct and any other officer of the law). Tod is always boozed up, high if not stumbling drunk. His habit is to come in, size up the joint, go out, come back minutes later, order something for himself, eat, go out, come back an hour later, place his big order, which it always takes Jesus an hour to prepare between other orders we take, while Tod cuts the bull with anyone he can find to cut it with, and sometimes comes back just before the shift change for a cup of coffee to sober up and go down to the unemployment office.

I jam Shurli about his order. "He comes in like that all the time. Who's all that stuff for?"

"Oh—that's his mother. She's got twelve kids, girl—still at home. Two girls are married. Tod makes fifteen. Tod's the oldest."

"How old is he?"

"Must be twenty-six by now. All the rest of 'em is still at home. It's pitiful child, pitiful. I ain't never seen folks so poor."

As the lull comes on, I immediately forget about Tod. My eyes go back to Tommy and I can tell he's warming more and more to the idea of waiting out the night and seeing me home after my shift is over. He keeps giving me approving looks as I move back and forth behind the counter. It's rough, trying to be a waitress and look sexy, but most of the girls manage it, me included. It's rough in them white uniforms and white brogans Chuck insists we wear, plus the heavy cloth aprons.

I'm built, no brag. Brothers keep telling me how I've got plenty of butter. A compliment to any black woman—cause our men, for the most part, like their women on the fleshy side. Skinny legs usually get a black gal laughed at although, as Shurli always says, "It ain't the beauty—it's the booty."

The place clears out about a quarter after two and we all settle in for the long haul. The guy whose old lady had died moves back to the counter and perches on a stool one down from my jazzy potential lay. Tod is still sitting on the service end of the room with Sharita and Kathy, cutting the bull and they accommodate him with their laughter. Li'l Bit is jawing with a youngster closer to her own age, which I figure to really be sixteen, although she swears by nineteen and one six-month-old son. Li'l Bit is a green-eyed sandy haired, sweet looking yellow-skinned girl with very small features, except for her eyes. Li'l Bit is married and her old man grumpily picks her up in their 1954 Chevy struggle buggy when shift is over. She doesn't like marriage and wants to leave her child to its grandparents (either set will do) and her old man to the dogs. I notice Li'l Bit is copping something from her friend. Must be some bush (marijuana) or white folks, I figure. But my attention is on my foxy gentleman catch who's listening to Ray talk again, continuing his story which he's managed to tell anyone he can collar.

We check out his loneliness. He just doesn't want to be by himself and we can appreciate his feelings. Tommy, Shurli and me, listening. It gets quieter and quieter, and pretty soon even Crazy Tod, Sharita and Kathy can hear him talking. Jesus has put down the ladle and is leaning against the griddle, listening. His two companeros have gone around back. Li'l Bit is in the jane.

"She bought me a Christmas present, you know? She showed it to me. We had had an argument that morning. She wanted to know what I was gonna get her—her having spent all that bread for me a present. She'll never know how doggish she made me feel. I been trying. I really been tryin'. But like you know how it is with the slump and alls goin' on." Shurli sighs deeply.

"I wanted to get her something. I planned to. I just hadn't figured on what, yet. And there she was, screaming at me and tossing my present around. She had got me a leather coat. It's really beautiful—all lined inside with red fur and got fur on the collar and cuffs. Real natty, you know? She liked to get her shoppin' done early—to avoid the rush. I wasn't even thinkin' 'bout it."

A beat down pause.

"I just can't get over her dying like that. So sudden. So quick. One minute and then—the next."

"Ah mannn, why don't you shut up all that sad talk! Ain't you got nothin' better to do than complain?" It was Tod. We bristle. I get up from the counter as a customer appears.

"Shut up Tod and let the man finish talkin'," Shurli chastises gently.

"Finish talkin'? He been talkin'all night and sayin' the same thing over and over again."

"Ah—go on," Shurli comes back. But the guy, Ray, had fallen into silence and is staring down into the coffee he was sipping. He pours sugar into it, takes a spoon and stirs slowly, his head bent. It aggravates all of us. Tommy stares a question at Tod.

A few people are coming in, a group of stragglers from the bar across the street. It is two o'clock. It's enough to keep everyone busy, with me and my man making eyes between orders. Tod catches us, then holds my glance for a second. I was giving the looks he wanted to someone else. He bristles, takes a sharp breath.

I signal my intentions and for him to back off. Tod ignores me. He looks at Tommy, then Ray.

Crazy Tod starts pacing, loud talking. "Yeah man, hush up all that whining. Be a man. Shows you a man. I'm a man! One hundred percent man! I don't do no whining, no complaining and no crying." He is pacing the length of the Taco House, going around to Tommy and tapping him on the shoulder at intervals. "Ain't that right, man?" He taps Tommy who smiles, puzzled, but friendly, and nods.

"Can't argue that, brother."

"Shit—a man has got to stand up, show no pain—ain't that right bruh?" He talks to Ray who is shriveled up on his stool.

"I proved I'm a man. See these here ribbons? I got this one for sharp shootin'. I can kill a niggah so dead so quick, quicker than the eye can see! You name it and I can fire it with deadly accuracy. If a man can't defend himself, he ain't a man. And I can always defend myself. I can do that if'n I can't never do nothin' else."

As he talks, Tod paces. His pace gets quicker. He waves his hands and his talk gets louder and louder. He keeps coming over to Tommy and tapping him. We can all see that Tommy don't like what is happening. It's getting on his nerves. He realizes that Tod is a taste unhinged.

"Come on, sit down and have some coffee." Shurli reaches out and grabs Tod by his overcoat, pulling him to her. He about-faces and slams into her huge torso.

"Emmm—Shurli, I loves yah!" Everybody laughs.

"Gimme a cup of coffee, Carol," Shurli orders.

I move to the coffee pot and pour a hot steaming cup, then slide the cup past Tommy and into Shurli's chunky outstretched hand. "Here, Tod, drink this and come to your senses."

Tod reaches awkwardly for the cup, knocking it out of her hand and into Tommy's lap. "Goddamn!" Tommy yells, jumping up, scalded, hastily brushing coffee from the lap of his fresh beige jumpsuit. "Shit, man—what's wrong with you?" He yells at Tod.

Tod, having gotten the desired response, spins, grabs up a handful of napkins and starts "helping" Tommy clean up.

"Oh, oh, sorry brother. I didn't mean to make a mess!"

Li'l Bit comes out of the jane and walks past the two. "Tod, what you done gone and did now?"

"Hey, man, I can help myself! You've done enough for one night!" Tommy snaps.

"I'm just trying to help." Tod's words are slippery.

"Back off bro-*ther*. You helped enough." We can see Tommy is short tempered and deeply pissed about his clothes. "If you was a man, as you claim you are, you'd offer to pay for my clothes. But that's all right, bro-*ther*, I understands."

"Hey, now—well, wait a minute bruh! I'm just bein' nice."

"Niggah, you can take your being nice 'n shove it!" Tommy's super pissed and moves to the door to leave. My heart does a slow painful sink. I'm getting pissed at Tod also.

Tod moves and halts Tommy at the door, hooking him at the elbow. "Don't run away, bruh! Don't run away from me like that!"

Tommy looks at Tod's hand on his elbow. "Man—is you crazy? What kind of fool is you? Let go of my elbow!"

Tod takes his hand away slowly, stepping back cautiously. "You think you man enough to take me?" Everybody groans. "Huh? You think you *man* enough?" Tod goes into a karate stance. "I gots my piece, man, and, like I say—I gots a deadly aim."

"Oh? You want to duel? I gots my piece too. It's out in the car. I'll be just a minute." He takes off his coat and goes through the door. Shurli turns to me, panic in her eyes.

"Girl, he always carries a .38 in his car. He'll kill Tod. I best go try and stop him." Shurli runs out into the night after Tommy.

Kathy takes her tall dark lithe healthy self and goes up to Tod. "Why don't you behave yourself, crazy, and quit actin' like everybody's a gook? Sit down and drink some coffee, take your order and go home!"

Tod turns to the counter. I hand him another cup of coffee. Shurli and Tommy come back in. She's mollified him, reasoned him down to a simmer.

She seats Tommy at the counter where he's left his coat. "I'll fix you a plate and you eat, okay?" He nods and turns up, spotting me, smiling, remembering our "date." I smile, then turn as another customer straggles through. "I'll get it," Li'l Bit slurs. Humph, I think—red devils.

Tod winds his drunken way over to Tommy, coffee in hand. "Like I said, man—I'm sorry." He stumbles and spills the coffee again. This time on Tommy's shoulder.

"Son-of-a-bitch!" Tommy jumps up screaming. "Sorry! You goddamned right you sorry. Now what you want to *do* sucker? Let's do it now!" Tommy tears off his hat, tossing it into one of the booths, revealing long matted brown hair. "Now do somethin', sucker, do somethin' now!"

"Aw niggah—I'm a black belt in karate. I'll kill your ass, sucker."

"Well, man, you better kill it then!" Tommy raises up his arms in a boxing stance, frustration in his eyes. I can see the thought traveling through his mind— images of being flipped through the plate glass window as he sizes up Tod. They are both about the same height, 6' 1", and frame. Tommy is worried about what his first move might be. He moves to hit Tod. Tod ducks. Tommy reverses, moves and swings again. Tommy misses. Tod grabs his extended arm, raises him up and flings him into the table next to the john. Everybody is out of the kitchen area now, watching. Not a sound but that of the two men fighting.

Tommy struggles up from the floor, beneath the confident Tod. "Get up niggah, get up and come and get me!" Tommy is feeling his way, blinded and dizzy from the impact of his head against the solid edge of the table which is bolted to the floor and the west wall. Tod turns away, mocking him, announcing to us: "That's how a man fights!"

Doggedly, Tommy is half way to his feet, leaning against the table for support, trying to get his focus. His hand brushes against the glass sugar canister. He secures it and pushes forward, stumbling after Tod, catching him by the flapping tail of his overcoat. "Okay, sucker, let's see you karate this!"

Wham, into Tod's skull. The scrunch of glass and blood spurting. Tod spins. Sugar everywhere. He reels under the impact. That is all Tommy needs. He rains blows down on Tod's neck and face. The sound of flesh pounding flesh. Jesus stands, awed. "Hey, man! Somebody call the cops. He's killing that man!" No one moves. Jesus hastily disappears around back to the pay phone.

"You's a man—huh? You's a man—huh?" Tommy screams like a chant. He's on top of Tod, slamming Tod's head into the floor with both of his hands. We all stand, frozen. Shurli finally runs from behind the counter, the unfinished plate still in her grasp. "Jesus is calling the cops. You best get outta here, quick!" She manages to pull him off of Tod with her free hand. Tommy stands, staggering—his eyes glazed, wild. He looks at me, through me, grabs the coat and hat Shurli hastily shoves at him, then stumbles through the door.

Silent, we all turn and look at Tod. He's struggling against the counter, trying to get to his feet. Blood everywhere, mixed with sugar and glass. Blood runs down from the gash in his head, in both directions, down his neck and down the front of his face. One eye seems to be partially out of its socket. His face torn, lumpy and jagged. I look away.

Shurli barks, "Carol—go get some cold wet towels and help me clean him up."

The ambulance and the cops arrive an hour later and Tod is taken away mumbling incoherently on the stretcher. The police sergeant lingers to take testimony, but nobody is talking, not even Jesus. No, we can't identify the assailant. No—we never seen him before. No one got his name.

It's five-thirty and the new shift is coming on in about ten more minutes. Chuck'll probably come in too, if I know K.P. He was sitting at one of the booths on the south wall and saw it all. Shurli and I are sitting at the counter along with Sharita, listening to Ray talk about his wife. He has that look in his eyes, it's fresh strong and sparkles. The one I mentioned at the jump, pain.

"That coat. I got it at the pad. All new and shiny. I just can't bear to go back to that empty room. All her stuff is still there. She'll be buried Sunday. Her sister is takin' over everything. She gave me a week to split."

I nod, trying to keep awake. The ten minutes crawl by. "She tried to tell me, you know? We were arguing and she threw the coat at me, and then clutched her heart sudden like. I asked her what was the matter and she said she was having a heart attack. I thought she was pretending."

Shurli and I look at each other.

It's sunup and Redd hits the door letting in the chilly morning. I reach down under the counter for my purse, go out back and get my jacket.

Outside, Ray is waiting for me. "Say, what's your name?"

"Carol."

"You know, I just can't stand being alone. How about coming over to my place. We'll have a drink, huh?"

I look at him and into Pain. "Thanks—but no thanks."

I turn away and shudder into the moist dawn. My struggle buggy, a tore down '69 Buick is de-icing behind the Taco House.

"Carol, wait up!"

It's Shurli. "I needs a lift, gal. My old man came and took the Cadillac. He has the duplicate keys. Just wait till I get my hands on that son-of-a-gun!"

We get into the car and I crank up. Shurli is grinning like a coon and plowing through that tremendous brown vinyl purse she always carries.

"Looka here what I gots," Shurli chuckles and shows me. It's about three pounds of hamburger meat. "I'm gonna feed my kids!" she announces.

We break into laughter. I neglect to mention the fifty dollar bill in my bra. I wonder what Chuck'll say when he totals up the take this morning.

Emerald City: Third & Pike

CHARLOTTE WATSON SHERMAN

This is Oya's corner. The pin-striped young executives and sleek-pumped clerk-typists, the lacquered-hair punk boys and bleached blondes with safety pins dangling from multi-holed earlobes, the frantic-eyed woman on the corner shouting obscenities, and the old timers rambling past new high-rise fantasy hotels all belong to Oya even though she's the only one who knows it.

Oya sits on this corner 365 days of the year, in front of the new McDonald's, with everything she needs bundled inside two plastic bags by her side. Most people pretend they don't even see Oya sitting there like a Buddha under that old green Salvation Army blanket.

Sometimes Oya's eyes look red and wild, but she won't say anything to anybody. Other times her eyes are flat, black and still as midnight outside the mission, and she talks up a furious wind.

She tells them about her family—her uncle who was a cowboy, her grandfather who fought in the Civil War, her mother who sang dirges and blues songs on the Chitlin Circuit, and her daddy who wouldn't "take no stuff from nobody," which is why they say some people got together and broke his back.

"Oh yeah, Oya be tellin them folks an earful if they'd ever stop to listen, but she don't pay em no mind. Just keeps right on talkin, keeps right on tellin it."

One day when Oya's eyes were flat and black and she was in a preaching mood, I walked down Third & Pike, passed her as if I didn't know her. Actually I didn't. But Oya turned her eyes on me and I could feel her looking at me and I knew I couldn't just walk past this woman without saying something. So I said, "Hello."

Oya looked at me with those flat black eyes and motioned for me to take a seat by her.

Now, usually I'm afraid of folks who sit on the sidewalks downtown and look as if they've never held a job or have no place to go, but something about her eyes made me sit.

I felt foolish. I felt my face growing warm and wondered what people walking by must think of me sitting on the street next to this woman who looked as if she had nowhere to go. But after sitting there for a few minutes, it seemed as if they didn't think more or less of me than when I was walking down the street. No one paid any attention to us. That bothered me. What if I really needed help or something? What if I couldn't talk, could only sit on that street?

"Don't pay them fools no mind, daughter. They wouldn't know Moses if he walked down Pike Street and split the Nordstrom Building right down the middle. You from round here?"

I nodded my head.

"I thought so. You look like one of them folks what's been up here all they lives, kinda soft-lookin like you ain't never knowed no hard work."

I immediately took offense because I could feel the inevitable speech coming on: "There ain't no real black people in Seattle."

"Calm down, daughter, I don't mean to hurt your feelings. It's just a fact, that's all. You folks up here too cushy, too soft. Can't help it. It's the rainwater does it to you, all that water can't help but make a body soggy and spineless."

I made a move to get up.

"Now wait a minute, just wait a minute. Let me show you somethin."

She reached in her pocket and pulled out a crumpled newspaper clipping. It held a picture of a grim-faced young woman and a caption that read: "DOMES-TIC TO SERVE TIME IN PRISON FOR NEAR-MURDER."

"That's me in that picture. Now ain't that somethin?"

Sure is, I thought and wondered how in the world I would get away from this woman before she hurt me.

"Them fools put me in the jail for protectin my dreams. Humph, they the only dreams I got, so naturally I'm gonna protect em. Nobody else gonna do it for me, is they?"

"But how could somebody put you in jail for protectin your dreams? That paper said you almost killed somebody."

I didn't want to seem combative but I didn't know exactly what this lady was talking about and I was feeling pretty uneasy after she'd almost insulted me then showed me evidence she'd been in jail for near-murder, no less.

"Now, I know you folks up here don't know much bout the importance of a body's dreams, but where I come from dreams was all we had. Seemed like a body got holt of a dream or a dream got holt of a body and wouldn't turn you loose. My dreams what got me through so many days of nothin, specially when it seemed like the only thing the future had to give was more of the same nothin, day after day."

She stopped abruptly and stared into space. I kept wondering what kind of dream would have forced her to try to kill somebody.

"Ain't nothin wrong with cleanin other folks' homes to make a livin. Nothin wrong with it at all. My mama had to do it and her mama had to do it at one time or nuther, so it didn't bother me none when it turned out I was gonna hafta do it too, least for a while. But my dream told me I wasn't gonna wash and scrub and shine behind other folks the rest of my life. Jobs like that was just temporary, you know what I mean?"

I nodded my head.

"Look at my hands. You never woulda knowed I danced in one of them fancy colored nightclubs and wore silk evenin gloves. Was in a sorority. Went to Xavier University."

As she reminisced, I looked at her hands. They looked rough and wide, like hands that had seen hard labor. I wondered if prison had caused them to look that way.

Oya's eyes pierced into mine. She seemed to know what I was thinking. She cackled.

"Daughter, they'd hafta put more than a prison on me to break my spirit. Don't you know it takes more than bars and beefy guards to break a fightin woman's spirit?"

She cackled some more.

"Un Un. Wouldn't never break me, and they damn sure tried. I spent fifteen years in that hellhole. Fifteen years of my precious life, all for a dreamkiller."

I looked at her and asked, "But what did you do? What did they try to do to your dreams?"

Oya leaned over to me and whispered, "I was gonna get into the space program. I was gonna be a astronaut and fly out into the universe, past all them stars. I was gonna meet up with some folks none of us never seen before, and be ambassador of goodwill; not like the fools bein sent out there now thinkin they own the universe. I was gonna be a real ambassador of goodwill and then that woman I scrubbed floors for had the nerve to tell me no black maid was ever gonna be no astronaut. Well, I could feel all the broken dreams of my mama and my grandmama and her mama swell up and start pulsin in my blood memory. I hauled off and beat that fool over the head with the mop I had in my hands till I couldn't raise up my arms no more. The chantin of my people's broken dreams died down and I looked and there was that dreamkiller in a mess of blood all over the clean floor I'd just scrubbed. And they turned round and put me in jail and never did say nothin bout that old dreamkiller. Just like my dreams never mattered. Like I didn't have no dreams. Like all I could ever think bout doin was cleanin up after nasty white folks for the rest of my life.

"Humph!" She snorted, and I almost eased to my feet so I could run if I had the cause to.

"You got any dreams, daughter?" Oya asked with a gleam in her eye.

I knew I better tell her yes, so I did.

"Well I don't care if you is from up here, you better fight for your dreams!"

Slowly, I reached out and held one of her rough hands. Then I asked, "But was your dream worth going to prison for all them years?"

Oya looked at me for a long, long time.

"I'm still gonna make it past all them stars," she said as she freed her hand and motioned for me to get to getting.

"Right now, this street b'longs to me and don't *nobody* mess with me or my dreams!" She was still shouting as I walked toward Pine Street.

And It's Called

PROGRESS???

$\mathbf{B}$eginning with "Elbow Room" and ending with "Amen," the stories in this section illustrate that the lure of the West continues and that black Westerners often fluctuate between hope and consternation. The mood of the Civil Rights movement, which pushed African Americans together while they battled racial discrimination and which established a bond toward a common causes remains. This strong sense of community and friendship is apparent in these stories about African Americans in the West. These stories also reflect relationships between blacks and whites, some expressing positive human connections, but others exposing racist attitudes that still exist in contemporary society. These stories confront social issues like oppression, racism, and economic exploitation. They illustrate both progress and regress, concerns relevant to African American lives in the West.

James Alan McPherson's "Elbow Room" epitomizes the lure of the West. This story characterizes an interracial couple. Paul, a white man from Kansas, and Virginia, a black woman from Tennessee, who move to San Francisco in search of personal and social freedom. The story deals with storytelling itself as well as Paul's parents' unwillingness to accept his interracial marriage. At the end of the story, Paul and Virginia return to Kansas, albeit remaining in the West.

Parental reluctance to accept marriages is also an issue in Jewell Parker Rhodes's "Long Distances," but it is not because of racial intolerance. Nate and Della leave Pittsburgh at midnight to move to Los Angeles because Della is in a hurry to seek the opportunities she believes await her. Della's father, who has never supported her relationship with Nate, follows them. Nate feels the urge to call his mother and tell her that he is moving to California, but he never gets the chance. While driving to Los Angeles, Nate considers the strength of his marriage to Della and recalls proverbs his mother and grandmother told him. The title "Long Distances" refers to the miles they travel, the positive strides their relationship takes, and the way Nate is able to learn from his ancestors' wisdom.

Cecil Brown's "Now Is the Time" involves a close bond between two African American comedians and an interracial romantic relationship. Jonah approaches his friend Billy, a famous comedian in Hollywood, for advice on how to be funny, and Billy explains that he has to learn to laugh at himself, that comedy is about real trouble and tragedy, as in the Greek tradition. Billy provides a summary of the history of black comedy that begins with Bert Williams, Ernest Hogan, Sam Lucas, and others who changed white stereotypes about blacks, and began the black comedic tradition. Billy explains that Dick Gregory, Bill Cosby, Redd Foxx, and Richard Pryor all built on the ideas of Bert Williams. He says a black comedian must be committed to black history and culture. References to Africa occur throughout the story. Billy says that he still faces racism even though he is famous, but the type of racism he experiences is different because he no longer lives in the ghetto and struggles with economic problems.

Like "Elbow Room," "Cry About a Nickel," by Percival Everett, shows both positive and negative relationships between blacks and whites. Joe Cooper, an African American, leaves South Carolina for the Cascades of Oregon, to work for Mr. Davis, who is white. Davis's young son, Charlie, helps Cooper take care of the horses, and Cooper becomes a father figure. Cooper tries to encourage Davis to communicate with his son, but Davis is unable to take his advice. One day, four men who have come to hunt on Davis's property interrogate Charlie about an alleged homosexual incident. When Cooper defends Charlie, the men mock Cooper with racial slurs. Upon his return from the store immediately following this encounter, Cooper notices Charlie standing in the rain beside a tree. When he realizes that Charlie is tied to the tree, he unties him and is fired by Davis. Charlie and Cooper experience a positive relationship; in fact, Cooper is more compassionate toward Charlie than Davis is, yet the hunters use racial slurs to attack Cooper and sexual slurs to attack Charlie because they are "different," demonstrating that they are as narrow-minded as Charlie's father.

As its title suggests, John Edgar Wideman's "Surfiction" represents the genre surfiction, fiction concerned with both the writing of fiction itself and challenging traditional narrative boundaries by exploring and expanding ways truth and reality counter fiction. The story defies plot summary but involves a professor of English in Wyoming who is teaching a married couple. The husband is a student in the professor's creative writing seminar and the wife, a student in his African American literature seminar. He learns about the man and the woman from comments they make about each other. Wideman, in referring to Barth, Barthes, and Barthelme, has created "Surfiction" as a sort of tribute to their achievements. He also mentions the notes he makes in the margins of Chesnutt's *Deep Sleeper* and the footnotes added to an editon of *The Short Fiction of Charles W. Chesnutt.* In his discussions of postmodernism and intertextuality, perhaps Wideman is mocking, tongue-in-cheek, the white male literary tradition and showing that deconstruction says little about African American texts in terms of black history and culture.

William Henry Lewis's "The Trip Back from Whidbey" exposes conflicts that frequently occur when African Americans subscribe to white middle-class values. Returning with her husband, Joseph, from a vacation at Whidbey Island, Maya struggles because her son has recently left home to attend a prestigious university and seems to have forsaken devotion to his black heritage. Although he has tried to explain to their son that possessions are not important, Joseph struggles with his own middle-class existence. Significantly, the family dog has died during this last visit to Whidbey. Joseph has lost his job, an event Maya feels is liberating because it will prompt Joseph to forgo middle-class values, such as the luxury of owning a beach cottage.

A concern relevant to both African American and white women is oppression based on gender. One manifestation of gender oppression is the social conditioning of women to conform to unreasonable standards of beauty, a notion expressed in Carolyn Ferrell's "Wonderful Teen." "Wonderful Teen," also the title of the magazine read by the twelve-year-old narrator, ironically captures her life when it is juxtaposed against that of the girls she reads about in the magazine. While the girls in the magazine fret over fashion, hairstyles, perfume, and getting dates, the narrator struggles to cope with abuse and her responsibility for nurturing her younger siblings. The narrator's mother takes the four children to a motel because her husband has abused her physically. While caring for the younger children and trying to console her mother, the narrator wonders why things could not have been different. When her father calls, she contemplates the cyclical pattern of domestic violence. Her epiphany is the complicated emotions that arise from her recognition that her lifestyle does not reflect that of the girls in the teen magazine.

In "The Kind of Light That Shines on Texas," by Reginald McKnight, three black children attend an otherwise all-white Texas school. The narrator recalls his experience when he attended grade school, where the teacher told racist jokes, never chose black children to perform class honors, and accused black children when something was stolen. The story is told from the perspective of the adult Clint, who is still haunted by his betrayal of one of the other black students. He has since realized the value of true friendship and fighting for one's convictions. He recalls his own behavior toward the teacher and realizes that he acted as an Uncle Tom and was not proud of his African American heritage.

Class and race discrimination is the major theme of Walter Mosley's "Equal Opportunity," a story from *Always Outnumbered, Always Outgunned,* a collection of stories about Socrates, who has recently been released from an Indiana prison and now lives in California. In this story, Socrates applies for a job at Bounty Supermarket. When he asks for an application and the clerk questions him, Socrates argues that discrimination is illegal. Socrates says that it is unfair not to hire him on the grounds that he has no phone or a car to drive to work. The catch-22 is that he cannot afford a phone or car until he has a job. After the police escort him out of the store for arguing with the management, Socrates makes further appeals and is finally given a job. After he is hired, he considers it ironic that, when he answered the question on the application about whether he had ever been convicted of a felony, he lied. Management pursued illegal forms of discrimination more than it did a legal reason for not hiring Socrates. "Equal Opportunity" raises questions concerning how poverty is perpetuated by denying jobs to people without economic means.

"Amen," by Sunny Nash, shows the bonds between African Americans in a religious community. It also shows an individual who departs from the community because she feels betrayed. The story is told from the point of view of Lacy, a seven-year-old girl who attends a church revival in a small Texas town with Dorsey, a woman acquaintance. Lacy hopes the evangelist will heal her brother, who cannot speak or walk. When the evangelist pays Dorsey to pretend she is healed, Lacy is disillusioned. After the ceremony, Lacy asks Dorsey why members of the community shouted "Amen" when they knew she was not sick. Dorsey replies that they were making fun of God. Lacy leaves the revival feeling disillusioned about God, religion, and her community, and she does not want to participate in such events.

These stories reflect ways in which contemporary western African Americans celebrate their cultural heritage while continuing to work toward equal opportunity. While some of the stories demonstrate that social progress has occurred—some African Americans have enjoyed career success—others illustrate that more progress is needed, for sometimes African Americans are still denied opportunities and are the victims of racist attitudes. These modern characters have a "fighting spirit" that refuses to relent to oppression. Reflecting social progress made since the late 1800s, when African Americans in the West first began publishing short fiction, the stories in this section continue to demonstrate the spirit, the courage, and the persistence of western African Americans in their search for "life with dignity."

Elbow Room

JAMES ALAN McPHERSON

"Boone's genius was to recognize the difficulty as neither material nor political but one purely moral and aesthetic."

—"The Discovery of Kentucky"
WILLIAM CARLOS WILLIAMS

Narrator is unmanageable. Demonstrates a disregard for form bordering on the paranoid. Questioned closely, he declares himself the open enemy of conventional narrative categories. When pressed for reasons, narrator became shrill in insistence that "borders," "structures," "frames," "order," and even "form" itself are regarded by him with the highest suspicion. Insists on unevenness as a virtue. Flaunts an almost barbaric disregard for the moral mysteries, or integrities, of traditional narrative modes. This flaw in his discipline is well demonstrated here. In order to save this narration, editor felt compelled to clarify slightly, not to censor but to impose at least the illusion of order. This was an effort toward preserving a certain morality of technique. Editor speaks here of a morality of morality, of that necessary corroboration between unyielding material and the discerning eye of absolute importance in the making of a final draft.

This is the essence of what he said:

I

Paul Frost was one of thousands of boys who came out of those little Kansas towns back during that time. He was one of the few who did not go back. When he came out it was easy moving forward by not going to the war. But after a while it got harder. Paul was in school up in Chicago when he determined to stand pat and take his blows. He returned home briefly and confronted his family and the members of a selective service committee. These were people who had watched him growing up. They were outraged at his refusal. Watching their outrage and remaining silent made Paul cry inside himself. He went back up to Chicago and did alternate service in a hospital for the insane. He began attending a Quaker meeting. Nights in the hospital, he read heavily in history, literature, and moral philosophy. Soon he began to see that many of the inmates were not insane. This frightened him enough to make him stop talking and begin watching things very closely. He was living, during this time, in a rented room out near Garfield Park. He went out only for work, meals, and to the library for more books. He knew no women and wanted none. Because he lived inside himself, he was soon taken by other people for an idiot. Their assumptions enabled Paul to maintain and nourish a secret self. He held conversations with it nights in his room. His first public speech, after many months of silence, was to a mental defective one evening at the hospital over a checkerboard down in the recreation room. "I don't think you're crazy," he whispered to the man. "So what are you *doing* here?" This patient looked warily at Paul and then smiled. He had that wistful, wide-eyed smile of the uncaring doomed. He leaned across the board and looked directly into Paul Frost's bright brown eyes. "What are *you* doing here?" he said. This question unsettled Paul. The more he thought about it the more nervous he became. He began walking LaSalle Street during his free time, picking conversations with total strangers. But everyone seemed to be in a great hurry. In the second year of his alternative service, he secured a transfer to another hospital out on the Coast. There, in Oakland, he did a number of wild things. Activity kept him from thinking about being crazy and going back to Kansas. His last act as a madman was to marry, in San Francisco, a black girl named Virginia Valentine, from a little town called Warren outside Knoxville, Tennessee.

II

Virginia Valentine had come out of Warren some ten years before, on the crest of that great wave of jailbreaking peasants. To people like her, imprisoned for generations, the outside world seemed absolutely clear in outline and full of sweet choices. Many could not cope with freedom and moved about crazily, much like long-chained pets anticipating the jerks of their leashes. Some committed suicide. Others, seeking safety, rushed into other prisons. But a few, like Virginia, rose and ranged far and wide in flight, like aristocratic eagles seeking high, free peaks on which to build their nests.

Virginia's quest was an epic of idealism. At nineteen she joined the Peace Corps and took the poor man's grand tour of the world. She was gregarious in a rough and country way. She had a talent for locating quickly the human core in people. And she had great humor. At twenty she was nursing babies in Ceylon. At twenty-one she stood watching people in a market in Jamshedpur, India, learning how to count the castes. Deciding then that Hindus were more "black" than anyone she had ever seen at home, she began calling herself "nigger" in an affirmative and ironic way. She developed a most subtle and delicious sense of humor. In Senegal, among the fishermen, she acquired the habit of eating with her hands. On holiday, in Kenya, she climbed up Kilimanjaro and stood on its summit, her hands on her hips in the country manner, her eyes looking up for more footholds. In the sweaty, spice-smelling markets of Cairo, Port Said, and Damascus she learned to outhaggle conniving traders. Seeing slaves and women still being sold, she developed the healthy habit of browbeating Arabs. There are stories she tells about old man Leakey, about squatting beside him in a Masai compound in north Tanzania, about helping herself to a drink of milk and cow's blood. The old man, she says, was curt, but eager to show his bones. The drink, she says, was not bad. The Masai did not dance. She entered the areas behind the smiles of Arabs, Asians, Africans, Israelis, Indians. In the stories they told she found implanted different ways of looking at the world.

When she returned home, at twenty-two, she was bursting with stories to tell. There were many like her. In Boston, New York, Philadelphia, Chicago, and all parts of California, people gathered in groups and told similar stories. They thought in terms new to them. In conversation they remarked on common points of reference in the four quarters of the world. The peasants among them had become aristocratic without any of the telling affectations. The aristocrats by birth had developed an easy, common touch. They considered themselves a new tribe.

But then their minds began to shift. In the beginning it was a subtle process. During conversation someone might say a casual "You know?" and there would be a hesitation, slight at first, denying affirmation. Virginia has painful stories to tell about increases in the periods of silence during the reacculturation. People began to feel self-conscious and guilty. If pushed, she will tell about the suicide in her group. People saw less and less of each other. Soon they were nodding on the street. Inevitably, many people in conversation began saying, "I don't understand!" At first this was tentative, then it became a defensive assertion. It took several months before they became black and white. Those who tried to fight grew confused and bitter. This was why Virginia, like many of the more stubborn, abandoned the East and ran off to California. Like a wounded bird fearful of landing with its wings still spread, she went out to the territory in search of some soft, personal space to cushion the impact of her grounding.

III

I went to the territory to renew my supply of stories. There were no new ones in the East at the time I left. Ideas and manners had coalesced into old and cobwebbed conventions. The old stories were still being told, but their tellers seemed to lack confidence in them. Words seemed to have become detached from emotion and no longer flowed on the rhythm of passion. Even the great myths floated apart from their rituals. Cynical salesmen hawked them as folklore. There was no more bite in humor. And language, mother language, was being whored by her best sons to suit the appetites of wealthy patrons. There were no new stories. Great energy was spent describing the technology of fucking. Black folk were back into entertaining with time-tested acts. Maupassant's whores bristled with the muscle of union organizers. The life-affirming peasants of Chekhov and Babel sat wasted and listless on their porches, oblivious to the beats in their own blood.

Even Pushkin's firebrands and noble brigands seemed content with the lackluster: mugging old ladies, killing themselves, snatching small change from dollar-and-dime grocers. During this time little men became afflicted with spells of swaggering. Men with greatness in them spoke on the telephone, and in private, as if bouncing safe clichés off the ear of a listener into an expectant and proprietary tape recorder. Everywhere there was this feeling of a grotesque sadness far, far past honest tears.

And the caste curtains were drawn, resegregating all imaginations. In restaurants, on airplanes, even in the homes of usually decent people, there was retrenchment, indifference, and fear. More than a million stories died in the East back during that time: confessions of fear, screams of hatred orchestrated into prayers, love and trust and need evolving, murders, retribution, redemption, honestly expressed rage. If I had approached a stranger and said, "Friend, I need your part of the story in order to complete my sense of self," I would have caused him to shudder, tremble, perhaps denounce me as an assailant. Yet to not do this was to default on my responsibility to narrate fully. There are stories that *must* be told, if only to be around when fresh dimensions are needed. But in the East, during that time, there was no thought of this. A narrator cannot function without new angles of vision. I needed new eyes, regeneration, fresh forms, and went hunting for them out in the territory.

A point of information. What has form to do with caste restrictions?
Everything.
You are saying you want to be white?
A narrator needs as much access to the world as the advocates of that mythology.
You are ashamed then of being black?
Only of not being nimble enough to dodge other people's straitjackets.
Are you not too much obsessed here with integration?
I was cursed with a healthy imagination.
What have caste restrictions to do with imagination?
Everything.
A point of information. What is your idea of personal freedom?
Unrestricted access to new stories forming.
Have you paid strict attention to the forming of this present one?
Once upon a time there was a wedding in San Francisco.

Virginia I valued for her stock of stories. I was suspicious of Paul Frost for claiming first right to these. They were a treasure I felt sure he would exploit. The girl was not at all pretty, and at first I could not see how he could love her. She was a little plump, had small breasts, and habitually wore Levi's and that flat, broad-brimmed type of cap popularized by movie gangsters in the forties. But the more I looked into her costume, the more I recognized it as the disguise of a person trying to deflect attention away from a secret self. When she laughed, it was loudly, and behind the laugh I heard a hand reaching out secretly to tug down loose corners of the costume. Even her affection of a swagger seemed contrived to conceal a softness of heart. Listening to the rough muscles of her voice, when she laughed, I sensed they were being flexed to keep obscure a sensitivity too finely tuned to risk exposure to the world. She employed a complicated kind of defensive irony. When her voice boomed, "Don't play with me now, nigger!" it said on the underside of the very same rhythm, *Don't come too close, I hurt easily.* Or when the voice said, "Come on in here and meet my fiancé, and if you don't like it you can go to hell!" the quick, dark eyes, watching closely for reactions, said in their silent language, *Don't hurt my baby! Don't hurt my baby!* She spiced her stories with this same delicious irony. Virginia Valentine was a country raconteur with a stock of stories flavored by international experience. Telling them, she spoke with her whole presence in very complicated ways. She was unique. She was a classic kind of narrator. Virginia Valentine was a magic woman.

Paul Frost seemed attracted to her by this outward display of strength. I am convinced he was by this time too mature to view her as just exotic. He was the second generation of a Kansas family successful in business matters, and he must have had keen eyes for value. But because of this, and perhaps for reasons still unclear to him, his family and the prairies were now in his past. I think he felt the need to redeem the family through works of great art, to release it from the hauntings of those lonely prairie towns. I know that when I looked I saw dead Indians living in his eyes. But I also saw a wholesome glow in their directness. They seemed in earnest need of answers to honest questions always on the verge of being asked. This aura of intense interest hung close to his face, like a bright cloud, or like a glistening second coat of skin not yet thick enough to be attached to him. It seemed to inquire of whomever his eyes addressed, "Who am I?" But this was only an outward essence. Whatever else he was eluded my inspection of his face. And as I grew aware of myself in pursuit of its definition, I began to feel embarrassed, and a little perverse. Because the thing that illuminated him, that provided the core of his mystery, might have been simple guilt, or outright lust, or a passion to dominate, or a need to submit to a fearful-seeming object. All such motives enter into the convention of love.

And yet at times, watching Virginia's eyes soften as they moved over his face, I could read in them the recognition of extraordinary spiritual forces, quietly commanded, but so self-assured as to be unafraid of advertising themselves. I am sure he was unaware of his innocence. And perhaps this is why Virginia's eyes pleaded, when he openly approached a soul-crushed stranger, *Don't hurt my baby! Don't hurt my baby!,* even while her voice laughed, teased, or growled. She employed her country wits with the finesse and style of a magic woman. And after I had come to understand them better, I began to see deeper into their bond. She was an eagle with broken wings spread, somewhat awkwardly, over the aristocratic soul of a simple farm boy. Having his soul intact made him a vulnerable human being. But having flown so high herself, and having been severely damaged, she still maintained too much grace, and too complete a sense of the treachery in the world, to allow any roughnesses to touch the naked thing. Paul Frost was a very lucky innocent. Virginia Valentine was protecting him to heal herself.

This wedding was a quiet affair in a judge's chambers. Paul's brother was best man. A tall, strapping fellow, he had flown out from Kansas to stand beside his brother. He held the ring with a gentle dignity. Paul's parents did not attend. They had called many times making the usual pleas. When these failed they sent a telegram saying BEST. But Virginia's parents were there from Tennessee. They were pleasant, country folk who had long begged her to come home. But when they saw they could not change her mind, they flew out with country-cured hams, a homemade cake, and a wedding quilt sewn by Virginia's grandmother, who was a full-blooded Cherokee living far back in the Tennessee woods. They also brought a handful of recipes from well-wishing neighbors. The mother wore a light blue dress and a white hat. A very dark-skinned little woman, she sat on the judge's leather chair looking as solemn as an usher at Sunday church service. Mr. Daniel Valentine, the father, a large-framed, handsome, brown man, smiled nervously when the judge had finished, and shook hands all around. He had the delicate facial features of an Indian, with curly black hair and high cheekbones. Virginia's color was deep reddish brown. She wore a simple white dress with a red sash. She smiled often and reassuringly at her brooding mother, as if to say, "It's all right. I told you so." Paul, in a black suit and black bow tie, looked as responsible and as sober as a banquet steward in a plush private club.

At the reception, in a sunny corner of Golden Gate Park, Mr. Daniel Valentine offered around cigars. Then he strolled slowly about the grounds, his hands in his pockets. It was a warm November afternoon, much warmer than his body said it had a right to be. He was out of his proper environment and was obviously ill at ease. I walked along with him, smoking my cigar. In his brown face I saw fear and pride and puzzlement. He felt obliged to explain to himself how one of the most certain things in the world had miscarried. He had assumed that color was the highest bond, and I think he must have felt ashamed for someone. "We told her many the time to come home," he said while we walked. He stared at the late-blooming flowers, the green trees just starting to brown, the shirtless young men throwing Frisbees. He said, "I don't pretend to know the world no more, but I know enough about the lay of the land to have me a good, long talk with him. I laid it *right on the line,* too. My baby come from a long line of family, and her mama and me's proud of that. Right there in the South, there's plenty white women that have chase me, so I know a little something about how the world go round. But I ain't nobody's pretty plaything, and my baby ain't neither." He swelled out his chest and breathed deeply, inspecting closely the greenness of the grass, the spread of the trees. I sensed that his body was trying desperately to remember the coolness of the Tennessee autumn. He was sweating a little. He said, "Now, I don't give a *damn* about *his* family. They can go to *hell* for all of me. But I care a lot about *mine!* And last night I told him, 'If you *ever* hurt my baby, if you *ever* make her cry about something that ain't the fault of her womanly ways, I'm gonna come *looking* for you.' I told him I'd wear out a stick on him." He said this to me as one black man to another, as if he owed me reassurance. And I had no way of telling him that his daughter, in her private mind and treasured, secret self, had long ago moved a world away from that small living room in which conventional opinion mattered. "That's just what I told him, too," Mr. Daniel Valentine said. Then he averted his eyes, puffed his cigar, and nodded toward where the others stood crowded around a eucalyptus tree. Mrs. Valentine was unpacking the lunch. Paul was laughing like a little boy and swinging Virginia's hand. "But they do make a fine couple, don't they now?" he asked me.

They made a very fine couple. Paul rented an apartment in the Mission district and brought all their possessions under one roof. Virginia's posters, paintings, and sculpture acquired while traveling were unpacked from their boxes and used to decorate the walls and end tables. Paul's many books were stacked neatly in high brown bookcases in the small living room. The few times I saw them after the wedding they seemed very happy. They seemed eager to pick up and mend the broken pieces of fragmented lives. Virginia worked as a clerk for a state agency. Paul worked for a construction company during the day and studied for his degree nights in a community college. Paul worked very hard, with the regularity and order of a determined man. I think the steady rhythms of the prairie were still in him, and he planned ahead with the memory of winter still in mind. But they made special efforts to live in cosmopolitan style. Both of them were learning Spanish from their Chicano neighbors. They chose their friends carefully with an eye on uniqueness and character. They were the most democratic people I have ever seen. They simply allowed people to present themselves, and they had relationships with Chicanos, Asians, French, Brazilians, black and white Americans. But they lived in a place where people were constantly coming and going. And they lived there at a time when a certain structure was settling in. It was not as brutal as it was in the East, but it was calculated to ensure the same results.

During this time Paul's father, back in Kansas, was putting on the pressure. I think the idea of Virginia had finally entered his imagination and he was frightened for the future of his name. He called long-distance periodically, vowing full support for Paul when he finally reconsidered. He seemed to have no doubt this would occur. They argued back and forth by telephone. The father accused the son of beginning to think like a Negro. The father accused the son of being deluded. The son accused the father of being narrow-minded. The son accused the father of being obtuse. Nothing was ever resolved, but the discussions were most rational. The father was simply a good businessman. In his mind he had a sharp impression of the market. I am sure he thought his son had made a bad investment that was bound to be corrected as soon as Virginia's stock declined. There was, after all, no permanent reification of color. From his point of view it was this simple. But from Paul's point of view it was not.

When they invited me to dinner in early December, Virginia said, "That old rascal thinks that one day he'll have to kiss a pickaninny. If I had a cold heart I'd send him one of them minstrel pictures." She laughed when she said this, but there was not the usual irony in her voice. She pushed her hands into the back pockets of her Levi's and leaned her butt against the kitchen stove.

Paul was at the kitchen table drinking wine. He seemed upset and determined. He said, "My father is a very decent man in his own way. He just knows a little part of the world. He's never talked seriously with anybody that's not like him. He doesn't understand black people, and he would have a hard time understanding Ginny." He laughed, his clear eyes flashing. "She's a bundle of contradictions. She breaks all the rules. All of you do."

I sat down at the table and poured myself a glass of the red wine. Virginia was baking a spicy Spanish dish, and the smell of it made me more relaxed than I should have been. After draining the glass I said, "I can understand your father's worry. According to convention, one of you is supposed to die, get crippled for life, or get struck down by a freak flash of lightning while making love on a sunny day."

Paul laughed. He sipped from his glass of wine. "This is real life," he said, "not the movies. And in any case, *I* don't have to worry."

Virginia was stirring a dish of red sauce on the stove. The air was heavy with the smell of pungent spices.

I said to Paul, "The producers in Hollywood are recycling."

Paul laughed again. "This is *real* life," he told me. But he was getting a little drunk. He sipped his wine and said, "In this house we pay close attention to reality. By public definition Ginny is black, but in fact she's a hybrid of African, European, and Indian bloodlines. Out in the world she roughhouses, but here at home she's gentle and sweet. Before anybody else she pretends to be tough, but with me she's a softy. It took me a long time to understand these contradictions, and it'll take my family longer. My father has a very unsubtle, orderly mind. I'm willing to wait. I see my marriage as an investment in the future. When my father has mellowed some, I'll take my wife home. As I said, *I* don't have to worry."

Virginia called from the stove, "That old rascal might at least *speak* to me when he calls."

Paul fingered his wineglass, looking guilty and cornered.

It was not my story, but I could not help intruding upon its materials. It seemed to me to lack perspective. I poured myself another glass of wine and looked across the table at Paul. Above us the naked light bulb reflected eerily in my glass of red wine. I said, "Time out here is different from time in the East. When we say 'Good afternoon' here, in the East people are saying 'Good night.' It's a matter of distance, not of values. Ideas that start in the East move very fast in media, but here the diversity tends to slow them down. Still, a mind needs media to reinforce a sense of self. There are no imaginations pure enough to be self-sustaining."

Paul looked hard at me. He looked irritated. He said, "I don't understand what you're talking about."

I said, "Someone is coming here to claim you. Soon you may surprise even yourself. While there is still time, you must force the reality of your wife into your father's mind and run toward whatever cover it provides."

He really did not understand. I think he still believed he was a free agent. He sat erect at the kitchen table, sipping from his glass of wine. He looked confused, hurt, almost on the edge of anger. I felt bad for having intruded into his story, but there was a point I wanted very much for him to see. I pointed toward a Nigerian ceremonial mask nailed to the wall just over the kitchen door. The white light from the bulb above us glowed on the brown, polished wood of the mask. "Do you think it's beautiful?" I asked.

Paul looked up and inspected the mask. It was an exaggeration of the human face, a celebration in carved wood of the mobile human personality. The eyes were mere slits. Teeth protruded from a broad mouth at unexpected angles. From the forehead of the face, curving upward, were appendages resembling a mountain goat's horns. Paul sipped his wine. He said, "It's very nice. Ginny bought it from a trader in Ibadan. There's a good story behind it."

I said, "But do you think it's beautiful?"

"The story or the mask?" Virginia called from the stove. She laughed with just a hint of self-derision, but the sound contained the image of a curtain being pulled across a private self.

"The mask, of course!" Paul called to her coolly. Then he looked at me with great emotion in his eyes. "It's nice," he said.

I said, "You are a dealer in art. You have extraordinary taste. But your shop is in a small town. You want to sell this mask by convincing your best customer it is beautiful and of interest to the eye. Every other dealer in town says it is ugly. How do you convince the customer and make a sale?"

Paul's eyes widened and flashed. He started to get up, then sat back down. "I don't like *condescension,*" he said. "I don't much like being talked down to!" He was angry, but in a controlled way. He started to get up again.

Virginia shouted, *"Dinner!"*

I said to Paul, "You have enlisted in a psychological war."

He looked trapped. He turned to face his wife. But she had her back to him, making great noises while opening the stove. I think she was singing an old Negro hymn. He turned toward me again, a great fear claiming control of his entire face. "Why don't you just *leave!*" he shouted. "Why don't you just *get out!*"

I looked past him and saw Virginia standing by the stove. She was holding a hot red dish with her bare hands. She was trembling like a bird. In her face was the recognition of a profound defeat. She cried, "Go away! Please, go away! No matter what you think, this is my husband!"

I left them alone with their dinner. It was not my story. It was not ripe for telling until they had got it under better control.

Analysis of this section is needed. It is too subtle and needs to be more clearly explained.
I tried to enter his mind and failed.
Explain.
I had confronted him with color and he became white.
Unclear. Explain.
There was a public area of personality in which his "I" existed. The nervous nature of this is the basis of what is miscalled arrogance. In reality it was the way his relationship with the world was structured. I attempted to challenge this structure by attacking its assumptions too directly and abruptly. He sensed the intrusion and reacted emotionally to protect his sense of form. He simply shut me out of his world.
Unclear. Explain.
I am I. I am we. You are.
Clarity is essential on this point. Explain.
More than a million small assumptions, reaffirmed year after year, had become as routine as brushing teeth. The totality guarded for him an area of personality he was under no obligation to develop. All necessary development preexisted for him, long before his birth, out there in the world, in the images, actions, power, and status of others. In that undefined "I" existed an ego that embraced the outlines, but only the outlines, of the entire world. This was an unconscious process over which he had little control. It defined his self for him. It was a formal structure that defined his sense of order. It was one geared unconsciously to the avoidance of personal experience challenging that order. I tried to enter this area uninvited and was pushed back. This was his right. A guest does not enter a very private room without knocking carefully. Nor does a blind man continue moving when he hears an unfamiliar sound.
Clarity is essential on this point. Please explain.
I think he understood enough to know that he was on a moral mission.

After Christmas, Virginia contacted me by telephone and said, "No matter what you think, he has a good heart and he's sorry. But you *did* provoke him. One thing I learned from traveling is you accept people the way they are and try to work from there. Africans can be a cruel people. Arabs I never *did* learn to trust. And there's a lot of us *niggers* that ain't so hot. But them raggedy-ass Indians taught me something about patience and faith. They ain't never had nothing, but they *still* going strong. In Calcutta you see crippled beggars out in the street, and people just walk on around them. Now a Westerner would say that's cruel, but them fucking Indians so damn complicated they probably look at that same beggar and see a reincarnated raja that lived in us a thousand years ago, ate too much of them hot spices, and died of gout. *Shit!* He don't *need* nothing else! So they don't worry about how he looks now. But patience is a Christmas-morning thing. You have to accept what's under the tree and keep on believing there's a Santa Claus. Both you *and* that nigger of mine have to learn that. I ain't giving up on *nothing!* I ain't giving up on *shit! So* why don't you heist up your raggedy ass and come with us to Mass on New Year's Eve?"

I have said Virginia Frost was a magic woman.

The cathedral was massive, chilly and dark. Huge arched stained-glass windows reflected the outlines of sacred images in the flickering lights of red and yellow candle flames. Two Episcopal priests, in flowing white albs, stood in the chancel and read invocations from their missals. Little boys in black cassocks paced reverently up and down the aisles, censing from gray-smoking thuribles. Seated on the benches around us were people—young and old and middle-aged, the well dressed and the shabby, the hopeful and the forlorn. Young men with great scraggly beards sat silently with lowered heads. Beside them were young women, pale and hard-faced, looking as beaten and worn as pioneer women after too many years of frontier life. Single girls wore sequined denim jackets over long frocks with ruffled bottoms. Many wore leather boots. Here and there, almost invisible in the crowd, men and men and women and women, segregated by sex, sat holding hands with heads bowed. Virginia was wearing her mug's cap, and it sat rakishly on her strong curly hair. I sat on her right, Paul on her left. We sat close together. The place projected the mood of a sanctuary.

Above us, in the balconies, two choirs in black and white robes sang a mass. Their voices cried like wounded angels bent on calling back to earth a delinquent God. The effort was magnificent. But all around us, people looked abstracted, beaten, drained of feeling. There was a desperate concentration on the choir, an effort of such intensity it almost made its own sound. It seemed to be asking questions of the songs floating down from the choir. We closed our eyes and said private prayers. It was nearing midnight, and we heard the faith of Bach insisted on in the collective voices of the choir. And in response, breathing in the stillness of the people, one sensed a profound imploring. But then a voice behind us imposed itself on the silence. "Young man," it rasped, "if you're too *dumb* to take your hat off in church, get out!" From all along the two rows came the sounds of stiff necks creaking. "Young man," the voice demanded of Virginia, "did you hear me? Or are you too *dumb* to know the English language?" I opened my eyes and turned. Beside me, Virginia was closing her eyes tighter. Beside her, I saw Paul lift his own head and turn fierce eyes on the old gentleman's face. In his voice was a familiar arrogance from a source he had just begun to consciously tap. "You old *fart!*" he said, his tone disrupting the harmony floating down from above us. "You old fart!" he said. "This is *my wife*. If you don't like what she's wearing, *that's tough!*"

The choir lifted their voices, as if bent on erasing the incident with the strength of their sound. Around us people coughed softly. Paul put his arm around Virginia's shoulder. He closed his eyes and whispered in her ear. I closed my own eyes and tried to lose myself in the music. But I was made humble and hopeful by that other thing, and I thought to myself, *This one's a man.*

From January on, Paul began confronting the hidden dimensions of his history. Something in his mind seemed to have opened, and he was hungry for information.

He read books hungrily for other points of view, sifting through propaganda for facts. He underlined a great deal, scribbled questions in the margins, asked questions openly. He discarded much of what he read, but what stuck in that private place in his mind made him pensive, and silent, and a little sad. I watched him closely, though I kept my distance. I admired him for his heroic attempt to look back.

But in early February, while he was with Virginia in the parking lot of a supermarket, a car full of children called him nigger. Their dog barked along with the singsong rhythm. "I just laughed at the little crumbsnatchers," Virginia said.

She said she could not understand why Paul became so upset.

In late February, when he was walking with Virginia in the rain through the Sunset district, two younger children called him nigger.

"What's a nigger?" he asked me on the telephone. "I mean, what does it *really* mean to you?"

I said, "A descendant of Proteus, an expression of the highest form of freedom."

He hung up on me.

I did not call him back. I was convinced he had to earn his own definitions.

In early March Virginia found out she was pregnant.

That same month Paul disclosed that his father, during one of their arguments, had mentioned to him the full name of the black janitor who swept out his office. But the old man was most upset about the baby.

During the months after Christmas I saw very little of them. I had become interested in a man recently paroled after more than fifty years in prison. He had many rich stories to tell. I visited him often in his room at a halfway-house, playing chess and listening while he talked. He sang eloquent praises to the luxuries of freedom. He detailed for me the epic nature of the effort that had got him sprung. He was alive with ambition, lust, large appetites. And yet, in his room, he seemed to regulate his movements by the beat of an invisible clock. He would begin walking toward the door, then stop and look puzzled, then return to his chair beside the bed. His window faced the evening sun just where it sank into the ocean, but the window shade was never lifted. He invited me once to have lunch with him, then opened a can of peaches and insisted that we share a single spoon. He invited me to attend a party with him, given in his honor by one of his benefactors. There, he sat on a chair in the corner of the room and smiled broadly only when a curious stranger expressed interest in his recollections. He told the same stories line for line. Late in the evening, I spoke briefly with the hostess. This woman looked me straight in the eye while denouncing prisons with a passionate indignation. Periodically, she swung her empty martini glass in a confident arc to the right of her body. There, as always, stood a servant holding a tray at just the point where, without ever having to look, my hostess knew a perfect arc and a flat surface were supposed to intersect. I saw my own face reflected roundly in the hostess's blue-tinted spectator's sunglasses, and I began to laugh.

The above section is totally unclear. It should be cut.

I would leave it in. It was attempting to suggest the nature of the times.

But here the narrative begins to drift. There is a shift in subject, mood, and focus of narration. Cutting is advised.

Back during that time there was little feeling and no focus.

Narrator has a responsibility to make things clear.

Narrator fails in this respect. There was no clarity. There was no focus. There was no control. The hands of a great clock seemed to be spinning wildly, and there was no longer any great difference between East and West.

This thing affected everyone. There was the feeling of a great giving up. I sensed a bombed-out place inside me. I watched people clutch at bottles, pills, the robes of Jesus, and I began to feel cynical and beaten. Inside myself, and out there in the world, I heard only sobs and sighs and moans. There was during this time a great nakedness, exposed everywhere, and people dared you to look. I looked. I saw. I saw Virginia Frost losing control of her stories. As her belly grew, her recollections began to lose their structure. The richness was still there, but her accounts became more anecdotal than like stories. They lacked clarity and order. She still knew the names, the accents, the personal quirks of individual Indians, Asians, Israelis, but more and more they fragmented into pieces of memory. There was no longer the sense of a personal epic. She no longer existed inside her own stories. They began bordering dangerously on the exotic and nostalgic. At times, telling them, she almost became a performer—one capable of brilliant flashes of recollection that stunned briefly, lived, and then were gone. She had inside her an epic adventure, multinational in scope, but the passion needed to give it permanent shape was obviously fading. One part of her was a resigned mother-to-be, but the other part was becoming a country teller of tall stories with an international cast.

I have said it was the nature of the times.

Something was also happening to Paul. In his mind, I think, he was trying desperately to unstructure and flesh out his undefined "I." But he seemed unable to locate the enemy and, a novice in thinking from the defensive point of view, had not yet learned the necessary tactics. Still, he seemed to sense there were some secrets to survival that could be learned from books, conversations, experiences with people who lived very close to the realities of life. He cut himself off from the company of most white males. He got a job with a landscaping crew and spent most of his days outdoors. His muscles hardened and his face grew brown. He grew a long black beard. He read the Bible, Sören Kierkegaard, abstract treatises on ethics. He underlined heavily. The beard merged with his intense, unblinking eyes to give him the appearance of a suffering, pain-accepting Christ. During this time he flirted with the clothing styles of the street-corner dandy. Often in conversation he spoke bitterly about the neglect of the poor. He quoted from memory long passages from Isaiah, Jeremiah, the book of Lamentations. He denounced his father as a moral coward. He was self-righteous, struggling, and abysmally alone.

But his face still maintained its aura. His large brown eyes still put the same question, though now desperately asked, "Who am I?"

And many times, watching him conceal his aloneness, I wanted to answer, "The abstract white man of mythic dimensions, if being that will make you whole again." But the story was still unfinished, and I did not want to intrude on its structure again. The chaos was his alone, as were the contents he was trying desperately to reclaim from an entrenched and determined form. But to his credit it must be said that, all during this time, I never once heard him say to Virginia, "I don't understand." For the stoic nature of this silence, considering the easy world waiting behind those words, one could not help but love him.

Then, in early June, both sets of parents began making gestures. Virginia's people called up often, proposing treasured family names for the baby. Paul's mother sent money for a bassinet. She hinted, in strictest confidence to Paul, that more than European bloodlines ran in her veins. But the father was still unyielding. His arguments had grown more complex: If he recognized the baby he would have to recognize Virginia's family, and if he ever visited the family they would have to visit him. From this new perspective the objection was grounded in a simple matter of class distinction. His mind lacked subtlety, but one had to admire its sense of order. On his personal initiative, he told his son, he had engineered the hiring of a black employee by his company. Paul told his father this would not do. The mother told Paul the father would think it over, and after he had thought it over Virginia and the baby would be welcome in their home. But Virginia told Paul this would not do either.

They had never seen the problem from her point of view.

Virginia said, "I don't want my baby to be an honorary white."

She said this to me toward midsummer, in the park, during a conversation at the Japanese Tea Garden. Around us under the pavilion sat tourists munching cookies, sipping warm tea, huddled against the coolness of the morning mist. Virginia now wore a maternity smock over her pants, but her mug's cap still rode defiantly atop her curly hair. Her belly protruded with the expanding child. Her brown cheeks were fleshy and her eyes looked very tired. She said, "I'm black. I've accepted myself as that. But didn't I make some elbow room, though?" She tapped her temple with her forefinger. "I mean up *here!*" Then she laughed bitterly and sipped her tea. "When times get tough, *anybody* can pass for white. Niggers been doing *that* for *centuries,* so it ain't nothing new. But shit, wouldn't it of been something to be a nigger that could relate to white and black and everything else in the world out of a self as big as the world is?" She laughed. Then she said, "That would have been *some* nigger!"

We sipped our tea and watched the mist lifting from the flowers. On the walkways below us the tourists kept taking pictures.

I said, "You were game. You were bold all right. *You* were some nigger."

She said, "I was *whiter* than white and *blacker* than black. Hell, at least I got to *see* through the fog."

I said, "You were game all right."

A tourist paused, smiled nervously, and snapped our picture.

Virginia said, "It's so *fucked up!* You get just two choices, and either one leaves you blind as a bat at noon. You want both, just for starters, and then you want everything else in the world. But what you wind up with is one eye and a bunch of memories. But I don't want my baby to be one-eyed and honorary white. At least the black eye can peep round corners."

Inside myself I suddenly felt a coolness as light as the morning mist against my skin. Then I realized that I was acting. I did not care about them and their problems any more. I did not think they had a story worth telling. I looked away from her and said, "Life is tough, all right."

Virginia was turning her teacup. She turned it around and around on the hand-painted tray. She looked out over the garden and said, "But I'm worried about that nigger of mine. I told you he had heart. In his mind he's still working through all that shit. Underneath that soft front he's strong as a mule, and he's stubborn. Right now both his eyes are a little open, but if he ever got his jaws tight he might close one eye and become blacker than I ever thought about being. That's the way it's rigged."

I did not feel I owed them anything more. But because she had once shared with me the richness of her stories, I felt obliged. I looked at the tourists moving clumsily between the hanging red and purple fuchsia. They knocked many of the delicate petals to the ground. The pavilion was completely surrounded by tramping tourists. I looked down at Virginia's belly and said, "Then for the sake of your child don't be black. Be more of a classic kind of nigger."

She laughed then and slapped my back.

I walked with Paul around the city before I returned East. This was in the late summer, several months before the baby was due, and I felt I owed him something. It was on a Sunday. Paul had attended a Quaker meeting that morning and seemed at peace with himself. We walked all afternoon. Along the avenues, on the sidewalk paralleling the beach, down the broad roads through the park, we strolled aimlessly and in silence. The people we saw seemed resigned, anomic, vaguely haunted by lackluster ghosts. My own eyes seemed drawn to black people. In Golden Gate Park I watched a black man, drunk or high on dope, making ridiculous gestures at a mother wheeling a baby in its carriage. The man seemed intent on parodying a thought already in the young mother's mind. I stopped and pointed and said to Paul, "That's a nigger." On the Panhandle we paused to study an overdressed black man, standing in a group of casually dressed whites, who smiled with all his teeth exposed. His smile seemed to be saying, even to strangers, "You know everything about me. I know you know I know I have nothing to hide." I nodded toward him and said to Paul, "That's a nigger." Paul looked about more freely. On Lincoln Way, walking back toward the bus stop, he directed my eyes to a passing car with stickers plastered on its bumpers. They boosted various mundane causes, motor lubricants, and the Second Coming of Jesus. In the middle of the back bumper there was a white sticker with great black letters reading, BE PROUD TO BE A NIGGER.

Paul laughed. I think he must have thought it a subtle joke. But a few blocks from the park I nodded toward a heavily bearded young white man on a sparkling, red ten-speed bike. He was red-faced and unwashed. His black pants and black sweatshirt seemed, even from a distance, infested with dirt and sweat and crawling things. As he pedaled, crusty, dirt-covered toes protruded from sandals made from the rubber casings of tires. He seemed conscious of himself as the survivor of something. He maneuvered through the afternoon traffic, against all lights, with a bemused arrogance etched into the creases of his red face. When he was far down the block, I said to Paul, "That one is only passing. He is a bad parody of a part-time nigger."

He did not laugh. He did not understand.

I said, "Imagine two men on this street. One is white and dressed like that. The other is black and seems to be a parading model for a gentleman's tailor. In your mind, or in your father's mind, which of them would seem unnatural?"

Paul stopped walking. He looked very hurt. He said, "Now it's finally out in the open. You think I'm a racist."

I felt very cool and spacious inside myself. I felt free of any obligation to find a new story. I felt free enough to say to Paul, "I think you were born in a lonely place where people value a certain order. I saw a picture on a calendar once of a man posed between the prairie and the sky. He seemed pressured by all that space, as if he were in a crucible. He seemed humbled by the simplistic rhythm of the place. I think that in his mind he must have to be methodical, to think in very simple terms, in order to abide with those rhythms."

But he still thought I was accusing him, or calling him to account. He said, "People *do* grow. You may not think much of *me*, but my children will be great!"

I said, "They will be black and blind or passing for white and self-blinded. Those are the only choices."

Paul walked on ahead of me, very fast.

On Nineteenth Avenue, at the bus stop, he turned to me and said, "Don't bother to come all the way back. Ginny's probably taking a nap." He looked away up the street to where several buses were waiting for the light to change. The fog had come in, it was getting darker, and in the light of the traffic his eyes looked red and tired. I was not standing close enough to him to see his face, but I am sure that by this time his aura had completely disappeared. He looked beaten and drained, like everything else in sight.

We shook hands and I began to walk away, convinced there were no new stories in the world.

Both buses passed me on their way to the corner. But above the squeaks and hissing of their brakes I heard Paul's voice calling, "At *least* I tried! At *least* I'm *fighting!* And I know what a *nigger* is, too. It's what you are when you begin thinking of yourself as a work of art!"

I did not turn to answer, although I heard him clearly. I am certain there was no arrogance at all left in his voice.

Almost two months later, when I called their apartment before leaving for the East, the telephone was disconnected. When I went there to say goodbye they were gone. A Chicano couple, just up from LA, was moving in. They spoke very poor English. When I described the couple I was looking for they shook their heads slowly. Then the husband, a big-bellied man with a handlebar mustache, rummaged in a pile of trash in the hall and pulled out a sign painted on a piece of cardboard. He held it up across his chest. The sign said, WE ARE PARENTS. GO AWAY.

I went back to the East resigned to telling the old stories.

But six months later, while I was trying to wrestle my imagination into the cold heart of a recalcitrant folktale, a letter from a small town in Kansas was forwarded to me by way of San Francisco. It was the announcement of a baby's birth, seven or eight months old. Also enclosed were three color pictures. The first, dated in October, was a mass of pink skin and curly black hair. The second, a more recent snapshot, was of a chubby brown boy, naked on his back, his dark brown eyes staring out at the world. On the back of this picture was printed: "Daniel P. Frost, four months, eight days." The third picture was of Virginia and Paul standing on either side of an elderly couple. Virginia was smiling triumphantly, wearing her mug's cap. The old man looked solemn. The woman, with purple-white hair, was holding the baby. Paul stood a little apart from the others, his arms crossed. His beard was gone and he looked defiant. There was a familiar intensity about his face. On the back of this picture someone had written: "He will be a classic kind of nigger."

Clarify the meaning of this comment.
I would find that difficult to do. It was from the beginning not my story. I lack the insight to narrate its complexities. But it may still be told. The mother is, after all, a country raconteur with cosmopolitan experience. The father sees clearly with both eyes. And when I called Kansas they had already left for the backwoods of Tennessee, where the baby has an odd assortment of relatives. I will wait. The mother is a bold woman. The father has a sense of how things should be. But while waiting, I will wager my reputation on the ambition, if not the strength, of the boy's story.

Comment is unclear. Explain. Explain.

Long Distances

JEWELL PARKER RHODES

Nate couldn't remember the moment when it had happened, let alone why. Was it in the supermarket buying kidney beans or touring through Allegheny Park with its man-made pond when he knew just from looking at her, he would have to go to California? Knew from fixed stares, drooping mouth, her restlessness.

Knew he'd have to leave his humid and river-choked valley with its steel-mill-sooted hills to drive across Plains, Rockies and desert until sand gave way to heaving ocean. And for what? Her dreaming?

Three thousand miles. A man could get lost.

Della showed him a postcard picture book of California. Flat-topped roofs and pastel stucco. Palm trees bent by breezes. He'd be trapped by distance. Sunshine.

"We'll be pioneers," Della said.

He wondered if he'd miss shoveling snow, crushing ice while sprinkling salt? If he'd miss the ugliness of brick homes with rain slicking off slant roofs into mud-packed gutters? He'd never see the three rivers overflow.

Would he miss driving over cobblestones, getting his wheels caught by street-car tracks the city was too cheap to dig up? Or parking on hills with the clutch in, the tires turned toward the curb?

He'd miss his mother.

For what? Della's dreaming? Or his fear she'd go with or without him? No matter.

Nate had traded in his muscle Chevy for a dreamboat Chrysler. A 300 with a red interior that wasn't as bright as the red metal outside and never would be. The skinny-ass man who sold him the car said it would get him around the world if that's where he wanted to go. He said he didn't. But Della had been sold with that line. And here he was driving on a stretch of highway about ready to cross into INDIANA WELCOME. A truck was coming out of Indiana, flicking its headlights to low. It started to rain. He turned on his windshield wipers, his high beams. Night driving was dangerous. But Della couldn't wait another day. Had to leave at midnight to make better time. Now she and the kids were sleeping.

He looked at the trip odometer: 270 miles. At least two more days and nights of driving. 800, 1,000 miles a day. No unnecessary stops. No motels. Della needed to get to Los Angeles fast, to make it big. Somehow. He'd drive until his mind warped and then maybe he'd forget his guilt. Forget his momma's unnatural quiet, forget her solemn shuffling about the house. Forget her leaning over a porch railing, watching them pack up as if she couldn't believe it. Forget her refusing to say or wave goodbye. Nate wished he had a drink. He'd promised to call his momma from Wheeling. But it'd seemed like too soon. He plain forgot to call at Dayton.

He looked in the side mirror and saw the Ford his father-in-law, Ben Williams, was driving. Ben was no comfort. For weeks, Ben told folks at the *Pier Point Bar,* "No way I'd allow my baby girl travel from Pittsburgh to L.A. alone."

"What you mean *alone,* Ben? Nate's going. He's her husband, ain't he?"

Then Ben Williams would puff his chest, suck his gut, and glare until the person nervously admitted, "Ain't right to let a woman travel alone. Not with two kids."

A dozen slicks and low-lifes had told Nate that Ben was drinking bourbon and calling him a faggot. But what was he supposed to do? Beat up on an old man? Have his wife holler? Nate gripped the steering wheel.

Since the first time he called on Della, the old man kept one-upping him. Nate remembered being seventeen, squirming on a plastic-covered sofa, his hands itching with sweat. Ben Williams, an ex-cop, had a bit of money. He had a bit of Irish too. He was a freckle-faced Negro and proud of it. Nate was just poor and black.

Ben Williams slipped in questions like artillery fire:

"Where you been, boy?"

"Home." He remembered how his plain, brown-faced momma could make a run-down house seem like the world. Make you never want to leave. He promised he'd never leave.

"Where you going, boy?"

"Uh, work, sir. I be wanting my own butcher shop." He liked the feel of a cleaver ripping away flesh from bone and the soft whishing sound of bloodied sawdust beneath his feet.

"What do you want with my girl?"

That one he couldn't answer.

Looking at Della with her head leaning up against the window and slightly cocked back, breathing through her nose in a slight snore—he still didn't know. Now she didn't look so pretty and when she was angry, she seemed less so. Maybe it was the old man that made him want her. Him with his attitude that his baby girl was so special and Nate was just another no-good hood from the streets.

Nate sighed, pressing the aching small of his back into the vinyl seat. He was twenty-eight. Still poor and black with a wife longing for the "opportunities" of California. She used to long for him.

At fifteen, Della was eager to do it anywhere. He remembered her hitching up her dress, begging him in the laundromat. Together they moaned; he had a kid.

Responsibilities. Della was smart—she finished school. He dropped out to cut beef full-time. God, how his momma screamed. Wasn't a man supposed to support his family? What choice did he have?

Another pretty baby. Della was less eager to do it. She started spreading her legs again when she started talking California. When he'd admitted he was scared that if the family couldn't make it in Pittsburgh, they couldn't make it anywhere, she pressed him down upon her breasts, reminding him while he suckled that he'd promised California. He rubbed himself between her thighs until the world and regrets faded.

Momma never liked Della. "She attracts men like bugs to flypaper. Her uppity dad is a yellow fool. Her momma is just as bad." Then she would grin, smack her hips, before uttering her final condemnation. "Spoiled."

The smell and sound of stale heat passing through vents sickened Nate. He felt like rolling down the window, but the cool wind would cut right back to the children. His two daughters, Carrie and Jackie, almost smothered beneath blankets, were two squirrelly balls in the back. He wondered when his momma would see her grandkids again? No more dressing them in white and carrying them to church to sing, shout and Praise the Lord. Who would she rock and sing lullabies to? It was his fault they were leaving. Dammit, why couldn't he say "no" to Della? He should've called his momma from Dayton.

A yellow sign with a vertical ripple told him the road up ahead was curved. Nate took one hand away from the wheel. His right hand adjusting the turn of the wheel was all he really needed. He loved the feel of cars. Even this one. And as the green fluorescent speedometer showed his increase in speed, the better he felt. 70, 75, 80. Without looking in the mirror, he knew the old man would be straining his car to keep up with him. He could just about hear Ben Williams cursing. Ben needed to be with his daughter more than he needed to breathe. What do I need? Nate thought.

As the asphalt turnpike straightened itself out, Nate lowered the speed. He didn't understand his feelings, but it didn't much matter. If he understood everything, he'd still hurt. Understanding didn't ease pain.

He was eight when his momma told him matter-of-factly his dad and Sondra were gone. They were at the kitchen table eating collard greens and rice. Even at eight, he'd understood the attraction of the neighbor woman with her flowery dresses and jasmine perfume. Him and his dad both laughed and smiled at her jokes. He understood his momma was too fat, awkward, and glum around Miss Sondra. Nonetheless he'd kicked the wall and tried to hide his crying. That night he slept on his daddy's side of the bed. Curled in the crook of his mother's arms, touching her round face, he promised he'd never leave. She didn't ask him to say it. But he was eight and thought words had power. For many nights thereafter, before uncoiling his wiry body against hers, he'd whisper, "I'll be here." And when he married, it was simple enough to live in the same house, two floors up, across the hall. Della hadn't threatened to take the kids. He couldn't even use that excuse.

The car was pulling him farther away from his mother.

At the point where the skyline met the road in his vision, Nate was sure he could see her. Her breasts sagging, her eyes dim. Was there a difference between what the two of them were feeling? His mother, flat in bed, hearing the sound of no one breathing; him, maneuvering through rain, hearing the car and bodies exhaling the same heated air. Who would care for his mother? He wished he could turn on the radio. There were buttons to push rather than knobs to turn. Too much noise though. Besides, he'd probably only get country.

Nate wanted to piss and buy some coffee. A red neon sign blinked, Food, Gas, 5 miles, Terre Haute. He would call his mother and tell her he loved her. He would get change. A hundred quarters. Call her every stop from a pay phone. First, Terre Haute. Then, St. Louis. Topeka. Denver. Would she weep?

He wanted to hit something. Wanted to run the car off the road. A twist to the right, and into the embankment. Kill them all. Metal, concrete, blood. The car would pleat like an accordion. He wished he could see Ben Williams's face then. Yeah. What would Ben say seeing his daughter smashed up? Her toes meeting her elbows; her head twisted off. What would Ben do?

Nate missed the exit. A dairy truck hauling cows rumbled past. The rain was easing. He looked at his watch: 4:28 A.M. His momma was probably asleep now. He should wait till morning. After he crossed the Mississippi. Columbia, Missouri, then. He'd call her there. Veins popped up like worms along his hands. What if she refused to talk to him? He stumbled a bent Kool out of his right pocket. He lit the cigarette, dragged deep, and smoke filled his lungs like a caress. He exhaled. Smoke blanketed the dash. He stubbed the cigarette out.

"Della," he whispered plaintively. "Della."

Her eyes opened. Disoriented, she registered the night, the bold headlights whizzing by, Route 70 heading across the Wabash River and into Illinois.

She turned her head to the left and looked at Nate. "What is it?"

He grit his teeth and stared straight ahead at the road.

"Would you have gone without me?" His voice was barely a whisper. The heater's fan kicked in again.

"Yes," she said.

He felt like the time a line drive hit him in the gut. Wind went right out of him. Driving was easy. Automatic. He concentrated on feeling the murmurs of the engine.

The sky was clear. He switched off the wipers and rear window defrost. Della was sleeping.

Kansas City. Maybe he'd call his mother then. She'd be up. 10:00 A.M. Monday was laundry day. She'd be gathering clothes, stuffing them into her basket to carry them down the first flight of steps. She needn't worry anymore about shaking out sawdust, starching his collars, or lifting bloodstains from his shirts. He'd probably miss her if he called. When the phone would ring, she'd already be racketing her way down the basement steps. He'd call her that evening. After dinner. In Wichita.

Maybe Colorado Springs? Yeah. She'd have more time to adjust to him being gone. Another 1,000 miles, he'd be in Los Angeles. His family needed him. Nate pressed his foot hard on the gas. Los Angeles. He'd call his mother there and tell her he loved her nonetheless.

"Pop?" It was Jackie.

"Sssh. You'll wake your momma and sister up."

"Carrie keeps kicking me."

"In her sleep, she don't mean it."

Nate watched his daughter scowl in the mirror. She was resting her chin on top of the front seat, next to his shoulder—her fuzzy blue blanket covering her head like a nun's cloth.

"Can I help drive?"

"Come on, but be careful."

Jackie lifted her tennis shoe foot over and onto the front seat. Nate, with his right hand, grabbed her by her collar and pulled her down between him and Della. Jackie shifted herself onto his lap. He relaxed, feeling her small hands gripping his two hands on the wheel.

"Wow. I ain't never drove on the turnpike before."

"You just keep your eyes on the road so none of us don't get killed."

Jackie tightly clutched her father's hands. "Can I turn on the radio?"

"No."

"Aw, Pop."

Nate nudged her head with the side of his jaw.

Together, they watched the road. A clear, straight line to the horizon. Him looking over the arch of the wheel, Jackie right beneath it. It felt good to have company. He needed the distraction.

"Look, there's a dog, Pop. Running across the road."

Nate didn't see anything but he pumped the brakes anyway so Jackie could be satisfied they wouldn't hit the animal.

"And there. It's a raccoon. See it? Scootin' across the road."

"Nothing's there."

"It *is*."

Nate pumped the brakes. He felt his heart lighten at his daughter's silliness. He slowed for deer, a wily old fox. Ben Williams must be thinking he's driving crazy. Nate didn't care. Jackie was the child most like himself. Carrie took after Della, feminine and sweet when she wanted something. Jackie was the one who should've been a boy.

Feeling her shoes bang his knees, her spine curling into his chest, and a stumpy braid tickling his chin, Nate felt more her father than any other time he could remember. They were alone in the car, driving to California. The sun was coming up.

"Angels are digging out the sun to wake up the world," said an awed Jackie. "Digging it right out of the earth."

"The sun doesn't come out of the earth."

"Does so," she said, fiercely whispering, staring at him through the mirror. "Right now, it's half in and half out."

"Who told you that?"

"Grandma."

Nate felt shaken. He remembered his momma telling him such things too. Telling him that stars were God's words in light. The moon, His mirror. Rainbows were the fluttering glow of angels' wings. The horizon was the blue gust of God's breath. All of a sudden his mother's presence was real.

"If Grandma said it, it must be true," Nate whispered.

Jackie tried burying her face in his shoulder. "I didn't want to leave," she said.

"I didn't want to go." Nate hugged his daughter closer, and hearing, feeling her soft shuddering sigh, he had a clear sense of what a damn fool he'd been.

"You think she'll forget me?" asked Jackie.

"Naw," he said. "Your grandma loves you."

"She wouldn't let me kiss her goodbye."

"She was just hurt."

Nate stared straight ahead at the gray roadway. He didn't want to look up and see Jackie's reflection in the overhead mirror. He didn't want to look up and see her looking at him. "There's a cat," he said. pumping the brakes, trying to stop his headlong drive. In his mind, he lost the image of a road map. He couldn't see a red-marked line named 70 winding its way to California. He saw him and his daughter marooned in a car, whispering secrets.

When the sun was halfway up in the sky, Jackie fell asleep. Her hands slipped off his hands and he could feel her fingers lightly touching the hair on his arms. "Jackie?" All the women in the car were sleeping.

In the side mirror, Nate looked yearningly at Ben Williams's car. He wished the old Ford would catch up with him. They could drive side by side past cornfields and wheat, at least until the Rockies.

Sunlight was baking him. He couldn't slip off his jacket without disturbing Jackie. He cursed under his breath. In the grease-slicked patches on the road, he saw shreds of rainbows. The sun loomed. He knew angels were moving it.

If Grandma said it, it must be true.

Now Is the Time

CECIL M. BROWN

I will admit that reason is a good thing. No argument about that. But reason is only reason, and it only satisfies man's rational requirements. Desire, on the other hand, is the manifestation of life itself—of all of life—and it encompasses everything from reason down to scratching oneself. And although, when we're guided by our desires, life very often turns into a messy affair, it's still life and not a series of extractions or square roots.

—Dostoyevsky, *Notes from Underground*

I parked my car in the courtyard just in front of the guest house. Facing west and looking beyond the guest house I could see the tennis court and bathhouses; to my right were the boxing gym, the dogs, and the cars. To my left was the main house. I remembered all this because I'd been to one of Billy's parties, where Billy entertained most of the party-goers in Hollywood. The comics have told me and I've observed it for myself that he liked nothing better than sharing his wealth with others and got the biggest pleasure out of seeing other people enjoying his estate.

I knocked at the back door of the main house and a Chicano maid opened it, greeted me politely, and said Billy was waiting for me upstairs. After leading me into the room, where I got a glimpse of the spacious kitchen with its slacked hardwood floors and stark simplicity, she led me up some stairs covered with two-inch carpeting to Billy's study.

When I entered the room I immediately saw Billy seated behind a large, modern Danish-style desk of books and mementoes and photos in an orderly hodge-podge. He was wearing a red T-shirt with *Hana* written across it, a pair of white ducks, and tennis shoes. On his head he wore one of those Hermes hats with silver wings. As I slowly sunk into the cushion and made my way to him he leaped up and started laughing. His infectious laughter seduced me immediately and though I wasn't aware of it, I realize, now that I look back on it, I was laughing too.

"Sit down, Partner," he said in a Western cowboy voice, "and rest your feet."

He'd done the voice so well that he rewarded himself with a chuckle.

"What you want to drink?" he asked me as I dropped into the chair adjoining his desk.

I knew he drank vodka, and I asked for it myself. He told this to the maid, who was still standing waiting for her orders, and she went away.

"Do you like fights?" my host asked and turned to the color video television of the Muhammad Ali–Frazier fight. Every time the champ hit Frazier, Billy would jump up and laugh like an excited child.

"Get 'im, Champ! Look at that! Look! The champ's got 'im down. He's knocked the shit out of Frazier! Sonabitch! Is that it? That's it!"

He clicked the television off with a remote control and announced to me, "That's it!" and then he said, almost to himself, "I've seen this fight a million times and each time I act just like a damn fool! It fucks me up to see anything that beautiful. I don't know why but it does!"

When he was watching the fight I took the time to drink in the room. It was the sort of room that could easily be an office when the occasion arose, and with the carpeting and soft-cushioned leather sofas and the video sets and sound systems (large impressive speakers stood ominously in the corners) it could easily be a playpen, a place to kick back in, entertain a half dozen intimate friends. A long glass window ran along the wall, just behind Billy's desk, and overlooked the courtyard, the guest house, gym, and garage; on the opposite wall a window overlooked moorish arches, a Spanish-styled fountain, a moorish plaza. This gave me an ancient, dark, soothing state of mind, like a bit of fantasy. This fantastic element seemed balanced with the realistic everywhere in the room itself. African sculptures, some standing in one corner as tall as an average man, added to this fantastic mood.

Along the walls perpendicular and adjacent to the two walls just described were the many plaques given to him commemorating his genius in comedy, movie posters advertising his cinematic pantomime, pictures and photographs capturing his social life at parties, his personal life in Hawaii, and his family life with his children. Then right in the middle of these (on the east wall) this touch of fantasy: a beautiful picture of an incredibly beautiful woman in an ancient Greek costume holding a spear and shield. This picture, though small, dominated the room. Who was the girl? And what role was she playing? And in what play? Did Billy also have an interest in drama? Was he in love with an actress, some true beauty of the drama stage? Was there a fantastic, hidden dimension to this already protean girl-crazy shape-shifter?

Making her entrance and exit as quietly as an unearthly sprite, the Chicano maid brought my vodka. It was like some weird, spooky magic. One moment I'm looking at the wall and the next there's this glass of vodka sitting right in front of me. I had to turn my head quick—real quick too—to see the last of her white, starched uniform disappearing behind the closed door. One day, I promised myself silently, I'll have servants fast like that. One minute they're here, the next minute they're gone. Off to some mysterious island to bring me back some strange, fantastic pleasure in the form of a drug which I'd serve as a vodka.

"Do you do this?" Billy asked and offered me the piece of paper with the White Girl on it.

"Of course," I said and accepted it, and, in the manner of an adept accepting from his guru some hip potion, a token of their deep and heavy pondering over the spiritual presences in life and death, I took a ceremonial snort. The thing about White Girl is that it just puts me to sleep. But not when I am doing it with my moral mentor! It was like smoking your first cigarette with your father: you are now taking the same moral assumptions about life that he has—you are, for better or worse, on the same level somehow and he knows you know this now and that's what is communicated between you by the smoking of the verboten cigarette or the snorting of the illegal White Girl.

At least that's the way I saw it that afternoon as all the light was leaving the sky. I was, after all, looking for help: I felt washed up as a comic, but I didn't want to face up to the truth. *I wasn't funny any more.* Even with jokes that I'd previously gotten laughs off, audiences would now, when I told them, look at me uncomprehendingly like I was a fool. Nobody would laugh at me. I was ashamed of my routine, my "show."

And then, as if he possessed a clairvoyant sense, Billy said, "I saw your show."

Oh, God, now! He had said it! With one word of condemnation he could make me a show-biz cripple for life! Don't you—the greatest comedian since the beginning of the world, not you whom I admire more than my very own father, not you whose records I listened to and admired when only three years old! Not you whom I compared to Dionysus in the *Bacchantes,* comparing your comedy to his savage divinity of wine in my college senior thesis, not you who is like a god to me—don't you be the one to tell me how unfunny my "show" was, please.

Quickly I interrupted him and condemned myself before he could. I'd much rather hear it from my own mouth, the lesser mouth, as it were, than his.

"I was lousy," I confessed. "I was terrible! I—"

"Yes," he said, "you were pretty bad."

"I don't know why I was so lousy," I went on in this pitiful voice, in a voice now that I look back on it, not unlike one of Billy's typical heroes, an utter loser, "Nobody laughed at me."

"You weren't funny. That's why," he said in a tone of voice that indicated that I'd offended him and his profession by declaring that I belonged to it. I kept shaking my head and looking depressed. When I wasn't shaking my bead in self-loathing I'd hang it down between my legs like a rock on the end of a string which I was about to drop into some dismal chasm below. Except I couldn't drop my head! If only I could disappear! If only I could become a fly! And buzz off!

"In fact," Billy went on, "I don't think I've ever seen anybody as bad as you were. There's something irritating about your work."

"That's the best thing anybody ever said to me," I confessed.

"Have you ever thought of giving it up?" he asked, peering into my face in such a manner as to suggest somebody searching into a dark, empty room and, finding nothing, closing the door.

Have I ever thought of giving it up? You mean, have I ever thought of killing myself?

How could I give it up? When there were so many funny people in the world to talk about, how could I not be a comic? When the corruption I saw all around me every day at the Beverly Hills Hotel, on the street corners, in the Polo Lounge, how could I not be a comic? And yet how could I explain this to him? Could he understand?

"Yes, I've thought of giving it up," I lied. "Right after this meeting with you I'm going to give it up and then kill myself."

"Why not?" He laughed. "You're already dead."

The pun didn't escape me and I rewarded his shrewdness with a laugh.

"So you've thought of giving it up?" he asked again.

"Yes," I lied again.

"Don't," he said.

"Don't . . . what?" I asked.

"Give it up," he muttered.

"But I'm living in misery," I challenged.

"I know, so did I. When I said a few minutes back that your show was the worst I'd ever seen I wasn't telling the complete truth. The worst show I'd ever seen was my first show. I was just like you. I was so bad I felt I'd offended the audience by just showing up. First I tried to be a singer, but the more I tried to be a singer, the worse I got. So I'd tell little jokes between songs. The people would boo my songs and laugh at my jokes. Clubs started hiring me for my jokes, and club managers would tell me, 'Billy, lay off the songs. Do more jokes,' until pretty soon I'd dropped the songs and was doing all jokes. Except, as soon as I started thinking hard about comedy, suddenly I wasn't funny. I started doing jokes from jokebooks, and other comics' jokes I'd heard get laughs, until I couldn't live with myself anymore. I wasn't being honest. I did one show once in Las Vegas that was worse than the show I saw you do at the Comedy Club. I'm not trying to pull rank on you by saying my show was worse than yours. But it was."

"It's hard to imagine a show worse than mine," I admitted to him without shame.

"You remind me of myself. I wasn't always funny when I *first* started."

I didn't believe this, but I went on nodding my head in agreement. Could anybody who'd ever seen Billy Badman believe he wasn't born funny?

"I know a little bit about comedy," he said in this typical understated manner. "To be funny, you have to learn to laugh at yourself. Laugh at your troubles!"

I know a little bit about comedy—under-fucking-statement of the century! Does he know a little bit about comedy!

Suddenly, silently, there stood this tall, svelte, attractive woman beside Billy. I recognized her lovely face as belonging to the girl holding the shield and sword in the picture. She was wearing a considerable bit more than a Grecian loincloth, dressed as she was in blue shorts and a pink tank top.

"Oh, this is my girlfriend, Tina," Billy said by way of introduction. "Tina, this is Jonah. He works at the Comedy Club."

"Hello." She smiled and extended a frail, suntanned hand for me to shake, which I did.

"We were talking about something," Billy said in a voice that succeeded in both informing her and dismissing her at once.

"I want to be with you, darling," Tina said and put her arm around his neck. I made a move in my chair that said, If you want to be alone I can leave, but Billy made a gesture with his hand that said, Don't move, I know how to handle this.

"I'm talking to a friend," Billy said with a slight annoyance in his voice.

"Nice meeting you, Jonah," Tina said and went back downstairs.

"Comedy," Billy went on, as if Tina hadn't interrupted him, "is about trouble. Everybody's in trouble, everybody's got to die. Death makes comedy possible! A comic makes people laugh at their problems and troubles, even though for that particular expression of the trouble, death is not so obvious, but it's always there. When somebody slips on a banana peel we laugh because he could also fall and kill himself."

Bert Williams! Bert-fucking-Williams! Did be know about Bert Williams or did he develop independently from him? Surely he knew they were kin, belonging to the same family? But even as I thought these thoughts, what I'm doing, see, is I'm leaned all over like a student or something. *Not one word* was going to escape my talking brain-box, is what I'm trying to get over by my pose. And I'm going to spend the balance of my days trying to live up to the wisdom that I'm about to receive from this great master!

"What about Bert Williams?" I finally had the courage to say.

"Bert Williams, the old mime artist? Ah, my friend Randell Young who lives in Berkeley told me about him. Somebody showed me a film about him once. He was able to come out and just stick his white-gloved hand out and make the audience laugh for forty minutes!"

"Were you influenced by him?"

"No, I was already a comic before I knew about him."

"But you belong to the same family, the same kin. I have this theory—well, it's not important."

"No, go on. Theory. I want to hear it."

"Well, first there was Williams. He studied black people. He was the first scientist of black culture. He said he looked at blacks as if he wasn't one of them! He learned their humor and their dialect. He studied with Petro in Europe to get the timing right. Because of his aesthetic distance, as it were, he became popular with whites like Al Jolson, Will Rogers, and W.C. Fields, who made money and career out of Negro impersonations. Then came the black side of his lineage: Ernest Hogan, Billy Kersands, Sam Lucas, Bailey and Fletcher, Coles and Johnson. They were the coon shouters. They were the early satirists who took the word 'coon' and turned it back on whites. Then came World War I. Then Stepin Fetchit and his gang. Then after World War II and the sixties, Dick Gregory, Bill Cosby, Redd Foxx. Then Richard Pryor. Then you. Don't you see? You're one family, but Bert stands at the head of the family."

"What about you?" he asked slyly.

"Me? I don't count. I'm nobody. I'm not even funny."

"*Nobody*. Isn't that the most famous of Bert Williams' songs?"

"Yes, yes it is."

"Isn't that the song that made him famous?"

"Yes."

"Then maybe you would be better off by being nobody. People like to laugh at a nobody. Especially a nobody that ain't funny. Maybe you should start laughing at what a nobody you are."

"I agree that I'm nobody," I said. I just remembered something. When I did that college senior paper the main point of comparison between the Greek god Dionysus and Bill's humor was first of all the divinity element, and second—the most important thing—was that Dionysus had taken the form of a human being. Billy often gave me the impression, especially in this part of our meeting, of being a spirit who had incarnated himself into the physical person of Billy Badman.

"Be a good nobody then," he said in the manner that suggested a guru speaking.

A God incarnate—like when I looked over the tall African statue that seemed to be guarding the portal against evil spirits, he seemed to have been reading my thoughts. I was thinking, *I've never been to Africa!*

"Have you ever been to Africa?" he asked.

"No."

"Go, Jonah. Go. It'll make you proud. Even the snakes hold their heads up in Africa."

I looked at the picture of Tina in the shield and sword.

"What play is that from?" I asked.

"I don't know," he said. "It's written down on the bottom of it," he said. "Look and see what it's from."

Crossing the room I looked at the picture frame: *Springfield College. Antigone, Summer, 1967.*

"Antigone," I said.

"Means nothing to me." He laughed.

"She rebels against her father and society and tradition."

He shook his head in the direction in which Tina had left and said, "That's her all right!"

"You don't think living with a white woman is a problem anymore?" I asked suddenly.

"No," he said, "I think we're beyond that now. Everybody feels that a black man and a white woman can have as many problems as anybody else."

"And as much happiness as anybody else," I bravely commented.

"That's right," he said.

"But-but-but everything you do, records, concerts, films, are all about black people, yet—and yet you don't live like a nigger, like the black people in your records or films. You don't live in a ghetto."

"Don't be naïve, Jonah! Don't think like a white boy! You have a lot more at stake than that! And a lot less to lose than you think! Listen, you're about to fall into their trap of making you think that you can be safe in America! You can't, brother! Do you think for a moment that if you are successful and live like Billy Badman you've escaped being black and are therefore safe? *Jesus!* I see now why you're not funny! Nobody can be funny who lives an illusion! Do you think I'm safe? All this you see"—he waved to his room and the swimming pool and guest house and gym—" is the price I've had to pay to do my work! I keep this bullshit going so they'll leave me the fuck alone! Sure, I'm happy, but not because of what I am but in spite of it."

"But you've at least escaped the ghetto!"

"The biggest ghetto in the world is show business."

"But you don't have to suffer in obscurity as millions of blacks still do."

"That's why I feel committed to them and why, I suppose, they don't feel so committed to me."

"At least the police leave you alone!"

"Says who? If I do the slightest thing it's in the newspaper. If I shit in the street, tomorrow the headlines'll say BILLY BADMAN SHITS IN THE STREET! and on top of that they're making money off it too!"

"But the studios will protect you."

"They do protect superstars, but since I'm a black superstar they could just change the rules. You see the situation I'm in—we're in?"

As with the statue and the picture of Tina as Antigone, so it was when I looked at the chess set on his desk: he read my mind.

"You like that chess set?" he asked.

"Where's it from?" I asked, impressed, for each of the pieces had been hand carved from wood like a miniature tribe of Zulu warriors, each piece representing somebody in the tribal army, with the King and Queen in these little skirts made out of straw and spears made out of toothpicks.

"We picked that up in Africa," he said. "Do you want to play some chess?"

"Sure."

"You have any money?"

"I got some. Not much."

"How much you got?"

I took out all of my money and put it on the table. It came to something like five dollars and some change.

"Pick up the change," he said. "I'll bet you a thousand dollars against the five I'll beat you."

"Okay," I said, accepting the challenge as if it were fair. My role as ingenu was to pretend that anything he said or did was perfectly normal.

There was nothing braggadocio about his challenge—what he meant by this was what he thought was fair.

"Hello, baby," Billy said to Tina as she came into the room. "We are playing a game of chess. Would you like some cocaine, dearie?"

She was so really pissed she was trembling. "You've ignored me all evening! And I'm fed up with it, goddam it!" Tina shouted, standing right over Billy.

"Baby, I'm sitting here enjoying a game of chess with my friend. Now what's the problem?"

"The problem is that you spend all your goddam time with your fucking friends and I wanna be with you!"

Her eyes were red with anger and it looked as if she'd been crying.

In a calm voice so different from the madman reputation his well-publicized fits of anger had earned him, Billy inquired into the origin of her dissatisfaction.

"All goddam evening, you've ignored me!" Tina stammered out, "And I'm sick of it!"

Billy turned to me and explained they'd had a big party just that afternoon and she was understandably tired. I nodded in agreement. With the same calm voice, he turned to Tina.

"Tina, we had a party. Many people were here. Now you were downstairs talking with the ladies and I was upstairs—"

"That's just it. I hated being downstairs talking with the ladies. You spend all of your goddam time up here enjoying yourself—"

She interrupted herself and picked up a box of cookies that were lying on the table and emptied them on Billy's head. Some of the cookies spilled over onto the chessboard.

"Now why did you do that?" Billy asked in a subdued voice. I expected, to be quite honest, for him to hit her upside her head, but he simply nodded his head.

"Because I wanted to! Damn you!"

Billy said, "Listen, I have a friend here and we are playing chess. Now if you wanted to tell me something that I did wrong, why can't you wait until my friend leaves, and then you can cuss me out or kick my ass or whatever. But I think you've gone too far."

"Fuck you, motherfucker, I'm leaving." She turned and started for the door.

"Wait a minute," Billy called out, still in that cool voice. "If you want to leave, why don't you do it right?"

He got up and went over to the wall and took down the picture of Tina in the role of Antigone, where she had a toga draped over her shoulder in the picture.

He took it down.

"This is the only thing you've given me in all the time we've been together."

He threw it across the room, and the glass shattered at her feet.

"Take that with you, if you want to leave," he said calmly, sitting back down in front of the chess game.

At this point I thought, This is a trick! a joke they both are playing on me! Any minute they'll turn to me and say, Ha! We caught you, didn't we? Knowing Billy's reputation as a prankster and remembering Dionysus as Euripides portrayed him (as a god who maliciously tricked mortals who didn't honor him by getting drunk and dressing up like a woman and worshiping him), I pictured some weird put-on. But if this was what was happening, they deserved the Academy Award for their acting, so convincing it was.

Tina picked the picture up and started for the door, but Billy picked up a photo on the desk.

"Oh, I forgot something." He threw it against the wall. "Take all the shit you gave me, okay. And get out of my life. I don't love you anymore. Do you understand?"

Tina stood there looking at him, her face red and streaked with tears and anger.

"You've fucked up our chess game, you've poured cookies all over my head. Look, Tina, you don't have to abuse me like that. I know how to abuse Billy. I'm very good at self-abuse. After all, I've done that all my life: Abuse myself."

"Look," Billy said, taking up a pencil can and knocking it against his head. "Look, I'm very good at self-abuse!"

Is this not comedy? I thought. I was dying with laughter but I held it in.

"Bastard!" Tina spat at him and went out the door again.

He turned his attention back to the chess board.

All the pieces had been covered with cookies. I started to pick the pieces of crumbs away from the pieces.

"Just look at that? What kind of person would do that?" he asked me.

"I think I should be leaving," I said.

"Leaving? Why? Because she's acting a fool? No, man, you're my friend. I want you to stay. I need for you to stay, Jonah. This bitch is trying to make me hit her. If I hit her the police will be up here in a minute. I don't want that. If the police come up here I'm going to the penitentiary. She knows this. She is trying to—"

Tina reappeared in the door.

Both Billy and I sat silent and watched her. She came across the room and over to us and swept the chess pieces off the board.

"Bastard!" she announced and started back for the door.

"No. Tina, I've had it with you. You took your clothes off in front of my son. My son came to me and he was crying and I said what's wrong but he wouldn't say anything. I made him tell me, Tina. He said you came out of your bedroom naked. You showed my son your pussy, woman."

"And you beat my face in," Tina accused him right in front of me.

"And you spit in my face and called me a nigger!" he shot back.

She came back. "And you beat me up."

"Well, just leave. I told you to leave. Now leave. I've done all I could for you, just leave. You would never treat Warren Beatty like you treated me. Or any of those other white boys you star-fucked."

He turned to me.

"Man, can you imagine her doing that to Warren Beatty?"

I said, "No!"

"That's right, because she doesn't respect me. I'm still a nigger to her. She told me so herself."

"No!" I replied incredulously—as I figured my part called for. I was like some weird straight man. "She called you a what? Where?"

"We were in Africa. I told her, I said, 'Tina, look up at the sky.' They got some skies in Africa that are a motherfucker, man! The stars glitter like diamonds on a piece of black velvet. I said, 'Look up at the sky,' I said. 'Do you see any star up there called nigger?' She got sassy on me and said, 'Yeah, there's one!' Do you think she do that to any of those white boys she fucked?"

In spite of all this—or perhaps because of it—Billy insisted on a drink. Trailing along behind him, I followed my host into the kitchen, where he took down from the cabinet a fifth of Stolichnaya vodka. No sooner had he poured us out a good portion in two tumblers than Tina appeared in the doorway. This time she was carrying a broom. With the broom as a weapon, she attacked us. We fell backwards through the dining room, falling and holding onto the vodka; we managed to make it back to the bedroom, where Billy locked the door.

"That bitch was trying to kill us." He laughed. "But we were trying to be cool, huh? Look," he said as if he'd thought my thoughts, "you're still holding your glass! Ha, ha, ha!" He laughed in that particular way he has. "You didn't even spill a drop!"

He was so busy telling me about my glass that he had forgotten his. He was holding his high over his head like Charlie Chaplin did in one of his films, as the waiter with the precariously balanced tray that keeps its equilibrium despite a knock-down-and-drag-out fight that takes place in the saloon.

"You know we some funny motherfuckers," he said, laughing deep inside his chest. "We try to be cool out here in Hollywood, but where we come from we've been hurt and abused, man. We never had a lot of liquor to spill. If we'd been white boys, we would've dropped the glasses and poured the liquor out. But we niggers, although we don't want to be, but way down deep in our souls we are still niggers who can't afford to spill the vodka. If Tina had a gun and had shot and killed us, we would've fell over each other and died, but when the undertaker came to get our dead asses, he'd have to take the vodka glasses out of our hands and pour the vodka out because there'd still be vodka in them. And some other nigger assistant undertaker would sneak up to our bodies when the white undertaker wasn't looking and steal that vodka. *That's good vodka,*' the nigger'd say. *'Gonna take that vodka home! Sheet, them niggers dead, they don't know no difference.'*"

Billy was up, faking the part of the white undertaker, the black assistant undertaker, and the two stiffs (us with the vodka glasses) all at once. "'Mister White Man, hehehe, you think we oughta take dese glasses outa these niggers' hands?' 'Naw, fool, I believe these boys' family gonna pay fo' the vodka, niggers gonna die with liquor on they bref!'"

I laughed hard, feeling relief briefly from the insistent, pounding, urgent knocking at the door. Apparently she'd taken off her shoe and was applying the heel of it to the wooden door. But Billy went on talking as if nobody was there, and I went on pretending that I didn't hear anybody either. His genius for making humor out of any situation, I learned that night, was his protection against hurt; it was his camouflage technique, the yellow and black spots on the butterfly's back that allows him to blend into the yellow leaves and black tree bark and prevents the predator from seeing him and devouring him in one hysterical gulp. His humor was his mimicking device, his cloud of black ink that the octopus uses to hide behind when an enemy attacks.

"Who is Randell?" I finally had the nerve to say.

"Randell?" he said, and his face lighted up. "That's a motherfucking genius. A literary genius. We would be fucking some bitches together and you know what he'd do, he'd turned over to me and say I was 'literary.' I'd say, 'What's literary about fucking a bitch?' and he'd say, 'You do it metaphorically.'"

"Was he there that night at the Hollywood Bowl?" I asked. I didn't have the nerve to ask him directly about the famous night when he told the gay community to kiss his rich, happy, black ass. I just didn't have the nerve and also I suppose I realized that there was really nothing he could say about it that he hadn't said on the stage that night.

"Was Randell there?" he asked himself. "Yes, Randell was there. He was there, now that I remember. He goes everywhere, man. He is the freest person I know. He never has any money but he just goes where he wants. He has curiosity. Real curiosity. I have that too. When I'm somewhere he just shows up. I was in Cannes at the Film Festival when my first big film came out and I got this note in my box one afternoon and the note said, *You better get out of France fucking our white women,* and I looked at the note and I said to myself, Who would send me a note like this? And I looked at the note again and at the bottom of it was this signature, *KKK,* and I said to myself, If this is not a joke played on me by Randell then my ass is in real trouble! I said this to myself as a prayer because at the time, man, I believed that the Ku Klux Klan had written it; it was the sort of prayer you sent up if you're Daniel in the lion's den, because I knew that Randell was still in Berkeley. The last time I saw him he was in Berkeley enjoying the royalties he made on his novel. *How could he get to Cannes and how did he know that I was here?* It turned out that the motherfucker knocked on my door later that night, and, man, was I glad to see him! When you leave America you're, at first, glad to be away from niggers, but then the first one you see, especially if he's a friend, you jump pass yourself with excitement. Man, me and Randell got some of the finest bitches in Cannes. He didn't have a nickel, he'd been living in Paris, man, with all the famous writers like James Jones, Irwin Shaw, James Baldwin, Carlos Fuentes, and the nigger didn't have a French franc on him, I'm not kidding—"

Boom! Boom! Boom! Tina was knocking on the door with something else. We couldn't figure out what it was she was knocking with this time but Billy, momentarily forgetting that he was supposed to be ignoring her ass, tilted his head back into a listening stance like the famous doe deer in one of his imitations, and I saw the origin of the doe deer imitation then, saw his curiosity he so much admired in his friend Randell.

Boom! Boom! Boom!—and Billy looked at me with an expression on his face that said, What the fuck is she hitting the door with now? But he silently let the question drop and took another hit of the coke and passed it to me and I took a hit.

"—Nigger was broker than a motherfucker, but it never bothered him any. He'd be talking shit just like he had a pocketful of money. Anyway, I gave him a whole handful of French money because French money don't look like real money, you know what I'm talking about? It's like play money. Big, oversized money, with no green in it. Who ever seen money with no green in it? This French money had a picture of a Frenchman on it, de Gaulle or one of them motherfuckers, and it was like a painting. So I gave half of what I had to Randell. He told me later that I gave him two thousand dollars! And I didn't know it. He told me that about two years later. And I told him—"

Boom! Boom! Krack! Now she had picked up something else to hit it with. Billy looked at the door again.

"If I opened that door—" He cut himself off. "That door is the door to the penitentiary."

I looked at the wooden door, at the fashionable woodwork around the handle, at the door of a famous rich superstar. How did he mean that? Suddenly I saw what he meant and the wooden door dissolved into the gray iron bars of a jail cell. *I am tired of beating her, man, I don't love her anymore, I don't want to beat her anymore, she wants me to beat her!* I thought of Tina as a vampire, a ghoulish vampire back from the dead, straight out of Edgar Allan Poe, beating at the door, I thought of the image of the door being knocked down and Tina, like Ligeia, appearing before us with the greenish, rotten flesh falling from her face, from her skull, rats and worms crawling out of her skin, back from the—fresh from the grave.

Krack! Krack! Krack!

"What about the Hollywood Bowl?" I started again. "I mean, Randell was there—"

Krack! Krack! Krack!

Tina's knocking was gathering momentum now.

"Yeah, Randell was there," Billy said. "Sent me this telegram. I'll never forget that. 'Cause I came home, I was scared a little. When they interviewed me in the gay press later, I said I wasn't scared. But I was scared. I was scared about what I'd done but I was so happy because I knew I'd done the right thing, I'd said what was in my heart. Somebody asked me, said, 'Do you fear your career is over?" and I said—I don't know what I said, but what I thought was this: 'If my career is over because I said what was in my heart, then I didn't have a career to start with. So fuck it!'"

We both laughed, genuinely, like friends, like brothers, and I felt very close to him then, and it was not with an effort, or pretext, or pretense that I ignored Tina's knocking at the door.

"Randell," he said, lighting a cigarette. I took one too. "Randell sent me a telegram. It said, CLASSIC JUVENAL SATIRE. But I was too ignorant to ask him who Juvenal was. Who is this motherfucker called Juvenal?"

"He was a writer that lived in Rome around the time of one of those evil emperors."

"Oh?" he answered and stretched and yawned with boredom.

Krack! Krack! Krack!

Billy said, "I had a dream about Tina. In this dream she's all in white and leads me with a blindfold on into hell. I take off the blindfold and see I'm in hell. I say to her, 'Why did you lead me here. I've been in hell before, and I'm used to it. I expected better from you—'"

"That was Dante's trip," I said. "Beatrice leads Dante out of hell."

"Dante?"

"The thirteenth-century poet. He wrote his dream up as a poem called the *Divine Comedy* in three parts. He had this broad, Beatrice, that led him around through places, except he wasn't blind."

"But a fool like me?"

"Yeah."

"Dante, eh? Well, I had the same dream. I'm going to use it in my movie, too."

He got up and went to the door, put his ear to it quietly.

"I think she's gone," he said, opening it just a little.

I expected to see Tina dead at the door from having committed suicide. But when he opened it she wasn't even there.

"Let's take a walk," he said.

As we came down the long hallway, Billy peeped into one of the rooms, then another.

He came to one door that was half closed, pushed the door open quietly, and walked in. He turned and beckoned silently for me to come see. I went over to the door and looked in. It was a bedroom and on the bed was Tina. What she'd done, she'd curled up in the bed without taking her clothes off. Her face was as quiet and calm and as beautiful as a sleeping child.

Billy reached down and kissed her on the cheek so softly that she didn't wake up. In her clenched hands was the Sukuma African sculpture she had been using to bang against the door with. Now we knew what she had been using.

We walked out by the swimming pool and he looked over at the tennis court. (I remember Randell telling me how avid a tennis player Billy was and how he was impressed by anybody who could beat him and since almost anybody could beat him he was impressed a lot. In fact, Randell said, one of the sure ways that white boys got to Billy was to beat him at a game of tennis.) As we passed it, Billy said, "I don't know why I built that tennis court. I can't stand the game now."

We walked around the swimming pool. The morning light was beginning to glow, a morning bird chirped, a rooster crowed.

Billy looked at his watch. "That rooster," he said laughing, "is never on time."

I felt very close to him now, and I'd lost a lot of my overearnestness.

"Let's talk about our business," he said. "I want you to warm them up for me tomorrow night, because you have a natural style. Don't worry about not being funny, just be natural and don't get pretentious. It's okay if you're not funny. I believe you understand what I mean by that. If you can master this about yourself you'll be the funniest person in this business. Except me."

We laughed.

"All the kidding aside," he said, "I need you for this. You have a voice in what you say to an audience that takes them into your confidence and speaks the truth. I need you to warm them up for me. Can I count on you?"

"Yes," I said.

"Meeting closed," he said and put something in my hand.

"I lost the game." He laughed. "I had to forfeit it."

We walked on toward my car. "Do you realize we stayed up all night?" I asked.

As a reply he suddenly laughed.

"I'm laughing at myself," he said. "I'm trying to figure out how to clean up the fact that you've seen my old lady pour cookies on my head."

We both laughed.

"You don't have to explain it to me," I said, like a man.

And he treated me like a man, too.

"I've been wondering how I was going to explain to you, how I could say what I said to her and then say I loved her, but I see I don't need to explain it to you."

He looked into my eyes and gave me a hug.

"We're friends now," he said.

"I know," I said. "Good morning."

"Good morning to you, Jonah."

I got in the car and pulled out of the yard. He was going into the house.

He waved, I waved, and I went out of the gate.

The world was just waking up when I pulled out of the gate and onto the highway. A blueness was giving way to a light gray haze. A few more cars hit the road carrying people to work. I felt exhilarated, not tired. Looking back on this now, I realize that that evening was the first time I'd laughed in a long time. True, I had laughed at my friend's misfortune, but I had laughed at it with my friend; and he had laughed at my misfortune with me. What this meant for me was that I was developing my sense of humor; what it meant for my friend was that he was learning to master his.

And what a guy that Billy was! How he could abuse himself. I laughed, thinking about him hitting himself across the head with that can. And the way he so sincerely cast himself as more sinned against than sinning! And Tina? What an actress! But who could write a script big enough for the two of them? Only God, probably.

And when Billy told me comedy was based on real trouble and tragedy, he wasn't kidding! And me! What an impostor! But what could I do: I loved him but was afraid of her. He was right about her, she would make him hurt her, but she knew that the greatest damage he could do to her would be what he would do to himself.

It was from this evening that I began to develop a sense of what it meant to be funny.

Cry About a Nickel

PERCIVAL EVERETT

Clouds hung like webs in the firs and a fine mist wet the air: Blackberry thickets sprawled wide and high, most of the berries withered past picking. Back home, on an autumn morning like this, we might be sharpening knives and boiling water to butcher a hog. But here I was in the wet Cascades. I pulled my pickup to the side of the road and got out. I looked down the steep slope at the Clackamas River tumbling at a good clip over and around rocks. I made my way down a path to the bank and found it littered with fishermen, shoulder to shoulder, casting lures and dragging them past a great many large fish just sitting in a pool as if parked in a lot. Being sincerely ignorant I figured I was running little risk of sounding so when I asked the man nearest me—

"What kind of fish are those?"

The man let his eyes find me slowly and his smile was a few beats behind. "Why, they're steelhead."

"They don't seem to be very interested," I said.

The man turned back to his line and said nothing.

I watched a bit longer, then climbed back to the road. In South Carolina fishing was done quietly, in private, for creatures hidden from view. At least a man could say, "Aw, there ain't no fish here." But this seemed like premeditated self-humiliation.

A boy at the house told me I'd find his father in one of the stables. I wandered into the near one, didn't see him, but I caught a mare nosing around her hock. I found a halter on a nail outside her stall and put it on her, tied her head up.

"What're you doing there?" a man yelled at me.

"She was nosin' around her hock and I saw it was capped and had ointment on it. I raised her head up so she wouldn't burn her nose."

"What do you know about capped hocks? Who are you?"

"Are you Mr. Davis?"

"Yeah. I'm waitin'."

"Name's Cooper. I heard you had a job open."

"What do you know about horses?"

"I know enough to tie a horse's head up when I'm trying to blister her."

"Where're you from?"

"Carolina."

"North?"

"No, the good one."

Davis rubbed his jaw and studied the mare. "We don't get many blacks around here."

"The horse said the same thing."

"Five hundred a month. Includes a two-room trailer and utilities."

Davis had twenty-three horses, most pretty good, and a lot of land. He rented rides to hunters and to anybody who just wanted to get wet in the woods.

The first thing was to clean out the medicine chest. The box was full of all sorts of old salves and liniments and I just had to say aloud to myself, "Pathetic."

Davis had stepped into the tack room without me noticing. "What's pathetic?" he asked.

I sat there on the floor, thinking oh no, but I couldn't back off. "All this stuff," I said. "Better to have nothing than all this useless trash."

He didn't like this. "What's wrong with it?"

I looked in the box. "Well, sir, I appreciate the fact that this thermometer is fairly clean, but better to have a roll of string in the chest than keep this crap-crusted one on all the time. This is ugly."

"So, you've got a weak stomach."

I shook my head. "You've got ointments in here twenty years old. Why don't you grab the good stuff for me. Where's the colic relief? You've got three bottles of Bluestone and they're all empty."

He didn't look directly at me, just sort of flipped me a glance. "Fix it," he said and left.

There were no crossties, so I had to set up some for grooming. I was currycombing a tall stallion when Davis's son came into the stable.

"Hey, Joe," the kid said.

"Charlie."

"Mind if I help?"

I looked at the teenager. It was really a question. As a boy, I would have been required to work the place. "I don't know," I said. "Your father might think I'm not earning my pay. Don't you have other chores?"

"No."

I didn't understand this at all. I looked around. "I tell you what. You comb out the hindquarters on Nib here and then dandy-brush his head. I'm gonna shovel out his stall real quick."

The boy took the comb, stood behind the horse, and began stroking.

"No," I said and I pulled him away. "Stand up here next to the shoulder, put your arm over his back, and do it like that. So, he won't kick the tar out of you."

Charlie laughed nervously and began working again. I shoveled at the stall and watched him. He was a nice boy. I couldn't tell if he was bright or not, he was so nervous. I stopped and listened to the rain on the roof.

"Does it ever stop raining?" I asked.

"One day last year."

I laughed, but he just stared at me. Then I thought he wasn't joking. "You're not saying—" Before I finished he was smiling.

"How'd you learn about horses?" he asked.

"Grew up with 'em. You don't spend much time with the animals?"

"Not really."

"People say that horses are stupid." I fanned some hay out of my face. "And they're right, you know. But at least it's something you can count on."

Then Davis showed up. "Charles."

The boy snapped to attention away from the horse and, glancing at the curry-comb in his hand, threw it down. "I asked Joe if I could help, Daddy."

"Get in the house."

The boy ran from the stable.

"He's a good boy," I said.

Davis picked up the comb and studied it. "I'd appreciate it if from now on you just sent him back to the house."

"All right." I leaned the pitchfork against the wall and moved to take the horse from the crossties. "He's got a bunch of chores in there to take care of, does he? Homework and stuff?"

"Yeah."

Davis looked around at the stable and at the horses, at the stallion in front of him. "The other stables look this good?"

"Gettin' there."

It was a full-time job, all right, and I went to bed sore every night. Finally, I took a weekend off and drove the hour to Portland. I got a hotel room downtown on Saturday and tried to figure out what I was going to do all day. I went to the zoo and a movie, ate at a restaurant, watched bizarrely made-up kids at Pioneer Square, saw another movie, shot pool at a tavern, and went to bed. I dreamed about women. You work ranches and you talk about women and you talk about going to town to get yourself a woman, but you end up watching movies in dark rooms and shooting pool with men.

After a big breakfast at the hotel restaurant, I headed back to the ranch. The weather in Portland had been nice and, to my surprise, the sun was out all during my drive home. I parked by my trailer. Charlie was splitting wood over beside the house. Seeing him doing this made me feel good. I went inside and stowed my gear. There was a knock.

"Come," I said.

Davis came in. He had a bottle with him and a couple of glasses. "How was your trip?"

"Oh, it was a trip."

"Mind if I sit?"

I nodded that he was welcome and watched him fill the glasses. "You like bourbon?"

"You bet."

"Here you go." He handed the drink over.

I took it and sat with him at the table. He knocked his back and I followed suit. He poured another round.

He cleared his throat and focused on me. He had already had a few. "You're all right, Cooper." He leaned back. "Naw, I mean it." He sipped from his glass. "You want to hear how I lost my wife?"

I didn't say anything. I just looked at him.

"Killed herself."

I had a headache.

"Know what she died of?"

"A sudden?"

He frowned off my joke. "She took pills. She was an alcoholic and a diabetic and a Catholic. All three, any one of which is fatal alone."

"I'm sorry," I said.

He drank more. "They said she was manic, too." He looked out the window at the sky which was growing overcast. "Charles is a good boy."

"He's quiet."

"That's my fault, I guess."

"That's not a problem."

"He's small, you know."

I just looked at him.

"I don't have a lot of patience. I don't have a lot of friends either. I guess the two go together."

"I reckon."

"Tell me something, Cooper. What do you think of a man who can't talk to his kid?"

I swirled my whiskey in the glass and held his eyes.

"I've got a temper. A bad one."

I nodded.

"You want to hear what happened at Charlie's school last year?"

"To tell the truth, no, I don't."

Davis pulled a pack of cigarettes from his shirt pocket and fumbled his way through lighting one, blew out a cloud of blue smoke and coughed. He stood and went to the window, watched as his son split wood. "Look at him. He could do that all day. He's small, though."

I polished off my drink.

"You think I'm crazy."

I shook my head. "No, I don't."

"Well, I ain't crazy. He ain't right." He was hot and I was beginning to think he *was* touched. "Don't tell me how to run things!"

"Sure thing."

I didn't know what he was talking about.

He snatched up his bottle and walked out.

I fell on my bunk and looked at the ceiling. I wanted to pack up and leave, but I needed the job and I wasn't the sort to leave a man in a lurch. He had a mare ready to drop and a couple of horses with thrush real bad. I didn't like what I had seen in Davis's eyes. He was slow-boiling and soon there wouldn't be anything left to scorch but the pot.

I fixed some grits and scrambled eggs and sausages and sat down to dinner by myself. An evening rain came and went and I could see the fuzzy glow of the moon behind the clouds. I felt bad for little Charlie. Funny, I hadn't thought of him as small before, but he was. I felt sorry for him and I didn't know why. I wasn't about to get involved, though. My mother had a number of hobbies, but raising fools wasn't one of them.

A couple of days later, four fellows rented horses and went into the hills for elk. I knew when they rode out that all they were going to get up there was drunk. They didn't deserve the weather that day. It was almost hot when they came back. I was trimming hooves. Charlie was in the stable with the pregnant mare.

"Woowee," said one man, "what a day."

"That was fun," said another, groaning and trying to work a kink out of his back as he climbed down. "That was more fun than huntin' coons."

They all dismounted and I took the horses. They'd ridden the animals hard right up to the end and they were sweating like crazy.

I called Charlie over. "Take these horses out and walk 'em around, get 'em cool." As he stepped away, I yelled for him to loosen the girths. His dad had let up a little and he was freer to hang about and help.

The men lined up along the fence and watched Charlie in the corral.

"Ain't he pretty?" I heard one of the men say. I thought he was talking about a horse, but another spoke up.

"Hey, I heard about that locker-room business," he said.

"Oh, this was the boy?"

"Yeah."

I stepped out and saw that Charlie was ignoring them pretty good. They said a few more things and I got fed up, started toward them.

"Looks like we got the nigger riled," one said.

I stopped at the crack of a rifle shot. Davis was out of his house and just yards from the corral.

"You boys paid?" Davis asked.

The leader, more or less, put his hands up and laughed a little. "Yeah, we paid."

"Then get along."

"Okay, Davis. We'll get along. Nice boy you got there." The man chuckled again. They got into their car and left.

Davis watched them roll away. "Charles," he said. "Go on inside."

I caught Davis by the arm. "Hey, just let him forget about it."

He pulled away, didn't even look at me.

I watched him disappear into the house. Things were becoming a little more clear. More reason to ignore it. My motto: Avoid shit.

It was raining real good when I came back from the grocery store. As I swept around the yard I saw Charlie standing by the tree behind the house. I parked at the trailer, got out of my truck, and went inside for lunch. I finished my coffee and shivered against the chill in the air. Outside, I found it warmer than in the trailer. I started to go check the horses when I noticed that Charlie was still standing by that tree. I went to him. At twenty yards I could see that he was tied to it.

"What's the story?" I asked, looking around.

The boy just cried and I was pretty damn close to it myself. Rain dripped from his hair and ran down his face.

"Your father do this?" I was looking at the house, but I knew Charlie was nodding. "Why? Did he say why?" I was hesitant about untying him. I thought Davis had flipped and might be waiting at a window to blow my head off. I shouted as I reached for the rope. "Davis! I'm untying the boy! Okay!" I undid the knots and led the kid back to the house.

Davis was sitting in a chair in front of the fireplace. He looked really spaced out. "Hey, Davis, you all right?"

He said nothing.

"I brought Charlie inside here."

"I heard you." He leaned forward and poked at the burning logs. "He wouldn't tell me who they were."

"He's a strong boy," I said.

"You could call it that." He sat back again. "Earl Pryor has a mare ready, wants to breed her with Nib. Be over tomorrow."

"I'll have him ready. What time?"

"Said eight-thirty. Maybe I should have Charlie watch."

"For the love of God, Davis, stop and think. Listen to yourself. Charlie's a good kid who got beat up—think of it like that. It's none of my business, but—"

Davis cut me off. He stood and faced me. "You're right. It's none of your business and you don't know what the hell you're talking about."

"Charlie didn't do anything."

"Pack up, drifter."

I looked at him for a second, but I'd heard him right "Okay. Fine. But listen up, you're gonna drive that boy away and for no good reason."

But he wasn't listening. He was at his desk. "I'm paying you for this month and next. Fair enough?"

I looked across the room at Charlie. He had settled on the sofa and was looking out the window. Davis waved the check in front of me. I wanted to tell him what he could do with his goddamn money, but I didn't. I didn't look at his face. I just took the check, went to the trailer, and started packing.

I kept waiting for a knock on the door; Charlie coming to say goodbye or Davis coming to tell me to have that stallion ready in the morning. But there was no knock. I climbed into my pickup and drove away.

Surfiction

JOHN EDGAR WIDEMAN

Among my notes on the first section of Charles Chesnutt's *Deep Sleeper* there are these remarks:

> Not reality but a culturally learned code—that is, out of the infinite number of ways one might apprehend, be conscious, be aware, a certain arbitrary pattern or finite set of indicators is sanctioned and over time becomes identical with reality. The signifier becomes the signified. For Chesnutt's contemporaries reality was *I* (eye) centered, the relationship between man and nature disjunctive rather than organic, time was chronological, linear, measured by man-made units—minutes, hours, days, months, etc. To capture this reality was then a rather mechanical procedure—a voice at the center of the story would begin to unravel reality: a catalog of sensuous detail, with the visual dominant, to indicate nature, *out there* in the form of clouds, birdsong, etc. A classical painting rendered according to the laws of perspective, the convention of the window frame through which the passive spectator observes. The voice gains its authority because it is literate, educated, perceptive, because it has aligned itself correctly with the frame, because it drops the cues, or elements of the code, methodically. The voice is reductive, as any code ultimately is; an implicit reinforcement occurs as the text elaborates itself through the voice: the voice gains authority because things are in order, the order gains authority because it is established by a voice we trust. For example the opening lines of *Deep Sleeper* . . .

> It was four o'clock on Sunday afternoon, in the month of July. The air had been hot and sultry, but a light, cool breeze had sprung up; and occasional cirrus clouds overspread the sun, and for a while subdued his fierceness. We were all out on the piazza—as the coolest place we could find—my wife, my sister-in-law and I. The only sounds that broke the Sabbath stillness were the hum of an occasional vagrant bumblebee, or the fragmentary song of a mockingbird in a neighboring elm . . .

Rereading, I realize my *remarks* are a pastiche of received opinions from Barthes, certain cultural anthropologists and linguistically oriented critics and Russian formalists, and if I am beginning a story rather than an essay, the whole stew suggests the preoccupations of Borges or perhaps a footnote in Barthelme. Already I have managed to embed several texts within other texts, already a rather unstable mix of genres and disciplines and literary allusion. Perhaps for all of this, already a grim exhaustion of energy and possibility, readers fall away as if each word is a well-aimed bullet.

More Chesnutt. This time from the text of the story, a passage unremarked upon except that in the margin of the Xeroxed copy of the story I am copying this passage from, several penciled comments appear. I'll reproduce the entire discussion.

Latin: secundus-tertius-quartus-quintus.

"Tom's gran'daddy wuz name' Skundus," he began. "He had a brudder name' Tushus en' ernudder name' Squinchus." The old man paused a moment and gave his leg another hitch.

"drawing out Negroes"—custom in old south, new north, a constant in America. Ignorance of one kind delighting ignorance of another. Mask to mask. The real joke.

My sister-in-law was shaking with laughter. "What remarkable names!" she exclaimed. "Where in the world did they get them?"

Naming: plantation owner usurps privilege of family. Logos. Word made flesh. Power. Slaves named in order of appearance. Language masks joke. Latin opaque to blacks.

Note: last laugh. Blacks (mis)pronounce secundus. Secundus = Skundus. Black speech takes over—opaque to white—subverts original purpose of name. Language (black) makes joke. Skundus has new identity.

"Dem names wuz gun ter 'em by ole Marse Dugal' McAdoo, w'at I use' ter b'long ter, en' dey use' ter b'long ter. Marse Dugal' named all de babies w'at wuz bawn on de plantation. Dese young un's mammy wanted ter call 'em sump'n plain en' simple, like *Rastus* er *Caesar* er *George Wash'n'ton,* but ole Marse say no, he want all de niggers on his place ter hab diffe'nt names, so he kin tell 'em apart. He'd done use' up all de common names, so he had ter take sump'n else. Dem names he gun Skundus en' his brudders is Hebrew names en' wuz tuk out'n de Bible."

I distinguish remarks from footnotes. Footnotes clarify specifics; they answer simple questions. You can always tell from a good footnote the question which it is answering. For instance: *The Short Fiction of Charles W. Chesnutt,* edited by Sylvia Lyons Render (Washington, D.C.: Howard University Press, 1974), 47. Clearly someone wants to know, Where did this come from? How might I find it? Tell me where to look. OK. Whereas remarks, at least my remarks, the ones I take the trouble to write out in my journal,* which is where the first long cogitation appears/appeared [the ambiguity here is not intentional but situational, not imposed for irony's sake but necessary because the first long cogitation—*my remark*—being referred to both *appears* in the sense that every time I open my journal, as I did a

---

Journal unpaginated. In progress. Unpublished. Many hands.

few moments ago, as I am doing NOW to check for myself and to exemplify for you the accuracy of my statement—the remark *appears* as it does/did just now. (Now?) But the remark (original), if we switch to a different order of time, treating the text diachronically rather than paradigmatically, the remark *appeared;* which poses another paradox. How language or words are both themselves and *Others,* but not always. Because the negation implied by *appearance,* the so-called "shadow within the rock," is *disappearance.* The reader correctly anticipates such an antiphony or absence suggesting presence (shadow play) between the text as realized and the text as shadow of its act. The dark side paradoxically is the absence, the nullity, the white space on the white page between the white words not stated but implied. Forever], are more complicated.

The story, then, having escaped the brackets, can proceed. In this story, *Mine,* in which Chesnutt replies to Chesnutt, remarks, comments, asides, allusions, foot-notes, quotes from Chesnutt have so far played a disproportionate role, and if this sentence is any indication, continue to play a grotesquely unbalanced role, will roll on.

It is four o'clock on Sunday afternoon, in the month of July. The air has been hot and sultry, but a light, cool breeze has sprung up; and occasional cirrus clouds (?) overspread the sun, and for a while subdue his fierceness. We were all out on the piazza (stoop?)—as the coolest place we could find—my wife, my sister-in-law and I. The only sounds that break the Sabbath stillness are the hum of an occasional bumblebee, or the fragmentary song of a mockingbird in a neighboring elm . . .

The reader should know now by certain unmistakable signs (codes) that a story is beginning. The stillness, the quiet of the afternoon tells us something is going to happen, that an event more dramatic than birdsong will rupture the static tableau. We expect, we know a payoff is forthcoming. We know this because we are put into the passive posture of readers or listeners (consumers) by the narra-tive unraveling of a reality which, because it is unfolding in time, slowly begins to take up our time and thus is obliged to give us something in return; the story enacts word by word, sentence by sentence in *real* time. Its moments will pass and our moments will pass simultaneously, hand in glove if you will. The literary, storytelling convention exacts this kind of relaxation or compliance or collaboration (con-spiracy). Sentences slowly fade in, substituting fictive sensations for those which normally constitute our awareness. The shift into the fictional world is made easier because the conventions by which we identify the real world are conventions shared with and often learned from our experience with fictive reality. What we are accus-tomed to acknowledging as awareness is actually a culturally learned, contingent condensation of many potential awarenesses. In this culture—American, Western, twentieth-century—an awareness that is eye centered, disjunctive as opposed to organic, that responds to clock time, calendar time more than biological cycles or seasons, that assumes nature is external, acting on us rather than through us, that tames space by manmade structures and with the *I* as center defines other people and other things by the nature of their relationship to the *I* rather than by the independent integrity of the order they may represent.

An immanent experience is being prepared for, is being framed. The experience will be real because the narrator produces his narration from the same set of conventions by which we commonly detect reality—dates, buildings, relatives, the noises of nature.

All goes swimmingly until a voice from the watermelon patch intrudes. Recall the dialect reproduced above. Recall Kilroy's phallic nose. Recall Earl and Cornbread, graffiti artists, their spray-paint cans notorious from one end of the metropolis to the other—from Society Hill to the Jungle, nothing safe from them and the artists uncatchable until hubris leads them to attempt the gleaming virgin flanks of a 747 parked on runway N-16 at the Philadelphia International Airport. Recall your own reflection in the fun house mirror and the moment of doubt when you turn away and it turns away and you lose sight of it and it naturally enough loses sight of you and you wonder where it's going and where you're going and the wrinkly reflecting plate still is laughing behind your back at someone.

The reader here pauses

Picks up in mid-

stream a totally irrelevant conversation:
. . . by accident twenty-seven double-
columned pages by accident?

I mean it started that way

started yeah I can see starting curiosity
whatever staring over somebody's shoulder or a letter maybe you think yours till
you see not meant for you at all

I'm not trying to excuse just understand
it was not premeditated your journal is
your journal that's not why I mean I
didn't forget your privacy or lose respect
on purpose
    it was just there and, well we sel-
dom talk and I was desperate we haven't
been going too well for a long time

and getting worse getting finished when
shit like this comes down

I wanted to stop but I needed something from you more than you've been
giving so when I saw it there I picked it
up you understand not to read but because it was you you and holding it was
all a part of you

you're breaking my heart

please don't dismiss

dismiss dismiss what I won't dismiss
your prying how you defiled how you
took advantage

don't try to make me a criminal the guilt
I feel it I know right from wrong and
accept whatever you need to lay on me
but I had to do it I was desperate for
something, anything, even if the cost

was rifling my personal life searching
through my guts for ammunition and
did you get any did you learn anything
you can use on me Shit I can't even remember the whole thing is a jumble I'm
blocking it all out my own journal and I
can't remember a word because it's not
mine anymore

I'm sorry I knew I shouldn't as soon as
I opened it I flashed on the Bergman
movie the one where she reads his diary
I flashed on how underhanded how evil
a thing she was doing but I couldn't
stop

A melodrama a god damned Swedish
subtitled melodrama you're going to
turn it around aren't you make it into

The reader can replay the tape at leisure. Can amplify or expand. There is
plenty of blank space on the pages. A sin really given the scarcity of trees, the
rapaciousness of paper companies in the forests which remain. The canny reader
will not trouble him/herself trying to splice the tape to what came before or after.
Although the canny reader would also be suspicious of the straightforward, absolute denial of relevance dismissing the tape.

Here is the main narrative again. In embryo. A professor of literature at a
university in Wyoming (the only university in Wyoming) by coincidence is teaching
two courses in which are enrolled two students (one in each of the professor's
seminars) who are husband and wife. They both have red hair. The male of the
couple aspires to write novels and is writing fast and furious a chapter a week his
first novel in the professor's creative writing seminar. The other redhead, there
are only two redheads in the two classes, is taking the professor's seminar in Afro-
American literature, one of whose stars is Charlie W. Chesnutt. It has come to the
professor's attention that both husband and wife are inveterate diary keepers, a
trait which like their red hair distinguishes them from the professor's other eigh-

teen students. Something old-fashioned, charming about diaries, about this pair of hip graduate students keeping them. A desire to keep up with his contemporaries (almost wrote *peers* but that gets complicated real quick) leads the professor, who is also a novelist, or as he prefers novelist who is also a professor, occasionally to assemble large piles of novels which he reads with bated breath. The novelist/ professor/reader bates his breath because he has never grown out of the awful habit of feeling praise bestowed on someone else lessens the praise which may find its way to him (he was eldest of five children in a very poor family—not an excuse perhaps an extenuation—never enough to go around breeds a fierce competitiveness and being for four years an only child breeds a selfishness and ego-centeredness that is only exacerbated by the shocking arrival of contenders, rivals, lower than dogshit pretenders to what is by divine right his). So he reads the bait and nearly swoons when the genuinely good appears. The relevance of this to the story is that occasionally the professor reads systematically and because on this occasion he is soon to appear on a panel at a neighboring university (Colorado) discussing *Surfiction* his stack of novels was culled from the latest, most hip, most avant-garde, new *Tel Quel* chic, anti, non-novel bibliographies he could locate. He has determined at least three qualities of these novels. *One*—you can stack ten in the space required for two traditional novels. *Two*—they are *au rebours* the present concern for ecology since they sometimes include as few as no words at all on a page and often no more than seven. *Three*—without authors whose last names begin with B, surfiction might not exist. B for Beckett, Barth, Burroughs, Barthes, Borges, Brautigan, Barthelme . . . (Which list further discloses a startling coincidence or perhaps the making of a scandal—one man working both sides of the Atlantic as a writer and critic explaining and praising his fiction as he creates it: *Barth Barthes Barthelme.*)

The professor's reading of these thin (not necessarily a dig—thin pancakes, watches, women for instance are *à la mode*) novels suggests to him that there may be something to what they think they have their finger on. All he needs then is a local habitation and some names. Hence the redheaded couple. Hence their diaries. Hence the infinite layering of the fiction he will never write (which is the subject of the fiction which he will never write). Boy meets Prof. Prof reads boy's novel. Girl meets Prof. Prof meets girl in boy's novel. Learns her pubic hair is as fiery red as what she wears short and stylish, flouncing just above her shoulders. (Of course it's all fiction. The fiction. The encounters.) What's real is how quickly the layers build, how like a spring snow in Laramie the drifts cover and obscure silently.

Boy keeps diary. Girl meets diary. Girl falls out of love with diary (his), retreats to hers. The suspense builds. Chesnutt is read. A conference with Prof in which she begins analyzing the multilayered short story *Deep Sleeper* but ends in tears reading from a diary (his? hers?). The professor recognizes her sincere compassion for the downtrodden (of which in one of his fictions he is one). He also recognizes a fiction in her husband's fiction (when he undresses her) and reads her diary. Which she has done previously (read her husband's). Forever.

The plot breaks down. It was supposed to break down. The characters disintegrate. Whoever claimed they were whole in the first place? The stability of the narrative voice is displaced into a thousand distracted madmen screaming in the dim corridors of literary history. Whoever insisted it should be more ambitious? The train doesn't stop here. Mistah Kurtz he dead. Godot ain't coming. Ecce Homo. Dat's all, folks. Sadness.

And so it goes.

The Trip Back From Whidbey

WILLIAM HENRY LEWIS

Without bitterness, Maya could remember watching the two on the beach with that dog. She thought of that time as she now sat on the sloop, watching the space of water widen between her and the island. It was a different beach back then, different driftwood, a younger tree line of blue spruce, and thousands of low tides ago. In those long ago mornings she watched Joe and little Terry trudge off through the fog, nettles, and ripening blackberry bluffs. Often she stepped out to the porch an hour later and charted their progress on the beach far below. From way off she could make out their figures, Terry in red galoshes stumbling after Otis, wet already, soon to deposit his canine smell in the pantry for the rest of the week. And Joe, ambling along hundreds of feet behind them, his smooth, deep-brown forehead to the sky. He had smoked pipes back then. When Terry and the dog circled back close enough, sometimes he would try to tackle them both and allow them the fun of barely escaping. Hours later they were back, boots full of water, grinning and tired as they peeked in at her over the sill of the kitchen window.

Otis was always immediately ushered to the back porch, barking for more play and with no ear for the light-hearted scolding she'd give the boys, father and son, for staying out too long. All three must have known she was faking it. By bedtime Joe would be standing on the porch petting Otis and making up excuses as to why Terry would sleep more comfortably with the dog in his room. That silly old brown dog: saliva everywhere, a coat of curious white splotches like he'd stumbled into some house painter's ladder. Laughable, enjoyable animals, the three of them.

Sometimes she thought Joe and Terry had forgotten that she, too, had come to the island for a vacation. Day after day, they'd be out there again, and she would be alone, watching, not even sad, just there, like the novel that stays in the beach bag the whole trip. It was a different beach then.

Now as the sloop headed for the mainland, she was thinking of that beach as she last saw it an hour ago from the water. As the sloop slid away from Whidbey, she hugged herself, remembering. She could hear Joe messing with his thermos.

"Maybe you shouldn't drink quite yet, Joseph." She wasn't looking at him; she focused on their wake. "The whitecaps are high all the way in."

But his hand stayed on the thermos of bourbon. Pressed against the starboard rail, his outline sharp in the gray of a spent sky, he maneuvered the sloop's tiller as an afterthought. *He will be like this all the way into Everett,* she thought, and decided that the nap she wanted would have to wait. She crossed the cockpit and stood next to him for a while, thinking she would be warmer there. Even in summer, these erratic Pacific inlet winds surprised her skin. Wind was insistent, the salty blast of the Puget Sound swirling around them.

Maya remembered another time Joseph and she had been on the sloop weathering the cool wind current that crept around the northeastern tip of Whidbey and picked up speed as it made its brisk race towards the mouth of the Columbia River. Terry had decided to stay on shore, collecting agate, so Maya and Joseph had taken this day sail alone. It was time to turn the sloop back in, but they had half a bottle of wine left and the sun hung above the horizon so brilliantly red that they felt it would be wrong to let it slip into the water unnoticed. Joseph had secured the tiller, taken off his shirt, and held her for a few moments, making her feel almost too warm, deep in her chest and at the edges of her ears. Smiling shyly, saying nothing, he lay her down onto spread quilts and undressed her slowly, exchanging her pullover for the blankets of cool mist that drifted over the sloop. But when he was inside her, she wasn't cold. She took in the silence of the open water, the warmth between their waists and again that fire in her ears. Amidst the lapping of the waves, she felt a thick, full sort of silence, and they warmed each other's faces with their breath, not moving or gyrating, but letting the sway and soft dip of the vessel, adrift on the waves, move them slowly in and out, apart and together. Their hips ground at some moments and, at others, were together, but motionless for long stretches, waiting for the next wave. They stayed like that until dark, and even after they were both tired and had been lulled in and out of sleep by the motion of the waves, she lay under him, warmed by his weight while he caressed her face, singing silly variations of old sailing songs from a cassette that she had bought him as a joke at the ferry port in Everett. On the way in she sat at the prow, giggling like a young girl at the soft whisper and random squeak of his singing voice.

Thinking of that time, she turned to him, offering the brush of her breast against his arm. He remained focused on the motion of the wheel and the thermos in his hand. Still, she tried to hold him.

"Please, Maya." His body braced.

She pulled away, zipped up her jacket to the chin and sat opposite him.

"Why don't you go below and check the bag," he said with a pulling in his voice. "The fur. It might be getting wet."

"I don't think I want to do that right now."

"It shouldn't get wet. The fur will smell."

She didn't answer, but again concentrated on the wake of the sloop, the foam lines quickly being rolled into themselves over autumn-eager Puget Sound waves.

He won't say "Otis," she thought. Otis as a name wouldn't do much good anymore. Otis had become an *it.* His smell would never linger in the pantry of the island house again.

Whidbey Island still was visible, beyond where the wake fanned out, and she convinced herself that she could make out the docks and beach fronts just north of Mukilteo. In and out of coming late-day gray, up and down among the waves, the green head of South Whidbey lulled her into visions of the driftwood in tide pools, agate scattered along the western beaches, salt-frosted evergreens, twisted and old, and a stinging realization that the summer had been cut short.

They had planned this as their last stay on Whidbey. The end of August was looming ahead and they were still recovering from the loss of Terry leaving early for college. She knew that their son's departure had been especially hard on Joseph. Terry left just months after Joseph's company had decided to cut back and had let him go first. She spent many nights since then alternating the direction of her support between her husband and her son, entertaining Joseph in the absence of their only child and reassuring him that the company didn't let him go because he was Black or because he wasn't good. She had held him sometimes as if he were her only child, and each time figured out new ways to say that even good people have bad times.

This was to be the last good summer or perhaps the last *rich* summer. Joseph had been persistent in pointing that out. He figured that his plan for a new job at a community center in Tacoma would not allow room for luxury expenditures, boats, summer homes, and unnatural airs.

Terry seemed to handle well the news of Joseph being let go. He was off to spend the first of his college years, and his parents had done well to save for it. The concern was not his. But Joseph had worried on the late nights of that summer. Waiting for Terry to come home from parties with his prep school friends, he would sit in the den, rubbing Otis' belly, feeling defeated. Where, *why* was Terry going, he would ask Maya, so far from him and breaking away from roots he had worked so hard to cultivate. He'll be Black whether he goes to Stanford, Oxford or Bob Jones University, Maya had told him. He wouldn't get any more aware of himself by living under Joe's arm forever. But she knew that the times father and son had spent together would not wash so easily from Joseph.

This trip to Whidbey had been truly liberating, just as they planned, she thought. Joseph was starting to accept Terry's absence and fall back into his yearning for the beach and the summer cottage. They even joked about the life that they had been living, her teasing him about their vacations being "convenient bourgeois departures" from their true selves. He laughed along with her, but she knew how hard it was for him. It had taken years for him to justify to *himself* a life that allowed things like the cottage on Whidbey Island, even as he was trying to impress upon Terry the danger in attaching too much importance to objects. It was difficult parenting for him. The Blacks Joseph knew—even Blacks he'd never known—just didn't sail off into the Puget Sound to beach houses.

With her acceptance of the cottage on Whidbey as being far from luxurious, but definitely not rustic, she took to playfully baiting him and his modified sensibilities. Joseph was the one who first mentioned the idea of the cottage. For all of his lessons to Terry in the ways of social class and the have-nots of life, the cottage's facilities offered chances for harmless satire for Maya. She had not minded it really, nor had Terry who, in their first summer at Whidbey, was too young to understand what irony was. Through the years Maya became quite accustomed to their accelerated sense of standards.

But that had been some years back and their luxury had become an uncomfortable garment to wear, especially now that she would have to remove it. She tried not to let herself get bitter, now leaving the island and a vacation stolen from her by the death of a dog and Joseph's strange preoccupation with getting it back home.

She looked from the island to the single mast of the sloop, now faded from its original brilliant white. Below it the carelessly stowed jib had been thrown. Gray and like an invalid creature it appeared now, tucked away from those younger years when they first bought the sloop and Terry was too young to be allowed anywhere above deck except between Joseph and the wheel. *We're not even using the wind on the way in,* Maya thought, *not even this last time,* and she felt cheated of that sensation. Seeing the age of the bare mast, how ironic and foolish this garment of luxury seemed to her now.

Sometimes she had to think for a moment to remember her old self, her legs still a soft, smooth brown, taut and unversed in the ways of a wet deck dancing with the Puget Sound currents. She stared at the barren mast and laughed quietly. She was remembering a dirty joke Terry made about his dating problems as he leaned against the mast a few years back during his confused summer of sixteen. Then, too, it was tall and bare, but less worn and, evidently by its presence and place in time, more humorous. She remembered how Joseph had laughed, giggling with his son, more as a good friend than a father. She allowed herself a soft, tickled laughter.

"You say something, Maya?"

"No, just remembering something." But she could see the inappropriateness of this. It would not help matters. Laughing. Or remembering. Earlier that summer, she had tried humor to lighten the preparation for how their life would be changing. Shed tried jokes about eating rice every night and having unframed pictures of the sailboat they *used* to have taped to their small economy refrigerator.

But Joseph, despite her kidding, held fast to his social commitment. He felt empowered in letting go of this romance of things to return to a world, his world, of serving necessity in people's lives more so than want in his own. She remembered the hurt he displayed when she teased him in front of Terry. It was important to Joseph that his son understand that being more wealthy and affluent never had to mean being less Black and that there was no shame in knowing your background, or as Joseph seemed proud in considering, returning to it. This was especially important. At random times Joseph held Terry gently by the wrist or shoulders, emphatically solid, telling him *don't forget me. Don't forget where you came from.* And in the summer before Terry's senior year of high school, Joseph had begun pressing into him the concept that you don't, *you can't,* run from your origins; it's not good to hide them. Even if you think you're secure in clothes or boats or houses. Or a well-paying job. Or at a prestigious college in California, far, far away from your parents.

She felt a private bitterness at Joe's stoicism and how the turn of events after he was fired did not come upon them unfortunate and overwhelming like some sudden squall, but more deliberately, planned out, and painfully prepared for by him. The summer and winter trips, the house, and even some of the furniture were to go; "necessary relinquishings," he termed them. He hadn't been eager in the job search and the prospect of service at the Tacoma community center loomed closer. Fate hadn't been dealt out to them. He had *chosen* it. They were to make room for the change.

She felt the wind in her face. Whidbey was no longer in sight, only him, framed in the gray sky. She turned her shoulders eastward toward Everett, where, if he had been more lighthearted and kept the sail up, they might have reached before the pier lights began to flicker in the coming dark. But he had lowered the main sail soon after they rounded the tip of Whidbey and resigned himself to a solemn stance at the wheel, guiding the sloop under auxiliary power through the choppy waves. It was hard to be bitter. That took energy. It was selfish; she knew he would say that if he could see the sullen look in her face.

Affirming this herself, she felt obligated to comfort him. She made a gesture with her arm towards the withered jib. "I remember when I didn't even know what a goddamned *jib* was." She tried a smile. "And *sloop.* Remember *that* one, Joe? You must have read up; you sounded like somebody's ole sea dog: '*Maya, go ahead and put*—' or was it 'stow?' Yes: stow . . . 'stow the bags in the sail locker . . .' and I said something like '*but I thought we're driving the boat out there.*'" She laughed loudly, pleased she could laugh at herself. "That was something."

But he had taken out a cigarette and was concentrating on cupping his hands to light it.

"And look at us now," she said, letting her laughter fade. Facing east again, she saw a few lights along the steely evergreen shore of the mainland.

He let the smoke curl around his head and he winced into the wind in a manner that she noticed he had taken on in the recent summers of sailing. "So you're really not going to go down and check on the bag?"

"No, I'm not. There's not much more we can do about him."

"It's just the fur, Maya. It shouldn't get wet. And if air gets to the skin . . ."

"Let's just not . . ." She closed her eyes tight with a knotted sense of resolve, an insulating kind of blocking out which she allowed as a necessity. "Let's not talk about it anymore."

"You'll have to do better than that when Terry sees him."

"You can't be serious about driving that dog's body all the way to Stanford."

He focused his eyes on Everett and reached under the wheel console for the thermos of bourbon.

"Are you going to check the bag for leaks at every rest stop?" She knew her voice might sound cruel right then to him. "And what about the smell? Are you going to keep Otis on ice for a *thousand* miles?" But she felt vindicated and fueled with the sense of being the more rational one.

He drank slowly from the thermos, heaving air out after the bourbon had gone down.

"Joe, please, it's rough all the way in. You know the current from Saratoga Pass. Why don't you rest and let me steer?"

He said nothing. He didn't move.

She heard the waves for the first time since they had left the island. She listened to their gentle pat and splash as she hadn't in years.

He finally spoke. "We'll fly him."

"Fly? Fly *Otis?!* Dammit, Joseph!"

He pulled his face back into that wince again. "Please, Maya . . ."

She decided that she hated his face with that wince. And the insipid *please Maya.* She felt that this was his way of pushing the pain onto her.

"Terry," he said.

"What?"

"We'll fly *Terry* up."

"So, Joseph, we're into flying again? Can our wallet stand that? What happened to commutes and treks in our soon-to-be acquired VW Bus? Or was it a rickshaw?"

"Jesus, think of Terry. He said he wanted to see . . ."

Otis had been old, and for his nine years had been the mellowed companion on all of their trips to Whidbey. She knew this. But Otis was gone now.

"A goddamned *dog* keeps us in luxury. I'll be damned."

"You don't have to help with the arrangements if you don't want to."

"Joe, you give up our only time together this year for a dead dog?"

His wince broke for a moment and she could see that too much had been said. His stoicism would not take that.

"I just want to do this." He drank again. "For Terry." His face set back into a gaze towards the shore.

It wasn't just the dog. It was difficult to have Terry leave early for school. But an apartment had to be found, a cheap place found early, and so Terry went. Maya could remember Joseph seeing the brighter side of their son's early departure. He told her that the last time on Whidbey would be theirs alone, echoing back to when she had first dated him and learned to love him there, when they could only afford the ferry and two days in a motel. This was to be a last good stay, not an event tainted by a slow, heavy trip back to mourn. But it wasn't just the dog.

Otis had passed away in a manner that, to her, seemed fitting. They had been on Whidbey for a day, good weather in the coming week promised by forecasters, and they had already begun an expedition for mussels. Otis had broken off in his regular fashion, forever enthused with being simply a dog and emphatically determined to herd seagulls from the beach. If one could assign emotion to a dog, or even importance, she felt that Otis was happiest trotting along the beaches of the Sound, his tongue hanging out. One moment Otis had been chasing gulls as Joseph and she were shoulder to shoulder, digging like children for a large mussel burrowing away from a future in their stew pot. They lost the mussel in wet, sliding sand and they slumped back on their heels. And there he was. Otis had collapsed without them even knowing, without sound, without struggle. She gasped first. Remembering that now, she thought of reminding Joseph of this, as if her shock then might impress upon him that, yes, she did care for Otis. But it was Joseph who walked over, picked up the body and walked slowly to the house. Even then, his face was sinking into the drawn, hard look it held now.

They didn't call a vet. That seemed fitting, too, and they sat in the kitchen that night, silent, drinking both of the bottles of wine they had brought. The oil lamp light punctuated the weight of Joseph's withdrawn appearance. His face, his hands, and even his clothes seemed to have taken on some silt or grime of gray after he carried the dog to the cottage. That night, Otis lay in a bag covered with ice on the porch.

They had been silent that night, but she had sensed that he was already thinking of Terry's reaction. The next morning she heard Joseph on the phone with his son. She heard talk of the dog for a brief time, but then Joseph focused more on the time passed and Terry, his son, so far away. She imagined Terry, tired, maybe even irritated, being treated like the son Joseph still wanted him to be. She sat on the bed, watching the deep blue of the morning lighten to gray and listened to Joseph in the kitchen trying not to cry. By noon he had packed, and she stumbled into him as he passed the front steps carrying a white styrofoam cooler down to the dinghy. He said he had walked to the store and bought it for Otis, for the trip back. For Terry, he had said.

It was more, she realized now. She had always been put off by his sensitivity that, in showing care for delicate issues, appeared impressive. Earlier, as he let down the main sail, she hated him for his look of resolve, just as she had hated how he would wear his frayed Peace Corps shirts to picnics and beach parties, signifying the sacrificial glory of his days in eastern Africa. He sometimes wore his pain like it was heavier upon him than her.

But she had heard a difference in his voice just then. . . . *for Terry.* It was now about more than the trip back. She thought of the day Joseph hugged Terry tight, longer than he would usually allow his son to take notice of, and watched Terry walk away to board his plane. Terry was now gone, left to the unknown design of his own life. Home became a desperate place, a little more silence in the house, and those still, lonely fall months coming. There was no way to know how much of their eighteen years together he would take and what he would leave.

"We can call Terry when we get in." She rose and took the bourbon from him. She saw tired pain on his face, and his shoulders loosened when she touched him.

Somewhere in California Terry was smiling and getting his brown skin darker, oblivious to the passing of a dog, the weight of things changed, life reverting.

"The piers are getting close, Joe," she said softly, letting him sit down. She no longer felt cold. She took the wheel and quieted the motor to let the sloop drift for a while towards the lights of Everett.

Wonderful Teen

CAROLYN FERRELL

It seemed to me that our motel room in Laguna Beach was only big enough for two people, like a mother and father, and here we were five. Mother picked up the phone and dialed for a plain cheese pizza. We protested, saying that we wanted a pizza with mushrooms and little fishes on it, and a bottle of orange soda as well, since it was so hot. The sun outside was turning roads back into tar, and the pool at the motel was as hot as a bath. A few minutes outside, and we could feel the light brown of our skin bake darker, like brownies with nuts in them. There was my baby sister Tess and me and the twins, Todd and Lee. Lee was named after my father, who was back at the house, probably cursing out loud to no one. We ran the bathroom sink full at the motel and soaked our arms up to the elbows in the cold hard water. Sometimes someone would say, "It's too hot here in this stinking room" or "I wish we were back at home." Mother would tell us to think about something else and to behave ourselves. That, and "I'm not made out of money! You eat what I say! If you're thirsty, fill yourself up a glass from that water you're playing with!"

Mother picked up the phone again and told us to be quiet. We all sat on the edge of the bed. I held Tess on my lap. I knew that she would be the first one to start bawling, no matter what. Mother twisted a strand of her ash-blond hair around her finger and put it in her mouth. The swelling around her eye had turned dark purple from the sky-blue it had been in the morning. When we walked into the motel office at eight A.M., Mother took off her sunglasses automatically, forgetting. The old lady behind the desk stared at us. Mother asked, "Do you give discounts for black eyes?" Then she started to cry, which made us all feel very wobbly. Mother put her sunglasses back on and touched each of us, one by one, with the tip of her hand, like she was making sure we were there. The old desk lady said, "Honey, we've seen everything." She gave us the room closest to the old highway because she said she didn't want to hear no trouble. She asked my mother if she was babysitting us kids. "They are mine," Mother announced. The old desk lady said she had never seen four colored kids come in with a white lady with a black eye before. She said she wasn't looking for no trouble. Mother sucked in her teeth and moved us out the door.

In the last issue of *Wonderful Teen,* it had said that most people don't really realize how grown-up and responsible their teens really are. "Today's youth," it said, "tomorrow's you." That made me feel different after I'd read it, even though I was only twelve. Now, on the way to our motel room, my hand was on Mother's shoulder, not like it used to be when I was a girl, when I used to hold on to her fingers with my whole hand. I'd brought the last issue of *Wonderful Teen* with me, because before we left, Mother made it clear to us: we will stay gone.

She was trying a new number. She said to me, "Hannah, get me a cigarette out of my bag." I pushed Tess off my lap and dug into her pocketbook for the twisted pack of Slims. *Wonderful Teen* was against cigarettes: it said that smoking could turn youthful skin not only older but darker as well. I knew this fact, and stiff, I never gave up my prayer with the pack of Slims in my hand that six years would hurry up and pass so that I would be able to smoke cigarettes legally, like Mother promised. It happened around the same time you could drink a chaser before your main drink and join the army and get married. My prayer was the same lines over and over: "And when I am a full woman . . . And when I am a full woman . . . thank you, heavenly God." I would start smoking nonfilters and I would be exactly like Mother anyway, who smoked all the time, and look: her skin was soft and youthful and not dark at all.

Mother lit up a cigarette and said, "Is that you, Lee?" Tess's lips began to shake so I whacked her on the head with Mother's bag, gently. Mother said, "You can't push me around now, Lee. You can't do that now! We're on the coast. Never mind where! One more word like that and I'll hang up for good!" The boys put their heads underneath the bedspread and began to howl like baby dogs. Tess was full-steam-ahead crying, just as I had predicted. I said, in the most mature adult whisper I could manage, "Shut up, you disgusting brats!"

Mother's voice was scratchy, like she was gargling with saltwater. She said, "You can't push me around now! No sir, there's not going to be a next time! There's a point I've reached, Lee, and that's called: *self-respect.*" She slammed down the phone and told us to go outside and wait for the pizza delivery truck. I shoved my brothers and sister out the door and said to my mother, still in that grown-up whisper, "You know I'm here if you need me, Ella." Mother put out her cigarette in the ashtray and said, "Just where did you learn talk like that? Go out and close the door!"

In the sun, our game was to put our hand on each other's foreheads to see who had the hottest skin. Tess wanted to change after a few minutes; she said she wanted to be a little white cloud that floated above the motel and looked at itself in the pool mirror. My brother Todd, who was only ten years old and just naturally thought he was the absolute Panama Cigar, said, "That's only something deluded baby girls think of. Me, I've had enough of delusions." Lee, still in the old game, jumped up and down and announced that his skin was on fire. I looked at them and folded my arms over my chest. Tess, Todd, and Lee were nothing but babies when you faced the cold, hard facts. I had been born two years before any of them, and in *Wonderful Teen* it had said, "Every year marks a difference." Lee said he wanted to go back in and tell Mother that he had a fever, but I said not to. I said she needed time to find herself, and Todd said, "Why, is she lost?" and he horse-laughed. I ignored him and pushed the others over to the pool.

There was a colored lady sitting next to the pool in a lounge chair. She was the first black person I'd seen all day, ever since we drove into Laguna Beach on the lam. She saw us and cried out, "Come and play your games over here by me!" She smiled. Her voice sounded like our grandma from the South, the one who wore an undershirt instead of a bra and who ate squirrel meat. The colored lady was beautiful. She had the same skin as Dad, the kind Mother had called "day-old coffee" in the old times when they used to laugh about it. The colored lady was just sitting there in broad daylight. She didn't have her arms or legs covered up in the sun. She kept batting her eyes. The look on her face was the kind that said *I'm never lonely*.

Todd and Lee went over to her and did cartwheels and rode upside-down bicycles with their legs. This colored lady's hair was made up into a thousand braids wrapped in one big twist at the back of her head. There were blue and gold beads woven into the braids. Blue and gold were my favorite colors. I suddenly remembered. Blue and gold were the national colors of *Wonderful Teen*. Todd and Lee were playing the Injured Cowboy and the Horse Who Could Dial for Help. She threw her head back and laughed. Her teeth could have been a full-page ad in *Wonderful Teen;* they had that unmistakable teen shine, although I guessed her to be a bit older. She looked over at Tess and me and said, "Are you feeling blue, girls?" Her voice was like a love story in the movies.

I shoved Tess behind me and said, "Our mother is under the weather. I am here to keep an eye out on the kids. You see, I'm almost a teen. And I'm here to keep an eye out."

The way the colored lady leaned forward in her chair, you could really see things if you looked. She tied the knot of her two-piece white-and-gold swimsuit tighter and said, "If you're going to be a teen, then you probably have all the reasons in the world for feeling blue." She winked at me. The boys ran to the highway edge to check for the delivery truck. My arms were hanging at my sides like long noodles, and suddenly I realized how amazing it was that I was going to be a teen.

The colored lady took Tess by the hand and said, "With this kind of hair, she'll have all the boys. All the boys who wouldn't want *us*." Tess had Mother's hair, the kind that was soft and went straight down. Not like mine, which didn't flow to the back when the wind hit it. My hair just stayed.

Then the colored lady asked, "What does your mother have?"

Tess said, "Dad slammed the phone down on Mother's hand, so that's why we're all here." She put her face in her hands, just like a grown-up, even though she was only five.

The colored lady turned and said to me, "Do you want me to start showing you the right way to be a teen?"

The boys came back and hung their legs over the side of the pool. The colored lady was braiding my hair. I sat on the ground in between her legs and looked into her compact mirror. She made five rows of braids on my head from front to back instead of the two that Mother usually did. She took out a jar of light blue grease and smoothed it through the rows over the hair that wouldn't stay put. I smelled like Dad in the morning. Tess said I looked like a star. I sat between the colored lady's legs on the hot cement and felt what *Wonderful Teen* would have called "The Evolution" come out.

The colored lady asked me, "Does your mama know what a beautiful baby she has here? You're going to get all the boys with your charm."

I said, "But what about my hair?" I asked her if I would still get all the boys with my hair. She smiled. Mother called for us from the door of the room. The colored lady wanted a goodbye kiss from the boys. I looked at myself one last time in the compact. I said to myself, "And when I am a full woman, I will always look like this. And when I am a full woman, I will always look like this. Thank you, heavenly God." Remembering our game, I shouted out to the others racing back, "Has anyone's skin reached the boiling point yet?"

Todd and Lee ran back into the bathroom to play with the water. Mother was flopped on the bed. Tess was flopped on Mother's chest and was trying to hide her face inside Mother's blouse. There were three cigarettes, all lit, in the ashtray. Mother's face looked tired and had red blobs all over it. She was wearing her sunglasses again, even though it was just us. When I sat next to her on the bed, I could smell the way our home smelled at night, when Mother smoked and cooked in the kitchen. The TV was on: it was our favorite show, *Day in Court.*

A man had returned home after twelve years of amnesia and now his wife's new husband was feeling pretty disgusted and was filing for divorce. The new husband called his wife a "black plague," and that made Todd laugh like crazy. The wife sat in the witness stand like a stone with its mouth open. She said she hadn't known. The judge said it was a clear-cut case of bigamy. The old husband just woke up in Las Vegas and adjusted to life as a children's librarian there. He'd married again, had a son, and gotten arrested for bad checks. But all that didn't matter now, now that he remembered who he really was. The new husband rolled his eyes at the camera and said, "Plague is right." The judge said it was a clear-cut case of mistaken identity.

When it came time for the wife to speak, Mother said, "Turn the set off. It's too damn late for her."

There was this ad in the last *Wonderful Teen* that I loved: a lady in a tanning studio applying a bottle of Wild Thing tanning oil to her silky legs. And she was dreaming of a man who had sun-streaked hair and closed eyes with a heavenly smile on his face. The ad said, "True Happiness." That was it. I tore it out of the magazine and kept it in my slacks pocket. Whenever I looked at it, I wanted to take off my shirt. Whenever I looked at it, first I would feel sexy, then sad.

I thought about the colored lady at the pool. I said to Mother, "Do you notice anything different about me?" I twirled the ends of my braids in my fingers.

Mother closed her eyes and said, "Not now, Hannah. Can't you see I'm think-ing?" One of her eyes was glued together by the lids in a purple ball.

I told her what I was thinking, though: that now I didn't look exactly like her anymore, but still, when people looked, they would be able to tell that I was hers. Mother laughed, "Oh yeah? You sure you're not shitting me?" Then after a minute she said, "To me, you're looking more like your father's side. Are you *sure* you're still mine?" And she laughed. And her laugh was the kind that meant: I might be serious.

I ran into the bathroom and looked into the mirror. I wanted to pull all the braids out. I wanted a hat or a scarf. I was ashamed. There were five braids where there used to be two and everything felt like it was gone and I was ashamed to death. Todd walked past the bathroom and whispered, "Plague" and with both hands I slammed the door. Shut.

Todd and Lee had been playing with the water, but now they came running out of the bathroom. The sink was overflowing. Todd announced, "I want to go home now."

Mother replied, "We can't right now, honey. Be good for a while. We'll check in on Dad later."

Lee said, "I want Dad to bring me my bike."

I said, "Now you two boys *behave!* I don't want to have to tell you again." I turned to Mother and I sighed. "What's a woman to do?"

Todd said, "Shut your face, black bitch." His voice was high and shaky. He kept his eyes on Mother's feet, long on the bed.

"Yeah, black bitch," Lee copied. He was smiling like an angel. He was clearly such a baby.

I shouted, "Mother! We don't have to stand for this!" I began to think of punishments for the boys.

She rubbed her eyes under the sunglasses and said, "Kids! That's the last thing I need! Nobody calls anybody else a black anything! Far as I am concerned, we are all *black.*"

She slid off the bed and put on her slippers and walked into the bathroom. No one said anything because it was just a feeling. Mother clicked the bathroom door locked. The only noise was from the highway. You could tell that inside, everything went frozen, frozen stiff, even our teeth hurt. You could tell we were alone.

Todd fell on the bed next to Tess and started bawling. Then Lee started in. Todd wriggled his body in the covers like a desert soldier. Mother shouted after a minute, "I have so many things to worry about, don't give me anything else on my plate, you hear?"

The toilet flushed. Then Mother resumed saying, "Boys, I'm doing all I can. Ask Hannah to read you a story."

I looked at my brothers on the bed. I was thinking: Yes, it was true. Even Mother had to admit I was the natural-born leader of the children. It was all up to me. I moved over and touched Todd's back with the flat of my hand and I let it stay there for a minute. Yes, it was true. He screamed at me to get my black bitch hand away. The toilet flushed again. I moved back for a moment. Then I slid underneath the bed like a sideways crab.

The doorbell to our room rang, and it was the old desk lady. She wanted to know whether Mother was interested in buying something to drink. She was selling bottles of Old Country Gentleman at a discount price. This was the stuff that would be good for someone like our mother, she said. I told her, "We are probably going to order a bottle of orange soda, which is rich in vitamin C."

Mother was back on the phone. "I told you how to get here," she was shouting. "Are you going to keep me waiting all damn day?" She slammed the phone down. We were all listening. "Who was that at the door?" Mother asked, going back into the bathroom.

Later, she made us wash our faces and brush our teeth even though it wasn't dark outside yet. She sat us down in a row in front of the TV and told us we could watch *Nature's Glorious Kingdom* and *The Gentle Giant*. We had to put on our pajamas. Mother combed out our hair. She asked me why mine was so greasy, but that was all. She didn't ask me where the braids came from. The doorbell rang. Lee said, "Maybe that's Dad." Todd replied, "Shut up, stupid dope."

It was the colored lady from the pool. Mother was peeking out from behind the front door. The way the lady stood in the doorway with her short white robe covering almost every important thing, I just knew she was a star. We were in Laguna Beach. That was home to the stars. The colored lady said she was selling cosmetics, natural cosmetics that didn't have any unnecessary chemicals or animal tests. They enhanced a woman's natural beauty without covering up or polluting what nature had put there in the first place.

Mother said she wasn't interested. The colored lady took out a small case from a huge bag that had "Only One You" on the side. It was a dark blue eye shadow. She said, "That one goes over big with ladies of your hue." She dabbed Mother's eyes, including the purple one. Then she said, "You'd be surprised to discover all the treasures that this particular tone can bring out." She showed Mother an orange lipstick called Debonair and a bottle of pink foundation. The colored lady said it would bring out the secret most beautiful woman that Mother had inside of her. Mother said, "I ain't in the market for that today, honey."

The colored lady gave her an eye pencil called Fire and Smoke and a mascara with a special lash-separating comb. She saw us through the door and waved. She pointed to my head and smiled. I felt my throat get thick. Mother kept her eyes down. She thanked her for the samples and then closed the door. Then the colored lady was gone, like that was all there was to it. Mother was silent. I knew that that meant *We are back in here together alone.*

She went back into the bathroom. When she came out, she had on the lipstick and the eye pencil. Her eyes looked like two wonderful stones. She asked us, "Is the treasure out?" and then burst into tears. We were all frozen again, but still we could run and put our arms around her.

Nature's Glorious Kingdom came on. I could tell that the day was ending because out the window, the bottom of the sky was turning pink. Tiny stars were popping out everywhere. *Wonderful Teen* said that the eveningtime would become a teen's best friend, what with the promise of corsages, candy, dates arriving at the door, cars, limousines, evening dresses. I sat on the edge of the bathtub and anticipated the universe as Mother scrubbed her feet and hands. She took moments out to dry her hands and smoke a cigarette. I said to her, "I wish I was eighteen already."

She answered, "Hannah, baby, when you're eighteen, you're going to wish yourself right back to twelve, believe you me." She smiled at me for the first time in days.

I thought about the car I would start driving when I hit the wonderful age, and all the men standing at street corners waiting for me to pick them up and drive them around. I would have on nylons, and instead of underwear, I would wear a white-and-gold bikini bottom. The men's hair would blow in the wind and they would have the best suntans. I would show Tess how to drive way before her time and how to hold a penny between her legs for posture. I would use Debonair.

I said, "I only want to keep getting older, Mother. I want to be exactly like you."

Mother said, "By the time I was twenty-nine, I had had all of my children. Grandmother used to call me and tell me that it was never too late. It didn't matter what I'd thought I wanted before. She just wished it could have been anything else—South American, Russian, even Chinese, for Christ's sake. I had four children, but my own freaking mother told me it was never too late to leave and come back and be twelve again."

Then Mother said, "Dad could've been anything, and still I would've fallen in love. It's not that love is blind, for Christ's sake. It's that love closes your eyes out of spite. Dad could've been anything, and still I would've gotten to right here." And then her cigarette fell out of her mouth and into the water.

I picked it up and said, "I don't care about all that other stuff, Mother. I just want to be like you."

Mother rubbed her eyes. She said, "At first your father called me his little drop of milk in his big bucket of tar."

Then she said, "And it's not like I ever became more than a drop of milk in the bucket of tar. I didn't spread out. I didn't evaporate. I just stayed a drop of milk and he just stayed a bucket."

Mother took a deep breath. I couldn't listen. I told her again that I wanted to be just like her, and she moaned, "Then be like me, Hannah."

The doorbell rang and it was the desk lady again. She said to tell Mother that there was a man around asking for her. She said she wasn't looking for no trouble, but facts were facts: someone had been sniffing around. Mother shouted from the bathroom, "Shut that damn door!" The desk lady asked me how long it was we were planning on staying. I smiled graciously to get her to leave, and then she did leave.

We turned the TV set low. We could hear Mother splashing water in the tub, saying, "It's not possible! How the hell could it be possible!" She got out of the tub and started throwing all our clothes in a big pile near the door.

The bell rang again, and this time we all looked out the window and saw the pizza delivery guy. Mother opened the door and said, "I called you hours ago! Do I need to make reservations a week in advance for a freaking pizza?"

The pizza guy said, "I got lost, that's all. No biggie." He placed a big soggy box on the floor next to our pile and began to chew his nails. He had streaked blond hair and legs with muscles. His shirt was open. He had what *Wonderful Teen* would call "that unmistakable surfer air."

The guy was eyeing Mother as she was fishing for some dollar bills. He asked her finally, "So what time do you knock off babysitting?" Mother was searching for her pocketbook. She was only wearing a towel. Tess moved over and started twirling her hair with her finger. She gave him a big smile. She was only five.

He rubbed the back of his neck with his hand. I suddenly realized that I was wearing feet pajamas, but I was praying he hadn't noticed. "And when I am a full woman, I will wear baby dolls. And when I am a full woman, I will wear baby dolls. Thank you, Father." Mother mumbled something at him and handed over a ten-dollar bill. He grinned and bent his head down to hers—did I mention that he was probably over six feet tall in his stocking feet and had five-o'clock shadow? He asked Mother if he could speak to her outside for a moment. "Why?" Mother asked, but she was already going into the bathroom with a sundress from the pile.

I sauntered over to the pizza guy. I put my hands on my hips and spread out my fingers wide so that it would look like something big and good was there. And then he stared into my eyes for a whole sixty seconds. They were as blue as Mother's new eye shadow. He put his warm hands on my shoulders, which were pulsating a feeling up to him. I was almost as tall as he was. I'd say he stared into my eyes for a good eighty seconds. I'd say that there was definitely love there.

Standing with me there, he said, *"Baby,"* and he said it so that I would have to follow his lips to really know the depth of his entire being. And I felt my whole essence get crushed and I knew that this had most certainly been a *Wonderful Teen* moment. I felt the beating of my rapid heart and all my favorite songs filling my head, like "Where Is My World." They were filling my soul. Baby. I wanted to sing. Heaven was really a place you could see before you died.

And then Mother came out of the bathroom with her yellow sundress on. The pizza guy pulled his hands away quickly and said, "That's a cute girl there. Where's her mother? I mean, I know you ain't their mother." Mother stopped a second, then she burst out laughing and said, "Of course they're mine, silly. I'm old enough." She pushed him gently out the door and followed, grinning gaily.

I went into the bathroom and turned on the water. The others were watching *Gentle Giant* and tearing off pieces of pizza from the box. I began scrubbing my face with cold water and the palms of my hands. Just water and hands. I looked up in the mirror over the sink after a minute, and I thought I saw myself going, but when I blinked my eyes, I was all there.

Out the window, the moon came out in full and the air was cooling down. I used our family-size jar of Vaseline for grease and did my hair again. I couldn't get the five braids, but I did smooth my hair out more, even my girl sideburns. I got two braids down the back of my head, Indian warrior fashion.

Mother came into the room after fifteen minutes. "That boy!" she said, giggling. Her face was red, and the blobs on it were even redder. "What a crazy *boy!*" She knelt near the pizza box and tore out a slice and stuffed it in her mouth. She said, when everyone kept on watching TV, "All he wanted to do was ask me out on a date! Now isn't that a crazy *boy?*" And she let out a string of giggles that sounded like they could've come from a cow. Todd said, "This pizza is too goddamn cold," but all Mother did was grab him and start hugging him. Her face was all lit up. She looked ugly. She didn't punish him for using the wrong language. Mother grabbed Tess and Lee and began hugging them too and kissing them and pretty soon they were all rolling on the floor, happy like puppies. They were all giggling in little lumps, like on a string, not laughing in one big laugh. Mother asked, "Where's Hannah?" but they were all too happy and giggling to answer. It was the first time in a long time.

Then Mother spread her arms out like wings around Tess and Todd and Lee and said, "My babies, you are all mine." And I could hear tears in her voice. It was the saddest time I ever knew. Mother rocked them like they were all back in the nest. I closed the door to the bathroom, where I was standing, looking, and I wondered if they would ever remember that I wasn't there, ever.

Before we went to bed, Mother called Dad again. She was still wearing her sundress and her new makeup. Dad picked up, saying it was pretty damn late to be calling and did she know she was facing possible kidnapping charges? Mother put Tess on the phone, then the boys. They all cried in no time. When you faced facts, they were all nothing but children, pure and simple. When I got on the phone, I told Dad, "I have everything under control. I'm not your baby." Then I said, "Yes. Yes,

I miss you. I already told you that before." Then I said calmly, *"Why couldn't you have been something different?"* Someone here needed to get to the bottom of things. Mother smacked me hard on the back and told me to mind my own freaking business. Then she took the phone into her own hands.

Back in the bathroom, I put on Mother's eye shadow and lipstick and pink foundation. I put it on seriously. There was this article in the last issue of *Wonderful Teen* called "Dress, But Don't Confess," which said that all wonderful teens had secrets in them that should only come out with the right man. Not just any man, the absolute right one. It said that lip gloss and eyeliner and a great tan were important, but the right man didn't need too much to see all the treasures that a wonderful teen possessed. I used to believe that. Only now I didn't know what to believe anymore. I studied my face in the mirror. From the side I could still pretend. From the side I knew for sure that I resembled Mother. That was a fact as plain as day, couldn't anyone deny it. But when I looked forward in the mirror, my face was homely and alone. I didn't know if I could fully believe *Wonderful Teen*. I realized, for example, that there were no treasures, not on the outside, not below.

When I looked straight in the mirror, all I could ask was *Why couldn't it have been anything else?* I sat down in the empty bathtub and cried and cried. Never again. Never again. Never again. Never again.

Milk tar. Mother knocked on the door of the bathroom and asked me if she could please give me a hug. "Never again!" I shouted, and nothing could change my mind, not even something to eat or drink, not even Mother's kisses, or her crying from the bed.

The Kind of Light That Shines on Texas

REGINALD McKNIGHT

I never liked Marvin Pruitt. Never liked him, never knew him, even though there were only three of us in the class. Three black kids. In our school there were fourteen classrooms of thirty-odd white kids (in '66, they considered Chicanos provisionally white) and three or four black kids. Primary school in primary colors. Neat division. Alphabetized. They didn't stick us in the back, or arrange us by degrees of hue, apartheidlike. This was real integration, a ten-to-one ratio as tidy as upper-class landscaping. If it all worked, you could have ten white kids all to yourself. They could talk to you, get the feel of you, scrutinize you bone deep if they wanted to. They seldom wanted to, and that was fine with me for two reasons. The first was that their scrutiny was irritating. How do you comb your hair—why do you comb your hair—may I please touch your hair—were the kinds of questions they asked. This is no way to feel at home. The second reason was Marvin. He embarrassed me. He smelled bad, was at least two grades behind, was hostile, dark skinned, homely, close-mouthed. I feared him for his size, pitied him for his dress, watched him all the time. Marveled at him, mystified, astonished, uneasy.

He had the habit of spitting on his right arm, juicing it down till it would glisten. He would start in immediately after taking his seat when we'd finished with the Pledge of Allegiance, "The Yellow Rose of Texas," "The Eyes of Texas Are upon You," and "Mistress Shady." Marvin would rub his spit-flecked arm with his left hand, rub and roll as if polishing an ebony pool cue. Then he would rest his head in the crook of his arm, sniffing, huffing deep like black-jacket boys huff bagsful of acrylics. After ten minutes or so, his eyes would close, heavy. He would sleep till recess. Mrs. Wickham would let him.

There was one other black kid in our class. A girl they called Ah-so. I never learned what she did to earn this name. There was nothing Asian about this big-shouldered girl. She was the tallest, heaviest kid in school. She was quiet, but I don't think any one of us was subtle or sophisticated enough to nickname our classmates according to any but physical attributes. Fat kids were called Porky or Butterball, skinny ones were called Stick or Ichabod. Ah-so was big, thick, and African. She would impassively sit, sullen, silent as Marvin. She wore the same dark blue pleated skirt every day, the same ruffled white blouse every day. Her skin always shone as if worked by Marvin's palms and fingers. I never spoke one word to her, nor she to me.

Of the three of us, Mrs. Wickham called only on Ah-so and me. Ah-so never answered one question, correctly or incorrectly, so far as I can recall. She wasn't stupid. When asked to read aloud she read well, seldom stumbling over long words, reading with humor and expression. But when Wickham asked her about Farmer Brown and how many cows, or the capital of Vermont, or the date of this war or that, Ah-so never spoke. Not one word. But you always felt she could have answered those questions if she'd wanted to. I sensed no tension, embarrassment, or anger in Ah-so's reticence. She simply refused to speak. There was something unshakable about her, some core so impenetrably solid, you got the feeling that if you stood too close to her she could eat your thoughts like a black star eats light. I didn't despise Ah-so as I despised Marvin. There was nothing malevolent about her. She sat like a great icon in the back of the classroom, tranquil, guarded, sealed up, watchful. She was close to sixteen, and it was my guess she'd given up on school. Perhaps she was just obliging the wishes of her family, sticking it out till the law could no longer reach her.

There were at least half a dozen older kids in our class. Besides Marvin and Ah-so there was Oakley, who sat behind me, whispering threats into my ear; Varna Willard with the large breasts; Eddie Limon, who played bass for a high school rock band; and Lawrence Ridderbeck, who everyone said had a kid and a wife. You couldn't expect me to know anything about Texan educational practices of the 1960s, so I never knew why there were so many older kids in my sixth-grade class. After all, I was just a boy and had transferred into the school around midyear. My father, an air force sergeant, had been sent to Viet Nam. The air force sent my mother, my sister, Claire, and me to Connolly Air Force Base, which during the war housed "unaccompanied wives." I'd been to so many different schools in my short life that I ceased wondering about their differences. All I knew about the Texas schools is that they weren't afraid to flunk you.

Yet though I was only twelve then, I had a good idea why Wickham never once called on Marvin, why she let him snooze in the crook of his polished arm. I knew why she would press her lips together, and narrow her eyes at me whenever I correctly answered a question, rare as that was. I know why she badgered Ah-so with questions everyone knew Ah-so would never even consider answering. Wickham didn't like us. She wasn't gross about it, but it was clear she didn't want us around. She would prove her dislike day after day with little stories and jokes. "I just want to share with you all," she would say, "a little riddle my daughter told me at the supper table th'other day. Now, where do you go when you injure your knee?" Then one, two, or all three of her pets would say for the rest of us, "We don't know, Miz Wickham," in that skin-chilling way suck-asses speak, "where?" "Why, to Africa," Wickham would say, "where the knee grows."

The thirty-odd white kids would laugh, and I would look across the room at Marvin. He'd be asleep. I would glance back at Ah-so. She'd be sitting still as a projected image, staring down at her desk. I, myself, would smile at Wickham's stupid jokes, sometimes fake a laugh. I tried to show her that at least one of us was alive and alert, even though her jokes hurt. I sucked ass, too, I suppose. But I wanted her to understand more than anything that I was not like her other nigra children, that I was worthy of more than the non-attention and the negative attention she paid Marvin and Ah-so. I hated her, but never showed it. No one could safely contradict that woman. She knew all kinds of tricks to demean, control, and punish you. And she could swing her two-foot paddle as fluidly as a big-league slugger swings a bat. You didn't speak in Wickham's class unless she spoke to you first. You didn't chew gum, or wear "hood" hair. You didn't drag your feet, curse, pass notes, hold hands with the opposite sex. Most especially, you didn't say anything bad about the Aggies, Governor Connolly, LBJ, Sam Houston, or Waco. You did the forbidden and she would get you. It was that simple.

She never got me, though. Never gave her reason to. But she could have invented reasons. She did a lot of that. I can't be sure, but I used to think she pitied me because my father was in Viet Nam and my uncle A.J. had recently died there. Whenever she would tell one of her racist jokes, she would always glance at me, preface the joke with, "Now don't you nigra children take offense. This is all in fun, you know. I just want to share with you all something Coach Gilchrest told me th'other day." She would tell her joke, and glance at me again. I'd giggle, feeling a little queasy. "I'm half Irish," she would chuckle, "and you should hear some of those Irish jokes." She never told any, and I never really expected her to. I just did my Tom-thing. I kept my shoes shined, my desk neat, answered her questions as best I could, never brought gum to school, never cursed, never slept in class. I wanted to show her we were not all the same.

I tried to show them all, all thirty-odd, that I was different. It worked to some degree, but not very well. When some article was stolen from someone's locker or desk, Marvin, not I, was the first accused. I'd be second. Neither Marvin, nor Ah-so nor I were ever chosen for certain classroom honors—"Pledge leader," "flag holder," "noise monitor," "paper passer outer," but Mrs. Wickham once let me be "eraser duster." I was proud. I didn't even care about the cracks my fellow students made about my finally having turned the right color. I had done something that Marvin, in the deeps of his never-ending sleep, couldn't even dream of doing. Jack Preston, a kid who sat in front of me, asked me one day at recess whether I was embarrassed about Marvin. "Can you believe that guy?" I said. "He's like a pig or something. Makes me sick."

"Does it make you ashamed to be colored?"

"No," I said, but I meant yes. Yes, if you insist on thinking us all the same. Yes, if his faults are mine, his weaknesses inherent in me.

"I'd be," said Jack.

I made no reply. I was ashamed. Ashamed for not defending Marvin and ashamed that Marvin even existed. But if it had occurred to me, I would have asked Jack whether he was ashamed of being white because of Oakley. Oakley, "Oak Tree," Kelvin "Oak Tree" Oakley. He was sixteen and proud of it. He made it clear to everyone, including Wickham, that his life's ambition was to stay in school one more year, till he'd be old enough to enlist in the army. "Them slopes got my brother," he would say. "I'mna sign up and git me a few slopes. Gonna kill them bastards deader'n shit." Oakley, so far as anyone knew, was and always had been the oldest kid in his family. But no one contradicted him. He would, as anyone would tell you, "snap yer neck jest as soon as look at you." Not a boy in class, excepting Marvin and myself, had been able to avoid Oakley's pink bellies, Texas titty twisters, moon pie punches, or worse. He didn't bother Marvin, I suppose, because Marvin was closer to his size and age, and because Marvin spent five sixths of the school day asleep. Marvin probably never crossed Oakley's mind. And to say that Oakley hadn't bothered me is not to say he had no intention of ever doing so. In fact, this haphazard sketch of hairy fingers, slash of eyebrow, explosion of acne, elbows, and crooked teeth, swore almost daily that he'd like to kill me.

Naturally, I feared him. Though we were about the same height, he outweighed me by no less than forty pounds. He talked, stood, smoked, and swore like a man. No one, except for Mrs. Wickham, the principal, and the coach, ever laid a finger on him. And even Wickham knew that the hot lines she laid on him merely amused him. He would smile out at the classroom, goofy and bashful, as she laid down the two, five, or maximum ten strokes on him. Often he would wink, or surreptitiously flash us the thumb as Wickham worked on him. When she was finished, Oakley would walk so cool back to his seat you'd think he was on wheels. He'd slide into his chair, sniff the air, and say, "Somethin's burnin. Do y'all smell smoke? I swanee, I smell smoke and fahr back here." If he had made these cracks and never threatened me, I might have grown to admire Oakley, even liked him a little. But he hated me, and took every opportunity during the six-hour school day to make me aware of this. "Some Sambo's gittin his ass broke open one of these days," he'd mumble. "I wanna fight somebody. Need to keep in shape till I git to Nam."

I never said anything to him for the longest time. I pretended not to hear him, pretended not to notice his sour breath on my neck and ear. "Yep," he'd whisper. "Coonies keep y'in good shape for slope killin." Day in, day out, that's the kind of thing I'd pretend not to hear. But one day when the rain dropped down like lead balls, and the cold air made your skin look plucked, Oakley whispered to me, "My brother tells me it rains like this in Nam. Maybe I oughta go out at recess and break your ass open today. Nice and cool so you don't sweat. Nice and wet to clean up the blood." I said nothing for at least half a minute, then I turned half right and said, "Thought you said your brother was dead." Oakley, silent himself, for a time, poked me in the back with his pencil and hissed, *"Yer* dead." Wickham cut her eyes our way, and it was over.

It was hardest avoiding him in gym class. Especially when we played murder-ball. Oakley always aimed his throws at me. He threw with unblinking intensity, his teeth gritting, his neck veining, his face flushing, his black hair sweeping over one eye. He could throw hard, but the balls were squishy and harmless. In fact, I found his misses more intimidating than his hits. The balls would whizz by, thunder against the folded bleachers. They rattled as though a locomotive were passing through them. I would duck, dodge, leap as if he were throwing grenades. But he always hit me, sooner or later. And after a while I noticed that the other boys would avoid throwing at me, as if I belonged to Oakley.

One day, however, I was surprised to see that Oakley was throwing at every-one else but me. He was uncommonly accurate, too; kids were falling like tin cans. Since no one was throwing at me, I spent most of the game watching Oakley cut this one and that one down. Finally, he and I were the only ones left on the court. Try as he would, he couldn't hit me, nor I him. Coach Gilchrest blew his whistle and told Oakley and me to bring the red rubber balls to the equipment locker. I was relieved I'd escaped Oakley's stinging throws for once. I was feeling triumphant, full of myself. As Oakley and I approached Gilchrest, I thought about saying something friendly to Oakley: Good game, Oak Tree, I would say. Before I could speak, though, Gilchrest said, "All right boys, there's five minutes left in the period. Y'all are so good, looks like, you're gonna have to play like men. No boundaries, no catch outs, and you gotta hit your opponent three times in order to win. Got me?"

We nodded.

"And you're gonna use these," said Gilchrest, pointing to three volleyballs at his feet. "And you better believe they're pumped full. Oates, you start at that end of the court. Oak Tree, you're at th'other end. Just like usual, I'll set the balls at mid-court, and when I blow my whistle I want y'all to haul your cheeks to the middle and th'ow for all you're worth. Got me?" Gilchrest nodded at our nods, then added, "Remember, no boundaries, right?"

I at my end, Oakley at his, Gilchrest blew his whistle. I was faster than Oakley and scooped up a ball before he'd covered three quarters of his side. I aimed, threw, and popped him right on the knee. "One–zip!" I heard Gilchrest shout. The ball bounced off his knee and shot right back into my hands. I hurried my throw and missed. Oakley bent down, clutched the two remaining balls. I remember being amazed that he could palm each ball, run full out, and throw left-handed or right-handed without a shade of awkwardness. I spun, ran, but one of Oakley's throws glanced off the back of my head. "One–one!" hollered Gilchrest. I fell and spun on my ass as the other ball came sailing at me. I caught it. "He's out!" I yelled. Gilchrest's voice boomed, "No catch outs. Three hits. Three hits." I leapt to my feet as Oakley scrambled across the floor for another ball. I chased him down, leapt, and heaved the ball hard as he drew himself erect. The ball hit him dead in the face, and he went down flat. He rolled around, cupping his hands over his nose. Gilchrest sped to his side, helped him to his feet, asked him whether he was OK. Blood flowed from Oakley's nose, dripped in startlingly bright spots on the floor, his shoes, Gilchrest's shirt. The coach removed Oakley's T-shirt and pressed it against the big kid's nose to stanch the bleeding. As they walked past me toward the office I mumbled an apology to Oakley, but couldn't catch his reply. "You watch your filthy mouth, boy," said Gilchrest to Oakley.

The locker room was unnaturally quiet as I stepped into its steamy atmosphere. Eyes clicked in my direction, looked away. After I was out of my shorts, had my towel wrapped around me, my shower kit in hand, Jack Preston and Brian Nailor approached me. Preston's hair was combed slick and plastic looking. Nailor's stood up like frozen flames. Nailor smiled at me with his big teeth and pale eyes. He poked my arm with a finger. "You fucked up," he said.

"I tried to apologize."

"Won't do you no good," said Preston.

"I swanee," said Nailor.

"It's part of the game," I said. "It was an accident. Wasn't my idea to use volleyballs."

"Don't matter," Preston said. "He's jest lookin for an excuse to fight you."

"I never done nothing to him."

"Don't matter," said Nailor. "He don't like you."

"Brian's right, Clint. He'd jest as soon kill you as look at you."

"I never done nothing to him."

"Look," said Preston, "I know him pretty good. And jest between you and me, it's 'cause you're a city boy—"

"Whadda you mean? I've never—"

"He don't like your clothes—"

"And he don't like the fancy way you talk in class."

"What fancy—"

"I'm tellin him, if you don't mind, Brian."

"Tell him then."

"He don't like the way you say 'tennis shoes' instead of sneakers. He don't like coloreds. A whole bunch a things, really."

"I never done nothing to him. He's got no reason—"

"And," said Nailor, grinning, *"and,* he says you're a stuck-up rich kid." Nailor's eyes had crow's-feet, bags beneath them. They were a man's eyes.

"My dad's a sergeant," I said.

"You chicken to fight him?" said Nailor.

"Yeah, Clint, don't be chicken. Jest go on and git it over with. He's whupped pert near ever'body else in the class. It ain't so bad."

"Might as well, Oates."

"Yeah, yer pretty skinny, but yer jest about his height. Jest git 'im in a headlock and don't let go."

"Goddamn," I said, "he's got no reason to—"

Their eyes shot right and I looked over my shoulder. Oakley stood at his locker, turning its tumblers. From where I stood I could see that a piece of cotton

was wedged up one of his nostrils, and he already had the makings of a good
shiner. His acne burned red like a fresh abrasion. He snapped the locker open and
kicked his shoes off without sitting. Then he pulled off his shorts, revealing two
paddle stripes on his ass. They were fresh red bars speckled with white, the white
speckles being the reverse impression of the paddle's suction holes. He must not
have watched his filthy mouth while in Gilchrest's presence. Behind me, I heard
Preston and Nailor pad to their lockers.

Oakley spoke without turning around. "Somebody's gonna git his skinny black
ass kicked, right today, right after school." He said it softly. He slipped his jock off,
turned around. I looked away. Out the corner of my eye I saw him stride off, his
hairy nakedness a weapon clearing the younger boys from his path. Just before he
rounded the corner of the shower stalls, I threw my toilet kit to the floor and
stammered, "I—I never did nothing to you, Oakley." He stopped, turned, stepped
closer to me, wrapping his towel around himself. Sweat streamed down my rib
cage. It felt like ice water. "You wanna go at it right now, boy?"

"I never did nothing to you." I felt tears in my eyes. I couldn't stop them even
though I was blinking like mad. "Never."

He laughed. "You busted my nose, asshole."

"What about before? What'd I ever do to you?"

"See you after school, Coonie." Then he turned away, flashing his acne-
spotted back like a semaphore. "Why?" I shouted. "Why you wanna fight me?"
Oakley stopped and turned, folded his arms, leaned against a toilet stall. "Why you
wanna fight *me,* Oakley?" I stepped over the bench. "What'd I do? Why me?" And
then unconsciously, as if scratching, as if breathing, I walked toward Marvin, who
stood a few feet from Oakley, combing his hair at the mirror. "Why not him?" I
said. "How come you're after *me* and not *him?*" The room froze. Froze for a
moment that was both evanescent and eternal, somewhere between an eye blink
and a week in hell. No one moved, nothing happened; there was no sound at all.
And then it was as if all of us at the same moment looked at Marvin. He just stood
there, combing away, the only body in motion, I think. He combed his hair and
combed it, as if seeing only his image, hearing only his comb scraping his scalp. I
knew he'd heard me. There's no way he could not have heard me. But all he did
was slide the comb into his pocket and walk out the door.

"I got no quarrel with Marvin," I heard Oakley say. I turned toward his voice,
but he was already in the shower.

I was able to avoid Oakley at the end of the school day. I made my escape by
asking Mrs. Wickham if I could go to the rest room.

"'Rest room,'" Oakley mumbled. "It's a damn toilet, sissy."

"Clinton," said Mrs. Wickham. "Can you *not* wait till the bell rings? It's almost
three o'clock."

"No ma'am," I said. "I won't make it."

"Well I should make you wait just to teach you to be more mindful about . . .
hygiene . . . uh things." She sucked in her cheeks, squinted. "But I'm feeling chari-

table today. You may go." I immediately left the building, and got on the bus. "Ain't you a little early?" said the bus driver, swinging the door shut. "Just left the office," I said. The driver nodded, apparently not giving me a second thought. I had no idea why I'd told her I'd come from the office, or why she found it a satisfactory answer. Two minutes later the bus filled, rolled, and shook its way to Connolly Air Base. When I got home, my mother was sitting in the living room, smoking her Slims, watching her soap opera. She absently asked me how my day had gone and I told her fine. "Hear from Dad?" I said.

"No, but I'm sure he's fine." She always said that when we hadn't heard from him in a while. I suppose she thought I was worried about him, or that I felt vulnerable without him. It was neither. I just wanted to discuss something with my mother that we both cared about. If I spoke with her about things that happened at school, or on my weekends, she'd listen with half an ear, say something like, "Is that so?" or "You don't say?" I couldn't stand that sort of thing. But when I mentioned my father, she treated me a bit more like an adult, or at least someone who was worth listening to. I didn't want to feel like a boy that afternoon. As I turned from my mother and walked down the hall I thought about the day my father left for Viet Nam. Sharp in his uniform, sure behind his aviator specs, he slipped a cigar from his pocket and stuck it in mine. "Not till I get back," he said. "We'll have us one when we go fishing. Just you and me, out on the lake all day, smoking and casting and sitting. Don't let Mama see it. Put it in y'back pocket." He hugged me, shook my hand, and told me I was the man of the house now. He told me he was depending on me to take good care of my mother and sister. "Don't you let me down, now, hear?" And he tapped his thick finger on my chest. "You almost as big as me. Boy, you something else." I believed him when he told me those things. My heart swelled big enough to swallow my father, my mother, Claire. I loved, feared, and respected myself, my manhood. That day I could have put all of Waco, Texas, in my heart. And it wasn't till about three months later that I discovered I really wasn't the man of the house, that my mother and sister, as they always had, were taking care of me.

For a brief moment I considered telling my mother about what had happened at school that day, but for one thing, she was deep down in the halls of *General Hospital,* and never paid you much mind till it was over. For another thing, I just wasn't the kind of person—I'm still not, really—to discuss my problems with anyone. Like my father I kept things to myself, talked about my problems only in retrospect. Since my father wasn't around I consciously wanted to be like him, doubly like him, I could say. I wanted to be the man of the house in some respect, even if it had to be in an inward way. I went to my room, changed my clothes, and laid out my homework. I couldn't focus on it. I thought about Marvin, what I'd said about him or done to him—I couldn't tell which. I'd done something to him, said something about him; said something about and done something to myself. *How come you're after* me *and not* him? I kept trying to tell myself I hadn't meant it that way. *That* way. I thought about approaching Marvin, telling him what I really meant was that he was more Oakley's age and weight than I. I would tell him I meant I was no match for Oakley. *See, Marvin, what I meant was that he wants to fight a colored guy, but is afraid to fight you 'cause you could beat him.* But try as I did, I couldn't for a moment convince myself that Marvin would believe me. I meant it *that* way and no other. Everybody heard. Everybody knew. That afternoon I forced myself to confront the notion that tomorrow I would probably have to fight both Oakley and Marvin. I'd have to be two men.

I rose from my desk and walked to the window. The light made my skin look orange, and I started thinking about what Wickham had told us once about light. She said that oranges and apples, leaves and flowers, the whole multicolored world, was not what it appeared to be. The colors we see, she said, look like they do only because of the light or ray that shines on them. "The color of the thing isn't what you see, but the light that's reflected off it." Then she shut out the lights and shone a white light lamp on a prism. We watched the pale splay of colors on the projector screen; some people oohed and aahed. Suddenly, she switched on a black light and the color of everything changed. The prism colors vanished, Wickham's arms were purple, the buttons of her dress were as orange as hot coals, rather than the blue they had been only seconds before. We were all very quiet. "Nothing," she said, after a while, "is really what it appears to be." I didn't really understand then. But as I stood at the window, gazing at my orange skin, I wondered what kind of light I could shine on Marvin, Oakley, and me that would reveal us as the same.

I sat down and stared at my arms. They were dark brown again. I worked up a bit of saliva under my tongue and spat on my left arm. I spat again, then rubbed the spittle into it, polishing, working till my arm grew warm. As I spat, and rubbed, I wondered why Marvin did this weird, nasty thing to himself, day after day. Was he trying to rub away the black, or deepen it, doll it up? And if he did this weird nasty thing for a hundred years, would he spit-shine himself invisible, rolling away the eggplant skin, revealing the scarlet muscle, blue vein, pink and yellow tendon, white bone? Then disappear? Seen through, all colors, no colors. Spitting and rubbing. Is this the way you do it? I leaned forward, sniffed the arm. It smelled vaguely of mayonnaise. After an hour or so, I fell asleep.

I saw Oakley the second I stepped off the bus the next morning. He stood outside the gym in his usual black penny loafers, white socks, high-water jeans, T-shirt, and black jacket. Nailor stood with him, his big teeth spread across his bottom lip like playing cards. If there was anyone I felt like fighting, that day, it was Nailor. But I wanted to put off fighting for as long as I could. I stepped toward the gymnasium, thinking that I shouldn't run, but if I hurried I could beat Oakley to the door and secure myself near Gilchrest's office. But the moment I stepped into the gym, I felt Oakley's broad palm clap down on my shoulder. "Might as well stay out here, Coonie," he said. "I need me a little target practice." I turned to face him and he slapped me, one-two, with the back, then the palm of his hand, as I'd seen Bogart

do to Peter Lorre in *The Maltese Falcon*. My heart went wild. I could scarcely breathe.
I couldn't swallow.

"Call me a nigger," I said. I have no idea what made me say this. All I know is
that it kept me from crying. "Call me a nigger, Oakley."

"Fuck you, ya black-ass slope." He slapped me again, scratching my eye. "I
don't do what coonies tell me."

"Call me a nigger."

"Outside, Coonie."

"Call me one. Go ahead!"

He lifted his hand to slap me again, but before his arm could swing my way,
Marvin Pruitt came from behind me and calmly pushed me aside. "Git out my
way, boy," he said. And he slugged Oakley on the side of his head. Oakley stumbled
back, stiff-legged. His eyes were big. Marvin hit him twice more, once again to the
side of the head, once to the nose. Oakley went down and stayed down. Though
blood was drawn, whistles blowing, fingers pointing, kids hollering, Marvin just
stood there, staring at me with cool eyes. He spat on the ground, licked his lips, and
just stared at me, till Coach Gilchrest and Mr. Calderon tackled him and violently
carried him away. He never struggled, never took his eyes off me.

Nailor and Mrs. Wickham helped Oakley to his feet. His already fattened nose
bled and swelled so that I had to look away. He looked around, bemused, wall-
eyed, maybe scared. It was apparent he had no idea how bad he was hurt. He didn't
blink. He didn't even touch his nose. He didn't look like he knew much of anything. He looked at me, looked me dead in the eye, in fact, but didn't seem to
recognize me.

That morning, like all other mornings, we said the Pledge of Allegiance, sang
"The Yellow Rose of Texas," "The Eyes of Texas Are upon You," and "Mistress
Shady." The room stood strangely empty without Oakley, and without Marvin, but
at the same time you could feel their presence more intensely somehow. I felt like
I did when I'd walk into my mother's room and could smell my father's cigars or
cologne. He was more palpable, in certain respects, than when there in actual flesh.
For some reason, I turned to look at Ah-so, and just this once I let my eyes linger
on her face. She had a very gentle-looking face, really. That surprised me. She must
have felt my eyes on her because she glanced up at me for a second and smiled,
white teeth, downcast eyes. Such a pretty smile. That surprised me too. She held it
for a few seconds, then let it fade. She looked down at her desk, and sat still as a
photograph.

Equal Opportunity

WALTER MOSLEY

1

Bounty Supermarket was on Venice Boulevard, miles and miles from Socrates' home. He gaped at the glittering palace as he strode across the hot asphalt parking lot. The front wall was made from immense glass panes with steel framing to hold them in place. Through the big windows he could see long lines of customers with baskets full of food. He imagined apples and T-bone steaks, fat hams and the extra large boxes of cereal that they only sold in supermarkets.

The checkers were all young women, some of them even girls. Most were black. Black women, black girls—taking money and talking back and forth between themselves as they worked; running the packages of food over the computer eye that rung in the price and added it to the total without them having to think a thing.

In between the check-out counters black boys and brown ones loaded up bags of food for the customers.

Socrates walked up to the double glass doors and they slid open moaning some deep machine blues. He came into the cool air and cocked his ear to that peculiar music of supermarkets; steel carts wheeling around, crashing together, resounding with the thuds of heavy packages. Children squealing and yelling. The foot steps and occasional conversation blended together until they made a murmuring sound that lulled the ex-convict.

There was a definite religious feel to being in the great store. The lofty ceilings, the abundance, the wealth.

Dozens of tens and twenties in between credit cards and bank cards, went back and forth over the counters. Very few customers used coupons. The cash seemed to be endless. How much money passed over those counters every day?

And what would they think if they knew that the man watching them had spent twenty-seven years doing hard time in prison? Socrates barked out a single syllable laugh. They didn't have to worry about him. He wasn't a thief. Or, if he was, the only thing he ever took was life.

'Sir, can I help you?' Anton Crier asked.

Socrates knew the name because it was right there, on a big badge on his chest. ANTON CRIER ASST. MGR. He wore tan pants and a blue blazer with the supermarket insignia over the badge.

'I came for an application,' Socrates said. It was a line that he spent a whole day thinking about; a week practicing. *I came for an application.* For a couple of days he had practiced saying *job application,* but after a while he dropped the word *job* to make his request sound more sure. But when he went to Stony Wile and told him that he planned to say, 'I came for a application,' Stony said that you had to say *an* application. 'If you got a word that starts with *a, e, i, o,* or *u* then you got to say an instead of a,' Stony had said.

Anton Crier's brow knitted and he stalled a moment before asking, 'An application for what?'

'A job.' There he'd said it. It was less than a minute and this short white man, just a boy really, had already made him beg.

'Oh,' said Anton Crier, nodding like a wise elder. 'Uh. How old are you, sir?'

'Ain't that against the law?' Like all other convicts Socrates was a student of the law.

'Huh?'

'Askin' me my age. That's against the law. You cain't discriminate against color or sex or religion or infirmity or against age. That's the law.'

'Uh, well, yes, of course it is. I know that. I'm not discriminating against you. It's just that we don't have any openings right now. Why don't you come in in the fall when the kids are back at school?'

Anton leaned to the side, intending to leave Socrates standing there.

'Hold on,' Socrates said. His hands were held up, loosely as fists, in a nonchalant sort of boxing stance.

Socrates had big hands.

Anton looked, and waited.

'I came for an application,' Socrates repeated.

'But I told you . . .'

'I know what you said. But first you looked at my clothes and at my bald head. First yo' eyes said that this is some kinda old hobo and what do he want here when it ain't bottle redemption time.'

'I did not . . .'

'It don't matter,' Socrates said quickly. He knew better than to let a white man in uniform finish a sentence. 'You got to give me a application. That's the law too.'

'Wait here,' young Mr. Crier said. He turned and strode away toward an elevated office that looked down along the line of cash registers.

Socrates watched him go. So did the checkers and bag boys. He was their boss and they knew when he was unhappy. They stole worried glances at Socrates.

Socrates stared back. He wondered if any of those young black women would stand up for him. Would they understand how far he'd come to get there?

He'd traveled more than fourteen miles from his little apartment down in Watts. They didn't have any supermarkets or jobs in his neighborhood. And all the stores along Crenshaw and Washington knew him as a bum who collected bottles and cans for a living.

They wouldn't hire him.

Socrates hadn't held a real job in over thirty-seven years. He'd been unemployed for twenty-five months before he'd murdered Shep Fogel and Murial. Then he'd spent twenty-seven years in prison. Now, eight years free, fifty-eight years old, he was starting life over again.

Not one of those girls, or Anton Crier, were alive when he started his journey. If they were lucky they wouldn't understand him.

2

There was a large electric clock above the office. The sweep hand reared back and then battered up against each second counting each one as drummer beating out time on a slave galley. Socrates could see the young assistant manager through the window under the clock. He said something to an older white woman sitting there. The woman looked down at Socrates and then swiveled in her chair to a file cabinet. She took out a piece of paper and held it while telling Anton something. He reached for the paper a couple of times but the woman kept it away from him and continued talking. Finally she said something and Crier nodded. He took the paper from her and left the office, coming down the external stairs at a fast step. Walking past the checkers he managed not to look at Socrates before he was standing there in front of him.

'Here,' he said, handing the single sheet application form to Socrates. Crier never stopped moving. As soon as Socrates had the form in his hand the younger man was walking past him.

Socrates touched the passing elbow and asked, 'You got a pencil?'

'What?'

'I need a pencil to fill out this form.'

'You, you, you can just send it in.'

'I didn't come all this way for a piece a paper, man. I come to apply for a job.'

Anton Crier stormed over to one of the checkers, demanded her pencil, and stormed back over to Socrates.

'Here,' he said.

Socrates answered, 'Thank you,' but the assistant manager was already on his way back to the elevated office.

Half an hour later Socrates was standing at the foot of the stairs leading up to Anton and his boss. He stood there waiting for one of them to come down. They could see him through the window.

They knew he was there.

So Socrates waited, holding the application and borrowed pencil in his killer hands.

After twenty minutes he was wondering if a brick could break the wall of windows at the front of the store.

After thirty minutes he decided that it might take a shotgun blast.

Thirty-nine minutes had gone by when the woman, who had bottled red hair, came down to meet Socrates. Anton Crier shadowed her. Socrates saw the anger in the boy's face.

'Yes? Can I help you?' Halley Grimes asked. She had a jail house smile—insincere and crooked.

'I wanted to ask a couple of things about my application.'

'All the information is right there at the top of the sheet.'

'But I had some questions.'

'We're very busy, sir,' Ms Grimes broadened her smile to show that she'd be willing to talk, if only there was time. 'What do you need to know?'

'It asks here if I got a car or a regular ride to work.'

'Yes,' beamed Ms Grimes. 'What is it exactly that you don't understand?'

'I understand what it *says* but I just don't get what it means.'

The look of confusion came into Halley Grimes's face. Socrates welcomed a real emotion.

He answered her unasked question. 'What I mean to say is that I don't have a car or a ride but I can take a bus to work.'

The store manager took his application form and fingered the address.

'Where is this street?' she asked.

'Down Watts.'

'That's pretty far to go by bus isn't it? There are stores closer than this one you know.'

'But I could get here.' Socrates noticed that his head wanted to move as if to the rhythm of a song. Then he heard it: 'Baby Love,' by Diana Ross and the Supremes. It was being played lightly over the loud speaker. 'I could get here.'

'Well,' Ms Grimes seemed to brighten. 'We'll send this in to the main office and, if it's clear with them, we'll put it on our files. When there's an opening we'll give you a call.'

'A what?'

'A call. We'll call you if you're qualified and if a job opens up.'

'Uh, well, we got to figure somethin' else than that out. You see, I don't have no phone.'

'Oh, well then,' Ms Grimes held up her hands in a gesture of helplessness. 'I don't see that there's anything we can do. The main office demands a phone number. That's how they check on your address. They call.'

'How do they know that they got my address just 'cause a some phone they call? Wouldn't it be better if they wrote me?'

'I'm very busy, sir. I've told you that we need a phone number to process this application.' Halley Grimes held out the form toward Socrates. 'Without that there really isn't anything I can do.'

Socrates kept his big hands down. He didn't want to take the application back—partly because he didn't want to break the pudgy white woman's fingers.

'Do me a favor and send it in,' he said.

'I told you . . .'

'Just send it in, okay? Send it in. I'll be back to find out what they said.'

'You don't . . .'

'Just send it in.' There was violence in this last request.

Halley Grimes pulled the application away from his face and said, 'All right. But it won't make any difference.'

3

Socrates had to transfer on three buses to get back home. His little apartment was ramshackle and run down. It was an ill-conceived add-on wedged in between two furniture stores that had long ago gone bust. There wasn't even a front door—just a back exit that entered out on a poor yard at the alley. It was a sad home for anyone but an ex-convict and Socrates was always happy to see it.

He was especially happy that day. Talking to Crier and Grimes had worn him out.

He boiled potatoes and eggs in a sauce pan on his single hot plate and then cut them together in the pot with two knives, adding mustard and sweet pickle relish. After the meal he had two shots of whiskey and one Camel cigarette.

He was asleep by nine o'clock.

His dream blared until dawn.

It was a realistic sort of dream; no magic, no impossible wish. It was Socrates in a nine-foot cell with a flickering fluorescent light from the walk way keeping him from sleeping and reading, giving him a headache, hurting his eyes.

'Mr Bennett,' the sleeping Socrates called out from his broad sofa. He shouted so loudly that the mouse in the kitchen jumped up and out of the potato pan pinging his tail against the thin tin as he went.

Socrates heard the sound in his sleep. He turned but then slipped back into the flickering, painful dream.

'What you want?' the guard asked. He was big and black and meaner than anyone Socrates had ever met.

'I cain't read. I cain't sleep. That light been like that for three days now.'

'Put the pillow on your head,' the big guard said. He was trying to be kind.

'I cain't breathe like that,' Socrates answered sensibly.

'Then don't,' Mr Bennett replied.

As the guard walked away Socrates knew, for the first time really, why they kept him in that jail. He would have killed Bennett if he could have right then; put his big hands around that fat neck and squeezed as if he were holding on for dear life. He was so mad that he balled his fists in his sleep twenty-five years after the fact.

He was a sleeping man wishing that he could sleep. And he was mad, killing mad. He couldn't rest because of the crackling, buzzing light and the more it shone the angrier he became. And the angrier he got the more scared he was. Scared that he'd kill Bennett the first chance he got.

The anger built for days in that dream. The sound of grinding teeth could be heard throughout Socrates' two rooms.

Finally, when he couldn't stand it any more, he took his rubber squeeze ball in his left hand and slipped his right hand through the bars. He passed the ball through the bars to his right hand and gauged its weight in the basket of his fingers. He blinked back at the angry light, felt the weight of his hard rubber ball. The violent jerk started from his belly button, traveled up through his chest and shoulder, and down until his fingers tensed like steel. The ball flew in a straight line that shattered the light, broke it into blackness.

And in the jet night he heard Bennett say, ' That's the last light you get from the state of Indiana. Now all you got is sounds.'

Socrates woke up in the morning knowing that he had cried. He could feel the strain in the muscles of his throat. He got out of bed thinking about Anton Crier and Halley Grimes.

4

'You what?' asked Stony Wile. He'd run into Socrates getting off a bus on Central and offered to buy his friend a beer. They went to Moody's bar on 109th Street where Socrates told his tale.

'I been down there ev'ry day for five days. An' ev'ry day I go in there I ask'em if they got my okay from the head office yet.'

'An' what they say about that?'

'Well, the first day that boy, that Anton Crier just said no. So I left. Next day he told me that I had to leave. But I said that I wanted to talk to his boss. She come down an' tell me that she done already said how I cain't work there if I don't have no phone.'

'Yeah,' asked Stony Wile. 'Then what'd you do?'

'I told'em that they should call downtown and get some kinda answer on me because I was gonna come back ev'ryday till I get some kinda answer.' There was a finality in Socrates' voice that opened Stony's eyes wide.

'You don't wanna do sumpin' dumb now, Socco,' he said.

'An' what would that be?'

'They could get you into all kindsa trouble, arrest you for trespassin' if you keep it up.'

'Maybe they could. Shit. Cops could come in here an' blow my head off too but you think I should kiss they ass?'

'But that's different. You got to stand up for yo' pride, yo' manhood. But I don't see it wit' this supermarket thing.'

'Well,' Socrates said. 'On Thursday Ms Grimes told me that the office had faxed her to say I wasn't qualified for the position. She said that she had called the cops and said that I'd been down there harassin' them. She said that they said that if I ever come over there again that they would come arrest me. Arrest me! Just for tryin' t'get my rights.'

'That was the fourth day?' Stony asked to make sure that he was counting right.

'Uh-huh. That was day number four. I asked her could I see that fax paper but she said that she didn't have it, that she threw it out. You ever heard a anything like that? White woman workin' for a white corporation throwin' out paper work?'

Stony was once a ship builder who now ran a fishing day boat out of San Pedro. He'd been in trouble before but never in jail. He never thought about the thousands of papers he'd signed over his life; never wondered where they went.

'Why wouldn't they throw them away?' Stony asked.

'Because they keep ev'ry scrap a paper they got just as long as it makes they case in court.'

Stony nodded. Maybe he understood.

'So I called Bounty's head office,' Socrates said. 'Over in Torrence.'

'"You lyin',' Stony said again.

'An' why not? I applied for that job, Stony. I should get my hearin' wit' them.'

'What'd they say?'

'That they ain't never heard a me.'

'You lyin',' Stony said again.

'Grimes an' Crier the liars. An' you know I went down there today t'tell'em so. I was up in Anton's face when he told me that Ms Grimes was out. I told him that they lied and that I had the right to get me a job.'

'An' what he say?'

'He was scared. He thought I might a hit'im. And I might a too except Ms Grimes comes on down.'

'She was there?'

Said that she was on a lunch break; said that she was gonna call the cops on me. Shit. I called her a liar. I said that she was a liar and that I had a right to be submitted to the main office and that they could call her.' Socrates jabbed his finger at Stony as if he were the one holding the job hostage. 'I told'er that I'd be back on Monday and that I expected some kinda fair treatment.'

'Well that sounds right,' Stony said. 'It ain't up to her who could apply an' who couldn't. She got to be fair.'

'Yeah,' Socrates answered. 'She said that the cops would be waitin' for me on Monday. Maybe Monday night you could come see me in jail.'

5

On Saturday Socrates took his canvas cart full of cans to the Boys Market on Adams. He waited three hours behind Calico, an older black woman who prowled the same streets he did, and two younger black men who worked as a team.

Calico and DJ and Bernard were having a good time waiting. DJ was from Oakland and had come down to LA to stay with his grandmother when he was fifteen. She died a year later and he'd had to live on the streets since then. But DJ didn't complain. He talked about how good life was and how much he was able to collect on the streets.

'Man,' DJ said. 'I wish they would let me up there in Beverly Hills just one week. Gimme one week with a pickup an' I could live for a year off a the good trash they got up there. They th'ow out stuff that still work up there.'

'How the fuck you know, man?' Bernard said. 'When you ever been up there?'

'When I was doin' day work. I helped a dude build a cinder block fence up on Hollandale. I saw what they th'owed out. I picked me up a portable TV right out the trash an' I swear that sucker get ev'ry channel.'

'I bet it don't get cable,' Bernard said.

'It would if I had a cable to hook it up wit'.'

They talked like that for three hours. Calico cooed and laughed with them, happy to be in the company of young men.

But Socrates was just mad.

Why the hell did he have to wait for hours? Who were they in that supermarket to make full grown men and women wait like they were children.

At two o'clock he got up and walked away from his canvas wagon.

'Hey,' Bernard called. 'You want us t'watch yo' basket?'

'You could keep it,' Socrates said. 'I ain't never gonna use the goddamned thing again.'

Calico let out a whoop, but Socrates didn't turn around to see her. He walked on so mad that he wanted to hit someone.

On Sunday Socrates sharpened his pocket knife on a graphite stone. He didn't keep a gun. If the cops caught him with a gun he would have spent the rest of his life in jail. But there was no law against a knife blade under three inches; and three inches was all a man, who knew how to use a knife, needed.

Socrates sharpened his knife but he didn't know why exactly. Grimes and Crier weren't going to harm him, at least not with violence. And if they called the cops a knife wouldn't be any use anyway. If the cops even thought that he had a knife they could shoot him and make a good claim for self defense.

But Socrates still practiced whipping out the knife and slashing with the blade sticking out of the back end of his fist.

'Hah!' he yelled.

6

He left the knife on the orange crate next to his sofa that morning before leaving for Bounty Supermarket. The RTD bus came right on time and he made his connections quickly, one after the other.

In half an hour he was back on that parking lot. It was a big building, he thought, but not as big as the penitentiary had been.

A smart man would have turned around and tried some other store, Socrates knew that. It didn't take a hero to make a fool out of himself.

It was before nine-thirty and the air still had the hint of a morning chill. The sky was a pearl gray and the parking lot was almost empty.

Socrates counted seven breaths and then walked toward the door with no knife in his hand. He cursed himself softly under his breath because he had no woman at home to tell him that he was a fool.

Nobody met him at the door. There was only one checker on duty while the rest of the workers went up and down the aisles restocking and straightening the shelves.

With nowhere else to go Socrates went toward the elevated office. He was half the way there when he saw Halley Grimes coming down the stairs. Seeing him she turned and went, actually ran, back up to the office.

Socrates was sure that she meant to call the police. He wanted to run but couldn't. All he could do was take one step after the other; the way he'd done in his cell sometimes, sometimes the way he did at home.

Two men appeared at the high door when Socrates reached the stairs. Salt and pepper, white and black. The older one, a white man, wore a tan wash and wear suit with a cheap maroon tie. The Negro had on black jeans, a black jacket, and a white turtle neck shirt. He was very light skinned but his nose and lips would always give him away.

The men came down to meet him. They were followed by Grimes and Crier.

"Mr Fortlow?" the white man said.

Socrates nodded and looked him in the eye.

'My name is Parker,' he continued. 'And this is Mr Weems.'

'Uh-huh,' Socrates answered.

The two men formed a wall behind which the manager and assistant manager slipped away.

'We work for Bounty,' Mr Weems said. 'Would you like to come upstairs for a moment?'

'What for?' Socrates wanted to know.

'We'd like to talk,' Parker answered.

The platform office was smaller than it looked from the outside. The two cluttered desks, that sat back to back, took up most of the space. Three sides were windows that gave a full panorama of the store. The back wall had a big blackboard on it with the chalked in time schedules of everyone who worked there. Beneath the blackboard was a safe door.

"Have a seat, Mr. Fortlow.' Parker gestured toward one of the two chairs. He sat in the other chair while Weems perched on a desk.

'Coffee?' asked Parker.

'What's this all about, man?' Socrates asked. He didn't have patience with false courtesy.

Smiling, Parker said, 'We want to know what your problem is with Ms Grimes. She called the head office on Friday and told us that she was calling the police because she was afraid of you.'

'I don't have no problem with Ms Grimes or Anton Crier or Bounty Supermarket. I need a job and I wanted to make a application. That's all.'

'But she told you that you had to have a phone number in order to complete your file,' said Weems.

'So? Just 'cause I don't have no phone then I cain't work? That don't make no sense at all. If I don't work I cain't afford no phone. If I don't have no phone then I cain't work. You might as well just put me in the ground.'

'It's not Bounty's problem that you don't have a phone.' Parker's face was placid but the threat was in his tone.

'All I want is to make a job application. All I want is to work,' Socrates said. Really he wanted to fight. He wanted his knife at close quarters with those private cops. But instead he went on, 'I ain't threatened nobody. I ain't said I was gonna do a thing. All I did was to come back ev'ry day an' ask if they had my okay from you guys yet. That's all. On the job application they asked if I had a car or a ride to work—to see if I could get here. Well, I come in ev'ry day for a week at nine-thirty or before. I come in an' asked if I been cleared yet. I didn't do nuthin' wrong. An' if that woman is scared it must be 'cause she knows she ain't been right by me. But I didn't do nuthin'.'

There was no immediate answer to Socrates' complaint. The men looked at him but kept silent. There was the hum of machinery coming from somewhere but Socrates couldn't figure out where. He concentrated on keeping his hands on his knees, on keeping them open.

'But how do you expect to get a job when you come in every day and treat the people who will be your bosses like they're doing something wrong?' Weems seemed really to want to know.

'If I didn't come in they woulda th'owed out my application, prob'ly did anyway. But at least she called in about me. At least the head office heard my name. I ain't no kid. I'm fifty-eight years old. I'm unemployed an' nowhere near benefits. If I don't find me some way t'get some money I'll starve. So, you see, I had to come. I couldn't let these people say that I cain't even apply. If I did that then I might as well die.'

Parker sighed. Weems scratched the top of his head and then rubbed his nose.

'You can't work here,' Parker said at last. 'If we tried to push you off on Ms Grimes she'd go crazy. She really thought that you were going to come in here guns blazing.'

'So 'cause she thought that I was a killer then I cain't have no job?' Socrates knew the irony of his words but he also knew their truth. He didn't care about a job just then. He was happy to talk, happy to say what he felt. Because he knew that he was telling the truth and that those men believed him.

'You could ask Pena to take a look at him,' Weeks said to Parker. 'You could tell'im up front what happened and see if he'd talk to him.'

Parker reached down under the desk and came out with a brief case. From this he brought out a sheet of paper; Socrates' application form.

'There's just one question,' Parker said.

7

'What he wanna know?' Stony Wile asked at Iula's bar and grill—two altered school buses that were welded together and suspended over Tony's open air garage. They were there with Right Burke, Markham Peal, and Howard Shakur. Iula gave Socrates a party when she heard that he got a job at the Bounty supermarket on Olympic. She made the food and his friends brought the liquor.

'He wanted to know why I had left one of the boxes blank.'

'What box?'

'The one that asks if I'd ever been arrested for or convicted of a felony.'

'Damn. What you say?'

'That I musta overlooked it.'

'An' then you lied?'

'Damn straight. But he knew I was lyin'. He was a cop before he went to work for Bounty. Both of'em was. He asked me that if they put through a check on me would it come up bad? An' I told him that he didn't need to put through no checks.'

'Mmm!' Stony hummed, shaking his head. 'That's always gonna be over your head, man. Always.'

Socrates laughed and grabbed his friend by the back of his head. He hugged Stony and then held him by the shoulders. 'I done had a lot worse hangin' over me, brother. At least I get a paycheck till they find out what I am.'

Amen

S U N N Y   N A S H

A blue moon etched Dorsey's long thin shadow in pitch black on the dirt road, exaggerating the length of her pencil legs and the height of her witchy hairdo. Stepping on sharp rocks that dug into the soles of my feet, I was unable to see my path as clearly as I could see the elongated shadow of my next-door neighbor, Dorsey. I remember hobbling along behind Dorsey and trying to keep the distance short between my tiny outline and her big one.

"Don't walk so fast, Dorsey. Rocks are cutting my feet."

"You better toughen up your tender feet, little girl," Dorsey called. "Cause the Lord done placed you in a mighty poor position to ever wear good shoes."

"Kids on television got good shoes," I said. "I don't know why Mama can't buy me a pair. I never get anything good."

"Seven years on earth don't earn you the right to complain about nothing," said Dorsey. "When you been around thirty-nine years like me, the bottoms of your feet will be just like mine, as thick as a pair of work boots."

Running a few steps over the crippling surface, I noticed dim light squeezing through shuttered windows at the funeral home. I imagined the McIntosh brothers hovering over a dead body doing whatever it was undertakers did to dead bodies before they buried them. One evening I ran home screaming that Miss Meg said the undertakers sucked blood out of live bodies and dead ones, too. That night, I stared at a bowl of beans and rice until my blurred vision made the food resemble mangled flesh.

"Undertakers don't suck out the blood with their mouths," Mama explained. "They pump it out and drain the bodies with a hose. Now, go to bed." Disoriented by her explanation, I took a bath in ice cold water, crawled into my cot in a daze and dreamed that the undertakers pumped blood from a screaming Miss Meg.

Miss Meg would never be out on a moonlit night without her husband, Mr. Jake. To Miss Meg, there was something evil about seeing her shadow in the dead of night. And to walk past the cemetery and the funeral home on a moonlit night was asking to be cursed for life! "If you point at a funeral home, your finger will fall off," Miss Meg had told me. Until I overheard that a nurse had cut off Old Otto's frostbitten fingers, I wondered if he'd lost them by pointing at the funeral home five times. A silhouette passed a shaded window. "Dorsey, you see that?"

"See what?"

"Someone carrying a dead body." I ran backwards trying to keep up with Dorsey and watch the window.

"It's a funeral home, Lacy! They keep dead bodies in there!"

I was still walking backwards when we reached the Durhams' house. Every light in the house was on. From the front window, a radio blared music through so much static it sounded like someone was frying bacon. And teenagers out front kicked up yard dirt trying to dance.

"Come on, Lacy!" Dorsey said.

Everyone, including Dorsey, considered the Durhams the lowlife of the neighborhood. The mother and big sisters brought men home and did to them for money what Dorsey did to Ray for free every Saturday night after drinking and fighting. But I overheard Mama tell Grandma that the Durham women brought men home and took their money without doing anything with them. Although Grandma disliked the Durhams as much as anyone, she said it served the men right. They had no business in a house on this side of town. Years later, I figured out what that meant.

"Come on, Lacy!" Dorsey said.

Before the glow and sound of the Durhams' party had faded, distant church music and preaching crept into my ears from the revival house—an abandoned rent house without electricity. Old Otto and some other bums used to sleep there before the owner chased them away.

"Dorsey," I called, walking a few steps behind her. "This sounds like church!"

"Don't worry, Lacy," Dorsey said. "You don't need no shoes to go see God. He takes you any kind of way."

"My bare feet don't bother me! I want to know if this is going to be like church."

"Don't start on me, Lacy," Dorsey said irritably.

"I ain't going in there if it's going to be like church."

"Lord, Lord." Dorsey moaned and threw her hands in the air. "I been cleaning up and cooking all day for old lady Larson's birthday party. I ain't wanting to hear no more whining cause that's the whiniest old bat I ever been around! Whining that the punch too sweet. Whining that her girdle too tight. Whining that her house going to be too hot cause her cake got so many candles. I say, if she put all the candles on that cake that's suppose to be on it, it burn down the house! Done listened to enough whining for one day, Lacy."

"Dorsey, I ain't whining! I'm telling you I don't want to go to nothing that's like church!"

"Your little sassy tail need to go to church," she said, turning around and sending me a wicked eye.

"Grandma say church can't help nobody," I screamed.

"Church surely can't help that mean woman you call Grandma!"

"Church can't help my brother get well," I said, lingering behind. "If it could, Mama would take him."

"Come on, Lacy!"

"Dorsey, I hate church!"

"Girl, it's a sin to say you hate church."

"Well, I won't say it. I'll hate it in my mind."

"Lacy, you going to burn up in hell!"

"Well, I just have to burn up in hell," I assured Dorsey. "Cause nothing makes me sicker than church!"

"It's a revival!" Dorsey yelled, grabbing my hand and dragging me toward the building. "Not church!"

"Only reason I'm going with you is cause you say the man can heal! Dorsey, can he really heal?"

"Yeah, Lacy, he can heal."

"Well, they sure can't sing," I said, listening to an odd mixture of bad voices trying to blend into a song. "Crows with a bad cold sound better than that."

"How I get stuck with you tonight?" Dorsey picked up the tail of her dress, wiped moisture from her face and then patted the frizzy ends of her hair, sticking up in every direction.

"Cause you're scared to walk at night by yourself," I said, following Dorsey up the dark steps of the tiny revival house.

"I know y'all see me," said a woman from the step smoking a cigarette and reeking of liquor, cheap perfume and armpit odor.

"Can't see nothing but your cigarette light," Dorsey said.

"You calling somebody black?" The woman jumped up from her seat on the step, her taffeta petty coats rustling.

"Puff so I can see!" shouted Dorsey, at least a whole head taller than the other woman. The woman's eyes bulged like a snake and her cheeks sank deeply inside her mouth as she dragged hard and long on the cigarette. "Ugly, too!" Dorsey said.

The woman pulled the cigarette butt out of her mouth with long glistening hooked red fingernails and inhaled slowly before releasing the hazy, rancid breath. Dorsey disappeared behind a veil of smoke and emerged coughing and clawing out of the cloud. Looking up at the two women and secretly hoping for a fight, I stepped back in case they started passing licks.

"You need to get your little drunk behind out of my way," Dorsey said, poking the woman in the chest with her finger. "I'm on a mission tonight. Got no time for your mess."

"If this wasn't church, I'd kick your ass," the woman slurred, throwing her cigarette in the dirt.

"You too little to be talking big woman trash," Dorsey said. "Better watch out," the little woman reeled. "Brother Magruder don't let nobody talk to Sister Magruder like that."

"Melroy Magruder do what any skirt tell him to do," Dorsey said. "Now, get away from me before I tear that store-bought hair off your head."

The woman grabbed her head. Dorsey laughed, pushed past her and went inside. Soft light from kerosene lamps licked people's tired faces. As soon as Dorsey and I got inside the building, she bent over and held her back. Confused, I watched her hold onto the back of the pew in front of her while she eased herself down and motioned for me to sit beside her.

"Faith, brothers and sisters!" yelled the six-foot-six overweight reverend–doctor–faith healer, Melroy Magruder, wearing flowing garments and a high white collar. "Y'all need faith!"

"Faith!" screeched Miss Meg's toothless mouth, smeared with bright red lipstick. Dressed up in a yellow dress and Red Fox stockings, sitting in a front-row seat, Miss Meg didn't look like herself. Powdered to chalky white, her sooty face was finished off with a red clown circle on each cheek. Her hair greased to a high gloss peeked from a white straw hat with limp yellow silk flowers and ribbons hanging off the back.

"Well, well, well, alright, Lord," Mr. Jake monotonically chanted from a corner full of old, tired men wearing secondhand, bad-fitting suits with heat melted fibers where the iron was too hot when they tried to press out the wrinkles. "We having us some good church tonight!"

"Dorsey, you said this wasn't church." "Hush up!" Dorsey hissed.

"I hate church!" I stuck my fingers in my ears and started singing a blues I'd heard on the radio. Dorsey elbowed me and slapped my fingers down.

"Yes, yes," Melroy said. "Me and my family glad to be here among y'all good people of Hearne, Texas tonight."

"Hearne, Texas," Miss Meg screeched and clapped her hands.

"Amen!" shouted a sweaty woman, fanning like crazy with the shopping section of a newspaper. Trying to avoid her rank breeze, I hid my face in my hands.

"When are they getting to the healing part, Dorsey?" I asked, staring through slits between my fingers. "If it works, maybe I can get Mama to bring Matthew."

"Don't get your hopes up about Matt," Dorsey said.

"But you said Melroy was a healing preacher."

"Your baby brother's five years old, Lacy, and can't walk and talk," Dorsey said. "Doctors don't know what's wrong with him. A healing preacher got his limits."

"I want to make y'all acquainted with my fine boys," Melroy said, pointing toward the door at his twin sons, mirror images of each other and younger versions of him. All heads turned to the twins who nodded from their usher positions. Coughing and fixing her wig, Sister Magruder stumbled in through the side door and plopped down on the piano stool.

Melroy glanced toward the choir stand. "My lovely wife, Sister Magruder."

"Amen!" shouted the congregation.

"We go to lots of towns," Melroy shouted, returning his attention to the congregation.

"Lots of towns," Miss Meg repeated.

"Big towns," he said.

"Yes, sir," Miss Meg repeated. "Big towns."

"Amen!" someone called from the congregation.

"And little towns, too," Melroy said.

"Little towns," Miss Meg repeated.

"All over this here great State of Texas in this fine preaching work," Melroy said.

"Amen!" shouted the woman sitting beside me.

"Well, well, well," chanted Old Otto from a corner where he sat alone. People chose to stand around the walls of the crowded room rather than share a pew with Old Otto who wore his home on his back—no place to bathe or sleep or eat or put his things. Even as a child, I knew it was his extraordinary singing voice that earned him toleration.

"Sing, Old Otto," I whispered. "Go on and sing the song out loud instead of humming. Sing!"

"Hush, Lacy," Dorsey scolded.

"But ain't no folks," Melroy yelled in his ugly singsong fashion, shaking his finger above his head.

"No folks," screeched Miss Meg like a parrot.

"In no town," Melroy shouted.

"In no town," repeated Miss Meg, clapping her hands.

"On the face of this whole earth," said Melroy.

"On the face of this whole earth," Miss Meg repeated.

"Well, well, well," Otto chanted and sort of sang in a rich bass voice. "Lord, Lord, I need you, Lord."

"Sing, Old Otto," I whispered. "Sing."

"Precious Lord," Old Otto began singing my favorite church song. "Take my hand."

"Amen," I screamed. "Sing it Old Otto!"

"Hush up!" Dorsey said. "You ain't suppose to like church!"

"Amen," came from somewhere in the congregation.

"No nicer," Melroy said.

"No nicer," repeated Miss Meg.

"Lead me on," Old Otto sang.

"No nicer than the folks," Melroy yelled.

"No nicer than the folks," Miss Meg repeated.

"Let me stand," Old Otto sang, holding the last note for an unnatural length of time.

"No nicer than the folks in Dallas!" Melroy shouted.

"Dallas?" Miss Meg shouted. "He say Dallas?"

"I am tired . . ." Old Otto's note trailed off.

Room noise dropped to shoe level, where worn soles and bare feet moved on loose grit. Throat clearing and grunting filled the room. Offended faces stared at Melroy who desperately sucked breath through coarse nasal hairs, clasped his hands together several times and twisted his fingers nervously.

Like a balloon about to burst, my suppressed laughter forced tears into my eyes. Little sounds I couldn't swallow rose in my throat when Melroy's eyeballs started darting about the room like a cartoon character who'd caught a glimpse of a ghost.

The woman next to me threw her newspaper on the floor and got up. "How can that fool heal somebody when he can't remember what town he's in," she shouted, stepping on toes and shoving her big behind in people's faces to make her way down the row to the aisle and out of the building. "She's right," said another woman, getting up and leaving. "This clown don't know what he's doing."

Sweat streamed from Melroy's tight, black, greasy curls. Speechless, he smacked his juicy lips and flung moist beads from his face with his dimpled and diamond fingers. He glanced at his enormous sons who were trying to convince the grumbling congregation to stay.

Pressure built up behind my ears. A snort escaped my nose. I lost control of my quivering lips. "Hearne," I yelled, breaking into full laughter. "You're in Hearne, fool!"

"Hearne!" Melroy finally managed to utter. "I meant Hearne. Y'all know I meant Hearne. Sister Magruder, let's have us a song, if you please." He ran his index finger into his collar, loosening it, while Sister Magruder fumbled with several books of music on the narrow ledge of the piano. Sheets of notes slid to the floor. Awkwardly, she went down to retrieve them.

"Dorsey," I said. "This is too much fun to be church." People looking around to see the source of my laughter started snickering and openly chuckling, too. What was left of the congregation was rapidly disintegrating into a heap of amusement.

"Come on, y'all," Dorsey yelled. "Give the man a chance!"

"I never had so much fun in my life!" I slapped my legs.

"Y'all ain't being fair," Dorsey said.

"That man may not know how to heal nobody!" I shouted, getting up. "But he sure know how to make people laugh. I can't stand it, Dorsey! I'm about to pee on myself."

"You set your butt down," she said, pulling me back in my seat. "Or I'm going to knock the pee out of you."

The congregation had broken into full laughter, pointing at Melroy and falling off their seats.

"Play something, woman!" Melroy yelled at his wife.

Sister Magruder was still busy picking up and sorting strewn sheet music.

Melroy pulled up his robe. Lamplight bounced off his gold watch chain and flitted around the room. He fished a white handkerchief from his pocket.

Finally, Sister Magruder selected a piece. She set the music in front of her and ceremoniously raised her hands high above the piano. When her fingers came down on the keys of the out-of-tune piano, a series of sour notes introduced a hymn that no one recognized. I knew I didn't. By the expressions on the confused faces around me, I knew they didn't recognize it either. Everyone turned to Old Otto for help but all he could do was shrug.

Sister Magruder's equally sour voice began croaking out lyrics. "There is a fountain," she strained to reach notes so high that she ran out of air and gagged. In all the years since, I have not yet heard stranger sounds than those squeezed from Sister Magruder's veiny neck. All the while, her feet stomped the floor and her skinny butt bounced around on the stool and her hands banged all the keys on the piano in no particular order. The congregation watched her in horror and no one joined in. "Sister Magruder," Melroy said, noticing the crowd's response to his wife's musical disability. "You can stop now."

She couldn't hear him.

"That's enough, darling," Melroy said, waving his hands.

She still didn't hear him. Finally, Melroy whistled! That got her attention.

"Darling, I'll take over the song from here," Melroy said and then sang, "There is a fountain."

The congregation sang reluctantly, "There is a fountain."

Sister Magruder got up and slammed the piano shut!

"Amen!" someone shouted.

Strings rang long after she had trampled out the side door.

"Drawn from Emanuel's veins," Old Otto took over the lead.

"Sing it, Old Otto," I screamed.

"Yes, Lordy!" Miss Meg screeched, clapping her hands.

"Dorsey," I whispered. "I have to go to the toilet."

Dorsey stared straight ahead and sang along.

"Dorsey," I pleaded.

"And sinners plunged beneath that flood," Old Otto led the congregation. "Lose all their guilty stains."

Dorsey rocked from side to side with her eyes closed. Listening to Old Otto's soothing voice, I leaned back in my seat, clamped my thighs tight and closed my eyes, too.

"Well, well, well," Mr. Jake chanted. "Now, let's get on with us some church tonight."

"Lose all their guilty stains," Old Otto led the congregation to a fine finish.

"Dorsey," I whispered. "Why everybody keep saying this is church if it ain't church?"

She didn't answer.

"Everybody need faith," Melroy said, raising open palms above his head and looking up at the ceiling.

"Yes, Lordy," screeched Miss Meg.

"Amen," several people in the congregation responded, working themselves into waves of infectious excitement. Emotions began running like a steamy river through the crowd. Some who had left came back into the cramped hot musty meeting place and new faces appeared as well. Body heat and the humble odor of overworked muscles created an atmosphere full of mystery. Desperate and despairing souls clung to the edges of hard benches waiting to see a miracle. More people squeezed into the room and joined into Old Otto's hymn.

"Y'all all knows there's plenty suffering out there in that mean old world," Melroy shouted. "Plenty of people sick!"

"Yes!" the congregation responded.

"Plenty evil!" he growled.

"Yes!" the congregation responded.

"Amen!"

"Plenty people trying to take away what you got!" he shouted. "Plenty suffering souls!"

"Yes!" the congregation responded.

"Plenty people needing a healing!" he yelled, looking around the audience and raising his hands toward the ceiling. "Won't y'all let me heal a poor suffering soul tonight?" Dorsey's hand went up.

"Yes, Sister, let me heal you!" Melroy yelled, motioning for Dorsey to come forward. "Come on up here."

Dorsey got up with her hands on the small of her back. I knew Dorsey wasn't sick. Dorsey and her old man Ray had lived on the other side of the duplex from us as long as I could remember. She'd never even had a cold. Everyone knew Dorsey wasn't sick.

"Can you make it?" Melroy asked. "Need some help?"

Shaking her head, Dorsey dragged toward the front.

"This sister is in a lot of pain," Melroy said. "Come on up here, sister, so I can heal you."

Dorsey stopped in front of Melroy's makeshift, wooden-box riser. "Yes, sir," Dorsey said.

"What's your name and your pain, sister?" Melroy asked.

"Dorsey Charles. Pain in my back."

Melroy blew his nose on the handkerchief and put it back in his pocket. Elevating his hand, he descended, stepping close to Dorsey. "Kneel, sister."

Dorsey knelt.

"Lord, I'm coming home," Old Otto began singing. "I wandered far away from God."

"Amen!" shouted Miss Meg, swaying back and forth like Humpty Dumpty and clapping her hands above her head. "Yes! Yes!"

"Now, I'm coming home," Old Otto led the congregation.

Melroy laid a sweaty palm on Dorsey's shoulder and with a lion's voice made the rafters rumble. "Lord, look down on us tonight." Melroy moaned something unintelligibly and ran his hands up and down Dorsey's back, then up and down her front.

"Amen!" shouted Miss Meg who—by this time—was crying and fanning with her hat. Real tears streamed down her face. When Mr. Jake walked over to Miss Meg to comfort her, she threw her fists aimlessly and hit him. Unoffended that she had landed a few punches in his chest, a tranced Mr. Jake sang and held Miss Meg's arms behind her. Real tears streamed from his eyes, too.

Dorsey stood transfixed under Melroy's touch. Her eyes rolled back until they were white marbles glowing in the sockets. The congregation murmured softly. Wishing for the skill, I wondered how Dorsey hid her eyeballs like that. For a few moments, I tried but the effort required to hide eyeballs gave me a headache. When I stopped, a little baby on the shoulder of a woman a row ahead was staring at me.

Melroy withdrew his hands from Dorsey. She went limp and released her eyeballs. The congregation finished singing. Melroy eased Dorsey to the floor.

"Amen!" the congregation screamed. Dorsey pretended to be asleep. I knew that was a trick, too. Dorsey's fluttering eyelids were visible all the way to the back row.

"Let the spirit come in me, Lord," Melroy cried over Dorsey and rubbed her breasts at the same time. "So, I can heal this poor ailing woman. Y'all want to see me heal this good sister?"

"Amen!"

"Well, y'all got to believe in me," Melroy said, running his fingers down the front of her body.

"Amen!" "If y'all don't believe in me hard enough, I can't heal her. And then it'll be y'all fault this good sister have to suffer the rest of her life. Y'all got to have faith in me."

"Amen!"

"You got faith in me, sister?" he asked Dorsey. She mumbled something through slightly smiling lips. Slowly, she got up and stood perfectly straight. The room fell dead in silence.

"This sister is healed," Melroy yelled. "Praise the Lord."

"Amen!" the congregation cried. "Amen!"

As Old Otto broke loose with an up-tempo rendition of "Never More to Roam," the congregation clapped in rhythm. Dorsey got up, lifted her skirt a little and danced in the aisle. Swishing the tail of her cotton work dress, she turned in circles on her toes. The backs of her worn shoes flopped up and down with each turn. Melroy sprinkled Dorsey with water from a small bottle as she whirled past him.

"Amen!"

The congregation was on the edge of frenzy, singing with Old Otto and dancing in the aisle with Dorsey. Melroy, turning in circles, sprinkled everybody with water.

"Amen," screeched Miss Meg, overtaken by a fit of emotion. She began screaming and crying and went as stiff as a board. Mr. Jake stretched Miss Meg out on the empty pew.

"Open now thine arms of love," Old Otto led everyone in song. "Lord, I'm coming home. Lord, I'm coming home. Open now thine arms of love."

Melroy stepped upon his riser and raised his open palms and shouted, "And open now thine pocketbooks!" The twins circulated through the crowd with collection baskets.

The congregation broke into the hymn "Steal away."

"Let's thank the Lord for this miracle tonight," Melroy shouted. "Let's thank him good! Let's dig deep in our pockets."

Singing "steal away," people went into impoverished pockets and purses pulling out their money. The baskets filled quickly.

"That's good," Melroy said, clapping his hands and closing his eyes. "Yes, that's real good."

"Steal away to Jesus," Old Otto sang, sneakily lifting a fistful of bills as the basket passed him. "Steal away. Steal away home."

One of Melroy's sons sold bottles of blessed healing fluid and the other sold wallet-size squares of blessed fabric.

"Friends," Melroy yelled, "Carry your prayer cloth with you at all times for good luck."

"Amen," someone cried from the congregation.

"If it's a money problem y'all having," Melroy said, "put my prayer cloth in your wallet and it'll help you come into money."

"Amen!" someone yelled. "I need two of them."

"If it's husband or wife trouble y'all having," Melroy began. "Put the prayer cloth in your . . ."

"Let me have one of them prayer cloths, too."

"Put my cloth in your . . . ," Melroy hesitated.

"I ain't got long to stay here," Old Otto led the congregation as Melroy's boys made their way up and down the aisles taking up money and passing out water and cloths. "If it's a husband or a wife problem, put the cloth in your . . . in your," Melroy searched for words.

"My Lord, he calls me," Old Otto led the congregation.

Sister Magruder sneaked back in through the side door and eased down on the piano bench.

"Put my prayer cloth between your . . . your," he searched.

"Amen!"

"He calls me by the thunder," Old Otto led while they gave their money to the fat Magruder twins.

Sister Magruder started playing the piano softly, looking around to see if anyone noticed her return. Everyone was caught up in the excitement.

"The trumpet sounds within my soul," sang the congregation. Sister Magruder croaked her way into the song.

"Amen!"

"Put the blasted thing between your legs," Melroy yelled, waving in Dorsey's direction before leaving the building through a side entrance.

Dorsey dashed down the aisle toward me. "Going to the toilet," she shouted from the door. "Stay here."

"I ain't got long to stay here," they sang.

"Well, well, well," Mr. Jake chanted and clapped his hands.

I got up and went outside. From the shadows, I saw Dorsey standing near the side door with her hand outstretched while Melroy pushed his hand deep into his pocket.

"Good take tonight," Dorsey said.

"Not too good," he said. "Seen better."

"Give me my money, Magruder," Dorsey said.

Melroy put something in her hand and turned to leave.

"Wait up, Melroy," Dorsey called, staring at the money in her palm. "This ain't what we agreed on."

"I told you, it wasn't that good of a night," he said.

"Well, I know it was better than this!"

"That's all you getting out of me."

"Then, I'm going to have to go in there and tell off on you, Mister," Dorsey said, walking away. "Then, you can forget coming back to The Hill stealing from my neighbors."

"OK," he said, grinning and reaching in his pocket.

"You better pull out another twenty dollars or else a gun to shoot me with," Dorsey said.

Melroy handed Dorsey some more money, which she took and stuffed in her bosom.

"Steal away," the congregation sang.

In a hurry, Dorsey almost ran over me. "Lacy, watch out."

"Why you fool the people, Dorsey?" I asked.

"I didn't fool them. They know I don't need healing. They know Melroy can't do it if I do need healing."

"Then what everybody in there praying and hollering about?" I watched Dorsey's stubby hair being raised by a strong breeze.

"That wasn't praying," Dorsey said through crooked lips.

"Then why y'all saying Amen!"

"Every time somebody say Amen don't mean they been praying."

"No, it mean they been poking fun at God!"

"You were laughing harder than anybody in there!"

"Dorsey," I whispered. "I wasn't poking fun at God."

"For goodness sake, Lacy, we were having a good time," she said, walking away. "You said you ain't never had so much fun."

"You told me the revival man could heal Matthew," I said sadly. "And you knew all the time he couldn't."

"No, he can't heal nobody! It's all a show! A show, Lacy!"

"You going to hell, Dorsey! You let that revival man rub your titties! I saw you!"

Afraid that God was somewhere up there behind the moon thinking I was part of that terrible joke, I hobbled down the dark street away from Dorsey as fast as I could.

Contributors

JULIAN ELIHU BAGLEY wrote short stories during the 1920s and 1930s. They appeared in African American journals such as *Opportunity* and *The Crisis*.

A significant writer of the Harlem Renaissance, ARNA BONTEMPS also served as a librarian and as executive assistant to the president at Fisk University. He wrote poetry, fiction, essays, and children's books and edited several anthologies. Among his works are *The Story of the Negro, 100 Years of Negro Freedom, Frederick Douglass: Slave Fighter and Freeman, Any Place but Here,* and his collection of short stories, *The Old South: "A Summer Tragedy" and Other Stories of the Thirties.* He won two Alexander Pushkin poetry prizes, Julius Rosenwald fellowships, and a Guggenheim fellowship for creative writing.

Screenwriter, novelist, and dramatist CECIL M. BROWN earned a master's degree from the University of Chicago, and as noted in *Contemporary Authors,* focuses on "black survival in a corrupt society" in his writings.

ED BULLINS, who also writes under the pseudonym Kingsley B. Bass Jr., began writing plays as a member of the Black Panther Party during the 1960s and soon emerged as a principal figure in the Black Arts movement. Primarily a dramatist, his plays include *In New England Winter, The Fabulous Miss Marie,* and *The Taking of Miss Janie,* each of which won an Obie Award. He has taught at several schools, including Columbia University and Dartmouth College.

A musician, North Carolinian J. C. "JACK" BURRIS moved to San Francisco where he performed his music with the help of wooden puppets. His short story in this collection is the only one by Burris we have located.

Often credited as the first major African American short story writer, CHARLES W. CHESNUTT published stories in distinguished magazines such as *Atlantic Monthly* at the turn of the twentieth century. Also a novelist and an essayist, Chesnutt wrote a biography, *Frederick Douglass;* the novels *The House Behind the Cedars* and *The Colonel's Dream;* and the short story collections *The Conjure Woman* and *The Wife of His Youth, and Other Stories of the Color Line.*

MAXINE CLAIR earned an MFA in creative writing from American University and currently teaches writing at George Washington University in Washington, D.C. Her short stories have appeared in *Antietam Review*, *Icarus*, and *Kenyon Review*. Her books include a collection of poetry, *Coping with Gravity*, and a short story collection, *Rattlebone*.

ELDRIDGE CLEAVER was most recognized for his essay collection *Soul on Ice*. Shortly after his release from prison, he joined the Black Panther Party and began touring America as their minister of information. Cleaver later ran for political office as a Republican. He became something of a recluse, and died in the spring of 1998.

ANITA SCOTT COLEMAN was a poet, short story writer, and essayist whose works appeared in African American journals during the 1920s and 1930s. She won second prize in the *Opportunity* literary contest for her nonfiction sketch "Dark Horse," an award sponsored by *The Crisis* for her essay "Unfinished Masterpieces" and another *Crisis* award for her short story "Three Dogs and a Rabbit." She published two books of poetry: *Reason for Singing* in 1948 and *Singing Bells* in 1961.

WANDA COLEMAN is the author of several poetry and short fiction collections and the recipient of prestigious awards such as a National Endowment for the Arts fellowship and a Guggenheim fellowship. Her works include *A War of Eyes and Other Stories*, *Heavy Daughter Blues: Poems & Stories*, *African Sleeping Sickness: Stories and Poems*, and *Hand Dance* (1993). She lives in Los Angeles.

AYA DE LEON is an Afro-Latina writer of fiction, nonfiction, poetry, and plays. Her work has appeared in *Essence* magazine as well as in various anthologies and journals. She is director of the Mothertongue Institute for Creative Development, which offers workshops on writing and creativity. She is currently at work on several projects, including a Madeline Moore mystery series, a nongenre novel, and a self-help memoir.

Former Poet Laureate of the United States **RITA DOVE** is also a recipient of the Pulitzer Prize for her poetry collection *Thomas and Beulah*. She is author of the poetry collections *The Yellow House on the Corner*, *Museum*, and *Grace Notes*, and a collection of short stories, *Fifth Sunday*. She is presently commonwealth professor of English at the University of Virginia and lives in Charlottesville, Virginia.

W.E.B. DuBois was a historian and essayist who challenged the views of Booker T. Washington and changed the study of African American history. In 1896 he became the first African American to receive a Ph.D. from Harvard; his dissertation, *The Suppression of the African Slave-Trade to the United States of America, 1638–1870*, was published that same year. He taught at several universities, including the University of Pennsylvania and Atlanta University; was a founding member of the NAACP; and founded and edited the periodical *The Crisis* and later *Phylon*. His publications include *The Souls of Black Folk* and *Black Reconstruction*.

Among the most successful of early African American writers, **PAUL LAURENCE DUNBAR** published six collections of poetry, four collections of short stories, and four novels. His collection of poems, *Lyrics of Lowly Life*, combines poems from his first two volumes of poetry, *Oak and Ivy* and *Majors and Minors*, and became a best-seller.

During the 1940s and 1950s, **RALPH ELLISON**'s stories and articles were featured in many of the best literary magazines. He was a writer-in-residence at many leading U.S. universities. He wrote *Invisible Man*, which has become a literary classic, and two essay collections, *Shadow and Act* and *Going to the Territory*. He received numerous awards, including the Medal of Freedom. His collection of short stories, *Flying Home and Other Stories,* was published posthumously in 1996.

PERCIVAL EVERETT is the author of *Suder, Walk Me to the Distance, Cutting Lisa, For Her Dark Skins, Zulus,* and *The Weather and Women Treat Me Fair.* He teaches in the department of English at the University of Notre Dame.

CAROLYN FERRELL's short stories have appeared in *Ploughshares, Fiction, Callaloo,* and other distinguished literary journals. Her story "Proper Library" also appears in *The Best American Short Stories 1994.* Her collection of short stories, *Don't Erase Me,* was recently published by Houghton Mifflin and received a John C. Zacharis First Book Award. She currently teaches creative writing at Sarah Lawrence College in New York City.

NICK AARON FORD coedited the anthology *Best Short Stories by Afro-American Writers (1925–1950),* which reprints selected stories that originally appeared in the *Baltimore Afro-American.* Along with the story reprinted in this anthology, "No Room in the Inn" appears in *Best Short Stories by Afro-American Writers.* Ford graduated with a Ph.D. from the University of Iowa in 1945, subsequently taught at Morgan State University and Coppin State, and until his death in 1982 published numerous books, stories, and scholarly essays.

EUGENE P. FRIERSON served as squadron sergeant major in the 10th Calvary (the famous "Buffalo Soldiers") of the U.S. Army. The story in this anthology was originally published in serialized parts in *Colored American Magazine* in 1905.

JOHN WESLEY GROVES, IV, graduated from Temple University. His short stories, collected in *Pyrrhic Victory: A Collection of Short Stories,* explore underprivileged African Americans in the 1950s from sociological and psychological perspectives.

One of the most prominent black American authors of the twentieth century, and a prolific writer during the 1940s and 1950s, **CHESTER HIMES** was recognized primarily for his detective novels, which include *The Real Cool Killers, The Crazy Kill,* and *Cotton Comes to Harlem.* He also published novels that bitingly comment on race relations in the United States. Himes published an informative two-volume autobiography, and his collection of short stories, *The Collected Stories of Chester Himes,* was published posthumously in 1991.

PAULINE E. HOPKINS's early short stories were published in *Colored American Magazine,* where she became literary editor after publication of her first novel, *Contending Forces: A Romance Illustrative of Negro Life North and South in 1900.* In 1916 she became editor of *New Era Magazine,* where she published her last work, the novella *Topsy Templeton.*

One of the seminal figures of the Harlem Renaissance, **LANGSTON HUGHES** inspired and encouraged two generations of black writers, including Margaret Walker and Gwendolyn Brooks, and later Ted Joans, Mari Evans, and Alice Walker. His poetry collections include *The Weary Blues, Fine Clothes to the Jew, Montage of a Dream Deferred, Ask Your Mama: 12 Moods for Jazz, The Panther and the Lash: Poems of Our Times,* and *Black Misery.* Although recognized primarily for his poetry, he also published in other genres, including the novel *Not Without Laughter,* the autobiography *The Big Sea: An Autobiography,* and the musical *The Sun Do Move.* Most of his short stories characterize Jesse B. Semple and were published as a series collectively known as The Simple Tales.

During World War II, **JOHN O. KILLENS** was a member of an amphibious unit in the South Pacific. He wrote three novels, *Youngblood, And Then We Heard the Thunder,* and *The Cotillion; or, One Good Bull Is Half the Herd;* a book of essays, *Black Man's Burden;* and the screen play for a motion picture, *Odds Against Tomorrow,* which starred Harry Belafonte. He taught at several universities and was chair of the Workshop of the Harlem Writers Guild.

Along with the story that appears in this anthology, **MARCH LACY'S** short story "Fighting Finish" appears in *Best Short Stories by Afro-American Writers (1925–1950),* a collection of stories that originally appeared in the *Baltimore Afro-American* between 1925 and 1950.

WILLIAM HENRY LEWIS'S fiction has appeared in *Ploughshares* and other literary journals, and his story "Shades" was selected for inclusion in *Best American Short Stories 1996.* The author of the short story collection *In the Arms of Our Elders,* he currently teaches at Trinity College in Hartford, Connecticut.

COLLEEN MCELROY'S work has appeared in *Short Story International, Callaloo, Confrontation,* and many other literary magazines and anthologies. Her volumes of poetry include *Lie and Say You Love Me, Winters Without Snow, Queen of the Ebony Isles,* and others. *Jesus and Fat Tuesday and Other Short Stories* and *Driving Under the Cardboard Pines* are among her short story collections. She has received numerous awards, including a Fulbright fellowship, and is currently a professor of English at the University of Washington in Seattle.

REGINALD MCKNIGHT teaches at the University of Maryland, College Park. Among his literary awards are a National Endowment for the Arts fellowship, a Whiting Writer's Award, a Drue Heinz Literature Prize, a Pushcart Prize, and an O. Henry Award. In addition to his novel *I Get on the Bus,* he has published three collections of short stories: *The Kind of Light That Shines on Texas, Moustapha's Eclipse,* and *White Boys: Stories.*

TERRY MCMILLAN'S first novel, *Mama,* received a National Book Award, and her novels *Waiting to Exhale* and *How Stella Got Her Groove Back* were recently adapted for film. She edited *Breaking Ice: An Anthology of Contemporary African-American Fiction* and lives in California.

Recipient of a Pulitzer Prize for fiction, **JAMES ALAN McPHERSON** has published two collections of stories, *Hue and Cry* and *Elbow Room*. He has been on the faculty at the University of Iowa Writer's Workshop for a number of years.

Among **WALTER MOSLEY**'s best-selling mysteries are *A Little Yellow Dog*, *Gone Fishin'*, *Black Betty*, and *Devil in a Blue Dress*, which was recently adapted for film. His work has been translated into twenty languages and appears in many anthologies. Among his writing awards are the Private Eye Writers of America's Shamus Award and a nomination for the Mystery Writers of America's Edgar Award. His collection of short stories, *Always Outnumbered, Always Outgunned*, was recently published by W. W. Norton. Born in Los Angeles, he now lives in New York City.

HARRYETTE MULLEN, who teaches English at the University of California, Los Angeles, is currently completing *Gender & the Subjugated Body*, a study of tropes of embodiment in the African American slave narrative tradition. Her next project, *Visionary Literacy*, is a study of cultural syncretism in African American visionary art and literature.

Native Texan **SUNNY NASH** recently moved to Southern California to seek film opportunities. Her works have appeared in *Houston Chronicle's Texas Magazine* and in the anthologies *New Growth/2* and *Common Bonds*.

WILLIAM PICKENS was an author, activist, government employee, and college teacher. Pickens wrote searing depictions of the relations between whites and blacks in U.S. society. For more on Pickens's views of western race relations, read his poignant story "The Vengeance of the Gods."

JOHN R. POSEY received a history degree from Dartmouth College. His novel *Charlatans* was a semifinalist for a Becking Foundation Novel-in-Progress Award. His works have appeared in publications such as *Texas Short Fiction: A World in Itself*, *The Texas Monthly*, *The Houston Post*, and *The Dallas Morning News*. He served as editor of *African-American Literary Review* as well as of the 1995 issue of *KenteCloth*.

JEWEL PARKER RHODES is the author of the novels *Voodoo Dreams* and *Magic City*. She lives in Arizona, where she is a professor of English and director of the MFA program in creative writing at Arizona State University.

JOHNIE SCOTT was one of the original "Angry Voices of Watts" on the NBC-TV special of the same name. His essays and poems have appeared in *Harper's*, *Time*, *Scholastic*, *Pageant*, and other magazines. Currently he is a professor in the Pan African studies department at California State University, Northridge.

Recognized primarily as the author of choreoplays, **NTOZAKE SHANGE** is also a poet, novelist, and short story writer. Her choreoplays include the critically acclaimed *for colored girls who have considered suicide/when the rainbow is enuf*. Her novels include *Sassafras, Cypress & Indigo,* and *Betsey Brown*. Her short stories and essays appear in *Ridin' the Moon in Texas*. She is the recipient of numerous awards and currently resides in Philadelphia.

CHARLOTTE WATSON SHERMAN's poems and short stories have appeared in *Obsidian, The Black Scholar, CALYX , Painted Bride Quarterly, Ikon*, and other distinguished literary journals. Her short story collection, *Killing Color*, received the King County Arts Commission Fiction Award. She currently lives in Seattle.

MIKE THELWELL was born in Jamaica and immigrated to the United States in 1959 to attend Howard University. Active in civil rights, he worked with the Student Non-Violent Coordinating Committee and was director of the Washington office of the Mississippi Freedom Democratic Party. He served as chair of the W. E. B. Du Bois Department of Afro-American Studies at the University of Massachusetts, Amherst. He is author of the novel *The Harder They Come*, several filmscripts, and stories that appeared in *Negro Digest, Short Story International*, and *Story* magazine.

JOYCE CAROL THOMAS won the National Book Award and the American Book Award for her novel *Marked by Fire;* her other novels include *Bright Shadow, Water Girl, The Golden Pasture*, and *Journey*. She is also editor of the anthology *A Gathering of Flowers: Stories About Being Young in America.*

Writer, producer, and educator **MALVIN WALD**'s filmscripts include *The Naked City, Al Capone, TV D-Day, Hollywood: The Golden Years, The Rafer Jounson Story, The Boy Who Owned an Elephant*, and *Around the World of Mike Todd*. He taught at the University of Southern California, Los Angeles, and served as a producer for Twentieth Century Fox Television. Awards for his filmscripts and film productions include a Writers Guild Award nomination, an Academy Award nomination, and a Gold Medal Award.

Rhodes scholar **JOHN EDGAR WIDEMAN** is the author of several novels, including the critically acclaimed trilogy *Sent for You Yesterday, Hiding Place*, and *The Lynchers*, and two memoirs, *Brothers and Keepers* and *Fatheralong*. His short story collections, including *Damballah* and *Fever*, have been collected in *The Short Stories of John Edgar Wideman*. He teaches at the University of Massachusetts and lives in Amherst.

JOHN A. WILLIAMS is author of several novels, including *The Angry Ones, Night Song, Sissie, The Man Who Cried I Am, Jacob's Ladder*, and *!Click Song*, which won an American Book Award. He is also author of the nonfiction book *This Is My Country*, an account of a journey across the United States in 1963. He received a National Institute of Arts and Letters Award, and some of his novels have been adapted for films and television. Currently, he is Paul Robeson Professor Emeritus at Rutgers University.

MARGARET WILLIAMS wrote fiction during the early 1940s. Her short story "Grazing in Good Pastures" first appeared in *The Crisis.*

FRANK YERBY is most recognized for historical romances such as *The Foxes of Harrow, The Devil's Laughter, Benton's Row*, and *Odor of Sanctity*. His novels have sold over 55 million copies and several have been adapted for film. The story that appears in this anthology was his first published fiction. It appeared originally in *Harper's* magazine and received an O. Henry Award.

Bibliography

Allen, Phyllis W. "The Crown." *Tex: A Magazine of Texas Fiction, Poetry, and Art* (1998): 4–5.

———. "Mama Minnie and Me." In *Texas Short Stories*. Edited by Billy Bob Hill. Dallas: Browder Springs Publishing, 1997. Pp. 306–314.

———. "The Red Swing." In *KenteCloth: Southwest Voices of the African Diaspora, The Oral Tradition Comes to the Page*. Edited by Jas. Mardis. Denton: University of North Texas Press, 1997. Pp. 141–146.

———. "The Shopping Trip." In *KenteCloth: African American Voices in Texas*. Edited by Sherry McGuire and John R. Posey. Denton: University of North Texas Press, 1995. Pp. 60–65.

Bagley, Julian Elihu. "Children of Chance." *The Crisis*, 29 (November 1924): 15–18.

———. "Moving Pictures in an Old Song Shop." *Opportunity*, 5 (December 1927): 369–372.

Ball, John. "Fido." In *Cop Cade*. Edited by John Ball. Garden City: Doubleday and Company, 1978. Pp. 86–90.

———. "Full Circle." In *Ellery Queen's Veils of Mystery*. Edited by Ellery Queen. New York: The Dial Press, 1980. Pp. 225–237.

———. "One for Virgil Tibbs." In *Ellery Queen's A Multitude of Sins*. Edited by Ellery Queen. New York: The Dial Press, 1975. Pp. 22–37.

———. "Virgil Tibbs and the Cocktail Napkin." In *Ellery Queen's Scenes of the Crime*. Edited by Ellery Queen. New York: The Dial Press, 1976. Pp. 56–65.

———. "Virgil Tibbs and the Fallen Body." In *Ellery Queen's Eyewitnesses*. Edited by Ellery Queen. New York: The Dial Press, 1982. Pp. 252–259.

Bernard, Jessie. "Alycia's Grandchildren." *The Crisis*, 24 (October 1933): 225, 238.

Bland, Eleanor Taylor. "The Man Who Said I'm Not." In *Spooks, Spies, and Private Eyes: Black Mystery, Crime, and Suspense Fiction*. Edited by Paula L. Woods. New York: Doubleday, 1995. Pp. 278–287.

———. "Nightfire." In *Women on the Case*. Edited by Sara Paretsky. New York: Delacorte Press, 1996. Pp. 61–70.

Bontemps, Arna. "3 Pennies for Luck." In *The Old South: "A Summer Tragedy" and Other Stories of the Thirties*. New York: Dodd, Mead, 1973. Pp. 221–238.

———. "The Cure." In *The Old South: "A Summer Tragedy" and Other Stories of the Thirties*. New York: Dodd, Mead, 1973. Pp. 27–40.

———. "Why I Returned." *Harper's Magazine*, 230 (April 1965): 176–182. Also in *The Old South: "A Summer Tragedy" and Other Stories of the Thirties*. New York: Dodd, Mead, 1973. Pp. 1–25.

Brister, Bob. "Moss, Mallards, and Mules." In *Moss, Mallards and Mules and Other Hunting and Fishing Stories*. New York: Winchester Press, 1973. Pp. 1–7.

———. "Of Perches and Pleasures." In *Moss, Mallards and Mules and Other Hunting and Fishing Stories*. New York: Winchester Press, 1973. Pp. 33–39.

Brooks, Gwendolyn. "Chicago Portraits." *Negro Story*, 1 (May–June 1944): 49–50.

Brown, Cecil M. "Now Is the Time." *The Black Scholar*, 12 (September—October 1981): 2–12.

Bullins, Ed. "The Drive." In *The Hungered One: Early Writings*. New York: William Morrow, 1971. Pp. 21–25.

———. "The Storekeeper." *Negro Digest*, 16 (May 1967): 55–58.

———. "Support Your Local Police." In *The Hungered One: Early Writings*. New York: William Morrow, 1971. Pp. 100–108.

Burris, Jack. "Judah's a Two-Way Street Running Out." *Negro Digest*, 15 (January 1966): 64–73.

Carpenter, Don. "The Crossroader." In *The Murder of the Frogs and Other Stories*. New York: Harcourt, Brace, and World, 1969. Pp. 15–26.

———. "Road Show." In *The Murder of the Frogs and Other Stories*. New York: Harcourt, Brace, and World, 1969. Pp. 3–14.

Carstarphen, Meta G. "Point of Departure." In *KenteCloth: African American Voices in Texas*. Edited by Sherry McGuire and John R. Posey. Denton: Center for Texas Studies, 1995. Pp. 151–157.

Cartier, Xam Wilson. "Muz and the Sphere of Memory." In *Breaking Ice: An Anthology of Contemporary African-American Fiction*. Edited by Terry McMillan. New York: Viking, 1990. Pp. 118–126.

Chesnutt, Charles W. "The Averted Strike." In *The Short Fiction of Charles W. Chesnutt*. Edited by Sylvia Lyons Render. Washington, D.C.: Howard University Press, 1974. Pp. 383–390.

———. "Mr. Taylor's Funeral." In *The Short Fiction of Charles W. Chesnutt*. Edited by Sylvia Lyons Render. Washington, D.C.: Howard University Press, 1974. Pp. 261–270.

Clair, Maxine. *Rattlebone*. New York: Farrar, Straus & Giroux, 1994.

Cleaver, Eldridge. "The Flashlight." *Playboy*, 16 (December 1969): 120–124, 287–302.

Coleman, Anita Scott. "The Brat." *The Messenger*, 8 (April 1926): 105–106, 126.

———. "El Tisico." *The Crisis*, 19 (March 1920): 252–253.

———. "Jack Arrives." *Half-Century Magazine*, 8 (February 1920): 5, 14.

———. "The Little Grey House." *Half-Century Magazine*, 13 (July–August 1922): 4, 17, 19; 13 (September–October 1922): 4, 21.

———. "Rich Man, Poor Man—." *Half-Century Magazine*, 8 (May 1920): 6, 14.

———. "Three Dogs and a Rabbit." *Crisis*, 31 (January 1926): 118–122.

Coleman, Wanda. "Big Dreams." In *A War of Eyes and Other Stories*. Santa Rosa: Black Sparrow Press, 1988. Pp. 137–158.

———. "The Big Little Gang." In *A War of Eyes and Other Stories*. Santa Rosa: Black Sparrow Press, 1988. Pp. 161–165.

———. "Dream 5281." In *A War of Eyes and Other Stories*. Santa Rosa: Black Sparrow Press, 1988. Pp. 85–91.

———. "The Dufus Rufus." In *A War of Eyes and Other Stories*. Santa Rosa: Black Sparrow Press, 1988. Pp. 223–227.

————. "Eyes and Teeth." In *A War of Eyes and Other Stories*. Santa Rosa: Black Sparrow Press, 1988. Pp. 81–84.

————. "The Friday Night Shift at the Taco House Blues (Wah-Wah)." In *A War of Eyes and Other Stories*. Santa Rosa: Black Sparrow Press, 1988. Pp. 103–116.

————. "Ladies." In *A War of Eyes and Other Stories*. Santa Rosa: Black Sparrow Press, 1988. Pp. 27–37.

————. "Lickety-Split." In *A War of Eyes and Other Stories*. Santa Rosa: Black Sparrow Press, 1988. Pp. 175–178.

————. "The Stare Down." In *A War of Eyes and Other Stories*. Santa Rosa: Black Sparrow Press, 1988. Pp. 41–57.

————. "Stashed." In *A War of Eyes and Other Stories*. Santa Rosa: Black Sparrow Press, 1988. Pp. 205–210.

————. "A War of Eyes." In *A War of Eyes and Other Stories*. Santa Rosa: Black Sparrow Press, 1988. Pp. 167–173.

Colter, Cyrus. "The Beach Umbrella." In *The Beach Umbrella*. Iowa City: University of Iowa Press, 1970. Pp. 199–225.

————. "Black for Dinner." In *The Beach Umbrella*. Iowa City: University of Iowa Press, 1970. Pp. 104–124.

Cooper, J. California. "Evergreen Grass." In *The Matter Is Life*. New York: Doubleday, 1991. Pp. 35–43.

————. "How, Why to Get Rich." In *The Matter Is Life*. New York: Doubleday, 1991. Pp. 17–31.

————. "Somebody for Everybody." In *Some Love, Some Pain, Sometime*. New York: Doubleday, 1995. Pp. 229–247.

————. "Vanity." In *The Matter Is Life*. New York: Doubleday, 1991. Pp. 71–110.

Corbin, Steven. "My Father's Son." In *Streetlights: Illuminating Tales of the Black Urban Experience*. Edited by DorisJean Austin and Martin Simmons. New York: Penguin Books, 1996. Pp. 61–76.

Crawford, Marc. "Willie T. Washington's Blues." *Black World*, 21 (May 1972): 54–66.

Daly, Carroll John. "Knights of the Open Palm." *The Black Mask*, 1 (June 1923): 22–47.

Davis, Marshall. "Booga Red: Part 1." *The Light: America's News Magazine* (February 4, 1928): 5–6.

————. "Booga Red: Part 2." *The Light: America's News Magazine* (February 11, 1928): 7–8, 19.

————. "Wreckage: A Faithless Wife Shattered Ferdol Jackson's Ideals." *The Light: America's News Magazine* (March 24, 1928): 5–6, 19.

Dawson, Curtis Dale. "Mayday at Northeast Mall." In *KenteCloth: African American Voices in Texas*. Edited by Sherry McGuire and John R. Posey. Denton: University of North Texas Press, 1995. Pp. 193–200.

de Leon, Aya. "Tell Me Moore." In *Spooks, Spies, and Private Eyes: Black Mystery, Crime, and Suspense Fiction*. Edited by Paula L. Woods. New York: Doubleday, 1995. Pp. 312– 327.

Dolan, Harry. "The Sand-Clock Day." In *From the Ashes: Voices of Watts*. Edited by Budd Schulberg. New York: World Publishing, 1969. Pp. 36–39.

Dove, Rita. "Damon and Vandalia." In *Fifth Sunday*. Charlottesville: University Press of Virginia, 1985. Pp. 30–39.

Dreiser, Theodore. "Nigger Jeff." In *The Best Short Stories of Theodore Dreiser*. Edited by Howard Fast. Cleveland: World Publishing Company, 1947. Pp. 157–182.

Du Bois, W. E. B. "Jesus Christ in Texas." In *Darkwater: Voices from the Veil*. New York: Schocken Books, 1969. Pp. 123–133.

———. "On Being Crazy." In *From the Roots: Short Stories by Black Americans*. Edited by Charles L. James. New York: Dodd, Mead, 1970. Pp. 43–45.

Dunbar, Paul Laurence. "The Ingrate." *The Strength of Gideon and Other Stories*. New York: Arno Press, 1969. Pp. 87–103.

———. "Little Billy." A. N. Kellogg Newspaper Agency, ca. 1891.

———. "The Tenderfoot." A. N. Kellogg Newspaper Agency, ca. 1891.

Edwards, Junius. "Mother Dear and Daddy." *The Angry Black*. Edited by John A. Williams. New York: Lancer Books, 1962. Pp. 23–33.

Ellison, Ralph. "Afternoon." *American Writing*. Edited by Hans Otto Storm et al. Prairie City, IL: Press of James A. Decker, 1940. Pp. 28–37. Also in *Negro Story*, 1 (March–April 1945): 3–8. Also in *Flying Home and Other Stories*. Edited by John F. Callahan. New York: Random House, 1996. Pp. 33–44.

———. "Boy on a Train." *New Yorker*, 72 (April 29 and May 6, 1996): 110–113. Also in *Flying Home and Other Stories*. Edited by John F. Callahan. New York: Random House, 1996. Pp. 12–32.

———. "A Coupla Scalped Indians." *New World Writing*, 9 (1956): 225–236. Also in *Flying Home and Other Stories*. Edited by John F. Callahan. New York: Random House, 1996. Pp. 63–81.

———. "I Did Not Learn Their Names." *New Yorker*, 72 (April 29 and May 6, 1996): 113–115. Also in *Flying Home and Other Stories*. Edited by John F. Callahan. New York: Random House, 1996. Pp. 89–96.

———. "Mister Toussan." *The New Masses*, 41 (November 4, 1941): 19–20. Also in *Flying Home and Other Stories*. Edited by John F. Callahan. New York: Random House, 1996. Pp. 22–32.

———. "That I Had Wings." *Common Ground*, 3 (Summer 1943): 30–37. Also in *Flying Home and Other Stories*. Edited by John F. Callahan. New York: Random House, 1996. Pp. 45–62.

Elman, Richard. "Law 'n Order Day." *Crossing Over, and Other Tales*. New York: Scribner, 1973. Pp. 162–176.

Everett, Percival. "Cry About a Nickel." In *The Weather and Women Treat Me Fair*. Little Rock: August House, 1987. Pp. 37–45.

———. "Esteban." In *The Weather and Women Treat Me Fair*. Little Rock: August House, 1987. Pp. 64–73.

———. "A Good Home for Hachita." In *The Weather and Women Treat Me Fair*. Little Rock: August House, 1987. Pp. 16–26.

Fahrenthold, Lisa. "Roberta." In *Common Bonds: Stories by and About Modern Texas Women*. Edited by Suzanne Comer. Dallas: Southern Methodist University Press, 1990. Pp. 12–25.

Farrell, James T. "For White Men Only." In *The Short Stories of James T. Farrell*. Garden City: Halcyon House, 1941. Pp. 238–249.

Faulk, John Henry. "A Glorious Fourth." *Unknown Texas*. Edited by Jonathan Eisen and Harold Straughn. New York: Collier Books, 1988. Pp. 208–215.

Ferrell, Carolyn. "Wonderful Teen." In *Don't Erase Me*. Boston: Houghton Mifflin, 1997. Pp. 109–124.

Fiedler, Leslie A. "The First Spade in the West." In *The Last Jew in America*. New York: Stein and Day, 1966. Pp. 121–191.

Fleming, David L. "The Sun Gone Down, Darkness Be Over Me." In *Careless Weeds: Six Texas Novellas*. Edited by Tom Pilkington. Dallas: Southern Methodist University Press, 1993. Pp. 141–186.

Ford, Nick Aaron. "Let the Church Roll On." In *Best Short Stories by Afro-American Writers (1925–1950)*. Edited by Nick Aaron Ford and H. L. Faggett. New York: Meador Publishing Company, 1950. Pp. 25–29.

———. "No Room in the Inn." In *Best Short Stories by Afro-American Writers (1925–1950)*. Edited by Nick Aaron Ford and H. L. Faggett. New York: Meador Publishing Company, 1950. Pp. 19–24.

French, Marie Louise. "There Never Fell a Night So Dark." *Crisis*, 31 (December 1925): 73–76.

Frierson, Eugene P. "An Adventure in the Big Horn Mountains; Or, the Trials and Tribulations of a Recruit." *Colored American Magazine*, 8 (April 1905): 196–199; 8 (May 1905): 277–279; 8 (June 1905): 338–340.

Gipson, Edna. "A Deep Blue Feeling." In *From the Ashes: Voices of Watts*. Edited by Budd Schulberg. New York: World Publishing, 1969. Pp. 189–193.

Glave, Thomas. "—And Love Them?" In *Children of the Night: The Best Short Stories by Black Writers, 1967 to the Present*. Edited by Gloria Naylor. Boston: Little, Brown, 1995. Pp. 502–520.

Gold, Herbert. "Song of the First and Last Beatnik." In *The Magic Will: Stories and Essays of a Decade*. New York: Random House, 1971. Pp. 170–189.

Greer, Robert O. "The Can Men." *Writer's Forum*, 16 (1990): 130–139.

Groves, John Wesley, IV. "Stop, Thief!" In *Pyrrhic Victory: A Collection of Short Stories*. Philadelphia: United Publishers, 1953. Pp. 27–44.

Harvey, Charles W. "To Taste Fire Once More." In *Go the Way Your Blood Beats: An Anthology of Lesbian and Gay Fiction by African-American Writers*. Edited by Shawn Stewart Ruff. New York: Henry Holt, 1996. Pp. 88–92.

———. "When Dogs Bark." In *Shade: An Anthology of Fiction by Gay Men of African Descent*. Edited by Bruce Morrow and Charles H. Rowell. New York: Avon Books, 1996. Pp. 290–302.

Haslam, Gerald. "Companeros." In *Okies: Selected Stories*. Santa Barbara: Peregrine Smith, 1975. Pp. 36–47.

———. "Rider." In *That Constant Coyote: California Stories*. Reno: University of Nevada Press, 1990. Pp. 23–33.

Haywood, Gar A. "And Pray Nobody Sees You." In *Spooks, Spies, and Private Eyes: Black Mystery, Crime, and Suspense Fiction*. Edited by Paula L. Woods. New York: Doubleday, 1995. Pp. 158–171.

Herbert, Helen. "The Masterpiece." *Negro Story*, 1 (May–June 1944): 32–43.

Hicks, A. Cinque. "Spice." In *Shade: An Anthology of Fiction by Gay Men of African Descent*. Edited by Bruce Morrow and Charles H. Rowell. New York: Avon Books, 1996. Pp. 1–13.

Himes, Chester. "Cotton Gonna Kill Me Yet." In *Black on Black: Baby Sister and Selected Writings*. New York: Doubleday and Company, 1973. Pp. 196–209. Originally published as "Let Me at the Enemy—an' George Brown." *Negro Story*, 1 (December–January 1944–45): 9–18. Also in *The Collected Stories of Chester Himes*. New York: Thunder's Mouth Press, 1990. Pp. 36–47.

———. "Da-Da-Dee." In *Black on Black: Baby Sister and Selected Writings*. New York: Doubleday and Company, 1973. Pp. 267–274. Also in *The Collected Stories of Chester Himes*. New York: Thunder's Mouth Press, 1992. Pp. 365–371.

———. "He Seen It in the Stars." *Negro Story*, 1 (July–August 1944): 5–9. Also in *The Collected Short Stories of Chester Himes*. New York: Thunder's Mouth Press, 1990. Pp. 105–109.

————. "In the Night." *Opportunity*, 20 (November 1942): 334–335, 348–349. Also in *The Collected Stories of Chester Himes*. New York: Thunder's Mouth Press, 1990. Pp. 340–345.

————. "Lunching at the Ritzmore." *The Crisis*, 49 (October 1942): 314–315, 331. Also in *The Collected Stories of Chester Himes*. New York: Thunder's Mouth Press, 1990. Pp. 16–21.

————. "Make with the Shape." *Negro Story*, 2 (1945): 3–6. Also in *The Collected Stories of Chester Himes*. New York: Thunder's Mouth Press, 1990. Pp. 110–113.

————. "A Night of Neuroses." *Negro Story*, 2 (1945): 10–14. Also in *The Collected Stories of Chester Himes*. New York: Thunder's Mouth Press, 1990. Pp. 126–130. Mistakenly called "A Night of New Roses" in original publication.

————. "One More Way to Die." *Negro Story*, 3 (1946): 10–14. Also in *The Collected Stories of Chester Himes*. New York: Thunder's Mouth Press, 1990. Pp. 375–380.

————. "A Penny for Your Thoughts." *Negro Story*, 1 (March–April 1945): 14–17. Also in *The Collected Stories of Chester Himes*. New York: Thunder's Mouth Press, 1990. Pp. 56–60.

————. "So Softly Smiling." *The Crisis*, 50 (October 1943): 302, 314–316, 318. Also in *The Collected Stories of Chester Himes*. New York: Thunder's Mouth Press, 1990. Pp. 65–73.

————. "The Something in a Colored Man." *Esquire*, 25 (January 1946): 120, 158. Also in *The Collected Stories of Chester Himes*. New York: Thunder's Mouth Press, 1990. Pp. 403–406.

————. "The Song Says 'Keep on Smiling.'" *The Crisis*, 52 (April 1945): 103–104. Also in *The Collected Stories of Chester Himes*. New York: Thunder's Mouth Press, 1990. Pp. 86–90.

Hodges, Frenchy. "Requiem for Willie Lee." *Ms. Magazine*, 8 (October 1979): 60–62, 75, 77–78.

Hopkins, Pauline E. "As the Lord Lives, He Is One of Our Mother's Children." *Colored American Magazine*, 6 (November 1903): 795–801.

Hughes, Langston. "Cora Unashamed." *American Mercury*, 30 (September 1933): 19–24. Also in *The Ways of White Folks*. New York: Alfred A. Knopf, 1973. Pp. 3–18.

————. "The Doors of Life." In *Afro-American Writing: An Anthology of Prose and Poetry*. Vol. 2. Edited by Richard A. Long and Eugenia W. Collier. New York: New York University Press, 1972. Pp. 429–433.

————. "The Gun." In *Something in Common and Other Stories*. New York: Hill and Wang, 1963. Pp. 154–161. Originally published as "Flora Belle."

————. "On the Road." *Esquire*, 3 (January 1935): 92, 154. Also in *Laughing to Keep from Crying*. New York: Henry Holt and Company, 1952. Pp. 183–189.

————. "One Friday Morning." *The Crisis*, 48 (July 1941): 216–218. Also in *Short Stories: Langston Hughes*. Edited by Akiba Sullivan Harper. New York: Hill and Wang, 1996. Pp. 153–162.

————. "Professor." In *Short Stories: Langston Hughes*. Edited by Akiba Sullivan Harper. New York: Hill and Wang, 1996. Pp. 101–107. First published as "Dr. Brown's Decision." *The Anvil* (May/June 1935): 5–8.

————. "Rock, Church." In *Soon, One Morning: New Writing by American Negroes, 1940–1962*. Edited by Herbert Hill. New York: Alfred A. Knopf, 1963. Pp. 231–241. Also in *Short Stories: Langston Hughes*. Edited by Akiba Sullivan Harper. New York: Hill and Wang, 1996 Pp. 262–271.

————. "Sailor Ashore." In *Short Stories: Langston Hughes*. Edited by Akiba Sullivan Harper. New York: Hill and Wang, 1996. Pp. 185–189.

————. "Slice Him Down." *Esquire*, 5 (May 1936): 44–45, 190–193. Also in *Laughing to Keep from Crying*. New York: Henry Holt and Company, 1952. Pp. 59–75.

————. "'Tain't So." *The Fight*, 5 (May 1937): 21, 29. Also in *Short Stories: Langston Hughes*. Edited by Akiba Sullivan Harper. New York: Hill and Wang, 1996. Pp. 149–152.

————. "Tragedy at the Baths." *Esquire*, 4 (October 1935): 80, 122. Also in *Laughing to Keep from Crying*. New York: Henry Holt and Company, 1952. Pp. 165–172.

Jackson, James Thomas. "Waiting in Line at the Drugstore." In *KenteCloth: Southwest Voices of the African Diaspora, The Oral Tradition Comes to the Page*. Edited by Jas. Mardis. Denton: University of North Texas Press, 1997. Pp. 117–120.

Johnson, Charles. "China." In *The Sorcerer's Apprentice*. New York: Atheneum, 1986. Pp. 61–95.

————. "Menagerie, A Child's Fable." In *The Sorcerer's Apprentice*. New York: Atheneum, 1986. Pp. 43–59.

Kidd, Harry, Jr. "Low Road Go Down." *Southwest Review*, 33 (Autumn 1948): 385–393.

Killens, John O. "God Bless America." *The California Quarterly* (1952): 37–40.

Lacy, March. "Fighting Finish." In *Best Short Stories by Afro-American Writers (1925–1950)*. Edited by Nick Aaron Ford and H. L. Faggett. New York: Meador Publishing Company, 1950. Pp. 140–145.

————. "No Fools, No Fun." In *Best Short Stories by Afro-American Writers (1925–1950)*. Edited by Nick Aaron Ford and H. L. Faggett. New York: Meador Publishing Company, 1950. Pp. 284–287.

Lee, Bob. "A Hunt in the Big Thicket." In *KenteCloth: Southwest Voices of the African Diaspora, The Oral Tradition Comes to the Page*. Edited by Jas. Mardis. Denton: University of North Texas Press, 1997. Pp. 121–124.

Lewis, Leslie Nia. "The Elixir." In *Streetlights: Illuminating Tales of the Black Urban Experience*. Edited by DorisJean Austin and Martin Simmons. New York: Penguin Books, 1996. Pp. 279–288.

Lewis, William Henry. "The Days the Light Stays On." In *In the Arms of Our Elders*. Durham: Carolina Wren Press, 1994. Pp. 1–15.

————. "Germinating." In *In the Arms of Our Elders*. Durham: Carolina Wren Press, 1994. Pp. 133–143.

————. "The Trip Back from Whidbey." In *In the Arms of Our Elders*. Durham: Carolina Wren Press, 1994. Pp. 65–76.

McCluskey, John A. "Lush Life." *Callaloo* 13 (Spring 1990). Reprinted in *Breaking Ice: An Anthology of Contemporary African-American Fiction*. Edited by Terry McMillan. New York: Penguin Books, 1990. Pp. 418–432.

————. "Nairobi Night." In *Ethnic American Short Stories*. Edited by Katharine D. Newman. New York: Washington Square Press, 1975. Pp. 59–65. Originally published as "A Short Story." *Black World*, 22 (1973): 54–58.

McElroy, Colleen. "A Brief Spell by the River." In *Jesus and Fat Tuesday, and Other Short Stories*. Berkeley: Creative Arts Book Company, 1987. Pp. 1–16.

————. "Driving Under the Cardboard Pines." In *Driving Under the Cardboard Pines and Other Stories*. Berkeley: Creative Arts Book Company, 1990. Pp. 121–134.

————. "The Edge of Night." In *Driving Under the Cardboard Pines and Other Stories*. Berkeley: Creative Arts Book Company, 1990. Pp. 201–221.

————. "Imogene." In *Jesus and Fat Tuesday, and Other Short Stories*. Berkeley: Creative Arts Book Company, 1987. Pp. 173–179.

————. "The Limitations of Jason Packard." In *Jesus and Fat Tuesday, and Other Short Stories*. Berkeley: Creative Arts Book Company, 1987. Pp. 17–34.

————. "The Losers." In *Driving Under the Cardboard Pines and Other Stories*. Berkeley: Creative Arts Book Company, 1990. Pp. 222–234.

————. "Sister Detroit." In *Jesus and Fat Tuesday, and Other Short Stories*. Berkeley: Creative Arts Book Company, 1987. Pp. 109–124. Also in *Breaking Ice: An Anthology of Contemporary African-American Literature*. Edited by Terry McMillan. New York: Penguin Books, 1990. Pp. 433–445.

————. "The Woman Who Would Eat Flowers." In *Driving Under the Cardboard Pines and Other Stories*. Berkeley: Creative Arts Book Company, 1990. Pp. 25–51.

McElroy, Njoki. "The Ninth Day of May." In *Common Bonds: Stories by and About Modern Texas Women*. Edited by Suzanne Comer. Dallas: Southern Methodist University Press, 1990. Pp. 40–42.

McKie, J. R. "Oda Rainbow." In *Streetlights: Illuminating Tales of the Black Urban Experience*. Edited by DorisJean Austin and Martin Simmons. New York: Penguin Books, 1996. Pp. 318–339.

McKnight, Reginald. "Boot." *Story*, 45 (Spring 1997): 106–123.

————. "First I Look at the Purse." In *Moustapha's Eclipse*. Pittsburgh: University of Pittsburgh Press, 1988. Pp. 17–26.

————. "The Honey Boys." In *Moustapha's Eclipse*. Pittsburgh: University of Pittsburgh Press, 1988. Pp. 79–101.

————. "The Kind of Light That Shines on Texas." In *The Kind of Light That Shines on Texas*. Boston: Little, Brown, 1992. Pp. 20–40.

————. "The More I Like Flies." *Kenyon Review*, 16 (Spring 1994): 43–55.

————. "Peacetime." In *The Kind of Light That Shines on Texas*. Boston: Little, Brown, 1992. Pp. 80–116.

————. "Peaches." In *Moustapha's Eclipse*. Pittsburgh: University of Pittsburgh Press, 1988. Pp. 27–35.

————. "Quitting Smoking." In *The Kind of Light That Shines on Texas*. Boston: Little, Brown, 1992. Pp. 139–174.

————. "Roscoe in Hell." In *The Kind of Light That Shines on Texas*. Boston: Little, Brown, 1992. Pp. 41–79.

————. "Who Big Bob?" In *Moustapha's Eclipse*. Pittsburgh: University of Pittsburgh Press, 1988. Pp. 37–42.

McMillan, Terry. "Quilting on the Rebound." In *Voices Louder Than Words: A Second Collection*. Edited by William Shore. New York: Vintage Books, 1991. Pp. 29–45.

McPherson, James Alan. "Elbow Room." In *Elbow Room*. Boston: Little, Brown, 1977. Pp. 215–241.

————. "On Trains." In *Hue and Cry*. Boston: Little, Brown, 1968. Pp. 33–40.

————. "A Solo Song: For Doc." In *Hue and Cry*. Boston: Little, Brown, 1968. Pp. 41–74. Also in *New Black Voices: An Anthology of Contemporary Afro-American Literature*. Edited by Abraham Chapman. New York: Mentor Books, 1972. Pp. 151–173.

————. "Widows and Orphans." In *Elbow Room*. Boston: Little, Brown, 1977. Pp. 133–153.

Majors, Michelle. "The Taxi Ride Home." In *KenteCloth: African American Voices in Texas*. Edited by Sherry McGuire and John R. Posey. Denton: Center for Texas Studies, 1995. Pp. 179–182.

Mardis, Jas. "The Arsenic Biscuits." *Tex: A Magazine of Texas Fiction, Poetry, and Art* (1998): 24–25.

Modupe, Talibah Folami. "Inmate 93274." In *Texas Short Fiction: A World in Itself II*. Edited by Mike Hennech and Billy Bob Hill. Redmond: ALE Publishing, 1995. Pp. 20–31.

———. "Is the Other Man's Ice Really Colder?" In *Texas Short Stories*. Edited by Billy Bob Hill. Dallas: Browder Springs Publishing, 1997. Pp. 361–363.

———. "The Right Reverend James." In *New Texas 94: Poetry and Fiction*. Edited by Kathryn S. McGuire and James Ward Lee. Denton: Center for Texas Studies, 1994. Pp. 159–162.

Morrow, Bruce. "Near the End of the World." In *Go the Way Your Blood Beats: An Anthology of Lesbian and Gay Fiction by African-American Writers*. Edited by Shawn Stewart Ruff. New York: Henry Holt, 1996. Pp. 122–133.

Mosley, Walter. *Always Outnumbered, Always Outgunned*. New York: W. W. Norton, 1997.

———. "Double Standard." *Gentlemen's Quarterly*, 65 (August 1995): 92, 94, 96–97.

———. "Equal Opportunity." *Critical Quarterly*, 37 (Winter 1995): 116–128.

———. "Fearless." In *Spooks, Spies, and Private Eyes: Black Mystery, Crime, and Suspense Fiction*. Edited by Paula L. Woods. New York: Doubleday, 1995. Pp. 135–157.

———. "Marvane Street." *Story*, 44 (Spring 1996): 109–120.

———. "Open House." In *The Henfield Prize Stories*. Edited by John Birmingham, Laura Gilpin, and Joseph F. McCrindle. New York: Warner Books, 1992. Pp. 60–67.

———. "The Thief." *Esquire*, 124 (July 1995): 74–80.

———. "The Watts Lions." In *The New Mystery: The International Association of Crime Writers' Essential Crime Writing of the Late 20th Century*. Edited by Jerome Charyn. New York: Dutton, 1993. Pp. 1–14.

Mowry, Jess. "Crusader Rabbit." *ZYZZYVA*, 6 (1990): 92–98.

———. "One Way." *ZYZZYVA*, 4 (1988): 45–61.

Mullen, Harryette. "Bad Girls." In *Her Work: Stories by Texas Women*. Edited by Lou Halsell Rodenberger. Bryan: Shearer Publishing, 1992. Pp. 204–206.

———. "Pica." In *Her Work: Stories by Texas Women*. Edited by Lou Halsell Rodenberger. Bryan: Shearer Publishing, 1992. Pp. 200–203.

———. "Tenderhead." In *Common Bonds: Stories by and About Modern Texas Women*. Edited by Suzanne Comer. Dallas: Southern Methodist University Press, 1990. Pp. 69–78.

———. "What Can't Be Measured." In *South by Southwest: 24 Stories from ModernTexas*. Edited by Don Graham. Austin: University of Texas Press, 1986. Pp. 203–213.

Nash, Sunny. "Amen." *Southwestern American Literature*, 20 (Spring 1995): 85–96.

———. "The Ladies' Room." In *Common Bonds: Stories by and About Modern Texas Women*. Edited by Suzanne Comer. Dallas: Southern Methodist University Press, 1990. Pp. 183–189.

———. "Too High for Birds." In *New Growth/2: Contemporary Short Stories by Texas Writers*. Edited by Mark Busby. San Antonio: Corona Publishing, 1993. Pp. 153–159.

Norris, Adrienne. "Dreams Befitting." In *KenteCloth: Southwest Voices of the African Diaspora, The Oral Tradition Comes to the Page*. Edited by Jas. Mardis. Denton: University of North Texas Press, 1997. Pp. 242–249.

Owens, William A. "Hangerman John." *Southwest Review*, 32 (Winter 1947): 124–132.

Patchett, Ann. "All Little Colored Children Should Play the Harmonica." *Paris Review*, 26 (Winter 1984): 180–192.

Patterson, Lindsay. "A New Understanding." In *KenteCloth: Southwest Voices of the African Diaspora, The Oral Tradition Comes to the Page*. Edited by Jas. Mardis. Denton: University of North Texas Press, 1997. Pp. 14–18. First published in *Tarnished Hero* (Modern Black Man, 1986).

Petesch, Natalie L. M. "L'il Britches." In *After the First Death There Is No Other*. Iowa City: University of Iowa Press, 1974. Pp. 65–71.

Phillips, Gary. "Dead Man's Shadow." In *Spooks, Spies, and Private Eyes: Black Mystery, Crime, and Suspense Fiction*. Edited by Paula L. Woods. New York: Doubleday, 1995. Pp. 218–237.

Pickens, William. "Jim Crow in Texas." *The Nation*, 117 (August 15, 1923): 155–156.

———. "The Vengeance of the Gods." In *The Vengeance of the Gods, and Three Other Stories of Real American Color Line Life*. Freeport: Books for Libraries Press, 1972. Pp. 11–86.

Pinson, Hermine. "Kris/Crack/Kyle." In *KenteCloth: African American Voices in Texas*. Edited by Sherry McGuire and John R. Posey. Denton: University of North Texas Press, 1995. Pp. 36–39.

———. "Someday My Prince." In *Common Bonds: Stories by and About Modern Texas Women*. Edited by Suzanne Comer. Dallas: Southern Methodist University Press, 1990. Pp. 294–298.

Posey, John R. "Ticket to Freedom." In *Texas Short Fiction: A World in Itself II*. Edited by Mike Hennech and Billy Bob Hill. Redmond: ALE Publishing, 1995. Pp. 203–217.

Poston, Ted. "Rat Joiner Routs the Klan." In *Soon, One Morning: New Writing by American Negroes, 1940–1962*. Edited by Herbert Hill. New York: Alfred A. Knopf, 1963. Pp. 379–388.

Priestley, Eric. "The Seed of a Slum's Eternity." In *What We Must See: Young Black Storytellers*. Edited by Orde Coombs. New York: Dodd, 1971. Pp. 137–147.

Reid, Jan. "Second Saddle." In *Texas Short Stories*. Edited by Billy Bob Hill. Dallas: Browder Springs Publishing, 1997. Pp. 267–278.

Rhodes, Jewell Parker. "Long Distances." In *Children of the Night: The Best Short Stories by Black Writers, 1967 to the Present*. Edited by Gloria Naylor. Boston: Little, Brown, 1995. Pp. 172–179.

Ruff, Shawn Stewart. "Meredith's Lie." In *Go the Way Your Blood Beats: An Anthology of Lesbian and Gay Fiction by African-American Writers*. Edited by Shawn Stewart Ruff. New York: Henry Holt, 1996. Pp. 53–78.

Scott, Darieck. "This City of Men." *Callaloo*, 17 (1994): 1035–1050.

Scott, Johnie. "The Coming of the Hoodlum." In *From the Ashes: Voices of Watts*. Edited by Budd Schulberg. New York: World Publishing, 1969. Pp. 97–116.

Shange, Ntozake. "Ridin' the Moon in Texas." In *Ridin' the Moon in Texas: Word Paintings*. New York: St. Martin's Press, 1987. Pp. 5–11.

Sherman, Charlotte Watson. "Emerald City: Third & Pike." In *Killing Color*. Corvallis: Calyx Books, 1992. Pp. 90–95.

Shockley, Ann Allen. "The Faculty Party." *Black World*, 21 (November 1971): 54–63.

Singley, Bernestine. "Heat." *Tex: A Magazine of Texas Fiction, Poetry, and Art* (1998): 18.

Smith, Andrea. "A Lesson in Murder." In *Women on the Case*. Edited by Sara Paretsky. New York: Delacorte Press, 1996. Pp. 143–161.

Stevens, R. L. "Five Rings in Reno." In *Ellery Queen's A Multitude of Sins*. Edited by Ellery Queen. New York: The Dial Press, 1975. Pp. 94–109.

Stewart, John. "Bloodstones." In *Curving Road*. Urbana: University of Illinois Press, 1975. Pp. 59–81.

———. "In the Winter Of." In *Curving Road*. Urbana: University of Illinois Press, 1975. Pp. 82–96.

———. "Letter to a Would-be Prostitute." In *Curving Road*. Urbana: University of Illinois Press, 1975. Pp. 25–34.

———. "The Pre-Jail Party." In *Curving Road*. Urbana: University of Illinois Press, 1975. Pp. 35–49.

————. "Satin's Dream." In *Curving Road*. Urbana: University of Illinois Press, 1975. Pp. 50–54.

Story, Rosalyn M. "Quiet as It's Kept." In *New Texas 94: Poetry and Fiction*. Edited by Kathryn S. McGuire and James Ward Lee. Denton: Center for Texas Studies, 1994. Pp. 67–86.

Straight, Susan. *Aquaboogie: A Novel in Stories*. Minneapolis: Milkweed Editions, 1990.

Taylor, Jeanne. "A House Divided." *Antioch Review*, 27 (1967): 298–305.

————. "The Stake-Out." In *From the Ashes: Voices of Watts*. Edited by Budd Schulberg. New York: World Publishing, 1969. Pp. 74–77.

Thelwell, Mike. "Direct Action." In *The Best Short Stories by Negro Writers: An Anthology from 1899 to the Present*. Edited by Langston Hughes. Boston: Little, Brown, 1967. Pp. 470–478.

Thomas, Joyce Carol. "Young Reverend Zelma Lee Moses." In *A Gathering of Flowers: Stories About Being Young in America*. Edited by Joyce Carol Thomas. New York: Harper and Row, 1990. Pp. 99–134.

Truvillion, Jesse Garfield. "A Child's Life in the Big Thicket: A Love of Blackberries." In *KenteCloth: Southwest Voices of the African Diaspora, The Oral Tradition Comes to the Page*. Edited by Jas. Mardis. Denton: University of North Texas Press, 1997. Pp. 136–140.

————. "A Stray Dog's Great Day." In *KenteCloth: Southwest Voices of the African Diaspora, The Oral Tradition Comes to the Page*. Edited by Jas. Mardis. Denton: University of North Texas Press, 1997. Pp. 113–116.

Twain, Mark. "A True Story." In *The Complete Short Stories of Mark Twain*. Edited by Charles Neider. New York: Bantam Books, 1957. Pp. 94–98.

————. "Which Was It." Unfinished manuscript, 1902.

Vickers, Jimmy. "Lead Roll." *Essence*, 8 (June 1977): 44, 46–47.

Wald, Malvin. "Keys to the City." *Negro Story*, 1 (December–January 1944–45): 19–22.

Watson, Henry. "The Educating of Exeter P. Jones." *Negro Story*, 1 (October–November 1944): 12–16.

Watt, Donley. "Caddo." In *Can You Get There From Here?* Dallas: Southern Methodist University Press, 1994. Pp. 83–96.

Wideman, John Edgar. "The Beginning of Homewood." In *The Stories of John Edgar Wideman*. New York: Pantheon Books, 1992. Pp. 420–432.

————. "Casa Grande." In *The Stories of John Edgar Wideman*. New York: Pantheon Books, 1992. Pp. 18–21.

————. "The Chinaman." In *The Stories of John Edgar Wideman*. New York: Pantheon Books, 1992. Pp. 331–342.

————. "Surfiction." In *The Stories of John Edgar Wideman*. New York: Pantheon Books, 1992. Pp. 189–197.

Wiley, Hugh. "Plated Goldfish." In *Fo' Meals a Day*. New York: Alfred A. Knopf, 1927. Pp. 109–145.

————. "The Pluvitor." In *Fo' Meals a Day*. New York: Alfred A. Knopf, 1927. Pp. 149–185.

————. "Sick Per Cent." In *Fo' Meals a Day*. New York: Alfred A. Knopf, 1927. Pp. 235–271.

Williams, John A. "Son in the Afternoon." In *The Angry Black*. New York: Lancer Books, 1962. Pp. 134–141.

Williams, Margaret. "Grazing in Good Pastures." *Crisis*, 48 (February 1941): 42–43, 59.

Wright, Lawrence. "Escape." In *Texas Bound:19 Texas Stories*. Edited by Kay Cattarulla. Dallas: Southern Methodist University Press, 1994. Pp. 211–236.

Wright, Richard. "Almos' a Man." *Negro Story*, 1 (May–June 1944): 51–59.

———. "The Man Who Was Almost a Man." In *Eight Men: Stories*. 1940. New York: Thunder's Mouth Press, 1987. Pp. 11–26.

———. "The Man Who Went to Chicago." In *Eight Men: Stories*. New York: Thunder's Mouth Press, 1987. Pp. 210–250.

Yerby, Frank. "Health Card." *Harper's Magazine*, 188 (May 1944): 548–553.

Young, Al. "Going for the Moon." In *A Gathering of Flowers: Stories About Being Young in America*. Edited by Joyce Carol Thomas. New York: Harper & Row, 1990. Pp. 37–62.

———. "Seduction by Light." In *Breaking Ice: An Anthology of Contemporary African-American Fiction*. Edited by Terry McMillan. New York: Viking, 1990. Pp. 671–681.

Permissions

DATE DUE			

OSSINING HIGH SCHOOL LIBRARY

OSSINING, NEW YORK   10562